The B

has been happe...
decades ago with the works of great artists
such as Wright and Ellison, whose prophetic
books defined the self-image of the Negro in
America.

In the powerful prose and poetry presented
here, each writer speaks with a distinctive voice
—each contributes to a growing body of work
which is one of the most important and vital
in American letters. The dynamic role of the
Negro in the artistic life of our nation is at
last being recognized: these are the spokesmen
of a potent new force at a time of great controversy and creativity.

About the Editor: Abraham Chapman is professor of English and Chairman of the American Literature survey courses at Wisconsin
State University-Stevens Point. His writings
include critical studies on American literature
of the 19th and 20th centuries, and book reviews for various leading periodicals. He is the
author of *The Negro In American Literature*.
In 1968 Professor Chapman received the bi-
ennial College Language Association Creative
Scholarship Award for his study *The Harlem
Renaissance in Literary History*, published in
CLA Journal.

BLACK VOICES

An Anthology of Afro-American Literature

EDITED, WITH AN INTRODUCTION AND BIO-
GRAPHICAL NOTES, BY ABRAHAM CHAPMAN

A MENTOR BOOK

NEW AMERICAN LIBRARY

A DIVISION OF PENGUIN BOOKS USA INC., NEW YORK
PUBLISHED IN CANADA BY
PENGUIN BOOKS CANADA LIMITED, MARKHAM, ONTARIO

Acknowledgments and Copyright Notices

JAMES BALDWIN, "Autobiographical Notes" copyright © 1955 by James Baldwin, and "Many Thousands Gone" copyright © 1951, 1955 by James Baldwin, from *Notes of a Native Son* by James Baldwin. Reprinted by permission of the Beacon Press.

LERONE BENNETT, JR., "Blues and Bitterness" from *New Negro Poets U.S.A.* ed. by Langston Hughes, Indiana University Press. Reprinted by permission of the author.

(The following pages constitute an extension of this copyright page.)

OWEN DODSON, "Guitar," "Black Mother Praying," "Drunken Lover," "The Reunion," and "Jonathan's Song" from *Powerful Long Ladder* by Owen Dodson. "Yardbird's Skull" and "Sailors on Leave" from *American Negro Poetry* ed. by Arna Bontemps. ALL reprinted by permission of the author.

PAUL LAURENCE DUNBAR, "We Wear the Mask," "A Death Song," "Sympathy," and "A Negro Love Song" from *The Complete Poems of Paul Laurence Dunbar*. Reprinted by permission of Dodd, Mead & Company, Inc.

RALPH ELLISON, "Prologue" from *Invisible Man* by Ralph Ellison, copyright 1947, 1948, 1952 by Ralph Ellison. Reprinted by permission of Random House, Inc.

MARI EVANS, "Coventry" from *Negro Digest*, "Status Symbol" from *Poets of Today* ed. by Walter Lowenfels, "The Emancipation of George-Hector (a colored turtle)" from *American Negro Poetry* ed. by Arna Bontemps, "My Man Let Me Pull Your Coat" and "Black Jam for Dr. Negro" from manuscripts, ALL reprinted by permission of the author.

RUDOLPH FISHER, "Common Meter" from *Best Short Stories by Afro-American Writers (1925-1950)* ed. by Nick Aaron Ford and H. L. Faggett, copyright by the *Afro-American*, reprinted by permission of Afro-American Newspapers.

DAN GEORGAKAS, "James Baldwin . . . in Conversation" from *Arts in Society*, Vol. 3, No. 4, copyright by Regents of The University of Wisconsin, reprinted by permission of *Arts in Society*, University Extension, The University of Wisconsin, and the author.

ROBERT HAYDEN, "Tour 5," "Figure," "In Light Half Nightmare and Half Vision," "Market," "Homage to the Empress of the Blues," "Mourning Poem for the Queen of Sunday," "Middle Passage," and "Frederick Douglass" from *Selected Poems* by Robert Hayden, copyright © 1966 by Robert Hayden; reprinted by permission of October House, Inc. "On the Coast of Maine" from *A Ballad of Remembrance* by Robert Hayden © 1962 by Robert Hayden, reprinted by permission of the author.

FRANK HORNE, "Kid Stuff" and "Nigger: A Chant for Children" from *American Negro Poetry* ed. by Arna Bontemps. Reprinted by permission of the author.

LANGSTON HUGHES, "Foreword: Who Is Simple?" "Feet Live Their Own Life," "Temptation," and "Bop" from *The Best of Simple* by Langston Hughes © 1961 by Langston Hughes; reprinted by permission of Hill and Wang, Inc. "Census," "Coffee Break," "Cracker Prayer," and "Promulgations" from *Simple's Uncle Sam* by Langston Hughes, copyright © 1965 by Langston Hughes; reprinted by permission of Hill and Wang, Inc. "Afro-American Fragment," from *Selected Poems of Langston Hughes*, © copyright 1959 by Langston Hughes, reprinted by permission of Alfred A. Knopf, Inc. "As I Grew Older," "Dream Variations," copyright 1926 by Alfred A. Knopf, Inc., and renewed 1954 by Langston Hughes. Reprinted from *Selected Poems of Langston Hughes* by permission of Alfred A. Knopf, Inc. "Daybreak in Alabama," copyright 1948 by Alfred A. Knopf, Inc. Reprinted from *Selected Poems of Langston Hughes* by permission of the publisher. "Dream Boogie," "Children's Rhymes," "Theme from English B," "Harlem," "Same in Blues," and "Ballad of the Landlord" from *Montage of a Dream De-*

MENTOR TRADEMARK REG. U.S. PAT. OFF. AND FOREIGN COUNTRIES
REGISTERED TRADEMARK—MARCA REGISTRADA
HECHO EN DRESDEN, TN, U.S.A.

SIGNET, SIGNET CLASSIC, MENTOR, ONYX, PLUME, MERIDIAN
and NAL BOOKS are published *in the United States* by
New American Library, a division of Penguin Books USA Inc.,
1633 Broadway, New York, New York 10019,
in Canada by Penguin Books Canada Limited,
2801 John Street, Markham, Ontario L3R 1B4

FIRST PRINTING, SEPTEMBER, 1968

20 21 22 23 24 25 26 27 28

PRINTED IN THE UNITED STATES OF AMERICA

TO BELLE

who has always shared
the explorations, the
trials, and the harvest,
with love

CONTENTS

II. AUTOBIOGRAPHY

III. POETRY

IV. LITERARY CRITICISM

INTRODUCTION

A rich and varied body of literature has been created by black Americans which has become an organic part of the literature of the United States.

The Africans torn away from their native languages and cultures and transported to colonial America began to use English as a written language of literary expression more than 220 years ago. A slave girl, Lucy Terry, from Deerfield, Massachusetts, is recognized as the first American Negro poet. In 1746, she wrote *Bars Fight*, a verse account of an Indian raid. Jupiter Hammon, a Long Island slave, was the first Negro poet to be published, in 1760 (an eighty-eight-line religious poem printed as a broadside). In 1773, Phyllis Wheatley, a Boston slave, was the first Negro in America to publish a volume of verse (124 pages, printed in London).

Of earlier and far greater literary significance than these first published poems is the great Afro-American folk literature in English created by the slaves in the plantation South. The folk poetry, with its striking imagery and metaphors, is wedded to the music of the spirituals and secular songs which proved to be the cradle of the most distinctive American music. The lyrics of these songs were only one literary manifestation of the Afro-American imagination. The profusion of oral narratives and folktales was another. Professor Richard M. Dorson, a scholarly authority on American folklore, has written in his book, *American Negro Folktales:*

> One of the memorable bequests by the Negro to American civilization is his rich and diverse store of folktales. . . . Only the Negro, as a distinct element of the English-speaking population, maintained a full-blown storytelling tradition. A separate Negro subculture formed within the shell of American life, missing the bounties of general education and material progress, remaining a largely oral, self-contained society with its own unwritten history and literature.

It was only in the 1880's, with the publication of the *Uncle Remus* stories by Joel Chandler Harris, that the American reading public began to get its first inklings of a small portion

21

of this very rich literature—as told by a white Southern journalist. And it was not very much earlier, in the 1860's, that some of the old spirituals and slave songs were published for the first time.

The poetic and rhythmic qualities of the spirituals and the dramatic qualities of the folktales were blended with added qualities of emotional intensity and psychological suggestiveness in the creation of still another current of oral literary expression: the sermons of the Negro preachers.

The rich variety of Afro-American folk imagination and expression made its impact on the consciousness and sensibility of both black and white American writers and has entered the written literature of the United States in many different shapes and ways. This incomparable cultural harvest of the black man's experience, anguish, humor, and creativity in the United States remains a viable and potent source of folk and shared emotional experience which Negro writers in the twentieth century draw upon in accordance with their individual needs, talents, and literary visions. How it can feed diverse individual artists in different ways is evident if you turn to the work of three poets in this anthology, each different from the other: James Weldon Johnson, Sterling Brown, and Langston Hughes. And James Baldwin, who has become a master of the modern American essay as a literary form, has mined nuggets of the Negro preacher's sermon style which he has woven into his high literary mode of individual expression.

The earliest published prose writing by an Afro-American, as far as we know, also dates back more than two centuries. In 1760, the same year that witnessed the publication in Hartford of Jupiter Hammon's first broadside in verse, another slave with the same surname, Briton Hammon, published a narrative in Boston. It was an autobiographical pamphlet entitled *A Narrative of the Uncommon Sufferings and Surprising Deliverance of Briton Hammon, a Negro Man.* Of historical rather than literary interest, this pamphlet foreshadowed a fact of Afro-American literary history: Autobiographical narratives were to become the first genre of prose writing of literary importance.

From the 1780's to the end of the Civil War there was a steady flow of a literature destined in advance to be stillborn, a literature "in spite of," created in defiance of the laws making literacy for slaves a crime. It consisted of autobiographies and narratives written, and sometimes told, by slaves who had escaped slavery. One of the earliest important works of this type is *The Interesting Narrative of the Life of Olondah*

Equiano, or Gustavas Vassa, the African. Vernon Loggins, in his book *The Negro Author in America,* affirmed: "At the time it was published, in 1789, few books had been produced in America which afford such vivid, concrete, and pictur-esque narrative."

Nineteenth-century peaks of this literary form are the nar-ratives by Frederick Douglass, William Wells Brown, and Samuel Ringgold Ward, leading Negroes in the antislavery movement. The Autobiography section of this anthology opens with selections from the 1845 *Narrative* of Frederick Douglass.

Another current of prose writing developed simultaneously with the slave narratives—protests against slavery and anti-slavery expository writing. The first noteworthy work in this field, an essay of unmistakable intellectual and stylistic im-portance, was "An Essay on Slavery" signed by "Othello," a Free Negro. This essay appeared in 1788 in two installments in the November and December issues of *American Museum,* one of the four major magazines founded in the United States after the American Revolution. From 1791 to 1796 Benjamin Banneker, the Negro of many talents who was ap-pointed by Thomas Jefferson to the commission which laid out the plans for the city of Washington, published his widely circulated annual *Almanacks.* On August 19, 1791, Banneker sent a letter to Jefferson, who was then Secretary of State, condemning the degradation and barbarism of slavery and ar-guing for recognition of the human worth and equality of "the African race." This letter was published in Philadelphia in 1792 and, until the Civil War, was reprinted countless times as a classic of Negro-American protest against slavery. Some believe that Benjamin Banneker was the author of the anonymous "Othello" essay.

From the first decade of the nineteenth century the protest writings of Lemuel Haynes and Peter Williams are remem-bered. In 1829, David Walker's famous abolitionist pamphlet *Walker's Appeal* was published in Boston and became, in the words of Vernon Loggins, "the most widely circulated work that came from the pen of an American Negro before 1840."

In 1827, *Freedom's Journal,* the first Negro newspaper in the United States, began publication in New York City, four years before the birth of Garrison's famous Abolitionist organ *The Liberator.* The opening editorial in the first issue of the first Negro newspaper (March 16, 1827) declared: "We wish to plead our own cause. Too long have others spo-ken for us. Too long has the publick been deceived by mis-representations, in things which concern us dearly. . . ."

A group of articulate writers, speakers, and fighters against slavery contributed to *Freedom's Journal*, including Samuel Ringgold Ward and William Wells Brown, who attracted public notice with their narratives. Poems by early Negro poets and versifiers were published in *Freedom's Journal* and in *The Liberator*.

We can detect a pattern in the development of Afro-American expression very similar to the general line of development of American writing. The real achievements in imaginative writing follow an initial period of expository, autobiographical, religious, and political writing. Significantly, the first fiction and first play by a Negro came from an active Abolitionist who contributed to *Freedom's Journal*. William Wells Brown, author of many important antislavery articles and books, also wrote the first novel by a Negro in the United States. The book, *Clotel*, was first published in London in 1853. A revised version was printed in the United States in 1864. William Wells Brown also wrote the first play by an American Negro, *The Escape; or, A Leap for Freedom*, published in 1858. Both his novel and play are of slight literary merit, but it is interesting that the Negro antislavery writings spill over into the first works of fiction and drama. Alain Locke, who is represented in the Literary Criticism section of this anthology with two essays, made an interesting point, in an article he wrote for *New World Writing* (1952):

> If slavery molded the emotional and folk life of the Negro, it was the anti-slavery struggle that developed his intellect and spurred him to disciplined, articulate expression. Up to the Civil War, the growing anti-slavery movement was the midwife of Negro political and literary talent.

The modern period of literature by Negro authors, marked by the mastery of literary craftsmanship, achievements in form, and the critical definition of specific literary and cultural problems of Negro Americans within American culture, opens with the 1890's. Paul Laurence Dunbar, Charles Waddell Chesnutt, and W. E. B. Du Bois loom large in these literary beginnings. Poems by Dunbar and Du Bois, a story by Chesnutt, and selections from Du Bois's *The Souls of Black Folk*, respectively, open the Poetry, Fiction, and Literary Criticism sections of this anthology. With the exception of the autobiography of Frederick Douglass, all of the writing by the forty-four Negro American writers in this book is from this "modern" period—predominantly from the 1920's and later—and the selections in all of the four categories into which this anthology is divided extend to prose and poetry of the 1960's.

Very much of the literature created by black American writers in the twentieth century is unknown to the general reading public and little known even to students of American literature. Before any meaningful debate can take place on conflicting critical approaches and interpretations and on analyses of distinctive forms, structures, images, and themes, the literature itself will have to become better known. All too often, and for far too long, it has been a spurned or neglected part of our literary heritage.

The climate of indifference, neglect, or rejection in which this literature has developed is easy to document. Many important books in this field are inaccessible and out of print. One of the finest collections of Negro literature in the world, the Schomburg Collection—which is part of the New York Public Library in Harlem—does not have the budget to maintain itself and its rare books and manuscripts properly. Many public and college libraries have but the sparsest sprinkling of imaginative literature by black Americans. You can form your own idea of this state of affairs by checking in your local library to see how many of the books listed in the Bibliography at the end of this volume are available. In American literature courses in a number of high schools and colleges, books by Ralph Ellison, James Baldwin, and Richard Wright are today assigned and taught. But in most schools the voices of the black writers remain unheard and unknown, and this also holds true for a very large proportion of the nonintegrated or resegregated schools, with their overwhelming numbers of black students.

It is a fact of life that in our day a teacher in a ghetto school in the great cultural center of Boston can be fired for teaching his black students a poem by Langston Hughes. Officially, of course, for teaching an unauthorized poem (what a horrible educational practice, anyhow, that poems need the seals and licenses of some board of approval before they can be read and discussed by students in a free society). But far beyond Boston's school procedures, the question remains: How come the poem of a leading Negro American poet is *not authorized* for teaching in the city's schools, and not only in the ghetto schools?

If you have any questions about the banned poem, "Ballad of the Landlord," you can find it with other poems by Hughes in the Poetry section of this anthology. Boston, of course, is well known for its excessive sensitivity to obscenity.

But the banned poem by Hughes doesn't have any sexual undertones or overtones. Its obscenity in the eyes of the respectable, it would appear, is its harsh illumination of the injustices of slum-life realities.

While the Boston school authorities made news with the severity of their action, the problem is not peculiar to Boston alone. I have taught a special course on the Negro in American literature to urban high school teachers from all over the country. These teachers maintain that there are school authorities in the urban centers who insist the teachers be very wary of, or ignore, works by black writers, because these writings are too disturbing, or too realistic, or too angry, when there are already enough "problems" with the ghetto students. This constitutes a kind of literary or cultural segregation, a stifling of the black literary voices, in addition to being wrong in educational principle. The black students know the confining and frustrating realities of ghetto life as lived experience and need not turn to books for that. But literature by black writers can give the black students a meaningful ordering and illumination of the black experience in this country; it can show them the creative and imaginative power and achievements of the black man and can prove very important psychologically.

I am well aware that many schools in a number of cities have been doing excellent pioneer work in teaching significant works by black writers as an indispensable component of the English curriculum. But this is still too rare in our schools today. The fact that work by Negro American writers can still encounter hostility, suspicion, or no recognition at all, in schools in every part of the country, is part of the problem of the neglect of Negro American literature for reasons which are very frequently not literary.

As a result of the various walls standing between many black writers and the reading audience, large numbers of literate and cultured Americans, including a high proportion of English majors and students of literature in the colleges, are not aware that many meaningful literary works have been created by black Americans and are an organic part of the American literary heritage. Unfortunately we still have to contend, in our study of American literature, with the long and harsh tradition of the rejection of the Negro in our society and the historically built-in tendencies in American culture to ignore or play down the importance of the black Americans as creators of cultural values and aesthetic forms in the United States.

This is not unexplored territory. Many important studies,

anthologies, and specialized collections of writings have been published over the years—predominantly but not exclusively by Negro scholars, critics, writers, and poets. But symptomatic of the long resistance to the proper recognition of the literary works created by black Americans is the fact that, even today, you will search in vain in definitive up-to-date American literary histories, for some of the elementary facts about Negro American writers and writing. You will search in vain in almost all of the standard American literary reference works of today for the "Negro Renaissance" or "Harlem Renaissance," interchangeable terms widely used by students of the Negro in American literature to denote the extensive literary creativity of the New Negro movement that arose in the 1920's. This was the literary explosion that brought into American literature the early works of such writers as Langston Hughes, Alain Locke, Jean Toomer, Claude McKay, Countee Cullen, Sterling Brown, Arna Bontemps, and others, that you will find in this anthology. But our literary histories, with very rare exceptions, simply do not recognize the existence of any flowering of Negro expression, or any specific literary movement of black Americans, worthy of special notice.

This is clear evidence of how much remains to be done to become aware of the full diversity and scope of American literature, to open our ears and eyes to the voices and imaginative creations of black humanity in our midst. That is a prime purpose of this anthology. To bring to the general reading public and to the students of American literature in the high schools and colleges a large and diverse collection of writing by black Americans at a popular price—literature worth reading as literature and worthy, in my opinion, of inclusion in the American literature curriculum in the schools.

I have no special thesis about Negro American literature to advance or prove. If there is anything I would like to emphasize, it is the plural *Voices* in the title of this book, the individuality of each and every black writer, the diversity of styles and approaches to literature, the conflict of ideas, values, and varying attitudes to life, within black America. In my reading and experience I simply have not found any such thing as "the Negro."

Even the name "Negro" is today the subject of intense debate among Negroes. The question has been posed as to whether or not the word "Negro" should be abandoned and replaced by the words "black" or "Afro-American." Lerone Bennett, Jr., in a lengthy and interesting article on this problem in *Ebony* in November, 1967 wrote:

This question is at the root of a bitter national controversy over the proper designation for *identifiable* Americans of African descent. (More than 40 million "white" Americans, according to some scholars, have African ancestors.) A large and vocal group is pressing an aggressive campaign for the use of the word "Afro-American" as the only historically accurate and humanly significant designation of this large and pivotal portion of the American population. This group charges that the word "Negro" is an inaccurate epithet which perpetuates the master-slave mentality in the minds of both black and white Americans. An equally large, but not so vocal, group says the word "Negro" is as accurate and as euphonious as the words "black" and "Afro-American." This group is scornful of the premises of the advocates of change. A Negro by any other name, they say, would be as black and as beautiful—and as segregated. The times, they add, are too crucial for Negroes to dissipate their energy in fratricidal strife over names. But the pro-black contingent contends . . . that names are of the essence of the game of power and control. And they maintain that a change in name will short-circuit the stereotyped thinking patterns that undergird the system of racism in America. To make things even more complicated, a third group, composed primarily of Black Power advocates, has adopted a new vocabulary in which the word "black" is reserved for "black brothers and sisters who are emancipating themselves," and the word "Negro" is used contemptuously for Negroes "who are still in Whitey's bag and who still think of themselves and speak of themselves as Negroes."

In a deeper sense the new challenge to the name "Negro" is a reflection of the challenge to the racist conditions of life identified with the reality of being a Negro in America. It is a part of the fight for new identities and new realities of life for black Americans. *Ebony* and other Negro publications have initiated polls of their readers as to which name they prefer. At this writing, early in 1968, the first incomplete results of these polls are reported and the first choice is for "Afro-American," second choice for "black," and third choice for "Negro."

Because life in the black American community, as in every human community, is characterized by diversity, divisions, and conflicts, there can be no single approach to Negro life, the black experience, or the literature and culture created by Afro-Americans. We would consider America as a whole a very static, drab, and regimented country without the very deep and fundamental differences of opinion which mark our national and cultural life. We would reject any single thesis or sweeping generalization to define the literature or culture of the United States. I don't know why the vigorous debates and sharp political and cultural differences within the black communities should evoke surprise and wonder. Conflict of opinions and values is the way of life of every thinking and human community. The great debates in the black communities of America today only confirm again what needs no confirmation—that the black communities are as human, argumentative, and divided in opinions as any thinking community. For an idea of the different approaches to the literature of black writers by Negro scholars, academic critics, and writers, I have included, as a special feature of this anthology, a section devoted to literary criticism by Negro Americans, ranging chronologically from 1903 to 1967.

American literary criticism largely ignores most of the works by the Afro-American writers. In the last few decades, a few individual Negro writers, namely Ralph Ellison and James Baldwin, have won critical recognition and acclaim as major American authors. To a lesser degree the critical spotlight has also shone on Richard Wright, frequently in terms of his power, drive, and searing anger—but quite often as a negative example, as the archetypal author of the "protest novel," which is so commonly dismissed as a subliterary species.

Rarely are Wright, Ellison, and Baldwin seen and treated, in our general American literary criticism, as part of a bigger and older current of literary expression—a literary tradition created by Americans of African descent, a literary reality which is both organically American, created on American soil in the American language, with the same rights to recognition for its American authenticity as the literature created by the descendants of the immigrants from England and Europe. Rarely is this literature of the Afro-Americans seen by our general literary criticism in its full light and complete complexity. On the one hand it is part of a literature and culture shared with white America as a whole, inevitably shaped in significant part by the dictates of the American language itself and by the forms of literary expression developed in the United States. At the same time, it is also a distinct and special body of literature, in the sense that the historical memories and myths, experiences, and conditions of life of the black Americans have been deliberately kept separate and apart, for generations, from the priority of conditions and values established for white Americans.

There is little general critical recognition of the fact that central metaphors and concepts of Ellison and Baldwin, like "the invisible man" and "nobody knows my name"—the in-

visibility and denial of identity, the facelessness and name-
lessness, which are associated with the Ellison and Baldwin
dramatizations of the alienated Negro in America—are actually
deeply rooted in the group or folk consciousness of black
America and were given literary expression long before Ellison and Baldwin ever appeared on the literary scene.

In the dawn of this century, in *The Souls of Black Folk*
(1903), a classic literary expression of the sensibility, consciousness, and dilemmas of a black American intellectual,
W. E. B. Du Bois wrote:

> After the Egyptian and Indian, the Greek and Roman, the
> Teuton and Mongolian, the Negro is a sort of seventh son,
> born with a veil, and gifted with second-sight in this Ameri-
> can world,—a world which yields him no true self-conscious-
> ness, but only lets him see himself through the revelation of
> the other world. It is a peculiar sensation, this double-con-
> sciousness, this sense of always looking at one's self through
> the eyes of others, of measuring one's soul by the tape of a
> world that looks on in amused contempt and pity. One ever
> feels his twoness,—an American, a Negro; two souls, two
> thoughts, two unreconciled strivings; two warring ideals in
> one dark body, whose dogged strength alone keeps it from
> being torn asunder.

Many years later, in his book *Dusk of Dawn* (1940), Du
Bois described the psychological impact of caste segregation
in the following words:

> It is as though one, looking out from a dark cave in a side
> of an impending mountain, sees the world passing and speaks
> to it; speaks courteously and persuasively, showing them how
> these entombed souls are hindered in their natural movement,
> expression, and development; and how their loosening from
> prison would be a matter not simply of courtesy, sympathy,
> and help to them, but aid to all the world. . . . It gradually
> permeates the minds of the prisoners that the people passing
> do not hear; that some thick sheet of invisible but horribly
> tangible plate glass is between them and the world. They get
> excited; they talk louder; they gesticulate. Some of the pass-
> ing world stop in curiosity; these gesticulations seem so point-
> less; they laugh and pass on. They still either do not hear at
> all, or hear but dimly, and even what they hear, they do not
> understand. Then the people within may become hysterical.

The sense of duality, powerlessness, and rejection by a hostile society and environment, as expressed by Du Bois, comes
from the core of the consciousness of black America and is

reiterated time and again, in a multitude of ways, by Negro American writers.

James Weldon Johnson published an article entitled "The Dilemma of the Negro Author" in *The American Mercury* in December, 1928. The title of the article itself sounds the note of duality we heard earlier in Du Bois. Observing that the Negro author faces all of the difficulties common to all writers, Johnson went on to say that "the Aframerican author faces a special problem which the plain American author knows nothing about—the problem of the double audience. It is more than a double audience; it is a divided audience, an audience made up of two elements with differing and often opposite and antagonistic points of view. His audience is always both white America and black America." The theme is insistent: two worlds, two Americas, two antagonistic points of view.

Langston Hughes voiced this sense of division in an early poem, "As I Grew Older," the full text of which you will find in the Poetry section of this anthology:

It was a long time ago
I have almost forgotten my dream
But it was there then,
In front of me,
Bright like a sun—
My dream.

And then the wall rose,
Rose slowly,
Slowly,
Between me and my dream.
Rose slowly, slowly,
Dimming,
Hiding,
The light of my dream.
Rose until it touched the sky—
The wall.

We hear the motif again in a late essay by Richard Wright, "The Literature of the Negro in the United States," articulated this way:

Held in bondage, stripped of his culture, denied family life for centuries, made to labor for others, the Negro tried to learn to live the life of the New World in an atmosphere of rejection and hate. . . . For the development of Negro expression—as well as the whole of Negro life in America—

hovers always somewhere between the rise of man from his ancient, rural way of life to the complex, industrial life of our time. Let me sum up these differences by contrasts; entity vs. identity; pre-individualism vs. individualism; the determined vs. the free. . . . Entity, men integrated with their culture; and identity, men who are at odds with their culture, striving for personal identification.

Richard Wright expressed the duality and the sense of two-ness as a "versus" and identified the search for personal identity with being at odds with the prevailing culture in the United States.

In a symposium of prominent Negro writers broadcast by a New York City radio station in 1961, the moderator, Nat Hentoff, asked the late playwright Lorraine Hansberry the following question:

Miss Hansberry, in writing *A Raisin in the Sun,* to what extent did you feel a double role, both as a kind of social actionist "protester," and as a dramatist?

Lorraine Hansberry answered:

Well, given the Negro writer, we are necessarily aware of a special situation in the American setting. . . . We are doubly aware of conflict, because of the special pressures of being a Negro in America. . . . In my play I was dealing with a young man who would have, I feel, been a compelling object of conflict as a young American of his class of whatever racial background, with the exception of the incident at the end of the play, and with the exception, of course, of character depth, because a Negro character is a reality; there is no such thing as saying that a Negro could be a white person if you just changed the lines or something like this. This is a very arbitrary and superficial approach to Negro character. . . . I started to write about this family as I knew them in the context of those realities which I remembered as being true for this particular given set of people; and, at one point, it was just inevitable that a problem of some magnitude which was racial would intrude itself, because this is one of the realities of Negro life in America. But it was just as inevitable that for a large part of the play, they would be excluded. Because the duality of consciousness is so complete that it is perfectly true to say that Negroes do not sit around twenty-four hours a day, thinking, "I am a Negro."

And Chester Himes, in an essay entitled "Dilemma of the Negro Novelist in U.S." published in 1966 in the miscellaneous collection by various writers, *Beyond the Angry Black,* wrote:

From the start the American Negro writer is beset by conflicts. He is in conflict with himself, with his environment, with his public. The personal conflict will be the hardest. He must decide at the outset the extent of his honesty. He will find it no easy thing to reveal the truth of his experience or even to discover it. He will derive no pleasure from the recounting of his hurts. He will encounter more agony by his explorations into his own personality than most non-Negroes realize. For him to delineate the degrading effects of oppression will be like inflicting a wound upon himself. He will have begun an intellectual crusade that will take him through the horrors of the damned. And this must be his reward for his integrity: he will be reviled by the Negroes and whites alike. Most of all, he will find no valid interpretation of his experiences in terms of human values until the truth be known.

If he does not discover this truth, his life will be forever veiled in mystery, not only to whites, but to himself; and he will be heir to all the weird interpretations of his personality.

Because this is an anthology of literature by black Americans, appearing at a time when the tensions and harsh realities of race relations in the United States are critical and high on the social, economic, and political agendas of the nation, it may also help serve a public function which literature is preeminently qualified to perform: to illuminate the human realities of black America. Without minimizing the value of the factual knowledge offered by history, sociology, anthropology, and economics, literature offers a depth of insight into the hearts and minds of black Americans which cannot be approximated by the social sciences.

The literature in this anthology takes us into the inner worlds of black Americans, as seen and felt from the *inside*. Literature as a way of knowing and perceiving probes beyond the conscious, the fully known, and the fully thought out. With contrast and analogy, imaginative ways of ordering images and values, with metaphor and symbol which suggest and imply the shapes and intimations of things and conditions sensed and known in the psychic subsoil, literature searches and captures human hopes and fears, dreams and nightmares, aspirations and frustrations, desires and resentments, which do not register on the computer cards, statistical surveys, and government reports. If America had only done something about the truths and literary revelations in Richard Wright's *Native Son*, published in 1940, with its profound psychological illumination of how the prison box of the big city ghetto was generating violence and destruction as the only language and means of action that had any validity for the hemmed in Bigger Thomas, living in a world without viable alternatives, moving in an incomprehensible mausoleum of dead dreams and hopes—then our past summers of discontent might have been very different.

There is still another special insight into American life that we get from black writers: the look and the feel and the psychological texture of the behavior of white Americans as it is manifest to black Americans. Here, too, we have an area of great human complexities, of codes of behavior and hidden emotional recesses, of cruelty and guilt, of cold calculation and the irrational, crime and conscience, hate and love. Here we find further illumination of a major concern of modern literature, the walls that isolate and separate man from man and the barriers to human connection and communication, with particular attention to what the "curtain of color" does to people on both sides of such a curtain. If, in addition to aesthetic delight, we turn to literature for its power of human illumination, both as mirror and lamp, then certainly the mirrors and lamps created by the black writers have a special value for America—if we are ready to look at the truths they expose.

2

A long time ago in the literary history of the United States, when the great debate was unfolding on whether and when and *how* a distinctively American literature would develop on this continent, the question of the Negro in American literature was an organic part of the whole discussion. Some of the highly original and nonconformist writers of that day, seeking to probe the uniqueness of America, thought that the United States differed most from England and all other countries in its human composition and evolution, its absorption of people from all the continents, races, and regions of mankind. A truly American literature, these writers believed, would somehow express the new fusion of peoples and races in the new continent, the new human realities and conditions of life in the United States.

This conception was clearly voiced in the dawn of the "Golden Age" of American literature by Margaret Fuller, first editor of the transcendentalist journal *The Dial*, who later joined the staff of the New York *Tribune* as the first professional book reviewer in America. In her landmark essay "American Literature: Its Position in the Present Time, and Prospects for the Future" (1846), a composite of reviews she had first written for the *Tribune*, later published in her two-volume collection of writings *Papers on Literature and Art,* Margaret Fuller wrote:

> We have no sympathy with national vanity. We are not anxious to prove that there is as yet much American literature. Of those who think and write among us in the methods and of the thoughts of Europe, we are not impatient; if their minds are still best adapted to such food and such action. . . . Yet there is often between child and parent a reaction from excessive influence having been exerted, and such a one we have experienced in behalf of our country against England. We use her language and receive in torrents the influence of her thought, yet it is in many respects uncongenial and injurious to our constitution. What suits Great Britain, with her insular position and consequent need to concentrate and intensify her life, her limited monarchy and spirit of trade, does not suit a mixed race continually enriched with new blood from other stocks the most unlike that of our first descent, with ample field and verge enough to range in and leave every impulse free, and abundant opportunity to develop a genius wide and full as our rivers. . . . That such a genius is to rise and work in this hemisphere we are confident; equally so that scarce the first faint streaks of that day's dawn are yet visible. . . . That day will not rise till the fusion of races among us is more complete. It will not rise till this nation shall attain sufficient moral and intellectual dignity to prize moral and intellectual no less highly than political freedom. . . .

A decade later, in the high tide of the "American Renaissance," Walt Whitman wrote in his Preface to the first (1855) edition of *Leaves of Grass:*

> Here is not merely a nation but a teeming nation of nations. . . . The American poets are to enclose old and new for America is the race of races. Of them a bard is to be commensurate with a people. To him the other continents arrive as contributions. . . . he gives them reception for their sake and his own sake.

Almost a century later, the American poet William Carlos Williams in his prose volume of poetic insights and interpretations of the American heritage, *In the American Grain,* wrote:

> The colored men and women whom I have known intimately have a racial character which has impressed me. I have not much bothered to know why, exactly, this has been so—
> The one thing that never seems to occur to anybody is that

the negroes have a quality which they have brought to America. . . . Poised against the *Mayflower* is the slave ship—manned by Yankees and Englishmen—bringing another race to try upon the New World. . . . There is a solidity, a racial irreducible minimum, which gives them poise in a world in which they have no authority.

The hopeful vision of Margaret Fuller, Walt Whitman, and many others—that the United States would realize the promise and potential of its genius by transcending racial exclusiveness and welcoming the contributions and qualities brought to this continent by all races and continents—clashed, and clashes to this day, with a tenacious, strong, and contrary current in American culture. It is in conflict with a cultural attitude and posture which Professor Horace M. Kallen, in his book *Cultural Pluralism and the American Idea* (1956), has designated as "a racism in culture":

It claimed that the American Idea and the American Way were hereditary to the Anglo-Saxon stock and to that stock only; that other stocks were incapable of producing them, learning them and living them. If, then, America is to survive as a culture of creed and code, it can do so only so long as the chosen Anglo-Saxon race retains its integrity of flesh and spirit and freely sustains and defends their American expression against alien contamination.

The famous Gunnar Myrdal study of the American Negro problem, published in 1944, dealt with this same reality in a strictly sociological context, and called it "the anti-amalgamation doctrine." This doctrine is the opposite of the "melting pot" theory, which envisaged the assimilation and amalgamation of the various streams of white immigrants to this country into an American synthesis. The "anti-amalgamation doctrine" works in reverse and is described as follows in the Myrdal report:

The Negroes, on the other hand, are commonly assumed to be unassimilable, and this is the reason why the Negro problem is different from the ordinary minority problem in America. The Negroes are set apart, together with other colored peoples, principally the Chinese and Japanese. While all other groups are urged to become Americanized as quickly and completely as possible, the colored peoples are excluded from assimilation. (*Quoted from the Condensed Version of the Myrdal study* The Negro in America *(1964) by Arnold Rose.*)

We can detect signs and echoes of this "racism in culture,"

this "anti-amalgamation doctrine," which is rooted so deeply in the American consciousness and American social practices, in white America's critical approaches to the Negro in American literature. I hasten to make clear that I am not saying that all American critics, writers, and readers are racists. What I am saying is that it is very difficult to maintain, in theory and practice, that the Negro is unassimilable, so different and inherently incapable of fitting into America like other people that he must be kept separate and apart, and at the same time see that this despised Negro has been, and is, a real and significant creator of American cultural values and aesthetic forms. Racism and currents of conflict with racism, including the resistance to racism of black America, are organic elements in the dynamics of American culture. And, since the pressures of racism in American life and thinking remain more powerful and pervasive than the significant but weaker currents of antiracism, inescapably racist attitudes often spill over into the literary domain and blur America's literary and critical vision.

Evidence of how the pressures of racism penetrate literature can be found in the crowded gallery of stereotyped Negro characters in American fiction and drama—certainly not all Negro characters by white writers, but quite predominantly: the servile Negro, the comic Negro, the savage Negro. The opening lines of Sterling Brown's book *The Negro in American Fiction* (1937) declare bluntly: "The treatment of the Negro in American fiction, since it parallels his treatment in American life, has naturally been noted for injustice. Like other oppressed and exploited minorities, the Negro has been interpreted in a way to justify his exploitation."

Ralph Ellison, in an early essay now included in his book *Shadow and Act,* wrote: "Thus it is unfortunate for the Negro that the most powerful formulations of modern American fictional works have been so slanted against him that when he approaches for a glimpse of himself he discovers an image drained of humanity."

The racist attitudes and feelings which have spawned the well-exposed stereotypes of Negro character in American imaginative literature have also been responsible for distortions of critical criteria and for the double standards and special criteria we often encounter in American literary criticism when the works of Afro-American writers are discussed. Whether it stems from a fear of looking at the blackness of the black experience in America and the human consequences of American racism or whether it stems from some cultural variation of the doctrine of the "unassimilability" of the Negro, the fact is that we do encounter in American literary criticism various forms of rejection and negation of the meaning and value of the human experience of the Negro in America.

I shall later offer the evidence on which I base this assertion, but first I want to contrast the very common sympathetic approaches of modern literary criticism to the particularity and otherness of regional and ethnic individuality, as primary proof of why I think there is a reverse tendency in American criticism, a tendency to reject the unique value of the ethnic individuality of the Negro. What seems to be frequently reversed when the Negro enters the picture are the critical criteria—commonly accepted by more than one school of modern literary criticism—that literature is the art of the particular and individual, that the universal in literature is most fully achieved in the depth and completeness with which the uniqueness of the individual is portrayed, and that human freedom is a valid subject for artistic and literary exploration.

Let us see how some modern critics and writers approach and appreciate the particular ethnic and regional literary worlds of writers who are not Negro.

Albert Camus, the French writer of Algerian birth, declared in an interview included in his book *Resistance, Rebellion, and Death:* "No one is more closely attached to his Algerian province than I, and yet I have no trouble feeling a part of French tradition. . . . Silone [the Italian writer] speaks to all of Europe, and the reason I feel so close to him is that he is also so unbelievably rooted in his national and even provincial tradition."

William Faulkner declared in his well-known *Paris Review* interview: "Beginning with *Sartoris* I discovered that my own little postage stamp of native soil was worth writing about and that I would never live long enough to exhaust it. . . ."

Isaac Bashevis Singer, the Jewish writer who came to the United States from Poland in 1935, writes in Yiddish and has been widely hailed as a significant figure in the contemporary literary scene since his works began appearing in English in the 1950's, wrote in an article published in *Book World* early in 1968: "But the masters of literary prose have seldom left their territorial and cultural frontiers. There is no such thing as the international novel or international drama. Literature is by its very nature bound to a people, a region, a language, even a dialect."

James Joyce, writing outside his native Ireland, created his

entire fictional world out of Dubliners, and this was no bar to
his universal recognition as a giant of modern fiction.

W. B. Yeats, recognized as a major poet of the twentieth
century, is not dismissed by any critic as "not universal" because he gave full expression to his Irish self, nor is he
dubbed a "protest" propagandist by any serious critic because
he stressed the thematic literary inspiration he derived from
the Irish freedom movement. Yeats shed much light on the
question I am now trying to examine in his essay "A General
Introduction For My Work," written in 1937 for a complete
edition of his works which did not appear, and later incorporated into his book *Essays and Introductions* (1961). Stating
as his "first principle" that "a poet writes always of his personal life, in his finest work out of its tragedy, whatever it be,
remorse, lost love, or loneliness," Yeats went on to say that
he found his subject matter in the Irish resistance movement.
He stated it in a very personal way: "It was through the old
Fenian leader John O'Leary I found my theme." He speaks
of O'Leary's long imprisonment, longer banishment, his
pride, his integrity, and his dream—the dream of Irish freedom—that nourished and attracted young Irishmen to him
and attracted the young Yeats too. He recalled that at the
time he read only romantic literature and the Irish poets,
some of which was not good poetry at all, and he added:
"But they had one quality I admired and admire: they were
not separated individual men; they spoke or tried to speak
out of a people to a people; behind them stretched the generations."

This is a quality we also find, in a different way, in the
works of the Negro writers in which we can also feel this
sense of a people speaking out to a people, with a sense of
the generations behind: mythic memories of the remote African past, memories of slavery and common experiences in
America.

Yeats, of course, as an artist, voiced his strong hatred of
didactic literature but at the same time took pains to disavow
any idea that his Irish self separated him from world literature and humanity as a whole. Later in this same essay Yeats
wrote:

> I hated and still hate with an ever growing hatred the liter-
> ature of the point of view. I wanted, if my ignorance permit-
> ted, to get back to Homer, to those that fed at his table. I
> wanted to cry as all men cried, to laugh as all men laughed,
> and the young Ireland poets when not writing mere politics
> had the same want, but they did not know that the common
> and its befitting language is the research of a lifetime, and

when found may lack popular recognition. . . . If Irish literature goes on as my generation planned it, it may do something to keep the "Irishry" living. . . .

In his poetic approach, Yeats united three components
which to others may seem irreconcilable or incompatible: to
express the personal and private self, to express the common
humanity the individual shares with all men, and to express
the ethnic or racial self with its particular mythology and cultural past. If for "Irishry" we substitute black or Negro consciousness we can see that the best of the Afro-American
writers have been struggling to express and blend the three
components Yeats speaks of and a fourth as well, which has
made the situation of the black writer in America even more
complex: their personal selves, their universal humanity, the
particular qualities and beauty of their blackness and ethnic
specificity, and their American selves. These are not separate
and boxed off compartments of the mind and soul, but the
inseparable and intermingled elements of a total human
being, of a whole person who blends diversities within himself. This is the rich blend we find in the best of the Negro
American artists.

The significance of Yeats' experience and point of view for
an understanding of certain aspects of American literature is
stressed, in a different way and in another context, by
Cleanth Brooks in his book *William Faulkner: The Yoknapatawpha Country*. Brooks writes:

> Any Southerner who reads Yeats' *Autobiographies* is
> bound to be startled, over and over again, by the analogies
> between Yeats' "literary situation" and that of the Southern
> author: the strength to be gained from the writer's sense of
> belonging to a living community and the special focus upon
> the world bestowed by one's having a precise location in time
> and history.

Certainly the Negro writer has this "sense of belonging to
a living community" which should be appreciated as a source
of strength. But the Negro writer and Negro community in
the United States have historically been denied the advantages "bestowed by one's having a precise location in time
and history." The Negro in America has been denied a
proper location and place, has been in perpetual motion
searching for a proper place he could call home. During slavery, the flight to freedom was the goal—the search for a
home, a haven, the search for a possibility of secure belonging. After the Civil War, and to this day, this historical real-

ity has expressed itself in the great migration from the South to the North and the patterns of flight and migration which are inherent in the spatial and plot movements in the novels of Richard Wright, Ralph Ellison, and James Baldwin. This opposite reality, of uprooting and dislocation, gave the Negro writer, to use the language of Brooks, a different "special focus upon the world," a focus of *denial* of a place, which we hear so clearly as far back as in the spirituals.

Here is how this theme is expressed time and again in lines chosen at random from different spirituals.

I'm rolling through an unfriendly worl'.

———

Sometimes I feel like a motherless child,
A long way from home. . . .

———

Swing low, sweet chariot,
Coming for to carry me home. . . .

———

I got a home in dat rock,
Don't you see? . . .
Poor man Laz'rus, poor as I,
When he died he found a home on high,
He had a home in dat rock,
Don't you see?

———

Deep river, my home is over Jordan.

———

I am a poor pilgrim of sorrow. . . .
I'm tryin' to make heaven my home.

Sometimes I am tossed and driven.
Sometimes I don't know where to roam.
I've heard of a city called heaven.
I've started to make it my home.

American literary criticism has still not come to terms with the "special focus upon the world" that the realities of being a black man in America have created for the Negro writers. And all too often the critical assumptions articulated by Camus, Faulkner, Singer, and Yeats are reversed into some kind of special critical doctrine for the black writer which seems to say or imply that to be meaningful for America, to be universal, the black writer has to be *other* than Negro, *other* than racial, *other* than what he actually and truly is.

What about the evidence for this statement? Let me begin with Louis Simpson, a fine contemporary American poet with a liberal and humane sensibility. When *Selected Poems* by Gwendolyn Brooks was published, he reviewed it among a group of new volumes of verse, in *Book Week* (October 27, 1963). Simpson wrote:

> Gwendolyn Brooks' *Selected Poems* contain some lively pictures of Negro life. I am not sure it is possible for a Negro to write well without making us aware he is a Negro; on the other hand, if being a Negro is the only subject, the writing is not important. . . . Miss Brooks must have had a devil of a time trying to write poetry in the United States, where there has been practically no Negro poetry worth talking about.

Why is writing about "being a Negro" a subject which "is not important"?—why, unless you somehow feel or believe that being a Negro is not important or that Negro life doesn't have values or meanings that are important? And why should there be anything wrong with our being aware of the Negro as author, anymore than it is wrong for us to be aware that Yeats is Irish and that Isaac Bashevis Singer is Jewish and that Ignazio Silone is Italian and that Dostoyevsky is unmistakably Russian and that Faulkner is very much a Mississippian? And why so cavalierly dismiss practically all Negro poetry in the United States with one fell swoop?

Or take another example, this one from academic criticism by Marcus Klein, a member of the Barnard College faculty. In his book *After Alienation: American Novels in Mid-Century* he devotes two chapters to Ralph Ellison and James Baldwin and considers them very seriously. He writes:

> But what seems characteristic of major Negro literature since mid-century is an urgency on the part of writers to be more than merely Negro. . . . The time has seemed to urge upon him [the Negro writer], rather, a necessity to discover his nonracial identity within the circumstances of race.

Why this emphasis on being more than "merely Negro" and "nonracial identity"? Perhaps the clearest answer is provided in a critical statement by William Faulkner. In the rich and complex fictional world of Faulkner we encounter many Negro characters, ranging from Negro stereotypes tainted by the racism of their Mississippi origin to Negro characters of great artistic stature, with depth and dignity and profound symbolic meaning, like Sam Fathers and Lucas Beauchamp in

Go Down, Moses. As man and critic, Faulkner, on numerous occasions, expressed the basic racist assumptions and attitudes of his society and his Mississippi environment, which Faulkner, the artist—at his best, but not always—succeeded in transcending. Let us look at one of his public nonliterary statements. In a speech delivered at the University of Virginia (February 20, 1958) and published in his book *Essays, Speeches and Public Letters,* Faulkner said:

Perhaps the Negro is not yet capable of more than second class citizenship. His tragedy may be that so far he is competent for equality only in the ratio of his white blood. . . . For the sake of argument, let us agree that as yet the Negro is incapable of equality for the reason that he could not hold and keep it even if it were forced on him with bayonets; that once the bayonets were removed, the first smart and ruthless man black or white who came along would take it away from him, because he, the Negro, is not yet capable of, or refuses to accept, the responsibilities of equality.

So we, the white man, must take him in hand and teach him that responsibility. . . . Let us teach him that, in order to be free and equal, he must first be worthy of it, and then forever afterward work to hold and keep and defend it. He must learn to cease forever more thinking like a Negro and acting like a Negro. This will not be easy for him.

Here we have the crux of the problem: the rejection by powerful forces in American life and thought of any positive qualities and values, in Negro life—the negation by cultivated people, by artists and poets, of the worth of "being a Negro" and "thinking like a Negro" and "acting like a Negro." In short, the repudiation of Negro identity and the vicious circle: on the one hand, the pressure to blot out the blackness of the black man, the pressure to make him like a white man —and, at the same time, the unrelenting pressure to slam the door of white society in his face and say: "Negro, keep out!"

These approaches to Negro life and literature contradict the critical premises voiced by T. S. Eliot in his famous review of James Joyce's *Ulysses,* which became axiomatic for much of modern criticism. Eliot declared that "in creation you are responsible for what you can do with material which you must simply accept. And in this material I include the emotions and feelings of the writer himself, which, for that writer, are simply material which he must accept—not virtues to be enlarged or vices to be diminished." Too much of American literary criticism is still not simply *accepting* the materials of the Negro writer—his subject matter and feelings and emotions, which are part of his material—and, in violation of well-established critical principles, is arguing with the material rather than addressing itself to how the writer has made artistic use of his particular material.

The underlying assumptions of Simpson, Klein, and Faulkner are the antitheses of the premises long held by Negro American writers.

Participating in a radio symposium in New York City in 1961, Langston Hughes said:

> My main material is the race problem—and I have found it most exciting and interesting and intriguing to deal with it in writing, and I haven't found the problem of being a Negro in any sense a hindrance to putting words on paper. It may be a hindrance sometimes to selling them. . . .
>
> Well now, I very often try to use social material in a humorous form and most of my writing from the very beginning has been aimed largely at a Negro reading public, because when I began to write I had no thought of achieving a wide public. My early work was always published in *The Crisis* of the N.A.A.C.P., and then in the *Opportunity* of the Urban League, and then the Negro papers like the Washington *Sentinel* and the Baltimore *Afro-American*, and so on. And I contend that since these things, which are Negro, largely for Negro readers, have in subsequent years achieved world-wide publication—my work has come out in South America, Japan, and all over Europe—that a regional Negro character like Simple, a character intended for the people who belong to his own race, if written about warmly enough, humanly enough, can achieve universality.
>
> And I don't see, as Jimmy Baldwin sometimes seems to imply, any limitations, in artistic terms, in being a Negro. I see none whatsoever. It seems to me that any Negro can write about anything he chooses, even the most narrow problems; if he can write about it forcefully and honestly and truly, it is very possible that that bit of writing will be read and understood, in Iceland or Uruguay.

Hughes was consistent in his position over a long period of years, a position which is really no more than not applying a reverse critical standard to the Negro writer. Some thirty-five years earlier, in his famous article "The Negro Artist and the Racial Mountain" published in *The Nation* (June 23, 1926), Hughes wrote:

> One of the most promising of the young Negro poets said to me once, "I want to be a poet—not a Negro poet," meaning, I believe, "I want to write like a white poet," meaning sub-consciously, "I would like to be a white poet," meaning behind that, "I would like to be white." And I was sorry the

young man said that, for no great poet has ever been afraid of being himself.

In one of his interesting essays, "The Literature of the Negro in the United States," which is included in his book *White Man, Listen!*, Richard Wright stated his views this way:

Around the turn of the century, two tendencies became evident in Negro expression. I'll call the first tendency: The Narcissistic Level, and the second tendency I'll call: The Forms of Things Unknown, which consists of folk utterances, spirituals, blues, work songs, and folklore.

These two main streams of Negro expression—The Narcissistic Level and The Forms of Things Unknown—remained almost distinctly apart until the depression struck our country in 1929. . . . Then there were those who hoped and felt that they would ultimately be accepted in their native land as free men, and they put forth their claims in a language that their nation had given them. These latter were more or less always middle class in their ideology. But it was among the migratory Negro workers that one found, rejected and ignorant though they were, strangely positive manifestations of expression, original contributions in terms of form and content.

Middle class Negroes borrowed the forms of the culture which they strove to make their own, but the migratory Negro worker improvised his cultural forms and filled those forms with a content wrung from a bleak and barren environment, an environment that stung, crushed, all but killed him. . . .

You remember the Greek legend of Narcissus who was condemned by Nemesis to fall in love with his own reflection which he saw in the water of a fountain? Well, the middle class Negro writers were condemned by America to stand before a Chinese Wall and wail that they were like other men, that they felt as others felt. It is this relatively static stance of emotion that I call The Narcissistic Level. These Negroes were in every respect the equal of whites; they were valid examples of personality types of Western culture; but they lived in a land where even insane white people were counted above them. They were men whom constant rejection had rendered impacted of feeling, choked of emotion. . . .

While this was happening in the upper levels of Negro life, a chronic and grinding poverty set in in the lower depths. Semi-literate black men and women drifted from city to city, ever seeking what was not to be found: jobs, homes, love—a chance to live as free men. . . .

Because I feel personally identified with the migrant Negro, his folk songs, his ditties, his wild tales of bad men; and because my own life was forged in the depths in which they live, I'll tell first of the Forms of Things Unknown. Numerically, this formless folk utterance accounts for the great majority of the Negro people in the United States, and it is my conviction that the subject matter of future novels resides in the lives of these nameless millions.

Wright affirmed not only the distinctive literary values and the rich forms and content forged in the depths and lower depths of urban Negro life, he also insisted on its value to America. Later in this same essay, Wright declared: "We write out of what life gives us in the form of experience. And there is a value in what we Negro writers say. Is it not clear to you that the American Negro is the only group in our nation that consistently and passionately raises the question of freedom?"

More recently, at the American Academy Conference on the Negro American which took place in 1965 and resulted in the two special issues of *Daedalus* devoted to "The Negro American," Ralph Ellison participated in the discussions and said:

> One thing that is not clear to me is the implication that Negroes have come together and decided that we want to lose our identity as quickly as possible. Where does that idea come from? . . . If one assumes that a group, which has existed within this complicated society as long as ours, has failed to develop cultural patterns, views, structures, or whatever other sociological terms one may want to use, then it is quite logical to assume that they would want to get rid of that inhuman condition as quickly as possible. But I, as a novelist looking at Negro life, in terms of its ceremonies, its rituals, and its rather complicated assertions and denials of identity, feel that there are many, many things we would fight to preserve. . . .
>
> There are great ideas of this society which are available to Negroes who have a little consciousness. . . . Contacts are being made. Judgments are being rendered. Choices are being made. I know that in the life styles of any number of groups in the nation, there are many things which Negroes would certainly reject, not because they held them in contempt, but because they do not satisfy our way of doing things and our feeling about things. Sociologists often assert that there is a Negro thing—a timbre of a voice, a style, a rhythm—in all of its positive and negative implications, the expression of a certain kind of American uniqueness. . . . If there is this uniqueness, why on earth would it not in some way be precious to the people who maintain it?

Later in the proceedings, which took the form of an elaborate exchange of views by a group of experts, Ellison added:

One concept that I wish we would get rid of is the concept of a main stream of American culture—which is an exact mirroring of segregation and second class citizenship. . . . The whole problem about whether there is a Negro culture might be cleared up if we said that there were many idioms of American culture, including, certainly, a Negro idiom of American culture in the South. We can trace it in many, many ways. We can trace it in terms of speech idioms, in terms of manners, in terms of dress, in terms of cuisine, and so on. But it is American, and it has existed a long time, it has refinements and crudities. It has all the aspects of a cultural reality. . . .

The feeling that I have about my own group is that it represents certain human values which are unique not in a Negritude sort of way, but in an American way. Because the group has survived, because it has maintained its sense of itself through all these years, it can be of benefit to the total society, the total culture.

John Oliver Killens, novelist and writer in residence at Fisk University, states another important view of a black writer in this way, in his volume of collected essays, *Black Man's Burden* (1965):

And now, in the middle of the twentieth century, I, the Negro, like my counterparts in Asia and Africa and South America and on the islands of the many seas, am refusing to be your "nigger" any longer. Even some of us "favored," "talented," "unusual," ones are refusing to be your educated, sophisticated, split-leveled "niggers" any more. We refuse to look at ourselves through the eyes of white America.

We are not fighting for the right to be like you. We respect ourselves too much for that. When we advocate freedom, we mean freedom for us to be black, or brown, and you to be white, and yet live together in a free and equal society. This is the only way that integration can bring dignity for both of us. . . . My fight is not for racial sameness but for racial equality and against racial prejudice and discrimination. I work for the day when black people will be free of the racist pressures to be white like you; a day when "good hair" and "high yaller" and bleaching cream and hair straighteners will be obsolete. What a tiresome place America would be if freedom meant we all had to think alike or be the same color or wear that same gray flannel suit! That road leads to the conformity of the graveyard!

The black cultural nationalists today not only take for granted the value and distinctness of their blackness but affirm a "black aesthetic" in literature and culture. Very revealing of the divergent and new currents of thinking among black writers today is the issue of the magazine *Negro Digest* for January, 1968. A large part of the magazine is devoted to a survey of the opinions of black writers, which is introduced in the following way by Hoyt W. Fuller, Managing Editor of the publication:

> There is a spirit of revolution abroad in the shadowy world of letters in black America. Not all black writers are attuned to it, of course, and some are even opposed to it which is to be expected also, one supposes. . . . There is, therefore, a wide divergence of opinion among black writers as to their role in society, as to their role in the Black Revolution, as to their role as artists—all these considerations tied into, and touching on, the others. *Negro Digest* polled some 38 black writers, both famous and unknown. . . . The questions elicited from the writers opinions relative to the books and writers which have influenced them, the writers who are "most important" to them in terms of achievement and promise, and what they think about the new movement toward "a black aesthetic" and the preoccupation with "the black experience," aspects of the larger Black Consciousness Movement.

Laurence P. Neal, a young black nationalist writer, expressed this view in the *Negro Digest* poll:

> There is no need to establish a "black aesthetic." Rather, it is important to understand that one already exists. The question is: where does it exist? . . . To explore the black experience means that we do not deny the reality and the power of the slave culture; the culture that produced the blues, spirituals, folk songs, work songs, and "jazz." It means that Afro-American life and its myriad of styles are expressed and examined in the fullest, most truthful manner possible. The models for what Black literature should be are found primarily in our folk culture, especially in the blues and jazz. . . .
>
> Strictly speaking it is not a matter of whether we write protest literature or not. I have written "love" poems that act to liberate the soul as much as any "war" poem I have written. No, it can't simply be about protest as such. Protest literature assumes that the people we are talking to do not understand the nature of their condition. In this narrow context, protest literature is finally a plea to white America for our human dignity. We cannot get it that way. We must address each other. We must touch each other's beauty, wonder, and pain.

Other Negro writers, like Saunders Redding and Robert Hayden, rejected the idea of a "black aesthetic." Redding asserted that "aesthetics has no racial, national or geographical boundaries," and Robert Hayden voiced sharp disagreement with the cultural black nationalism of LeRoi Jones. Poet and novelist Margaret Walker, on the other hand, wrote:

> The "black aesthetic" has a rich if undiscovered past. This goes back in time to the beginning of civilization in Egypt, Babylonia, India, China, Persia, and all the Islamic world that precedes the Renaissance of the Europeans. We have lived too long excluded by the Anglo-Saxon aesthetic. . . . Where else should the journey lead? The black writer IS the black experience. How can the human experience transcend humanity? It's the same thing.

The contemporary black writers polled by *Negro Digest* were asked who, in their opinions, was the most important black writer. Richard Wright headed the choices, with Langston Hughes and James Baldwin in second and third place and Ralph Ellison trailing Baldwin.

In reply to the question on "the most important living black poet" LeRoi Jones came out first, with Robert Hayden and Gwendolyn Brooks in second and third place and Margaret Walker in fourth.

This is a time of great liveliness, controversy, and creativity in the black literary world in the United States. The pages of *Negro Digest* month after month reflect the vitality of the black literary scene, and new literary publications are coming forward, like *The Journal of Black Poetry* and the Broadsides Press, which publishes black poetry. New literary voices are being heard, like those in *From the Ashes,* the collection of writing by the writers in Budd Schulberg's workshop in Watts, and in *ex umbra,* the magazine of the arts produced by the black students at North Carolina College at Durham.

I close this anthology reluctantly with the feeling that so much is happening and being born that it would be good to keep the book open and bring in still more of the new. But the end of this anthology is not conclusion, I hope, but further beginnings: greater appreciation of what black writers have contributed and are contributing to the diversity of American literature, and movement towards greater inclusion of works by Negro writers in our American literature courses in the high schools and colleges.

ABRAHAM CHAPMAN

Wisconsin State University—Stevens Point

1.

Fiction

CHARLES W. CHESNUTT (1858–1932)

American Negroes were writing and publishing fiction for nearly four decades before Charles Waddell Chesnutt's first short story appeared in The Atlantic Monthly *in 1887. But Chesnutt is commonly considered the first Negro writer in the United States to master the short story form and the craft of fiction. He succeeded during his lifetime in establishing national literary reputation as a novelist and short story writer. Born in Cleveland, Ohio, his biography first reverses, then reenacts, the dominant south-to-north migratory pattern of Negro life in the United States. He lived in North Carolina from the age of eight until he was twenty-five and dug deep into the Negro folklore and folkways of the South, which later found literary expression in his fiction. He left North Carolina in 1883 for New York, where he worked as a stenographer for Dow Jones, the commercial reporting agency. Chesnutt finally returned to Cleveland for the rest of his life,*

*where he worked as a commercial and legal stenographer.
During the early part of his writing career his identity as a
Negro was concealed. Walter Hines Page, editor of* The Atlantic Monthly *when Chesnutt's stories were first being published there, believed that revealing the author's race
would harm the reception of his work and so kept it a secret
for close to a decade. In* The Atlantic Monthly *of May, 1900,
William Dean Howells published an article entitled "Mr.
Charles W. Chesnutt's Stories." The tone of the article
reflects what a novelty fiction by an American Negro was to
the American reading public of that day, though Howells emphasized that Chesnutt merited critical acclaim for his
achievement as an artist and not for any reasons of race. As
Howells put it:*

> Now, however, it is known that the author of this story
> ["The Wife of His Youth"] is of Negro blood—diluted, in-
> deed, in such measure that if he did not admit this descent
> few would imagine it, but still quite of that middle world,
> which lies next, though wholly outside, our own. Since his
> first story appeared he has contributed several others to these
> pages, and he now makes a showing palpable to criticism in a
> volume called The Wife of His Youth, and Other Stories of
> the Color Line; a volume of Southern sketches called The
> Conjure Woman; and a short life of Frederick Douglass in
> the Beacon Series of biographies. . . . But the volumes of fic-
> tion *are* remarkable above many, above most short stories by
> people entirely white. . . . It is not from their racial interest
> that we could first wish to speak of them, though that must
> have a very great and very just claim upon the critic. It is
> much more simply and directly, as works of art, that they
> make their appeal, and we must allow the force of this quite
> independently of the other interest.

*Chesnutt studied law and passed the Ohio bar examination in
1887, with unusually high scores, but never practiced law because he found legal stenography a more lucrative profession.
From 1905 until his death in 1932 Chesnutt wrote no further
fiction. The Spingarn Gold Medal was awarded to Chesnutt
in 1928 for his "pioneer work as a literary artist depicting the
life and struggle of Americans of African descent." He is represented here by one of his last stories, "Baxter's Procrustes,"
taken from* The Atlantic Monthly, *June, 1904.*

Baxter's Procrustes

Baxter's Procrustes is one of the publications of the Bodleian Club. The Bodleian Club is composed of gentlemen of culture, who are interested in books and book-collecting. It was named, very obviously, after the famous library of the same name, and not only became in our city a sort of shrine for local worshipers of fine buildings and rare editions, but was visited occasionally by pilgrims from afar. The Bodleian has entertained Mark Twain, Joseph Jefferson, and other literary and histrionic celebrities. It possesses quite a collection of personal mementos of distinguished authors, among them a paperweight which once belonged to Goethe, a lead pencil used by Emerson, an autograph letter of Matthew Arnold, and a chip from a tree felled by Mr. Gladstone. Its library contains a number of rare books, including a fine collection on chess, of which game several of the members are enthusiastic devotees.

The activities of the club are not, however, confined entirely to books. We have a very handsome clubhouse, and much taste and discrimination have been exercised in its adornment. There are many good paintings, including portraits of the various presidents of the club, which adorn the entrance hall. After books, perhaps the most distinctive feature of the club is our collection of pipes. In a large rack in the smoking-room—really a superfluity, since smoking is permitted all over the house—is as complete an assortment of pipes as perhaps exists in the civilized world. Indeed, it is an unwritten rule of the club that no one is eligible for membership who cannot produce a new variety of pipe, which is filed with his application for membership, and, if he passes, deposited with the club collection, he, however, retaining the title in himself. Once a year, upon the anniversary of the death of Sir Walter Raleigh, who, it will be remembered, first introduced tobacco into England, the full membership of the club, as a rule, turns out. A large supply of the very best smoking mixture is laid in. At nine o'clock sharp each member takes his pipe from the rack, fills it with tobacco, and then the whole club, with the president at the head, all smoking furiously, march in solemn procession from room to room, upstairs and downstairs, making the tour of the clubhouse and returning to the smoking-room. The president then delivers an address, and each member is called upon to say something, either by way of a quotation or an original sentiment, in praise of the virtues of nicotine. This ceremony—facetiously known as "hitting the pipe"—being thus concluded, the membership pipes are carefully cleaned out and replaced in the club rack.

As I have said, however, the *raison d'être* of the club, and the feature upon which its fame chiefly rests, is its collection of rare books, and of these by far the most interesting are its own publications. Even its catalogues are works of art, published in numbered editions, and sought by libraries and book-collectors. Early in its history it began the occasional publication of books which should meet the club standard— books in which emphasis should be laid upon the qualities that make a book valuable in the eyes of collectors. Of these, age could not, of course, be imparted, but in the matter of fine and curious bindings, of hand-made linen papers, of uncut or deckle edges, of wide margins and limited editions, the club could control its own publications. The matter of contents was, it must be confessed, a less important consideration. At first it was felt by the publishing committee that nothing but the finest products of the human mind should be selected for enshrinement in the beautiful volumes which the club should issue. The length of the work was an important consideration,—long things were not compatible with wide margins and graceful slenderness. For instance, we brought out Coleridge's Ancient Mariner, an essay by Emerson, and another by Thoreau. Our Rubáiyát of Omar Khayyám was Heron-Allen's translation of the original MS. in the Bodleian Library at Oxford, which, though less poetical than Fitz-Gerald's, was not so common. Several years ago we began to publish the works of our own members. Bascom's Essay on Pipes was a very creditable performance. It was published in a limited edition of one hundred copies, and since it had not previously appeared elsewhere and was copyrighted by the club, it was sufficiently rare to be valuable for that reason. The second publication of local origin was Baxter's Procrustes.

I have omitted to say that once or twice a year, at a meeting of which notice has been given, an auction is held at the Bodleian. The members of the club send in their duplicate copies, or books they for any reason wish to dispose of, which are auctioned off to the highest bidder. At these sales, which are well attended, the club's publications have of recent years formed the leading feature. Three years ago, number three of Bascom's Essay on Pipes sold for fifteen dollars;—the original cost of publication was one dollar and seventy-five cents.

Later in the evening an uncut copy of the same brought thirty dollars. At the next auction the price of the cut copy was run up to twenty-five dollars, while the uncut copy was knocked down at seventy-five dollars. The club had always appreciated the value of uncut copies, but this financial indorsement enhanced their desirability immensely. This rise in the Essay on Pipes was not without a sympathetic effect upon all the club publications. The Emerson essay rose from three dollars to seventeen, and the Thoreau, being an author less widely read, and by his own confession commercially unsuccessful, brought a somewhat higher figure. The prices, thus inflated, were not permitted to come down appreciably. Since every member of the club possessed one or more of these valuable editions, they were all manifestly interested in keeping up the price. The publication, however, which brought the highest prices, and, but for the sober second thought, might have wrecked the whole system, was Baxter's Procrustes.

Baxter was, perhaps, the most scholarly member of the club. A graduate of Harvard, he had traveled extensively, had read widely, and while not so enthusiastic a collector as some of us, possessed as fine a private library as any man of his age in the city. He was about thirty-five when he joined the club, and apparently some bitter experience—some disappointment in love or ambition—had left its mark upon his character. With light, curly hair, fair complexion, and gray eyes, one would have expected Baxter to be genial of temper, with a tendency toward wordiness of speech. But though he had occasional flashes of humor, his ordinary demeanor was characterized by a mild cynicism, which, with his gloomy pessimistic philosophy, so foreign to the temperament that should accompany his physical type, could only be accounted for upon the hypothesis of some secret sorrow such as I have suggested. What it might be no one knew. He had means and social position, and was an uncommonly handsome man. The fact that he remained unmarried at thirty-five furnished some support for the theory of a disappointment in love, though this the several intimates of Baxter who belonged to the club were not able to verify.

It had occurred to me, in a vague way, that perhaps Baxter might be an unsuccessful author. That he was a poet we knew very well, and typewritten copies of his verses had occasionally circulated among us. But Baxter had always expressed such a profound contempt for modern literature, had always spoken in terms of such unmeasured pity for the slaves of the pen, who were dependent upon the whim of an undiscriminating public for recognition and a livelihood, that no one of us had ever suspected him of aspirations toward publication, until, as I have said, it occurred to me one day that Baxter's attitude with regard to publication might be viewed in the light of effect as well as of cause,—that his scorn of publicity might as easily arise from failure to achieve it, as his never having published might be due to his preconceived disdain of the vulgar popularity which one must share with the pugilist or balloonist of the hour.

The notion of publishing Baxter's Procrustes did not emanate from Baxter,—I must do him the justice to say this. But he had spoken to several of the fellows about the theme of his poem, until the notion that Baxter was at work upon something fine had become pretty well disseminated throughout our membership. He would occasionally read brief passages to a small coterie of friends in the sitting-room or library,—never more than ten lines at once, or to more than five people at a time,—and these excerpts gave at least a few of us a pretty fair idea of the motive and scope of the poem. As I, for one, gathered, it was quite along the line of Baxter's philosophy. Society was the Procrustes which, like the Greek bandit of old, caught every man born into the world, and endeavored to fit him to some preconceived standard, generally to the one for which he was least adapted. The world was full of men and women who were merely square pegs in round holes, and *vice versa.* Most marriages were unhappy because the contracting parties were not properly mated. Religion was mostly superstition, science for the most part sciolism, popular education merely a means of forcing the stupid and repressing the bright, so that all the youth of the rising generation might conform to the same dull, dead level of democratic mediocrity. Life would soon become so monotonously uniform and so uniformly monotonous as to be scarce worth the living.

It was Smith, I think, who first proposed that the club publish Baxter's Procrustes. The poet himself did not seem enthusiastic when the subject was broached; he demurred for some little time, protesting that the poem was not worthy of publication. But when it was proposed that the edition be limited to fifty copies he agreed to consider the proposition. When I suggested, having in mind my secret theory of Baxter's failure in authorship, that the edition would at least be in the hands of friends, that it would be difficult for a hostile critic to secure a copy, and that if it should not achieve success from a literary point of view, the extent of the failure would be limited to the size of the edition, Baxter was visibly impressed. When the literary committee at length decided to request formally of Baxter the privilege of publishing his Pro-

crustes, he consented, with evident reluctance, upon condition
that he should supervise the printing, binding, and delivery of
the books, merely submitting to the committee, in advance,
the manuscript, and taking their views in regard to the bookmaking.

The manuscript was duly presented to the literary committee. Baxter having expressed the desire that the poem be
not read aloud at a meeting of the club, as was the custom,
since he wished it to be given to the world clad in suitable
garb, the committee went even farther. Having entire confidence in Baxter's taste and scholarship, they, with great delicacy, refrained from even reading the manuscript, contenting
themselves with Baxter's statement of the general theme and
the topics grouped under it. The details of the bookmaking,
however, were gone into thoroughly. The paper was to be of
hand-made linen, from the Kelmscott Mills; the type black-
letter, with rubricated initials. The cover, which was Baxter's
own selection, was to be of dark green morocco, with a cap-
and-bells border in red inlays, and doublures of maroon morocco with a blind-tooled design. Baxter was authorized to
contract with the printer and superintend the publication.
The whole edition of fifty numbered copies was to be disposed of at auction, in advance, to the highest bidder, only
one copy to each, the proceeds to be devoted to paying for
the printing and binding, the remainder, if any, to go into the
club treasury, and Baxter himself to receive one copy by way
of remuneration. Baxter was inclined to protest at this, on the
ground that his copy would probably be worth more than the
royalties on the edition, at the usual ten per cent, would
amount to, but was finally prevailed upon to accept an author's copy.

While the Procrustes was under consideration, some one
read, at one of our meetings, a note from some magazine,
which stated that a sealed copy of a new translation of Cam-
panella's Sonnets, published by the Grolier Club, had been
sold for three hundred dollars. This impressed the members
greatly. It was a novel idea. A new work might thus be en-
shrined in a sort of holy of holies, which, if the collector so
desired, could be forever sacred from the profanation of any
vulgar or unappreciative eye. The possessor of such a treasure
could enjoy it by the eye of imagination, having at the same
time the exaltation of grasping what was for others the unat-
tainable. The literary committee were so impressed with this
idea that they presented it to Baxter in regard to the Procrustes. Baxter making no objection, the subscribers who
might wish their copies delivered sealed were directed to no-

tify the author. I sent in my name. A fine book, after all, was an investment, and if there was any way of enhancing its rarity, and therefore its value, I was quite willing to enjoy such an advantage.

When the Procrustes was ready for distribution, each subscriber received his copy by mail, in a neat pasteboard box. Each number was wrapped in a thin and transparent but very strong paper, through which the cover design and tooling were clearly visible. The number of the copy was indorsed upon the wrapper, the folds of which were securely fastened at each end with sealing-wax, upon which was impressed, as a guaranty of its inviolateness, the monogram of the club.

At the next meeting of the Bodleian a great deal was said about the Procrustes, and it was unanimously agreed that no finer specimen of bookmaking had ever been published by the club. By a curious coincidence, no one had brought his copy with him, and the two club copies had not yet been received from the binder, who, Baxter had reported, was retaining them for some extra fine work. Upon resolution, offered by a member who had not subscribed for the volume, a committee of three was appointed to review the Procrustes at the next literary meeting of the club. Of this committee it was my doubtful fortune to constitute one.

In pursuance of my duty in the premises, it of course became necessary for me to read the Procrustes. In all probability I should have cut my own copy for this purpose, had not one of the club auctions intervened between my appointment and the date set for the discussion of the Procrustes. At this meeting a copy of the book, still sealed, was offered for sale, and bought by a non-subscriber for the unprecedented price of one hundred and fifty dollars. After this a proper regard for my own interests would not permit me to spoil my copy by opening it, and I was therefore compelled to procure my information concerning the poem from some other source. As I had no desire to appear mercenary, I said nothing about my own copy, and made no attempt to borrow. I did, however, casually remark to Baxter that I should like to look at his copy of the proof sheets, since I wished to make some extended quotations for my review, and would rather not trust my copy to a typist for that purpose. Baxter assured me, with every evidence of regret, that he had considered them of so little importance that he had thrown them into the fire. The indifference of Baxter to literary values struck me as just a little overdone. The proof sheets of Hamlet, corrected in Shakespeare's own hand, would be well-nigh priceless.

At the next meeting of the club I observed that Thompson and Davis, who were with me on the reviewing committee, very soon brought up the question of the Procrustes in conversation in the smoking-room, and seemed anxious to get from the members their views concerning Baxter's production, I supposed upon the theory that the appreciation of any book review would depend more or less upon the degree to which it reflected the opinion of those to whom the review should be presented. I presumed, of course, that Thompson and Davis had each read the book,—they were among the subscribers,—and I was desirous of getting their point of view.

"What do you think," I inquired, "of the passage on Social Systems?" I have forgotten to say that the poem was in blank verse, and divided into parts, each with an appropriate title.

"Well," replied Davis, it seemed to me a little cautiously, "it is not exactly Spencerian, although it squints at the Spencerian view, with a slight deflection toward Hegelianism. I should consider it an harmonious fusion of the best views of all the modern philosophers, with a strong Baxterian flavor."

"Yes," said Thompson, "the charm of the chapter lies in this very quality. The style is an emanation from Baxter's own intellect,—he has written himself into the poem. By knowing Baxter we are able to appreciate the book, and after having read the book we feel that we are so much the more intimately acquainted with Baxter,—the real Baxter."

Baxter had come in during this colloquy, and was standing by the fireplace smoking a pipe. I was not exactly sure whether the faint smile which marked his face was a token of pleasure or cynicism; it was Baxterian, however, and I had already learned that Baxter's opinions upon any subject were not to be gathered always from his facial expression. For instance, when the club porter's crippled child died Baxter remarked, it seemed to me unfeelingly, that the poor little devil was doubtless better off, and that the porter himself had certainly been relieved of a burden; and only a week later the porter told me in confidence that Baxter had paid for an expensive operation, undertaken in the hope of prolonging the child's life. I therefore drew no conclusions from Baxter's somewhat enigmatical smile. He left the room at this point in the conversation, somewhat to my relief.

"By the way, Jones," said Davis, addressing me, "are you impressed by Baxter's view on Degeneration?"

Having often heard Baxter express himself upon the general downward tendency of modern civilization, I felt safe in discussing his views in a broad and general manner.

"I think," I replied, "that they are in harmony with those of Schopenhauer, without his bitterness; with those of Nordau, without his flippancy. His materialism is Haeckel's, presented with something of the charm of Omar Khayyám."

"Yes," chimed in Davis, "it answers the strenuous demand of our day—dissatisfaction with an unjustified optimism—and voices for us the courage of human philosophy facing the unknown."

I had a vague recollection of having read something like this somewhere, but so much has been written, that one can scarcely discuss any subject of importance without unconsciously borrowing, now and then, the thoughts or the language of others. Quotation, like imitation, is a superior grade of flattery.

"The Procrustes," said Thompson, to whom the metrical review had been apportioned, "is couched in sonorous lines, of haunting melody and charm; and yet so closely inter-related as to be scarcely quotable with justice to the author. To be appreciated the poem should be read as a whole,—I shall say as much in my review. What shall you say of the letter-press?" he concluded, addressing me. I was supposed to discuss the technical excellence of the volume from the connoisseur's viewpoint.

"The setting," I replied judicially, "is worthy of the gem. The dark green cover elaborately tooled, the old English lettering, the heavy linen paper, mark this as one of our very choicest publications. The letter-press is of course De Vinne's best,—there is nothing better on this side of the Atlantic. The text is a beautiful, slender stream, meandering gracefully through a wide meadow of margin."

For some reason I left the room for a minute. As I stepped into the hall, I almost ran into Baxter, who was standing near the door, facing a hunting print of a somewhat humorous character, hung upon the wall, and smiling with an immensely pleased expression.

"What a ridiculous scene!" he remarked. "Look at that fat old squire on that tall hunter! I'll wager dollars to doughnuts that he won't get over the first fence!"

It was a very good bluff, but did not deceive me. Under his mask of unconcern, Baxter was anxious to learn what we thought of his poem, and had stationed himself in the hall that he might overhear our discussion without embarrassing us by his presence. He had covered up his delight at our appreciation by this simulated interest in the hunting print.

When the night came for the review of the Procrustes there was a large attendance of members, and several visitors, among them a young English cousin of one of the members, on his first visit to the United States; some of us had met him at other clubs, and in society, and had found him a very jolly boy, with a youthful exuberance of spirits and a naïve ignorance of things American, that made his views refreshing and, at times, amusing.

The critical essays were well considered, if a trifle vague. Baxter received credit for poetic skill of a high order.

"Our brother Baxter," said Thompson, "should no longer bury his talent in a napkin. This gem, of course, belongs to the club, but the same brain from which issued this exquisite emanation can produce others to inspire and charm an appreciative world."

"The author's view of life," said Davis, "as expressed in these beautiful lines, will help us to fit our shoulders for the heavy burden of life, by bringing to our realization those profound truths of philosophy which find hope in despair and pleasure in pain. When he shall see fit to give to the wider world, in fuller form, the thoughts of which we have been vouchsafed this foretaste, let us hope that some little ray of his fame may rest upon the Bodleian, from which can never be taken away the proud privilege of saying that he was one of its members."

I then pointed out the beauties of the volume as a piece of bookmaking. I knew, from conversation with the publication committee, the style of type and rubrication, and could see the cover through the wrapper of my sealed copy. The dark green morocco, I said, in summing up, typified the author's serious view of life, as a thing to be endured as patiently as might be. The cap-and-bells border was significant of the shams by which the optimist sought to delude himself into the view that life was a desirable thing. The intricate blind-tooling of the doublure shadowed forth the blind fate which left us in ignorance of our future and our past, or of even what the day itself might bring forth. The black-letter type, with rubricated initials, signified a philosophic pessimism enlightened by the conviction that in duty one might find, after all, an excuse for life and a hope for humanity. Applying this test to the club, this work, which might be said to represent all that the Bodleian stood for, was in itself sufficient to justify the club's existence. If the Bodleian had done nothing else, if it should do nothing more, it had produced a masterpiece.

There was a sealed copy of the Procrustes, belonging, I believe, to one of the committee, lying on the table by which I stood, and I had picked it up and held it in my hand for a moment, to emphasize one of my periods, but had laid it down immediately. I noted, as I sat down, that young Hunkin, our English visitor, who sat at the other side of the table, had picked up the volume and was examining it with interest. When the last review was read, and the generous applause had subsided, there were cries for Baxter.

"Baxter! Baxter! Author! Author!"

Baxter had been sitting over in a corner during the reading of the reviews, and had succeeded remarkably well, it seemed to me, in concealing, under his mask of cynical indifference, the exulatation which I was sure he must feel. But this outburst of enthusiasm was too much even for Baxter, and it was clear that he was struggling with strong emotion when he rose to speak.

"Gentlemen, and fellow members of the Bodleian, it gives me unaffected pleasure—sincere pleasure—some day you may know how much pleasure—I cannot trust myself to say it now—to see the evident care with which your committee have read my poor verses, and the responsive sympathy with which my friends have entered into my views of life and conduct. I thank you again, and again, and when I say that I am too full for utterance,—I'm sure you will excuse me from saying any more."

Baxter took his seat, and the applause had begun again when it was broken by a sudden exclamation.

"By Jove!" exclaimed our English visitor, who still sat behind the table, "what an extraordinary book!"

Every one gathered around him.

"You see," he exclaimed, holding up the volume, "you fellows said so much about the bally book that I wanted to see what it was like; so I untied the ribbon, and cut the leaves with the paper knife lying there, and found—and found that there wasn't a single line in it, don't you know!"

Blank consternation followed this announcement, which proved only too true. Every one knew instinctively, without further investigation, that the club had been badly sold. In the resulting confusion Baxter escaped, but later was waited upon by a committee, to whom he made the rather lame excuse that he had always regarded uncut and sealed books as tommy-rot, and that he had merely been curious to see how far the thing could go; and that the result had justified his belief that a book with nothing in it was just as useful to a book-collector as one embodying a work of genius. He offered to pay all the bills for the sham Procrustes, or to replace the blank copies with the real thing, as we might choose. Of course, after such an insult, the club did not care for the poem. He was permitted to pay the expense, however, and it was more than hinted to him that his resignation from the club would be favorably acted upon. He never sent it in, and, as he went to Europe shortly afterwards, the affair had time to blow over.

In our first disgust at Baxter's duplicity, most of us cut our copies of the Procrustes, some of us mailed them to Baxter with cutting notes, and others threw them into the fire. A few wiser spirits held on to theirs, and this fact leaking out, it began to dawn upon the minds of the real collectors among us that the volume was something unique in the way of a publication.

"Baxter," said our president one evening to a select few of us who sat around the fireplace, "was wiser than we knew, or than he perhaps appreciated. His Procrustes, from the collector's point of view, is entirely logical, and might be considered as the acme of bookmaking. To the true collector, a book is a work of art, of which the contents are no more important than the words of an opera. Fine binding is a desideratum, and, for its cost, that of the Procrustes could not be improved upon. The paper is above criticism. The true collector loves wide margins, and Procrustes, being all margin, merely touches the vanishing point of the perspective. The smaller the edition, the greater the collector's eagerness to acquire a copy. There are but six uncut copies left, I am told, of the Procrustes, and three sealed copies, of one of which I am the fortunate possessor."

After this deliverance, it is not surprising that, at our next auction, a sealed copy of Baxter's Procrustes was knocked down, after spirited bidding, for two hundred and fifty dollars, the highest price ever brought by a single volume published by the club.

JEAN TOOMER (1894–1967)

With his single book Cane *(1923), a mosaic of poems, short stories, and intense sketches, Jean Toomer raised the innovation of the literary experimentation of the 20's and the modernist mode to new levels of artistic achievement in racial expression by an American Negro. Profoundly appreciated by other American writers, Toomer's new artistic ways did not win the audience and public recognition merited by his contribution to American writing at that time. The most promising of the talents and original voices of the Negro Renaissance, he died in the obscurity of a rest home near Philadelphia on March 30, 1967. Toomer was born in Washington, D. C., and attended the University of Wisconsin and the City College of New York. He began his literary career in 1918 with poems, sketches and reviews in a variety of national magazines. In 1922 he went to Georgia, where he worked for a while as principal of a school. It was from his contact with Negro life in the deep South that he created the most striking stories and poems in* Cane. *After* Cane, *as Professor Darwin T. Turner noted in a memorial tribute to Toomer: "He wrote; editors refused. Seeking an excuse for failure, he blamed his identification as a Negro. He denied that he came from Negro ancestry. Still the editors refused. . . . He continued to write and rewrite; two novels, two books of poems, a collection of stories, books of nonfiction, two books of aphorisms. But editors never again accepted a book for publication." He lived for a time in the artistic community of Carmel, California, later moving to Taos, New Mexico. Toomer finally settled in Bucks County, Pennsylvania, where he became a "literary ghost," a living writer remembered and revered for over forty years by a small group of critics and literary historians for his literary past. We present two stories from* Cane, *"Karintha," which opens the book as the first in a cycle of stories set in Georgia, and "Blood-Burning Moon," the story which concludes the Georgia cycle.*

Karintha

Her skin is like dusk on the eastern horizon,
O cant you see it, O cant you see it,
Her skin is like dusk on the eastern horizon
. . . When the sun goes down.

Men always wanted her, this Karintha, even as a child, Karintha carrying beauty, perfect as dusk when the sun goes
down. Old men rode her hobby-horse upon their knees.
Young men danced with her at frolics when they should have
been dancing with their grown-up girls. God grant us youth,
secretly prayed the old men. The young fellows counted the
time to pass before she would be old enough to mate with
them. This interest of the male, who wishes to ripen a growing thing too soon, could mean no good to her.

Karintha, at twelve, was a wild flash that told the other
folks just what it was to live. At sunset, where there was no
wind, and the pine-smoke from over by the sawmill hugged
the earth, and you couldnt see more than a few feet in front,
her sudden darting past you was a bit of vivid color, like a
black bird that flashes in light. With the other children one
could hear, some distance off, their feet flopping in the two-
inch dust. Karintha's running was a whir. It had the sound of
the red dust that sometimes makes a spiral in the road. At
dusk, during the hush just after the sawmill had closed down,
and before any of the women had started their supper-getting-
ready songs, her voice, high-pitched, shrill, would put one's
ears to itching. But no one ever thought to make her stop because of it. She stoned the cows, and beat her dog, and
fought the other children. . . . Even the preacher, who
caught her at mischief, told himself that she was as innocently lovely as a November cotton flower. Already, rumors
were out about her. Homes in Georgia are most often built
on the two-room plan. In one, you cook and eat, in the other
you sleep, and there love goes on. Karintha had seen or
heard, perhaps she had felt her parents loving. One could but
imitate one's parents, for to follow them was the way of God.
She played "home" with a small boy who was not afraid to
do her bidding. That started the whole thing. Old men could
no longer ride her hobby-horse upon their knees. But young
men counted faster.

Her skin is like dusk,
O cant you see it,
Her skin is like dusk,
When the sun goes down.

Karintha is a woman. She who carries beauty, perfect as dusk when the sun goes down. She has been married many times. Old men remind her that a few years back they rode her hobby-horse upon their knees. Karintha smiles, and indulges them when she is in the mood for it. She has contempt for them. Karintha is a woman. Young men run stills to make her money. Young men go to the big cities and run on the road. Young men go away to college. They all want to bring her money. These are the young men who thought that all they had to do was to count time. But Karintha is a woman, and she has had a child. A child fell out of her womb onto a bed of pine-needles in the forest. Pine-needles are smooth and sweet. They are elastic to the feet of rabbits . . . A sawmill was nearby. Its pyramidal sawdust pile smouldered. It is a year before one completely burns. Meanwhile, the smoke curls up and hangs in odd wraiths about the trees, curls up, and spreads itself out over the valley . . . Weeks after Karintha returned home the smoke was so heavy you tasted it in water. Some one made a song:

Smoke is on the hills. Rise up.
Smoke is on the hills, O rise
And take my soul to Jesus.

Karintha is a woman. Men do not know that the soul of her was a growing thing ripened too soon. They will bring their money; they will die not having found it out . . . Karintha at twenty, carrying beauty, perfect as dusk when the sun goes down. Karintha. . .

Her skin is like dusk on the eastern horizon,
O cant you see it, O cant you see it,
Her skin is like dusk on the eastern horizon
. . . When the sun goes down.

Goes down . . .

Blood-Burning Moon

Up from the skeleton stone walls, up from the rotting floor boards and the solid hand-hewn beams of oak of the pre-war cotton factory, dusk came. Up from the dusk the full moon came. Glowing like a fired pine-knot, it illumined the great door and soft showered the Negro shanties aligned along the single street of factory town. The full moon in the great door was an omen. Negro women improvised songs against its spell.

Louisa sang as she came over the crest of the hill from the white folks' kitchen. Her skin was the color of oak leaves on young trees in fall. Her breasts, firm and up-pointed like ripe acorns. And her singing had the low murmur of winds in fig trees. Bob Stone, younger son of the people she worked for, loved her. By the way the world reckons things, he had won her. By measure of that warm glow which came into her mind at thought of him, he had won her. Tom Burwell, whom the whole town called Big Boy, also loved her. But working in the fields all day, and far away from her, gave him no chance to show it. Though often enough of evenings he had tried to. Somehow, he never got along. Strong as he was with his hands upon the ax or plow, he found it difficult to hold her. Or so he thought. But the fact was that he held her to factory town more firmly than he thought, for his black balanced, and pulled against, the white of Stone, when she thought of them. And her mind was vaguely upon them as she came over the crest of the hill, coming from the white folks' kitchen. As she sang softly at the evil face of the full moon.

A strange stir was in her. Indolently, she tried to fix upon Bob or Tom as the cause of it. To meet Bob in the cane-brake, as she was going to do an hour or so later, was nothing new. And Tom's proposal which she felt on its way to her could be indefinitely put off. Separately, there was no unusual significance to either one. But for some reason, they jumbled when her eyes gazed vacantly at the rising moon. And from the jumble came the stir that was strangely within her. Her lips trembled. The slow rhythm of her song grew agitant and restless. Rusty black and tan spotted hounds, lying in the dark corners of porches or prowling around back yards, put their noses in the air and caught its tremor. They began plaintively to yelp and howl. Chickens woke up and cackled.

Intermittently, all over the countryside dogs barked and roosters crowed as if heralding a weird dawn or some ungodly awakening. The women sang lustily. Their songs were cotton-wads to stop their ears. Louisa came down into factory town and sank wearily upon the step before her home. The moon was rising towards a thick cloud-bank which soon would hide it.

Red nigger moon. Sinner!
Blood-burning moon. Sinner!
Come out that fact'ry door.

2

Up from the deep dusk of a cleared spot on the edge of the forest a mellow glow arose and spread fan-wise into the low-hanging heavens. And all around the air was heavy with the scent of boiling cane. A large pile of cane-stalks lay like ribboned shadows upon the ground. A mule, harnessed to a pole, trudged lazily round and round the pivot of the grinder. Beneath a swaying oil lamp, a Negro alternately whipped out at the mule, and fed cane-stalks to the grinder. A fat boy waddled pails of fresh-ground juice between the grinder and the boiling stove. Steam came from the copper boiling pan. The scent of cane came from the copper pan and drenched the forest and the hill that sloped to factory town, beneath its fragrance. It drenched the men in the circle seated around the stove. Some of them chewed at the white pulp of stalks, but there was no need for them to, if all they wanted was to taste the cane. One tasted it in factory town. And from factory town one could see the soft haze thrown by the glowing stove upon the low-hanging heavens.

Old David Georgia stirred the thickening syrup with a long ladle, and ever so often drew it off. Old David Georgia tended his stove and told tales about the white folks, about moonshining and cotton picking, and about sweet nigger gals, to the men who sat there about his stove to listen to him. Tom Burwell chewed cane-stalk and laughed with the others till someone mentioned Louisa. Till someone said something about Louisa and Bob Stone, about the silk stockings she must have gotten from him. Blood ran up Tom's neck hotter than the glow that flooded from the stove. He sprang up. Glared at the men and said, "She's my gal." Will Manning laughed. Tom strode over to him. Yanked him up and knocked him to the ground. Several of Manning's friends got up to fight for him. Tom whipped out a long knife and would have cut them to shreds if they hadnt ducked into the woods. Tom had had enough. He nodded to Old David Georgia and swung down the path to factory town. Just then, the dogs started barking and the roosters began to crow. Tom felt funny. Away from the fight, away from the stove, chill got to him. He shivered. He shuddered when he saw the full moon rising towards the cloud-bank. He who didnt give a godam for the fears of old women. He forced his mind to fasten on Louisa. Bob Stone. Better not be. He turned into the street and saw Louisa sitting before her home. He went towards her, ambling, touched the brim of a marvelously shaped, spotted, felt hat, said he wanted to say something to her, and then found that he didnt know what he had to say, or if he did, that he couldnt say it. He shoved his big fists in his overalls, grinned, and started to move off.

"Youall want me, Tom?"

"Thats what us wants, sho, Louisa."

"Well, here I am—"

"An here I is, but that aint ahelpin none, all th same."

"You wanted to say somthing?"

"I did that, sho. But the words is like th spots on dice: no matter how y fumbles em, there's times when they jes wont come. I dunno why. Seems like th love I feels fo yo done stole m tongue. I got it now. Whee! Louisa, honey, I oughtnt tell y, I feel I oughtnt cause yo is young an goes t church an I has had other gals, but Louisa I sho do love y. Lil gal, Ise watched y from them first days when youall sat right there befo yo door befo th well an sang sometimes in a way that like t broke m heart. Ise carried y with me into th fields, day after day, and after that, an' I sho can plow when yo is there, an I can pick cotton. Yassur! Come near beatin Barlo yesterday. I sho did. Yassur! An next year if ole Stone'll trust me, I'll have a farm. My own. My bales will buy yo what y gets from white folks now. Silk stockings an purple dresses —course I dont believe what some folks been whisperin' as t how y gets them things now. White folks always did do for niggers what they likes. An they jes cant help alikin yo, Louisa. Bob Stone likes y. Course he does. But not th way folks is awhisperin. Does he, hon?"

"I dont know what you mean, Tom."

"Course y dont. Ise already cut two niggers. Had t hon, t tell em so. Niggers always tryin t make somethin outa nothin. An then besides, white folks aint up t them tricks so much nowadays. Godam better not be. Leastawise not with you. Cause I wouldnt stand f it. Nassur."

"What would you do, Tom?"

"Cut him jes like I cut a nigger."

"No, Tom—"

"I said I would an there ain't no mo to it. But that aint th talk f now. Sing, honey Louisa, an while I'm listenin t y I'll be makin love."

Tom took her hand in his. Against the tough thickness of his own, hers felt soft and small. His huge body slipped down to the step beside her. The full moon sank upward into the deep purple of the cloud-bank. An old woman brought a lighted lamp and hung it on the common well whose bulky shadow squatted in the middle of the road, opposite Tom and Louisa. The old woman lifted the well-lid, took hold the chain, and began drawing up the heavy bucket. As she did so, she sang. Figures shifted, restless-like, between lamp and window in the front rooms of the shanties. Shadows of the figures fought each other on the gray dust of the road. Figures raised the windows and joined the old woman in song. Louisa and Tom, the whole street, singing:

Red nigger moon. Sinner!
Blood-burning moon. Sinner!
Come out that fact'ry door.

3

Bob Stone sauntered from his veranda out into the gloom of fir trees and magnolias. The clear white of his skin paled, and the flush of his cheeks turned purple. As if to balance this outer change, his mind became consciously a white man's. He passed the house with its huge open hearth which, in the days of slavery, was the plantation cookery. He saw Louisa bent over that hearth. He went in as a master should and took her. Direct, honest, bold. None of this sneaking that he had to go through now. The contrast was repulsive to him. His family had lost ground. Hell no, his family still owned the niggers, practically. Damned if they did, or he wouldnt have to duck around so. What would they think if they knew? His mother? His sister? He shouldnt mention them, shouldnt think of them in this connection. There in the dark he blushed at doing so. Fellows about town were all right, but how about his friends up North? He could see them, incredible, repulsed. They didnt know. The thought first made him laugh. Then, with their eyes still upon him, he began to feel embarrassed. He felt the need of explaining things to them. Explain hell. They wouldnt understand, and moreover, who ever heard of a Southerner getting on his knees to any Yankee, or anyone. No sir. He was going to see Louisa to-night, and love

her. She was lovely—in her way. Nigger way. What way was
that? Damned if he knew. Must know. He'd known her long
enough to know. Was there something about niggers that you
couldnt know? Listening to them at church didnt tell you
anything. Looking at them didnt tell you anything. Talking to
them didnt tell you anything—unless it was gossip, unless
they wanted to talk. Of course, about farming, and licker,
and craps—but those werent nigger. Nigger was something
more. How much more? Something to be afraid of, more?
Hell no. Who ever heard of being afraid of a nigger? Tom
Burwell. Cartwell had told him that Tom went with Louisa
after she reached home. No sir. No nigger had ever been
with his girl. He'd like to see one try. Some position for him
to be in. Him, Bob Stone, of the Stone family, in a scrap with
a nigger over a nigger girl. In the good old days . . . Ha!
Those were the days. His family had lost ground. Not so
much, though. Enough for him to have to cut through old
Lemon's canefield by way of the woods, that he might meet
her. She was worth it. Beautiful nigger gal. Why nigger? Why
not, just gal? No, it was because she was nigger that he went
to her. Sweet . . . The scent of boiling cane came to him.
Then he saw the rich glow of the stove. He heard the voices
of the men circled around it. He was about to skirt the clearing when he heard his own name mentioned. He stopped.
Quivering. Leaning against a tree, he listened.

"Bad nigger. Yassur, he sho is one bad nigger when he gets
started."

"Tom Burwell's been on th gang three times fo cuttin
men."

"What y think he's a gwine t do t Bob Stone?"

"Dunno yet. He aint found out. When he does— Baby!"

"Young Stone aint no quitter an I ken tell y that. Blood of
th old uns in his veins."

"Thats right. He'll scrap, sho."

"Be gettin too hot f niggers round this away."

"Shut up, nigger. Y dont know what y talkin bout."

Bob Stone's ears burned as though he had been holding
them over the stove. Sizzling heat welled up within him. His
feet felt as if they rested on red-hot coals. They stung him to
quick movement. He circled the fringe of the glowing. Not a
twig cracked beneath his feet. He reached the path that led to
factory town. Plunged furiously down it. Halfway along, a
blindness within him veered him aside. He crashed into the
bordering canebrake. Cane leaves cut his face and lips. He
tasted blood. He threw himself down and dug his fingers in
the ground. The earth was cool. Cane-roots took the fever

from his hands. After a long while, or so it seemed to him, the thought came to him that it must be time to see Louisa. He got to his feet and walked calmly to their meeting place. No Louisa. Tom Burwell had her. Veins in his forehead bulged and distended. Saliva moistened the dried blood on his lips. He bit down on his lips. He tasted blood. Not his own blood; Tom Burwell's blood. Bob drove through the cane and out again upon the road. A hound swung down the path before him towards factory town. Bob couldn't see it. The dog loped aside to let him pass. Bob's blind rushing made him stumble over it. He fell with a thud that dazed him. The hound yelped. Answering yelps came from all over the countryside. Chickens cackled. Roosters crowed, heralding the bloodshot eyes of southern awakening. Singers in the town were silenced. They shut their windows down. Palpitant between the rooster crows, a chill hush settled upon the huddled forms of Tom and Louisa. A figure rushed from the shadow and stood before them. Tom popped to his feet.

"Whats y want?"

"I'm Bob Stone."

"Yassur—and I'm Tom Burwell. Whats y want?"

Bob lunged at him. Tom side-stepped, caught him by the shoulder, and flung him to the ground. Straddled him.

"Let me up."

"Yassur—but watch yo doins, Bob Stone."

A few dark figures, drawn by the sound of scuffle, stood about them. Bob sprang to his feet.

"Fight like a man, Tom Burwell, an I'll lick y."

Again he lunged. Tom side-stepped and flung him to the ground. Straddled him.

"Get off me, you godam nigger you."

"Yo sho has started somethin now. Get up."

Tom yanked him up and began hammering at him. Each blow sounded as if it smashed into a precious, irreplaceable soft something. Beneath them, Bob staggered back. He reached in his pocket and whipped out a knife. "That's my game, sho."

Blue flash, a steel blade slashed across Bob Stone's throat. He had a sweetish sick feeling. Blood began to flow. Then he felt a sharp twitch of pain. He let his knife drop. He slapped one hand against his neck. He pressed the other on top of his head as if to hold it down. He groaned. He turned, and staggered towards the crest of the hill in the direction of white town. Negroes who had seen the fight slunk into their homes and blew the lamps out. Louisa, dazed, hysterical, refused to go indoors. She slipped, crumpled, her body loosely propped against the woodwork of the well. Tom Burwell leaned against it. He seemed rooted there.

Bob reached Broad Street. White men rushed up to him. He collapsed in their arms.

"Tom Burwell. . . ."

White men like ants upon a forage rushed about. Except for the taut hum of their moving, all was silent. Shotguns, revolvers, rope, kerosene, torches. Two high-powered cars with glaring search-lights. They came together. The taut hum rose to a low roar. Then nothing could be heard but the flop of their feet in the thick dust of the road. The moving body of their silence preceded them over the crest of the hill into factory town. It flattened the Negroes beneath it. It rolled to the wall of the factory, where it stopped. Tom knew that they were coming. He couldnt move. And then he saw the searchlights of the two cars glaring down on him. A quick shock went through him. He stiffened. He started to run. A yell went up from the mob. Tom wheeled about and faced them. They poured down on him. They swarmed. A large man with dead-white face and flabby cheeks came to him and almost jabbed a gun-barrel through his guts.

"Hands behind y, nigger."

Tom's wrists were bound. The big man shoved him to the well. Burn him over it, and when the woodwork caved in, his body would drop to the bottom. Two deaths for a godam nigger.

Louisa was driven back. The mob pushed in. Its pressure, its momentum was too great. Drag him to the factory. Wood and stakes already there. Tom moved in the direction indicated. But they had to drag him. They reached the great door. Too many to get in there. The mob divided and flowed around the walls to either side. The big man shoved him through the door. The mob pressed in from the sides. Taut humming. No words. A stake was sunk into the ground. Rotting floor boards piled around it. Kerosene poured on the rotting floor boards. Tom bound to the stake. His breast was bare. Nails scratches let little lines of blood trickle down and mat into the hair. His face, his eyes were set and stony. Except for irregular breathing, one would have thought him already dead. Torches were flung onto the pile. A great flare muffled in black smoke shot upward. The mob yelled. The mob was silent. Now Tom could be seen within the flames. Only his head, erect, lean, like a blackened stone. Stench of burning flesh soaked the air. Tom's eyes popped. His head settled downward. The mob yelled. Its yell echoed against the skeleton stone walls and sounded like a hundred yells. Like a

hundred mobs yelling. Its yell thudded against the thick front
wall and fell back. Ghost of a yell slipped through the
flames and out the great door of the factory. It fluttered like
a dying thing down the single street of factory town. Louisa,
upon the step before her home, did not hear it, but her eyes
opened slowly. They saw the full moon glowing in the great
door. The full moon, an evil thing, an omen, soft showering
the homes of folks she knew. Where were they, these people?
She'd sing, and perhaps they'd come out and join her. Perhaps Tom Burwell would come. At any rate, the full moon in
the great door was an omen which she must sing to:

Red nigger moon. Sinner!
Blood-burning moon. Sinner!
Come out that fact'ry door.

RUDOLPH FISHER (1897–1934)

*Prominently associated with the "Negro Renaissance," the lit-
erary movement and fictional portrayal of Harlem in the
1920's, Rudolph Fisher was born in Washington, D. C., and
received degrees from Brown University and Howard University Medical School. Fisher completed his medical studies at
Columbia University, and became a physician-author practic-
ing roentgenology and writing in New York City. His first
short story was published in* The Atlantic Monthly. *Fisher
published two novels and many short stories and sketches of
Harlem during his lifetime. Several of his short stories were
included in annual anthologies of* Best Short Stories. *He is
represented in this anthology by a story he first published in
the Baltimore Afro-American, the famous Negro newspaper.
The story subsequently appeared in* Best Short Stories by
Afro-American Writers (1925–1950), *selected and edited by
Nick Aaron Ford and H. L. Faggett (Boston, 1950).*

Common Meter

The Arcadia, on Harlem's Lenox Avenue, is "The World's Largest and Finest Ballroom—Admission Eighty-Five Cents." Jazz is its holy spirit, which moves it continuously from nine till two every night. Observe above the brilliant entrance this legend in white fire:

TWO — ORCHESTRAS — TWO

Below this in red:

FESS BAXTER'S FIREMEN

Alongside in blue:

BUS WILLIAMS' BLUE DEVILS

Still lower in gold:

HEAR THEM OUTPLAY EACH OTHER

So much outside. Inside, a blazing lobby, flanked by marble stairways. Upstairs, an enormous dance hall the length of a city block. Low ceilings blushing pink with rows of inverted dome-lights. A broad dancing area, bounded on three sides by a wide soft-carpeted promenade, on the fourth by an ample platform accommodating the two orchestras.

People. Flesh. A fly-thick jam of dancers on the floor, grimly jostling each other; a milling herd of thirsty-eyed boys, moving slowly, searchingly over the carpeted promenade; a congregation of languid girls, lounging in rows of easy chairs here and there, bodies and faces unconcerned, dark eyes furtively alert. A restless multitude of empty, romance-hungry lives.

Bus Williams' jolly round brown face beamed down on the crowd as he directed his popular hit—*She's Still My Baby:*

You take her out to walk
And give her baby-talk,
But talk or walk, walk or talk —
    She's still my baby!

But the cheese-colored countenance of Fessenden Baxter, his professional rival, who with his orchestra occupied the adjacent half of the platform, was totally oblivious to *She's Still My Baby.*

Baxter had just caught sight of a girl, and catching sight of girls was one of his special accomplishments. Unbelief, wonder, amazement registered in turn on his blunt, bright features. He passed a hand over his straightened brown hair and bent to Perry Parker, his trumpetist.

"P.P., do you see what I see, or is it only the gin?"

"Both of us had the gin," said P.P., "so both of us sees the same thing."

"Judas Priest! Look at that figure, boy!"

"Never was no good at figures," said P.P.

"I've got to get me an armful of that baby."

"Lay off, papa," advised P.P.

"What do you mean, lay off?"

"Lay off. You and your boy got enough to fight over already, ain't you?"

"My boy?"

"Your boy, Bus."

"You mean that's Bus Williams' folks?"

"No lie. Miss Jean Ambrose, lord. The newest hostess. Bus got her the job."

Fess Baxter's eyes followed the girl. "Oh, he got her the job, did he?—Well, I'm going to fix it so she won't need any job. Woman like that's got no business working anywhere."

"Gin," murmured P.P.

"Gin hell," said Baxter. "Gunpowder wouldn't make a mama look as good as that."

"Gunpowder wouldn't make *you* look so damn good, either."

"You hold the cat's tail," suggested Baxter.

"I'm tryin' to save yours," said P.P.

"Save your breath for that horn."

"Maybe," P.P. insisted, "she ain't so possible as she looks."

"Huh. They can all be taught."

"I've seen some that couldn't."

"Oh you have?—Well, P.P., my boy, remember, that's you."

Beyond the brass rail that limited the rectangular dance area at one lateral extreme there were many small round tables and clusters of chairs. Bus Williams and the youngest hostess occupied one of these tables while Fess Baxter's Firemen strutted their stuff.

Bus ignored the tall glass before him, apparently endeavoring to drain the girl's beauty with his eyes; a useless effort, since it lessened neither her loveliness nor his thirst. Indeed the more he looked the less able was he to stop looking. Oblivious, the girl was engrossed in the crowd. Her amber skin grew clearer and the roses imprisoned in it brighter as her merry black eyes danced over the jostling company.

"Think you'll like it?" he asked.

"Like it?" She was a child of Harlem and she spoke its language. "Boy, I'm having the time of my life. Imagine getting paid for this!"

"You ought to get a bonus for beauty."

"Nice time to think of that—after I'm hired."

"You look like a full course dinner—and I'm starved."

"Hold the personalities, papa."

"No stuff. Wish I could raise a loan on you. Baby—what a roll I'd tote."

"Thanks. Try that big farmer over there hootin' it with Sister Full-bosom. Boy, what a side-show they'd make!"

"Yea. But what I'm lookin' for is a leadin' lady."

"Yea? I got a picture of any lady leadin' you anywhere."

"You could, Jean."

"Be yourself, brother."

"I ain't bein' nobody else."

"Well, be somebody else, then."

"Remember the orphanage?"

"Time, papa. Stay out of my past."

"Sure—if you let me into your future."

"Speaking of the orphanage—?"

"You wouldn't know it now. They got new buildings all over the place."

"Somehow that fails to thrill me."

"You always were a knock-out, even in those days. You had the prettiest hair of any of the girls out there—and the sassiest hip-switch."

"Look at Fred and Adele Astaire over there. How long they been doing blackface?"

"I used to watch you even then. Know what I used to say?"

"Yea. 'Toot-a-toot-toot' on a bugle."

"That ain't all. I used to say to myself, 'Boy, when that sister grows up, I'm going to—'."

Her eyes grew suddenly onyx and stopped him like an abruptly reversed traffic signal.

"What's the matter?" he said.

She smiled and began nibbling the straw in her glass.

"What's the matter, Jean?"

"Nothing, Innocence. Nothing. Your boy plays a devilish one-step, doesn't he?"

"Say. You think I'm jivin', don't you?"

"No, darling. I think you're selling insurance."

"Think I'm gettin' previous, just because I got you the job."

"Funny, I never have much luck with jobs."

"Well, I don't care what you think, I'm going to say it."

"Let's dance."

"I used to say to myself, 'When that kid grows up, I'm going to ask her to marry me.'"

She called his bluff. "Well, I'm grown up."

"Marry me, will you, Jean?"

Her eyes relented a little in admiration of his audacity. Rarely did a sober aspirant have the courage to mention marriage.

"You're good, Bus. I mean, you're good."

"Every guy ain't a wolf, you know, Jean."

"No. Some are just ordinary meat-hounds."

From the change in his face she saw the depth of the thrust, saw pain where she had anticipated chagrin.

"Let's dance," she suggested again, a little more gently.

They had hardly begun when the number ended, and Fess Baxter stood before them, an ingratiating grin on his Swiss-cheese-colored face.

"Your turn, young fellow," he said to Bus.

"Thoughtful of you, reminding me," said Bus. "This is Mr. Baxter, Miss Ambrose."

"It's always been one of my ambitions," said Baxter, "to dance with a sure-enough angel."

"Just what I'd like to see you doin'," grinned Bus.

"Start up your stuff and watch us," said Baxter. "Step on it, brother. You're holding up traffic."

"Hope you get pinched for speedin'," said Bus, departing.

The Blue Devils were in good form tonight, were really "bearin' down" on their blues. Bus, their leader, however, was only going through the motions, waving his baton idly. His eyes followed Jean and Baxter, and it was nothing to his credit that the jazz maintained its spirit. Occasionally he lost the pair: a brace of young wild birds double-timed through the forest, miraculously avoiding the trees: an extremely ardent couple, welded together, did a decidedly localized mess-around; that gigantic black farmer whom Jean had pointed out sashayed into the line of vision, swung about, backed off, being fancy. . . .

Abruptly, as if someone had caught and held his right arm, Bus' baton halted above his head. His men kept on playing under the impulse of their own momentum, but Bus was a creature apart. Slowly his baton drooped, like the crest of a proud bird, beaten. His eyes died on their object and all his features sagged. On the floor forty feet away, amid the surrounding clot of dancers, Jean and Baxter had stopped moving and were standing perfectly still. The girl had clasped her partner close about the shoulders with both arms. Her face was buried in his chest.

Baxter, who was facing the platform, looked up and saw Bus staring. He drew the girl closer, grinned, and shut one eye.

They stood so a moment or an hour till Bus dragged his eyes away. Automatically he resumed beating time. Every moment or so his baton wavered, slowed, and hurried to catch up. The blues were very low-down, the nakedest of jazz, a series of periodic wails against a background of steady, slow rhythm, each pounding pulse descending inevitably, like leaden strokes of fate. Bus found himself singing the words of this grief-stricken lamentation:

Trouble—trouble has followed me all my days,
Trouble—trouble has followed my all my days—
Seems like trouble's gonna follow me always.

The mob demanded an encore, a mob that knew its blues and liked them blue. Bus complied. Each refrain became bluer as it was caught up by a different voice: the wailing clarinet, the weeping C sax, the moaning B-flat sax, the trombone, and Bus' own plaintive tenor:

Baby—baby—my baby's gone away.
Baby—baby—my baby's gone away—
Seems like baby—my baby's gone to stay.

Presently the thing beat itself out, and Bus turned to acknowledge applause. He broke a bow off in half. Directly before the platform stood Jean alone, looking up at him.

He jumped down. "Dance?"

"No. Listen. You know what I said at the table?"

"At the table?"

"About—wolves?"

"Oh—that—?"

"Yea. I didn't mean anything personal. Honest, I didn't." Her eyes besought his. "You didn't think I meant anything personal, did you?"

"Course not," he laughed. "I know now you didn't mean anything." He laughed again. "Neither one of us meant anything."

With a wry little smile, he watched her slip off through the crowd.

From his side of the platform Bus overheard Fess Baxter talking to Perry Parker. Baxter had a custom of talking while he conducted, the jazz serving to blanket his words. The blanket was not quite heavy enough tonight.

"P. P., old pooter, she fell."

Parker was resting while the C sax took the lead. "She did?"

"No lie. She says, 'You don't leave me any time for cash customers.' "

"Yea?"

"Yea. And I says, 'I'm a cash customer, baby. Just name your price.' "

Instantly Bus was across the platform and at him, clutched him by the collar, bent him back over the edge of the platform; and it was clear from the look in Bus's eyes that he wasn't just being playful.

"Name her!"

"Hey—what the hell you doin'!"

"Name her or I'll drop you and jump in your face. I swear to—"

"Nellie!" gurgled Fessenden Baxter.

"Nellie who—damn it?"

"Nellie—Gray!"

"All right then!"

Baxter found himself again erect with dizzy suddenness.

The music had stopped, for the players had momentarily lost their breath. Baxter swore and impelled his men into action, surreptitiously adjusting his ruffled plumage.

The crowd had an idea what it was all about and many good-naturedly derided the victim as they passed:

" 'Smatter, Fess? Goin' in for toe-dancin'?"

"Nice back-dive, papa, but this ain't no swimmin'-pool."

Curry, the large, bald, yellow manager, also had an idea what it was all about and lost no time accosting Bus.

"Tryin' to start somethin'?"

"No. Tryin' to stop somethin'."

"Well, if you gonna stop it with your hands, stop it outside. I ain't got no permit for prize fights in here— 'Course, if you guys can't get on together I can maybe struggle along without one of y' till I find somebody."

Bus said nothing.

"Listen. You birds fight it out with them jazz sticks, y' hear? Them's your weapons. Nex' Monday night's the jazz contest. You'll find out who's the best man next Monday night. Might win more'n a lovin' cup. And y' might lose more. Get me?"

He stood looking sleekly sarcastic a moment, then went to give Baxter like counsel.

Rumor spread through the Arcadia's regulars as night succeeded night.

A pair of buddies retired to the men's room to share a half-pint of gin. One said to the other between gulps:

"Lord today! Ain't them two roosters bearin' down on the jazz!"

"No lie. They mussa had some this same licker."

"Licker hell. Ain't you heard 'bout it?"

" 'Bout what?"

"They fightin', Oscar, fightin'."

"Gimme that bottle 'fo' you swaller it. Fightin'? What you mean, fightin'?"

"Fightin' over that new mama."

"The honey-dew?"

"Right. They can't use knives and they can't use knucks. And so they got to fight it out with jazz."

"Yea? Hell of a way to fight."

"That's the only way they'd be any fight. Bus Williams'd knock that yaller boy's can off in a scrap."

"I know it. Y'ought-a-seen him grab him las' night."

"I did. They tell me she promised it to the one 'at wins this cup nex' monday night."

"Yea? Wisht I knowed some music."

"Sho-nuff sheba all right. I got a long shout with her last night, Papa, an' she's got ever'thing!"

"Too damn easy on the eyes. Women like that ain't no good 'cep'n to start trouble."

"She sho' could start it for me. I'd 'a' been dancin' with her yet, but my two-bitses give out. Spent two hardearned bucks dancin' with her, too."

"Shuh! Might as well th'ow yo' money in the street. What you git dancin' with them hostesses?"

"You right there, brother. All I got out o' that one was two dollars worth o' disappointment."

Two girl friends, lounging in adjacent easy chairs, discussed the situation.

"I can't see what she's got so much more'n anybody else."

"Me neither. I could look a lot better'n that if I didn't have to work all day."

"No lie. Scrubbin' floors never made no bathin' beauties."

"I heard Fess Baxter jivin' her while they was dancin'. He's got a line, no stuff."

"He'd never catch me with it."

"No, dearie. He's got two good eyes too, y'know."

"Maybe that's why he couldn't see you flaggin' 'im."

"Be yourself, sister. He says to her, 'Baby, when the boss hands me that cup—'."

"Hates hisself, don't he?"

" 'When the boss hands me that cup,' he says, 'I'm gonna put it right in your arms.' "

"Yea. And I suppose he goes with the cup."

"So she laughs and says, 'Think you can beat him?' So he says, 'Beat him? Huh, that bozo couldn't play a hand organ.' "

"He don't mean her no good though, this Baxter."

"How do you know?"

"A kack like that never means a woman no good. The other one ast her to step off with him."

"What!"

"Etta Pipp heard him. They was drinkin' and she was at the next table."

"Well, ain't that somethin'! Ast her to step off with him! What'd she say?"

"Etta couldn't hear no more."

"Jus' goes to show ya. What chance has a honest workin' girl got?"

Bus confided in Tappen, his drummer.

"Tap," he said, "ain't it funny how a woman always seems to fall for a wolf?"

"No lie," Tap agreed. "When a guy gets too deep, he's long-gone."

"How do you account for it, Tap?"

"I don't. I jes' play 'em light. When I feel it gettin' heavy —boy, I run like hell."

"Tap, what would you do if you fell for a girl and saw her neckin' another guy?"

"I wouldn't fall," said Tappen, "so I wouldn't have to do nothin'."

"Well, but s'posin' you did?"

"Well, if she was my girl, I'd knock the can off both of 'em."

"S'posin' she wasn't your girl?"

"Well, if she wasn't my girl, it wouldn't be none of my business."

"Yea, but a guy kind o' hates to see an old friend gettin' jived."

"Stay out, papa. Only way to protect yourself."

"S'posin' you didn't want to protect yourself? S'posin' you wanted to protect the woman?"

"Hmph! Who ever heard of a woman needin' protection?"

"Ladies and gentlemen!" sang Curry to the tense crowd that gorged the Arcadia. "Tonight is the night of the only contest of its kind in recorded history! On my left, Mr. Bus Williams, chief of the Blue Devils. On my right, Mr. Fessenden Baxter, leader of the Firemen. On this stand, the solid gold loving-cup. The winner will claim the jazz championship of the world!"

"And the sweet mama too, how 'bout it?" called a wag.

"Each outfit will play three numbers: a one-step, a fox-trot, and a blues number. With this stop watch which you see in my hand, I will time your applause after each number. The leader receiving the longest total applause wins the loving-cup!"

"Yea—and some lovin'-up wid it!"

"I will now toss a coin to see who plays the first number!"

"Toss it out here!"

"Bus Williams's Blue Devils, ladies and gentlemen, will play the first number!"

Bus's philosophy of jazz held tone to be merely the vehicle of rhythm. He spent much time devising new rhythmic patterns with which to vary his presentations. Accordingly he depended largely on Tappen, his master percussionist, who knew every rhythmic monkey-shine with which to delight a gaping throng.

Bus had conceived the present piece as a chase, in which an agile clarinet eluded impetuous and turbulent traps. The other instruments were to be observers, chorusing their excitement while they urged the principals on.

From the moment the piece started something was obviously wrong. The clarinet was elusive enough, but its agility was without purpose. Nothing pursued it. People stopped dancing in the middle of the number and turned puzzled faces toward the platform. The trap-drummer was going through the motions faithfully but to no avail. His traps were voiceless, emitted mere shadows of sound. He was a deaf mute making a speech.

Brief, perfunctory, disappointed applause rose and fell at the number's end. Curry announced its duration:

"Fifteen seconds flat!"

Fess Baxter, with great gusto, leaped to his post.

"The Firemen will play their first number!"

Bus was consulting Tappen.

"For the love o' Pete, Tap—?"

"Love o' hell. Look a' here."

Bus looked—first at the trapdrum, then at the bass; snapped them with a finger, thumped them with his knuckles. There was almost no sound; each drum-sheet was dead, lax instead of taut, and the cause was immediately clear: each bore a short curved knife-cut following its edge a brief distance, a wound unnoticeable at a glance, but fatal to the instrument.

Bus looked at Tappen, Tappen looked at Bus.

"The cream-colored son of a buzzard!"

Fess Baxter, gleeful and oblivious, was directing a whirlwind number, sweeping the crowd about the floor at an exciting, exhausting pace, distorting, expanding, etherealizing their emotions with swift-changing dissonances. Contrary to Bus Williams's philosophy, Baxter considered rhythm a mere rack upon which to hang his tonal tricks. The present piece was dizzy with sudden disharmonies, unexpected twists of phrase, successive false resolutions. Incidentally, however, there was nothing wrong with Baxter's drums.

Boiling over, Bus would have started for him, but Tappen grabbed his coat.

"Hold it, papa. That's a sure way to lose. Maybe we can choke him yet."

"Yea—?"

"I'll play the wood. And I still got cymbals and sandpaper."

"Yea—and a triangle. Hell of a lot o' good they are."

"Can't quit," said Tappen.

"Well," said Bus.

Baxter's number ended in a furor.

"Three minutes and twenty seconds!" bellowed Curry as the applause eventually died out.

Bus began his second number, a fox-trot. In the midst of it he saw Jean dancing, beseeching him with bewildered dismay in her eyes, a look that at once crushed and crazed him. Tappen rapped on the rim of his trap drum, tapped his triangle, stamped the pedal that clapped the cymbals, but the result was a toneless and hollow clatter, a weightless noise that bounced back from the multitude instead of penetrating into it. The players also, distracted by the loss, were operating far below par, and not all their leader's frantic false enthusiasm could compensate for the gaping absence of bass. The very spine had been ripped out of their music, and Tappen's desperate efforts were but the hopeless flutterings of a stricken, limp, pulseless heart.

"Forty-five seconds!" Curry announced. "Making a total so

far of one minute flat for the Blue Devils! The Firemen will now play their second number!"

The Firemen's fox-trot was Baxter's re-arrangement of Burleigh's "Jean, My Jean," and Baxter, riding his present advantage hard, stressed all that he had put into it of tonal ingenuity. The thing was delirious with strange harmonies, iridescent with odd color-changes, and its very flamboyance, its musical fine-writing and conceits delighted the dancers.

But it failed to delight Jean Ambrose, whom by its title it was intended to flatter. She rushed to Bus.

"What is it?" She was a-quiver.

"Drums gone. Somebody cut the pigskin the last minute."

"What? Somebody? Who?"

"Cut 'em with a knife close to the rim."

"Cut? He cut—? Oh, Bus!"

She flashed Baxter a look that would have crumpled his assurance had he seen it. "Can't you— Listen." She was at once wild and calm. "It's the bass. You got to have—I know! Make 'em stamp their feet! Your boys, I mean. That'll do it. All of 'em. Turn the blues into a shout."

"Yea? Gee. Maybe—"

"Try it! You've got to win this thing."

An uproar that seemed endless greeted Baxter's version of "Jean." The girl, back out on the floor, managed to smile as Baxter acknowledged the acclaim by gesturing toward her.

"The present score, ladies and gentlemen, is—for the Blue Devils, one minute even; for the Firemen, six minutes and thirty seconds! The Devils will now play their last number!" Curry's intonation of "last" moved the mob to laughter.

Into that laughter Bus grimly led his men like a captain leading his command into fire. He had chosen the parent of blue songs, the old St. Louis Blues, and he adduced every device that had ever adorned that classic. Clarinets wailed, saxophones moaned, trumpets wept wretchedly, trombones laughed bitterly, even the great bass horn sobbed dismally from the depths. And so perfectly did the misery in the music express the actual despair of the situation that the crowd was caught from the start. Soon dancers closed their eyes, forgot their jostling neighbors, lost themselves bodily in the easy sway of that slow, fateful measure, vaguely aware that some quality hitherto lost had at last been found. They were too wholly absorbed to note just how that quality had been found: that every player softly dropped his heel where each bass-drum beat would have come, giving each major impulse a body and breadth that no drum could have achieved. Zoom-zoom-zoom-zoom. It was not a mere sound; it was a vibrant throb that took hold of the crowd and rocked it.

They had been rocked thus before, this multitude. Two hundred years ago they had swayed to that same slow fateful measure, lifting their lamentation to heaven, pounding the earth with their feet, seeking the mercy of a new God through the medium of an old rhythm, zoom-zoom. They had rocked so a thousand years ago in a city whose walls were jungle, forfending the wrath of a terrible black God who spoke in storm and pestilence, had swayed and wailed to that same slow period, beaten on a wild boar's skin stretched over the end of a hollow tree-trunk. Zoom-zoom-zoom-zoom. Not a sound but an emotion that laid hold on their bodies and swung them into the past. Blues—low-down blues indeed —blues that reached their souls' depths.

But slowly the color changed. Each player allowed his heel to drop less and less softly. Solo parts faded out, and the orchestra began to gather power as a whole. The rhythm persisted, the unfaltering common meter of blues, but the blueness itself, the sorrow, the despair, began to give way to hope. Ere long hope came to the verge of realization— mounted it—rose above it. The deep and regular impulses now vibrated like nearing thunder, a mighty, inescapable, all-embracing dominance, stressed by the contrast of wind-tone; an all-pervading atmosphere through which soared wild-winged birds. Rapturously, rhapsodically, the number rose to madness and at the height of its madness, burst into sudden silence.

Illusion broke. Dancers awoke, dropped to reality with a jolt. Suddenly the crowd appreciated that Bus Williams had returned to form, had put on a comeback, had struck off a masterpiece. And the crowd showed its appreciation. It applauded its palms sore.

Curry's suspense-ridden announcement ended:

"Total—for the Blue Devils, seven minutes and forty seconds! For the Firemen, six minutes and thirty seconds! Maybe that wasn't the Devils' last number after all! The Firemen will play their last number!"

It was needless for Baxter to attempt the depths and heights just attained by Bus Williams's Blue Devils. His speed, his subordination of rhythm to tone, his exotic coloring, all were useless in a low-down blues song. The crowd moreover, had nestled upon the broad, sustaining bosom of a shout. Nothing else warmed them. The end of Baxter's last piece left them chilled and unsatisfied.

But if Baxter realized that he was beaten, his attitude failed to reveal it. Even when the major volume of applause died out in a few seconds, he maintained his self-assured grin. The reason was soon apparent: although the audience as a whole had stopped applauding, two small groups of assiduous handclappers, one at either extreme of the dancing-area, kept up a diminutive, violent clatter.

Again Bus and Tappen exchanged sardonic stares.

"Damn' if he ain't paid somebody to clap!"

Only the threatening hisses and boos of the majority terminated this clatter, whereupon Curry summed up:

"For Bus Williams's Blue Devils—seven minutes and forty seconds! For Fess Baxter's Firemen—eight minutes flat!"

He presented Baxter the loving-cup amid a hubbub of murmurs, handclaps, shouts, and hisses that drowned whatever he said. Then the hubbub hushed. Baxter was assisting Jean Ambrose to the platform. With a bow and a flourish he handed the girl the cup.

She held it for a moment in both arms, uncertain, hesitant. But there was nothing uncertain or hesitant in the mob's reaction. Feeble applause was overwhelmed in a deluge of disapprobation. Cries of "Crooked!" "Don't take it!" "Crown the cheat!" "He stole it!" stood out. Tappen put his finger in the slit in his trap-drum, ripped it to a gash, held up the mutilated instrument, and cried, "Look what he done to my traps!" A few hardboiled ruffians close to the platform moved menacingly toward the victor. "Grab 'im! Knock his can off!"

Jean's uncertainty abruptly vanished. She wheeled with the trophy in close embrace and sailed across the platform toward the defeated Bus Williams. She smiled into his astonished face and thrust the cup into his arms.

"Hot damn, mama! That's the time!" cried a jubilant voice from the floor, and instantly the gathering storm of menace broke into a cloudburst of delight. That romance-hungry multitude saw Bus Williams throw his baton into the air and gather the girl and the loving-cup into his arms. And they went utterly wild—laughed, shouted, yelled and whistled till the walls of the Arcadia bulged.

Jazz emerged as the mad noise subsided: Bus Williams's Blue Devils playing *"She's Still My Baby."*

ARNA BONTEMPS (1902--)

As poet, novelist, author of short stories and juvenile litera-
ture, critic, anthologist, playwright, librarian, and educator,
Arna Bontemps is a central figure in the creation, dissemina-
tion, and teaching of Negro American literature. He was
born in Alexandria, Louisiana, raised and educated in Cali-
fornia, and graduated from Pacific Union College in 1923.
He came to Harlem at the beginning of the "Harlem Renais-
sance" and became one of its best known writers. His poetry
first appeared in The Crisis, *in the summer of 1924. In 1926*
and 1927 his poems "Golgotha Is a Mountain" and "The Re-
turn" won the Alexander Pushkin Awards for Poetry offered
by Opportunity: Journal of Negro Life. *In 1927 he also won*
first prize in the poetry contest sponsored by The Crisis.
Since then he has been primarily writing prose. He pursued
graduate studies in English at the University of Chicago during
the Depression years and later earned an M.A. in librarianship.
Bontemps became University Librarian at Fisk University in
1943, a position he held for twenty-two years before joining
the faculty of the University of Illinois, Chicago Circle, in the
fall of 1966. His anthologies (some edited in collaboration with
Langston Hughes), his books for young people, and his non-
fiction, have become even more widely known than his three
novels. His Story of the Negro *received the Jane Addams*
Children's Book Award in 1956. His Anyplace but Here
(written in collaboration with Jack Conroy) won the James L.
Dow Award of the Society of Midland Authors in 1967. He
has also received citations and special recognition for Lonesome
Boy *(1955),* Frederick Douglass *(1958),* 100 Years of Negro
Freedom *(1961), and* American Negro Poetry *(1963). The*
following short story, "A Summer Tragedy," was written in
1933. Bontemps is also represented in other sections of this
anthology with poems and an autobiographical essay.

A Summer Tragedy

Old Jeff Patton, the black share farmer, fumbled with his bow tie. His fingers trembled and the high stiff collar pinched his throat. A fellow loses his hand for such vanities after thirty or forty years of simple life. Once a year, or maybe twice if there's a wedding among his kinfolks, he may spruce up; but generally fancy clothes do nothing but adorn the wall of the big room and feed the moths. That had been Jeff Patton's experience. He had not worn his stiff-bosomed shirt more than a dozen times in all his married life. His swallow-tailed coat lay on the bed beside him, freshly brushed and pressed, but it was as full of holes as the overalls in which he worked on weekdays. The moths had used it badly. Jeff twisted his mouth into a hideous toothless grimace as he contended with the obstinate bow. He stamped his good foot and decided to give up the struggle.

"Jennie," he called.

"What's that, Jeff?" His wife's shrunken voice came out of the adjoining room like an echo. It was hardly bigger than a whisper.

"I reckon you'll have to he'p me wid this heah bow tie, baby," he said meekly. "Dog if I can hitch it up."

Her answer was not strong enough to reach him, but presently the old woman came to the door, feeling her way with a stick. She had a wasted, dead-leaf appearance. Her body, as scrawny and gnarled as a string bean, seemed less than nothing in the ocean of frayed and faded petticoats that surrounded her. These hung an inch or two above the tops of her heavy unlaced shoes and showed little grotesque piles where the stockings had fallen down from her negligible legs.

"You oughta could do a heap mo' wid a thing like that'n me—beingst as you got yo' good sight."

"Looks like I oughta could," he admitted. "But ma fingers is gone democrat on me. I get all mixed up in the looking glass an' can't tell wicha way to twist the devilish thing."

Jennie sat on the side of the bed and old Jeff Patton got down on one knee while she tied the bow knot. It was a slow and painful ordeal for each of them in this position. Jeff's bones cracked, his knee ached, and it was only after a half dozen attempts that Jennie worked a semblance of a bow into the tie.

"I got to dress maself now," the old woman whispered.

"These is ma old shoes an' stockings, and I ain't so much as unwrapped ma dress."

"Well, don't worry 'bout me no mo', baby," Jeff said. "That 'bout finishes me. All I gotta do now is slip on that old coat 'n ves' an' I'll be fixed to leave."

Jennie disappeared again through the dim passage into the shed room. Being blind was no handicap to her in that black hole. Jeff heard the cane placed against the wall beside the door and knew that his wife was on easy ground. He put on his coat, took a battered top hat from the bedpost and hobbled to the front door. He was ready to travel. As soon as Jennie could get on her Sunday shoes and her old black silk dress, they would start.

Outside the tiny log house, the day was warm and mellow with sunshine. A host of wasps were humming with busy excitement in the trunk of a dead sycamore. Gray squirrels were searching through the grass for hickory nuts and blue jays were in the trees, hopping from branch to branch. Pine woods stretched away to the left like a black sea. Among them were scattered scores of log houses like Jeff's, houses of black share farmers. Cows and pigs wandered freely among the trees. There was no danger of loss. Each farmer knew his own stock and knew his neighbor's as well as he knew his neighbor's children.

Down the slope to the right were the cultivated acres on which the colored folks worked. They extended to the river, more than two miles away, and they were today green with the unmade cotton crop. A tiny thread of a road, which passed directly in front of Jeff's place, ran through these green fields like a pencil mark.

Jeff, standing outside the door, with his absurd hat in his left hand, surveyed the wide scene tenderly. He had been forty-five years on these acres. He loved them with the unexplained affection that others have for the countries to which they belong.

The sun was hot on his head, his collar still pinched his throat, and the Sunday clothes were intolerably hot. Jeff transferred the hat to his right hand and began fanning with it. Suddenly the whisper that was Jennie's voice came out of the shed room.

"You can bring the car round front whilst you's waitin'," it said feebly. There was a tired pause; then it added, "I'll soon be fixed to go."

"A'right, baby," Jeff answered. "I'll get it in a minute."

But he didn't move. A thought struck him that made his mouth fall open. The mention of the car brought to his mind,

with new intensity, the trip he and Jennie were about to take.
Fear came into his eyes; excitement took his breath. Lord,
Jesus!

"Jeff . . . O Jeff," the old woman's whisper called.

He awakened with a jolt. "Hunh, baby?"

"What you doin'?"

"Nuthin. Jes studyin'. I jes been turnin' things round'n
round in ma mind."

"You could be gettin' the car," she said.

"Oh yes, right away, baby."

He started round to the shed, limping heavily on his bad
leg. There were three frizzly chickens in the yard. All his
other chickens had been killed or stolen recently. But the
frizzly chickens had been saved somehow. That was fortunate
indeed, for these curious creatures had a way of devouring
"Poison" from the yard and in that way protecting against
conjure and black luck and spells. But even the frizzly chickens seemed now to be in a stupor. Jeff thought they had some
ailment; he expected all three of them to die shortly.

The shed in which the old T-model Ford stood was only a
grass roof held up by four corner poles. It had been built by
tremulous hands at a time when the little rattletrap car had
been regarded as a peculiar treasure. And, miraculously, despite wind and downpour it still stood.

Jeff adjusted the crank and put his weight upon it. The en-
gine came to life with a sputter and bang that rattled the old
car from radiator to taillight. Jeff hopped into the seat and
put his foot on the accelerator. The sputtering and banging
increased. The rattling became more violent. That was good.
It was good banging, good sputtering and rattling, and it
meant that the aged car was still in running condition. She
could be depended on for this trip.

Again Jeff's thought halted as if paralyzed. The suggestion
of the trip fell into the machinery of his mind like a wrench.
He felt dazed and weak. He swung the car out into the yard,
made a half turn and drove around to the front door. When
he took his hands off the wheel, he noticed that he was trembling violently. He cut off the motor and climbed to the
ground to wait for Jennie.

A few minutes later she was at the window, her voice rattling against the pane like a broken shutter.

"I'm ready, Jeff."

He did not answer, but limped into the house and took her
by the arm. He led her slowly through the big room, down
the step and across the yard.

"You reckon I'd oughta lock the do'?" he asked softly.

They stopped and Jennie weighed the question. Finally she shook her head.

"Ne' mind the do'," she said. "I don't see no cause to lock up things."

"You right," Jeff agreed. "No cause to lock up."

Jeff opened the door and helped his wife into the car. A quick shudder passed over him. Jesus! Again he trembled.

"How come you shaking so?" Jennie whispered.

"I don't know," he said.

"You mus' be scairt, Jeff."

"No, baby, I ain't scairt."

He slammed the door after her and went around to crank up again. The motor started easily. Jeff wished that it had not been so responsive. He would have liked a few more minutes in which to turn things around in his head. As it was, with Jennie chiding him about being afraid, he had to keep going. He swung the car into the little pencil-mark road and started off toward the river, driving very slowly, very cautiously.

Chugging across the green countryside, the small battered Ford seemed tiny indeed. Jeff felt a familiar excitement, a thrill, as they came down the first slope to the immense levels on which the cotton was growing. He could not help reflecting that the crops were good. He knew what that meant, too; he had made forty-five of them with his own hands. It was true that he had worn out nearly a dozen mules, but that was the fault of old man Stevenson, the owner of the land. Major Stevenson had the odd notion that one mule was all a share farmer needed to work a thirty-acre plot. It was an expensive notion, the way it killed mules from overwork, but the old man held to it. Jeff thought it killed a good many share farmers as well as mules, but he had no sympathy for them. He had always been strong, and he had been taught to have no patience with weakness in men. Women or children might be tolerated if they were puny, but a weak man was a curse. Of course, his own children—

Jeff's thought halted there. He and Jennie never mentioned their dead children any more. And naturally he did not wish to dwell upon them in his mind. Before he knew it, some remark would slip out of his mouth and that would make Jennie feel blue. Perhaps she would cry. A woman like Jennie could not easily throw off the grief that comes from losing five grown children within two years. Even Jeff was still staggered by the blow. His memory had not been much good recently. He frequently talked to himself. And, although he had kept it a secret, he knew that his courage had left him. He was terrified by the least unfamiliar sound at night. He was reluctant to venture far from home in the daytime. And that habit of trembling when he felt fearful was now far beyond his control. Sometimes he became afraid and trembled without knowing what had frightened him. The feeling would just come over him like a chill.

The car rattled slowly over the dusty road. Jennie sat erect and silent, with a little absurd hat pinned to her hair. Her useless eyes seemed very large, very white in their deep sockets. Suddenly Jeff heard her voice, and he inclined his head to catch the words.

"Is we passed Delia Moore's house yet?" she asked.

"Not yet," he said.

"You must be drivin' mighty slow, Jeff."

"We might just as well take our time, baby."

There was a pause. A little puff of steam was coming out of the radiator of the car. Heat wavered above the hood. Delia Moore's house was nearly half a mile away. After a moment Jennie spoke again.

"You ain't really scairt, is you, Jeff?"

"Nah, baby, I ain't scairt."

"You know how we agreed—we gotta keep on goin'."

Jewels of perspiration appeared on Jeff's forehead. His eyes rounded, blinked, became fixed on the road.

"I don't know," he said with a shiver. "I reckon it's the only thing to do."

"Hm."

A flock of guinea fowls, pecking in the road, were scattered by the passing car. Some of them took to their wings; others hid under bushes. A blue jay, swaying on a leafy twig, was annoying a roadside squirrel. Jeff held an even speed till he came near Delia's place. Then he slowed down noticeably.

Delia's house was really no house at all, but an abandoned store building converted into a dwelling. It sat near a crossroads, beneath a single black cedar tree. There Delia, a cattish old creature of Jennie's age, lived alone. She had been there more years than anybody could remember, and long ago had won the disfavor of such women as Jennie. For in her young days Delia had been gayer, yellower and saucier than seemed proper in those parts. Her ways with menfolks had been dark and suspicious. And the fact that she had had as many husbands as children did not help her reputation.

"Yonder's old Delia," Jeff said as they passed.

"What she doin'?"

"Jes sittin' in the do'," he said.

"She see us?"

"Hm," Jeff said. "Musta did."

That relieved Jennie. It strengthened her to know that her old enemy had seen her pass in her best clothes. That would give the old she-devil something to chew her gums and fret about, Jennie thought. Wouldn't she have a fit if she didn't find out? Old evil Delia! This would be just the thing for her. It would pay her back for being so evil. It would also pay her, Jennie thought, for the way she used to grin at Jeff— long ago when her teeth were good.

The road became smooth and red, and Jeff could tell by the smell of the air that they were nearing the river. He could see the rise where the road turned and ran along parallel to the stream. The car chugged on monotonously. After a long silent spell, Jennie leaned against Jeff and spoke.

"How many bale o' cotton you think we got standin'?" she said.

Jeff wrinkled his forehead as he calculated.

" 'Bout twenty-five, I reckon."

"How many you make las' year?"

"Twenty-eight," he said. "How come you ask that?"

"I's jes thinkin'," Jennie said quietly.

"It don't make a speck o' difference though," Jeff reflected. "If we get much or if we get little, we still gonna be in debt to old man Stevenson when he gets through counting up agin us. It's took us a long time to learn that."

Jennie was not listening to these words. She had fallen into a trance-like meditation. Her lips twitched. She chewed her gums and rubbed her gnarled hands nervously. Suddenly she leaned forward, buried her face in the nervous hands and burst into tears. She cried aloud in a dry cracked voice that suggested the rattle of fodder on dead stalks. She cried aloud like a child, for she had never learned to suppress a genuine sob. Her slight old frame shook heavily and seemed hardly able to sustain such violent grief.

"What's the matter, baby?" Jeff asked awkwardly. "Why you cryin' like all that?"

"I's jes thinkin'," she said.

"So you the one what's scairt now, hunh?"

"I ain't scairt, Jeff. I's jes thinkin' 'bout leavin' eve'thing like this—eve'thing we been used to. It's right sad-like."

Jeff did not answer, and presently Jennie buried her face again and cried.

The sun was almost overhead. It beat down furiously on the dusty wagon-path road, on the parched roadside grass and the tiny battered car. Jeff's hands, gripping the wheel, became wet with perspiration; his forehead sparkled. Jeff's lips parted. His mouth shaped a hideous grimace. His face suggested the face of a man being burned. But the torture passed and his expression softened again.

"You mustn't cry, baby," he said to his wife. "We gotta be strong. We can't break down."

Jennie waited a few seconds, then said, "You reckon we oughta do it, Jeff? You reckon we oughta go 'head an' do it, really?"

Jeff's voice choked; his eyes blurred. He was terrified to hear Jennie say the thing that had been in his mind all morning. She had egged him on when he had wanted more than anything in the world to wait, to reconsider, to think things over a little longer. Now she was getting cold feet. Actually there was no need of thinking the question through again. It would only end in making the same painful decision once more. Jeff knew that. There was no need of fooling around longer.

"We jes as well to do like we planned," he said. "They ain't nothin' else for us now—it's the bes' thing."

Jeff thought of the handicaps, the near impossibility, of making another crop with his leg bothering him more and more each week. Then there was always the chance that he would have another stroke, like the one that had made him lame. Another one might kill him. The least it could do would be to leave him helpless. Jeff gasped—Lord, Jesus! He could not bear to think of being helpless, like a baby, on Jennie's hands. Frail, blind Jennie.

The little pounding motor of the car worked harder and harder. The puff of steam from the cracked radiator became larger. Jeff realized that they were climbing a little rise. A moment later the road turned abruptly and he looked down upon the face of the river.

"Jeff."

"Hunh?"

"Is that the water I hear?"

"Hm. Tha's it."

"Well, which way you goin' now?"

"Down this-a way," he said. "The road runs 'long 'side o' the water a lil piece."

She waited a while calmly. Then she said, "Drive faster."

"A'right, baby," Jeff said.

The water roared in the bed of the river. It was fifty or sixty feet below the level of the road. Between the road and the water there was a long smooth slope, sharply inclined. The slope was dry, the clay hardened by prolonged summer heat. The water below, roaring in a narrow channel, was noisy and wild.

"Jeff."

"Hunh?"

"How far you goin'?"

"Jes a lil piece down the road."

"You ain't scairt, is you, Jeff?"

"Nah, baby," he said trembling. "I ain't scairt."

"Remember how we planned it, Jeff. We gotta do it like we said. Brave-like."

"Hm."

Jeff's brain darkened. Things suddenly seemed unreal, like figures in a dream. Thoughts swam in his mind foolishly, hysterically, like little blind fish in a pool within a dense cave. They rushed, crossed one another, jostled, collided, retreated and rushed again. Jeff soon became dizzy. He shuddered violently and turned to his wife.

"Jennie, I can't do it. I can't." His voice broke pitifully.

She did not appear to be listening. All the grief had gone from her face. She sat erect, her unseeing eyes wide open, strained and frightful. Her glossy black skin had become dull. She seemed as thin, as sharp and bony, as a starved bird. Now, having suffered and endured the sadness of tearing herself away from beloved things, she showed no anguish. She was absorbed with her own thoughts, and she didn't even hear Jeff's voice shouting in her ear.

Jeff said nothing more. For an instant there was light in his cavernous brain. The great chamber was, for less than a second, peopled by characters he knew and loved. They were simple, healthy creatures, and they behaved in a manner that he could understand. They had quality. But since he had already taken leave of them long ago, the remembrance did not break his heart again. Young Jeff Patton was among them, the Jeff Patton of fifty years ago who went down to New Orleans with a crowd of country boys to the Mardi Gras doings. The gay young crowd, boys with candy-striped shirts and rouged-brown girls in noisy silks, was like a picture in his head. Yet it did not make him sad. On that very trip Slim Burns had killed Joe Beasley—the crowd had been broken up. Since then Jeff Patton's world had been the Greenbriar Plantation. If there had been other Mardi Gras carnivals, he had not heard of them. Since then there had been no time; the years had fallen on him like waves. Now he was old, worn out. Another paralytic stroke (like the one he had already suffered) would put him on his back for keeps. In that condition, with a frail blind woman to look after him, he would be worse off than if he were dead.

Suddenly Jeff's hands became steady. He actually felt

brave. He slowed down the motor of the car and carefully pulled off the road. Below, the water of the stream boomed, a soft thunder in the deep channel. Jeff ran the car onto the clay slope, pointed it directly toward the stream and put his foot heavily on the accelerator. The little car leaped furiously down the steep incline toward the water. The movement was nearly as swift and direct as a fall. The two old black folks, sitting quietly side by side, showed no excitement. In another instant the car hit the water and dropped immediately out of sight.

A little later it lodged in the mud of a shallow place. One wheel of the crushed and upturned little Ford became visible above the rushing water.

LANGSTON HUGHES (1902–1967)

The most prolific and perhaps best-known of modern Negro American writers, Langston Hughes was the only Negro poet who lived entirely on the professional earnings of his literary activities in a long and diverse literary career. He was born in Joplin, Missouri, but for most of his childhood Hughes lived with his grandmother in Lawrence, Kansas. Hughes recalled that his Kansas grandmother was the last surviving widow of John Brown's Raid—in his words, "her first husband having been one of the five colored men to die so gloriously at Harper's Ferry." She died when he was thirteen and he then went to live with his mother in Lincoln, Illinois. A year later they moved to Cleveland, where he attended Central High School and began writing poetry. After graduation he spent fifteen months in Mexico with his father, who had been living there for some years. Here Hughes learned Spanish and wrote "The Negro Speaks of Rivers," which was published in The Crisis *(1921). He attended Columbia University for a year in 1921, leaving to work as a seaman for almost two years. His travels brought him to the West Coast of Africa and Northern Europe. In 1924 he went to Paris, where he worked in nightclubs, and then on to Italy. By the end of the year*

Hughes worked his way back to New York on a tramp steamer, painting and scrubbing decks. He spent the next year in Washington, employed in the office of the Association for the Study of Negro Life and History, and later as a busboy at the Wardman Park Hotel. It was there that Vachel Lindsay read some of his poems and Hughes (as he recalled) "was discovered by the newspapers." He received his first prize for poetry in 1925 from Opportunity *magazine and went on to become a major figure of the "Harlem Renaissance." He resumed his college education at Lincoln University, in Pennsylvania, where he wrote his first novel,* Not Without Laughter *(1930). More than twelve volumes of his poems were published during his lifetime and a final collection,* The Panther and the Lash *(1967), was issued posthumously. He was frequently introduced to audiences as "the Poet Laureate of Harlem." He won the Witter Bynner undergraduate prize for excellence in poetry in 1926 and was awarded Rosenwald and Guggenheim fellowships and a grant from the American Academy of Arts and Letters. He received the Anisfield Wolfe award in 1959 and the Spingarn Medal in 1960. His prodigious literary activities and versatility are evident in the large number of books listed in the Bibliography at the end of this volume. A favorite fictional character created by Hughes is Jesse B. Semple of Harlem. As the Simple tales grew in number and were assembled periodically in book form, they ultimately filled four volumes. Seven tales of Simple are presented here, preceded by the author's Foreword explaining who Simple is. More of Hughes' work will be found in the Poetry and Literary Criticism sections of this anthology.*

Tales of Simple

Foreword: Who Is Simple?

I cannot truthfully state, as some novelists do at the beginnings of their books, that these stories are about "nobody living or dead." The facts are that these tales are about a great many people—although they are stories about no specific persons as such. But it is impossible to live in Harlem and not know at least a hundred Simples, fifty Joyces, twenty-five Zaritas, a number of Boyds, and several Cousin Minnies—or reasonable facsimiles thereof.

"Simple Speaks His Mind" had hardly been published when I walked into a Harlem cafe one night and the proprietor said, "Listen, I don't know where you got that character, Jesse B. Semple, but I want you to meet one of my customers who is *just* like him." He called to a fellow at the end of the bar. "Watch how he walks," he said, "exactly like Simple. And I'll bet he won't be talking to you two minutes before he'll tell you how long he's been standing on his feet, and how much his bunions hurt—just like your book begins."

The barman was right. Even as the customer approached, he cried, "Man, my feet hurt! If you want to see me, why don't you come over here where I am? I stands on my feet all day."

"And I stand on mine all night," said the barman. Without me saying a word, a conversation began so much like the opening chapter in my book that even I was a bit amazed to see how nearly life can be like fiction—or vice versa.

Simple, as a character, originated during the war. His first words came directly out of the mouth of a young man who lived just down the block from me. One night I ran into him in a neighborhood bar and he said, "Come on back to the booth and meet my girl friend." I did and he treated me to a beer. Not knowing much about the young man, I asked where he worked. He said, "In a war plant."

I said, "What do you make?"

He said, "Cranks."

I said, "What kind of cranks?"

He said, "Oh, man, I don't know what kind of cranks."

I said, "Well, do they crank cars, tanks, buses, planes or what?"

He said, "I don't know what them cranks crank."

Whereupon, his girl friend, a little put out at this ignorance of his job, said, "You've been working there long enough. Looks like by now you ought to know what them cranks crank."

"Aw, woman," he said, "you know white folks don't tell colored folks what cranks crank."

That was the beginning of Simple. I have long since lost track of the fellow who uttered those words. But out of the mystery as to what the cranks of this world crank, to whom they belong and why, there evolved the character in this book, wondering and laughing at the numerous problems of white folks, colored folks, and just folks—including himself. He talks about the wife he used to have, the woman he loves today, and his one-time play-girl, Zarita. Usually over a glass of beer, he tells me his tales, mostly in high humor, but sometimes with a pain in his soul as sharp as the occasional hurt of that bunion on his right foot. Sometimes, as the old blues says, Simple might be "laughing to keep from crying." But even then, he keeps you laughing, too. If there were not a lot of genial souls in Harlem as talkative as Simple, I would never have these tales to write down that are "just like him." He is my ace-boy, Simple. I hope you like him, too.

LANGSTON HUGHES

New York City
August, 1961

Feet Live Their Own Life

"If you want to know about my life," said Simple as he blew the foam from the top of the newly filled glass the bartender put before him, "don't look at my face, don't look at my hands. Look at my feet and see if you can tell how long I been standing on them."

"I cannot see your feet through your shoes," I said.

"You do not need to see through my shoes," said Simple. "Can't you tell by the shoes I wear—not pointed, not rocking-chair, not French-toed, not nothing but big, long, broad, and flat—that I been standing on these feet a long time and carrying some heavy burdens? They ain't flat from standing at no bar, neither, because I always sets at a bar. Can't you tell that? You know I do not hang out in a bar unless it has stools, don't you?"

"That I have observed," I said, "but I did not connect it with your past life."

"Everything I do is connected up with my past life," said Simple. "From Virginia to Joyce, from my wife to Zarita, from my mother's milk to this glass of beer, everything is connected up."

"I trust you will connect up with that dollar I just loaned you when you get paid," I said. "And who is Virginia? You never told me about her."

"Virginia is where I was borned," said Simple. "I *would* be borned in a state named after a woman. From that day on, women never give me no peace."

"You, I fear, are boasting. If the women were running after you as much as you run after them, you would not be able to sit here on this bar stool in peace. I don't see any women coming to call you out to go home, as some of these fellows' wives do around here."

"Joyce better not come in no bar looking for me," said Simple. "That is why me and my wife busted up—one reason. I do not like to be called out of no bar by a female. It's a man's perogative to just set and drink sometimes."

"How do you connect that prerogative with your past?" I asked.

"When I was a wee small child," said Simple, "I had no place to set and think in, being as how I was raised up with three brothers, two sisters, seven cousins, one married aunt, a common-law uncle, and the minister's grandchild—and the house only had four rooms. I never had no place just to set and think. Neither to set and drink—not even much my milk before some hongry child snatched it out of my hand. I were not the youngest, neither a girl, nor the cutest. I don't know why, but I don't think nobody liked me much. Which is why I was afraid to like anybody for a long time myself. When I did like somebody, I was full-grown and then I picked out the wrong woman because I had no practice in liking anybody before that. We did not get along."

"Is that when you took to drink?"

"Drink took to me," said Simple. "Whiskey just naturally likes me but beer likes me better. By the time I got married I had got to the point where a cold bottle was almost as good as a warm bed, especially when the bottle could not talk and the bed-warmer could. I do not like a woman to talk to me too much—I mean about me. Which is why I like Joyce. Joyce most in generally talks about herself."

"I am still looking at your feet," I said, "and I swear they do not reveal your life to me. Your feet are no open book."

"You have eyes but you see not," said Simple. "These feet have stood on every rock from the Rock of Ages to 135th and Lenox. These feet have supported everything from a cotton bale to a hongry woman. These feet have walked ten thousand miles working for white folks and another ten thousand keeping up with colored. These feet have stood at altars, crap tables, free lunches, bars, graves, kitchen doors, betting windows, hospital clinics, WPA desks, social security railings, and in all kinds of lines from soup lines to the draft. If I just had four feet, I could have stood in more places longer. As it is, I done wore out seven hundred pairs of shoes, eighty-nine tennis shoes, twelve summer sandals, also six loafers. The socks that these feet have bought could build a knitting mill. The corns I've cut away would dull a German razor. The bunions I forgot would make you ache from now till Judgment Day. If anybody was to write the history of my life, they should start with my feet."

"Your feet are not all that extraordinary," I said. "Besides, everything you are saying is general. Tell me specifically some one thing your feet have done that makes them different from any other feet in the world, just one."

"Do you see that window in that white man's store across the street?" asked Simple. "Well, this right foot of mine broke out that window in the Harlem riots right smack in the middle. Didn't no other foot in the world break that window but mine. And this left foot carried me off running as soon as my right foot came down. Nobody else's feet saved me from the cops that night but these *two* feet right here. Don't tell me these feet ain't had a life of their own."

"For shame," I said, "going around kicking out windows. Why?"

"Why?" said Simple. "You have to ask my great-great-grandpa why. He must of been simple—else why did he let them capture him in Africa and sell him for a slave to breed my great-grandpa in slavery to breed my grandpa in slavery to breed my pa to breed me to look at that window and say, 'It ain't mine! Bam-mmm-mm-m!' and kick it out?"

"This bar glass is not yours either," I said. "Why don't you smash it?"

"It's got my beer in it," said Simple.

Just then Zarita came in wearing her Thursday-night rabbit-skin coat. She didn't stop at the bar, being dressed up, but went straight back to a booth. Simple's hand went up, his beer went down, and the glass back to its wet spot on the bar.

"Excuse me a minute," he said, sliding off the stool.

Just to give him pause, the dozens, that old verbal game of maligning a friend's female relatives, came to mind. "Wait," I said. "You have told me about what to ask your great-great-grandpa. But I want to know what to ask your great-great-*grandma*."

"I don't play the dozens that far back," said Simple, following Zarita into the smoky juke-box blue of the back room.

Temptation

"When the Lord said, 'Let there be light,' and there was light, what I want to know is where was us colored people?"

"What do you mean, 'Where were we colored people?' " I said.

"We must *not* of been there," said Simple, "because we are still dark. Either He did not include me or else I were not there."

"The Lord was not referring to people when He said, 'Let there be light.' He was referring to the elements, the atmosphere, the air."

"He must have included some people," said Simple, "because white people are light, in fact, *white*, whilst I am dark. How come? I say, we were not there."

"Then where do you think we were?"

"Late as usual," said Simple, "old C. P. Time. We must have been down the road a piece and did not get back on time."

"There was no C. P. Time in those days," I said. "In fact, no people were created—so there couldn't be any Colored People's Time. The Lord God had not yet breathed the breath of life into anyone."

"No?" said Simple.

"No," said I, "because it wasn't until Genesis 2 and 7 that God 'formed man of the dust of the earth and breathed into his nostrils the breath of life and man became a living soul.' His name was Adam. Then He took one of Adam's ribs and made a woman."

"Then trouble began," said Simple. "Thank God, they was both white."

"How do you know Adam and Eve were white?" I asked.

"When I was a kid I seen them on the Sunday school cards," said Simple. "Ever since I been seeing a Sunday School card, they was white. That is why I want to know where was us Negroes when the Lord said, 'Let there be light'?"

"Oh, man, you have a color complex so bad you want to trace it back to the Bible."

"No, I don't. I just want to know how come Adam and Eve was white. If they had started out black, this world might not be in the fix it is today. Eve might not of paid that serpent no attention. I never did know a Negro yet that liked a snake."

"That snake is a symbol," I said, "a symbol of temptation and sin. And that symbol would be the same, no matter what the race."

"I am not talking about no symbol," said Simple. "I am talking about the day when Eve took that apple and Adam et. From then on the human race has been in trouble. There ain't a colored woman living what would take no apple from a snake—and she better not give no snake-apples to her husband!"

"Adam and Eve are symbols, too," I said.

"You are simple yourself," said Simple. "But I just wish we colored folks had been somewhere around at the start. I do not know where we was when Eden was a garden, but we sure didn't get in' on none of the crops. If we had, we would not be so poor today. White folks started out ahead and they are still ahead. Look at me!"

"I am looking," I said.

"Made in the image of God," said Simple, "but I never did see anybody like me on a Sunday school card."

"Probably nobody looked like you in Biblical days," I said. "The American' Negro did not exist in B.C. You're a product of Caucasia and Africa, Harlem and Dixie. You've been conditioned entirely by our environment, our modern times."

"Times have been hard," said Simple, "but still I am a child of God."

"In' the cosmic sense, we are all children of God."

"I have been baptized," said Simple, "also anointed with oil. When I were a child I come through at the mourners' bench. I was converted. I have listened to Daddy Grace and et with Father Divine, moaned with Elder Lawson' and prayed with Adam Powell. Also I have been to the Episcopalians with Joyce. But if a snake were to come up to me and offer *me* an apple, I would say, 'Varmint, be on your way! No fruit today! Bud, you got the wrong stud now, so get along somehow, be off down the road because you're lower than a toad!' Then that serpent would respect me as a wise man—and this world would not be where it is—all on account of an apple. That apple has turned into an' atom now."

"To hear you talk, if you had been in the Garden of Eden, the world would still be a Paradise," I said. "Man would not have fallen into sin."

"Not *this* man," said Simple. "I would have stayed in that garden making grape wine, singing like Crosby, and feeling fine! I would not be scuffling out in this rough world, neither would I be in Harlem. If I was Adam I would just stay in Eden in that garden with no rent to pay, no landladies to dodge, no time clock to punch—and *my* picture on a Sunday school card. I'd be a *real gone guy* even if I didn't have but one name—Adam—and no initials."

"You would be *real gone* all right. But you were not there. So, my dear fellow, I trust you will not let your rather late arrival on our contemporary stage distort your perspective."

"No," said Simple.

Bop

Somebody upstairs in Simple's house had the combination turned up loud with an old Dizzy Gillespie record spinning like mad filling the Sabbath with Bop as I passed.

"Set down here on the stoop with me and listen to the music," said Simple.

"I've heard your landlady doesn't like tenants sitting on her stoop," I said.

"Pay it no mind," said Simple. "Ool-ya-koo," he sang. "Hey Ba-Ba-Re-Bop! Be-Bop! Mop!"

"All that nonsense singing reminds me of Cab Calloway back in the old *scat* days," I said, "around 1930 when he was chanting, 'Hi-de-*hie*-de-ho! Hee-de-*hee*-de-hee!'"

"Not at all," said Simple, "absolutely not at all."

"Re-Bop certainly sounds like scat to me," I insisted.

"No," said Simple, "Daddy-o, you are wrong. Besides, it was not *Re*-Bop. It is *Be*-bop."

"What's the difference," I asked, "between *Re* and *Be?*"

"A lot," said Simple. "Re-Bop was an imitation like most of the white boys play. Be-Bop is the real thing like the colored boys play."

"You bring race into everything," I said, "even music."

"It is in everything," said Simple.

"Anyway, Be-Bop is passé, gone, finished."

"It may be gone, but its riffs remain behind," said Simple. "Be-Bop music was certainly colored folks' music—which is why white folks found it so hard to imitate. But there are some few white boys that latched onto it right well. And no wonder, because they sat and listened to Dizzy, Thelonius, Tad Dameron, Charlie Parker, also Mary Lou, all night long every time they got a chance, and bought their records by the dozen to copy their riffs. The ones that sing tried to make up new Be-Bop words, but them white folks don't know what they are singing about, even yet."

"It all sounds like pure nonsense syllables to me."

"Nonsense, nothing!" cried Simple. "Bop makes plenty of sense."

"What kind of sense?"

"You must not know where Bop comes from," said Simple, astonished at my ignorance.

"I do not know," I said. "Where?"

"From the police," said Simple.

"What do you mean, from the police?"

"From the police beating Negroes' heads," said Simple. "Every time a cop hits a Negro with his billy club, that old club say, 'BOP! BOP! . . . BE-BOP! . . . MOP! . . . BOP!'"

"That Negro hollers, 'Ooool-ya-koo! Ou-o-o!'"

"Old Cop just keeps on, 'MOP! MOP! . . . BE-BOP! . . . MOP!' That's where Be-Bop came from, beaten right out of some Negro's head into them horns and saxophones and piano keys that plays it. Do you call that nonsense?"

"If it's true, I do not," I said.

"That's why so many white folks don't dig Bop," said Simple. "White folks do not get their heads beat *just for being white*. But me—a cop is liable to grab me almost any time and beat my head—*just* for being colored.

"In some parts of this American country as soon as the polices see me, they say, 'Boy, what are you doing in this neighborhood?'

"I say, 'Coming from work, sir.'

"They say, 'Where do you work?'

"Then I have to go into my whole pedigree because I am a black man in a white neighborhood. And if my answers do not satisfy them, BOP! MOP! . . . BE-BOP! . . . MOP! If they do not hit me, they have already hurt my soul. *A dark man shall see dark days.* Bop comes out of them dark days. That's why real Bop is mad, wild, frantic, crazy—and not to be dug unless you've seen dark days, too. Folks who ain't suffered much cannot play Bop, neither appreciate it. They think Bop is nonsense—like you. They think it's just *crazy* crazy. They do not know Bop is also MAD crazy, SAD crazy, FRANTIC WILD CRAZY—beat out of somebody's head! That's what Bop is. Them young colored kids who started it, they know what Bop is."

"Your explanation depresses me," I said.

"Your nonsense depresses me," said Simple.

Census

"I have had so many hardships in this life," said Simple, "that it is a wonder I'll live until I die. I was born young, black, voteless, poor, and hungry, in a state where white folks did not even put Negroes on the census. My daddy said he were never counted in his life by the United States government. And nobody could find a birth certificate for me nowhere. It were not until I come to Harlem that one day a census taker dropped around to my house and asked me where were I born and why, also my age and if I was still living. I said, 'Yes, I am here, in spite of all.'

" 'All of what?' asked the census taker. 'Give me the data.'

" 'All my corns and bunions, for one,' I said. 'I were borned with corns. Most colored peoples get corns so young, they must be inherited. As for bunions, they seem to come natural, we stands on our feet so much. These feet of mine have stood in everything from soup lines to the draft board. They have supported everything from a packing trunk to a hongry woman. My feet have walked ten thousand miles running errands for white folks and another ten thousand trying to keep up with colored. My feet have stood before altars, at crap tables, bars, graves, kitchen doors, welfare windows, and social security railings. Be sure and include my feet on that census you are taking,' I told that man.

"Then I went on to tell him how my feet have helped to keep the American shoe industry going, due to the money I have spent on my feet. 'I have wore out seven hundred pairs of shoes, eight-nine tennis shoes, forty-four summer sandals, and two hundred and two loafers. The socks my feet have bought could build a knitting mill. The razor blades I have used cutting away my corns could pay for a razor plant. Oh, my feet have helped to make America rich, and I am still standing on them.

" 'I stepped on a rusty nail once, and mighty near had lockjaw. And from my feet up, so many other things have happened to me, since, it is a wonder I made it through this world. In my time, I have been cut, stabbed, run over, hit by a car, tromped by a horse, robbed, fooled, deceived, double-crossed, dealt seconds, and mighty near blackmailed—but I am still here! I have been laid off, fired and not rehired, Jim Crowed, segregated, insulted, eliminated, locked in, locked out, locked up, left holding the bag, and denied relief. I have been caught in the rain, caught in jails, caught short with my rent, and caught with the wrong woman—but I am still here!

" 'My mama should have named me Job instead of Jesse B. Semple. I have been underfed, underpaid, undernourished, and everything but undertaken—yet I am still here. The only thing I am afraid of now—is that I will die before my time. So man, put me on your census now this year, because I may not be here when the next census comes around.'

"The census man said, 'What do you expect to die of—complaining?'

" 'No,' I said, 'I expect to ugly away.' At which I thought the man would laugh. Instead you know he nodded his head, and wrote it down. He were white and did not know I was making a joke. Do you reckon that man really thought I am homely?"

Coffee Break

"My boss is white," said Simple.

"Most bosses are," I said.

"And being white and curious, my boss keeps asking me just what does THE Negro want. Yesterday he tackled me during the coffee break, talking about THE Negro. He always says 'THE Negro,' as if there was not 50-11 different kinds of Negroes in the U.S.A.," complained Simple. "My boss says, 'Now that you-all have got the Civil Rights Bill and the Supreme Court, Adam Powell in Congress, Ralph Bunche in the United Nations, and Leontyne Price singing in the Metropolitan Opera, plus Dr. Martin Luther King getting the Nobel Prize, what more do you want? I am asking you, just what does THE Negro want?'"

" 'I am not THE Negro,' I says. 'I am *me*.'

" 'Well,' says my boss, 'you represent THE Negro.'

" 'I do not,' I says. 'I represent my own self.'

" 'Ralph Bunche represents you, then,' says my boss, 'and Thurgood Marshall and Martin Luther King. Do they not?'

" 'I am proud to be represented by such men, if you say they represent me,' I said. 'But all them men you name are *way* up there, and they do not drink beer in my bar. I have never seen a single one of them mens on Lenox Avenue in my natural life. So far as I know, they do not even live in Harlem. I cannot find them in the telephone book. They all got private numbers. But since you say they represent THE Negro, why do you not ask them what THE Negro wants?'

" 'I cannot get to them,' says my boss.

" 'Neither can I,' I says, 'so we both is in the same boat.'

" 'Well then, to come nearer home,' says my boss, 'Roy Wilkins fights your battles, also James Farmer.'

" 'They do not drink in my bar, neither,' I said.

" 'Don't Wilkins and Farmer live in Harlem?' he asked.

" 'Not to my knowledge,' I said. 'And I bet they have not been to the Apollo since Jackie Mabley cracked the first joke.'

" 'I do not know him,' said my boss, 'but I see Nipsey Russell and Bill Cosby on TV.'

" 'Jackie Mabley is no *him*,' I said. 'She is a *she*—better known as Moms.'

" 'Oh,' said my boss.

" 'And Moms Mabley has a story on one of her records about Little Cindy Ella and the magic slippers going to the Junior Prom at Ole Miss which tells all about what THE Negro wants.'

" 'What's its conclusion?' asked my boss.

" 'When the clock strikes midnight, Little Cindy Ella is dancing with the President of the Ku Klux Klan, says Moms, but at the stroke of twelve, Cindy Ella turns back to her natural self, black, and her blonde wig turns to a stocking cap —and her trial comes up next week.'

" 'A symbolic tale,' says my boss, 'meaning, I take it, that THE Negro is in jail. But you are not in jail.'

" 'That's what you think,' I said.

" 'Anyhow, you claim you are not THE Negro,' said my boss.

" 'I am not,' I said. 'I am *this* Negro.'

" 'Then what do *you* want?' asked my boss.

" 'To get out of jail,' I said.

" 'What jail?'

" 'The jail you got me in.'

" 'Me?' yells my boss. 'I have not got you in jail. Why, boy, I like you. I am a liberal. I voted for Kennedy. And this time for Johnson. I believe in integration. Now that you got it, though, what more do you want?'

" 'Reintegration,' I said.

" 'Meaning by that, what?'

" 'That you be integrated with *me,* not me with you.'

" 'Do you mean that I come and live in Harlem?' asked my boss. 'Never!'

" 'I live in Harlem,' I said.

" 'You are adjusted to it,' said my boss. 'But there is so much crime in Harlem.'

" 'There are no two-hundred-thousand-dollar bank robberies, though,' I said, 'of which there was three lately *elsewhere* —all done by white folks, and nary one in Harlem. The biggest and best crime is outside of Harlem. We never has no half-million-dollar jewelry robberies, no missing star sapphires. You better come uptown with me and reintegrate.'

" 'Negroes are the ones who want to be integrated,' said my boss.

" 'And white folks are the ones who do *not* want to be,' I said.

" 'Up to a point, we do,' said my boss.

" 'That is what THE Negro wants,' I said, 'to remove that *point.*'

" 'The coffee break is over,' said my boss."

Cracker Prayer

"Well," said Simple, "this other old cracker down in Virginia who acted like Mr. Winclift what kicked my shins, one night he were down on his knees praying. Since he were getting right ageable, he wanted to be straight with God before he departed his life and headed for the Kingdom. So he lifted his voice and said, 'Oh, Lord, help me to get right, do right, be right, and die right before I ascends to Thy sight. Help me to make my peace with Nigras, Lord, because I have hated them all my life. If I do not go to heaven, Lord, I certainly do not want to go to hell with all them Nigras down there waiting to meet me. I hear the Devil is in league with Nigras, and if the Devil associates with Nigras, he must be a Yankee who would not give me protection. Lord, take me to Thy Kingdom where I will not have to associate with a hell full of Nigras. Do You hear me, Lord?'

"The Lord answered and said, 'I hearest thee, Colonel Cushenberry. What else wilst thou have of me?'

"The old cracker prayed on, 'Lord, Lord, dear Lord, since I did not have a nice old colored mammy in my childhood, give me one in heaven, Lord. My family were too poor to afford a black mammy for any of my father's eight children. I were mammyless as a child. Give me a mammy in heaven, Lord. Also a nice old Nigress to polish my golden slippers and keep the dust off of my wings. But, Lord, if there be educated Nigras in heaven, keep them out of my sight. The only thing I hate worse than an educated Nigra is an integrated one. Do not let me meet no New York Nigras in heaven, Lord, nor none what ever flirted with the NAACP or Eleanor Roosevelt. As You is my Father, Lord, lead me not into black pastures, but deliver me from integration, for Thine is the power to make all men as white as snow. But I would still know a Nigra even though he were white, by the way he sings, also by certain other characteristics which I will not go into now because a prayer is no place to explain everything. But You understand as well as I do, Lord, why a Nigra is something special.

" 'Lord, could I ask You one question? Did You make Nigras just to bedevil white folks? Was they put here on earth to be a trial and tribulation to the South? Did You create the NAACP to add fire to brimstone? You know, Lord, as soon as a Nigra gets an inch he wants an el. Give him an el, and he wants it ALL. Pretty soon a white man will not be able to sing "Come to Jesus" without a Nigra wanting to sing along with him. And you know Nigras can outsing us, Lord.

" 'Lord, You know I think it would be a good idea if You would send Christ down to earth again. It is about time for the Second Coming, because I don't believe Christ knows what Nigras is up to in this modern day and age. They is up to devilment, Lord—riding in the same train coaches with us, setting beside us on busses, sending their little Nigra children to school with our little white children. Even talking about they do not like to be segregated in jail no more—that a jail is a public place for which they also pay taxes.

" 'Lord, separate the black taxes from the white taxes, black sheep from white sheep, and Nigra soldiers from white soldiers before the next war comes around. I do not want my grandson atomized with no Nigra. Lord, dispatch Christ down here before it is too late. Great Lord God, Jehovah, Father, send Your Only Begotten Son in a Cloud of Fire to straighten out this world again and put Nigras back in their places before that last trumpet sounds. When I get ready to go to Glory, Lord, and put on my white robe and prepare to step into Thy chariot, I do not want no Nigras lined up telling me the Supreme Court has decreed integrated seats in the Celestial Chariot, too. If I hear tell of such, Lord, I elect to stay right here on earth where at least Faubus is on my side.' "

Promulgations

"If I was setting in the High Court in Washington," said Simple, "where they do not give out no sentences for crimes, but where they gives out promulgations, I would promulgate. Up them long white steps behind them tall white pillars in that great big marble hall with the eagle of the U.S.A., where at I would bang my gavel and promulgate."

"Promulgate what?" I asked.

"Laws," said Simple. "After that I would promulgate the promulgations that would take place if people did not obey my laws. I see no sense in passing laws if nobody pays them any mind."

"What would happen if people did not obey your promulgations?" I asked.

"Woe be unto them," said Simple. "I would not be setting in that High Court paid a big salary just to read something off a paper. I would be there with a robe on to see that what I read was carried out. I would gird on my sword, like in the Bible, and prepare to do battle. For instant, 'Love thy neighbor as thyself.' The first man I caught who did not love his neighbor as hisself, I would make him change places with his neighbor—the rich with the poor, the white with the black, and Governor Faubus with me."

"I know you have lost your mind," I said. "How could you accomplish such an objective?"

"With education," said Simple, "which white folks favors. I would make Governor Faubus go to school again in Little Rock and study with them integrated students there and learn all over again the facts of life."

"You are telling me *what* you would do," I said, "not *how* you would do it. How could you make Faubus do anything?"

"I would say, 'Faubus! Faubus! Come out of that clothes closet or wherever you are hiding and face me. *Me,* Jesse B., who has promulgated your attendance in my presence! I decrees now and from here on out that you straighten up and fly right. Cast off your mask of ignorance and hate and go study your history. You have not yet learned that "taxation without representation is tyranny," which I learned in grade school. You have also not learned that "all men are created equal," which I learned before I quit school. Educate yourself, Faubus, so that you can better rule your state.' "

"Suppose he paid you no attention?" I said.

"Then I would whisper something in his ear," said Simple. "I would tell him that the secret records in the hands of my committee show that he has got colored blood. Whilst he was trying to recover from that shock, I would continue with some facts I made up.

" 'Governor Faubus, did you know your great-great-grandfather were black?'

"He would say, 'What?'

"I would say, 'Look at me, Governor, I am your third cousin.' Whereupon Faubus would faint. Whilst he was fainted, I would pick him up and take him to a mixed school. When he come to, he would be integrated. That is the way I would work my promulgations," said Simple.

"I should think you would rapidly become a national figure," I said, "with your picture in *Time, Life, Newsweek, Ebony,* and *Jet.*"

"Yes," said Simple. "Then in my spare time I would take up the international situation. I would call a Summit Meeting and get together with all the big heads of state in the world."

"I gather you would drop your judgeship for the nonce and become a diplomat."

"A hip-to-mat," said Simple, "minding everybody's business but my own. I would call my valet to tell my confidential secretary to inform my aide to bring me my attaché case. I would put on my swallowtail coat, striped trousers, and high hat, get into my limousine, and ride to the Summit looking like an Englishman. But what would be different about me is I would be black. I would take my black face, black hands, and black demands right up to the top and set down and say, 'Gimme a microphone, turn on the TVs, and hook up the national hookups. I want the world to hear my message.' Then I would promulgate at large as I proceeded to chair the agenda."

"Proceed," I said.

"Which I would do," said Simple, "no sooner than the audience got settled, the diplomats got their earphones strapped on, and the translators got their dictionaries out, also the stenographers got their machines ready to take my message from Harlem down for the record. The press galleries would be full of reporters waiting to wire my words around the world, and I would be prepared to send them, Jack. I would be ready."

"Give forth," I said.

"Bread and meat come first," said Simple. " 'Gentlemens of the Summit, I want you-all to think how you can provide everybody in the world with bread and meat. Civil rights comes next. Let everybody have civil rights, white, black, yellow, brown, gray, grizzle, or green. No Jim-Crow-take-low can't go for anybody! Let Arabs go to Israel and Israels go to Egypt, Chinese come to America and Negroes live in Australia, if any be so foolish as to want to. Let Willie Mays live in Levittown and Casey Stengel live in Ghana if he so desires. And let me drink at the Stork Club if I get tired of Small's Paradise. Open house before open skies. After which comes peace, which you can't have nohow as long as peoples and nations is snatching and grabbing over pork chops and payola so as not to starve to death. No peace could be had nowhow with white nations against dark.

" 'You big countries of the world has got to wake up to the sense your leaders wasn't born with, and the peoples has got to reach out their hands to each others' over the leaders' heads, just like I am talking over your leaders' heads now, because so many leaders is in the game for payola and say-ola, not *do*-ola. But me, self-appointed, I am beholden to nobody. Right now I cannot do much, but I can say *all*.

" 'I therefore say to you, gentlemens of the Summit, you may not pay attention to me now, but some sweet day you will. I will get tired of your stuff and your bluff. I will take your own golf stick and wham the world so far up into orbit until you will be shaken off the surface of the earth and everybody will wonder where have all the white folks gone. Gentlemens of the Summit, you-all had better get together and straighten up and fly right—else in due time you will have to contend with what Harlem thinks. Do I hear some of you-all say, "It do not matter what Harlem thinks"?

" 'I regret to inform you, gentlemens of the Summit, that IT DO!' "

RICHARD WRIGHT (1908–1960)

Going far beyond the "protest novel" label which has been tagged to his fiction by some critics, Richard Wright brought into American literature in a radically new way, the feeling and the texture of the complex psychological tensions simmering in the black ghetto of urban America. Bigger Thomas in Native Son *is a literary archetype of the hemmed-in, frustrated, and rejected black American in the ghetto who is propelled into violence by overwhelming conditions and forces. Wright was born on a plantation near Natchez, Mississippi, spent his youth in Memphis, Tennessee, and reached Chicago in his teens where he worked at odd jobs while experiencing his genesis as a writer. He participated in the traumatic mass migration of Negroes from the South to the North which produced the great centers of urban Negro life in the North. In his fiction he gave literary expression to the human and psychological meanings of this complex process of uprooting and rerooting. When he was born, about ninety per cent of the Negroes in the United States lived in the South. He was one of the many who made the northward trek which resulted in a quadrupling of the proportion of Negroes in the North during his lifetime. As he wrote in the last years of his life: "I feel personally identified with the migrant Negro, his folk songs, his ditties, his wild tales of bad men . . . because my own life was forged in the depths in which they live." He found his voice in the literary and political ferment of the Left in the 30's. His first writing was published in the Communist press, and for a while he was Harlem correspondent of* The Daily Worker; *later he voiced sharp conflict with Communist policies. His first book, a collection of short stories entitled* Uncle Tom's Children *(1938), won the annual award of* Story *magazine. His novel* Native Son, *published in 1940, became the first novel by an American Negro to enter the full mainstream of American literature, both in terms of its mass audience and its subsequent influence. It was a best* seller, the first novel by a Negro to become a Book-of-the-Month Club selection, and became the first novel by a Negro to appear in the Modern Library editions. In 1945 he published Black Boy, an autobiographical account of his childhood and youth in the South. LeRoi Jones has written: "The most completely valid social novels and social criticisms of South and North, nonurban and urban Negro life, are Wright's Black Boy and Native Son." After the publication of Black Boy, Wright went to Paris. He lived there as an expatriate for about fifteen years until his death in 1960. He traveled in Europe and Africa and continued to write fiction and nonfiction during his long exile, but critical opinion recognizes his earlier pre-Paris fiction as his most significant work. The short story that follows, with its obvious allusion in the title to the Dostoyevskyan Underground—redefined and applied here to the nightmarish hell of an urban Negro —was written at the peak of Wright's literary activity in America. An earlier draft was first published in Accent magazine in 1942. The present revised and enlarged version was published in Cross-Section 1944 and later included in his posthumously published collection of short stories, Eight Men. Other works by Richard Wright appear in the Autobiography, Poetry, and Literary Criticism sections.

The Man Who Lived Underground

I've got to hide, he told himself. His chest heaved as he waited, crouching in a dark corner of the vestibule. He was tired of running and dodging. Either he had to find a place to hide, or he had to surrender. A police car swished by through the rain, its siren rising sharply. They're looking for me all over . . . He crept to the door and squinted through the fogged plate glass. He stiffened as the siren rose and died in the distance. Yes, he had to hide, but where? He gritted his teeth. Then a sudden movement in the street caught his attention. A throng of tiny columns of water snaked into the air from the perforations of a manhole cover. The columns stopped abruptly, as though the perforations had become clogged; a gray spout of sewer water jutted up from underground and lifted the circular metal cover, juggled it for a moment, then let it fall with a clang.

He hatched a tentative plan: he would wait until the siren sounded far off, then he would go out. He smoked and waited, tense. At last the siren gave him his signal; it wailed, dying, going away from him. He stepped to the sidewalk, then paused and looked curiously at the open manhole, half expecting the cover to leap up again. He went to the center of the street and stooped and peered into the hole, but could see nothing. Water rustled in the black depths.

He started with terror; the siren sounded so near that he had the idea that he had been dreaming and had awakened to find the car upon him. He dropped instinctively to his knees and his hands grasped the rim of the manhole. The siren seemed to hoot directly above him and with a wild gasp of exertion he snatched the cover far enough off to admit his body. He swung his legs over the opening and lowered himself into watery darkness. He hung for an eternal moment to the rim by his finger tips, then he felt rough metal prongs and at once he knew that sewer workmen used these ridges to lower themselves into manholes. Fist over fist, he let his body sink until he could feel no more prongs. He swayed in dank space; the siren seemed to howl at the very rim of the manhole. He dropped and was washed violently into an ocean of warm, leaping water. His head was battered against a wall and he wondered if this were death. Frenziedly his fingers clawed and sank into a crevice. He steadied himself and measured the strength of the current with his own muscular tension. He stood slowly in water that dashed past his knees with fearful velocity.

He heard a prolonged scream of brakes and the siren broke off. Oh, God! They had found him! Looming above his head in the rain a white face hovered over the hole. "How did this damn thing get off?" he heard a policeman ask. He saw the steel cover move slowly until the hole looked like a quarter moon turned black. "Give me a hand here," someone called. The cover clanged into place, muffling the sights and sounds of the upper world. Knee-deep in the pulsing current, he breathed with aching chest, filling his lungs with the hot stench of yeasty rot.

From the perforations of the manhole cover, delicate lances of hazy violet sifted down and wove a mottled pattern upon the surface of the streaking current. His lips parted as a car swept past along the wet pavement overhead, its heavy rumble soon dying out, like the hum of a plane speeding through a dense cloud. He had never thought that cars could sound like that; everyting seemed strange and unreal under here. He stood in darkness for a long time, knee-deep in rustling water, musing.

The odor of rot had become so general that he no longer smelled it. He got his cigarettes, but discovered that his matches were wet. He searched and found a dry folder in the pocket of his shirt and managed to strike one; it flared weirdly in the wet gloom, glowing greenishly, turning red, orange, then yellow. He lit a crumpled cigarette; then, by the flickering light of the match, he looked for support so that he would not have to keep his muscles flexed against the pouring water. His pupils narrowed and he saw to either side of him two steaming walls that rose and curved inward some six feet above his head to form a dripping, mouse-colored dome. The bottom of the sewer was a sloping V-trough. To the left, the sewer vanished in ashen fog. To the right was a steep downcurve into which water plunged.

He saw now that had he not regained his feet in time, he would have been swept to death, or had he entered any other manhole he would have probably drowned. Above the rush of the current he heard sharper juttings of water; tiny streams were spewing into the sewer from smaller conduits. The match died; he struck another and saw a mass of debris sweep past him and clog the throat of the down-curve. At once the water began rising rapidly. Could he climb out before he drowned? A long hiss sounded and the debris was sucked from sight; the current lowered. He understood now what had made the water toss the manhole cover; the downcurve had become temporarily obstructed and the perforations had become clogged.

He was in danger; he might slide into a down-curve; he might wander with a lighted match into a pocket of gas and blow himself up; or he might contract some horrible disease . . . Though he wanted to leave, an irrational impulse held him rooted. To the left, the convex ceiling swooped to a height of less than five feet. With cigarette slanting from pursed lips, he waded with taut muscles, his feet sloshing over the slimy bottom, his shoes sinking into spongy slop, the slate-colored water cracking in creamy foam against his knees. Pressing his flat left palm against the lowered ceiling, he struck another match and saw a metal pole nestling in a niche of the wall. Yes, some sewer workman had left it. He reached for it, then jerked his head away as a whisper of scurrying life whisked past and was still. He held the match close and saw a huge rat, wet with slime, blinking beady eyes and baring tiny fangs. The light blinded the rat and the frizzled head moved aimlessly. He grabbed the pole and let it fly against the rat's soft body; there was shrill piping and the grizzly body splashed into the dun-colored water and was snatched out of sight, spinning in the scuttling stream.

He swallowed and pushed on, following the curve of the

misty cavern, sounding the water with the pole. By the faint light of another manhole cover he saw, amid loose wet brick, a hole with walls of damp earth leading into blackness. Gingerly he poked the pole into it; it was hollow and went beyond the length of the pole. He shoved the pole before him, hoisted himself upward, got to his hands and knees, and crawled. After a few yards he paused, struck to wonderment by the silence; it seemed that he had traveled a million miles away from the world. As he inched forward again he could sense the bottom of the dirt tunnel becoming dry and lowering slightly. Slowly he rose and to his astonishment he stood erect. He could not hear the rustling of the water now and he felt confoundingly alone, yet lured by the darkness and silence.

He crept a long way, then stopped, curious, afraid. He put his right foot forward and it dangled in space; he drew back in fear. He thrust the pole outward and it swung in emptiness. He trembled, imagining the earth crumbling and burying him alive. He scratched a match and saw that the dirt floor sheered away steeply and widened into a sort of cave some five feet below him. An old sewer, he muttered. He cocked his head, hearing a feathery cadence which he could not identify. The match ceased to burn.

Using the pole as a kind of ladder, he slid down and stood in darkness. The air was a little fresher and he could still hear vague noises. Where was he? He felt suddenly that someone was standing near him and he turned sharply, but there was only darkness. He poked cautiously and felt a brick wall; he followed it and the strange sounds grew louder. He ought to get out of here. This was crazy. He could not remain here for any length of time; there was no food and no place to sleep. But the faint sounds tantalized him; they were strange but familiar. Was it a motor? A baby crying? Music? A siren? He groped on, and the sounds came so clearly that he could feel the pitch and timbre of human voices. Yes, singing! That was it! He listened with open mouth. It was a church service. Enchanted, he groped toward the waves of melody.

Jesus, take me to your home above
And fold me in the bosom of Thy love......

The singing was on the other side of a brick wall. Excited, he wanted to watch the service without being seen. Whose church was it? He knew most of the churches in this area above ground, but the singing sounded too strange and detached for him to guess. He looked to the left, to the right, down to the black dirt, then upward and was startled to see a bright sliver of light slicing the darkness like the blade of a razor. He struck one of his two remaining matches and saw rusty pipes running along an old concrete ceiling. Photographically he located the exact position of the pipes in his mind. The match flame sank and he sprang upward; his hands clutched a pipe. He swung his legs and tossed his body onto the bed of pipes and they creaked, swaying up and down; he thought that the tier was about to crash, but nothing happened. He edged to the crevice and saw a segment of black men and women, dressed in white robes, singing, holding tattered songbooks in their black palms. His first impulse was to laugh, but he checked himself.

What was he doing? He was crushed with a sense of guilt. Would God strike him dead for that? The singing swept on and he shook his head, disagreeing in spite of himself. They oughtn't to do that, he thought. But he could think of no reason *why* they should not do it. Just singing with the air of the sewer blowing in on them . . . He felt that he was gazing upon something abysmally obscene, yet he could not bring himself to leave.

After a long time he grew numb and dropped to the dirt. Pain throbbed in his legs and a deeper pain, induced by the sight of those black people groveling and begging for something they could never get, churned in him. A vague conviction made him feel that those people should stand unrepentant and yield no quarter in singing and praying, yet *he* had run away from the police, had pleaded with them to believe in *his* innocence. He shook his head, bewildered.

How long had he been down here? He did not know. This was a new kind of living for him; the intensity of feelings he had experienced when looking at the church people sing made him certain that he had been down here a long time, but his mind told him that the time must have been short. In this darkness the only notion he had of time was when a match flared and measured time by its fleeting light. He groped back through the hole toward the sewer and the waves of song subsided and finally he could not hear them at all. He came to where the earth hole ended and he heard the noise of the current and time lived again for him, measuring the moments by the wash of water.

The rain must have slackened, for the flow of water had lessened and came only to his ankles. Ought he to go up into the streets and take his chances on hiding somewhere else? But they would surely catch him. The mere thought of dodging and running again from the police made him tense. No, he would stay and plot how to elude them. But what could he do down here? He walked forward into the sewer and came to another manhole cover; he stood beneath it, debating. Fine pencils of gold spilled suddenly from the little circles in the manhole cover and trembled on the surface of the current. Yes, street lamps . . . It must be night . . .

He went forward for about a quarter of an hour, wading aimlessly, poking the pole carefully before him. Then he stopped, his eyes fixed and intent. What's that? A strangely familiar image attracted and repelled him. Lit by the yellow stems from another manhole cover was a tiny nude body of a baby snagged by debris and half-submerged in water. Thinking that the baby was alive, he moved impulsively to save it, but his roused feelings told him that it was dead, cold, nothing, the same nothingness he had felt while watching the men and women singing in the church. Water blossomed about the tiny legs, the tiny arms, the tiny head, and rushed onward. The eyes were closed, as though in sleep; the fists were clenched, as though in protest; and the mouth gaped black in a soundless cry.

He straightened and drew in his breath, feeling that he had been staring for all eternity at the ripples of veined water skimming impersonally over the shriveled limbs. He felt as condemned as when the policemen had accused him. Involuntarily he lifted his hand to brush the vision away, but his arm fell listlessly to his side. Then he acted; he closed his eyes and reached forward slowly with the soggy shoe of his right foot and shoved the dead baby from where it had been lodged. He kept his eyes closed, seeing the little body twisting in the current as it floated from sight. He opened his eyes, shivered, placed his knuckles in the sockets, hearing the water speed in the somber shadows.

He tramped on, sensing at times a sudden quickening in the current as he passed some conduit whose waters were swelling the stream that slid by his feet. A few minutes later he was standing under another manhole cover, listening to the faint rumble of noises above ground. Streetcars and trucks, he mused. He looked down and saw a stagnant pool of gray-green sludge; at intervals a balloon pocket rose from the scum, glistening a bluish-purple, and burst. Then another. He turned, shook his head, and tramped back to the dirt cave by the church, his lips quivering.

Back in the cave, he sat and leaned his back against a dirt wall. His body was trembling slightly. Finally his senses quieted and he slept. When he awakened he felt stiff and cold. He had to leave this foul place, but leaving meant facing those policemen who had wrongly accused him. No, he could not go back aboveground. He remembered the beating they had given him and how he had signed his name to a confession, a confession which he had not even read. He had been too tired when they had shouted at him, demanding that he sign his name; he had signed it to end his pain.

He stood and groped about in the darkness. The church singing had stopped. How long had he slept? He did not know. But he felt refreshed and hungry. He doubled his fist nervously, realizing that he could not make a decision. As he walked about he stumbled over an old rusty iron pipe. He picked it up and felt a jagged edge. Yes, there was a brick wall and he could dig into it. What would he find? Smiling, he groped to the brick wall, sat, and began digging idly into damp cement. I can't make any noise, he cautioned himself. As time passed he grew thirsty, but there was no water. He had to kill time or go aboveground. The cement came out of the wall easily; he extracted four bricks and felt a soft draft blowing into his face. He stopped, afraid. What was beyond? He waited a long time and nothing happened; then he began digging again, soundlessly, slowly; he enlarged the hole and crawled through into a dark room and collided with another wall. He felt his way to the right; the wall ended and his fingers toyed in space, like the antennae of an insect.

He fumbled on and his feet struck something hollow, like wood. What's this? He felt with his fingers. Steps . . . He stooped and pulled off his shoes and mounted the stairs and saw a yellow chink of light shining and heard a low voice speaking. He placed his eye to a keyhole and saw the nude waxen figure of a man stretched out upon a white table. The voice, low-pitched and vibrant, mumbled indistinguishable words, neither rising nor falling. He craned his neck and squinted to see the man who was talking, but he could not locate him. Above the naked figure was suspended a huge glass container filled with a blood-red liquid from which a white rubber tube dangled. He crouched closer to the door and saw the tip end of a black object lined with pink satin. A coffin, he breathed. This is an undertaker's establishment . . . A fine-spun lace of ice covered his body and he shuddered. A throaty chuckle sounded in the depths of the yellow room.

He turned to leave. Three steps down it occurred to him that a light switch should be nearby; he felt along the wall, found an electric button, pressed it, and a blinding glare smote his pupils so hard that he was sightless, defenseless. His pupils contracted and he wrinkled his nostrils at a pecu-

liar odor. At once he knew that he had been dimly aware of
this odor in the darkness, but the light had brought it sharply
to his attention. Some kind of stuff they use to embalm, he
thought. He went down the steps and saw piles of lumber,
coffins, and a long workbench. In one corner was a tool
chest. Yes, he could use tools, could tunnel through walls
with them. He lifted the lid of the chest and saw nails, a
hammer, a crowbar, a screwdriver, a light bulb, a long length
of electric wire. Good! He would lug these back to his cave.

He was about to hoist the chest to his shoulders when he
discovered a door behind the furnace. Where did it lead? He
tried to open it and found it securely bolted. Using the crowbar so as to make no sound, he pried the door open; it swung
on creaking hinges, outward. Fresh air came to his face and
he caught the faint roar of faraway sound. Easy now, he told
himself. He widened the door and a lump of coal rattled toward him. A coalbin . . . Evidently the door led into another
basement. The roaring noise was louder now, but he could
not identify it. Where was he? He groped slowly over the
coal pile, then ranged in darkness over a gritty floor. The
roaring noise seemed to come from above him, then below,
His fingers followed a wall until he touched a wooden ridge.
A door, he breathed.

The noise died to a low pitch; he felt his skin prickle. It
seemed that he was playing a game with an unseen person
whose intelligence outstripped his. He put his ear to the flat
surface of the door. Yes, voices . . . Was this a prize fight
stadium? The sound of the voices came near and sharp, but
he could not tell if they were joyous or despairing. He twisted
the knob until he heard a soft click and felt the springy
weight of the door swinging toward him. He was afraid to
open it, yet captured by curiosity and wonder. He jerked the
door wide and saw on the far side of the basement a furnace
glowing red. Ten feet away was still another door, half ajar.
He crossed and peered through the door into an empty,
high-ceilinged corridor that terminated in a dark complex of
shadow. The belling voices rolled about him and his eagerness mounted. He stepped into the corridor and the voices
swelled louder. He crept on and came to a narrow stairway
leading circularly upward; there was no question but what he
was going to ascend those stairs.

Mounting the spiraled staircase, he heard the voices roll in
a steady wave, then leap to crescendo, only to die away, but
always remaining audible. Ahead of him glowed red letters:
E—X—I—T. At the top of the steps he paused in front of a
black curtain that fluttered uncertainly. He parted the folds

and looked into a convex depth that gleamed with clusters of shimmering lights. Sprawling below him was a stretch of human faces, tilted upward, chanting, whistling, screaming, laughing. Dangling before the faces, high upon a screen of silver, were jerking shadows. A movie, he said with slow laughter breaking from his lips.

He stood in a box in the reserved section of a movie house and the impulse he had had to tell the people in the church to stop their singing seized him. These people were laughing at their lives, he thought with amazement. They were shouting and yelling at the animated shadows of themselves. His compassion fired his imagination and he stepped out of the box, walked out upon thin air, walked on down to the audience; and, hovering in the air just above them, he stretched out his hand to touch them . . . His tension snapped and he found himself back in the box, looking down into the sea of faces. No; it could not be done; he could not awaken them. He sighed. Yes, these people were children, sleeping in their living, awake in their dying.

He turned away, parted the black curtain, and looked out. He saw no one. He started down the white stone steps and when he reached the bottom he saw a man in trim blue uniform coming toward him. So used had he become to being underground that he thought that he could walk past the man, as though he were a ghost. But the man stopped. And he stopped.

"Looking for the men's room, sir?" the man asked, and, without waiting for an answer, he turned and pointed. "This way, sir. The first door to your right."

He watched the man turn and walk up the steps and go out of sight. Then he laughed. What a funny fellow! He went back to the basement and stood in the red darkness, watching the glowing embers in the furnace. He went to the sink and turned the faucet and the water flowed in a smooth silent stream that looked like a spout of blood. He brushed the mad image from his mind and began to wash his hands leisurely, looking about for the usual bar of soap. He found one and rubbed it in his palms until a rich lather bloomed in his cupped fingers, like a scarlet sponge. He scrubbed and rinsed his hands meticulously, then hunted for a towel; there was none. He shut off the water, pulled off his shirt, dried his hands on it; when he put it on again he was grateful for the cool dampness that came to his skin.

Yes, he was thirsty; he turned on the faucet again, bowled his fingers and when the water bubbled over the brim of his cupped palms, he drank in long, slow swallows. His bladder grew tight; he shut off the water, faced the wall, bent his head, and watched a red stream strike the floor. His nostrils wrinkled against acrid wisps of vapor; though he had tramped in the waters of the sewer, he stepped back from the wall so that his shoes, wet with sewer slime, would not touch his urine.

He heard footsteps and crawled quickly into the coalbin. Lumps rattled noisily. The footsteps came into the basement and stopped. Who was it? Had someone heard him and come down to investigate? He waited, crouching, sweating. For a long time there was silence, then he heard the clang of metal and a brighter glow lit the room. Somebody's tending the furnace, he thought. Footsteps came closer and he stiffened. Looming before him was a white face lined with coal dust, the face of an old man with watery blue eyes. Highlights spotted his gaunt cheekbones, and he held a huge shovel. There was a screechy scrape of metal against stone, and the old man lifted a shovelful of coal and went from sight.

The room dimmed momentarily, then a yellow glare came as coal flared at the furnace door. Six times the old man came to the bin and went to the furnace with shovels of coal, but not once did he lift his eyes. Finally he dropped the shovel, mopped his face with a dirty handkerchief, and sighed: "Wheeew!" He turned slowly and trudged out of the basement, his footsteps dying away.

He stood, and lumps of coal clattered down the pile. He stepped from the bin and was startled to see the shadowy outline of an electric bulb hanging above his head. Why had not the old man turned it on? Oh, yes . . . He understood. The old man had worked here for so long that he had no need for light; he had learned a way of seeing in his dark world, like those sightless worms that inch along underground by a sense of touch.

His eyes fell upon a lunch pail and he was afraid to hope that it was full. He picked it up; it was heavy. He opened it. *Sandwiches!* He looked guiltily around; he was alone. He searched farther and found a folder of matches and a half-empty tin of tobacco; he put them eagerly into his pocket and clicked off the light. With the lunch pail under his arm, he went through the door, groped over the pile of coal, and stood again in the lighted basement of the undertaking establishment. I've got to get those tools, he told himself. And turn off that light. He tiptoed back up the steps and switched off the light; the invisible voice still droned on behind the door. He crept down and, seeing with his fingers, opened the lunch pail and tore off a piece of paper bag and brought out the tin and spilled grains of tobacco into the makeshift concave. He rolled it and wet it with spittle, then inserted one end into his mouth and lit it: he sucked smoke that bit his lungs. The nicotine reached his brain, went out along his arms to his finger tips, down to his stomach, and over all the tired nerves of his body.

He carted the tools to the hole he had made in the wall. Would the noise of the falling chest betray him? But he would have to take a chance; he had to have those tools. He lifted the chest and shoved it; it hit the dirt on the other side of the wall with a loud clatter. He waited, listening; nothing happened. Head first, he slithered through and stood in the cave. He grinned, filled with a cunning idea. Yes, he would now go back into the basement of the undertaking establishment and crouch behind the coal pile and dig another hole. Sure! Fumbling, he opened the tool chest and extracted a crowbar, a screwdriver, and a hammer; he fastened them securely about his person.

With another lumpish cigarette in his flexed lips, he crawled back through the hole and over the coal pile and sat, facing the brick wall. He jabbed with the crowbar and the cement sheered away; quicker than he thought, a brick came loose. He worked an hour; the other bricks did not come easily. He sighed, weak from effort. I ought to rest a little, he thought. I'm hungry. He felt his way back to the cave and stumbled along the wall till he came to the tool chest. He sat upon it, opened the lunch pail, and took out two thick sandwiches. He smelled them. Pork chops . . . His mouth watered. He closed his eyes and devoured a sandwich, savoring the smooth rye bread and juicy meat. He ate rapidly, gulping down lumpy mouthfuls that made him long for water. He ate the other sandwich and found an apple and gobbled that up too, sucking the core till the last trace of flavor was drained from it. Then, like a dog, he ground the meat bones with his teeth, enjoying the salty, tangy marrow. He finished and stretched out full length on the ground and went to sleep. . . .

. . . His body was washed by cold water that gradually turned warm and he was buoyed upon a stream and swept out to sea where waves rolled gently and suddenly he found himself walking upon the water how strange and delightful to walk upon the water and he came upon a nude woman holding a nude baby in her arms and the woman was sinking into the water holding the baby above her head and screaming *help* and he ran over the water to the woman and he reached her just before she went down and he took the baby from her hands and stood watching the breaking bubbles where the woman sank and he called *lady* and still no answer yes dive down there and rescue that woman but he could not take this baby with him and he stooped and laid the baby tenderly upon the surface of the water expecting it to sink but it floated and he leaped into the water and held his breath and strained his eyes to see through the gloomy volume of water but there was no woman and he opened his mouth and called *lady* and the water bubbled and his chest ached and his arms were tired but he could not see the woman and he called again *lady lady* and his feet touched sand at the bottom of the sea and his chest felt as though it would burst and he bent his knees and propelled himself upward and water rushed past him and his head bobbed out and he breathed deeply and looked around where was the baby the baby was gone and he rushed over the water looking for the baby calling *where is it* and the empty sky and sea threw back his voice *where is it* and he began to doubt that he could stand upon the water and then he was sinking and as he struggled the water rushed him downward spinning dizzily and he opened his mouth to call for help and water surged into his lungs and he choked . . .

He groaned and leaped erect in the dark, his eyes wide. The images of terror that thronged his brain would not let him sleep. He rose, made sure that the tools were hitched to his belt, and groped his way to the coal pile and found the rectangular gap from which he had taken the bricks. He took out the crowbar and hacked. Then dread paralyzed him. How long had he slept? Was it day or night now? He had to be careful. Someone might hear him if it were day. He hewed softly for hours at the cement, working silently. Faintly quivering in the air above him was the dim sound of yelling voices. Crazy people, he muttered. They're still there in that movie . . .

Having rested, he found the digging much easier. He soon had a dozen bricks out. His spirits rose. He took out another brick and his fingers fluttered in space. Good! What lay ahead of him? Another basement? He made the hole larger, climbed through, walked over an uneven floor and felt a metal surface. He lighted a match and saw that he was standing behind a furance in a basement; before him, on the far side of the room, was a door. He crossed and opened it; it was full of odds and ends. Daylight spilled from a window above his head.

Then he was aware of a soft, continuous tapping. What was it? A clock? No, it was louder than a clock and more irregular. He placed an old empty box beneath the window, stood upon it, and looked into an areaway. He eased the window up and crawled through; the sound of the tapping came clearly now. He glanced about; he was alone. Then he looked upward at a series of window ledges. The tapping identified itself. That's a typewriter, he said to himself. It seemed to be coming from just above. He grasped the ridges of a rain pipe and lifted himself upward; through a half-inch opening of window he saw a doorknob about three feet away. No, it was not a doorknob; it was a small circular disk made of stainless steel with many fine markings upon it. He held his breath: an eerie white hand, seemingly detached from its arm, touched the metal knob and whirled it, first to the left, then to the right. It's a safe! . . . Suddenly he could see the dial no more; a huge metal door swung slowly toward him and he was looking into a safe filled with green wads of paper money, rows of coins wrapped in brown paper, and glass jars and boxes of various sizes. His heart quickened. Good Lord! The white hand went in and out of the safe, taking wads of bills and cylinders of coins. The hand vanished and he heard the muffled click of the big door as it closed. Only the steel dial was visible now. The typewriter still tapped in his ears, but he could not see it. He blinked, wondering if what he had seen was real. There was more money in that safe than he had seen in all his life.

As he clung to the rain pipe, a daring idea came to him and he pulled the screwdriver from his belt. If the white hand twirled that dial again, he would be able to see how far to the left and right it spun and he would have the combination! His blood tingled. I can scratch the numbers right here, he thought. Holding the pipe with one hand, he made the sharp edge of the screwdriver bite into the brick wall. Yes, he could do it. Now, he was set. Now, he had a reason for staying here in the underground. He waited for a long time, but the white hand did not return. Goddamn! Had he been more alert, he would have counted the twirls and he would have had the combination. He got down and stood in the areaway, sunk in reflection.

How could he get into that room? He climbed back into the basement and saw wooden steps leading upward. Was that the room where the safe stood? Fearing that the dial was now being twirled, he clambered through the window, hoisted himself up the rain pipe, and peered; he saw only the naked gleam of the steel dial. He got down and doubled his fists. Well, he would explore the basement. He returned to the basement room and mounted the steps to the door and squinted through the keyhole; all was dark, but the tapping was still somewhere near, still faint and directionless. He pushed the door in; along one wall of a room was a table piled with radios and electrical equipment. A radio shop, he muttered.

Well, he could rig up a radio in his cave. He found a sack, slid the radio into it, and slung it across his back. Closing the door, he went down the steps and stood again in the basement, disappointed. He had not solved the problem of the steel dial and he was irked. He set the radio on the floor and again hoisted himself through the window and up the rain pipe and squinted; the metal door was swinging shut. Goddamn! He's worked the combination again. If I had been patient, I'd have had it! How could he get into that room? He *had* to get into it. He could jimmy the window, but it would be much better if he could get in without any traces. To the right of him, he calculated, should be the basement of the building that held the safe; therefore, if he dug a hole right *here*, he ought to reach his goal.

He began a quiet scraping; it was hard work, for the bricks were not damp. He eventually got one out and lowered it softly to the floor. He had to be careful; perhaps people were beyond this wall. He extracted a second layer of brick and found still another. He gritted his teeth, ready to quit. I'll dig one more, he resolved. When the next brick came out he felt air blowing into his face. He waited to be challenged, but nothing happened.

He enlarged the hole and pulled himself through and stood in quiet darkness. He scratched a match to flame and saw steps; he mounted and peered through a keyhole: Darkness . . . He strained to hear the typewriter, but there was only silence. Maybe the office had closed? He twisted the knob and swung the door in; a frigid blast made him shiver. In the shadows before him were halves and quarters of hogs and lambs and steers hanging from metal hooks on the low ceiling, red meat encased in folds of cold white fat. Fronting him was frost-coated glass from behind which came indistinguishable sounds. The odor of fresh raw meat sickened him and he backed away. A meat market, he whispered.

He ducked his head, suddenly blinded by light. He narrowed his eyes; the red-white rows of meat were drenched in yellow glare. A man wearing a crimson-spotted jacket came in and took down a bloody meat clever. He eased the door to, holding it ajar just enough to watch the man, hoping that the darkness in which he stood would keep him from being seen. The man took down a hunk of steer and placed it upon a bloody wooden block and bent forward and whacked with the cleaver. The man's face was hard, square, grim; a jet of mustache smudged his upper lip and a glistening cowlick of hair fell over his left eye. Each time he lifted the cleaver and brought it down upon the meat, he let out a short, deep-chested grunt. After he had cut the meat, he wiped blood off the wooden block with a sticky wad of gunny sack and hung the cleaver upon a hook. His face was proud as he placed the chunk of meat in the crook of his elbow and left.

The door slammed and the light went off; once more he stood in shadow. His tension ebbed. From behind the frosted glass he heard the man's voice: "Forty-eight cents a pound, ma'am." He shuddered, feeling that there was something he had to do. But what? He stared fixedly at the cleaver, then he sneezed and was terrified for fear that the man had heard him. But the door did not open. He took down the cleaver and examined the sharp edge smeared with cold blood. Behind the ice-coated glass a cash register rang with a vibrating, musical tinkle.

Absent-mindedly holding the meat cleaver, he rubbed the glass with his thumb and cleared a spot that enabled him to see into the front of the store. The shop was empty, save for the man who was now putting on his hat and coat. Beyond the front window a wan sun shone in the streets; people passed and now and then a fragment of laughter or the whir of a speeding auto came to him. He peered closer and saw on the right counter of the shop a mosquito netting covering pears, grapes, lemons, oranges, bananas, peaches, and plums. His stomach contracted.

The man clicked out the light and he gritted his teeth, muttering, Don't lock the icebox door . . . The man went through the door of the shop and locked it from the outside. Thank God! Now, he would eat some more! He waited, trembling. The sun died and its rays lingered on in the sky, turning the streets to dusk. He opened the door and stepped inside the shop. In reverse letters across the front window was: NICK'S FRUITS AND MEATS. He laughed, picked up a soft ripe yellow pear and bit into it; juice squirted; his mouth ached as his saliva glands reacted to the acid of the fruit. He ate three pears, gobbled six bananas, and made away with several oranges, taking a bite out of their tops and holding them to his lips and squeezing them as he hungrily sucked the juice.

He found a faucet, turned it on, laid the cleaver aside, pursed his lips under the stream until his stomach felt about to burst. He straightened and belched, feeling satisfied for the

first time since he had been underground. He sat upon the
floor, rolled and lit a cigarette, his bloodshot eyes squinting
against the film of drifting smoke. He watched a patch of sky
turn red, then purple; night fell and he lit another cigarette,
brooding. Some part of him was trying to remember the
world he had left, and another part of him did not want to
remember it. Sprawling before him in his mind was his wife,
Mrs. Wooten for whom he worked, the three policemen who
had picked him up . . . He possessed them now more completely than he had ever possessed them when he had lived
aboveground. How this had come about he could not say, but
he had no desire to go back to them. He laughed, crushed the
cigarette, and stood up.

He went to the front door and gazed out. Emotionally he
hovered between the world aboveground and the world underground. He longed to go out, but sober judgment urged
him to remain here. Then impulsively he pried the lock loose
with one swift twist of the crowbar; the door swung outward.
Through the twilight he saw a white man and a white woman
coming toward him. He held himself tense, waiting for them
to pass; but they came directly to the door and confronted
him.

"I want to buy a pound of grapes," the woman said.

Terrified, he stepped back into the store. The white man
stood to one side and the woman entered.

"Give me a pound of dark ones," the woman said.

The white man came slowly forward, blinking his eyes.

"Where's Nick?" the man asked.

"Were you just closing?" the woman asked.

"Yes, ma'am," he mumbled. For a second he did not
breathe, then he mumbled again: "Yes, ma'am."

"I'm sorry," the woman said.

The street lamps came on, lighting the store somewhat.
Ought he run? But that would raise an alarm. He moved
slowly, dreamily, to a counter and lifted up a bunch of grapes
and showed them to the woman.

"Fine," the woman said. "But isn't that more than a
pound?"

He did not answer. The man was staring at him intently.

"Put them in a bag for me," the woman said, fumbling
with her purse.

"Yes, ma'am."

He saw a pile of paper bags under a narrow ledge; he
opened one and put the grapes in.

"Thanks," the woman said, taking the bag and placing a
dime in his dark palm.

"Where's Nick?" the man asked again. "At supper?"

"Sir? Yes, sir," he breathed.

They left the store and he stood trembling in the doorway. When they were out of sight, he burst out laughing and crying. A trolley car rolled noisily past and he controlled himself quickly. He flung the dime to the pavement with a gesture of contempt and stepped into the warm night air. A few shy stars trembled above him. The look of things was beautiful, yet he felt a lurking threat. He went to an unattended newsstand and looked at a stack of papers. He saw a headline: HUNT NEGRO FOR MURDER.

He felt that someone had slipped up on him from behind and was stripping off his clothes; he looked about wildly, went quickly back into the store, picked up the meat cleaver where he had left it near the sink, then made his way through the icebox to the basement. He stood for a long time, breathing heavily. They know I didn't do anything, he muttered. But how could he prove it? He had signed a confession. Though innocent, he felt guilty, condemned. He struck a match and held it near the steel blade, fascinated and repelled by the dried blotches of blood. Then his fingers gripped the handle of the cleaver with all the strength of his body, he wanted to fling the cleaver from him, but he could not. The match flame wavered and fled; he struggled through the hole and put the cleaver in the sack with the radio. He was determined to keep it, for what purpose he did not know.

He was about to leave when he remembered the safe. Where was it? He wanted to give up, but felt that he ought to make one more try. Opposite the last hole he had dug, he tunneled again, plying the crowbar. Once he was so exhausted that he lay on the concrete floor and panted. Finally he made another hole. He wriggled through and his nostrils filled with the fresh smell of coal. He struck a match; yes, the usual steps led upward. He tiptoed to a door and eased it open. A fair-haired white girl stood in front of a steel cabinet, her blue eyes wide upon him. She turned chalky and gave a high-pitched scream. He bounded down the steps and raced to his hole and clambered through, replacing the bricks with nervous haste. He paused, hearing loud voices.

"What's the matter, Alice?"

"A man . . ."

"What man? Where?"

"A man was at that door . . ."

"Oh nonsense!"

"He was looking at me through the door!"

"Aw, you're dreaming."

"I *did* see a man!"

The girl was crying now.

"There's nobody here."

Another man's voice sounded.

"What is it, Bob?"

"Alice says she saw a man in here, in that door!"

"Let's take a look."

He waited, poised for flight. Footsteps descended the stairs.

"There's nobody down here."

"The window's locked."

"And there's no door."

"You ought to fire that dame."

"Oh, I don't know. Women are that way."

"She's too hysterical."

The men laughed. Footsteps sounded again on the stairs. A door slammed. He sighed, relieved that he had escaped. But he had not done what he had set out to do; his glimpse of the room had been too brief to determine if the safe was there. He had to know. Boldly he groped through the hole once more; he reached the steps and pulled off his shoes and tip-toed up and peered through the keyhole. His head accidentally touched the door and it swung silently in a fraction of an inch; he saw the girl bent over the cabinet, her back to him. Beyond her was the safe. He crept back down the steps, thinking exultingly: I found it!

Now he had to get the combination. Even if the window in the areaway was locked and bolted, he could gain entrance when the office closed. He scoured through the hole he had dug and stood again in the basement where he had left the radio and the clever. Again he crawled out of the window and lifted himself up the rain pipe and peered. The steel dial showed lonely and bright, reflecting the yellow glow of an unseen light. Resigned to a long wait, he sat and leaned against a wall. From far off came the faint sounds of life aboveground; once he looked with a baffled expression at the dark sky. Frequently he rose and climbed the pipe to see the white hand spin the dial, but nothing happened. He bit his lip with impatience. It was not the money that was luring him, but the mere fact that he could get it with impunity. Was the hand now twirling the dial? He rose and looked, but the white hand was not in sight.

Perhaps it would be better to watch continuously? Yes; he clung to the pipe and watched the dial until his eyes thickened with tears. Exhausted, he stood again in the areaway. He heard a door being shut and he clawed up the pipe and looked. He jerked tense as a vague figure passed in front of

him. He stared unblinkingly, hugging the pipe with one hand
and holding the screwdriver with the other, ready to etch the
combination upon the wall. His ears caught: *Dong* . . .
Dong . . . *Dong* . . . *Dong* . . . *Dong* . . . *Dong* . . . *Dong* . . .
Seven o'clock, he whispered Maybe they were closing now?
What kind of a store would be open as late as this? he wondered. Did anyone live in the rear? Was there a night watchman? Perhaps the safe was *already* locked for the night!
Goddamn! While he had been eating in that shop, they had
locked up everything . . . Then, just as he was about to give
up, the white hand touched the dial and turned it once to the
right and stopped at six. With quivering fingers, he etched
1—R—6 upon the brick wall with the tip of the screwdriver.
The hand twirled the dial twice to the left and stopped at
two, and he engraved 2—L—2 upon the wall. The dial was
spun four times to the right and stopped at six again; he
wrote 4—R—6. The dial rotated three times to the left and
was centered straight up and down; he wrote 3—L—0. The
door swung open and again he saw the piles of green money
and the rows of wrapped coins. I got it, he said grimly.

Then he was stone still, astonished. There were two hands
now. A right hand lifted a wad of green bills and deftly
slipped it up the sleeve of a left arm. The hands trembled;
again the right hand slipped a packet of bills up the left
sleeve. He's stealing, he said to himself. He grew indignant,
as if the money belonged to him. Though *he* had planned to
steal the money, he despised and pitied the man. He felt that
his stealing the money and the man's stealing were two entirely different things. He wanted to steal the money merely
for the sensation involved in getting it, and he had no intention whatever of spending a penny of it; but he knew that the
man who was now stealing it was going to spend it, perhaps
for pleasure. The huge steel door closed with a soft click.

Though angry, he was somewhat satisfied. The office would
close soon. I'll clean the place out, he mused. He imagined
the entire office staff cringing with fear; the police would
question everyone for a crime they had not committed, just
as they had questioned him. And they would have no idea of
how the money had been stolen until they discovered the
holes, he had tunneled in the walls of the basements. He lowered himself and laughed mischievously, with the abandoned
glee of an adolescent.

He flattened himself against the wall as the window above
him closed with rasping sound. He looked; somebody was
bolting the window securely with a metal screen. That won't
help you, he snickered to himself. He clung to the rain pipe

until the yellow light in the office went out. He went back into the basement, picked up the sack containing the radio and cleaver, and crawled through the two holes he had dug and groped his way into the basement of the building that held the safe. He moved in slow motion, breathing softly. Be careful now, he told himself. There might be a night watchman . . . In his memory was the combination written in bold white characters as upon a blackboard. Eel-like he squeezed through the last hole and crept up the steps and put his hand on the knob and pushed the door in about three inches. Then his courage ebbed; his imagination wove dangers for him.

Perhaps the night watchman was waiting in there, ready to shoot. He dangled his cap on a forefinger and poked it past the jamb of the door. If anyone fired, they would hit his cap; but nothing happened. He widened the door, holding the crowbar high above his head, ready to beat off an assailant. He stood like that for five minutes; the rumble of a streetcar brought him to himself. He entered the room. Moonlight floated in from a wide window. He confronted the safe, then checked himself. Better take a look around first . . . He stepped about and found a closed door. Was the night watchman in there? He opened it and saw a washbowl, a faucet, and a commode. To the left was still another door that opened into a huge dark room that seemed empty; on the far side of that room he made out the shadow of still another door. Nobody's here, he told himself.

He turned back to the safe and fingered the dial; it spun with ease. He laughed and twirled it just for fun. Get to work, he told himself. He turned the dial to the figures he saw on the blackboard of his memory; it was so easy that he felt that the safe had not been locked at all. The heavy door eased loose and he caught hold of the handle and pulled hard, but the door swung open with a slow momentum of its own. Breathless, he gaped at wads of green bills, rows of wrapped coins, curious glass jars full of white pellets, and many oblong green metal boxes. He glanced guiltily over his shoulder; it seemed impossible that someone should not call to him to stop.

They'll be surprised in the morning, he thought. He opened the top of the sack and lifted a wad of compactly tied bills; the money was crisp and new. He admired the smooth, clean-cut edges. The fellows in Washington sure know how to make this stuff, he mused. He rubbed the money with his fingers, as though expecting it to reveal hidden qualities. He lifted the wad to his nose and smelled the fresh odor of ink.

Just like any other paper, he mumbled. He dropped the wad into the sack and picked up another. Holding the bag, he thought and laughed.

There was in him no sense of possessiveness; he was intrigued with the form and color of the money, with the manifold reactions which he knew that men aboveground held toward it. The sack was one-third full when it occurred to him to examine the denominations of the bills; without realizing it, he had put many wads of one-dollar bills into the sack, Aw, nuts, he said in disgust. Take the big ones . . . He dumped the one-dollar bills onto the floor and swept all the hundred-dollar bills he could find into the sack, then he raked in rolls of coins with crooked fingers.

He walked to a desk upon which sat a typewriter, the same machine which the blond girl had used. He was fascinated by it; never in his life had he used one of them. It was a queer instrument of business, something beyond the rim of his life. Whenever he had been in an office where a girl was typing, he had almost always spoken in whispers. Remembering vaguely what he had seen others do, he inserted a sheet of paper into the machine; it went in lopsided and he did not know how to straighten it. Spelling in a soft diffident voice, he pecked out his name on the keys: *freddaniels.* He looked at it and laughed. He would learn to type correctly one of these days.

Yes, he would take the typewriter too. He lifted the machine and placed it atop the bulk of money in the sack. He did not feel that he was stealing, for the cleaver, the radio, the money, and the typewriter were all on the same level of value, all meant the same thing to him. They were the serious toys of the men who lived in the dead world of sunshine and rain he had left, the world that had condemned him, branded him guilty.

But what kind of a place is this? He wondered. What was in that dark room to his rear? He felt for his matches and found that he had only one left. He leaned the sack against the safe and groped forward into the room, encountering smooth, metallic objects that felt like machines. Baffled, he touched a wall and tried vainly to locate an electric switch. Well, he *had* to strike his last match. He knelt and struck it, cupping the flame near the floor with his palms. The place seemed to be a factory, with benches and tables. There were bulbs with green shades spaced about the tables; he turned on a light and twisted it low so that the glare was limited. There were stools at the benches and he concluded that men worked here at some trade. He wandered and found a few half-used folders of matches. If only he could find more cigarettes! But there were none.

But what kind of a place was this? On a bench he saw a pad of paper captioned: PEER'S—MANUFACTURING JEWELERS. His lips formed an "O," then he snapped off the light and ran back to the safe and lifted one of the glass jars and stared at the tiny white pellets. Gingerly he picked up one and found that it was wrapped in tissue paper. He peeled the paper and saw a glittering stone that looked like glass, glinting white and blue sparks. Diamonds, he breathed.

Roughly he tore the paper from the pellets and soon his palm quivered with precious fire. Trembling, he took all four glass jars from the safe and put them into the sack. He grabbed one of the metal boxes, shook it, and heard a tinny rattle. He pried off the lid with the screwdriver. Rings! Hundreds of them . . . Were they worth anything? He scooped up a handful and jets of fire shot fitfully from the stones. These are diamonds too, he said. He pried open another box. Watches! A chorus of soft, metallic ticking filled his ears. For a moment he could not move, then he dumped all the boxes into the sack.

He shut the safe door, then stood looking around, anxious not to overlook anything. Oh! He had seen a door in the room where the machines were. What was in there? More valuables? He re-entered the room, crossed the floor, and stood undecided before the door. He finally caught hold of the knob and pushed the door in; the room beyond was dark. He advanced cautiously inside and ran his fingers along the wall for the usual switch, then he was stark still. *Something had moved in the room!* What was it? Ought he to creep out, taking the rings and diamonds and money? Why risk what he already had? He waited and the ensuing silence gave him confidence to explore further. Dare he strike a match? Would not a match flame make him a good target? He tensed again as he heard a faint sigh; he was now convinced that there was something alive near him, something that lived and breathed. On tiptoe he felt slowly along the wall, hoping that he would not collide with anything. Luck was with him; he found the light switch.

No; don't turn the light on . . . Then suddenly he realized that he did not know in what direction the door was. Goddamn! He had to turn the light on or strike a match. He fingered the switch for a long time, then thought of an idea. He knelt upon the floor, reached his arm up to the switch and flicked the button, hoping that if anyone shot, the bullet would go above his head. The moment the light came on he narrowed his eyes to see quickly. He sucked in his breath and his body gave a violent twitch and was still. In front of him, so close that it made him want to bound up and scream, was a human face.

He was afraid to move lest he touch the man. If the man had opened his eyes at that moment, there was no telling what he might have done. The man—long and rawboned—was stretched out on his back upon a little cot, sleeping in his clothes, his head cushioned by a dirty pillow; his face, clouded by a dark stubble of beard, looked straight up to the ceiling. The man sighed, and he grew tense to defend himself; the man mumbled and turned his face away from the light. I've got to turn off that light, he thought. Just as he was about to rise, he saw a gun and cartridge belt on the floor at the man's side. Yes, he would take the gun and cartridge belt, not to use them, but just to keep them, as one takes a memento from a country fair. He picked them up and was about to click off the light when his eyes fell upon a photograph perched upon a chair near the man's head; it was the picture of a woman, smiling, shown against a background of open fields; at the woman's side were two young children, a boy and a girl. He smiled indulgently; he could send a bullet into that man's brain and time would be over for him . . .

He clicked off the light and crept silently back into the room where the safe stood; he fastened the cartridge belt about him and adjusted the holster at his right hip. He strutted about the room on tiptoe, lolling his head nonchalantly, then paused abruptly, pulled the gun, and pointed it with grim face toward an imaginary foe. "Boom!" he whispered fiercely. Then he bent forward with silent laughter. That's just like they do it in the movies, he said.

He contemplated his loot for a long time, then got a towel from the washroom and tied the sack securely. When he looked up he was momentarily frightened by his shadow looming on the wall before him. He lifted the sack, dragged it down the basement steps, lugged it across the basement, gasping for breath. After he had struggled through the hole, he clumsily replaced the bricks, then tussled with the sack until he got it to the cave. He stood in the dark, wet with sweat, brooding about the diamonds, the rings, the watches, the money; he remembered the singing in the church, the people yelling in the movie, the dead baby, the nude man stretched out upon the white table . . . He saw these items hovering before his eyes and felt that some dim meaning linked them together, that some magical relationship made them kin. He stared with vacant eyes, convinced that all of these images, with their tongueless reality, were striving to tell him something . . .

Later, seeing with his fingers, he untied the sack and set each item neatly upon the dirt floor. Exploring, he took the bulb, the socket, and the wire out of the tool chest; he was elated to find a double socket at one end of the wire. He crammed the stuff into his pockets and hoisted himself upon the rusty pipes and squinted into the church; it was dim and empty. Somewhere in this wall were live electric wires; but where? He lowered himself, groped and tapped the wall with the butt of the screwdriver, listening vainly for hollow sounds. I'll just take a chance and dig, he said.

For an hour he tried to dislodge a brick, and when he struck a match, he found that he had dug a depth of only an inch! No use in digging here, he sighed. By the flickering light of a match, he looked upward, then lowered his eyes, only to glance up again, startled. Directly above his head, beyond the pipes, was a wealth of electric wiring. I'll be damned, he snickered.

He got an old dull knife from the chest and, seeing again with his fingers, separated the two strands of wire and cut away the insulation. Twice he received a slight shock. He scraped the wiring clean and managed to join the two twin ends, then screwed in the bulb. The sudden illumination blinded him and he shut his lids to kill the pain in his eyeballs. I've got that much done, he thought jubilantly.

He placed the bulb on the dirt floor and the light cast a blatant glare on the bleak clay walls. Next he plugged one end of the wire that dangled from the radio into the light socket and bent down and switched on the button; almost at once there was the harsh sound of static, but no words or music. Why won't it work? he wondered. Had he damaged the mechanism in any way? Maybe it needed grounding? Yes . . . He rummaged in the tool chest and found another length of wire, fastened it to the ground of the radio, and then tied the opposite end to a pipe. Rising and growing distinct, a slow strain of music entranced him with its measured sound. He sat upon the chest, deliriously happy.

Later he searched again in the chest and found a half-gallon can of glue; he opened it and smelled a sharp odor. Then he recalled that he had not even looked at the money. He took a wad of green bills and weighed it in his palm, then broke the seal and held one of the bills up to the light and studied it closely. *The United States of America will pay to the bearer on demand one hundred dollars,* he read in slow speech; then: *This note is legal tender for all debts, public*

and private. . . . He broke into a musing laugh, feeling that
he was reading of the doings of people who lived on some
far-off planet. He turned the bill over and saw on the other
side of it a delicately beautiful building gleaming with paint
and set amidst green grass. He had no desire whatever to
count the money; it was what it stood for—the various currents of life swirling aboveground—that captivated him. Next
he opened the rolls of coins and let them slide from their
paper wrappings to the ground; the bright, new gleaming
pennies and nickels and dimes piled high at his feet, a glowing mound of shimmering copper and silver. He sifted them
through his fingers, listening to their tinkle as they struck the
conical heap.

Oh, yes! He had forgotten. He would now write his name
on the typewriter. He inserted a piece of paper and poised his
fingers to write. But what was his name? He stared, trying to
remember. He stood and glared about the dirt cave, his name
on the tip of his lips. But it would not come to him. Why was
he here? Yes, he had been running away from the police. But
why? His mind was blank. He bit his lips and sat again, feeling a vague terror. But why worry? He laughed, then pecked
slowly: *itwasalonghotday.* He was determined to type the sentence without making any mistakes. How did one make capital letters? He experimented and luckily discovered how to
lock the machine for capital letters and then shift it back to
lower case. Next he discovered how to make spaces, then he
wrote neatly and correctly: *It was a long hot day.* Just why
he selected that sentence he did not know; it was merely the
ritual of performing the thing that appealed to him. He took
the sheet out of the machine and looked around with stiff
neck and hard eyes and spoke to an imaginary person:

"Yes, I'll have the contracts ready tomorrow."

He laughed. That's just the way they talk, he said. He grew
weary of the game and pushed the machine aside. His eyes
fell upon the can of glue, and a mischievous idea bloomed in
him, filling him with nervous eagerness. He leaped up and
opened the can of glue, then broke the seals on all the wads
of money. I'm going to have some wallpaper, he said with a
luxurious, physical laugh that made him bend at the knees.
He took the towel with which he had tied the sack and balled
it into a swab and dipped it into the can of glue and dabbed
glue onto the wall; then he pasted one green bill by the side
of another. He stepped back and cocked his head. Jesus!
That's funny . . . He slapped his thighs and guffawed. He
had triumphed over the world aboveground! He was free! If

only people could see this! He wanted to run from this cave and yell his discovery to the world.

He swabbed all the dirt walls of the cave and pasted them with green bills; when he had finished the walls blazed with a yellow-green fire. Yes, this room would be his hide-out; between him and the world that had branded him guilty would stand this mocking symbol. He had not stolen the money; he had simply picked it up, just as a man would pick up firewood in a forest. And that was how the world aboveground now seemed to him, a wild forest filled with death.

The walls of money finally palled on him and he looked about for new interests to feed his emotions. The cleaver! He drove a nail into the wall and hung the bloody cleaver upon it. Still another idea welled up. He pried open the metal boxes and lined them side by side on the dirt floor. He grinned at the gold and fire. From one box he lifted up a fistful of ticking gold watches and dangled them by their gleaming chains. He stared with an idle smile, then began to wind them up; he did not attempt to set them at any given hour, for there was no time for him now. He took a fistful of nails and drove them into the papered walls and hung the watches upon them, letting them swing down by their glittering chains, trembling and ticking busily against the backdrop of green with the lemon sheen of the electric light shining upon the metal watch casings, converting the golden disks into blobs of liquid yellow. Hardly had he hung up the last watch than the idea extended itself; he took more nails from the chest and drove them into the green paper and took the boxes of rings and went from nail to nail and hung up the golden bands. The blue and white sparks from the stones filled the cave with brittle laughter, as though enjoying his hilarious secret. People certainly can do some funny things, he said to himself.

He sat upon the tool chest, alternately laughing and shaking his head soberly. Hours later he became conscious of the gun sagging at his hip and he pulled it from the holster. He had seen men fire guns in movies, but somehow his life had never led him into contact with firearms. A desire to feel the sensation others felt in firing came over him. But someone might hear . . . Well, what if they did? They would not know where the shot had come from. Not in their wildest notions would they think that it had come from under the streets! He tightened his finger on the trigger; there was a deafening report and it seemed that the entire underground had caved in upon his eardrums; and in the same instant there flashed an orange-blue spurt of flame that died quickly but lingered on as a vivid after-image. He smelled the acrid stench of burnt powder filling his lungs and he dropped the gun abruptly.

The intensity of his feelings died and he hung the gun and cartridge belt upon the wall. Next he lifted the jars of diamonds and turned them bottom upward, dumping the white pellets upon the ground. One by one he picked them up and peeled the tissue paper from them and piled them in a neat heap. He wiped his sweaty hands on his trousers, lit a cigarette, and commenced playing another game. He imagined that he was a rich man who lived aboveground in the obscene sunshine and he was strolling through a park of a summer morning, smiling, nodding to his neighbors, sucking an after-breakfast cigar. Many times he crossed the floor of the cave, avoiding the diamonds with his feet, yet subtly gauging his footsteps so that his shoes, wet with sewer slime, would strike the diamonds at some undetermined moment. After twenty minutes of sauntering, his right foot smashed into the heap and diamonds lày scattered in all directions, glinting with a million tiny chuckles of icy laughter. Oh, shucks, he mumbled in mock regret, intrigued by the damage he had wrought. He continued walking, ignoring the brittle fire. He felt that he had a glorious victory locked in his heart.

He stooped and flung the diamonds more evenly over the floor and they showered rich sparks, collaborating with him. He went over the floor and trampled the stones just deep enough for them to be faintly visible, as though they were set delicately in the prongs of a thousand rings. A ghostly light bathed the cave. He sat on the chest and frowned. Maybe *any*thing's right, he mumbled. Yes, if the world as men had made it was right, then anything else was right, any act a man took to satisfy himself, murder, theft, torture.

He straightened with a start. What was happening to him? He was drawn to these crazy thoughts, yet they made him feel vaguely guilty. He would stretch out upon the ground, then get up; he would want to crawl again through the holes he had dug, but would restrain himself; he would think of going again up into the streets, but fear would hold him still. He stood in the middle of the cave, surrounded by green walls and a laughing floor, trembling. He was going to do something, but what? Yes, he was afraid of himself, afraid of doing some nameless thing.

To control himself, he turned on the radio. A melancholy piece of music rose. Brooding over the diamonds on the floor was like looking up into a sky full of restless stars; then the illusion turned into its opposite: he was high up in the air looking down at the twinkling lights of a sprawling city. The music ended and a man recited news events. In the same attitude in which he had contemplated the city, so now, as he heard the cultivated tone, he looked down upon land and sea as men fought, as cities were razed, as planes scattered death upon open towns, as long lines of trenches wavered and broke. He heard the names of generals and the names of mountains and the names of countries and the names and numbers of divisions that were in action on different battle fronts. He saw black smoke billowing from the stacks of warships as they neared each other over wastes of water and he heard their huge guns thunder as red-hot shells screamed across the surface of night seas. He saw hundreds of planes wheeling and droning in the sky and heard the clatter of machine guns as they fought each other and he saw planes falling in plumes of smoke and blaze of fire. He saw steel tanks rumbling across fields of ripe wheat to meet other tanks and there was a loud clang of steel as numberless tanks collided. He saw troops with fixed bayonets charging in waves against other troops who held fixed bayonets and men groaned as steel ripped into their bodies and they went down to die . . . The voice of the radio faded and he was staring at the diamonds on the floor at his feet.

He shut off the radio, fighting an irrational compulsion to act. He walked aimlessly about the cave, touching the walls with his finger tips. Suddenly he stood still. *What was the matter with him?* Yes, he knew . . . It was these walls; these crazy walls were filling him with a wild urge to climb out into the dark sunshine aboveground. Quickly he doused the light to banish the shouting walls, then sat again upon the tool chest. Yes, he was trapped. His muscles were flexed taut and sweat ran down his face. He knew now that he could not stay here and he could not go out. He lit a cigarette with shaking fingers; the match flame revealed the green-papered walls with militant distinctness; the purple on the gun barrel glinted like a threat; the meat cleaver brooded with its eloquent splotches of blood; the mound of silver and copper smoldered angrily; the diamonds winked at him from the floor; and the gold watches ticked and trembled, crowning time the king of consciousness, defining the limits of living . . . The match blaze died and he bolted from where he stood and collided brutally with the nails upon the walls. The spell was broken. He shuddered, feeling that, in spite of his fear, sooner or later he would go up into that dead sunshine and somehow say something to somebody about all this.

He sat again upon the tool chest. Fatigue weighed upon his

forehead and eyes. Minutes passed and he relaxed. He dozed, but his imagination was alert. He saw himself rising, wading again in the sweeping water of the sewer; he came to a manhole and climbed out and was amazed to discover that he had hoisted himself into a room filled with armed policemen who were watching him intently. He jumped awake in the dark; he had not moved. He sighed, closed his eyes, and slept again; this time his imagination designed a scheme of protection for him. His dreaming made him feel that he was standing in a room watching over his own nude body lying stiff and cold upon a white table. At the far end of the room he saw a crowd of people huddled in a corner, afraid of his body. Though lying dead upon the table, he was standing in some mysterious way at his side, warding off the people, guarding his body, and laughing to himself as he observed the situation. They're scared of me, he thought.

He awakened with a start, leaped to his feet, and stood in the center of the black cave. It was a full minute before he moved again. He hovered between sleeping and waking, unprotected, a prey of wild fears. He could neither see nor hear. One part of him was asleep; his blood coursed slowly and his flesh was numb. On the other hand he was roused to a strange, high pitch of tension. He lifted his fingers to his face, as though about to weep. Gradually his hands lowered and he struck a match, looking about, expecting to see a door through which he could walk to safety: but there was no door, only the green walls and the moving floor. The match flame died and it was dark again.

Five minutes later he was still standing when the thought came to him that he had been asleep. Yes . . . But he was not yet fully awake; he was still queerly blind and deaf. How long had he slept? Where was he? Then suddenly he recalled the green-papered walls of the cave and in the same instant he heard loud singing coming from the church beyond the wall. Yes, they woke me up, he muttered. He hoisted himself and lay atop the bed of pipes and brought his face to the narrow slit. Men and women stood here and there between pews. A song ended and a young black girl tossed back her head and closed her eyes and broke plaintively into another hymn:

Glad, glad, glad, oh, so glad
I got Jesus in my soul . . .

Those few words were all she sang, but what her words did not say, her emotions said as she repeated the lines, varying the mood and tempo, making her tone express meanings which her conscious mind did not know. Another woman melted her voice with the girl's, and then an old man's voice merged with that of the two women. Soon the entire congregation was singing:

Glad, glad, glad, oh, so glad
I got Jesus in my soul . . .

They're wrong, he whispered in the lyric darkness. He felt that their search for a happiness they could never find made them feel that they had committed some dreadful offense which they could not remember or understand. He was now in possession of the feeling that had gripped him when he had first come into the underground. It came to him in a series of questions: Why was this sense of guilt so seemingly innate, so easy to come by, to think, to feel, so verily physical? It seemed that when one felt this guilt one was retracing in one's feelings a faint pattern designed long before; it seemed that one was always trying to remember a gigantic shock that had left a haunting impression upon one's body which one could not forget or shake off, but which had been forgotten by the conscious mind, creating in one's life a state of eternal anxiety.

He had to tear himself away from this; he got down from the pipes. His nerves were so taut that he seemed to feel his brain pushing through his skull. He felt that he had to do something, but he could not figure out what it was. Yet he knew that if he stood here until he made up his mind, he would never move. He crawled through the hole he had made in the brick wall and the exertion afforded him respite from tension. When he entered the basement of the radio store, he stopped in fear, hearing loud voices.

"Come on, boy! Tell us what you did with the radio!"

"Mister, I didn't steal the radio! I swear!"

He heard a dull thumping sound and he imagined a boy being struck violently.

"Please, mister!"

"Did you take it to a pawn shop?"

"No, sir! I didn't steal the radio! I got a radio at home," the boy's voice pleaded hysterically. "Go to my home and look!"

There came to his ears the sound of another blow. It was so funny that he had to clap his hand over his mouth to keep from laughing out loud. They're beating some poor boy, he whispered to himself, shaking his head. He felt a sort of distant pity for the boy and wondered if he ought to bring back the radio and leave it in the basement. No. Perhaps it was a good thing that they were beating the boy; perhaps the beating would bring to the boy's attention, for the first time in his life, the secret of his existence, the guilt that he could never get rid of.

Smiling, he scampered over a coal pile and stood again in the basement of the building where he had stolen the money and jewelry. He lifted himself into the areaway, climbed the rain pipe, and squinted through a two-inch opening of window. The guilty familiarity of what he saw made his muscles tighten. Framed before him in a bright tableau of daylight was the night watchman sitting upon the edge of a chair, stripped to the waist, his head sagging forward, his eyes red and puffy. The watchman's face and shoulders were stippled with red and black welts. Back of the watchman stood the safe, the steel door wide open showing the empty vault. Yes, they think he did it, he mused.

Footsteps sounded in the room and a man in a blue suit passed in front of him, then another, then still another. Policemen, he breathed. Yes, they were trying to make the watchman confess, just as they had once made him confess to a crime he had not done. He stared into the room, trying to recall something. Oh . . . Those were the same policemen who had beaten him, had made him sign that paper when he had been too tired and sick to care. Now, they were doing the same thing to the watchman. His heart pounded as he saw one of the policemen shake a finger into the watchman's face.

"Why don't you admit it's an inside job, Thompson?" the policeman said.

"I've told you all I know," the watchman mumbled through swollen lips.

"But nobody was here but you!" the policeman shouted.

"I was sleeping," the watchman said. "It was wrong, but I was sleeping all that night!"

"Stop telling us that lie!"

"It's the truth!"

"When did you get the combination?"

"I don't know how to open the safe," the watchman said.

He clung to the rain pipe, tense; he wanted to laugh, but he controlled himself. He felt a great sense of power; yes, he could go back to the cave, rip the money off the walls, pick up the diamonds and rings, and bring them here and write a note, telling them where to look for their foolish toys. No . . . What good would that do? It was not worth the effort. The watchman was guilty; although he was not guilty of the crime of which he had been accused, he was guilty, had always been guilty. The only thing that worried him was that the man who had been really stealing was not being accused. But he consoled himself: they'll catch him sometime during his life.

He saw one of the policemen slap the watchman across the mouth.

"Come clean, you bastard!"

"I've told you all I know," the watchman mumbled like a child.

One of the police went to the rear of the watchman's chair and jerked it from under him; the watchman pitched forward upon his face.

"Get up!" a policeman said.

Trembling, the watchman pulled himself up and sat limply again in the chair.

"Now, are you going to talk?"

"I've told you all I know," the watchman gasped.

"Where did you hide the stuff?"

"I didn't take it!"

"Thompson, your brains are in your feet," one of the policemen said. "We're going to string you up and get them back into your skull."

He watched the policemen clamp handcuffs on the watchman's wrists and ankles; then they lifted the watchman and swung him upside-down and hoisted his feet to the edge of a door. The watchman hung, head down, his eyes bulging. They're crazy, he whispered to himself as he clung to the ridges of the pipe.

"You going to talk?" a policeman shouted into the watchman's ear.

He heard the watchman groan.

"We'll let you hang there till you talk, see?"

He saw the watchman close his eyes.

"Let's take 'im down. He passed out," a policeman said.

He grinned as he watched them take the body down and dump it carelessly upon the floor. The policeman took off the handcuffs.

"Let 'im come to. Let's get a smoke," a policeman said.

The three policemen left the scope of his vision. A door slammed. He had an impulse to yell to the watchman that he could escape through the hole in the basement and live with him in the cave. But he wouldn't understand, he told himself. After a moment he saw the watchman rise and stand swaying from weakness. He stumbled across the room to a desk, opened a drawer, and took out a gun. He's going to kill himself, he thought, intent, eager, detached, yearning to see the end of the man's actions. As the watchman stared vaguely about he lifted the gun to his temple; he stood like that for some minutes, biting his lips until a line of blood etched its way down a corner of his chin. No, he oughtn't do that, he said to himself in a mood of pity.

"Don't!" he half whispered and half yelled.

The watchman looked wildly about; he had heard him. But it did not help; there was a loud report and the watchman's head jerked violently and he fell like a log and lay prone, the gun clattering over the floor.

The three policemen came running into the room with drawn guns. One of the policemen knelt and rolled the watchman's body over and stared at a ragged, scarlet hole in the temple.

"Our hunch was right," the kneeling policeman said. "He was guilty, all right."

"Well, this ends the case," another policeman said .

"He knew he was licked," the third one said with grim satisfaction.

He eased down the rain pipe, crawled back through the holes he had made, and went back into his cave. A fever burned in his bones. He had to act, yet he was afraid. His eyes stared in the darkness as though propped open by invisible hands, as though they had become lidless. His muscles were rigid and he stood for what seemed to him a thousand years.

When he moved again his actions were informed with precision, his muscular system reinforced from a reservoir of energy. He crawled through the hole of earth, dropped into the gray sewer current, and sloshed ahead. When his right foot went forward at a street intersection, he fell backward and shot down into water. In a spasm of terror his right hand grabbed the concrete ledge of a down-curve and he felt the streaking water tugging violently at his body. The current reached his neck and for a moment he was still. He knew that if he moved clumsily he would be sucked under. He held onto the ledge with both hands and slowly pulled himself up. He sighed, standing once more in the sweeping water, thankful that he had missed death.

He waded on through sludge, moving with care, until he came to a web of light sifting down from a manhole cover. He saw steel hooks running up the side of the sewer wall; he caught hold and lifted himself and put his shoulder to the cover and moved it an inch. A crash of sound came to him

as he looked into a hot glare of sunshine through which
blurred shapes moved. Fear scalded him and he dropped
back into the pallid current and stood paralyzed in the shadows. A heavy car rumbled past overhead, jarring the pavement, warning him to stay in his world of dark light, knock-
ing the cover back into place with an imperious clang.

He did not know how much fear he felt, for fear claimed
him completely; yet it was not a fear of the police or of people, but a cold dread at the thought of the actions he knew he
would perform if he went out into that cruel sunshine. His
mind said no; his body said yes; and his mind could not understand his feelings. A low whine broke from him and he
was in the act of uncoiling. He climbed upward and heard
the faint honking of auto horns. Like a frantic cat clutching a
rag, he clung to the steel prongs and heaved his shoulder
against the cover and pushed it off halfway. For a split second his eyes were drowned in the terror of yellow light and
he was in a deeper darkness than he had ever known in the
underground.

Partly out of the hole, he blinked, regaining enough sight
to make out meaningful forms. An odd thing was happening:
No one was rushing forward to challenge him. He had imagined the moment of his emergence as a desperate tussle with
men who wanted to cart him off to be killed; instead, life
froze about him as the traffic stopped. He pushed the cover
aside, stood, swaying in a world so fragile that he expected it
to collapse and drop him into some deep void. But nobody
seemed to pay him heed. The cars were now swerving to
shun him and the gaping hole.

"Why in hell don't you put up a red light, dummy?" a raucous voice yelled.

He understood; they thought that he was a sewer workman. He walked toward the sidewalk, weaving unsteadily
through the moving traffic.

"Look where you're going, nigger!"

"That's right! Stay there and get killed!"

"You blind, you bastard?"

"Go home and sleep your drunk off!"

A policeman stood at the curb, looking in the opposite direction. When he passed the policeman, he feared that he
would be grabbed, but nothing happened. Where was he?
Was this real? He wanted to look about to get his bearings,
but felt that something awful would happen to him if he did.
He wandered into a spacious doorway of a store that sold
men's clothing and saw his reflection in a long mirror: his
cheekbones protruded from a hairy black face; his greasy cap

was perched askew upon his head and his eyes were red and glassy. His shirt and trousers were caked with mud and hung loosely. His hands were gummed with a black stickiness. He threw back his head and laughed so loudly that passers-by stopped and stared.

He ambled on down the sidewalk, not having the merest notion of where he was going. Yet, sleeping within him, was the drive to go somewhere and say something to somebody. Half an hour later his ears caught the sound of spirited singing.

The Lamb, the Lamb, the Lamb
  I hear thy voice a-calling
The Lamb, the Lamb, the Lamb
  I feel thy grace a-falling

A church! he exclaimed. He broke into a run and came to brick steps leading downward to a subbasement. This is it! The church into which he had peered. Yes, he was going in and tell them. What? He did not know; but, once face to face with them, he would think of what to say. Must be Sunday, he mused. He ran down the steps and jerked the door open; the church was crowded and a deluge of song swept over him.

The Lamb, the Lamb, the Lamb
  Tell me again your story
The Lamb, the Lamb, the Lamb
  Flood my soul with your glory

He stared at the singing faces with a trembling smile.

"Say!" he shouted.

Many turned to look at him, but the song rolled on. His arm was jerked violently.

"I'm sorry, Brother, but you can't do that in here," a man said.

"But, mister!"

"You can't act rowdy in God's house," the man said.

"He's filthy," another man said.

"But I want to tell 'em," he said loudly.

"He stinks," someone muttered.

The song had stopped, but at once another one began.

Oh, wondrous sight upon the cross
  Vision sweet and divine
Oh, wondrous sight upon the cross
  Full of such love sublime

He attempted to twist away, but other hands grabbed him and rushed him into the doorway.

"Let me alone!" he screamed, struggling.

"Get out!"

"He's drunk," somebody said. "He ought to be ashamed!"

"He acts crazy!"

He felt that he was failing and he grew frantic.

"But, mister, let me tell—"

"Get away from this door, or I'll call the police!"

He stared, his trembling smile fading in a sense of wonderment.

"The police," he repeated vacantly.

"Now, get!"

He was pushed toward the brick steps and the door banged shut. The waves of song came.

Oh, wondrous sight, wondrous sight
  Lift my heavy heart above
Oh, wondrous sight, wondrous sight
  Fill my weary soul with love

He was smiling again now. Yes, the police . . . That was it! Why had he not thought of it before? The idea had been deep down in him, and only now did it assume supreme importance. He looked up and saw a street sign: COURT STREET—HARTSDALE AVENUE. He turned and walked northward, his mind filled with the image of the police station. Yes, that was where they had beaten him, accused him, and had made him sign a confession of his guilt. He would go there and clear up everything, make a statement. What statement? He did not know. He was the statement, and since it was all so clear to him, surely he would be able to make it clear to others.

He came to the corner of Hartsdale Avenue and turned westward. Yeah, there's the station . . . A policeman came down the steps and walked past him without a glance. He mounted the stone steps and went through the door, paused; he was in a hallway where several policemen were standing, talking, smoking. One turned to him.

"What do you want, boy?"

He looked at the policeman and laughed.

"What in hell are you laughing about?" the policeman asked.

He stopped laughing and stared. His whole being was full of what he wanted to say to them, but he could not say it.

"Are you looking for the Desk Sergeant?"

"Yes, sir," he said quickly; then: "Oh, no, sir."

"Well, make up your mind, now."

Four policemen grouped themselves around him.

"I'm looking for the men," he said.

"What men?"

Peculiarly, at that moment he could not remember the names of the policemen; he recalled their beating him, the confession he had signed, and how he had run away from them. He saw the cave next to the church, the money on the walls, the guns, the rings, the cleaver, the watches, and the diamonds on the floor.

"They brought me here," he began.

"When?"

His mind flew back over the blur of the time lived in the underground blackness. He had no idea of how much time had elapsed, but the intensity of what had happened to him told him that it could not have transpired in a short space of time, yet his mind told him that time must have been brief.

"It was a long time ago." He spoke like a child relating a dimly remembered dream. "It was a long time," he repeated, following the promptings of his emotions. "They beat me . . . I was scared . . . I ran away."

A policeman raised a finger to his temple and made a derisive circle.

"Nuts," the policeman said.

"Do you know what place this is, boy?"

"Yes, sir. The police station," he answered sturdily, almost proudly.

"Well, who do you want to see?"

"The men," he said again, feeling that surely they knew the men. "You know the men," he said in a hurt tone.

"What's your name?"

He opened his lips to answer and no words came. He had forgotten. But what did it matter if he had? It was not important.

"Where do you live?"

Where did he live? It had been so long ago since he had lived up here in this strange world that he felt it was foolish even to try to remember. Then for a moment the old mood that had dominated him in the underground surged back. He leaned forward and spoke eagerly.

"They said I killed the woman."

"What woman?" a policeman asked.

"And I signed a paper that said I was guilty," he went on, ignoring their questions. "Then I ran off . . ."

"Did you run off from an institution?"

"No, sir," he said, blinking and shaking his head. "I came

from under the ground. I pushed off the manhole cover and climbed out . . ."

"All right, now," a policeman said, placing an arm about his shoulder. "We'll send you to the psycho and you'll be taken care of."

"Maybe he's a Fifth Columnist!" a policeman shouted.

There was laughter and, despite his anxiety, he joined in. But the laughter lasted so long that it irked him.

"I got to find those men," he protested mildly.

"Say, boy, what have you been drinking?"

"Water," he said. "I got some water in a basement."

"Were the men you ran away from dressed in white, boy?"

"No, sir," he said brightly. "They were men like you."

An elderly policeman caught hold of his arm.

"Try and think hard. Where did they pick you up?"

He knitted his brows in an effort to remember, but he was blank inside. The policeman stood before him demanding logical answers and he could no longer think with his mind; he thought with his feelings and no words came.

"I was guilty," he said. "Oh, no, sir. I wasn't then, I mean, mister!"

"Aw, talk sense. Now, where did they pick you up?"

He felt challenged and his mind began reconstructing events in reverse; his feelings ranged back over the long hours and he saw the cave, the sewer, the bloody room where it was said that a woman had been killed.

"Oh, yes, sir," he said, smiling. "I was coming from Mrs. Wooten's."

"Who is she?"

"I work for her."

"Where does she live?"

"Next door to Mrs. Peabody, the woman who was killed."

The policemen were very quiet now, looking at him intently.

"What do you know about Mrs. Peabody's death, boy?"

"Nothing, sir. But they said I killed her. But it doesn't make any difference. I'm guilty!"

"What are you talking about, boy?"

His smile faded and he was possessed with memories of the underground; he saw the cave next to the church and his lips moved to speak. But how could he say it? The distance between what he felt and what these men meant was vast. Something told him, as he stood there looking into their faces, that he would never be able to tell them, that they would never believe him even if he told them.

"All the people I saw was guilty," he began slowly.

"Aw, nuts," a policemen muttered.

"Say," another policeman said, "that Peabody woman was killed over on Winewood. That's Number Ten's beat."

"Where's Number Ten?" a policeman asked.

"Upstairs in the swing room," someone answered.

"Take this boy up, Sam," a policeman ordered.

"O.K. Come along, boy."

An elderly policeman caught hold of his arm and led him up a flight of wooden stairs, down a long hall, and to a door.

"Squad Ten!" the policeman called through the door.

"What?" a gruff voice answered.

"Someone to see you!"

"About what?"

The old policeman pushed the door in and then shoved him into the room.

He stared, his lips open, his heart barely beating. Before him were the three policemen who had picked him up and had beaten him to extract the confession. They were seated about a small table, playing cards. The air was blue with smoke and sunshine poured through a high window, lighting up fantastic smoke shapes. He saw one of the policemen look up; the policeman's face was tired and a cigarette dropped limply from one corner of his mouth and both of his fat, puffy eyes were squinting and his hands gripped his cards.

"Lawson!" the man exclaimed.

The moment the man's name sounded he remembered the names of all of them: Lawson, Murphy, and Johnson. How simple it was. He waited, smiling, wondering how they would react when they knew that he had come back.

"Looking for me?" the man who had been called Lawson mumbled, sorting his cards. "For what?"

So far only Murphy, the red-headed one, had recognized him.

"Don't you-all remember me?" he blurted, running to the table.

All three of the policemen were looking at him now. Lawson, who seemed the leader, jumped to his feet.

"Where in hell have you been?"

"Do you know 'im, Lawson?" the old policeman asked.

"Huh?" Lawson frowned. "Oh, yes. I'll handle 'im." The old policeman left the room and Lawson crossed to the door and turned the key in the lock. "Come here, boy," he ordered in a cold tone.

He did not move; he looked from face to face. Yes, he would tell them about his cave.

"He looks batty to me," Johnson said, the one who had not spoken before.

"Why in hell did you come back here?" Lawson said.

"I—I just didn't want to run away no more," he said. "I'm all right, now." He paused; the men's attitude puzzled him.

"You've been hiding, huh?" Lawson asked in a tone that denoted that he had not heard his previous words. "You told us you were sick, and when we left you in the room, you jumped out of the window and ran away."

Panic filled him. Yes, they were indifferent to what he would say! They were waiting for him to speak and they would laugh at him. He had to rescue himself from this bog; he had to force the reality of himself upon them.

"Mister, I took a sackful of money and pasted it on the walls . . ." he began.

"I'll be damned," Lawson said.

"Listen," said Murphy, "let me tell you something for your own good. We don't want you, see? You're free, free as air. Now go home and forget it. It was all a mistake. We caught the guy who did the Peabody job. He wasn't colored at all. He was an Eyetalian."

"Shut up!" Lawson yelled. "Have you no sense!"

"But I want to tell 'im," Murphy said.

"We can't let this crazy fool go," Lawson exploded. "He acts nuts, but this may be a stunt . . ."

"I was down in the basement," he began in a childlike tone as though repeating a lesson learned by heart; "and I went into a movie . . ." His voice failed. He was getting ahead of his story. First, he ought to tell them about the singing in the church, but what words could he use? He looked at them appealingly. "I went into a shop and took a sackful of money and diamonds and watches and rings . . . I didn't steal 'em; I'll give 'em all back. I just took 'em to play with . . ." He paused, stunned by their disbelieving eyes.

Lawson lit a cigarette and looked at him coldly.

"What did you do with the money?" he asked in a quiet, waiting voice.

"I pasted the hundred-dollar bills on the walls."

"What walls?" Lawson asked.

"The walls of the dirt room," he said, smiling, "the room next to the church. I hung up the rings and the watches and I stamped the diamonds into the dirt . . ." He saw that they were not understanding what he was saying. He grew frantic to make them believe, his voice tumbled on eagerly. "I saw a dead baby and a dead man . . ."

"Aw, you're nuts," Lawson snarled, shoving him into a chair.

"But, mister . . ."

"Johnson, where's the paper he signed?" Lawson asked.

"What paper?"

"The confession, fool!"

Johnson pulled out his billfold and extracted a crumpled piece of paper.

"Yes, sir, mister," he said, stretching forth his hand. "That's the paper I signed . . ."

Lawson slapped him and he would have toppled had his chair not struck a wall behind him. Lawson scratched a match and held the paper over the flame; the confession burned down to Lawson's fingertips.

He stared, thunderstruck; the sun of the underground was fleeing and the terrible darkness of the day stood before him. They did not believe him, but he *had* to make them believe him!

"But, mister . . ."

"It's going to be all right, boy," Lawson said with a quiet, soothing laugh. "I've burned your confession, see? You didn't sign anything." Lawson came close to him with the black ashes cupped in his palm. "You don't remember a thing about this, do you?"

"Don't you-all be scared of me," he pleaded, sensing their uneasiness. "I'll sign another paper, if you want me to. I'll show you the cave."

"What's your game, boy?" Lawson asked suddenly.

"What are you trying to find out?" Johnson asked.

"Who sent you here?" Murphy demanded.

"Nobody sent me, mister," he said. "I just want to show you the room . . ."

"Aw, he's plumb bats," Murphy said. "Let's ship 'im to the psycho."

"No," Lawson said. "He's playing a game and I wish to God I knew what it was."

There flashed through his mind a definite way to make them believe him; he rose from the chair with nervous excitement.

"Wister, I saw the night watchman blow his brains out because you accused him of stealing," he told them. "But he didn't steal the money and diamonds. I took 'em."

Tigerishly Lawson grabbed his collar and lifted him bodily. *"Who told you about that?"*

"Don't get excited, Lawson," Johnson said. "He read about it in the papers."

Lawson flung him away.

"He couldn't have," Lawson said, pulling papers from his pocket. "I haven't turned in the reports yet."

"Then how *did* he find out?" Murphy asked.

"Let's get out of here," Lawson said with quick resolution. "Listen, boy, we're going to take you to a nice, quiet place, see?"

"Yes, sir," he said. "And I'll show you the underground."

"Goddamn," Lawson muttered, fastening the gun at his hip. He narrowed his eyes at Johnson and Murphy. "Listen," he spoke just above a whisper, "say nothing about this, you hear?"

"O.K.," Johnson said.

"Sure," Murphy said.

Lawson unlocked the door and Johnson and Murphy led him down the stairs. The hallway was crowded with policemen.

"What have you got there, Lawson?"

"What did he do, Lawson?"

"He's psycho, ain't he, Lawson?"

Lawson did not answer; Johnson and Murphy led him to the car parked at the curb, pushed him into the back seat. Lawson got behind the steering wheel and the car rolled forward.

"What's up, Lawson?" Murphy asked.

"Listen," Lawson began slowly, "we tell the papers that he spilled about the Peabody job, then he escapes. The Wop is caught and we tell the papers that we steered them wrong to trap the real guy, see? Now this dope shows up and acts nuts. If we let him go, he'll squeal that we framed him, see?"

"I'm all right, mister," he said, feeling Murphy's and Johnson's arms locked rigidly into his. "I'm guilty . . . I'll show you everything in the underground. I laughed and laughed . . ."

"Shut that fool up!" Lawson ordered.

Johnson tapped him across the head with a blackjack and he fell back against the seat cushion, dazed.

"Yes, sir," he mumbled. "I'm all right."

The car sped along Hartsdale Avenue, then swung onto Pine Street and rolled to State Street, then turned south. It slowed to a stop, turned in the middle of a block, and headed north again.

"You're going around in circles, Lawson," Murphy said.

Lawson did not answer; he was hunched over the steering wheel. Finally he pulled the car to a stop at the curb.

"Say, boy, tell us the truth," Lawson asked quietly. "Where did you hide?"

"I didn't hide, mister."

The three policemen were staring at him now; he felt that for the first time they were willing to understand him.

"Then what happened?"

"Mister, when I looked through all of those holes and saw how people were living, I loved 'em. . . ."

"Cut out that crazy talk!" Lawson snapped. "Who sent you back here?"

"Nobody, mister."

"Maybe he's talking straight," Johnson ventured.

"All right," Lawson said. "Nobody hid you. Now, tell us *where* you hid."

"I went underground . . ."

"What goddamn underground do you keep talking about?"

"I just went . . ." He paused and looked into the street, then pointed to a manhole cover. "I went down in there and stayed."

"In the *sewer?*"

"Yes, sir."

The policemen burst into a sudden laugh and ended quickly. Lawson swung the car around and drove to Woodside Avenue; he brought the car to a stop in front of a tall apartment building.

"What're we going to do, Lawson?" Murphy asked.

"I'm taking him up to my place," Lawson said. "We've got to wait until night. There's nothing we can do now."

They took him out of the car and led him into a vestibule.

"Take the steps," Lawson muttered.

They led him up four flights of stairs and into the living room of a small apartment. Johnson and Murphy let go of his arms and he stood uncertainly in the middle of the room.

"Now, listen, boy," Lawson began, "forget those wild lies you've been telling us. Where did you hide?"

"I just went underground, like I told you."

The room rocked with laughter. Lawson went to a cabinet and got a bottle of whisky; he placed glasses for Johnson and Murphy. The three of them drank.

He felt that he could not explain himself to them. He tried to muster all the sprawling images that floated in him; the images stood out sharply in his mind, but he could not make them have the meaning for others that they had for him. He felt so helpless that he began to cry.

"He's nuts, all right," Johnson said. "All nuts cry like that."

Murphy crossed the room and slapped him.

"Stop that raving!"

A sense of excitement flooded him; he ran to Murphy and grabbed his arm.

"Let me show you the cave," he said. "Come on, and you'll see!"

Before he knew it a sharp blow had clipped him on the chin; darkness covered his eyes. He dimly felt himself being lifted and laid out on the sofa. He heard low voices and struggled to rise, but hard hands held him down. His brain was clearing now. He pulled to a sitting posture and stared with glazed eyes. It had grown dark. How long had he been out?

"Say, boy," Lawson said soothingly, "will you show us the underground?"

His eyes shone and his heart swelled with gratitude. Lawson believed him! He rose, glad; he grabbed Lawson's arm, making the policeman spill whisky from the glass to his shirt.

"Take it easy, goddammit," Lawson said.

"Yes, sir."

"O.K. We'll take you down. But you'd better be telling us the truth, you hear?"

He clapped his hands in wild joy.

"I'll show you everything!"

He had triumphed at last! He would now do what he had felt was compelling him all along. At last he would be free of his burden.

"Take 'im down," Lawson ordered.

They led him down to the vestibule; when he reached the sidewalk he saw that it was night and a fine rain was falling.

"It's just like when I went down," he told them.

"What?" Lawson asked.

"The rain," he said, sweeping his arm in a wide arc. "It was raining when I went down. The rain made the water rise and lift the cover off."

"Cut it out," Lawson snapped.

They did not believe him now, but they would. A mood of high selflessness throbbed in him. He could barely contain his rising spirits. They would see what he had seen; they would feel what he had felt. He would lead them through all the holes he had dug and . . . He wanted to make a hymn, prance about in physical ecstasy, throw his arms about the policemen in fellowship.

"Get into the car," Lawson ordered.

He climbed in and Johnson and Murphy sat at either side

of him; Lawson slid behind the steering wheel and started the
motor.

"Now, tell us where to go," Lawson said.

"It's right around the corner from where the lady was
killed," he said.

The car rolled slowly and he closed his eyes, remembering
the song he had heard in the church, the song that had
wrought him to such a high pitch of terror and pity. He sang
softly, lolling his head:

Glad, glad, glad, oh, so glad
I got Jesus in my soul . . .

"Mister," he said, stopping his song, "you ought to see how
funny the rings look on the wall." He giggled. "I fired a pistol, too. Just once, to see how it felt."

"What do you suppose he's suffering from?" Johnson
asked.

"Delusions of grandeur, maybe," Murphy said.

"Maybe it's because he lives in a white man's world," Lawson said.

"Say, boy, what did you eat down there?" Murphy asked,
prodding Johnson anticipatorily with his elbow.

"Pears, oranges, bananas, and pork chops," he said.

The car filled with laughter.

"You didn't eat any watermelon?" Lawson asked, smiling.

"No, sir," he answered calmly. "I didn't see any."

The three policemen roared harder and louder.

"Boy, you're sure some case," Murphy said, shaking his
head in wonder.

The car pulled to a curb.

"All right, boy," Lawson said. "Tell us where to go."

He peered through the rain and saw where he had gone
down. The streets, save for a few dim lamps glowing softly
through the rain, were dark and empty.

"Right there, mister," he said, pointing.

"Come on; let's take a look," Lawson said.

"Well, suppose he did hide down there," Johnson said,
"what is that supposed to prove?"

"I don't believe he hid down there," Murphy said.

"It won't hurt to look," Lawson said. "Leave things to
me."

Lawson got out of the car and looked up and down the
street.

He was eager to show them the cave now. If he could
show them what he had seen, then they would feel what he

had felt and they in turn would show it to others and those others would feel as they had felt, and soon everybody would be governed by the same impulse of pity.

"Take 'im out," Lawson ordered.

Johnson and Murphy opened the door and pushed him out; he stood trembling in the rain, smiling. Again Lawson looked up and down the street; no one was in sight. The rain came down hard, slanting like black wires across the wind-swept air.

"All right," Lawson said. "Show us."

He walked to the center of the street, stopped and inserted a finger in one of the tiny holes of the cover and tugged, but he was too weak to budge it.

"Did you really go down in there, boy?" Lawson asked; there was a doubt in his voice.

"Yes, sir. Just a minute. I'll show you."

"Help 'im get that damn thing off," Lawson said.

Johnson stepped forward and lifted the cover; it clanged against the wet pavement. The hole gaped round and black.

"I went down in there," he announced with pride.

Lawson gazed at him for a long time without speaking, then he reached his right hand to his holster and drew his gun.

"Mister, I got a gun just like that down there," he said, laughing and looking into Lawson's face. "I fired it once then hung it on the wall. I'll show you."

"Show us how you went down," Lawson said quietly.

"I'll go down first, mister, and then you-all can come after me, hear?" He spoke like a little boy playing a game.

"Sure, sure," Lawson said soothingly. "Go ahead. We'll come."

He looked brightly at the policemen; he was bursting with happiness. He bent down and placed his hands on the rim of the hole and sat on the edge, his feet dangling into watery darkness. He heard the familiar drone of the gray current. He lowered his body and hung for a moment by his fingers, then he went downward on the steel prongs, hand over hand, until he reached the last rung. He dropped and his feet hit the water and he felt the stiff current trying to suck him away. He balanced himself quickly and looked back upward at the policemen.

"Come on, you-all!" he yelled, casting his voice above the rustling at his feet.

The vague forms that towered above him in the rain did not move. He laughed, feeling that they doubted him. But, once they saw the things he had done, they would never doubt again.

"Come on! The cave isn't far!" he yelled. "But be careful when your feet hit the water, because the current's pretty rough down here!"

Lawson still held the gun. Murphy and Johnson looked at Lawson quizzically.

"What are we going to do, Lawson?" Murphy asked.

"We are not going to follow that crazy nigger down into that sewer, are we?" Johnson asked.

"Come on, you-all!" he begged in a shout.

He saw Lawson raise the gun and point it directly at him. Lawson's face twitched, as though he were hesitating.

Then there was a thunderous report and a streak of fire ripped through his chest. He was hurled into the water, flat on his back. He looked in amazement at the blurred white faces looming above him. They shot me, he said to himself. The water flowed past him, blossoming in foam about his arms, his legs, and his head. His jaw sagged and his mouth gaped soundless. A vast pain gripped his head and gradually squeezed out consciousness. As from a great distance he heard hollow voices.

"What did you shoot him for, Lawson?"

"I had to."

"Why?"

"You've got to shoot his kind. They'd wreck things."

As though in a deep dream, he heard a metallic clank; they had replaced the manhole cover, shutting out forever the sound of wind and rain. From overhead came the muffled roar of a powerful motor and the swish of a speeding car. He felt the strong tide pushing him slowly into the middle of the sewer, turning him about. For a split second there hovered before his eyes the glittering cave, the shouting walls, and the laughing floor . . . Then his mouth was full of thick, bitter water. The current spun him around. He sighed and closed his eyes, a whirling object rushing alone in the darkness, veering, tossing, lost in the heart of the earth.

´ANN PETRY (1911–)

Mrs. Ann Petry, born and raised in Old Saybrook, Connecticut, made a striking literary debut with her first novel, The Street *(1946), set in Harlem and completed on a Houghton Mifflin Literary Fellowship. That same year Martha Foley dedicated her annual volume* The Best American Short Stories 1946 *to Ann Petry and included a short story Mrs. Petry had first published in* The Crisis. *It was only after her marriage in 1938 that Ann Petry left New England to live in Harlem, where she began a newspaper career, first with the* Amsterdam News *and later with* The People's Voice. *After some years of journalism, she went into experimental education in a Harlem grade school. Her first novel drew upon her life and experiences in Harlem. She has written two additional novels, short stories, books for children, and a biography of Harriet Tubman. "In Darkness and Confusion," which follows, is a novella which grew imaginatively out of the Harlem riot of 1943. It is reprinted from* Cross-Section 1947, *a collection of new American writing edited by Edwin Seaver.*

In Darkness and Confusion

William Jones took a sip of coffee and then put his cup down on the kitchen table. It didn't taste right and he was annoyed because he always looked forward to eating breakfast. He usually got out of bed as soon as he woke up and hurried into the kitchen. Then he would take a long time heating the corn bread left over from dinner the night before, letting the coffee brew until it was strong and clear, frying bacon and scrambling eggs. He would eat very slowly—savoring the early-morning quiet and the just-rightness of the food he'd fixed.

There was no question about early morning being the best

part of the day, he thought. But this Saturday morning in July it was too hot in the apartment. There were too many nagging worries that kept drifting through his mind. In the heat he couldn't think clearly—so that all of them pressed in against him, weighed him down.

He pushed his plate away from him. The eggs had cooked too long; much as he liked corn bread it tasted like sand this morning—grainy and coarse inside his throat. He couldn't help wondering if it scratched the inside of his stomach in the same way.

Pink was moving around in the bedroom. He cocked his head on one side, listening to her. He could tell exactly what she was doing, as though he were in there with her. The soft heavy sound of her stockinged feet as she walked over to the dresser. The dresser drawer being pulled out. That meant she was getting a clean slip. Then the thud of her two hundred pounds landing in the rocker by the window. She was sitting down to comb her hair. Untwisting the small braids she'd made the night before. She would unwind them one by one, putting the hairpins in her mouth as she went along. Now she was brushing it, for he could hear the creak of the rocker; she was rocking back and forth, humming under her breath as she brushed.

He decided that as soon as she came into the kitchen he would go back to the bedroom, get dressed, and go to work. For his mind was already on the mailbox. He didn't feel like talking to Pink. There simply had to be a letter from Sam today. There had to be.

He was thinking about it so hard that he didn't hear Pink walk toward the kitchen.

When he looked up she was standing in the doorway. She was a short, enormously fat woman. The only garment she had on was a bright pink slip that magnified the size of her body. The skin on her arms and shoulders and chest was startlingly black against the pink material. In spite of the brisk brushing she had given her hair, it stood up stiffly all over her head in short wiry lengths, as though she wore a turban of some rough dark-gray material.

He got up from the table quickly when he saw her. "Hot, ain't it?" he said, and patted her arm as he went past her toward the bedroom.

She looked at the food on his plate. "You didn't want no breakfast?" she asked.

"Too hot," he said over his shoulder.

He closed the bedroom door behind him gently. If she saw the door was shut, she'd know that he was kind of low in his mind this morning and that he didn't feel like talking. At first he moved about with energy—getting a clean work shirt, giving his shoes a hasty brushing, hunting for a pair of clean socks. Then he stood still in the middle of the room, holding his dark work pants in his hand while he listened to the rush and roar of water running in the bathtub.

Annie May was up and taking a bath. And he wondered if that meant she was going to work. Days when she went to work she used a hot comb on her hair before she ate her breakfast, so that before he left the house in the morning it was filled with the smell of hot irons sizzling against hair grease.

He frowned. Something had to be done about Annie May. Here she was only eighteen years old and staying out practically all night long. He hadn't said anything to Pink about it, but Annie May crept into the house at three and four and five in the morning. He would hear her key go in the latch and then the telltale click as the lock drew back. She would shut the door very softly and turn the bolt. She'd stand there awhile, waiting to see if they woke up. Then she'd take her shoes off and pad down the hall in her stockinged feet.

When she turned the light on in the bathroom, he could see the clock on the dresser. This morning it was four-thirty when she came in. Pink, lying beside him, went on peacefully snoring. He was glad that she didn't wake up easy. It would only worry her to know that Annie May was carrying on like that.

Annie May put her hands on her hips and threw her head back and laughed whenever he tried to tell her she had to come home earlier. The smoky smell of the hot irons started seeping into the bedroom and he finished dressing quickly.

He stopped in the kitchen on his way out. "Got to get to the store early today," he explained. He was sure Pink knew he was hurrying downstairs to look in the mailbox. But she nodded and held her face up for his kiss. When he brushed his lips against her forehead he saw that her face was wet with perspiration. He thought with all that weight she must feel the heat something awful.

Annie May nodded at him without speaking. She was hastily swallowing a cup of coffee. Her dark thin hands made a pattern against the thick white cup she was holding. She had pulled her hair out so straight with the hot combs that, he thought, it was like a shiny skullcap fitted tight to her head. He was surprised to see that her lips were heavily coated with lipstick. When she was going to work she didn't use any, and he wondered why she was up so early if she wasn't working.

He could see the red outline of her mouth on the cup.

He hadn't intended to say anything. It was the sight of the lipstick on the cup that forced the words out. "You ain't workin' today?"

"No," she said lazily. "Think I'll go shopping." She winked at Pink, and it infuriated him.

"How you expect to keep a job when you don't show up half the time?" he asked.

"I can always get another one." She lifted the coffee cup to her mouth with both hands and her eyes laughed at him over the rim of the cup.

"What time did you come home last night?" he asked abruptly.

She stared out of the window at the blank brick wall that faced the kitchen. "I dunno," she said finally. "It wasn't late."

He didn't know what to say. Probably she was out dancing somewhere. Or maybe she wasn't. He was fairly certain that she wasn't. Yet he couldn't let Pink know what he was thinking. He shifted his feet uneasily and watched Annie May swallow the coffee. She was drinking it fast.

"You know you ain't too big to get your butt whipped," he said finally.

She looked at him out of the corner of her eyes. And he saw a deep smoldering sullenness in her face that startled him. He was conscious that Pink was watching both of them with a growing apprehension.

Then Annie May giggled. "You and who else?" she said lightly. Pink roared with laughter. And Annie May laughed with her.

He banged the kitchen door hard as he went out. Striding down the outside hall, he could still hear them laughing. And even though he knew Pink's laughter was due to relief because nothing unpleasant had happened, he was angry. Lately every time Annie May looked at him there was open, jeering laughter in her eyes, as though she dared him to say anything to her. Almost as though she thought he was a fool for working so hard.

She had been a nice little girl when she first came to live with them six years ago. He groped in his mind for words to describe what he thought Annie May had become. A Jezebel, he decided grimly. That was it.

And he didn't want Pink to know what Annie May was really like. Because Annie May's mother, Lottie, had been Pink's sister. And when Lottie died, Pink took Annie May. Right away she started finding excuses for anything she did that was wrong. If he scolded Annie May he had to listen to a sharp lecture from Pink. It always started off the same way: "Don't care what she done, William. You ain't goin' to lay a finger on her. She ain't got no father and mother except us. . . ."

The quick spurt of anger and irritation at Annie May had sent him hurrying down the first flight of stairs. But he slowed his pace on the next flight because the hallways were so dark that he knew if he wasn't careful he'd walk over a step. As he trudged down the long flights of stairs he began to think about Pink. And the hot irritation in him disappeared as it usually did when he thought about her. She was so fat she couldn't keep on climbing all these steep stairs. They would have to find another place to live—on a first floor where it would be easier for her. They'd lived on this top floor for years, and all the time Pink kept getting heavier and heavier. Every time she went to the clinic the doctor said the stairs were bad for her. So they'd start looking for another apartment and then because the top floors cost less, why, they stayed where they were. And——

Then he stopped thinking about Pink because he had reached the first floor. He walked over to the mailboxes and took a deep breath. Today there'd be a letter. He knew it. There had to be. It had been too long a time since they had had a letter from Sam. The last ones that came he'd said the same thing. Over and over. Like a refrain. "Ma, I can't stand this much longer." And then the letters just stopped.

As he stood there, looking at the mailbox, half afraid to open it for fear there would be no letter, he thought back to the night Sam graduated from high school. It was a warm June night. He and Pink got all dressed up in their best clothes. And he kept thinking me and Pink have got as far as we can go. But Sam—he made up his mind Sam wasn't going to earn his living with a mop and a broom. He was going to earn it wearing a starched white collar, and a shine on his shoes and a crease in his pants.

After he finished high school Sam got a job redcapping at Grand Central. He started saving his money because he was going to go to Lincoln—a college in Pennsylvania. It looked like it was no time at all before he was twenty-one. And in the army. Pink cried when he left. Her huge body shook with her sobbing. He remembered that he had only felt queer and lost. There was this war and all the young men were being drafted. But why Sam—why did he have to go?

It was always in the back of his mind. Next thing Sam was in a camp in Georgia. He and Pink never talked about his being in Georgia. The closest they ever came to it was one night when she said, "I hope he gets used to it quick down there. Bein' born right here in New York there's lots he won't understand."

Then Sam's letters stopped coming. He'd come home from work and say to Pink casually, "Sam write today?" She'd shake her head without saying anything.

The days crawled past. And finally she burst out. "What you keep askin' for? You think I wouldn't tell you?" And she started crying.

He put his arm around her and patted her shoulder. She leaned hard against him. "Oh, Lord," she said. "He's my baby. What they done to him?"

Her crying like that tore him in little pieces. His mind kept going around in circles. Around and around. He couldn't think what to do. Finally one night after work he sat down at the kitchen table and wrote Sam a letter. He had written very few letters in his life because Pink had always done it for him. And now standing in front of the mailbox he could even remember the feel of the pencil in his hand; how the paper looked—blank and challenging—lying there in front of him; that the kitchen clock was ticking and it kept getting louder and louder. It was hot that night, too, and he held the pencil so tight that the inside of his hand was covered with sweat.

He had sat and thought a long time. Then he wrote: "Is you all right? Your Pa." It was the best he could do. He licked the envelope and addressed it with the feeling that Sam would understand.

He fumbled for his key ring, found the mailbox key, and opened the box quickly. It was empty. Even though he could see it was empty he felt around inside it. Then he closed the box and walked toward the street door.

The brilliant sunlight outside made him blink after the darkness of the hall. Even now, so early in the morning, it was hot in the street. And he thought it was going to be a hard day to get through, what with the heat and its being Saturday and all. Lately he couldn't seem to think about anything but Sam. Even at the drugstore where he worked as a porter, he would catch himself leaning on the broom or pausing in his mopping to wonder what had happened to him.

The man who owned the store would say to him sharply, "Boy, what the hell's the matter with you? Can't you keep your mind on what you're doing?" And he would go on washing windows, or mopping the floor, or sweeping the sidewalk. But his thoughts, somehow, no matter what he was doing, drifted back to Sam.

As he walked toward the drugstore he looked at the houses

on both sides of the street. He knew this street as he knew the creases in the old felt hat he wore the year round. No matter how you looked at it, it wasn't a good street to live on. It was a long cross-town street. Almost half of it on one side consisted of the backs of the three theaters on One Hundred Twenty-fifth Street—a long blank wall of gray brick. There were few trees on the street. Even these were a source of danger, for at night shadowy, vague shapes emerged from the street's darkness, lurking near the trees, dodging behind them. He had never been accosted by any of those disembodied figures, but the very stealth of their movements revealed a dishonest intent that frightened him. So when he came home at night he walked an extra block or more in order to go through One Hundred Twenty-fifth Street and enter the street from Eighth Avenue.

Early in the morning like this, the street slept. Window shades were drawn down tight against the morning sun. The few people he passed were walking briskly on their way to work. But in those houses where the people still slept, the window shades would go up about noon, and radios would blast music all up and down the street. The bold-eyed women who lived in these houses would lounge in the open windows and call to each other back and forth across the street.

Sometimes when he was on his way home to lunch they would call out to him as he went past, "Come on in, Poppa!" And he would stare straight ahead and start walking faster.

When Sam turned sixteen it seemed to him the street was unbearable. After lunch he and Sam went through this block together—Sam to school and he on his way back to the drugstore. He'd seen Sam stare at the lounging women in the windows. His face was expressionless, but his eyes were curious.

"I catch you goin' near one of them women and I'll beat you up and down the block," he'd said grimly.

Sam didn't answer him. Instead he looked down at him with a strangely adult look, for even at sixteen Sam had been a good five inches taller than he. After that when they passed through the block, Sam looked straight ahead. And William got the uncomfortable feeling that he had already explored the possibilities that the block offered. Yet he couldn't be sure. And he couldn't bring himself to ask him. Instead he walked along beside him, thinking desperately, We gotta move. I'll talk to Pink. We gotta move this time for sure.

That Sunday after Pink came home from church they looked for a new place. They went in and out of apartment houses along Seventh Avenue and Eighth Avenue, One Hundred Thirty-fifth Street, One Hundred Forty-fifth Street. Most

of the apartments they didn't even look at. They just asked
the super how much the rents were.

It was late when they headed for home. He had irritably
agreed with Pink that they'd better stay where they were.
Twenty-two dollars a month was all they could afford.

"It ain't a fit place to live, though," he said. They were
walking down Seventh Avenue. The street looked wide to
him, and he thought with distaste of their apartment. The
rooms weren't big enough for a man to move around in without bumping into something. Sometimes he thought that was
why Annie May spent so much time away from home. Even
at thirteen she couldn't stand being cooped up like that in
such a small amount of space.

And Pink said, "You want to live on Park Avenue? With a
doorman bowin' you in and out. 'Good mornin', Mr. William
Jones. Does the weather suit you this mornin'?' " Her voice
was sharp, like the crack of a whip.

That was five years ago. And now again they ought to
move on account of Pink not being able to stand the stairs
any more. He decided that Monday night after work he'd
start looking for a place.

It was even hotter in the drugstore than it was in the street.
He forced himself to go inside and put on a limp work coat.
Then broom in hand he went to stand in the doorway. He
waved to the superintendent of the building on the corner.
And watched him as he lugged garbage cans out of the areaway and rolled them to the curb. Now, that's the kind of
work he didn't want Sam to have to do. He tried to decide
why that was. It wasn't just because Sam was his boy and it
was hard work. He searched his mind for the reason. It didn't
pay enough for a man to live on decently. That was it. He
wanted Sam to have a job where he could make enough to
have good clothes and a nice home.

Sam's being in the army wasn't so bad, he thought. It was
his being in Georgia that was bad. They didn't treat colored
people right down there. Everybody knew that. If he could
figure out some way to get him farther north Pink wouldn't
have to worry about him so much.

The very sound of the word "Georgia" did something to
him inside. His mother had been born there. She had talked
about it a lot and painted such vivid pictures of it that he felt
he knew the place—the heat, the smell of the earth, how cotton looked. And something more. The way her mouth had
folded together whenever she had said, "They hate niggers
down there. Don't you never none of you children go down
there."

That was years ago, yet even now, standing here on Fifth Avenue, remembering the way she said it turned his skin clammy cold in spite of the heat. And of all the places in the world, Sam had to go to Georgia. Sam, who was born right here in New York, who had finished high school here—they had to put him in the army and send him to Georgia.

He tightened his grip on the broom and started sweeping the sidewalk in long, even strokes. Gradually the rhythm of the motion stilled the agitation in him. The regular back-and-forth motion was so pleasant that he kept on sweeping long after the sidewalk was clean. When Mr. Yudkin, who owned the store, arrived at eight-thirty he was still outside with the broom. Even now he didn't feel much like talking, so he only nodded in response to the druggist's brisk, "Good morning! Hot today!"

William followed him into the store and began polishing the big mirror in back of the soda fountain. He watched the man out of the corner of his eye as he washed his hands in the back room and exchanged his suit coat for a crisp white laboratory coat. And he thought maybe when the war is over Sam ought to study to be a druggist instead of a doctor or a lawyer.

As the morning wore along, customers came in in a steady stream. They got Bromo-Seltzers, cigarettes, aspirin, cough medicine, baby bottles. He delivered two prescriptions that cost five dollars. And the cash register rang so often it almost played a tune. Listening to it he said to himself, yes, Sam ought to be a druggist. It's clean work and it pays good.

A little after eleven o'clock three young girls came in. "Cokes," they said, and climbed up on the stools in front of the fountain. William was placing new stock on the shelves and he studied them from the top of the stepladder. As far as he could see, they looked exactly alike. All three of them. And like Annie May. Too thin. Too much lipstick. Their dresses were too short and too tight. Their hair was piled on top of their heads in slicked set curls.

"Aw, I quit that job," one of them said. "I wouldn't get up that early in the morning for nothing in the world."

That was like Annie May, too. She was always changing jobs. Because she could never get to work on time. If she was due at a place at nine she got there at ten. If at ten, then she arrived about eleven. He knew, too, that she didn't earn enough money to pay for all the cheap, bright-colored dresses she was forever buying.

Her girl friends looked just like her and just like these girls. He'd seen her coming out of the movie houses on One

Hundred Twenty-fifth Street with two or three of them. They were all chewing gum and they nudged each other and talked too loud and laughed too loud. They stared hard at every man who went past them.

Mr. Yudkin looked up at him sharply, and he shifted his glance away from the girls and began putting big bottles of Father John's medicine neatly on the shelf in front of him. As he stacked the bottles up he wondered if Annie May would have been different if she'd stayed in high school. She had stopped going when she was sixteen. He had spoken to Pink about it. "She oughtn't to stop school. She's too young," he'd said.

And because Annie May was Pink's sister's child all Pink had done had been to shake her head comfortably. "She's tired of going to school. Poor little thing. Leave her alone."

So he hadn't said anything more. Pink always took up for her. And he and Pink didn't fuss at each other like some folks do. He didn't say anything to Pink about it, but he took the afternoon off from work to go to see the principal of the school. He had to wait two hours to see her. And he studied the pictures on the walls in the outer office, and looked down at his shoes while he tried to put into words what he'd say—and how he wanted to say it.

The principal was a large-bosomed white woman. She listened to him long enough to learn that he was Annie May's uncle. "Ah, yes, Mr. Jones," she said. "Now in my opinion——"

And he was buried under a flow of words, a mountain of words, that went on and on. Her voice was high-pitched and loud, and she kept talking until he lost all sense of what she was saying. There was one phrase she kept using that sort of jumped at him out of the mass of words—"a slow learner."

He left her office feeling confused and embarrassed. If he could only have found the words he could have explained that Annie May was bright as a dollar. She wasn't any "slow learner." Before he knew it he was out in the street, conscious only that he'd lost a whole afternoon's pay and he never had got to say what he'd come for. And he was boiling mad with himself. All he'd wanted was to ask the principal to help him persuade Annie May to finish school. But he'd never got the words together.

When he hung up his soiled work coat in the broom closet at eight o'clock that night he felt as though he'd been sweeping floors, dusting fixtures, cleaning fountains, and running errands since the beginning of time itself. He looked at himself in the cracked mirror that hung on the door of the closet.

There was no question about it; he'd grown older-looking since Sam went in the army. His hair was turning a frizzled gray at the temples. His jawbones showed up sharper. There was a stoop in his shoulders.

"Guess I'll get a haircut," he said softly. He didn't really need one. But on a Saturday night the barbershop would be crowded. He'd have to wait a long time before Al got around to him. It would be good to listen to the talk that went on— the arguments that would get started and never really end. For a little while all the nagging worry about Sam would be pushed so far back in his mind, he wouldn't be aware of it.

The instant he entered the barbershop he could feel himself begin to relax inside. All the chairs were full. There were a lot of customers waiting. He waved a greeting to the barbers. "Hot, ain't it?" he said and mopped his forehead.

He stood there a minute, listening to the hum of conversation, before he picked out a place to sit. Some of the talk, he knew, would be violent, and he always avoided those discussions because he didn't like violence—even when it was only talk. Scraps of talk drifted past him.

"White folks got us by the balls——"

"Well, I dunno. It ain't just white folks. There's poor white folks gettin' their guts squeezed out, too——"

"Sure. But they're white. They can stand it better."

"Sadie had two dollars on 546 yesterday and it came out and——"

"You're wrong, man. Ain't no two ways about it. This country's set up so that——"

"Only thing to do, if you ask me, is shoot all them crackers and start out new——"

He finally settled himself in one of the chairs in the corner —not too far from the window and right in the middle of a group of regular customers who were arguing hotly about the war. It was a good seat. By looking in the long mirror in front of the barbers he could see the length of the shop.

Almost immediately he joined in the conversation. "Them Japs ain't got a chance——" he started. And he was feeling good. He'd come in at just the right time. He took a deep breath before he went on. Most every time he started talking about the Japs the others listened with deep respect. Because he knew more about them than the other customers. Pink worked for some Navy people and she told him what they said.

He looked along the line of waiting customers, watching their reaction to his words. Pretty soon they'd all be listening to him. And then he stopped talking abruptly. A soldier was sitting in the far corner of the shop, staring down at his shoes. Why, that's Scummy, he thought. He's at the same camp where Sam is. He forgot what he was about to say. He got up and walked over to Scummy. He swallowed all the questions about Sam that trembled on his lips.

"Hiya, son," he said. "Sure is good to see you."

As he shook hands with the boy he looked him over carefully. He's changed, he thought. He was older. There was something about his eyes that was different than before. He didn't seem to want to talk. After that first quick look at William he kept his eyes down, staring at his shoes.

Finally William couldn't hold the question back any longer. It came out fast. "How's Sam?"

Scummy picked up a newspaper from the chair beside him. "He's all right," he mumbled. There was a long silence. Then he raised his head and looked directly at William. "Was the las' time I seen him." He put a curious emphasis on the word "las'."

William was conscious of a trembling that started in his stomach. It went all through his body. He was aware that conversation in the barbership had stopped. There was a cone of silence in which he could hear the scraping noise of the razors—a harsh sound, loud in the silence. Al was putting thick oil on a customer's hair and he turned and looked with the hair-oil bottle still in his hand, tilted up over the customer's head. The men sitting in the tilted-back barber's chairs twisted their necks around—awkwardly, slowly—so they could look at Scummy.

"What you mean—the las' time?" William asked sharply. The words beat against his ears. He wished the men in the barbershop would start talking again, for he kept hearing his own words. "What you mean—the las' time?" Just as though he were saying them over and over again. Something had gone wrong with his breathing, too. He couldn't seem to get enough air in through his nose.

Scummy got up. There was something about him that William couldn't give a name to. It made the trembling in his stomach worse.

"The las' time I seen him he was O.K." Scummy's voice made a snarling noise in the barbershop.

One part of William's mind said, yes, that's it. It's hate that makes him look different. It's hate in his eyes. You can see it. It's in his voice, and you can hear it. He's filled with it.

"Since I seen him las'," he went on slowly, "he got shot by a white MP. Because he wouldn't go to the nigger end of a bus. He had a bullet put through his guts. He took the MP's gun away from him and shot the bastard in the shoulder." He put the newspaper down and started toward the door; when he reached it he turned around. "They court-martialed him," he said softly. "He got twenty years at hard labor. The notice was posted in the camp the day I left." Then he walked out of the shop. He didn't look back.

There was no sound in the barbershop as William watched him go down the street. Even the razors had stopped. Al was still holding the hair-oil bottle over the head of his customer. The heavy oil was falling on the face of the man sitting in the chair. It was coming down slowly—one drop at a time.

The men in the shop looked at William and then looked away. He thought, I mustn't tell Pink. She mustn't ever get to know. I can go down to the mailbox early in the morning and I can get somebody else to look in it in the afternoon, so if a notice comes I can tear it up.

The barbers started cutting hair again. There was the murmur of conversation in the shop. Customers got up out of the tilted-back chairs. Someone said to him, "You can take my place."

He nodded and walked over to the empty chair. His legs were weak and shaky. He couldn't seem to think at all. His mind kept dodging away from the thought of Sam in prison. Instead the familiar details of Sam's growing up kept creeping into his thoughts. All the time the boy was in grammar school he made good marks. Time went so fast it seemed like it was just overnight and he was in long pants. And then in high school.

He made the basketball team in high school. The whole school was proud of him, for his picture had been in one of the white papers. They got two papers that day. Pink cut the pictures out and stuck one in the mirror of the dresser in their bedroom. She gave him one to carry in his wallet.

While Al cut his hair he stared at himself in the mirror until he felt as though his eyes were crossed. First he thought, maybe it isn't true. Maybe Scummy was joking. But a man who was joking didn't look like Scummy looked. He wondered if Scummy was AWOL. That would be bad. He told himself sternly that he mustn't think about Sam here in the barbershop—wait until he got home.

He was suddenly angry with Annie May. She was just plain no good. Why couldn't something have happened to her? Why did it have to be Sam? Then he was ashamed. He tried to find an excuse for having wanted harm to come to her. It looked like all his life he'd wanted a little something for himself and Pink and then when Sam came along he forgot about those things. He wanted Sam to have all the things that he and Pink couldn't get. It got to be too late for them to have them. But Sam—again he told himself not to think about him. To wait until he got home and in bed.

Al took the cloth from around his neck, and he got up out of the chair. Then he was out on the street, heading toward home. The heat that came from the pavement seeped through the soles of his shoes. He had forgotten how hot it was. He forced himself to wonder what it would be like to live in the country. Sometimes on hot nights like this, after he got home from work, he went to sit in the park. It was always cooler there. It would probably be cool in the country. But then it might be cold in winter—even colder than the city.

The instant he got in the house he took off his shoes and his shirt. The heat in the apartment was like a blanket—it made his skin itch and crawl in a thousand places. He went into the living room, where he leaned out of the window, trying to cool off. Not yet, he told himself. He mustn't think about it yet.

He leaned farther out of the window, to get away from the innumerable odors that came from the boxlike rooms in back of him. They cut off his breath, and he focused his mind on them. There was the greasy smell of cabbage and collard greens, smell of old wood and soapsuds and disinfectant, a lingering smell of gas from the kitchen stove, and over it all Annie May's perfume.

Then he turned his attention to the street. Up and down as far as he could see, folks were sitting on the stoops. Not talking. Just sitting. Somewhere up the street a baby wailed. A woman's voice rose sharply as she told it to shut up.

Pink wouldn't be home until late. The white folks she worked for were having a dinner party tonight. And no matter how late she got home on Saturday night she always stopped on Eighth Avenue to shop for her Sunday dinner. She never trusted him to do it. It's a good thing, he thought. If she ever took a look at me tonight she'd know there was something wrong.

A key clicked in the lock, and he drew back from the window. He was sitting on the couch when Annie May came in the room.

"You're home early, ain't you?" he asked.

"Oh, I'm going out again," she said.

"You shouldn't stay out so late like you did last night," he said mildly. He hadn't really meant to say it. But what with Sam—

"What you think I'm going to do? Sit here every night and make small talk with you?" Her voice was defiant. Loud.

"No," he said, and then added, "but nice girls ain't runnin' around the streets at four o'clock in the mornin'." Now that he'd started he couldn't seem to stop. "Oh, I know what time you come home. And it ain't right. If you don't stop it you can get some other place to stay."

"It's O.K. with me," she said lightly. She chewed the gum in her mouth so it made a cracking noise. "I don't know what Auntie Pink married a little runt like you for, anyhow. It wouldn't bother me a bit if I never saw you again." She walked toward the hall. "I'm going away for the week end," she added over her shoulder. "And I'll move out on Monday."

"What you mean for the week end?" he asked sharply. "Where you goin'?"

"None of your damn business," she said, and slammed the bathroom door hard.

The sharp sound of the door closing hurt his ears so that he winced, wondering why he had grown so sensitive to sounds in the last few hours. What'd she have to say that for, anyway, he asked himself. Five feet five wasn't so short for a man. He was taller than Pink, anyhow. Yet compared to Sam, he supposed he was a runt, for Sam had just kept on growing until he was six feet tall. At the thought he got up from the chair quickly, undressed, and got in bed. He lay there trying to still the trembling in his stomach; trying even now not to think about Sam, because it would be best to wait until Pink was in bed and sound asleep so that no expression on his face, no least little motion, would betray his agitation.

When he heard Pink come up the stairs just before midnight he closed his eyes. All of him was listening to her. He could hear her panting outside on the landing. There was a long pause before she put her key in the door. It took her all that time to get her breath back. She's getting old, he thought. I mustn't let her know about Sam.

She came into the bedroom, and he pretended to be asleep. He made himself breathe slowly. Evenly. Thinking, I can get through tomorrow all right. I won't get up much before she goes to church. She'll be so busy getting dressed she won't notice me.

She went out of the room and he heard the soft murmur of her voice talking to Annie May. "Don't you pay no attention, honey. He don't mean a word of it. I know menfolks. They's always tired and out of sorts by the time Saturdays come around."

"But I'm not going to stay here any more."

"Yes, you is. You think I'm goin' to let my sister's child be turned out? You goin' to be right here."

They lowered their voices. There was laughter. Pink's deep and rich and slow. Annie May's high-pitched and nervous. Pink said, "You looks lovely, honey. Now, have a good time."

The front door closed. This time Annie May didn't slam it. He turned over on his back, making the springs creak. Instantly Pink came into the bedroom to look at him. He lay still, with his eyes closed, holding his breath for fear she would want to talk to him about what he'd said to Annie May and would wake him up. After she moved away from the door he opened his eyes.

There must be some meaning in back of what had happened to Sam. Maybe it was some kind of judgment from the Lord, he thought. Perhaps he shouldn't have stopped going to church. His only concession to Sunday was to put on his best suit. He wore it just that one day, and Pink pressed the pants late on Saturday night. But in the last few years it got so that every time he went to church he wanted to stand up and yell, "You Goddamn fools! How much more you goin' to take?"

He'd get to thinking about the street they lived on, and the sight of the minister with his clean white collar turned hind side to and the sound of his buttery voice were too much. One Sunday he'd actually gotten on his feet, for the minister was talking about the streets of gold up in heaven; the words were right on the tip of his tongue when Pink reached out and pinched his behind sharply. He yelped and sat down. Someone in back of him giggled. In spite of himself a slow smile had spread over his face. He stayed quiet through the rest of the service, but after that he didn't go to church at all.

This street where he and Pink lived was like the one where his mother had lived. It looked like he and Pink ought to have gotten further than his mother had. She had scrubbed floors, washed, and ironed in the white folks' kitchens. They were doing practically the same thing. That was another reason he stopped going to church. He couldn't figure out why these things had to stay the same, and if the Lord didn't intend it like that, why didn't He change it?

He began thinking about Sam again, so he shifted his attention to the sounds Pink was making in the kitchen. She was getting the rolls ready for tomorrow. Scrubbing the sweet potatoes. Washing the greens. Cutting up the chicken. Then the thump of the iron. Hot as it was, she was pressing his pants. He resisted the impulse to get up and tell her not to do it.

A little later, when she turned the light on in the bathroom, he knew she was getting ready for bed. And he held his eyes tightly shut, made his body rigidly still. As long as he could make her think he was sound asleep she wouldn't take a real good look at him. One real good look and she'd know there was something wrong. The bed sagged under her weight as she knelt down to say her prayers. Then she was lying down beside him. She sighed under her breath as her head hit the pillow.

He must have slept part of the time, but in the morning it seemed to him that he had looked up at the ceiling most of the night. He couldn't remember actually going to sleep.

When he finally got up, Pink was dressed and ready for church. He sat down in a chair in the living room away from the window, so the light wouldn't shine on his face. As he looked at her he wished that he could find relief from the confusion of his thoughts by taking part in the singing and the shouting that would go on in church. But he couldn't. And Pink never said anything about his not going to church. Only sometimes like today, when she was ready to go, she looked at him a little wistfully.

She had on her Sunday dress. It was made of a printed material—big red and black poppies splashed on a cream-colored background. He wouldn't let himself look right into her eyes, and in order that she wouldn't notice the evasiveness of his glance he stared at the dress. It fit snugly over her best corset, and the corset in turn constricted her thighs and tightly encased the rolls of flesh around her waist. She didn't move away, and he couldn't keep on inspecting the dress, so he shifted his gaze up to the wide cream-colored straw hat she was wearing far back on her head. Next he noticed that she was easing her feet by standing on the outer edges of the high-heeled patent-leather pumps she wore.

He reached out and patted her arm. "You look nice," he said, picking up the comic section of the paper.

She stood there looking at him while she pulled a pair of white cotton gloves over her roughened hands. "Is you all right, honey?" she asked.

"Course," he said, holding the paper up in front of his face.

"You shouldn't talk so mean to Annie May," she said gently.

"Yeah, I know," he said, and hoped she understood that he was apologizing. He didn't dare lower the paper while she was standing there looking at him so intently. Why doesn't she go, he thought.

"There's grits and eggs for breakfast."

"O.K." He tried to make his voice sound as though he were so absorbed in what he was reading that he couldn't give her all of his attention. She walked toward the door, and he lowered the paper to watch her, thinking that her legs looked too small for her body under the vastness of the printed dress, that womenfolks sure were funny—she's got that great big pocketbook swinging on her arm and hardly anything in it. Sam used to love to tease her about the size of the handbags she carried.

When she closed the outside door and started down the stairs, the heat in the little room struck him in the face. He almost called her back so that he wouldn't be there by himself—left alone to brood over Sam. He decided that when she came home from church he would make love to her. Even in the heat the softness of her body, the smoothness of her skin, would comfort him.

He pulled his chair up close to the open window. Now he could let himself go. He could begin to figure out something to do about Sam. There's gotta be something, he thought. But his mind wouldn't stay put. It kept going back to the time Sam graduated from high school. Nineteen seventy-five his dark-blue suit had cost. He and Pink had figured and figured and finally they'd managed it. Sam had looked good in the suit; he was so tall and his shoulders were so broad it looked like a tailor-made suit on him. When he got his diploma everybody went wild—he'd played center on the basketball team, and a lot of folks recognized him.

The trembling in his stomach got worse as he thought about Sam. He was aware that it had never stopped since Scummy had said those words "the las' time." It had gone on all last night until now there was a tautness and a tension in him that left him feeling as though his eardrums were strained wide open, listening for sounds. They must be a foot wide open, he thought. Open and pulsing with the strain of being open. Even his nostrils were stretched open like that. He could feel them. And a weight behind his eyes.

He went to sleep sitting there in the chair. When he woke up his whole body was wet with sweat. It musta got hotter while I slept, he thought. He was conscious of an ache in his jawbones. It's from holding 'em shut so tight. Even his tongue —he'd been holding it so still in his mouth it felt like it was glued there.

Attracted by the sound of voices, he looked out of the window. Across the way a man and a woman were arguing. Their voices rose and fell on the hot, still air. He could look directly into the room where they were standing, and he saw that they were half undressed.

The woman slapped the man across the face. The sound was like a pistol shot, and for an instant William felt his jaw relax. It seemed to him that the whole block grew quiet and waited. He waited with it. The man grabbed his belt and lashed out at the woman. He watched the belt rise and fall against her brown skin. The woman screamed with the regularity of clockwork. The street came alive again. There was the sound of voices, the rattle of dishes. A baby whined. The woman's voice became a murmur of pain in the background.

"I gotta get me some beer," he said aloud. It would cool him off. It would help him to think. He dressed quickly, telling himself that Pink wouldn't be home for hours yet and by that time the beer smell would be gone from his breath.

The street outside was full of kids playing tag. They were all dressed up in their Sunday clothes. Red socks, blue socks, danced in front of him all the way to the corner. The sight of them piled up the quivering in his stomach. Sam used to play in this block on Sunday afternoons. As he walked along, women thrust their heads out of the opened windows, calling to the children. It seemed to him that all the voices were Pink's voice saying, "You, Sammie, stop that runnin' in your good cloes!"

He was so glad to get away from the sight of the children that he ignored the heat inside the barroom of the hotel on the corner and determinedly edged his way past girls in sheer summer dresses and men in loud plaid jackets and tight-legged cream-colored pants until he finally reached the long bar.

There was such a sense of hot excitement in the place that he turned to look around him. Men with slicked, straightened hair were staring through half-closed eyes at the girls lined up at the bar. One man sitting at a table close by kept running his hand up and down the bare arm of the girl leaning against him. Up and down. Down and up. William winced and looked away. The jukebox was going full blast, filling the room with high, raw music that beat about his ears in a queer mixture of violence and love and hate and terror. He stared at the brilliantly colored moving lights on the front of the jukebox as he listened to it, wishing that he had stayed at home, for the music made the room hotter.

"Make it a beer," he said to the bartender.

The beer glass was cold. He held it in his hand, savoring the chill of it, before he raised it to his lips. He drank it down fast. Immediately he felt the air grow cooler. The smell of beer and whisky that hung in the room lifted.

"Fill it up again," he said. He still had that awful trembling in his stomach, but he felt as though he were really beginning to think. Really think. He found he was arguing with himself.

"Sam mighta been like this. Spendin' Sunday afternoons whorin'."

"But he was part of me and part of Pink. He had a chance——"

"Yeah. A chance to live in one of them hell-hole flats. A chance to get himself a woman to beat."

"He woulda finished college and got a good job. Mebbe been a druggist or a doctor or a lawyer——"

"Yeah. Or mebbe got himself a stable of women to rent out on the block——"

He licked the suds from his lips. The man at the table nearby had stopped stroking the girl's arm. He was kissing her—forcing her closer and closer to him.

"Yeah," William jeered at himself. "That coulda been Sam on a hot Sunday afternoon——"

As he stood there arguing with himself he thought it was getting warmer in the bar. The lights were dimmer. I better go home, he thought. I gotta live with this thing some time. Drinking beer in this place ain't going to help any. He looked out toward the lobby of the hotel, attracted by the sound of voices. A white cop was arguing with a frowzy-looking girl who had obviously had too much to drink.

"I got a right in here. I'm mindin' my own business," she said with one eye on the bar.

"Aw, go chase yourself." The cop gave her a push toward the door. She stumbled against a chair.

William watched her in amusement. "Better than a movie," he told himself.

She straightened up and tugged at her girdle. "You white son of a bitch," she said.

The cop's face turned a furious red. He walked toward the woman, waving his nightstick. It was then that William saw the soldier. Tall. Straight. Creases in his khaki pants. An overseas cap cocked over one eye. Looks like Sam looked that one time he was home on furlough, he thought.

The soldier grabbed the cop's arm and twisted the nightstick out of his hand. He threw it half the length of the small lobby. It rattled along the floor and came to a dead stop under a chair.

"Now what'd he want to do that for?" William said softly.

He knew that night after night the cop had to come back to this hotel. He's the law, he thought, and he can't let— Then he stopped thinking about him, for the cop raised his arm. The soldier aimed a blow at the cop's chin. The cop ducked and reached for his gun. The soldier turned to run.

It's happening too fast, William thought. It's like one of those horse-race reels they run over fast at the movies. Then he froze inside. The quivering in his stomach got worse. The soldier was heading toward the door. Running. His foot was on the threshold when the cop fired. The soldier dropped. He folded up as neatly as the brown-paper bags Pink brought home from the store, emptied, and then carefully put in the kitchen cupboard.

The noise of the shot stayed in his eardrums. He couldn't get it out. "Jesus Christ!" he said. Then again, "Jesus Christ!" The beer glass was warm. He put it down on the bar with such violence some of the beer slopped over on his shirt. He stared at the wet place, thinking Pink would be mad as hell. Him out drinking in a bar on Sunday. There was a stillness in which he was conscious of the stink of the beer, the heat in the room, and he could still hear the sound of the shot. Somebody dropped a glass, and the tinkle of it hurt his ears.

Then everybody was moving toward the lobby. The doors between the bar and the lobby slammed shut. High, excited talk broke out.

The tall, thin black man standing next to him said, "That ties it. It ain't even safe here where we live. Not no more. I'm goin' to get me a white bastard of a cop and nail his hide to a street sign."

"Is the soldier dead?" someone asked.

"He wasn't movin' none," came the answer.

They pushed hard against the doors leading to the lobby. The doors stayed shut.

He stood still, watching them. The anger that went through him was so great that he had to hold on to the bar to keep from falling. He felt as though he were going to burst wide open. It was like having seen Sam killed before his eyes. Then he heard the whine of an ambulance siren. His eardrums seemed to be waiting to pick it up.

"Come on, what you waitin' for?" he snarled the words at the people milling around the lobby doors. "Come on!" he repeated, running toward the street.

The crowd followed him to the One Hundred Twenty-sixth Street entrance of the hotel. He got there in time to see a stretcher bearing a limp khaki-clad figure disappear inside the ambulance in front of the door. The ambulance pulled away fast, and he stared after it stupidly.

He hadn't known what he was going to do, but he felt cheated. Let down. He noticed that it was beginning to get dark. More and more people were coming into the street. He wondered where they'd come from and how they'd heard about the shooting so quickly. Every time he looked around there were more of them. Curious, eager voices kept asking, "What happened? What happened?" The answer was always the same. Hard. Angry. "A white cop shot a soldier."

Someone said, "Come on to the hospital. Find out what happened to him."

In front of the hotel he had been in the front of the crowd. Now there were so many people in back of him and in front of him that when they started toward the hospital, he moved along with them. He hadn't decided to go—the forward movement picked him up and moved him along without any intention on his part. He got the feeling that he had lost his identity as a person with a free will of his own. It frightened him at first. Then he began to feel powerful. He was surrounded by hundreds of people like himself. They were all together. They could do anything.

As the crowd moved slowly down Eighth Avenue, he saw that there were cops lined up on both sides of the street. Mounted cops kept coming out of the side streets, shouting, "Break it up! Keep moving. Keep moving."

The cops were scared of them. He could tell. Their faces were dead white in the semidarkness. He started saying the words over separately to himself. Dead. White. He laughed. White cops. White MP's. They got us coming and going, he thought. He laughed again. Dead. White. The words were funny said separately like that. He stopped laughing suddenly because a part of his mind repeated: twenty years, twenty years.

He licked his lips. It was hot as all hell tonight. He imagined what it would be like to be drinking swallow after swallow of ice-cold beer. His throat worked and he swallowed audibly.

The big black man walking beside him turned and looked down at him. "You all right, brother?" he asked curiously.

"Yeah," he nodded. "It's them sons of bitches of cops. They're scared of us." He shuddered. The heat was terrible. The tide of hate quivering in his stomach made him hotter. "Wish I had some beer," he said.

The man seemed to understand not only what he had said but all the things he had left unsaid. For he nodded and smiled. And William thought this was an extraordinary night. It was as though, standing so close together, so many of them like this—as though they knew each other's thoughts. It was a wonderful thing.

The crowd carried him along. Smoothly. Easily. He wasn't really walking. Just gliding. He was aware that the shuffling feet of the crowd made a muffled rhythm on the concrete sidewalk. It was slow, inevitable. An ominous sound, like a funeral march. With the regularity of a drumbeat. No. It's more like a pulse beat, he thought. It isn't a loud noise. It just keeps repeating over and over. But not that regular, because it builds up to something. It keeps building up.

The mounted cops rode their horses into the crowd. Trying to break it up into smaller groups. Then the rhythm was broken. Seconds later it started again. Each time the tempo was a little faster. He found he was breathing the same way. Faster and faster. As though he were running. There were more and more cops. All of them white. They had moved the colored cops out.

"They done that before," he muttered.

"What?" said the man next to him.

"They moved the colored cops out," he said.

He heard the man repeat it to someone standing beside him. It became part of the slow shuffling rhythm on the sidewalk. "They moved the colored cops." He heard it go back and back through the crowd until it was only a whisper of hate on the still, hot air. "They moved the colored cops."

As the crowd shuffled back and forth in front of the hospital, he caught snatches of conversation. "The soldier was dead when they put him in the ambulance." "Always tryin' to fool us." "Christ! Just let me get my hands on one of them cops."

He was thinking about the hospital and he didn't take part in any of the conversations. Even now across the long span of years he could remember the helpless, awful rage that had sent him hurrying home from this same hospital. Not saying anything. Getting home by some kind of instinct.

Pink had come to this hospital when she had had her last child. He could hear again the cold contempt in the voice of the nurse as she listened to Pink's loud grieving. "You people have too many children anyway," she said.

It left him speechless. He had his hat in his hand and he remembered how he wished afterward that he'd put it on in front of her to show her what he thought of her. As it was, all the bitter answer that finally surged into his throat seemed to choke him. No words would come out. So he stared at her lean, spare body. He let his eyes stay a long time on her flat breasts. White uniform. White shoes. White stockings. White skin.

Then he mumbled, "It's too bad your eyes ain't white, too." And turned on his heel and walked out.

It wasn't any kind of answer. She probably didn't even know what he was talking about. The baby dead, and all he could think of was to tell her her eyes ought to be white. White shoes, white stockings, white uniform, white skin, and blue eyes.

Staring at the hospital, he saw with satisfaction that frightened faces were appearing at the windows. Some of the lights went out. He began to feel that this night was the first time he'd ever really been alive. Tonight everything was going to be changed. There was a growing, swelling sense of power in him. He felt the same thing in the people around him.

The cops were aware of it, too, he thought. They were out in full force. Mounties, patrolmen, emergency squads. Radio cars that looked like oversize bugs crawled through the side streets. Waited near the curbs. Their white tops stood out in the darkness. "White folks riding in white cars." He wasn't aware that he had said it aloud until he heard the words go through the crowd. "White folks in white cars." The laughter that followed the words had a rough, raw rhythm. It repeated the pattern of the shuffling feet.

Someone said, "They got him at the station house. He ain't here." And the crowd started moving toward One Hundred Twenty-third Street.

Great God in the morning, William thought, everybody's out here. There were girls in thin summer dresses, boys in long coats and tight-legged pants, old women dragging kids along by the hand. A man on crutches jerked himself past to the rhythm of the shuffling feet. A blind man tapped his way through the center of the crowd, and it divided into two separate streams as it swept by him. At every street corner William noticed someone stopped to help the blind man up over the curb.

The street in front of the police station was so packed with people that he couldn't get near it. As far as he could see they weren't doing anything. They were simply standing there. Waiting for something to happen. He recognized a few of them: the woman with the loose, rolling eyes who sold shopping bags on One Hundred Twenty-fifth Street; the lucky-number peddler—the man with the white parrot on his shoulder; three sisters of the Heavenly Rest for All movement—barefooted women in loose white robes.

Then, for no reason that he could discover, everybody moved toward One Hundred Twenty-fifth Street. The motion of the crowd was slower now because it kept increasing in size as people coming from late church services were drawn into it. It was easy to identify them, he thought. The women wore white gloves. The kids were all slicked up. Despite the more gradual movement he was still being carried along effortlessly, easily. When someone in front of him barred his way, he pushed against the person irritably, frowning in annoyance because the smooth forward flow of his progress had been stopped.

It was Pink who stood in front of him. He stopped frowning when he recognized her. She had a brown-paper bag tucked under her arm, and he knew she had stopped at the corner store to get the big bottle of cream soda she always brought home on Sundays. The sight of it made him envious, for it meant that this Sunday had been going along in an orderly, normal fashion for her while he— She was staring at him so hard he was suddenly horribly conscious of the smell of the beer that had spilled on his shirt. He knew she had smelled it, too, by the tighter grip she took on her pocketbook.

"What you doing out here in this mob? A Sunday evening and you drinking beer," she said grimly.

For a moment he couldn't answer her. All he could think of was Sam. He almost said, "I saw Sam shot this afternoon," and he swallowed hard.

"This afternoon I saw a white cop kill a colored soldier," he said. "In the bar where I was drinking beer. I saw it. That's why I'm here. The glass of beer I was drinking went on my clothes. The cop shot him in the back. That's why I'm here."

He paused for a moment, took a deep breath. This was how it ought to be, he decided. She had to know sometime and this was the right place to tell her. In this semidarkness, in this confusion of noises, with the low, harsh rhythm of the footsteps sounding against the noise of the horses' hoofs.

His voice thickened. "I saw Scummy yesterday," he went on. "He told me Sam's doing time at hard labor. That's why we ain't heard from him. A white MP shot him when he wouldn't go to the nigger end of a bus. Sam shot the MP. They gave him twenty years at hard labor."

He knew he hadn't made it clear how to him the soldier in the bar was Sam; that it was like seeing his own son shot before his very eyes. I don't even know whether the soldier was dead, he thought. What made me tell her about Sam out here in the street like this, anyway? He realized with a sense of shock that he really didn't care that he had told her. He felt strong, powerful, aloof. All the time he'd been talking he wouldn't look right at her. Now, suddenly, he was looking at her as though she were a total stranger. He was coldly wondering what she'd do. He was prepared for anything.

But he wasn't prepared for the wail that came from her throat. The sound hung in the hot air. It made the awful quivering in his stomach worse. It echoed and re-echoed the length of the street. Somewhere in the distance a horse whinnied. A woman standing way back in the crowd groaned as though the sorrow and the anguish in that cry were more than she could bear.

Pink stood there for a moment. Silent. Brooding. Then she lifted the big bottle of soda high in the air. She threw it with all her might. It made a wide arc and landed in the exact center of the plate-glass window of a furniture store. The glass crashed in with a sound like a gunshot.

A sigh went up from the crowd. They surged toward the broken window. Pink followed close behind. When she reached the window, all the glass had been broken in. Reaching far inside, she grabbed a small footstool and then turned to hurl it through the window of the dress shop next door. He kept close behind her, watching her as she seized a new missile from each store window that she broke.

Plate-glass windows were being smashed all up and down One Hundred Twenty-fifth Street—on both sides of the street. The violent, explosive sound fed the sense of power in him. Pink had started this. He was proud of her, for she had shown herself to be a fit mate for a man of his type. He stayed as close to her as he could. So in spite of the crashing, splintering sounds and the swarming, violent activity around him, he knew the exact moment when she lost her big straw hat; when she took off the high-heeled patent-leather shoes and flung them away, striding swiftly along in her stockinged feet. That her dress was hanging crooked on her.

He was right in back of her when she stopped in front of a hat store. She carefully appraised all the hats inside the broken window. Finally she reached out, selected a small hat covered with purple violets, and fastened it securely on her head.

"Woman's got good sense," a man said.

"Man, oh, man! Let me get in there," said a rawboned woman who thrust her way forward through the jam of people to seize two hats from the window.

A roar of approval went up from the crowd. From then on

when a window was smashed it was bare of merchandise when the people streamed past it. White folks owned these stores. They'd lose and lose and lose, he thought with satisfaction. The words "twenty years" re-echoed in his mind. I'll be an old man, he thought. Then: I may be dead before Sam gets out of prison.

The feeling of great power and strength left him. He was so confused by its loss that he decided this thing happening in the street wasn't real. It was so dark, there were so many people shouting and running about, that he almost convinced himself he was having a nightmare. He was aware that his hearing had now grown so acute he could pick up the tiniest sounds: the quickened breathing and the soft, gloating laughter of the crowd; even the sound of his own heart beating. He could hear these things under the noise of the breaking glass, under the shouts that were coming from both sides of the street. They forced him to face the fact that this was no dream but a reality from which he couldn't escape. The quivering in his stomach kept increasing as he walked along.

Pink was striding through the crowd just ahead of him. He studied her to see if she, too, was feeling as he did. But the outrage that ran through her had made her younger. She was tireless. Most of the time she was leading the crowd. It was all he could do to keep up with her, and finally he gave up the attempt—it made him too tired.

He stopped to watch a girl who was standing in a store window, clutching a clothes model tightly around the waist. "What's she want that for?" he said aloud. For the model had been stripped of clothing by the passing crowd, and he thought its pinkish torso was faintly obscene in its resemblance to a female figure.

The girl was young and thin. Her back was turned toward him, and there was something so ferocious about the way her dark hands gripped the naked model that he resisted the onward movement of the crowd to stare in fascination. The girl turned around. Her nervous hands were tight around the dummy's waist. It was Annie May.

"Ah, no!" he said, and let his breath come out with a sigh.

Her hands crept around the throat of the model and she sent it hurtling through the air above the heads of the crowd. It landed short of a window across the street. The legs shattered. The head rolled toward the curb. The waist snapped neatly in two. Only the torso remained whole and in one piece.

Annie May stood in the empty window and laughed with the crowd when someone kicked the torso into the street. He

stood there, staring at her. He felt that now for the first time
he understood her. She had never had anything but badly
paying jobs—working for young white women who probably
despised her. She was like Sam on that bus in Georgia. She
didn't want just the nigger end of things, and here in Harlem
there wasn't anything else for her. All along she'd been trying
the only way she knew how to squeeze out of life a little
something for herself.

He tried to get closer to the window where she was standing. He had to tell her that he understood. And the crowd,
tired of the obstruction that he had made by standing still,
swept him up and carried him past. He stopped thinking and
let himself be carried along on a vast wave of feeling. There
was so much plate glass on the sidewalk that it made a grinding noise under the feet of the hurrying crowd. It was a dull,
harsh sound that set his teeth on edge and quickened the
trembling of his stomach.

Now all the store windows that he passed were broken.
The people hurrying by him carried tables, lamps, shoeboxes,
clothing. A woman next to him held a wedding cake in her
hands—it went up in tiers of white frosting with a small
bride and groom mounted at the top. Her hands were bleeding, and he began to look closely at the people nearest him.
Most of them, too, had cuts on their hands and legs. Then he
saw there was blood on the sidewalk in front of the windows;
blood dripping down the jagged edges of the broken windows. And he wanted desperately to go home.

He was conscious that the rhythm of the crowd had
changed. It was faster, and it had taken on an ugly note. The
cops were using their nightsticks. Police wagons drew up to
the curbs. When they pulled away, they were full of men and
women who carried loot from the stores in their hands.

The police cars slipping through the streets were joined by
other cars with loudspeakers on top. The voices coming
through the loudspeakers were harsh. They added to the
noise and the confusion. He tried to listen to what the voices
were saying. But the words had no meaning for him. He
caught one phrase over and over: "Good people of Harlem."
It made him feel sick.

He repeated the words "of Harlem." We don't belong anywhere, he thought. There ain't no room for us anywhere.
There wasn't no room for Sam in a bus in Georgia. There
ain't no room for us here in New York. There ain't no place
but top floors. The top-floor black people. And he laughed,
and the sound stuck in his throat.

After that he snatched a suit from the window of a men's

clothing store. It was a summer suit. The material felt crisp and cool. He walked away with it under his arm. He'd never owned a suit like that. He simply sweated out the summer in the same dark pants he wore in winter. Even while he stroked the material, a part of his mind sneered—you got summer pants; Sam's got twenty years.

He was surprised to find that he was almost at Lenox Avenue, for he hadn't remembered crossing Seventh. At the corner the cops were shoving a group of young boys and girls into a police wagon. He paused to watch. Annie May was in the middle of the group. She had a yellow-fox jacket dangling from one hand.

"Annie May!" he shouted. "Annie May!" The crowd pushed him along faster and faster. She hadn't seen him. He let himself be carried forward by the movement of the crowd. He had to find Pink and tell her that the cops had taken Annie May.

He peered into the dimness of the street ahead of him, looking for her; then he elbowed his way toward the curb so that he could see the other side of the street. He forgot about finding Pink, for directly opposite him was the music store that he passed every night coming home from work. Young boys and girls were always lounging on the sidewalk in front of it. They danced a few steps while they listened to the records being played inside the shop. All the records sounded the same—a terribly magnified woman's voice bleating out a blues song in a voice that sounded to him like that of an animal in heat—an old animal, tired and beaten, but with an insinuating know-how left in her. The white men who went past the store smiled as their eyes lingered on the young girls swaying to the music.

"White folks got us comin' and goin'. Backwards and forwards," he muttered. He fought his way out of the crowd and walked toward a no-parking sign that stood in front of the store. He rolled it up over the curb. It was heavy, and the effort made him pant. It took all his strength to send it crashing through the glass on the door.

Almost immediately an old woman and a young man slipped inside the narrow shop. He followed them. He watched them smash the records that lined the shelves. He hadn't thought of actually breaking the records, but once he started he found the crisp, snapping noise pleasant. The feeling of power began to return. He didn't like these records, so they had to be destroyed.

When they left the music store there wasn't a whole record left. The old woman came out of the store last. As he hurried off up the street he could have sworn he smelled the sharp, acrid smell of smoke. He turned and looked back. He was right. A thin wisp of smoke was coming through the store door. The old woman had long since disappeared in the crowd.

Farther up the street he looked back again. The fire in the record shop was burning merrily. It was making a glow that lit up that part of the street. There was a new rhythm now. It was faster and faster. Even the voices coming from the loud-speakers had taken on the urgency of speed.

Fire trucks roared up the street. He threw his head back and laughed when he saw them. That's right, he thought. Burn the whole damn place down. It was wonderful. Then he frowned. "Twenty years at hard labor." The words came back to him. He was a fool. Fire wouldn't wipe that out. There wasn't anything that would wipe it out.

He remembered then that he had to find Pink. To tell her about Annie May. He overtook her in the next block. She's got more stuff, he thought. She had a table lamp in one hand, a large enamel kettle in the other. The lightweight summer coat drapped across her shoulders was so small it barely covered her enormous arms. She was watching a group of boys assault the steel gates in front of a liquor store. She frowned at them so ferociously he wondered what she was going to do. Hating liquor the way she did, he half expected her to cuff the boys and send them on their way up the street.

She turned and looked at the crowd in back of her. When she saw him she beckoned to him. "Hold these," she said. He took the lamp, the kettle, and the coat she held out to him, and he saw that her face was wet with perspiration. The print dress was darkly stained with it.

She fastened the hat with the purple flowers securely on her head. Then she walked over to the gate. "Git out the way," she said to the boys. Bracing herself in front of the gate, she started tugging at it. The gate resisted. She pulled at it with a sudden access of such furious strength that he was frightened. Watching her, he got the feeling that the resistance of the gate had transformed it in her mind. It was no longer a gate—it had become the world that had taken her son, and she was wreaking vengeance on it.

The gate began to bend and sway under her assault. Then it was down. She stood there for a moment, staring at her hands—big drops of blood oozed slowly over the palms. Then she turned to the crowd that had stopped to watch.

"Come on, you niggers," she said. Her eyes were little and evil and triumphant. "Come on and drink up the white man's liquor." As she strode off up the street, the beflowered hat dangled precariously from the back of her head.

When he caught up with her she was moaning, talking to herself in husky whispers. She stopped when she saw him and put her hand on his arm.

"It's hot, ain't it?" she said, panting.

In the midst of all this violence, the sheer commonplaceness of her question startled him. He looked at her closely. The rage that had been in her was gone, leaving her completely exhausted. She was breathing too fast in uneven gasps that shook her body. Rivulets of sweat streamed down her face. It was as though her triumph over the metal gate had finished her. The gate won anyway, he thought.

"Let's go home, Pink," he said. He had to shout to make his voice carry over the roar of the crowd, the sound of breaking glass.

He realized she didn't have the strength to speak, for she only nodded in reply to his suggestion. Once we get home she'll be all right, he thought. It was suddenly urgent that they get home, where it was quiet, where he could think, where he could take something to still the tremors in his stomach. He tried to get her to walk a little faster, but she kept slowing down until, when they entered their own street, it seemed to him they were barely moving.

In the middle of the block she stood still. "I can't make it," she said. "I'm too tired."

Even as he put his arm around her she started going down. He tried to hold her up, but her great weight was too much for him. She went down slowly, inevitably, like a great ship capsizing. Until all of her huge body was crumpled on the sidewalk.

"Pink," he said. "Pink. You gotta get up," he said it over and over again.

She didn't answer. He leaned over and touched her gently. Almost immediately afterward he straightened up. All his life, moments of despair and frustration had left him speechless—strangled by the words that rose in his throat. This time the words poured out.

He sent his voice raging into the darkness and the awful confusion of noises. "The sons of bitches," he shouted. "The sons of bitches."

RALPH ELLISON (1914–   )

With a single novel, Invisible Man—*honored with the National Book Award in 1952 and judged, in 1965, "the most distinguished single work" published in the last twenty years by a Book Week poll of some two hundred critics, authors, and editors—Ralph Ellison reached the summit of the American literary establishment. Never before had a Negro writer been so accepted by the dominant critical circles, discussed as a major figure of contemporary American literature rather than as a "race" writer. Ellison was born in Oklahoma City and originally intended to be a musician. He majored in music at Tuskegee Institute, and when he came to New York City in 1936, he planned to study music and sculpture. Ellison has had a lifelong interest in jazz, and among his numerous jobs before he established himself as a writer, he was a jazz trumpeter. Ellison has been Writer in Residence at Rutgers University, Visiting Fellow at Yale, and has lectured and read from his works at colleges, universities, and academic gatherings throughout the United States. He has published a volume of critical essays,* Shadow and Act, *and excerpts from a second novel, on which he has been working for a number of years, have appeared in the literary journals. He is represented here with the Prologue to* Invisible Man, *the best possible introduction to his literary world. His views on literature are expressed in an interview with him in the Literary Criticism section.*

Invisible Man: Prologue

I am an invisible man. No, I am not a spook like those who haunted Edgar Allan Poe; nor am I one of your Hollywood-movie ectoplasms. I am a man of substance, of flesh and bone, fiber and liquids—and I might even be said to possess a

mind. I am invisible, understand, simply because people refuse to see me. Like the bodiless heads you see sometimes in
circus sideshows, it is as though I have been surrounded by
mirrors of hard, distorting glass. When they approach me
they see only my surroundings, themselves, or figments of
their imagination—indeed, everything and anything except
me.

Nor is my invisibility exactly a matter of a bio-chemical
accident to my epidermis. That invisibility to which I refer
occurs because of a peculiar disposition of the eyes of those
with whom I come in contact. A matter of the construction
of their *inner* eyes, those eyes with which they look through
their physical eyes upon reality. I am not complaining, nor
am I protesting either. It is sometimes advantageous to be unseen, although it is most often rather wearing on the nerves.
Then too, you're constantly being bumped against by those of
poor vision. Or again, you often doubt if you really exist.
You wonder whether you aren't simply a phantom in other
people's minds. Say, a figure in a nightmare which the sleeper
tries with all his strength to destroy. It's when you feel like
this that, out of resentment, you begin to bump people back.
And, let me confess, you feel that way most of the time. You
ache with the need to convince yourself that you do exist in
the real world, that you're a part of all the sound and anguish, and you strike out with your fists, you curse and you
swear to make them recognize you. And, alas, it's seldom
successful.

One night I accidentally bumped into a man, and perhaps
because of the near darkness he saw me and called me an
insulting name. I sprang at him, seized his coat lapels and demanded that he apologize. He was a tall blond man, and as
my face came close to his he looked insolently out of his blue
eyes and cursed me, his breath hot in my face as he struggled. I pulled his chin down sharp upon the crown of my
head, butting him as I had seen the West Indians do, and I
felt his flesh tear and the blood gush out, and I yelled, "Apologize! Apologize!" But he continued to curse and struggle,
and I butted him again and again until he went down heavily,
on his knees, profusely bleeding. I kicked him repeatedly, in
a frenzy because he still uttered insults though his lips were
frothy with blood. Oh yes, I kicked him! And in my outrage
I got out my knife and prepared to slit his throat, right there
beneath the lamplight in the deserted street, holding him by
the collar with one hand, and opening the knife with my
teeth—when it occurred to me that the man had not *seen* me,
actually; that he, as far as he knew, was in the midst of a

walking nightmare! And I stopped the blade, slicing the air as
I pushed him away, letting him fall back to the street. I
stared at him hard as the lights of a car stabbed through the
darkness. He lay there, moaning on the asphalt; a man almost killed by a phantom. It unnerved me. I was both dis-
gusted and ashamed. I was like a drunken man myself, wavering about on weakened legs. Then I was amused. Something in this man's thick head had sprung out and beaten him
within an inch of his life. I began to laugh at this crazy discovery. Would he have awakened at the point of death?
Would Death himself have freed him for wakeful living? But
I didn't linger. I ran away into the dark, laughing so hard I
feared I might rupture myself. The next day I saw his picture
in the *Daily News*, beneath a caption stating that he had been
"mugged." Poor fool, poor blind fool, I thought with sincere
compassion, mugged by an invisible man!

Most of the time (although I do not choose as I once did
to deny the violence of my days by ignoring it) I am not so
overtly violent. I remember that I am invisible and walk
softly so as not to awaken the sleeping ones. Sometimes it is
best not to awaken them; there are few things in the world as
dangerous as sleepwalkers. I learned in time though that it is
possible to carry on a fight against them without their realizing it. For instance, I have been carrying on a fight with
Monopolated Light & Power for some time now. I use their
service and pay them nothing at all, and they don't know it.
Oh, they suspect that power is being drained off, but they
don't know where. All they know is that according to the
master meter back there in their power station a hell of a lot
of free current is disappearing somewhere into the jungle of
Harlem. The joke, of course, is that I don't live in Harlem
but in a border area. Several years ago (before I discovered
the advantage of being invisible) I went through the routine
process of buying service and paying their outrageous rates.
But no more. I gave up all that, along with my apartment,
and my old way of life: That way based upon the fallacious
assumption that I, like other men, was visible. Now, aware of
my invisibility, I live rent-free in a building rented strictly to
whites, in a section of the basement that was shut off and forgotten during the nineteenth century, which I discovered
when I was trying to escape in the night from Ras the Destroyer. But that's getting too far ahead of the story, almost
to the end, although the end is in the beginning and lies far
ahead.

The point now is that I found a home—or a hole in the
ground, as you will. Now don't jump to the conclusion that

because I call my home a "hole" it is damp and cold like a grave; there are cold holes and warm holes. Mine is a warm hole. And remember, a bear retires to his hole for the winter and lives until spring; then he comes strolling out like the Easter chick breaking from its shell. I say all this to assure you that it is incorrect to assume that, because I'm invisible and live in a hole, I am dead. I am neither dead nor in a state of suspended animation. Call me Jack-the-Bear, for I am in a state of hibernation.

My hole is warm and full of light. Yes, *full* of light. I doubt if there is a brighter spot in all New York than this hole of mine, and I do not exclude Broadway. Or the Empire State Building on a photographer's dream night. But that is taking advantage of you. Those two spots are among the darkest of our whole civilization—pardon me, our whole *culture* (an important distinction, I've heard)—which might sound like a hoax, or a contradiction, but that (by contradiction, I mean) is how the world moves: Not like an arrow, but a boomerang. (Beware of those who speak of the *spiral* of history; they are preparing a boomerang. Keep a steel helmet handy.) I know; I have been boomeranged across my head so much that I now can see the darkness of lightness. And I love light. Perhaps you'll think it strange that an invisible man should need light, desire light, love light. But maybe it is exactly because I *am* invisible. Light confirms my reality, gives birth to my form. A beautiful girl once told me of a recurring nightmare in which she lay in the center of a large dark room and felt her face expand until it filled the whole room, becoming a formless mass while her eyes ran in bilious jelly up the chimney. And so it is with me. Without light I am not only invisible, but formless as well; and to be unaware of one's form is to live a death. I myself, after existing some twenty years, did not become alive until I discovered my invisibility.

That is why I fight my battle with Monopolated Light & Power. The deeper reason, I mean: It allows me to feel my vital aliveness. I also fight them for taking so much of my money before I learned to protect myself. In my hole in the basement there are exactly 1,369 lights. I've wired the entire ceiling, every inch of it. And not with fluorescent bulbs, but with the older, more-expensive-to-operate kind, the filament type. An act of sabotage, you know. I've already begun to wire the wall. A junk man I know, a man of vision, has supplied me with wire and sockets. Nothing, storm or flood, must get in the way of our need for light and ever more and brighter light. The truth is the light and light is the truth.

When I finish all four walls, then I'll start on the floor. Just how that will go, I don't know. Yet when you have lived invisible as long as I have you develop a certain ingenuity. I'll solve the problem. And maybe I'll invent a gadget to place my coffeepot on the fire while I lie in bed, and even invent a gadget to warm my bed—like the fellow I saw in one of the picture magazines who made himself a gadget to warm his shoes! Though invisible, I am in the great American tradition of tinkers. That makes me kin to Ford, Edison and Franklin. Call me, since I have a theory and a concept, a "thinker-tinker." Yes, I'll warm my shoes; they need it, they're usually full of holes. I'll do that and more.

Now I have one radio-phonograph; I plan to have five. There is a certain acoustical deadness in my hole, and when I have music I want to *feel* its vibration, not only with my ear but with my whole body. I'd like to hear five recordings of Louis Armstrong playing and singing "What Did I Do to Be so Black and Blue"—all at the same time. Sometimes now I listen to Louis while I have my favorite dessert of vanilla ice cream and sloe gin. I pour the red liquid over the white mound, watching it glisten and the vapor rising as Louis bends that military instrument into a beam of lyrical sound. Perhaps I like Louis Armstrong because he's made poetry out of being invisible. I think it must be because he's unaware that he *is* invisible. And my own grasp of invisibility aids me to understand his music. Once when I asked for a cigarette, some jokers gave me a reefer, which I lighted when I got home and sat listening to my phonograph. It was a strange evening. Invisibility, let me explain, gives one a slightly different sense of time, you're never quite on the beat. Sometimes you're ahead and sometimes behind. Instead of the swift and imperceptible flowing of time, you are aware of its nodes, those points where time stands still or from which it leaps ahead. And you slip into the breaks and look around. That's what you hear vaguely in Louis' music.

Once I saw a prizefighter boxing a yokel. The fighter was swift and amazingly scientific. His body was one violent flow of rapid rhythmic action. He hit the yokel a hundred times while the yokel held up his arms in stunned surprise. But suddenly the yokel, rolling about in the gale of boxing gloves, struck one blow and knocked science, speed and footwork as cold as a well-digger's posterior. The smart money hit the canvas. The long shot got the nod. The yokel had simply stepped inside of his opponent's sense of time. So under the spell of the reefer I discovered a new analytical way of listening to music. The unheard sounds came through, and each melodic line existed of itself, stood out clearly from all the rest, said its piece, and waited patiently for the other voices to speak. That night I found myself hearing not only in time, but in space as well. I not only entered the music but descended, like Dante, into its depths. And *beneath the swiftness of the hot tempo there was a slower tempo and a cave and I entered it and looked around and heard an old woman singing a spiritual as full of Weltschmerz as flamenco, and beneath that lay a still lower level on which I saw a beautiful girl the color of ivory pleading in a voice like my mother's as she stood before a group of slave owners who bid for her naked body, and below that I found a lower level and a more rapid tempo and I heard someone shout:*

"Brothers and sisters, my text this morning is the 'Blackness of Blackness.'"

And a congregation of voices answered: "That blackness is most black, brother, most black . . ."

"In the beginning . . ."

"At the very start," they cried.

". . . there was blackness . . ."

"Preach it . . ."

". . . and the sun . . ."

"The sun, Lawd . . ."

". . . was bloody red . . ."

"Red . . ."

"Now black is . . ." the preacher shouted.

"Bloody . . ."

"I said black is . . ."

"Preach it, brother . . ."

". . . an' black ain't . . ."

"Red, Lawd, red: He said it's red!"

"Amen, brother . . ."

"Black will git you . . ."

"Yes, it will . . ."

". . . an' black won't . . ."

"Naw, it won't!"

"It do . . ."

"It do, Lawd . . ."

". . . an' it don't."

"Halleluiah . . ."

". . . It'll put you, glory, glory, Oh my Lawd, in the WHALE'S BELLY."

"Preach it, dear brother . . ."

". . . an' make you tempt . . ."

"Good God a-mighty!"

"Old Aunt Nelly!"

"Black will make you . . ."

"Black . . ."

". . . or black will un-make you."

"Ain't it the truth, Lawd?"

And at that point a voice of trombone timbre screamed at me, "Git out of here, you fool! Is you ready to commit treason?"

And I tore myself away, hearing the old singer of spirituals moaning, "Go curse your God, boy, and die."

I stopped and questioned her, asked her what was wrong.

"I dearly loved my master, son," she said.

"You should have hated him," I said.

"He gave me several sons," she said, "and because I loved my sons I learned to love their father though I hated him too."

"I too have become acquainted with ambivalence," I said. "That's why I'm here."

"What's that?"

"Nothing, a word that doesn't explain it. Why do you moan?"

"I moan this way 'cause he's dead," she said.

"Then tell me, who is that laughing upstairs?"

"Them's my sons. They glad."

"Yes, I can understand that too," I said.

"I laughs too, but I moans too. He promised to set us free but he never could bring hisself to do it. Still I loved him . . ."

"Loved him? You mean . . ."

"Oh yes, but I loved something else even more."

"What more?"

"Freedom."

"Freedom," I said. "Maybe freedom lies in hating."

"Naw, son, it's in loving. I loved him and give him the poison and he withered away like a frost-bit apple. Them boys woulda tore him to pieces with they homemake knives."

"A mistake was made somewhere," I said, "I'm confused." And I wished to say other things, but the laughter upstairs became too loud and moan-like for me and I tried to break out of it, but I couldn't. Just as I was leaving I felt an urgent desire to ask her what freedom was and went back. She sat with her head in her hands, moaning softly; her leather-brown face was filled with sadness.

"Old woman, what is this freedom you love so well?" I asked around a corner of my mind.

She looked surprised, then thoughtful, then baffled. "I done forgot, son. It's all mixed up. First I think it's one thing, then

*I think it's another. It gits my head to spinning. I guess now
it ain't nothing but knowing how to say what I got up in my
head. But it's a hard job, son. Too much is done happen to
me in too short a time. Hit's like I have a fever. Ever' time I
starts to walk my head gits swirling and I falls down. Or if
it ain't that, it's the boys; they gits to laughing and wants to
kill up the white folks. They's bitter, that's what they is . . ."*

"But what about freedom?"

"Leave me 'lone, boy; my head aches!"

I left her, feeling dizzy myself. I didn't get far.

*Suddenly one of the sons, a big fellow six feet tall, ap-
peared out of nowhere and struck me with his fist.*

"What's the matter, man?" I cried.

"You made Ma cry!"

"But how?" I said, dodging a blow.

"Askin' her them questions, that's how. Git outa here and
stay, and next time you got questions like that, ask yourself!"*

*He held me in a grip like cold stone, his fingers fastening
upon my windpipe until I thought I would suffocate before
he finally allowed me to go. I stumbled about dazed, the
music beating hysterically in my ears. It was dark. My head
cleared and I wandered down a dark narrow passage, thinking I heard his footsteps hurrying behind me. I was sore, and
into my being had come a profound craving for tranquillity, for
peace and quiet, a state I felt I could never achieve. For one
thing, the trumpet was blaring and the rhythm was too hectic. A tom-tom beating like heart-thuds began drowning out
the trumpet, filling my ears. I longed for water and I heard it
rushing through the cold mains my fingers touched as I felt
my way, but I couldn't stop to search because of the footsteps behind me.*

"Hey, Ras," I called. "Is it you, Destroyer? Rinehart?"

*No answer, only the rhythmic footsteps behind me. Once I
tried crossing the road, but a speeding machine struck me,
scraping the skin from my leg as it roared past.*

Then somehow I came out of it, ascending hastily from
this underworld of sound to hear Louis Armstrong innocently
asking,

*What did I do
To be so black
And blue?*

At first I was afraid; this familiar music had demanded action, the kind of which I was incapable, and yet had I lingered there beneath the surface, I might have attempted to

act. Nevertheless, I know now that few really listen to this
music. I sat on the chair's edge in a soaking sweat, as though
each of my 1,369 bulbs had everyone become a klieg light in
an individual setting for a third degree with Ras and Rinehart
in charge. It was exhausting—as though I had held my breath
continuously for an hour under the terrifying serenity that
comes from days of intense hunger. And yet, it was a
strangely satisfying experience for an invisible man to hear
the silence of sound. I had discovered unrecognized compul-
sions of my being—even though I could not answer "yes" to
their promptings. I haven't smoked a reefer since, however;
not because they're illegal, but because to *see* around corners
is enough (that is not unusual when you are invisible). But to
hear around them is too much; it inhibits action. And despite
Brother Jack and all that sad, lost period of the Brotherhood, I believe in nothing if not in action.

Please, a definition: A hibernation is a covert preparation
for a more overt action.

Besides, the drug destroys one's sense of time completely.
If that happened, I might forget to dodge some bright morning and some cluck would run me down with an orange and
yellow street car, or a bilious bus! Or I might forget to leave
my hole when the moment for action presents itself.

Meanwhile I enjoy my life with the compliments of Monopolated Light & Power. Since you never recognize me even
when in closest contact with me, and since, no doubt, you'll
hardly believe that I exist, it won't matter if you know that I
tapped a power line leading into the building and ran it into
my hole in the ground. Before that I lived in the darkness
into which I was chased, but now I see. I've illuminated the
blackness of my invisibility—and vice versa. And so I play
the invisible music of my isolation. The last statement doesn't
seem just right, does it? But it is; you hear this music simply
because music is heard and seldom seen, except by musicians.
Could this compulsion to put invisibility down in black and
white be thus an urge to make music of invisibility? But I am
an orator, a rabble rouser—Am? I *was*, and perhaps shall be
again. Who knows? All sickness is not unto death, neither is
invisibility.

I can hear you say, "What a horrible, irresponsible bastard!" And you're right. I leap to agree with you. I am one of
the most irresponsible beings that ever lived. Irresponsibility
is part of my invisibility; any way you face it, it is a denial.
But to whom can I be responsible, and why should I be,
when you refuse to see me? And wait until I reveal how truly
irresponsible I am. Responsibility rests upon recognition, and

recognition is a form of agreement. Take the man whom I almost killed: Who was responsible for that near murder—I? I don't think so, and I refuse it. I won't buy it. You can't give it to me. *He* bumped *me*, *he* insulted *me*. Shouldn't he, for his own personal safety, have recognized my hysteria, my "danger potential"? He, let us say, was lost in a dream world. But didn't *he* control that dream world—which, alas, is only too real!—and didn't *he* rule me out of it? And if he had yelled for a policeman, wouldn't *I* have been taken for the offending one? Yes, yes, yes! Let me agree with you, I was the irresponsible one; for I should have used my knife to protect the higher interests of society. Some day that kind of foolishness will cause us tragic trouble. All dreamers and sleepwalkers must pay the price, and even the invisible victim is responsible for the fate of all. But I shirked that responsibility; I became too snarled in the incompatible notions that buzzed within my brain. I was a coward.

But what did *I* do to be so blue? Bear with me.

FRANK LONDON BROWN (1927–1962)

An urban literary voice of the 50's and 60's, Frank London Brown was born in Kansas City, Missouri, attended Wilberforce University and the Chicago Kent College of Law and received his B.A. at Roosevelt University in Chicago. He worked as a machinist, union organizer, government employee, jazz singer, journalist, and editor. He reached the higher echelons of modern jazz and appeared with Thelonius Monk at the Gate of Horn in Chicago and the Five Spot in New York. Trumbull Park, his first novel, was published in 1959. Brown published many articles and short stories in Downbeat, the Chicago Review, Ebony, the Negro Digest, the Chicago Tribune, the Chicago Sun-Times, and the Southwest Review. He was Associate Editor of Ebony magazine. Brown was the first to read short stories, rather than poetry, to jazz accompaniment. He received the John Hay Whitney Foundation Award for creative writing and a University of

*Chicago Fellowship. At the time of his death, at the age of
thirty-four, he was working on a revised draft of his second
novel and was director of the Union Leadership Program of
the University of Chicago, while completing his doctorate in
political science at the University of Chicago. His short story
"McDougal," rooted in his experience in the world of jazz, is
reprinted from the Chicago literary review* Phoenix Magazine
*(Fall, 1961). A critical evaluation of Frank London Brown's
literary work, by Sterling Stuckey, appears in the Literary
Criticism section of this anthology.*

McDougal

The bass was walking. Nothing but the bass. And the rhythm
section waited, counting time with the tap of a foot or the tip
of a finger against the piano top. Pro had just finished his
solo and the blood in his neck was pumping so hard it made
his head hurt. Sweat shone upon the brown backs of his fingers and the moisture stained the bright brass of his tenor
where he held it. Jake, young eyeglass-wearing boy from
Dallas, had stopped playing the drums, and he too was sweating, and slight stains were beginning to appear upon his thin
cotton coat, and his dark skin caught the purple haze from
the overhead spotlight and the sweat that gathered on his flat
cheekbones seemed purple. Percy R. Brookins bent over the
piano tapping the black keys but not hard enough to make a
sound.

Everybody seemed to be waiting.

And the bass was walking. Doom-de-doom-doom-doom-
doom-doom!

A tall thin white man whose black hair shone with sweat
stood beside the tenorman, lanky, ginger-brown Pro.

Pro had wailed—had blown choruses that dripped with the
smell of cornbread and cabbage and had roared like a late "L"
and had cried like a blues singer on the last night of a good
gig.

Now it was the white man's turn, right after the bass solo
was over . . . and he waited and Pro waited and so did Jake
the drummer, and Percy R. Brookins. Little Jug was going
into his eighth chorus and showed no sign of letting up.

DOOM-DE-DOOM-DOOM-DOOM-DOOM-DOOM!

Jake looked out into the audience. And the shadowy faces
were hard to see behind the bright colored lights that ringed
the bandstand. Yet he felt that they too waited . . . Pro had

laid down some righteous sound—he had told so much truth
—told it so plainly, so passionately that it had scared everybody in the place, even Pro, and now he waited for the affirming bass to finish so that he could hear what the white
man had to say.

McDougal was his name. And his young face had many
wrinkles and his young body slouched and his shoulders hung
round and loose. He was listening to Little Jug's bass yet he
also seemed to be listening to something else, almost as if he
were still listening to the truth Pro had told.

And the bass walked.

Jake leaned over his drums and whispered to Percy R.
Brookins.

"That cat sure looks beat don't he?"

Percy R. Brookins nodded, and then put his hand to the
side of his mouth, and whispered back.

"His old lady's pregnant again."

"Again?! What's that? Number three?"

"Number four," Percy R. Brookins answered.

"Hell I'd look sad too . . . Is he still living on Forty Seventh Street?"

The drums slid in underneath the bass and the bass
dropped out amid strong applause and a few "Yeahs!" And
Jake, not having realized it, cut in where McDougal was to
begin his solo. He smiled sheepishly at Percy R. Brookins and
the piano player hunched his shoulders and smiled.

McDougal didn't look around, he didn't move from his
slouched one-sided stance, he didn't stop staring beyond the
audience and beyond the room itself. Yet his left foot kept
time with the light bombs the drummer dropped and the
husky soft scrape of the brushes.

Little Jug pulled a handkerchief from his back pocket and
wiped his cheeks and around the back of his neck, then he
stared at the black, glistening back of McDougal's head and
then leaned down and whispered to Percy R. Brookins.

"Your boy sure could stand a haircut. He looks as bad as
Ol' Theo." And they both knew how bad Ol' Theo looked
and they both frowned and laughed.

Percy R. Brookins touched a chord lightly to give some
color to Jake's solo and then he said.

"Man, that cat has suffered for that brownskin woman."
Little Jug added.

"And those . . . three little brownskin crumb-crushers."

Percy R. Brookins, hit another chord and then

"Do you know none of the white folks'll rent to him
now?"

Little Jug laughed.

"Why hell yes . . . will they rent to me?"

"Sure they will, down on Forty Seventh Street."

Little Jug nodded at Jake and Jake made a couple of breaks that meant that he was about to give in to McDougal.

Percy R. Brookins turned to face his piano and then he got an idea and he turned to Little Jug and spoke with a serious look behind the curious smile on his face.

"You know that cat's after us? I mean he's out to blow the real thing. You know what I mean? Like he's no Harry James? Do you know that?"

Little Jug ran into some triplets and skipped a couple of beats and brought McDougal in right on time.

At the same time McDougal rode in on a long, hollow, gut bucket note that made Percy R. Brookins laugh, and caused Pro to cock his head and rub his cheek. The tall worried looking white man bent his trumpet to the floor and hunched his shoulders and closed his eyes and blew.

Little Jug answered Percy R. Brookins question about McDougal.

"I been knowing that . . . he knows the happenings . . . I mean about where we get it, you dig? I mean like with Leola and those kids and Forty Seventh Street and those jive landlords, you dig? The man's been burnt, Percy. Listen to that somitch—listen to him!"

McDougal's eyes were closed and he did not see the dark woman with the dark cotton suit that ballooned away from the great bulge of her stomach. He didn't see her ease into a chair at the back of the dark smoky room. He didn't see the smile on her face or the sweat upon her flat nose.

PAULE MARSHALL (1929–)

Winning critical recognition as a significant and accomplished writer of the newer generation, Paule Marshall was born in Brooklyn, of West Indian parents who emigrated from Barbados to the United States shortly after World War

1. She began writing sketches and poems before she was ten years old. After graduating Phi Beta Kappa from Brooklyn College, Mrs. Marshall worked in libraries and was a feature writer for the magazine Our World, *for which she traveled on assignments to the West Indies and Brazil. In her writing she has captured the idiom and patterns of Barbadian speech and has drawn on her experiences in the Caribbean as well as in the United States. In a letter to the editor of this anthology she has written: "As you know, my work falls beween two stools and is both West Indian and American."* Brown Girl, Brownstones, *her first novel, was published in 1959. In 1961 her collection of four novellas,* Soul Clap Hands and Sing, *was published. She is a Guggenheim Fellow and has received grants from the American Academy of Arts and Letters and the Ford Foundation. At present she is at work on her second novel,* Ceremonies at the Guesthouse. *Her autobiographical story "To Da-duh, In Memoriam," which appeared initially in the West Indian magazine* New World *in 1967, is published here for the first time in the United States.*

To Da-duh, In Memoriam

"... Oh Nana! all of you is not involved in this evil business
Death,
Nor all of us in Life."
—From "At My Grandmother's Grave," by Lebert Bethune

I did not see her at first I remember. For not only was it dark inside the crowded disembarkation shed in spite of the daylight flooding in from outside, but standing there waiting for her with my mother and sister I was still somewhat blinded from the sheen of tropical sunlight on the water of the bay which we had just crossed in the landing boat, leaving behind us the ship that had brought us from New York lying in the offing. Besides, being only nine years of age at the time and knowing nothing of islands I was busy attending to the alien sights and sounds of Barbados, the unfamiliar smells.

I did not see her, but I was alerted to her approach by my mother's hand which suddenly tightened around mine, and looking up I traced her gaze through the gloom in the shed until I finally made out the small, purposeful, painfully erect figure of the old woman headed our way.

Her face was drowned in the shadow of an ugly rolled-brim brown felt hat, but the details of her slight body and of the struggle taking place within it were clear enough—an intense, unrelenting struggle between her back which was beginning to bend ever so slightly under the weight of her eighty odd years and the rest of her which sought to deny those years and hold that back straight, keep it in line. Moving swiftly toward us (so swiftly it seemed she did not intend stopping when she reached us but would sweep past us out the doorway which opened onto the sea and like Christ walk upon the water!), she was caught between the sunlight at her end of the building and the darkness inside—and for a moment she appeared to contain them both: the light in the long severe old-fashioned white dress she wore which brought the sense of a past that was still alive into our bustling present and in the snatch of white at her eye; the darkness in her black high-top shoes and in her face which was visible now that she was closer.

It was as stark and fleshless as a death mask, that face. The maggots might have already done their work, leaving only the framework of bone beneath the ruined skin and deep wells at the temple and jaw. But her eyes were alive, unnervingly so for one so old, with a sharp light that flicked out of the dim clouded depths like a lizard's tongue to snap up all in her view. Those eyes betrayed a child's curiosity about the world, and I wondered vaguely seeing them, and seeing the way the bodice of her ancient dress had collapsed in on her flat chest (what had happened to her breasts?), whether she might not be some kind of child at the same time that she was a woman, with fourteen children, my mother included, to prove it. Perhaps she was both, both child and woman, darkness and light, past and present, life and death—all the opposites contained and reconciled in her.

"My Da-duh," my mother said formally and stepped forward. The name sounded like thunder fading softly in the distance.

"Child," Da-duh said, and her tone, her quick scrutiny of my mother, the brief embrace in which they appeared to shy from each other rather than touch, wiped out the fifteen years my mother had been away and restored the old relationship. My mother, who was such a formidable figure in my eyes, had suddenly with a word been reduced to my status.

"Yes, God is good," Da-duh said with a nod that was like a tic. "He has spared me to see my child again."

We were led forward then, apologetically because not only did Da-duh prefer boys but she also liked her grandchildren to be "white," that is, fair-skinned; and we had, I was to discover, a number of cousins, the outside children of white estate managers and the like, who qualified. We, though, were as black as she.

My sister being the oldest was presented first. "This one takes after the father," my mother said and waited to be reproved.

Frowning, Da-duh tilted my sister's face toward the light. But her frown soon gave way to a grudging smile, for my sister with her large mild eyes and little broad winged nose, with our father's high-cheeked Barbadian cast to her face, was pretty.

"She's goin' be lucky," Da-duh said and patted her once on the cheek. "Any girl-child that takes after the father does be lucky."

She turned then to me. But oddly enough she did not touch me. Instead leaning close, she peered hard at me, and then quickly drew back. I thought I saw her hand start up as though to shield her eyes. It was almost as if she saw not only me, a thin truculent child who it was said took after no one but myself, but something in me which for some reason she found disturbing, even threatening. We looked silently at each other for a long time there in the noisy shed, our gaze locked. She was the first to look away.

"But Adry," she said to my mother and her laugh was cracked, thin, apprehensive. "Where did you get this one here with this fierce look?"

"We don't know where she came out of, my Da-duh," my mother said, laughing also. Even I smiled to myself. After all I had won the encounter. Da-duh had recognized my small strength—and this was all I ever asked of the adults in my life then.

"Come, soul," Da-duh said and took my hand. "You must be one of those New York terrors you hear so much about."

She led us, me at her side and my sister and mother behind, out of the shed into the sunlight that was like a bright driving summer rain and over to a group of people clustered beside a decrepit lorry. They were our relatives, most of them from St. Andrews although Da-duh herself lived in St. Thomas, the women wearing bright print dresses, the colors vivid against their darkness, the men rusty black suits that encased them like straitjackets. Da-duh, holding fast to my hand, became my anchor as they circled round us like a nervous sea, exclaiming, touching us with their calloused hands, embracing us shyly. They laughed in awed bursts: "But look Adry got big-big children!"/ "And see the nice things they wearing, wrist watch and all!/ "I tell you, Adry has done all right for sheself in New York. . . ."

Da-duh, ashamed at their wonder, embarrassed for them, admonished them the while. "But oh Christ," she said, "why you all got to get on like you never saw people from 'Away' before? You would think New York is the only place in the world to hear wunna. That's why I don't like to go anyplace with you St. Andrews people, you know. You all ain't been colonized."

We were in the back of the lorry finally, packed in among the barrels of ham, flour, cornmeal and rice and the trunks of clothes that my mother had brought as gifts. We made our way slowly through Bridgetown's clogged streets, part of a funereal procession of cars and open-sided buses, bicycles and donkey carts. The dim little limestone shops and offices along the way marched with us, at the same mournful pace, toward the same grave ceremony—as did the people, the women balancing huge baskets on top their heads as if they were no more than hats they wore to shade them from the sun. Looking over the edge of the lorry I watched as their feet slurred the dust. I listened, and their voices, raw and loud and dissonant in the heat, seemed to be grappling with each other high overhead.

Da-duh sat on a trunk in our midst, a monarch amid her court. She still held my hand, but it was different now. I had suddenly become her anchor, for I felt her fear of the lorry with its asthmatic motor (a fear and distrust, I later learned, she held of all machines) beating like a pulse in her rough palm.

As soon as we left Bridgetown behind though, she relaxed, and while the others around us talked she gazed at the canes standing tall on either side of the winding marl road. "C'dear," she said softly to herself after a time. "The canes this side are pretty enough."

They were too much for me. I thought of them as giant weeds that had overrun the island, leaving scarcely any room for the small tottering houses of sunbleached pine we passed or the people, dark streaks as our lorry hurtled by. I suddenly feared that we were journeying, unaware that we were, toward some dangerous place where the canes, grown as high and thick as a forest, would close in on us and run us through with their stiletto blades. I longed then for the familiar: for the street in Brooklyn where I lived, for my father who had refused to accompany us ("Blowing out good money on foolishness," he had said of the trip), for a game of tag with my friends under the chestnut tree outside our aging brownstone house.

"Yes, but wait till you see St. Thomas canes," Da-duh was saying to me. "They's canes father, bo," she gave a proud arrogant nod. "Tomorrow, God willing, I goin' take you out in the ground and show them to you."

True to her word Da-duh took me with her the following day out into the ground. It was a fairly large plot adjoining her weathered board and shingle house and consisting of a small orchard, a good-sized canepiece and behind the canes, where the land sloped abruptly down, a gully. She had purchased it with Panama money sent her by her eldest son, my uncle Joseph, who had died working on the canal. We entered the ground along a trail no wider than her body and as devious and complex as her reasons for showing me her land. Da-duh strode briskly ahead, her slight form filled out this morning by the layers of sacking petticoats she wore under her working dress to protect her against the damp. A fresh white cloth, elaborately arranged around her head, added to her height, and lent her a vain, almost roguish air.

Her pace slowed once we reached the orchard, and glancing back at me occasionally over her shoulder, she pointed out the various trees.

"This here is a breadfruit," she said. "That one yonder is a papaw. Here's a guava. This is a mango. I know you don't have anything like these in New York. Here's a sugar apple [the fruit looked more like artichokes than apples to me]. This one bears limes. . . ." She went on for some time, intoning the names of the trees as though they were those of her gods. Finally, turning to me, she said, "I know you don't have anything this nice where you come from." Then, as I hesitated: "I said I know you don't have anything this nice where you come from. . . ."

"No," I said and my world did seem suddenly lacking.

Da-dau nodded and passed on. The orchard ended and we were on the narrow cart road that led through the canepiece, the canes clashing like swords above my cowering head. Again she turned and her thin muscular arms spread wide, her dim gaze embracing the small field of canes, she said—and her voice almost broke under the weight of her pride, "Tell me, have you got anything like these in that place where you were born?"

"No."

"I din' think so. I bet you don't even know that these canes here and the sugar you eat is one and the same thing. That they does throw the canes into some damn machine at the factory and squeeze out all the little life in them to make sugar for you all so in New York to eat. I bet you don't know that."

"I've got two cavities and I'm not allowed to eat a lot of sugar."

But Da-duh didn't hear me. She had turned with an inexplicably angry motion and was making her way rapidly out of the canes and down the slope at the edge of the field which led to the gully below. Following her apprehensively down the incline amid a stand of banana plants whose leaves flapped like elephants ears in the wind, I found myself in the middle of a small tropical wood—a place dense and damp and gloomy and tremulous with the fitful play of light and shadow as the leaves high above moved against the sun that was almost hidden from view. It was a violent place, the tangled foliage fighting each other for a chance at the sunlight, the branches of the trees locked in what seemed an immemorial struggle, one both necessary and inevitable. But despite the violence, it was pleasant, almost peaceful in the gully, and beneath the thick undergrowth the earth smelled like spring.

This time Da-duh didn't even bother to ask her usual question, but simply turned and waited for me to speak.

"No," I said, my head bowed. "We don't have anything like this in New York."

"Ah," she cried, her triumph complete. "I din' think so. Why, I've heard that's a place where you can walk till you near drop and never see a tree."

"We've got a chestnut tree in front of our house," I said.

"Does it bear?" She waited. "I ask you, does it bear?"

"Not anymore," I muttered. "It used to, but not anymore."

She gave the nod that was like a nervous twitch. "You see," she said. "Nothing can bear there." Then, secure behind her scorn, she added, "But tell me, what's this snow like that you hear so much about?"

Looking up, I studied her closely, sensing my chance, and then I told her, describing at length and with as much drama as I could summon not only what snow in the city was like, but what it would be like here, in her perennial summer kingdom.

". . . And you see all these trees you got here," I said. "Well, they'd be bare. No leaves, no fruit, nothing. They'd be covered in snow. You see your canes. They'd be buried under tons of snow. The snow would be higher than your head, higher than your house, and you wouldn't be able to come down into this here gully because it would be snowed under. . . ."

She searched my face for the lie, still scornful but intrigued. "What a thing, huh?" she said finally, whispering it softly to herself.

"And when it snows you couldn't dress like you are now," I said. "Oh no, you'd freeze to death. You'd have to wear a hat and gloves and galoshes and ear muffs so your ears wouldn't freeze and drop off, and a heavy coat. I've got a Shirley Temple coat with fur on the collar. I can dance. You wanna see?"

Before she could answer I began, with a dance called the Truck which was popular back then in the 1930's. My right forefinger waving, I trucked around the nearby trees and around Da-duh's awed and rigid form. After the Truck I did the Suzy-Q, my lean hips swishing, my sneakers sidling zigzag over the ground. "I can sing," I said and did so, starting with "I'm Gonna Sit Right Down and Write Myself a Letter," then without pausing, "Tea For Two," and ending with "I Found a Million Dollar Baby in a Five and Ten Cent Store."

For long moments afterwards Da-duh stared at me as if I were a creature from Mars, an emissary from some world she did not know but which intrigued her and whose power she both felt and feared. Yet something about my performance must have pleased her, because bending down she slowly lifted her long skirt and then, one by one, the layers of petticoats until she came to a drawstring purse dangling at the end of a long strip of cloth tied round her waist. Opening the purse she handed me a penny. "Here," she said half-smiling against her will. "Take this to buy yourself a sweet at the shop up the road. There's nothing to be done with you, soul."

From then on, whenever I wasn't taken to visit relatives, I accompanied Da-duh out into the ground, and alone with her amid the canes or down in the gully I told her about New York. It always began with some slighting remark on her part: "I know they don't have anything this nice where you come from," or "Tell me, I hear those foolish people in New York does do such and such. . . ." But as I answered, re-creating my towering world of steel and concrete and machines for her, building the city out of words, I would feel her give way. I came to know the signs of her surrender: the total stillness that would come over her little hard dry form, the probing gaze that like a surgeon's knife sought to cut through my skull to get at the images there, to see if I were lying; above all, her fear, a fear nameless and profound, the same one I had felt beating in the palm of her hand that day in the lorry.

Over the weeks I told her about refrigerators, radios, gas

stoves, elevators, trolley cars, wringer washing machines, movies, airplanes, the cyclone at Coney Island, subways, toasters, electric lights: "At night, see, all you have to do is flip this little switch on the wall and all the lights in the house go on. Just like that. Like magic. It's like turning on the sun at night."

"But tell me," she said to me once with a faint mocking smile, "do the white people have all these things too or it's only the people looking like us?"

I laughed. "What d'ya mean," I said. "The white people have even better." Then: "I beat up a white girl in my class last term."

"Beating up white people!" Her tone was incredulous.

"How you mean!" I said, using an expression of hers. "She called me a name."

For some reason Da-duh could not quite get over this and repeated in the same hushed, shocked voice, "Beating up white people now! Oh, the lord, the world's changing up so I can scarce recognize it anymore."

One morning toward the end of our stay, Da-duh led me into a part of the gully that we had never visited before, an area darker and more thickly overgrown than the rest, almost impenetrable. There in a small clearing amid the dense bush, she stopped before an incredibly tall royal palm which rose cleanly out of the ground, and drawing the eye up with it, soared high above the trees around it into the sky. It appeared to be touching the blue dome of sky, to be flaunting its dark crown of fronds right in the blinding white face of the late morning sun.

Da-duh watched me a long time before she spoke, and then she said very quietly, "All right, now, tell me if you've got anything this tall in that place you're from."

I almost wished, seeing her face, that I could have said no. "Yes," I said. "We've got buildings hundreds of times this tall in New York. There's one called the Empire State building that's the tallest in the world. My class visited it last year and I went all the way to the top. It's got over a hundred floors. I can't describe how tall it is. Wait a minute. What's the name of that hill I went to visit the other day, where they have the police station?"

"You mean Bissex?"

"Yes, Bissex. Well, the Empire State Building is way taller than that."

"You're lying now!" she shouted, trembling with rage. Her hand lifted to strike me.

"No, I'm not," I said. "It really is, If you don't believe me

I'll send you a picture postcard of it soon as I get back home so you can see for yourself. But it's way taller than Bissex."

All the fight went out of her at that. The hand poised to strike me fell limp to her side, and as she stared at me, seeing not me but the building that was taller than the highest hill she knew, the small stubborn light in her eyes (it was the same amber as the flame in the kerosene lamp she lit at dusk) began to fail. Finally, with a vague gesture that even in the midst of her defeat still tried to dismiss me and my world, she turned and started back through the gully, walking slowly, her steps groping and uncertain, as if she was suddenly no longer sure of the way, while I followed triumphant yet strangely saddened behind.

The next morning I found her dressed for our morning walk but stretched out on the Berbice chair in the tiny drawing room where she sometimes napped during the afternoon heat, her face turned to the window beside her. She appeared thinner and suddenly indescribably old.

"My Da-duh," I said.

"Yes, nuh," she said. Her voice was listless and the face she slowly turned my way was, now that I think back on it, like a Benin mask, the features drawn and almost distorted by an ancient abstract sorrow.

"Don't you feel well?" I asked.

"Girl, I don't know."

"My Da-duh, I goin' boil you some bush tea," my aunt, Da-duh's youngest child, who lived with her, called from the shed roof kitchen.

"Who tell you I need bush tea?" she cried, her voice assuming for a moment its old authority. "You can't even rest nowadays without some malicious person looking for you to be dead. Come girl," she motioned me to a place beside her on the old-fashioned lounge chair, "give us a tune."

I sang for her until breakfast at eleven, all my brash irreverent Tin Pan Alley songs, and then just before noon we went out into the ground. But it was a short, dispirited walk. Da-duh didn't even notice that the mangoes were beginning to ripen and would have to be picked before the village boys got to them. And when she paused occasionally and looked out across the canes or up at her trees it wasn't as if she were seeing them but something else. Some huge, monolithic shape had imposed itself, it seemed, between her and the land, obstructing her vision. Returning to the house she slept the entire afternoon on the Berbice chair.

She remained like this until we left, languishing away the mornings on the chair at the window gazing out at the land as if it were already doomed; then, at noon, taking the brief stroll with me through the ground during which she seldom spoke, and afterwards returning home to sleep till almost dusk sometimes.

On the day of our departure she put on the austere, ankle length white dress, the black shoes and brown felt hat (her town clothes she called them), but she did not go with us to town. She saw us off on the road outside her house and in the midst of my mother's tearful protracted farewell, she leaned down and whispered in my ear, "Girl, you're not to forget now to send me the picture of that building, you hear."

By the time I mailed her the large colored picture postcard of the Empire State building she was dead. She died during the famous '37 strike which began shortly after we left. On the day of her death England sent planes flying low over the island in a show of force—so low, according to my aunt's letter, that the downdraft from them shook the ripened mangoes from the trees in Da-duh's orchard. Frightened, everyone in the village fled into the canes. Except Da-duh. She remained in the house at the window so my aunt said, watching as the planes came swooping and screaming like monstrous birds down over the village, over her house, rattling her trees and flattening the young canes in her field. It must have seemed to her lying there that they did not intend pulling out of their dive, but like the hardback beetles which hurled themselves with suicidal force against the walls of the house at night, those menacing silver shapes would hurl themselves in an ecstasy of self-immolation onto the land, destroying it utterly.

When the planes finally left and the villagers reurned they found her dead on the Berbice chair at the window.

She died and I lived, but always, to this day even, within the shadow of her death. For a brief period after I was grown I went to live alone, like one doing penance, in a loft above a noisy factory in downtown New York and there painted seas of sugarcane and huge swirling Van Gogh suns and palm trees striding like brightly-plumed Watussi across a tropical landscape, while the thunderous tread of the machines downstairs jarred the floor beneath my easel, mocking my efforts.

DIANE OLIVER (1943-1966)

Death in an automobile accident at the age of twenty-three brought a tragic end to the promising literary talent of Diane Alene Oliver, a student at the famous Writer's Workshop of the University of Iowa. She was born in Charlotte, North Carolina, and graduated from the University of North Carolina at Greensboro in 1964. She served as feature editor and later as managing editor of the student newspaper The Carolinian. *In 1964 she was selected as a guest editor of* Mademoiselle *magazine, and during the summer of that year spent eight weeks in Switzerland with the Experiment in International Living. She published short stories in* Red Clay Reader, Negro Digest, The Sewanee Review, *and* New Writing of the Sixties. *The University of Iowa conferred the Master of Fine Arts degree on Miss Oliver posthumously. Her story "Neighbors," which follows, was published in* The Sewanee Review *(Spring, 1966) and was selected for inclusion in* Prize Stories 1967: The O. Henry Awards.

Neighbors

The bus turning the corner of Patterson and Talford Avenue was dull this time of evening. Of the four passengers standing in the rear, she did not recognize any of her friends. Most of the people tucked neatly in the double seats were women, maids and cooks on their way from work or secretaries who had worked late and were riding from the office building at the mill. The cotton mill was out from town, near the house where she worked. She noticed that a few men were riding too. They were obviously just working men, except for one gentleman dressed very neatly in a dark grey suit and carrying what she imagined was a push-button umbrella.

He looked to her as though he usually drove a car to work.

She immediately decided that the car probably wouldn't start this morning so he had to catch the bus to and from work. She was standing in the rear of the bus, peering at the passengers, her arms barely reaching the over-head railing, trying not to wobble with every lurch. But every corner the bus turned pushed her head toward a window. And her hair was coming down too, wisps of black curls swung between her eyes. She looked at the people around her. Some of them were white, but most of them were her color. Looking at the passengers at least kept her from thinking of tomorrow. But really she would be glad when it came, then everything would be over.

She took a firmer grip on the green leather seat and wished she had on her glasses. The man with the umbrella was two people ahead of her on the other side of the bus, so she could see him between other people very clearly. She watched as he unfolded the evening newspaper, craning her neck to see what was on the front page. She stood, impatiently trying to read the headlines, when she realized he was staring up at her rather curiously. Biting her lips she turned her head and stared out of the window until the downtown section was in sight.

She would have to wait until she was home to see if they were in the newspaper again. Sometimes she felt that if another person snapped a picture of them she would burst out screaming. Last Monday reporters were already inside the pre-school clinic when she took Tommy for his last polio shot. She didn't understand how anyone could be so heartless to a child. The flashbulb went off right when the needle went in and all the picture showed was Tommy's open mouth.

The bus pulling up to the curb jerked to a stop, startling her and confusing her thoughts. Clutching in her hand the paper bag that contained her uniform, she pushed her way toward the door. By standing in the back of the bus, she was one of the first people to step to the ground. Outside the bus, the evening air felt humid and uncomfortable and her dress kept sticking to her. She looked up and remembered that the weatherman had forecast rain. Just their luck—why, she wondered, would it have to rain on top of everything else?

As she walked along, the main street seemed unnaturally quiet but she decided her imagination was merely playing tricks. Besides, most of the stores had been closed since five o'clock.

She stopped to look at a reversible raincoat in Ivey's window, but although she had a full time job now, she couldn't keep her mind on clothes. She was about to continue walking when she heard a horn blowing. Looking around, half-scared but also curious, she saw a man beckoning to her in a grey car. He was nobody she knew but since a nicely dressed woman was with him in the front seat, she walked to the car.

"You're Jim Mitchell's girl, aren't you?" he questioned. "You Ellie or the other one?"

She nodded yes, wondering who he was and how much he had been drinking.

"Now honey," he said leaning over the woman, "you don't know me but your father does and you tell him that if anything happens to that boy of his tomorrow we're ready to set things straight." He looked her straight in the eye and she promised to take home the message.

Just as the man was about to step on the gas, the woman reached out and touched her arm. "You hurry up home, honey, it's about dark out here."

Before she could find out their names, the Chevrolet had disappeared around a corner. Ellie wished someone would magically appear and tell her everything that had happened since August. Then maybe she could figure out what was real and what she had been imagining for the past couple of days.

She walked past the main shopping district up to Tanner's where Saraline was standing in the window peeling oranges. Everything in the shop was painted orange and green and Ellie couldn't help thinking that poor Saraline looked out of place. She stopped to wave to her friend who pointed the knife to her watch and then to her boyfriend standing in the rear of the shop. Ellie nodded that she understood. She knew Sara wanted her to tell her grandfather that she had to work late again. Neither one of them could figure out why he didn't like Charlie. Saraline had finished high school three years ahead of her and it was time for her to be getting married. Ellie watched as her friend stopped peeling the orange long enough to cross her fingers. She nodded again but she was afraid all the crossed fingers in the world wouldn't stop the trouble tomorrow.

She stopped at the traffic light and spoke to a shrivelled woman hunched against the side of a building. Scuffing the bottom of her sneakers on the curb she waited for the woman to open her mouth and grin as she usually did. The kids used to bait her to talk, and since she didn't have but one tooth in her whole head they called her Doughnut Puncher. But the woman was still, the way everything else had been all week.

From where Ellie stood, across the street from the Sears and Roebuck parking lot, she could see their house, all of the

houses on the single street white people called Welfare Row.
Those newspaper men always made her angry. All of their
articles showed how rough the people were on their street.
And the reporters never said her family wasn't on welfare,
the papers always said the family lived on that street. She
paused to look across the street at a group of kids pouncing
on one rubber ball. There were always white kids around their
neighborhood mixed up in the games, but playing with them
was almost an unwritten rule. When everybody started going
to school nobody played together any more.

She crossed at the corner ignoring the cars at the stop
light and the closer she got to her street the more she realized
that the newspaper was right. The houses were ugly, there
were not even any trees, just patches of scraggly bushes and
grasses. As she cut across the sticky asphalt pavement covered with cars she was conscious of the parking lot floodlights
casting a strange glow on her street. She stared from habit at
the house on the end of the block and except for the way the
paint was peeling they all looked alike to her. Now at twilight
the flaking grey paint had a luminous glow and as she walked
down the dirt sidewalk she noticed Mr. Paul's pipe smoke
added to the hazy atmosphere. Mr. Paul would be sitting in
that same spot waiting until Saraline came home. Ellie slowed
her pace to speak to the elderly man sitting on the porch.

"Evening, Mr. Paul," she said. Her voice sounded clear
and out of place on the vacant street.

"Eh, who's that?" Mr. Paul leaned over the rail. "What
you say, girl?"

"How are you?" she hollered louder. "Sara said she'd be
late tonight, she has to work." She waited for the words to
sink in.

His head had dropped and his eyes were facing his lap.
She could see that he was disappointed. "Couldn't help it," he
said finally. "Reckon they needed her again." Then as if he
suddenly remembered he turned toward her.

"You people be ready down there? Still gonna let him go
tomorrow?"

She looked at Mr. Paul between the missing rails on his
porch, seeing how his rolled up trousers seemed to fit exactly
in the vacant banister space.

"Last I heard this morning we're still letting him go," she
said.

Mr. Paul had shifted his weight back to the chair. "Don't
reckon they'll hurt him," he mumbled, scratching the side of
his face. "Hope he don't mind being spit on though. Spitting
ain't like cutting. They can spit on him and nobody'll ever

know who did it," he said, ending his words with a quiet chuckle.

Ellie stood on the sidewalk grinding her heel in the dirt waiting for the old man to finish talking. She was glad somebody found something funny to laugh at. Finally he shut up.

"Goodbye, Mr. Paul," she waved. Her voice sounded loud to her own ears. But she knew the way her head ached intensified noises. She walked home faster, hoping they had some aspirin in the house and that those men would leave earlier tonight.

From the front of her house she could tell that the men were still there. The living room light shone behind the yellow shades, coming through brighter in the patched places. She thought about moving the geranium pot from the porch to catch the rain but changed her mind. She kicked a beer can under a car parked in the street and stopped to look at her reflection on the car door. The tiny flowers of her printed dress made her look as if she had a strange tropical disease. She spotted another can and kicked it out of the way of the car, thinking that one of these days some kid was going to fall and hurt himself. What she wanted to do she knew was kick the car out of the way. Both the station wagon and the Ford had been parked in front of her house all week, waiting. Everybody was just sitting around waiting.

Suddenly she laughed aloud. Reverend Davis' car was big and black and shiny just like, but no, the smile disappeared from her face, her mother didn't like for them to say things about other people's color. She looked around to see who else came, and saw Mr. Moore's old beat up blue car. Somebody had torn away half of his NAACP sign. Sometimes she really felt sorry for the man. No matter how hard he glued on his stickers somebody always yanked them off again.

Ellie didn't recognize the third car but it had an Alabama license plate. She turned around and looked up and down the street, hating to go inside. There were no lights on their street, but in the distance she could see the bright lights of the parking lot. Slowly she did an about face and climbed the steps.

She wondered when her mama was going to remember to get a yellow bulb for the porch. Although the lights hadn't been turned on, usually June bugs and mosquitoes swarmed all around the porch. By the time she was inside the house she always felt like they were crawling in her hair. She pulled on the screen and saw that Mama finally had made Hezekiah patch up the holes. The globs of white adhesive tape scattered over the screen door looked just like misshapen butterflies.

She listened to her father's voice and could tell by the tone that the men were discussing something important again. She rattled the door once more but nobody came.

"Will somebody please let me in?" Her voice carried through the screen to the knot of men sitting in the corner.

"The door's open," her father yelled. "Come on in."

"The door is not open," she said evenly. "You know we stopped leaving it open." She was feeling tired again and her voice had fallen an octave lower.

"Yeah, I forgot, I forgot," he mumbled walking to the door.

She watched her father almost stumble across a chair to let her in. He was shorter than the light bulb and the light seemed to beam down on him, emphasizing the wrinkles around his eyes. She could tell from the way he pushed open the screen that he hadn't had much sleep either. She'd overheard him telling Mama that the people down at the shop seemed to be piling on the work harder just because of this thing. And he couldn't do anything or say anything to his boss because they probably wanted to fire him.

"Where's Mama?" she whispered. He nodded toward the back.

"Good evening, everybody," she said looking at the three men who had not looked up since she entered the room. One of the men half stood, but his attention was geared back to something another man was saying. They were sitting on the sofa in their shirt sleeves and there was a pitcher of ice water on the window sill.

"Your mother probably needs some help," her father said. She looked past him trying to figure out who the white man was sitting on the end. His face looked familiar and she tried to remember where she had seen him before. The men were paying no attention to her. She bent to see what they were studying and saw a large sheet of white drawing paper. She could see blocks and lines and the man sitting in the middle was marking a trail with the eraser edge of the pencil.

The quiet stillness of the room was making her head ache more. She pushed her way through the red embroidred curtains that led to the kitchen.

"I'm home, Mama," she said, standing in front of the back door facing the big yellow sun Hezekiah and Tommy had painted on the wall above the iron stove. Immediately she felt a warmth permeating her skin. "Where is everybody?" she asked, sitting at the table where her mother was peeling potatoes.

"Mrs. McAllister is keeping Helen and Teenie," her

mother said. "Your brother is staying over with Harry to-night." With each name she uttered, a slice of potato peeling tumbled to the newspaper on the table. "Tommy's in the bed-room reading that Uncle Wiggily book."

Ellie looked up at her mother but her eyes were straight ahead. She knew that Tommy only read the Uncle Wiggily book by himself when he was unhappy. She got up and walked to the kitchen cabinet.

"The other knives dirty?" she asked.

"No," her mother said, "look in the next drawer."

Ellie pulled open the drawer, flicking scraps of white paint with her fingernail. She reached for the knife and at the same time a pile of envelopes caught her eye.

"Any more come today?" she asked, pulling out the knife and slipping the envelopes under the dish towels.

"Yes, seven more came today," her mother accentuated each word carefully. "Your father has them with him in the other room."

"Same thing?" she asked picking up a potato and wishing she could think of some way to change the subject.

The white people had been threatening them for the past three weeks. Some of the letters were aimed at the family, but most of them were directed to Tommy himself. About once a week in the same handwriting somebody wrote that he'd better not eat lunch at school because they were going to poison him.

They had been getting those letters ever since the school board made Tommy's name public. She sliced the potato and dropped the pieces in the pan of cold water. Out of all those people he had been the only one the board had accepted for transfer to the elementary school. The other children, the members said, didn't live in the district. As she cut the eyes out of another potato she thought about the first letter they had received and how her father just set fire to it in the ash-tray. But then Mr. Belk said they'd better save the rest, in case anything happened, they might need the evidence for court.

She peeped up again at her mother, "Who's that white man in there with Daddy?"

"One of Lawyer Belk's friends," she answered. "He's pas-tor of the church that's always on television Sunday morning. Mr. Belk seems to think that having him around will do some good." Ellie saw that her voice was shaking just like her hand as she reached for the last potato. Both of them could hear Tommy in the next room mumbling to himself. She was afraid to look at her mother.

Suddenly Ellie was aware that her mother's hands were

trembling violently. "He's so little," she whispered and suddenly the knife slipped out of her hands and she was crying and breathing at the same time.

Ellie didn't know what to do but after a few seconds she cleared away the peelings and put the knives in the sink. "Why don't you lie down?" she suggested. "I'll clean up and get Tommy in bed." Without saying anything her mother rose and walked to her bedroom.

Ellie wiped off the table and draped the dishcloth over the sink. She stood back and looked at the rusting pipes powdered with a whitish film. One of these days they would have to paint the place. She tiptoed past her mother who looked as if she had fallen asleep from exhaustion.

"Tommy," she called softly, "come in and get ready for bed."

Tommy sitting in the middle of the floor did not answer. He was sitting the way she imagined he would be, crosslegged, pulling his ear lobe as he turned the ragged pages of *Uncle Wiggily at the Zoo.*

"What you doing, Tommy?" she said squatting on the floor beside him. He smiled and pointed at the picture of the ducks.

"School starts tomorrow," she said, turning a page with him. "Don't you think it's time to go to bed?"

"Oh Ellie, do I have to go now?" She looked down at the serious brown eyes and the closely cropped hair. For a minute she wondered if he questioned having to go to bed now or to school tomorrow.

"Well," she said, "aren't you about through with the book?" He shook his head. "Come on," she pulled him up, "you're a sleepy head." Still he shook his head.

"When Helen and Teenie coming home?"

"Tomorrow after you come home from school they'll be here."

She lifted him from the floor thinking how small he looked to be facing all those people tomorrow.

"Look," he said breaking away from her hand and pointing to a blue shirt and pair of cotton twill pants, "Mama got them for me to wear tomorrow."

While she ran water in the tub, she heard him crawl on top of the bed. He was quiet and she knew he was untying his sneakers.

"Put your shoes out," she called through the door, "and maybe Daddy will polish them."

"Is Daddy still in there with those men? Mama made me be quiet so I wouldn't bother them."

He padded into the bathroom with bare feet and crawled into the water. As she scrubbed him they played Ask Me A Question, their own version of Twenty Questions. She had just dried him and was about to have him step into his pajamas when he asked: "Are they gonna get me tomorrow?"

"Who's going to get you?" She looked into his eyes and began rubbing him furiously with the towel.

"I don't know," he answered. "Somebody I guess."

"Nobody's going to get you," she said, "who wants a little boy who gets bubblegum in his hair anyway—but us?" He grinned but as she hugged him she thought how much he looked like his father. They walked to the bed to say his prayers and while they were kneeling she heard the first drops of rain. By the time she covered him up and tucked the spread off the floor the rain had changed to a steady downpour.

When Tommy had gone to bed her mother got up again and began ironing clothes in the kitchen. Something, she said, to keep her thoughts busy. While her mother folded and sorted the clothes Ellie drew up a chair from the kitchen table. They sat in the kitchen for a while listening to the voices of the men in the next room. Her mother's quiet speech broke the stillness in the room.

"I'd rather," she said making sweeping motions with the iron, "that you stayed home from work tomorrow and went with your father to take Tommy. I don't think I'll be up to those people."

Ellie nodded. "I don't mind," she said, tracing circles on the oil cloth covered table.

"Your father's going," her mother continued. "Belk and Reverend Davis are too. I think that white man in there will probably go."

"They may not need me," Ellie answered.

"Tommy will," her mother said, folding the last dish towel and storing it in the cabinet.

"Mama, I think he's scared," the girl turned toward the woman. "He was so quiet while I was washing him."

"I know," she answered sitting down heavily. "He's been that way all day." Her brown wavy hair glowed in the dim lighting of the kitchen. "I told him he wasn't going to school with Jakie and Bob any more but I said he was going to meet some other children just as nice."

Ellie saw that her mother was twisting her wedding band around and around on her finger.

"I've already told Mrs. Ingraham that I wouldn't be able to come out tomorrow." Ellie paused. "She didn't say very much. She didn't even say anything about his pictures in the newspaper. Mr. Ingraham said we were getting right crazy but even he didn't say anything else."

She stopped to look at the clock sitting near the sink. "It's almost time for the cruise cars to begin," she said. Her mother followed Ellie's eyes to the sink. The policemen circling their block every twenty minutes was supposed to make them feel safe, but hearing the cars come so regularly and that light flashing through the shade above her bed only made her nervous.

She stopped talking to push a wrinkle out of the shiny red cloth, dragging her finger along the table edges. "How long before those men going to leave?" she asked her mother. Just as she spoke she heard one of the men say something about getting some sleep. "I didn't mean to run them away," she said smiling. Her mother half-smiled too. They listened for the sound of motors and tires and waited for her father to shut the front door.

In a few seconds her father's head pushed through the curtain. "Want me to turn down your bed now, Ellie?" She felt uncomfortable staring up at him, the whole family looked drained of all energy.

"That's all right," she answered. "I'll sleep in Helen and Teenie's bed tonight."

"How's Tommy?" he asked looking toward the bedroom. He came in and sat down at the table with them.

They were silent before he spoke. "I keep wondering if we should send him." He lit a match and watched the flame disappear into the ashtray, then he looked into his wife's eyes. "There's no telling what these fool white folks will do."

Her mother reached over and patted his hand. "We're doing what we have to do, I guess," she said. "Sometimes though I wish the others weren't so much older than him."

"But it seems so unfair," Ellie broke in, "sending him there all by himself like that. Everybody keeps asking me why the MacAdams didn't apply for their children."

"Eloise." Her father's voice sounded curt. "We aren't answering for the MacAdams, we're trying to do what's right for your brother. He's not old enough to have his own say so. You and the others could decide for yourselves, but we're the ones that have to do for him."

She didn't say anything but watched him pull a handful of envelopes out of his pocket and tuck them in the cabinet drawer. She knew that if anyone had told him in August that Tommy would be the only one going to Jefferson Davis they would not have let him go.

"Those the new ones?" she asked. "What they say?"

"Let's not talk about the letters," her father said. "Let's go to bed."

Outside they heard the rain become heavier. Since early evening she had become accustomed to the sound. Now it blended in with the rest of the noises that had accumulated in the back of her mind since the whole thing began.

As her mother folded the ironing board they heard the quiet wheels of the police car. Ellie noticed that the clock said twelve-ten and she wondered why they were early. Her mother pulled the iron cord from the switch and they stood silently waiting for the police car to turn around and pass the house again, as if the car's passing were a final blessing for the night.

Suddenly she was aware of a noise that sounded as if everything had broken loose in her head at once, a loudness that almost shook the foundation of the house. At the same time the lights went out and instinctively her father knocked them to the floor. They could hear the tinkling of glass near the front of the house and Tommy began screaming.

"Tommy, get down," her father yelled.

She hoped he would remember to roll under the bed the way they had practiced. She was aware of objects falling and breaking as she lay perfectly still. Her breath was coming in jerks and then there was a second noise, a smaller explosion but still drowning out Tommy's cries.

"Stay still," her father commanded. "I'm going to check on Tommy. They may throw another one."

She watched him crawl across the floor, pushing a broken flower vase and an iron skillet out of his way. All of the sounds, Tommy's crying, the breaking glass, everything was echoing in her ears. She felt as if they had been crouching on the floor for hours but when she heard the police car door slam, the luminous hands of the clock said only twelve-fifteen.

She heard other cars drive up and pairs of heavy feet trample on the porch. "You folks all right in there?"

She could visualize the hands pulling open the door, because she knew the voice. Sergeant Kearns had been responsible for patrolling the house during the past three weeks. She heard him click the light switch in the living room but the darkness remained intense.

Her father deposited Tommy in his wife's lap and went to what was left of the door. In the next fifteen minutes policemen were everywhere. While she rummaged around underneath the cabinet for a candle, her mother tried to hush up

Tommy. His cheek was cut where he had scratched himself on the springs of the bed. Her mother motioned for her to dampen a cloth and put some petroleum jelly on it to keep him quiet. She tried to put him to bed again but he would not go, even when she promised to stay with him for the rest of the night. And so she sat in the kitchen rocking the little boy back and forth on her lap.

Ellie wandered around the kitchen but the light from the single candle put an eerie glow on the walls making her nervous. She began picking up pans, stepping over pieces of broken crockery and glassware. She did not want to go into the living room yet, but if she listened closely, snatches of the policemen's conversation came through the curtain.

She heard one man say that the bomb landed near the edge of the yard, that was why it had only gotten the front porch. She knew from their talk that the living room window was shattered completely. Suddenly Ellie sat down. The picture of the living room window kept flashing in her mind and a wave of feeling invaded her body making her shake as if she had lost all muscular control. She slept on the couch, right under that window.

She looked at her mother to see if she too had realized, but her mother was looking down at Tommy and trying to get him to close his eyes. Ellie stood up and crept toward the living room trying to prepare herself for what she would see. Even that minute of determination could not make her control the horror that she felt. There were jagged holes all along the front of the house and the sofa was covered with glass and paint. She started to pick up the picture that had toppled from the book shelf, then she just stepped over the broken frame.

Outside her father was talking and, curious to see who else was with him, she walked across the splinters to the yard. She could see pieces of the geranium pot and the red blossoms turned face down. There were no lights in the other houses on the street. Across from their house she could see forms standing in the door and shadows being pushed back and forth. "I guess the MacAdams are glad they just didn't get involved." No one heard her speak, and no one came over to see if they could help; she knew why and did not really blame them. They were afraid their house could be next.

Most of the policemen had gone now and only one car was left to flash the revolving red light in the rain. She heard the tall skinny man tell her father they would be parked outside for the rest of the night. As she watched the reflection of the police cars returning to the station, feeling sick on her stomach, she wondered now why they bothered.

Ellie went back inside the house and closed the curtain behind her. There was nothing anyone could do now, not even to the house. Everything was scattered all over the floor and poor Tommy still would not go to sleep. She wondered what would happen when the news spread through their section of town, and at once remembered the man in the grey Chevrolet. It would serve them right if her father's friends got one of them.

Ellie pulled up an overturned chair and sat down across from her mother who was crooning to Tommy. What Mr. Paul said was right, white people just couldn't be trusted. Her family had expected anything but even though they had practiced ducking, they didn't really expect anybody to try tearing down the house. But the funny thing was the house belonged to one of them. Maybe it was a good thing her family were just renters.

Exhausted, Ellie put her head down on the table. She didn't know what they were going to do about tomorrow, in the day time they didn't need electricity. She was too tired to think any more about Tommy, yet she could not go to sleep. So, she sat at the table trying to sit still, but every few minutes she would involuntarily twitch. She tried to steady her hands, all the time listening to her mother's sing-songy voice and waiting for her father to come back inside the house.

She didn't know how long she lay hunched against the kitchen table, but when she looked up, her wrists bore the imprints of her hair. She unfolded her arms gingerly, feeling the blood rush to her fingertips. Her father sat in the chair opposite her, staring at the vacant space between them. She heard her mother creep away from the table, taking Tommy to his room.

Ellie looked out the window. The darkness was turning to grey and the hurt feeling was disappearing. As she sat there she could begin to look at the kitchen matter-of-factly. Although the hands of the clock were just a little past five-thirty, she knew somebody was going to have to start clearing up and cook breakfast.

She stood and tipped across the kitchen to her parents' bedroom. "Mama," she whispered, standing near the door of Tommy's room. At the sound of her voice, Tommy made a funny throaty noise in his sleep. Her mother motioned for her to go out and be quiet. Ellie knew then that Tommy had just fallen asleep. She crept back to the kitchen and began picking up the dishes that could be salvaged, being careful not to go into the living room.

She walked around her father, leaving the broken glass underneath the kitchen table. "You want some coffee?" she asked.

He nodded silently, in strange contrast she thought to the water faucet that turned with a loud gurgling noise. While she let the water run to get hot she measured out the instant coffee in one of the plastic cups. Next door she could hear people moving around in the Williams' kitchen, but they too seemed much quieter than usual.

"You reckon everybody knows by now?" she asked, stirring the coffee and putting the saucer in front of him.

"Everybody will know by the time the city paper comes out," he said. "Somebody was here last night from the *Observer*. Guess it'll make front page."

She leaned against the cabinet for support watching him trace endless circles in the brown liquid with the spoon. "Sergeant Kearns says they'll have almost the whole force out there tomorrow," he said.

"Today," she whispered.

Her father looked at the clock and then turned his head. "When's your mother coming back in here?" he asked, finally picking up the cup and drinking the coffee.

"Tommy's just off to sleep," she answered. "I guess she'll be in here when he's asleep for good."

She looked out the window of the back door at the row of tall hedges that had separated their neighborhood from the white people for as long as she remembered. While she stood there she heard her mother walk into the room. To her ears the steps seemed much slower than usual. She heard her mother stop in front of her father's chair.

"Jim," she said, sounding very timid, "what we going to do?" Yet as Ellie turned toward her she noticed her mother's face was strangely calm as she looked down on her husband.

Ellie continued standing by the door listening to them talk. Nobody asked the question to which they all wanted an answer.

"I keep thinking," her father said finally, "that the policemen will be with him all day. They couldn't hurt him inside the school building without getting some of their own kind."

"But he'll be in there all by himself," her mother said softly. "A hundred policemen can't be a little boy's only friends."

She watched her father wrap his calloused hands, still

splotched with machine oil, around the salt shaker on the table.

"I keep trying," he said to her, "to tell myself that somebody's got to be the first one and then I just think how quiet he's been all week."

Ellie listened to the quiet voices that seemed to be a room apart from her. In the back of her mind she could hear phrases of a hymn her grandmother used to sing, something about trouble, her being born for trouble.

"Jim, I cannot let my baby go." Her mother's words, although quiet, were carefully pronounced.

"Maybe," her father answered, "it's not in our hands. Reverend Davis and I were talking day before yesterday how God tested the Israelites, maybe he's just trying us."

"God expects you to take care of your own," his wife interrupted. Ellie sensed a trace of bitterness in her mother's voice.

"Tommy's not going to understand why he can't go to school," her father replied. "He's going to wonder why, and how are we going to tell him we're afraid of them?" Her father's hand clutched the coffee cup. "He's going to be fighting them the rest of his life. He's got to start sometime."

"But he's not on their level. Tommy's too little to go around hating people. One of the others, they're bigger, they understand about things."

Ellie still leaning against the door saw that the sun covered part of the sky behind the hedges and the light slipping through the kitchen window seemed to reflect the shiny red of the table cloth.

"He's our child," she heard her mother say. "Whatever we do, we're going to be the cause." Her father had pushed the cup away from him and sat with his hands covering part of his face. Outside Ellie could hear a horn blowing.

"God knows we tried but I guess there's just no use." Her father's voice forced her attention back to the two people sitting in front of her. "Maybe when things come back to normal, we'll try again."

He covered his wife's chunky fingers with the palm of his hand and her mother seemed to be enveloped in silence. The three of them remained quiet, each involved in his own thoughts, but related, Ellie knew, to the same thing. She was the first to break the silence.

"Mama," she called after a long pause, "do you want me to start setting the table for breakfast?"

Her mother nodded.

Ellie turned the clock so she could see it from the sink

while she washed the dishes that had been scattered over the floor.

"You going to wake up Tommy or you want me to?"

"No," her mother said, still holding her father's hand, "let him sleep. When you wash your face, you go up the street and call Hezekiah. Tell him to keep up with the children after school, I want to do something to this house before they come home."

She stopped talking and looked around the kitchen, finally turning to her husband. "He's probably kicked the spread off by now," she said. Ellie watched her father, who without saying anything walked toward the bedroom.

She watched her mother lift herself from the chair and automatically push in the stuffing underneath the cracked plastic cover. Her face looked set, as it always did when she was trying hard to keep her composure.

"He'll need something hot when he wakes up. Hand me the oatmeal," she commanded, reaching on top of the icebox for matches to light the kitchen stove.

2.
Autobiography

FREDERICK DOUGLASS (1817?–1895)

Born a slave in Talbot County, Maryland, Frederick Doug-
lass escaped from bondage in 1838 to become the leading
Negro in the antislavery movement and, after the Civil War,
in the fight for Negro rights. He wrote three autobiographies
at different stages of his life, classics of the rich, extensive,
and still not fully mined body of writing known as "slave
narratives." The first, Narrative of the Life of Frederick
Douglass, An American Slave, *was published in 1845 at the*
Anti-Slavery Office in Boston. It was written when his memo-
ries of the realities of his life as a slave were sharpest and
most vivid. Ten years later his enlarged autobiography, My
Bondage and My Freedom, *was published in New York. His*
third autobiography, Life and Times of Frederick Douglass,
was first published in 1881 and was then revised, expanded,
and published in its final form in 1892. He was famous as an
antislavery orator and, during the Civil War, helped recruit

Negro soldiers for the 54th and 55th Massachusetts Regiments. A consistent proponent of the emancipation of the slaves, after the war he remained active in the fight to secure and protect the rights of Negro freemen. In his later life he held various official offices, including Secretary of the Santo Domingo Commission, Marshal and Recorder of the Deeds of the District of Columbia, and Minister of the United States to Haiti. The selections that follow are from his 1845 autobiography.

Narrative of the Life of Frederick Douglass, An American Slave

Chapter I

I was born in Tuckahoe, near Hillsborough, and about twelve miles from Easton, in Talbot county, Maryland. I have no accurate knowledge of my age, never having seen any authentic record containing it. By far the larger part of the slaves know as little of their ages as horses know of theirs, and it is the wish of most masters within my knowledge to keep their slaves thus ignorant. I do not remember to have ever met a slave who could tell of his birthday. They seldom come nearer to it than planting-time, harvest-time, cherry-time, spring-time, or fall-time. A want of information concerning my own was a source of unhappiness to me even during childhood. The white children could tell their ages. I could not tell why I ought to be deprived of the same privilege. I was not allowed to make any inquiries of my master concerning it. He deemed all such inquiries on the part of a slave improper and impertinent, and evidence of a restless spirit. The nearest estimate I can give makes me now between twenty-seven and twenty-eight years of age. I come to this, from hearing my master say, some time during 1835, I was about seventeen years old.

My mother was named Harriet Bailey. She was the daughter of Isaac and Betsey Bailey, both colored, and quite dark. My mother was of a darker complexion than either my grandmother or grandfather.

My father was a white man. He was admitted to be such by all I ever heard speak of my parentage. The opinion was also whispered that my master was my father; but of the correctness of this opinion, I know nothing; the means of knowing was withheld from me. My mother and I were separated when I was but an infant—before I knew her as my mother. It is a common custom, in the part of Maryland from which I ran away, to part children from their mothers at a very early age. Frequently, before the child has reached its twelfth month, its mother is taken from it, and hired out on some farm a considerable distance off, and the child is placed under the care of an old woman, too old for field labor. For what this separation is done, I do not know, unless it be to hinder the development of the child's affection toward its mother, and to blunt and destroy the natural affection of the mother for the child. This is the inevitable result.

I never saw my mother, to know her as such, more than four or five times in my life; and each of these times was very short in duration, and at night. She was hired by a Mr. Stewart, who lived about twelve miles from my home. She made her journeys to see me in the night, travelling the whole distance on foot, after the performance of her day's work. She was a field hand, and a whipping is the penalty of not being in the field at sunrise, unless a slave has special permission from his or her master to the contrary—a permission which they seldom get, and one that gives to him that gives it the proud name of being a kind master. I do not recollect of ever seeing my mother by the light of day. She was with me in the night. She would lie down with me, and get me to sleep, but long before I waked she was gone. Very little communication ever took place between us. Death soon ended what little we could have while she lived, and with it her hardships and suffering. She died when I was about seven years old, on one of my master's farms near Lee's Mill. I was not allowed to be present during her illness, at her death, or burial. She was gone long before I knew any thing about it. Never having enjoyed, to any considerable extent, her soothing presence, her tender and watchful care, I received the tidings of her death with much the same emotions I should have probably felt at the death of a stranger.

Called thus suddenly away, she left me without the slightest intimation of who my father was. The whisper that my master was my father, may or may not be true; and, true or false, it is of but little consequence to my purpose whilst the fact remains, in all its glaring odiousness, that slaveholders have ordained, and by law established, that the children of slave women shall in all cases follow the condition of their mothers; and this is done too obviously to administer to their own lusts, and make a gratification of their wicked desires profitable as well as pleasurable; for by this cunning arrangement, the slaveholder, in cases not a few, sustains to his slaves the double relation of master and father.

I know of such cases; and it is worthy of remark that such slaves invariably suffer greater hardships, and have more to contend with, than others. They are, in the first place, a constant offence to their mistress. She is ever disposed to find fault with them; they can seldom do any thing to please her; she is never better pleased than when she sees them under the lash, especially when she suspects her husband of showing to his mulatto children favors which he withholds from his black slaves. The master is frequently compelled to sell this class of his slaves, out of deference to the feelings of his white wife; and, cruel as the deed may strike any one to be, for a man to sell his own children to human flesh-mongers, it is often the dictate of humanity for him to do so; for, unless he does this, he must not only whip them himself, but must stand by and see one white son tie up his brother, of but few shades darker complexion than himself, and ply the gory lash to his naked back; and if he lisp one word of disapproval, it is set down to his parental partiality, and only makes a bad matter worse, both for himself and the slave whom he would protect and defend.

Every year brings with it multitudes of this class of slaves. It was doubtless in consequence of a knowledge of this fact, that one great statesman of the south predicted the downfall of slavery by the inevitable laws of population. Whether this prophecy is ever fulfilled or not, it is nevertheless plain that a very different-looking class of people are springing up at the south, and are now held in slavery, from those originally brought to this country from Africa; and if their increase will do no other good, it will do away the force of the argument, that God cursed Ham, and therefore American slavery is right. If the lineal descendants of Ham are alone to be scripturally enslaved, it is certain that slavery at the south must soon become unscriptural; for thousands are ushered into the world, annually, who, like myself, owe their existence to white fathers, and those fathers most frequently their own masters.

I have had two masters. My first master's name was Anthony. I do not remember his first name. He was generally called Captain Anthony—a title which, I presume, he acquired by sailing a craft on the Chesapeake Bay. He was not considered a rich slaveholder. He owned two or three farms, and about thirty slaves. His farms and slaves were under the care of an overseer. The overseer's name was Plummer. Mr. Plummer was a miserable drunkard, a profane swearer, and a

savage monster. He always went armed with a cowskin and a
heavy cudgel. I have known him to cut and slash the
women's heads so horribly, that even master would be enraged at his cruelty, and would threaten to whip him if he
did not mind himself. Master, however, was not a humane
slaveholder. It required extraordinary barbarity on the part of
an overseer to affect him. He was a cruel man, hardened by a
long life of slaveholding. He would at times seem to take
great pleasure in whipping a slave. I have often been awakened at the dawn of day by the most heart-rending shrieks of
an own aunt of mine, whom he used to tie up to a joist, and
whip upon her naked back till she was literally covered with
blood. No words, no tears, no prayers, from his gory victim,
seemed to move his iron heart from its bloody purpose. The
louder she screamed, the harder he whipped; and where the
blood ran fastest, there he whipped longest. He would whip
her to make her scream, and whip her to make her hush; and
not until overcome by fatigue, would he cease to swing the
blood-clotted cowskin. I remember the first time I ever witnessed this horrible exhibition. I was quite a child, but I well
remember it. I never shall forget it whilst I remember any
thing. It was the first of a long series of such outrages, of
which I was doomed to be a witness and a participant. It
struck me with awful force. It was the blood-stained gate, the
entrance to the hell of slavery, through which I was about to
pass. It was a most terrible spectacle. I wish I could commit
to paper the feelings with which I beheld it.

This occurrence took place very soon after I went to live
with my old master, and under the following circumstances.
Aunt Hester went out one night,—where or for what I do not
know,—and happened to be absent when my master desired
her presence. He had ordered her not to go out evenings, and
warned her that she must never let him catch her in company
with a young man, who was paying attention to her belonging
to Colonel Lloyd. The young man's name was Ned Roberts,
generally called Lloyd's Ned. Why master was so careful of
her, may be safely left to conjecture. She was a woman of
noble form, and of graceful proportions, having very few
equals, and fewer superiors, in personal appearance, among
the colored or white women of our neighborhood.

Aunt Hester had not only disobeyed his orders in going
out, but had been found in company with Lloyd's Ned; which
circumstance, I found, from what he said while whipping her,
was the chief offence. Had he been a man of pure morals
himself, he might have been thought interested in protecting
the innocence of my aunt; but those who knew him will not

suspect him of any such virtue. Before he commenced whipping Aunt Hester, he took her into the kitchen, and stripped her from neck to waist, leaving her neck, shoulders, and back, entirely naked. He then told her to cross her hands, calling her at the same time a d——d b——h. After crossing her hands, he tied them with a strong rope, and led her to a stool under a large hook in the joist, put in for the purpose. He made her get upon the stool, and tied her hands to the hook. She now stood fair for his infernal purpose. Her arms were stretched up at their full length, so that she stood upon the ends of her toes. He then said to her, "Now, you d——d b——h, I'll learn you how to disobey my orders!" and after rolling up his sleeves, he commenced to lay on the heavy cowskin, and soon the warm, red blood (amid heart-rending shrieks from her, and horrid oaths from him) came dripping to the floor. I was so terrified and horror-stricken at the sight, that I hid myself in a closet, and dared not venture out till long after the bloody transaction was over. I expected it would be my turn next. It was all new to me. I have never seen any thing like it before. I had always lived with my grandmother on the outskirts of the plantation, where she was put to raise the children of the younger women. I had therefore been, until now, out of the way of the bloody scenes that often occurred on the plantation.

Chapter VI

My new mistress proved to be all she appeared when I first met her at the door,—a woman of the kindest heart and finest feelings. She had never had a slave under her control previously to myself, and prior to her marriage she had been dependent upon her own industry for a living. She was by trade a weaver; and by constant application to her business, she had been in a good degree preserved from the blighting and dehumanizing effects of slavery. I was utterly astonished at her goodness. I scarcely knew how to behave towards her. She was entirely unlike any other white woman I had ever seen. I could not approach her as I was accustomed to approach other white ladies. My early instruction was all out of place. The crouching servility, usually so acceptable a quality in a slave, did not answer when manifested toward her. Her favor was not gained by it; she seemed to be disturbed by it. She did not deem it impudent or unmannerly for a slave to look her in the face. The meanest slave was put fully at east in her presence, and none left without feeling better for having seen her. Her face was made of heavenly smiles, and her voice of tranquil music.

But, alas! this kind heart had but a short time to remain such. The fatal poison of irresponsible power was already in her hands, and soon commenced its infernal work. That cheerful eye, under the influence of slavery, soon became red with rage; that voice, made all of sweet accord, changed to one of harsh and horrid discord; and that angelic face gave place to that of a demon.

Very soon after I went to live with Mr. and Mrs. Auld, she very kindly commenced to teach me the A, B, C. After I had learned this, she assisted me in learning to spell words of three or four letters. Just at this point of my progress, Mr. Auld found out what was going on, and at once forbade Mrs. Auld to instruct me further, telling her, among other things, that it was unlawful, as well as unsafe, to teach a slave to read. To use his own words, further, he said, "If you give a nigger an inch, he will take an ell. A nigger should know nothing but to obey his master—to do as he is told to do. Learning would *spoil* the best nigger in the world. Now," said he, "if you teach that nigger (speaking of myself) how to read, there would be no keeping him. It would forever unfit him to be a slave. He would at once become unmanageable, and of no value to his master. As to himself, it could do him no good, but a great deal of harm. It would make him discontented and unhappy." These words sank deep into my heart, stirred up sentiments within that lay slumbering, and called into existence an entirely new train of thought. It was a new and special revelation, explaining dark and mysterious things, with which my youthful understanding had struggled, but struggled in vain. I now understood what had been to me a most perplexing difficulty—to wit, the white man's power to enslave the black man. It was a grand achievement, and I prized it highly. From that moment, I understood the pathway from slavery to freedom. It was just what I wanted, and I got it at a time when I the least expected it. Whilst I was saddened by the thought of losing the aid of my kind mistress, I was gladdened by the invaluable instruction which, by the merest accident, I had gained from my master. Though conscious of the difficulty of learning without a teacher, I set out with high hope, and a fixed purpose, at whatever cost of trouble, to learn how to read. The very decided manner with which he spoke, and strove to impress his wife with the evil consequences of giving me instruction, served to convince me that he was deeply sensible of the truths he was uttering. It gave me the best assurance that I might rely with the utmost confidence on' the results which, he said, would flow from teaching me to read. What he most dreaded, that I most desired. What he most loved, that I most hated. That which to him was a great evil, to be carefully shunned, was to me a great good, to be diligently sought; and the argument which he so warmly urged, against my learning to read, only served to inspire me with a desire and determination to learn. In learning to read, I owe almost as much to the bitter opposition of my master, as to the kindly aid of my mistress. I acknowledge the benefit of both.

I had resided but a short time in Baltimore before I observed a marked difference, in the treatment of slaves, from that which I had witnessed in the country. A city slave is almost a freeman, compared with a slave on the plantation. He is much better fed and clothed, and enjoys privileges altogether unknown to the slave on the plantation. There is a vestige of decency, a sense of shame, that does much to curb and check those outbreaks of atrocious cruelty so commonly enacted upon the plantation. He is a desperate slaveholder, who will shock the humanity of his non-slaveholding neighbors with the cries of his lacerated slave. Few are willing to incur the odium attaching to the reputation of being a cruel master; and above all things, they would not be known as not giving a slave enough to eat. Every city slaveholder is anxious to have it known of him, that he feeds his slaves well; and it is due to them to say, that most of them do give their slaves enough to eat. There are, however, some painful exceptions to this rule. Directly opposite to us, on Philpot Street, lived Mr. Thomas Hamilton. He owned two slaves. Their names were Henrietta and Mary. Henrietta was about twenty-two years of age, Mary was about fourteen; and of all the mangled and emaciated creatures I ever looked upon, these two were the most so. His heart must be harder than stone, that could look upon these unmoved. The head, neck, and shoulders of Mary were literally cut to pieces. I have frequently felt her head, and found it nearly covered with festering sores, caused by the lash of her cruel mistress. I do not know that her master ever whipped her, but I have been an eye-witness to the cruelty of Mrs. Hamilton. I used to be in Mr. Hamilton's house nearly every day. Mrs. Hamilton used to sit in' a large chair in the middle of the room, with a heavy cowskin always by her side, and scarce an hour passed during the day but was marked by the blood of one of these slaves. The girls seldom passed her without her saying, "Move faster, you *black gip!*" at the same time giving them a blow with the cowskin over the head or shoulders, often drawing the blood.

She would then say, "Take that, you *black gip!*"—continuing, "If you don't move faster, I'll move you!" Added to the cruel lashings to which these slaves were subjected, they were kept nearly half-starved. They seldom knew what it was to eat a full meal. I have seen Mary contending with the pigs for the offal thrown into the street. So much was Mary kicked and cut to pieces, that she was oftener called *"pecked"* than by her name.

Chapter VII

I lived in Master Hugh's family about seven years. During this time, I succeeded in learning to read and write. In accomplishing this, I was compelled to resort to various stratagems. I had no regular teacher. My mistress, who had kindly commenced to instruct me, had, in compliance with the advice and direction of her husband, not only ceased to instruct, but had set her face against my being instructed by any one else. It is due, however, to my mistress to say of her, that she did not adopt this course of treatment immediately. She at first lacked the depravity indispensable to shutting me up in mental darkness. It was at least necessary for her to have some training in the exercise of irresponsible power, to make her equal to the task of treating me as though I were a brute.

My mistress was, as I have said, a kind and tender-hearted woman; and in the simplicity of her soul she commenced, when I first went to live with her, to treat me as she supposed one human being ought to treat another. In entering upon the duties of a slaveholder, she did not seem to perceive that I sustained to her the relation of a mere chattel, and that for her to treat me as a human being was not only wrong, but dangerously so. Slavery proved as injurious to her as it did to me. When I went there, she was a pious, warm, and tenderhearted woman. There was no sorrow or suffering for which she had not a tear. She had bread for the hungry, clothes for the naked, and comfort for every mourner that came within her reach. Slavery soon proved its ability to divest her of these heavenly qualities. Under its influence, the tender heart became stone, and the lamblike disposition gave way to one of tiger-like fierceness. The first step in her downward course was in her ceasing to instruct me. She now commenced to practise her husband's precepts. She finally became even more violent in her opposition than her husband himself. She was not satisfied with simply doing as well as he had commanded; she seemed anxious to do better. Nothing seemed to make her more angry than to see me with a newspaper. She seemed to think that here lay the danger. I have had her rush at me with a face made all up of fury, and snatch from me a newspaper, in a manner that fully revealed her apprehension. She was an apt woman; and a little experience soon demonstrated, to her satisfaction, that education and slavery were incompatible with each other.

From this time I was most narrowly watched. If I was in a separate room any considerable length of time, I was sure to be suspected of having a book, and was at once called to give an account of myself. All this, however, was too late. The first step had been taken. Mistress, in teaching me the alphabet, had given me the *inch*, and no precaution could prevent me from taking the *ell*.

The plan which I adopted, and the one by which I was most successful, was that of making friends of all the little white boys whom I met in the street. As many of these as I could, I converted into teachers. With their kindly aid, obtained at different times and in different places, I finally succeeded in learning to read. When I was sent on errands, I always took my book with me, and by going one part of my errand quickly, I found time to get a lesson before my return. I used also to carry bread with me, enough of which was always in the house, and to which I was always welcome; for I was much better off in this regard than many of the poor white children in our neighborhood. This bread I used to bestow upon the hungry little urchins, who, in return, would give me that more valuable bread of knowledge. I am strongly tempted to give the names of two or three of those little boys, as a testimonial of the gratitude and affection I bear them; but prudence forbids;—not that it would injure me, but it might embarrass them; for it is almost an unpardonable offence to teach slaves to read in this Christian country. It is enough to say of the dear little fellows, that they lived on Philpot Street, very near Durgin and Bailey's shipyard. I used to talk this matter of slavery over with them. I would sometimes say to them, I wished I could be as free as they would be when they got to be men. "You will be free as soon as you are twenty-one, *but I am a slave for life!* Have not I as good a right to be free as you have?" These words used to trouble them; they would express for me the liveliest sympathy, and console me with the hope that something would occur by which I might be free.

I was now about twelve years old, and the thought of being *a slave for life* began to bear heavily upon my heart. Just about this time, I got hold of a book entitled "The Columbian Orator." Every opportunity I got, I used to read this book. Among much of other interesting matter, I found in it a dialogue between a master and his slave. The slave was represented as having run away from his master three times. The dialogue represented the conversation which took place between them, when the slave was retaken the third time. In this dialogue, the whole argument in behalf of slavery was brought forward by the master, all of which was disposed of by the slave. The slave was made to say some very smart as well as impressive things in reply to his master—things which had the desired though unexpected effect; for the conversation resulted in the voluntary emancipation of the slave on the part of the master.

In the same book, I met with one of Sheridan's mighty speeches on and in behalf of Catholic emancipation. These were choice documents to me. I read them over and over again with unabated interest. They gave tongue to interesting thoughts of my own soul, which had frequently flashed through my mind, and died away for want of utterance. The moral which I gained from the dialogue was the power of truth over the conscience of even a slaveholder. What I got from Sheridan was a bold denunciation of slavery, and a powerful vindication of human rights. The reading of these documents enabled me to utter my thoughts, and to meet the arguments brought forward to sustain slavery; but while they relieved me of one difficulty, they brought on another even more painful than the one of which I was relieved. The more I read, the more I was led to abhor and detest my enslavers. I could regard them in no other light than a band of successful robbers, who had left their homes, and gone to Africa, and stolen us from our homes, and in a strange land reduced us to slavery. I loathed them as being the meanest as well as the most wicked of men. As I read and contemplated the subject, behold! that very discontentment which Master Hugh had predicted would follow my learning to read had already come, to torment and sting my soul to unutterable anguish. As I writhed under it, I would at times feel that learning to read had been a curse rather than a blessing. It had given me a view of my wretched condition, without the remedy. It opened my eyes to the horrible pit, but to no ladder upon which to get out. In moments of agony, I envied my fellow-slaves for their stupidity. I have often wished myself a beast. I preferred the condition of the meanest reptile to my own. Any thing, no matter what, to get rid of thinking! It was this everlasting thinking of my condition that tormented me. There was no getting rid of it. It was pressed upon me by every object within sight or hearing, animate or inanimate. The silver trump of freedom had roused my soul to eternal wakefulness. Freedom now appeared, to disappear no more forever. It was heard in every sound, and seen in every thing. It was ever present to torment me with a sense of my wretched condition. I saw nothing without seeing it, I heard nothing without hearing it, and felt nothing without feeling it. It looked from every star, it smiled in every calm, breathed in every wind, and moved in every storm.

I often found myself regretting my own existence, and wishing myself dead; and but for the hope of being free, I have no doubt but that I should have killed myself, or done something for which I should have been killed. While in this state of mind, I was eager to hear any one speak of slavery. I was a ready listener. Every little while, I could hear something about the abolitionists. It was some time before I found what the word meant. It was always used in such connections as to make it an interesting word to me. If a slave ran away and succeeded in getting clear, or if a slave killed his master, set fire to a barn, or did any thing very wrong in the mind of a slaveholder, it was spoken of as the fruit of *abolition*. Hearing the word in this connection very often, I set about learning what it meant. The dictionary afforded me little or no help. I found it was "the act of abolishing"; but then I did not know what was to be abolished. Here I was perplexed. I did not dare to ask any one about its meaning, for I was satisfied that it was something they wanted me to know very little about. After a patient waiting, I got one of our city papers, containing an account of the number of petitions from the north, praying for the abolition of slavery in the District of Columbia, and of the slave trade between the States. From this time I understood the words *abolition* and *abolitionist*, and always drew near when that word was spoken, expecting to hear something of importance to myself and fellow-slaves. The light broke in upon me by degrees. I went one day down on the wharf of Mr. Waters; and seeing two Irishmen unloading a scow of stone, I went, unasked, and helped them. When we had finished, one of them came to me and asked, "Are ye a slave for life?" I told him that I was. The good Irishman seemed to be deeply affected by the statement. He said to the other that it was a pity so fine a little fellow as myself should be a slave for life. He said it was a shame to hold me. They both advised me to run away to the north; that I should find friends there, and that I should be free. I pretended not to be interested in what they said, and treated them as if I did not understand them; for I feared they might be treacherous. White men have been known to encourage slaves to escape, and then, to get the reward, catch them and return them to their masters. I was afraid that these seemingly good men might use me so; but I nevertheless remembered their advice, and from that time I resolved to run away. I looked forward to a time at which it would be safe for me to escape. I was too young to think of doing so immediately; besides, I wished to learn how to write, as I might have occasion to write my own pass. I consoled myself with the hope that I should one day find a good chance. Meanwhile, I would learn to write.

The idea as to how I might learn to write was suggested to me by being in Durgin and Bailey's ship-yard, and frequently seeing the ship carpenters, after hewing, and getting a piece of timber ready for use, write on the timber the name of that part of the ship for which it was intended. When a piece of timber was intended for the larboard side, it would be marked thus—"L." When a piece was for the starboard side, it would be marked thus—"S." A piece for the larboard side forward, would be marked thus—"L. F." When a piece was for starboard side forward, it would be marked thus— "S. F." For larboard aft, it would be marked thus— "L. A." For starboard aft, it would be marked thus—"S. A." I soon learned the names of these letters, and for what they were intended when placed upon a piece of timber in the ship-yard. I immediately commenced copying them, and in a short time was able to make the four letters named. After that, when I met with any boy who I knew could write, I would tell him I could write as well as he. The next word would be, "I don't believe you. Let me see you try it." I would then make the letters which I had been so fortunate as to learn, and ask him to beat that. In this way I got a good many lessons in writing, which it is quite possible I should never have gotten in any other way. During this time, my copy-book was the board fence, brick wall, and pavement; my pen and ink was a lump of chalk. With these, I learned mainly how to write. I then commenced and continued copying the Italics in Webster's Spelling Book, until I could make them all without looking on the book. By this time, my little Master Thomas had gone to school, and learned how to write, and had written over a number of copy-books. These had been brought home, and shown to some of our near neighbors, and then laid aside. My mistress used to go to class meeting at the Wilk Street meetinghouse every Monday afternoon, and leave me to take care of the house. When left thus, I used to spend this time writing in the spaces left in

Master Thomas's copy-book, copying what he had written. I continued to do this until I could write a hand very similar to that of Master Thomas. Thus, after a long, tedious effort for years, I finally succeeded in learning how to write.

Chapter X

I left Master Thomas's house, and went to live with Mr. Covey, on the 1st of January, 1833. I was now, for the first time in my life, a field hand. In my new employment, I found myself even more awkward than a country boy appeared to be in a large city. I had been at my new home but one week before Mr. Covey gave me a severe whipping, cutting my back, causing the blood to run, and raising ridges on my flesh as large as my little finger. The details of this affair are as follows: Mr. Covey sent me, very early in the morning of one of our coldest days in the month of January, to the woods, to get a load of wood. He gave me a team of unbroken oxen. He told me which was the in-hand ox, and which the off-hand one. He then tied the end of a large rope around the horns of the in-hand ox, and gave me the other end of it, and told me, if the oxen started to run, that I must hold on upon the rope. I had never driven oxen before, and of course I was very awkward. I, however, succeeded in getting to the edge of the woods with little difficulty; but I had got a very few rods into the woods, when the oxen took fright, and started full tilt, carrying the cart against trees, and over stumps, in the most frightful manner. I expected every moment that my brains would be dashed out against the trees. After running thus for a considerable distance, they finally upset the cart, dashing it with great force against a tree, and threw themselves into a dense thicket. How I escaped death, I do not know. There I was, entirely alone, in a thick wood, in a place new to me. My cart was upset and shattered, my oxen were entangled among the young trees, and there was none to help me. After a long spell of effort, I succeeded in getting my cart righted, my oxen disentangled, and again yoked to the cart. I now proceeded with my team to the place where I had, the day before, been chopping wood, and loaded my cart pretty heavily, thinking in this way to tame my oxen. I then proceeded on my way home. I had now consumed one half of the day. I got out of the woods safely, and now felt out of danger. I stopped my oxen to open the woods gate; and just as I did so, before I could get hold of my ox-rope, the oxen again started, rushed through the gate, catching it between the wheel and the body of the cart, tearing it to pieces, and coming within a few inches of crushing me against the gate-post. Thus twice, in one short day, I escaped death by the merest chance. On my return, I told Mr. Covey what had happened, and how it happened. He ordered me to return to the woods again immediately. I did so, and he followed on after me. Just as I got into the woods, he came up and told me to stop my cart, and that he would teach me how to trifle away my time, and break gates. He then went to a large gum-tree, and with his axe cut three large switches, and, after trimming them up neatly with his pocket-knife, he ordered me to take off my clothes. I made him no answer, but stood with my clothes on. He repeated his order. I still made him no answer, nor did I move to strip myself. Upon this he rushed at me with the fierceness of a tiger, tore off my clothes, and lashed me till he had worn out his switches, cutting me so savagely as to leave the marks visible for a long time after. This whipping was the first of a number just like it, and for similar offenses.

I lived with Mr. Covey one year. During the first six months, of that year, scarce a week passed without his whipping me. I was seldom free from a sore back. My awkwardness was almost always his excuse for whipping me. We were worked fully up to the point of endurance. Long before day we were up, our horses fed, and by the first approach of day we were off to the field with our hoes and ploughing teams. Mr. Covey gave us enough to eat, but scarce time to eat it. We were often less than five minutes taking our meals. We were often in the field from the first approach of day till its last lingering ray had left us; and at saving-fodder time, midnight often caught us in the field binding blades.

Covey would be out with us. The way he used to stand it, was this. He would spend the most of his afternoons in bed. He would then come out fresh in the evening, ready to urge us on with his words, example, and frequently with the whip. Mr. Covey was one of the few slaveholders who could and did work with his hands. He was a hard-working man. He knew by himself just what a man or a boy could do. There was no deceiving him. His work went on in his absence almost as well as in his presence; and he had the faculty of making us feel that he was ever present with use. This he did by surprising us. He seldom approached the spot where we were at work openly, if he could do it secretly. He always aimed at taking us by surprise. Such was his cunning, that we used to call him, among ourselves, "the snake." When we were at work in the cornfield, he would sometimes crawl on his hands and knees to avoid detection, and all at once he

would rise nearly in our midst, and scream out, "Ha, ha!
Come, come! Dash on, dash on!" This being his mode of attack, it was never safe to stop a single minute. His comings
were like a thief in the night. He appeared to us as being ever
at hand. He was under every tree, behind every stump, in
every bush, and at every window, on the plantation. He
would sometimes mount his horse, as if bound to St. Michael's, a distance of seven miles, and in half an hour afterwards you would see him coiled up in the corner of the
wood-fence, watching every motion of the slaves. He would,
for this purpose, leave his horse tied up in the woods. Again,
he would sometimes walk up to us, and give us orders as
though he was upon the point of starting on a long journey,
turn his back upon us, and make as though he was going to
the house to get ready; and, before he would get half way
thither, he would turn short and crawl into a fence-corner, or
behind some tree, and there watch us till the going down of
the sun.

Mr. Covey's *forte* consisted in his power to deceive. His
life was devoted to planning and perpetrating the grossest de-
ceptions. Every thing he possessed in the shape of learning or
religion, he made conform to his disposition to deceive. He
seemed to think himself equal to deceiving the Almighty. He
would make a short prayer in the morning, and a long prayer
at night; and, strange as it may seem, few men would at
times appear more devotional than he. The exercises of his
family devotions were always commenced with singing; and,
as he was a very poor singer himself, the duty of raising the
hymn generally came upon me. He would read his hymn, and
nod at me to commence. I would at times do so; at others, I
would not. My non-compliance would almost always produce
much confusion. To show himself independent of me, he
would start and stagger through with his hymn in the most
discordant manner. In this state of mind, he prayed with
more than ordinary spirit. Poor man! such was his disposition, and success at deceiving, I do verily believe that he
sometimes deceived himself into the solemn belief, that he
was a sincere worshipper of the most high God; and this, too,
at a time when he may be said to have been guilty of compelling his woman slave to commit the sin of adultery. The facts
in the case are these: Mr. Covey was a poor man; he was just
commencing in life; he was only able to buy one slave; and,
shocking as is the fact, he bought her, as he said, for *a
breeder*. This woman was named Caroline. Mr. Covey bought
her from Mr. Thomas Lowe, about six miles from St. Michael's. She was a large, able-bodied woman, about twenty

years old. She had already given birth to one child, which proved her to be just what he wanted. After buying her, he hired a married man of Mr. Samuel Harrison, to live with him one year; and him he used to fasten up with her every night! The result was, that, at the end of the year, the miserable woman gave birth to twins. At this result Mr. Covey seemed to be highly pleased, both with the man and the wretched woman. Such was his joy, and that of his wife, that nothing they could do for Caroline during her confinement was too good, or too hard, to be done. The children were regarded as being quite an addition to his wealth.

If at any one time of my life more than another, I was made to drink the bitterest dregs of slavery, that time was during the first six months of my stay with Mr. Covey. We were worked in all weathers. It was never too hot or too cold; it could never rain, blow, hail, or snow, too hard for us to work in the field. Work, work, work, was scarcely more the order of the day than of the night. The longest days were too short for him, and the shortest nights too long for him. I was somewhat unmanageable when I first went there, but a few months of this discipline tamed me. Mr. Covey succeeded in breaking me. I was broken in body, soul, and spirit. My natural elasticity was crushed, my intellect languished, the disposition to read departed, the cheerful spark that lingered about my eye died; the dark night of slavery closed in upon me; and behold a man transformed into a brute!

Sunday was my only leisure time. I spent this in a sort of beast-like stupor, between sleep and wake, under some large tree. At times I would rise up, a flash of energetic freedom would dart through my soul, accompanied with a faint beam of hope, that flickered for a moment, and then vanished. I sank down again, mourning over my wretched condition. I was sometimes prompted to take my life, and that of Covey, but was prevented by a combination of hope and fear. My sufferings on this plantation seem now like a dream rather than a stern reality.

Our house stood within a few rods of the Chesapeake Bay, whose broad bosom was ever white with sails from every quarter of the habitable globe. Those beautiful vessels, robed in the purest white, so delightful to the eye of freemen, were to me so many shrouded ghosts, to terrify and torment me with thoughts of my wretched condition. I have often, in the deep stillness of summer's Sabbath, stood all alone upon the lofty banks of that noble bay, and traced, with saddened heart and tearful eye, the countless number of sails moving off to the mighty ocean. The sight of these always affected me powerfully. My thoughts would compel utterance; and there, with no audience but the Almighty, I would pour out my soul's complaint, in my rude way, with an apostrophe to the moving multitude of ships:—

"You are loosed from your moorings, and are free; I am fast in my chains, and am a slave! You move merrily before the gentle gale, and I sadly before the bloody whip! You are freedom's swift-winged angels, that fly round the world; I am confined in bands of iron! O that I were free! O, that I were on one of your gallant decks, and under your protecting wing! Alas! betwixt me and you, the turbid waters roll. Go on, go on. O that I could also go! Could I but swim! If I could fly! O, why was I born a man, of whom to make a brute! The glad ship is gone; she hides in the dim distance. I am left in the hottest hell of unending slavery. O God, save me! God, deliver me! Let me be free! Is there any God? Why am I a slave? I will run away. I will not stand it. Get caught, or get clear, I'll try it. I had as well die with ague as the fever. I have only one life to lose. I had as well be killed running as die standing. Only think of it; one hundred miles straight north, and I am free! Try it? Yes! God helping me, I will. It cannot be that I shall live and die a slave. I will take to the water. This very bay shall yet bear me to freedom. The steamboats steered in a north-east course from North Point. I will do the same; and when I get to the head of the bay, I will turn my canoe adrift, and walk straight through Delaware into Pennsylvania. When I get there, I shall not be required to have a pass; I can travel without being disturbed. Let but the first opportunity offer, and, come what will, I am off. Meanwhile, I will try to bear up under the yoke. I am not the only slave in the world. Why should I fret? I can bear as much as any of them. Besides, I am but a boy, and all boys are bound to some one. It may be that my misery in slavery will only increase my happiness when I get free. There is a better day coming."

Thus I used to think, and thus I used to speak to myself; goaded almost to madness at one moment, and at the next reconciling myself to my wretched lot.

I have already intimated that my condition was much worse, during the first six months of my stay at Mr. Covey's, than in the last six. The circumstances leading to the change in Mr. Covey's course toward me form an epoch in my humble history. You have seen how a man was made a slave; you shall see how a slave was made a man. On one of the hottest days of the month of August 1833, Bill Smith, William Hughes, a slave named Eli, and myself, were engaged in fan-

ning wheat. Hughes was clearing the fanned wheat from before the fan. Eli was turning. Smith was feeding, and I was
carrying wheat to the fan. The work was simple, requiring
strength rather than intellect; yet, to one entirely unused to
such work, it came very hard. About three o'clock of that
day, I broke down; my strength failed me; I was seized with
a violent aching of the head, attended with extreme dizziness;
I trembled in every limb. Finding what was coming, I nerved
myself up, feeling it would never do to stop work. I stood as
long as I could stagger to the hopper with grain. When I
could stand no longer, I fell, and felt as if held down by an
immense weight. The fan of course stopped; every one had
his own work to do; and no one could do the work of the
other, and have his own go on at the same time.

Mr. Covey was at the house, about one hundred yards
from the treading-yard where we were fanning. On hearing
the fan stop, he left immediately, and came to the spot where
we were. He hastily inquired what the matter was. Bill answered that I was sick, and there was no one to bring wheat
to the fan. I had by this time crawled away under the side of
the post and rail-fence by which the yard was enclosed, hoping to find relief by getting out of the sun. He then asked
where I was. He was told by one of the hands. He came to
the spot, and, after looking at me awhile, asked me what was
the matter. I told him as well as I could, for I scarce had
strength to speak. He then gave me a savage kick in the side,
and told me to get up. I tried to do so, but fell back in the
attempt. He gave me another kick, and again told me to rise.
I again tried, and succeeded in gaining my feet; but, stoop-
ing to get the tub with which I was feeding the fan, I again
staggered and fell. While down in this situation, Mr. Covey
took up the hickory slat with which Hughes had been striking
off the half-bushel measure, and with it gave me a heavy
blow upon the head, making a large wound, and the blood
ran freely; and with this again told me to get up. I made no
effort to comply, having now made up my mind to let him do
his worst. In a short time after receiving this blow, my head
grew better. Mr. Covey had now left me to my fate. At this
moment I resolved, for the first time, to go to my master,
enter a complaint, and ask his protection. In order to do this,
I must that afternoon walk seven miles; and this, under the
circumstances, was truly a severe undertaking. I was exceed-
ingly feeble; made so as much by the kicks and blows which
I received, as by the severe fit of sickness to which I had
been subjected. I, however, watched my chance, while Covey
was looking in an opposite direction, and started for St. Mi-

chael's. I succeeded in getting a considerable distance on my way to the woods, when Covey discovered me and called after me to come back, threatening what he would do if I did not come. I disregarded both his calls and his threats, and made my way to the woods as fast as my feeble state would allow; and thinking I might be overhauled by him if I kept the road, I walked through the woods, keeping far enough from the road to avoid detection, and near enough to prevent losing my way. I had not gone far before my little strength again failed me. I could go no farther. I fell down, and lay for a considerable time. The blood was yet oozing from the wound on my head. For a time I thought I should bleed to death; and think now that I should have done so, but that the blood so matted my hair as to stop the wound. After lying there about three quarters of an hour, I nerved myself up again, and started on my way, through bogs and briers, barefooted and bareheaded, tearing my feet sometimes at nearly every step; and after a journey of about seven miles, occupying some five hours to perform it, I arrived at master's store. I then presented an appearance enough to affect any but a heart of iron. From the crown of my head to my feet, I was covered with blood; my shirt was stiff with blood. My legs and feet were torn in sundry places with briers and thorns, and were also covered with blood. I suppose I looked like a man who had escaped a den of wild beasts, and barely escaped them. In this state I appeared before my master, humbly entreating him to interpose his authority for my protection. I told him all the circumstances as well as I could, and it seemed, as I spoke, at times to affect him. He would then walk the floor, and seek to justify Covey by saying he expected I deserved it. He asked me what I wanted. I told him, to let me get a new home; that as sure as I lived with Mr. Covey again, I should live with but to die with him; that Covey would surely kill me; he was in a fair way for it. Master Thomas ridiculed the idea that there was any danger of Mr. Covey's killing me, and said that he knew Mr. Covey; that he was a good man, and that he could not think of taking me from him; that, should he do so, he would lose the whole year's wages; that I belonged to Mr. Covey for one year, and that I must go back to him, come what might; and that I must not trouble him with any more stories, or that he would himself *get hold of me*. After threatening me thus, he gave me a very large dose of salts, telling me that I might remain in St. Michael's that night, (it being quite late,) but that I must be off back to Mr. Covey's early in the morning; and that if I did not, he would *get hold of me*, which meant that he would whip me. I remained all night, and, according to his orders, I started off to Covey's in the morning, (Saturday morning,) wearied in body and broken in spirit. I got no supper that night, or breakfast that morning. I reached Covey's about nine o'clock; and just as I was getting over the fence that divided Mrs. Kemp's fields from ours, out ran Covey with his cowskin, to give me another whipping. Before he could reach me, I succeeded in getting to the cornfield and as the corn was very high, it afforded me the means of hiding. He seemed very angry, and searched for me a long time. My behavior was altogether unaccountable. He finally gave up the chase, thinking, I suppose, that I must come home for something to eat; he would give himself no further trouble in looking for me. I spent that day mostly in the woods, having the alternative before me,—to go home and be whipped to death, or stay in the woods and be starved to death. That night, I fell in with Sandy Jenkins, a slave with whom I was somewhat acquainted. Sandy had a free wife who lived about four miles from Mr. Covey's; and it being Saturday, he was on his way to see her. I told him my circumstances, and he very kindly invited me to go home with him. I went home with him, and talked this whole matter over, and got his advice as to what course it was best for me to pursue. I found Sandy an old adviser. He told me, with great solemnity, I must go back to Covey; but that before I went, I must go with him into another part of the woods, where there was a certain *root,* which, if I would take some of it with me, carrying it *always on my right side,* would render it impossible for Mr. Covey, or any other white man, to whip me. He said he had carried it for years; and since he had done so, he had never received a blow, and never expected to while he carried it. I at first rejected the idea, that the simple carrying of a root in my pocket would have any such effect as he had said, and was not disposed to take it; but Sandy impressed the necessity with much earnestness, telling me it could do no harm, if it did no good. To please him, I at length took the root, and, according to his direction, carried it upon my right side. This was Sunday morning. I immediately started for home; and upon entering the yard gate, out came Mr. Covey on his way to meeting. He spoke to me very kindly, bade me drive the pigs from a lot near by, and passed on towards the church. Now, this singular conduct of Mr. Covey really made me begin to think that there was something in the *root* which Sandy had given me; and had it been on any other day than Sunday, I could have attributed the conduct to no other cause than the influence of that root; and as it was, I was half inclined to think the root to be something more than I at first had taken it to be. All went well till Monday morning. On this morning, the virtue of the *root* was fully tested. Long before daylight, I was called to go and rub, curry, and feed, the horses. I obeyed, and was glad to obey. But whilst thus engaged, whilst in the act of throwing down some blades from the loft, Mr. Covey entered the stable with a long rope; and just as I was half out of the loft, he caught hold of my legs, and was about tying me. As soon as I found what he was up to, I gave a sudden spring, and as I did so, he holding to my legs, I was brought sprawling on the stable floor. Mr. Covey seemed now to think he had me, and could do what he pleased; but at this moment —from whence came the spirit I don't know—I resolved to fight; and, suiting my action to the resolution, I seized Covey hard by the throat; and as I did so, I rose. He held on to me, and I to him. My resistance was so entirely unexpected, that Covey seemed taken all aback. He trembled like a leaf. This gave me assurance, and I held him uneasy, causing the blood to run where I touched him with the ends of my fingers. Mr. Covey soon called out to Hughes for help. Hughes came, and, while Covey held me, attempted to tie my right hand. While he was in the act of doing so, I watched my chance, and gave him a heavy kick close under the ribs. This kick fairly sickened Hughes, so that he left me in the hands of Mr. Covey. This kick had the effect of not only weakening Hughes, but Covey also. When he saw Hughes bending over with pain, his courage quailed. He asked me if I meant to persist in my resistance. I told him I did, come what might; that he had used me like a brute for six months, and that I was determined to be used so no longer. With that, he strove to drag me to a stick that was lying just out of the stable door. He meant to knock me down. But just as he was leaning over to get the stick, I seized him with both hands by his collar, and brought him by a sudden snatch to the ground. By this time, Bill came. Covey called upon him for assistance. Bill wanted to know what he could do. Covey said, "Take hold of him, take hold of him!" Bill said his master hired him out to work, and not to help to whip me; so he left Covey and myself to fight our own battle out. We were at it for nearly two hours. Covey at length let me go, puffing and blowing at a great rate, saying that if I had not resisted, he would not have whipped me half so much. The truth was, that he had not whipped me at all. I considered him as getting entirely the worst end of the bargain; for he had drawn no blood from me, but I had from him. The whole six months afterwards, that I spent with Mr. Covey, he never laid the weight of his finger upon me in anger. He would occasionally say, he didn't want to get hold of me again. "No," thought I, "you need not; for you will come off worse than you did before."

This battle with Mr. Covey was the turning-point in my career as a slave. It rekindled the few expiring embers of freedom, and revived within me a sense of my own manhood. It recalled the departed self-confidence, and inspired me again with a determination to be free. The gratification afforded by the triumph was a full compensation for whatever else might follow, even death itself. He only can understand the deep satisfaction which I experienced, who has himself repelled by force the bloody arm of slavery. I felt as I never felt before. It was a glorious resurrection, from the tomb of slavery, to the heaven of freedom. My long-crushed spirit rose, cowardice departed, bold defiance took its place; and I now resolved that, however long I might remain a slave in form, the day had passed forever when I could be a slave in fact. I did not hesitate to let it be known of me, that the white man who expected to succeed in whipping, must also succeed in killing me.

From this time I was never again what might be called fairly whipped, though I remained a slave four years afterwards. I had several fights, but was never whipped.

It was for a long time a matter of surprise to me why Mr. Covey did not immediately have me taken by the constable to the whipping-post, and there regularly whipped for the crime of raising my hand against a white man in defence of myself. And the only explanation I can now think of does not entirely satisfy me; but such as it is, I will give it. Mr. Covey enjoyed the most unbounded reputation for being a first-rate overseer and negro-breaker. It was of considerable importance to him. That reputation was at stake; and had he sent me—a boy about sixteen years old—to the public whipping-post, his reputation would have been lost; so, to save his reputation, he suffered me to go unpunished.

My term of actual service to Mr. Edward Covey ended on Christmas day, 1833. The days between Christmas and New Year's day are allowed as holidays; and, accordingly, we were not required to perform any labor, more than to feed and take care of the stock. This time we regarded as our own, by the grace of our masters; and we therefore used or abused it nearly as we pleased. Those of us who had families at a distance, were generally allowed to spend the whole six days in

their society. This time, however, was spent in various ways.
The staid, sober, thinking and industrious ones of our number would employ themselves in making corn-brooms, mats,
horse-collars, and baskets; and another class of us would
spend the time in hunting opossums, hares, and coons. But by
far the larger part engaged in such sports and merriments as
playing ball, wrestling, running foot-races, fiddling, dancing,
and drinking whisky; and this latter mode of spending the
time was by far the most agreeable to the feelings of our
masters. A slave who would work during the holidays was
considered by our masters as scarcely deserving them. He
was regarded as one who rejected the favor of his master. It
was deemed a disgrace not to get drunk at Christmas; and he
was regarded as lazy indeed, who had not provided himself
with the necessary means, during the year, to get whisky
enough to last him through Christmas.

From what I know of the effect of these holidays upon the
slave, I believe them to be among the most effective means in
the hands of the slaveholder in keeping down the spirit of insurrection. Were the slaveholders at once to abandon this
practice, I have not the slightest doubt it would lead to an
immediate insurrection among the slaves. These holidays
serve as conductors, or safety-valves, to carry off the rebellious spirit of enslaved humanity. But for these, the slave
would be forced up to the wildest desperation; and woe be-
tide the slaveholder, the day he ventures to remove or hinder
the operation of those conductors! I warn him that, in such
an event, a spirit will go forth in their midst, more to be
dreaded than the most appalling earthquake.

The holidays are part and parcel of the gross fraud, wrong,
and inhumanity of slavery. They are professedly a custom
established by the benevolence of the slaveholders; but I under-
take to say, it is the result of selfishness, and one of the grossest frauds committed upon the down-trodden slave. They do
not give the slaves this time because they would not like to
have their work during its continuance, but because they
know it would be unsafe to deprive them of it. This will be
seen by the fact, that the slaveholders like to have their slaves
spend those days just in such a manner as to make them as
glad of their ending as of their beginning. Their object seems
to be, to disgust their slaves with freedom, by plunging them
into the lowest depths of dissipation. For instance, the slaveholders not only like to see the slave drink of his own accord,
but will adopt various plans to make him drunk. One plan is,
to make bets on their slaves, as to who can drink the most
whisky without getting drunk; and in this way they succeed

in getting whole multitudes to drink to excess. Thus, when the slave asks for virtuous freedom, the cunning slaveholder, knowing his ignorance, cheats him with a dose of vicious dissipation, artfully labelled with the name of liberty. The most of us used to drink it down, and the result was just what might be supposed: many of us were led to think that there was little to choose between liberty and slavery. We felt, and very properly too, that we had almost as well be slaves to man as to rum. So, when the holidays ended, we staggered up from the filth of our wallowing, took a long breath, and marched to the field,—feeling, upon the whole, rather glad to go, from what our master had deceived us into a belief was freedom, back to the arms of slavery.

I have said that this mode of treatment is a part of the whole system of fraud and inhumanity of slavery. It is so. The mode here adopted to disgust the slave with freedom, by allowing him to see only the abuse of it, is carried out in other things. For instance, a slave loves molasses; he steals some. His master, in many cases, goes off to town, and buys a large quantity; he returns, takes his whip, and commands the slave to eat the molasses, until the poor fellow is made sick at the very mention of it. The same mode is sometimes adopted to make the slaves refrain from asking for more food than their regular allowance. A slave runs through his allowance and applies for more. His master is enraged at him; but, not willing to send him off without food, gives him more than is necessary, and compels him to eat it within a given time. Then, if he complains that he cannot eat it, he is said to be satisfied neither full nor fasting, and is whipped for being hard to please! I have an abundance of such illustrations of the same principle, drawn from my own observation, but think the cases I have cited sufficient. The practice is a very common one.

On the first of January, 1834, I left Mr. Covey, and went to live with Mr. William Freeland, who lived about three miles from St. Michael's. I soon found Mr. Freeland a very different man from Mr. Covey. Thought not rich, he was what would be called an educated southern gentleman. Mr. Covey, as I have shown, was a well-trained negro-breaker and slave-driver. The former (slaveholder though he was) seemed to possess some regard for honor, some reverence for justice, and some respect for humanity. The latter seemed totally insensible to all such sentiments. Mr. Freeland had many of the faults peculiar to slaveholders, such as being very passionate and fretful; but I must do him the justice to say, that he was exceedinly free from those degrading vices to which Mr. Covey was constantly addicted. The one was open and frank, and we always knew where to find him. The other was a most artful deceiver, and could be understood only by such as were skilful enough to detect his cunningly-devised frauds. Another advantage I gained in my new master was, he made no pretensions to, or profession of, religion; and this, in my opinion, was truly a great advantage. I assert most unhesitatingly, that the religion of the south is a mere covering for the most horrid crimes,—a justifier of the most appalling barbarity,—a sanctifer of the most hateful frauds,—and a dark shelter under which the darkest, foulest, grossest, and most infernal deeds of slaveholders find the strongest protection. Were I to be again reduced to the chains of slavery, next to that enslavement, I should regard being the slave of a religious master the greatest calamity that could befall me. For of all slaveholders with whom I have ever met, religious slaveholders are the worst. I have ever found them the meanest and basest, the most cruel and cowardly, of all others. It was my unhappy lot not only to belong to a religious slaveholder, but to live in a community of such religionists. Very near Mr. Freeland lived the Rev. Daniel Weeden, and in the same neighborhood lived the Rev. Rigby Hopkins. These were members and ministers in the Reformed Methodist Church. Mr. Weeden owned, among others, a woman slave, whose name I have forgotten. This woman's back, for weeks, was kept literally raw, made so by the lash of this merciless, *religious* wretch. He used to hire hands. His maxim was, Behave well or behave ill, it is the duty of a master occasionally to whip a slave, to remind him of his master's authority. Such was his theory, and such his practice.

Mr. Hopkins was even worse than Mr. Weeden. His chief boast was his ability to manage slaves. The peculiar feature of his government was that of whipping slaves in advance of deserving it. He always managed to have one or more of his slaves to whip every Monday morning. He did this to alarm their fears, and strike terror into those who escaped. His plan was to whip for the smallest offences, to prevent the commission of large ones. Mr. Hopkins could always find some excuse for whipping a slave. It would astonish one, unaccustomed to a slaveholding life, to see with what wonderful ease a slaveholder can find things, of which to make occasion to whip a slave. A mere look, word, or motion,—a mistake, accident, or want of power,—are all matters for which a slave may be whipped at any time. Does a slave look dissatisfied? It is said, he has the devil in him, and it must be whipped out. Does he speak loudly when spoken to by his master?

Then he is getting high-minded, and should be taken down a button-hole lower. Does he forget to pull off his hat at the approach of a white person? Then he is wanting in reverence, and should be whipped for it. Does he ever venture to vindicate his conduct, when censured for it? Then he is guilty of impudence,—one of the greatest crimes of which a slave can be guilty. Does he ever venture to suggest a different mode of doing things from that pointed out by his master? He is indeed presumptuous, and getting above himself; and nothing less than a flogging will do for him. Does he, while ploughing, break a plough,—or, while hoeing, break a hoe? It is owing to his carelessness, and for it a slave must always be whipped. Mr. Hopkins could always find something of this sort to justify the use of the lash, and he seldom failed to embrace such opportunities. There was not a man in the whole county, with whom the slaves who had the getting their own home, would not prefer to live, rather than with this Rev. Mr. Hopkins. And yet there was not a man any where round, who made higher professions of religion, or was more active in revivals,—more attentive to the class, love-feast, prayer and preaching meetings, or more devotional in his family,— that prayed earlier, later, louder, and longer,—than this same reverend slave-driver, Rigby Hopkins.

But to return to Mr. Freeland, and to my experience while in his employment. He, like Mr. Covey, gave us enough to eat; but, unlike Mr. Covey, he also gave us sufficient time to take our meals. He worked us hard, but always between sunrise and sunset. He required a good deal of work to be done, but gave us good tools with which to work. His farm was large, but he employed hands enough to work it, and with ease, compared with many of his neighbors. My treatment, while in his employment, was heavenly, compared with what I experienced at the hands of Mr. Edward Covey.

Mr. Freeland was himself the owner of but two slaves. Their names were Henry Harris and John Harris. The rest of his hands he hired. These consisted of myself, Sandy Jenkins,* and Handy Caldwell. Henry and John were quite intelligent, and in a very little while after I went there, I succeeded in creating in them a strong desire to learn how to read. This desire soon sprang up in the others also. They very

---

*This is the same man who gave me the roots to prevent my being whipped by Mr. Covey. He was "a clever soul." We used frequently to talk about the fight with Covey, and as often as we did so, he would claim my success as the result of the roots which he gave me. This superstition is very common among the more ignorant slaves. A slave seldom dies but that his death is attributed to trickery.

soon mustered up some old spelling-books, and nothing would do but that I must keep a Sabbath school. I agreed to do so, and accordingly devoted my Sundays to teaching these my loved fellow-slaves how to read. Neither of them knew his letters when I went there. Some of the slaves of the neighboring farms found what was going on, and also availed themselves of the little opportunity to learn to read. It was understood, among all who came, that there must be as little display about it as possible. It was necessary to keep our religious masters at St. Michael's unacquainted with the fact, that, instead of spending the Sabbath in wrestling, boxing, and drinking whisky, we were trying to learn how to read the will of God; for they had much rather see us engaged in those degrading sports, than to see us behaving like intellectual, moral, and accountable beings. My blood boils as I think of the bloody manner in which Messrs. Wright Fairbanks and Garrison West, both class-leaders, in connection with many others, rushed in upon us with sticks and stones, and broke up our virtuous little Sabbath school, at St. Michael's—all calling themselves Christians! humble followers of the Lord Jesus Christ! But I am again digressing.

I held my Sabbath school at the house of a free colored man, whose name I deem it imprudent to mention; for should it be known, it might embarrass him greatly, though the crime of holding the school was committed ten years ago. I had at one time over forty scholars, and those of the right sort, ardently desiring to learn. They were of all ages, though mostly men and women. I look back to those Sundays with an amount of pleasure not to be expressed. They were great days to my soul. The work of instructing my dear fellow-slaves was the sweetest engagement with which I was ever blessed. We loved each other, and to leave them at the close of the Sabbath was a severe cross indeed. When I think that these precious souls are to-day shut up in the prison-house of slavery, my feelings overcome me, and I am almost ready to ask, "Does a righteous God govern the universe? and for what does he hold the thunders in his right hand, if not to smite the oppressor, and deliver the spoiled out of the hand of the spoiler?" These dear souls came not to Sabbath school because it was reputable to be thus engaged. Every moment they spent in that school, they were liable to be taken up, and given thirty-nine lashes. They came because they wished to learn. Their minds had been starved by their cruel masters. They had been shut up in mental darkness. I taught them, because it was the delight of my soul to be doing something that looked like bettering the condition of my race. I kept up my school nearly the whole year I lived with Mr. Freeland; and, beside my Sabbath school, I devoted three evenings in the week, during the winter, to teaching the slaves at home. And I have the happiness to know, that several of those who came to Sabbath school learned how to read; and that one, at least, is now free through my agency.

The year passed off smoothly. It seemed only about half as long as the year which preceded it. I went through it without receiving a single blow. I will give Mr. Freeland the credit of being the best master I ever had, *till I became my own master.* For the ease with which I passed the year, I was, however, somewhat indebted to the society of my fellow-slaves. They were noble souls; they not only possessed loving hearts, but brave ones. We were linked and interlinked with each other. I loved them with a love stronger than any thing I have experienced since. It is sometimes said that we slaves do not love and confide in each other. In answer to this assertion, I can say, I never loved any or confided in any people more than my fellow-slaves, and especially those with whom I lived at Mr. Freeland's. I believe we would have died for each other. We never undertook to do any thing, of any importance, without a mutual consultation. We never moved separately. We were one; and as much so by our tempers and dispositions, as by the mutual hardships to which we were necessarily subjected by our condition as slaves.

At the close of the year 1834, Mr. Freeland again hired me of my master, for the year 1835. But, by this time, I began to want to live *upon free land* as well as *with Freeland;* and I was no longer content, therefore, to live with him or any other slave-holder. I began, with the commencement of the year, to prepare myself for a final struggle, which should decide my fate one way or the other. My tendency was upward. I was fast approaching manhood, and year after year had passed, and I was still a slave. These thoughts roused me—I must do something. I therefore resolved that 1835 should not pass without witnessing an attempt, on my part, to secure my liberty. But I was not willing to cherish this determination alone. My fellow-slaves were dear to me. I was anxious to have them participate with me in this, my life-giving determination. I therefore, though with great prudence, commenced early to ascertain their views and feelings in regard to their condition, and to imbue their minds with thoughts of freedom. I bent myself to devising ways and means for our escape, and meanwhile strove, on all fitting occasions, to impress them with the gross fraud and inhumanity of slavery. I went first to Henry, next to John, then to the others. I found, in them all, warm hearts and noble spirits. They were ready to hear, and ready to act when a feasible plan should be proposed. This was what I wanted. I talked to them of our want of manhood, if we submitted to our enslavement without at least one noble effort to be free. We met often, and consulted frequently, and told our hopes and fears, recounted the difficulties, real and imagined, which we should be called on to meet. At times we were almost disposed to give up, and try to content ourselves with our wretched lot; at others, we were firm and unbending in our determination to go. Whenever we suggested any plan, there was shrinking —the odds were fearful. Our path was beset with the greatest obstacles; and if we succeeded in gaining the end of it, our right to be free was yet questionable—we were yet liable to be returned to bondage. We could see no spot, this side of the ocean, where we could be free. We knew nothing about Canada. Our knowledge of the north did not extend farther than New York; and to go there, and be forever harassed with the frightful liability of being returned to slavery—with the certainty of being treated tenfold worse than before—the thought was truly a horrible one, and one which it was not easy to overcome. The case sometimes stood thus: At every gate through which we were to pass, we saw a watchman—at every ferry a guard—on every bridge a sentinel—and in every wood a patrol. We were hemmed in upon every side. Here were the difficulties, real or imagined—the good to be sought, and the evil to be shunned. On the one hand, there stood slavery, a stern reality, glaring frightfully upon us—its robes already crimsoned with the blood of millions, and even now feasting itself greedily upon our own flesh. On the other hand, away back in the dim distance, under the flickering light of the north star, behind some craggy hill or snow-covered mountain, stood a doubtful freedom—half frozen—beckoning us to come and share its hospitality. This in itself was sometimes enough to stagger us; but when we permitted ourselves to survey the road, we were frequently appalled. Upon either side we saw grim death, assuming the most horrid shapes. Now it was starvation, causing us to eat our own flesh;—now we were contending with the waves, and were drowned;—now we were overtaken, and torn to pieces by the fangs of the terrible bloodhound. We were stung by scorpions, chased by wild beasts, bitten by snakes, and finally, after having nearly reached the desired spot,—after swimming rivers, encountering wild beasts, sleeping in the woods, suffering hunger and nakedness,—we were overtaken by our pursuers, and, in our resistance, we were shot dead upon the spot! I say, this picture sometimes appalled us, and made us

"rather bear those ills we had,
Than fly to others, that we knew not of."

In coming to a fixed determination to run away, we did more than Patrick Henry, when he resolved upon liberty or death. With us it was a doubtful liberty at most, and almost certain death if we failed. For my part, I should prefer death to hopeless bondage.

Sandy, one of our number, gave up the notion, but still encouraged us. Our company then consisted of Henry Harris, John Harris, Henry Bailey, Charles Roberts, and myself. Henry Bailey was my uncle, and belonged to my master. Charles married my aunt: he belonged to my master's father-in-law, Mr. William Hamilton.

The plan we finally concluded upon was, to get a large canoe belonging to Mr. Hamilton, and upon the Saturday night previous to Easter holidays, paddle directly up the Chesapeake Bay. On our arrival at the head of the bay, a distance of seventy or eighty miles from where we lived, it was our purpose to turn our canoe adrift, and follow the guidance of the north star till we got beyond the limits of Maryland. Our reason for taking the water route was, that we were less liable to be suspected as runaways; we hoped to be regarded as fishermen; whereas, if we should take the land route, we should be subjected to interruptions of almost every kind. Any one having a white face, and being so disposed, could stop us, and subject us to examination.

The week before our intended start, I wrote several protections, one for each of us. As well as I can remember, they were in the following words, to wit:—

"This is to certify that I, the undersigned, have given the bearer, my servant, full liberty to go to Baltimore, and spend the Easter holidays. Written with mine own hand, &c., 1835.
"WILLIAM HAMILTON,
"Near St. Michael's, in Talbot county, Maryland."

We were not going to Baltimore; but, in going up the bay, we went toward Baltimore, and these protections were only intended to protect us while on the bay.

As the time drew near for our departure, our anxiety became more and more intense. It was truly a matter of life and death with us. The strength of our determination was about to be fully tested. At this time, I was very active in explaining every difficulty, removing every doubt, dispelling every fear, and inspiring all with the firmness indispensable to success in our undertaking; assuring them that half was gained the instant we made the move; we had talked long enough; we were now ready to move; if not now, we never should be; and if we did not intend to move now, we had as well fold our arms, sit down, and acknowledge ourselves fit only to be slaves. This none of us were prepared to acknowledge. Every man stood firm; and at our last meeting, we pledged ourselves afresh, in the most solemn manner, that, at the time appointed, we would certainly start in pursuit of freedom. This was in the middle of the week, at the end of which we were to be off. We went, as usual, to our several fields of labor, but with bosoms highly agitated with thoughts of our truly hazardous undertaking. We tried to conceal our feelings as much as possible; and I think we succeeded very well.

After a painful waiting, the Saturday morning, whose night was to witness our departure, came. I hailed it with joy, bring what of sadness it might. Friday night was a sleepless one for me. I probably felt more anxious than the rest, because I was, by common consent, at the head of the whole affair. The responsibility of success or failure lay heavily upon me. The glory of the one, and the confusion of the other, were alike mine. The first two hours of that morning were such as I never experienced before, and hope never to again. Early in the morning, we went, as usual, to the field. We were spreading manure; and all at once, while thus engaged, I was overwhelmed with an indescribable feeling, in the fulness of which I turned to Sandy, who was near by, and said, "We are betrayed!" "Well," said he, "that thought has this moment struck me." We said no more. I was never more certain of any thing.

The horn was blown as usual, and we went up from the field to the house for breakfast. I went for the form more than for want of any thing to eat that morning. Just as I got to the house, in looking out at the lane gate, I saw four white men, with two colored men. The white men were on horseback, and the colored ones were walking behind, as if tied. I watched them a few moments till they got up to our lane gate. Here they halted, and tied the colored men to the gatepost. I was not yet certain as to what the matter was. In a few moments, in rode Mr. Hamilton, with a speed betokening great excitement. He came to the door, and inquired if Master William was in. He was told he was at the barn. Mr. Hamilton, without dismounting, rode up to the barn with extraordinary speed. In a few moments, he and Mr. Freeland returned to the house. By this time, the three constables rode up, and in great haste dismounted, tied their horses, and met Master William and Mr. Hamilton returning from the barn; and after talking awhile, they all walked up to the kitchen door. There was no one in the kitchen but myself and John. Henry and Sandy were up at the barn. Mr. Freeland put his head in at the door, and called me by name, saying, there were some gentlemen at the door who wished to see me. I stepped to the door, and inquired what they wanted. They at once seized me, and, without giving me any satisfaction, tied me—lashing my hands closely together. I insisted upon knowing what the matter was. They at length said, that they had learned I had been in a "scrape," and that I was to be examined before my master; and if their information proved false, I should not be hurt.

In a few moments, they succeeded in tying John. They then turned to Henry, who had by this time returned, and commanded him to cross his hands. "I won't!" said Henry, in a firm tone indicating his readiness to meet the consequences of his refusal. "Won't you?" said Tom Graham, the constable. "No, I won't!" said Henry, in a still stronger tone. With this, two of the constables pulled out their shining pistols, and swore, by their Creator, that they would make him cross his hands or kill him. Each cocked his pistol, and, with fingers on the trigger, walked up to Henry, saying, at the same time, if he did not cross his hands, they would blow his damned heart out. "Shoot me, shoot me!" said Henry; "you can't kill me but once. Shoot, shoot,—and be damned! *I won't be tied!*" This he said in a tone of loud defiance; and at the same time, with a motion as quick as lightning, he with one single stroke dashed the pistols from the hand of each constable. As he did this, all hands fell upon him, and after beating him some time, they finally overpowered him, and got him tied.

During the scuffle, I managed, I know not how, to get my pass out, and, without being discovered, put it into the fire. We were all now tied; and just as we were to leave for Easton jail, Betsy Freeland, mother of William Freeland, came to the door with her hands full of biscuits, and divided them between Henry and John. She then delivered herself of a speech, to the following effect:—addressing herself to me, she said, *"You devil! You yellow devil!* it was you that put it into the heads of Henry and John to run away. But for you, you long-legged mulatto devil! Henry nor John would never have thought of such a thing." I made no reply, and was immediately hurried off towards St. Michael's. Just a moment previous to the scuffle with Henry, Mr. Hamilton suggested the propriety of making a search for the protections which he had understood Frederick had written for himself and the rest. But, just at the moment he was about carrying his proposal into effect, his aid was needed in helping to tie Henry; and the excitement attending the scuffle caused them either to forget, or to deem it unsafe, under the circumstances, to search. So we were not yet convicted of the intention to run away.

When we got about half way to St. Michael's, while the constables having us in charge were looking ahead, Henry inquired of me what he should do with his pass. I told him to eat it with his biscuit, and own nothing; and we passed the word around, *"Own nothing"*; and *"Own nothing!"* said we all. Our confidence in each other was unshaken. We were resolved to succeed or fail together, after the calamity had befallen us as much as before. We were now prepared for any thing. We were to be dragged that morning fifteen miles behind horses, and then to be placed in the Easton jail. When we reached St. Michael's, we underwent a sort of examination. We all denied that we ever intended to run away. We did this more to bring out the evidence against us, than from any hope of getting clear of being sold; for, as I have said, we were ready for that. The fact was, we cared but little where we went, so we went together. Our greatest concern was about separation. We dreaded that more than any thing this side of death. We found the evidence against us to be the testimony of one person; our master would not tell who it was; but we came to a unanimous decision among ourselves as to who their informant was. We were sent off to the jail at Easton. When we got there, we were delivered up to the sheriff, Mr. Joseph Graham, and by him placed in jail. Henry, John, and myself, were placed in one room together —Charles, and Henry Bailey, in another. Their object in separating us was to hinder concert.

We had been in jail scarcely twenty minutes, when a swarm of slave traders, and agents for slave traders, flocked into jail to look at us, and to ascertain if we were for sale. Such a set of beings I never saw before! I felt myself surrounded by so many fiends from perdition. A band of pirates never looked more like their father, the devil. They laughed and grinned over us, saying, "Ah, my boys! we have got you, haven't we?" And after taunting us in various ways, they one by one went into an examination of us, with intent to ascertain our value. They would impudently ask us if we would not like to have them for our masters. We would make them no answer, and leave them to find out as best they could.

Then they would curse and swear at us, telling us that they could take the devil out of us in a very little while, if we were only in their hands.

While in jail, we found ourselves in much more comfortable quarters than we expected when we went there. We did not get much to eat, nor that which was very good; but we had a good clean room, from the windows of which we could see what was going on in the street, which was very much better than though we had been placed in one of the dark, damp cells. Upon the whole, we got along very well, so far as the jail and its keeper were concerned. Immediately after the holidays were over, contrary to all our expectations, Mr. Hamilton and Mr. Freeland came up to Easton, and took Charles, the two Henrys, and John, out of jail, and carried them home, leaving me alone. I regarded this separation as a final one. It caused me more pain than any thing else in the whole transaction. I was ready for any thing rather than separation. I supposed that they had consulted together, and had decided that, as I was the whole cause of the intention of the others to run away, it was hard to make the innocent suffer with the guilty; and that they had, therefore, concluded to take the others home, and sell me, as a warning to the others that remained. It is due to the noble Henry to say, he seemed almost as reluctant at leaving the prison as at leaving home to come to the prison. But we knew we should, in all probability, be separated, if we were sold; and since he was in their hands, he concluded to go peaceably home.

I was now left to my fate. I was all alone, and within the walls of a stone prison. But a few days before, and I was full of hope. I expected to have been safe in a land of freedom; but now I was covered with gloom, sunk down to the utmost despair. I thought the possibility of freedom was gone. I was kept in this way about one week, at the end of which, Captain Auld, my master, to my surprise and utter astonishment, came up, and took me out, with the intention of sending me, with a gentleman of his acquaintance, into Alabama. But, from some cause or other, he did not send me to Alabama, but concluded to send me back to Baltimore, to live again with his brother Hugh, and to learn a trade.

Thus, after an absence of three years and one month, I was once more permitted to return to my old home at Baltimore. My master sent me away, because there existed against me a very great prejudice in the community, and he feared I might be killed.

In a few weeks after I went to Baltimore, Master Hugh hired me to Mr. William Gardner, an extensive ship-builder, on Fell's Point. I was put there to learn how to calk. It, however, proved a very unfavorable place for the accomplishment of this object. Mr. Gardner was engaged that spring in building two large man-of-war brigs, professedly for the Mexican government. The vessels were to be launched in the July of that year, and in failure thereof, Mr. Gardner was to lose a considerable sum; so that when I entered, all was hurry. There was no time to learn any thing. Every man had to do that which he knew how to do. In entering the shipyard, my orders from Mr. Gardner were, to do whatever the carpenters commanded me to do. This was placing me at the beck and call of about seventy-five men. I was to regard all these as master. Their word was to be my law. My situation was a most trying one. At times I needed a dozen pair of hands. I was called a dozen ways in the space of a single minute. Three or four voices would strike my ear at the same moment. It was—"Fred., come help me to cant this timber here."—Fred., come carry this timber yonder."—Fred., bring that roller here."—"Fred, go get a fresh can of water."—Fred., come help saw off the end of this timber."—"Fred., go quick, and get the crowbar."—"Fred., hold on the end of this fall."—"Fred., go to the blacksmith's shop, and get a new punch."—"Hurra, Fred.! run and bring me a cold chisel."—"I say, Fred., bear a hand, and get up a fire as quick as lightning under that steam-box."—"Halloo, nigger! come, turn this grindstone."—"Come, come! move, move! and *bowse* this timber forward."—"I say, darky, blast your eyes, why don't you heat up some pitch?"—"Halloo! halloo! halloo!" (Three voices at the same time.) "Come here!—Go there!—Hold on where you are! Damn you, if you move, I'll knock your brains out!"

This was my school for eight months; and I might have remained there longer, but for a most horrid fight I had with four of the white apprentices, in which my left eye was nearly knocked out, and I was horribly mangled in other respects. The facts in the case were these: Until a very little while after I went there, white and black ship-carpenters worked side by side, and no one seemed to see any impropriety in it. All hands seemed to be very well satisfied. Many of the black carpenters were freemen. Things seemed to be going on very well. All at once, the white carpenters knocked off, and said they would not work with free colored workmen. Their reason for this, as alleged, was, that if free colored carpenters were encouraged, they would soon take the trade into their own hands, and poor white men would be thrown out of employment. They therefore felt called upon at once to put a stop to it. And, taking advantage of Mr. Gardner's necessities, they broke off, swearing they would work no longer, unless he would discharge his black carpenters. Now, though this did not extend to me in form, it did reach me in fact. My fellow-apprentices very soon began to feel it degrading to them to work with me. They began to put on airs, and talk about the "niggers" taking the country, saying we all ought to be killed; and, being encouraged by the journeymen, they commenced making my condition as hard as they could, by hectoring me around, and sometimes striking me. I, of course, kept the vow I made after the fight with Mr. Covey, and struck back again, regardless of consequences; and while I kept them from combining, I succeeded very well; for I could whip the whole of them, taking them separately. They, however, at length combined, and came upon me, armed with sticks, stones, and heavy handspikes. One came in front with a half brick. There was one at each side of me, and one behind me. While I was attending to those in front, and on either side, the one behind ran up with the handspike, and struck me a heavy blow upon the head. It stunned me. I fell, and with this they all ran upon me, and fell to beating me with their fists. I let them lay on for a while, gathering strength. In an instant, I gave a sudden surge, and rose to my hands and knees. Just as I did that, one of their number gave me, with his heavy boot, a powerful kick in the left eye. My eyeball seemed to have burst. When they saw my eye closed, and badly swollen, they left me. With this I seized the handspike, and for a time pursued them. But here the carpenters interfered, and I thought I might as well give it up. It was impossible to stand my hand against so many. All this took place in sight of not less than fifty white ship-carpenters, and not one interposed a friendly word; but some cried, "Kill the damned nigger! Kill him! kill him! He struck a white person." I found my only chance for life was in flight. I succeeded in getting away without an additional blow, and barely so; for to strike a white man is death by Lynch law,—and that was the law in Mr. Gardner's shipyard nor is there much of any other out of Mr. Gardner's ship-yard.

I went directly home, and told the story of my wrongs to Master Hugh; and I am happy to say of him, irreligous as he was, his conduct was heavenly, compared with that of his brother Thomas under similar circumstances. He listened attentively to my narration of the circumstances leading to the savage outrage, and gave many proofs of his strong indignation at it. The heart of my once overkind mistress was again melted into pity. My puffed-out eye and blood-covered face moved her to tears. She took a chair by me, washed the blood from my face, and, with a mother's tenderness, bound up my head, covering the wounded eye with a lean piece of fresh beef. It was almost compensation for my suffering to witness, once more, a manifestation of kindness from this, my once affectionate old mistress. Master Hugh was very much enraged. He gave expression to his feelings by pouring out curses upon the heads of those who did the deed. As soon as I got a little the better of my bruises, he took me with him to Esquire Watson's, on Bond Street, to see what could be done about the matter. Mr. Watson inquired who saw the assault committed. Master Hugh told him it was done in Mr. Gardner's ship-yard, at midday, where there were a large company of men at work. "As to that," he said, "the deed was done, and there was no question as to who did it." His answer was, he could do nothing in the case, unless some white man would come forward and testify. He could issue no warrant on my word. If I had been killed in the presence of a thousand colored people, their testimony combined would have been insufficient to have arrested one of the murderers. Master Hugh, for once, was compelled to say this state of things was too bad. Of course, it was impossible to get any white man to volunteer his testimony in my behalf, and against the white young men. Even those who may have sympathized with me were not prepared to do this. It required a degree of courage unknown to them to do so; for just at that time, the slightest manifestation of humanity toward a colored person was denounced as abolitionism, and that name subjected its bearer to frightful liabilities. The watchwords of the bloody-minded in that region, and in those days were, "Damn the abolitionists!" and "Damn the niggers!" There was nothing done, and probably nothing would have been done if I had been killed. Such was, and such remains, the state of things in the Christian city of Baltimore.

Master Hugh, finding he could get no redress, refused to let me go back again to Mr. Gardner. He kept me himself, and his wife dressed my wound till I was again restored to health. He then took me into the ship-yard of which he was foreman, in the employment of Mr. Walter Price. There I was immediately set to calking, and very soon learned the art of using my mallet and irons. In the course of one year from the time I left Mr. Gardner's, I was able to command the highest wages given to the most experienced calkers. I was now of some importance to my master. I was bringing him from six to seven dollars per week. I sometimes brought him nine dollars per week: my wages were a dollar and a half a day. After learning how to calk, I sought my own employment, made my own contracts, and collected the money which I earned. My pathway became much more smooth than before; my condition was now much more comfortable. When I could get no calking to do, I did nothing. During these leisure times, those old notions about freedom would steal over me again. When in Mr. Gardner's employment, I was kept in such a perpetual whirl of excitement, I could think of nothing, scarcely, but my life; and in thinking of my life, I almost forgot my liberty. I have observed this in my experience of slavery,—that whenever my condition was improved, instead of its increasing my contentment, it only increased my desire to be free, and set me to thinking of plans to gain my freedom. I have found that, to make a contented slave, it is necessary to make a thoughtless one. It is necessary to darken his moral and mental vision, and, as far as possible, to annihilate the power of reason. He must be able to detect no inconsistencies in slavery; he must be made to feel that slavery is right; and he can be brought to that only when he ceases to be a man.

I was now getting, as I have said, one dollar and fifty cents per day. I contracted for it; I earned it; it was paid to me; it was rightfully my own; yet, upon each returning Saturday night, I was compelled to deliver every cent of that money to Master Hugh. And why? Not because he earned it,—not because he had any hand in earning it,—not because I owed it to him,—nor because he possessed the slightest shadow of a right to it; but solely because he had the power to compel me to give it up. The right of the grim-visaged pirate upon the high seas is exactly the same.

JAMES WELDON JOHNSON (1871–1938)

A major figure in the creation and development of Negro American literature and culture, James Weldon Johnson contributed in many ways: as a poet and songwriter, novelist, es-

sayist and critic, collector of spirituals, pioneer anthologist and interpreter of Negro poetry, pioneer student of the history of the Negro in the drama, educator, and active participant in the early development of the civil rights movement. He was born in Jacksonville, Florida, went to Atlanta University, and returned to Jacksonville as a teacher and public-school principal. He was the first Negro to pass the Florida bar examination but did not devote his energies to the practice of law. He wrote songs which his composer brother, Rosamond, set to music. They both went to New York in 1901 and achieved success in musical comedy. Johnson also pursued the study of literature and drama at Columbia University. From 1906 to 1913 he was in the U.S. diplomatic service as a consul, first in Venezuela and later in Nicaragua, and, while in the consular service, he wrote his landmark novel The Autobiography of an Ex-Colored Man *(1912). On returning to the United States, he became associated with the National Association for the Advancement of Colored People. He served as Field Secretary of the N.A.A.C.P. from 1916 to 1920, and as General Secretary from 1920 to 1930. During these years he became a recognized poet, collected and published* The Book of American Negro Poetry *and, with his brother, edited* The Books of American Negro Spirituals. *In 1930 he was appointed Professor of Creative Literature at Fisk University, in Nashville, Tennessee, and also served as a visiting professor at New York University. His autobiography,* Along This Way, *from which we present selected episodes, was published in 1933.*

Along This Way (Selected Episodes)

I was born June 17, 1871, in the old house on the corner; but I have no recollection of having lived in it. Before I could be aware of such a thing my father had built a new house near the middle of his lot. In this new house was formed my first consciousness of home. My childish idea of it was that it was a great mansion. I saw nothing in the neighborhood that surpassed it in splendor. Of course, it was only a neat cottage. The house had three bedrooms, a parlor, and a kitchen. The four main rooms were situated, two on each side of a hall that ran through the center of the house. The kitchen, used also as a room in which the family ate, was at the rear of the house and opened on a porch that was an extension of the hall. On the front a broad piazza ran the width of the house.

Under the roof was an attic to which a narrow set of steps in one of the back rooms gave access.

But the house was painted, and there were glass windows and green blinds. Before long there were some flowers and trees. One of the first things my father did was to plant two maple trees at the front gate and a dozen or more orange trees in the yard. The maples managed to live; the orange trees, naturally, flourished. The hallway of the house was covered with a strip of oilcloth and the floors of the rooms with matting. There were curtains at the windows and some pictures on the walls. In the parlor there were two or three dozen books and a cottage organ. When I was seven or eight years old, the organ gave way to a square piano. It was a tinkling old instrument, but a source of rapturous pleasure. It is one of the indelible impressions on my mind. I can still remember just how the name "Bacon" looked, stamped in gold letters above the keyboard. There was a center marble-top table on which rested a big, illustrated Bible and a couple of photograph albums. In a corner stood a what-not filled with bric-a-brac and knickknacks. On a small stand was a glass-domed receptacle in which was a stuffed canary perched on a diminutive tree; on this stand there was also kept a stereoscope and an assortment of views photographed in various parts of the world. For my brother and me, in our childhood (my brother, John Rosamond, was born in the new house August 11, 1873), this room was an Aladdin's cave. We used to stand before the what-not and stake out our claims to the objects on its shelves with a "that's mine" and a "that's mine." We never tired of looking at the stereoscopic scenes, examining the photographs in the album, or putting the big Bible and other books on the floor and exploring for pictures. Two large conch shells decorated the ends of the hearth. We greatly admired their pink, polished inner surface; and loved to put them to our ears to hear the "roar of the sea" from their cavernous depths. But the undiminishing thrill was derived from our experiments on the piano.

When I was born, my mother was very ill, too ill to nurse me. Then she found a friend and neighbor in an unexpected quarter. Mrs. McCleary, her white neighbor who lived a block away, had a short while before given birth to a girl baby. When this baby was christened she was named Angel. The mother of Angel, hearing of my mother's plight, took me and nursed me at her breast until my mother had recovered sufficiently to give me her own milk. So it appears that in the land of black mammies I had a white one. Between her and me there existed an affectionate relation through all my childhood; and even in after years when I had grown up and moved away I never, up to the time of her death, went back to my old home without paying her a visit and taking her some small gift.

I do not intend to boast about a white mammy, for I have perceived bad taste in those Southern white people who are continually boasting about their black mammies. I know the temptation for them to do so is very strong, because the honor point on the escutcheon of Southern aristocracy, the *sine qua non* of a background of family, of good breeding and social prestige, in the South is the Black Mammy. Of course, many of the white people who boast of having had black mammies are romancing. Naturally, Negroes had black mammies, but black mammies for white people were expensive luxuries, and comparatively few white people had them.

When I was about a year old, my father made a trip to New York, taking my mother and me with him. It was during this visit that I developed from a creeping infant into a walking child. Without doubt, my mother welcomed this trip. She was, naturally, glad to see again the city and friends of her girlhood; and it is probable that she brought some pressure on my father to make another move—back to New York. If she did, it was without effect. I say she probably made some such effort because I know what a long time it took her to become reconciled to life in the South; in fact, she never did entirely. The New York of her childhood and youth was all the United States she knew. Latterly she had lived in a British colony under conditions that rendered the weight of race comparatively light. During the earlier days of her life in Jacksonville she had no adequate conception of her "place."

And so it was that one Sunday morning she went to worship at St. John's Episcopal Church. As one who had been a member of the choir of Christ Church Cathedral she went quite innocently. She went, in fact, not knowing any better. In the chanting of the service her soprano voice rang out clear and beautiful, and necks were craned to discover the singer. On leaving the church she was politely but definitely informed that the St. John's congregation would prefer to have her worship the Lord elsewhere. Certainly she never went back to St. John's nor to any other Episcopal church; she followed her mother and joined Ebenezer, the colored Methodist Episcopal Church in Jacksonville, and became the choir leader.

Racially she continued to be a nonconformist and a rebel.

A decade or so after the St. John's Church incident Lemuel W. Livingston, a student at Cookman Institute, the Negro school in Jacksonville founded and maintained by the Methodist Church (North), was appointed as a cadet to West Point. Livingston passed his written examinations, and the colored people were exultant. The members of Ebenezer Church gave a benefit that netted for him a purse of several hundred dollars. There was good reason for a show of pride; Livingston was a handsome, bronze-colored boy with a high reputation as a student, and appeared to be ideal material for a soldier and officer. But at the Academy he was turned down. The examining officials there stated that his eyesight was in some manner defective. The news that Livingston had been denied admission to West Point was given out at a Sunday service at Ebenezer Church. When at the same service the minister announced "America" as a hymn, my mother refused to sing it.

My mother was artistic and more or less impractical and in my father's opinion had absolutely no sense about money. She was a splendid singer and she had a talent for drawing. One day when I was about fifteen years old, she revealed to me that she had written verse, and showed me a thin sheaf of poems copied out in her almost perfect handwriting. She was intelligent and possessed a quick though limited sense of humor. But the limitation of her sense of humor was quite the normal one: she had no relish for a joke whose butt was herself or her children; my father had the rarer capacity for laughing even at himself. . . .

My father was a quiet, unpretentious man. He was naturally conservative and cautious, and generally displayed common sense in what he said and did. He never went to school; such education as he had was self-acquired. Later in life, I appreciated the fact that his self-development was little less than remarkable. He had a knowledge of general affairs and was familiar with many of the chief events and characters in the history of the world. I have the old sheepskin bound volume of *Plutarch's Lives* which he owned before I was born. He had gained by study a working knowledge of the Spanish language; this he had done to increase his value as a hotel employee. When he was a young man in New York, he attended the theater a good deal, and, before I was aware of where the lines came from or of what they meant, I used to go around the house parroting after him certain snatches from the Shakespearean plays. I particularly recall: "To be or not to be; that is the question" and "A horse! a horse! my kingdom for a horse!"

The quality in my father that impressed me most was his high and rigid sense of honesty. I simply could not conceive of him as a party to any monetary transaction that was questionable in the least. I think he got his greatest satisfaction in life out of the reputation he had built up as a man of probity, and took his greatest pride in the consequent credit standing that he enjoyed. This element in his character was a source of gratification to my pride and also, more than once, to my needs. One instance of double gratification was when I was at home in Jacksonville in 1910, just a few weeks before I was to be married. My father and mother discussed an appropriate gift to me and, finally, to my undisguised joy, decided upon a check for a thousand dollars. My father, excusably, did not have a thousand dollars in cash; but he said to me, "My boy, we'll go down town tomorrow and see if we can get the money." We went the next morning to one of the principal banks and my father spoke with John C. L'Engle, the president. The transaction was put through without any delay; he got the money on his note, without collateral security, without even an endorser. I was as proud to see him able to do such a thing as I was glad to have the money. . . .

Atlanta disappointed me. It was a larger city than Jacksonville, but did not seem to me to be nearly so attractive. Many of the thoroughfares were still red clay roads. It was a long time before I grew accustomed to the bloody aspect of Atlanta's highways. Trees were rare and there was no city park or square within walking distance. The city was neither picturesque nor smart; it was merely drab. Atlanta University was a pleasant relief. The Confederate ramparts on the hill where the school was built had been leveled, the ground terraced, and grass and avenues of trees planted. The three main buildings were ivy-covered. Here was a spot fresh and beautiful, a rest for the eyes from what surrounded it, a green island in a dull, red sea. The University, as I was soon to learn, was a little world in itself, with ideas of social conduct and of the approach to life distinct from those of the city within which it was situated. When students or teachers stepped off the campus into West Mitchell Street, they underwent as great a transition as would have resulted from being instantaneously shot from a Boston drawing room into the wilds of Borneo. They had to make an immediate readjustment of many of their fundamental notions about life. When I was at the University, there were twenty-odd teachers, of whom all, except four, were white. These white teachers by eating at table with the students rendered themselves "unclean," not fit to sit at table with any Atlanta white family. The president was Horace Bumstead, a cultured gentleman, educated at Yale and in Germany, yet there was only one white door in all Atlanta thrown open to him socially, the door of a German family. No observance of caste in India was more cruelly rigid. The year before I entered, the state of Georgia had cut off its annual appropriation of $8000 because the school stood by its principles and refused to exclude the children of the white teachers from the regular classes.

I was at the University only a short time before I began to get an insight into the ramifications of race prejudice and an understanding of the American race problem. Indeed, it was in this early period that I received my initiation into the arcana of "race." I perceived that education for me meant, fundamentally: preparation to meet the tasks and exigencies of life as a Negro, a realization of the peculiar responsibilities due to my own racial group, and a comprehension of the application of American democracy to Negro citizens. Of course, I had not been entirely ignorant of these conditions and requirements, but now they rose before me in such sudden magnitude as to seem absolutely new knowledge. This knowledge was no part of classroom instruction—the college course at Atlanta University was practically the old academic course at Yale; the founder of the school was Edmund Asa Ware, a Yale man, and the two following presidents were graduates of Yale—it was simply in the spirit of the institution; the atmosphere of the place was charged with it. Students talked "race." It was the subject of essays, orations, and debates. Nearly all that was acquired, mental and moral, was destined to be fitted into a particular system of which "race" was the center. . . .

I now began to get my bearings with regard to the world and particularly with regard to my own country. I began to get the full understanding of my relationship to America, and to take on my share of the peculiar responsibilities and burdens additional to those of the common lot, which every Negro in the United States is compelled to carry. I began my mental and spiritual training to meet and cope not only with the hardships that are common, but with planned wrong, concerted injustice, and applied prejudice. Here was a deepening, but narrowing experience; an experience so narrowing that the inner problem of a Negro in America becomes that of not allowing it to choke and suffocate him. I am glad that this fuller impact of the situation came to me as late as it did, when my apprehension of it could be more or less objective.

As an American Negro, I consider the most fortunate thing
in my whole life to be the fact that through childhood I was
reared free from undue fear of or esteem for white people as
a race; otherwise, the deeper implications of American race
prejudice might have become a part of my subconscious as
well as of my conscious self.

I began also in this period to find myself, to think of life
not only as it touched me from without but also as it moved
me from within. I went in for reading, and spent many of the
winter afternoons that settle down so drearily on the bleak
hills of North Georgia absorbed in a book. The university library was then the Graves Memorial Library. It contained
ten thousand or so volumes, an array of books that seemed
infinite to me. Many of the titles snared me, but I was often
disappointed to find that the books were written from the
point of view of divine revelation and Christian dogma or
with a bald moral purpose. Among all the books in the
Graves Library it was from books of fiction that I gained the
greatest satisfaction. I read more Dickens; I read George
Eliot; I read *Vanity Fair*, and that jewel among novels, *Lorna
Doone*. It was during this period that I also read with burning interest Alphonse Daudet's *Sapho*, a book which was not
in the library but was owned by one of the boys and circulated until it was all but worn out. The episode in which
Sapho is carried up the flight of stairs left a disquieting
impression on my mind that lingered long.

Before I left Stanton I had begun to scribble. I had written
a story about my first plug (derby) hat. Mr. Artrell thought
it was fine, and it made a hit when I read it before the
school. Now an impulse set me at writing poetry, and I filled
several notebooks with verses. I looked over these juvenilia
recently and noted that the first of my poems opened with
these three lines:

Miserable, miserable, weary of life,
Worn with its turmoil, its din and its strife,
And with its burden of grief.

I did not follow this vein. Perhaps even then I sensed that
there was already an over-supply of poetry by people who
mistake a torpid liver for a broken heart, and frustrated sex
desires for yearnings of the soul. I wrote a lot of verses lam-
pooning certain students and teachers and conditions on the
campus. However, the greater part of my output consisted of
rather ardent love poems. A number of these latter circulated
with success in North Hall, and brought me considerable
prestige as a gallant. It has struck me that the potency pos-

sessed by a few, fairly well written lines of passionate poetry is truly astounding, and altogether disproportionate to what really goes into the process of producing them. It is probable that the innate hostility of the average man toward the poet has its basis in this fact. . . .

In the fall Rosamond * and I went back to our teaching in Jacksonville and to do more writing. Before we left New York we met Bob Cole. Bob was one of the most talented and versatile Negroes ever connected with the stage. He could write a play, stage it, and play a part. Although he was not a trained musician, he was the originator of a long list of catchy songs. We also met Williams and Walker and Ernest Hogan, the comedians; Will Marion Cook, the Negro composer; Harry T. Burleigh, the musician and singer; and a number of others, doing pioneer work in Negro theatricals. I attended rehearsals of two Negro companies that were preparing for the coming season, and I took in something of night life in Negro Bohemia, then flourishing in the old Tenderloin District. Into one of the rehearsals I was attending walked Paul Laurence Dunbar, the Negro poet. The year before he had written in collaboration with Cook an operetta called, *Clorindy—The Origin of the Cakewalk,* which had been produced with an all-Negro cast and Ernest Hogan as star by George Lederer at the Casino Theater Roof Garden, and had run with great success the entire summer. Mr. Lederer was the principal and most skillful musical play producer of the period. His production, *The Belle of New York,* with Dan Daly and Edna May, was one of the greatest successes the American stage had seen. But he learned some new things from *Clorindy.* He judged correctly that the practice of the Negro chorus, to dance strenuously and sing at the same time, if adapted by the white stage would be a profitable novelty; so he departed considerably from the model of the easy, leisurely movements of the English light opera chorus. He also judged that some injection of Negro syncopated music would produce a like result. Mr. Lederer was, at least, the grandfather of the modern American musical play. Ironi-

---

*James Weldon Johnson's brother, a composer and musician. They collaborated on many occasions as a songwriting team, producing popular tunes and songs for Broadway musicals. They worked together as co-editors of *The Book of American Negro Spirituals* (1925) and *The Second Book of Negro Spirituals* (1926), which included the words and music (voice and piano arrangement) for 124 spirituals—*Ed.*

cally, these adaptations from the Negro stage, first made years ago, give many present-day critics reason for condemning Negro musical comedy on the ground that it is too slavish an imitation of the white product. I had met Dunbar five years before, when he was almost unknown; now he was at the height of his fame. When he walked into the hall, those who knew him rushed to welcome him; among those who did not know him personally there were awed whispers. But it did not appear that celebrity had puffed him up; he did not meet the homage that was being shown him with anything but friendly and hearty response. There was no hint of vainglory in his bearing. He sat quiet and unassuming while the rehearsal proceeded. He was then twenty-seven years old, of medium height and slight of figure. His black, intelligent face was grave, almost sad, except when he smiled or laughed. But notwithstanding this lack of ostentation, there was on him the hallmark of distinction. He had an innate courtliness of manner, his speech was unaffectedly polished and brilliant, and he carried himself with that dignity of humility which never fails to produce a sense of the presence of greatness. Paul and I were together a great deal during those last few weeks. I was drawn to him and he to me; and a friendship that grew closer and lasted until his death. A day or two before I left he took me into Dutton's on 23rd Street, where he bought a copy of his *Lyrics of Lowly Life* and inscribed it for me. It is one of my most treasured books.

These glimpses of life that I caught during our last two or three weeks in New York were not wholly unfamiliar to Rosamond, but they showed me a new world—an alluring world, a tempting world, a world of greatly lessened restraints, a world of fascinating perils; but, above all, a world of tremendous artistic potentialities. Up to this time, outside of polemical essays on the race question, I had not written a single line that had any relation to the Negro. I now began to grope toward a realization of the importance of the American Negro's cultural background and his creative folk-art, and to speculate on the superstructure of conscious art that might be reared upon them. My first step in this general direction was taken in a song that Bob Cole, my brother, and I wrote in conjunction during the last days in New York. It was an attempt to bring a higher degree of artistry to Negro songs, especially with regard to the text. The Negro songs then the rage were known as "coon songs" and were concerned with jamborees of various sorts and the play of razors, with the gastronomical delights of chicken, pork chops and watermelon, and with the experiences of red-hot "mammas"

and their never too faithful "papas." These songs were for
the most part crude, raucous, bawdy, often obscene. Such elements frequently are excellencies in folk-songs, but rarely so
in conscious imitations. The song we did was a little love
song called *Louisiana Lize* and was forerunner of a style that
displaced the old "coon songs." We sold the singing rights to
May Irwin for fifty dollars—our first money earned. With the
check the three of us proceeded joyfully to the Garfield National Bank, then at Sixth Avenue and 23rd Street, where
Bob was slightly known. The paying teller looked at the
check and suggested we take it over on the next corner to the
Fifth Avenue Bank, on which it was drawn and have it
O.K.'d It is always disconcerting to have a bank teller shove
a check back to you, whatever his reasons may be, so we
went over to the other bank not without some misgivings.
The teller there looked at it and said, "Tell them over at the
Garfield Bank that the check would be good if it was for fifty
thousand dollars." Bob delivered the message. Next, we took
the manuscript to Jos. W. Stern and Co., who published the
song.

When I got back to Jacksonville I found that my artistic
ideas and plans were undergoing a revolution. Frankly, I was
floundering badly: the things I had been trying to do seemed
vapid and nonessential, and the thing I felt a yearning to do
was so nebulous that I couldn't take hold of it or even quite
make it out. In this state, satisfactory expression first came
through writing a short dialect poem. One night, just after I
had finished the poem, I was at Mr. McBeath's house talking
about school matters; then about books and literature. He
read me a long poem he had written on Lincoln—a Lincoln
poem, the expression of a Southern white man. I thought it
was good and told him so. I also thought but did not say that
there was yet to be written a great poem on Lincoln, the
expression of a Negro. Aloud, I repeated for him my dialect
poem, *Sence You Went Away*. He thought it was good
enough for me to try it on one of the important magazines. I
sent it to *Century*, and it was promptly accepted and printed.
Outside of what had appeared in Atlanta University periodicals and in the local newspapers, this was my first published
poem. Some years later my brother set this little poem to
music. It has proved to be one of the most worthwhile and
lasting songs he has written. It was first sung by Amato, the
Metropolitan Opera baritone; it was afterwards recorded for
the phonograph by John McCormack, with a violin obbligato
played by Kreisler; and was again recorded by Louis Grav-
eure and still again by Paul Robeson. It continues to find a

place on concert programs.

During the winter I wrote more dialect poems, some of them very trite, written with an eye on Broadway. Rosamond made some pretty songs out of these trivialities and put them aside for our next migration to New York. In the same winter Rosamond planned a concert such as had not before been given by or for colored people in Jacksonville. He brought Sidney Woodward down from Boston. The affair was successful, artistically and financially, beyond our expectations. The concert sent the level of musical entertainment among the colored people many degrees higher. Nor were its effects limited to the colored people; it was a treat for the hundred or so local white music lovers who were present, for, indeed, not all of them had before heard a tenor with Woodward's voice and technical finish.

A group of young men decided to hold on February 12 a celebration of Lincoln's birthday. I was put down for an address, which I began preparing; but I wanted to do something else also. My thoughts began buzzing round a central idea of writing a poem on Lincoln, but I couldn't net them. So I gave up the project as beyond me; at any rate, beyond me to carry out in so short a time; and my poem on Lincoln is still to be written. My central idea, however, took on another form. I talked over with my brother the thought I had in mind, and we planned to write a song to be sung as a part of the exercises. We planned, better still, to have it sung by schoolchildren—a chorus of five hundred voices.

I got my first line:—Lift ev'ry voice and sing. Not a startling line; but I worked along grinding out the next five. When, near the end of the first stanza, there came to me the lines:

Sing a song full of the faith that the dark past has taught us
Sing a song full of the hope that the present has brought us.

the spirit of the poem had taken hold of me. I finished the stanza and turned it over to Rosamond.

In composing the two other stanzas I did not use pen and paper. While my brother worked at his musical setting I paced back and forth on the front porch, repeating the lines over and over to myself, going through all of the agony and ecstasy of creating. As I worked through the opening and middle lines of the last stanza:

God of our weary years,
God of our silent tears,
Thou who hast brought us thus far on our way,

Thou who hast by Thy might
Let us into the light,
Keep us forever in the path, we pray;
Lest our feet stray from the places, our God, where we met Thee,
Lest, our hearts drunk with the wine of the world, we forget
    Thee . . . .

I could not keep back the tears, and made no effort to do so.
I was experiencing the transports of the poet's ecstasy. Fever-
ish ecstasy was followed by that contentment—that sense
of serene joy—which makes artistic creation the most complete of all human experiences.

When I had put the last stanza down on paper I at once
recognized the Kiplingesque touch in the two longer lines
quoted above; but I knew that in the stanza the American
Negro was, historically and spiritually, immanent; and I decided to let it stand as it was written.

As soon as Rosamond had finished his noble setting of the
poem he sent a copy of the manuscript to our publishers in
New York, requesting them to have a sufficient number of
mimeographed copies made for the use of the chorus. The
song was taught to the children and sung very effectively at
the celebration; and my brother and I went on with other
work. After we had permanently moved away from Jacksonville, both the song and the occasion passed out of our minds.
But the schoolchildren of Jacksonville kept singing the song;
some of them went off to other schools and kept singing it;
some of them became schoolteachers and taught it to their
pupils. Within twenty years the song was being sung in
schools and churches and on special occasions throughout the
South and in some other parts of the country. Within that
time the publishers had recopyrighted it and issued it in several arrangements. Later it was adopted by the National Association for the Advancement of Colored People, and is now
quite generally used throughout the country as the "Negro
National Hymn." The publishers consider it a valuable piece
of property; however, in traveling round I have commonly
found printed or typewritten copies of the words pasted in
the backs of hymnals and the songbooks used in Sunday
schools, Y.M.C.A.'s, and similar institutions; and I think that
is the method by which it gets its widest circulation. Recently
I spoke for the summer labor school at Bryn Mawr College
and was surprised to hear it fervently sung by the white students there and to see it in their mimeographed folio of
songs.

Nothing that I have done has paid me back so fully in satisfaction as being the part creator of this song. I am always

thrilled deeply when I hear it sung by Negro children. I am
lifted up on their voices, and I am also carried back and enabled to live through again the exquisite emotions I felt at the
birth of the song. My brother and I, in talking, have often
marveled at the results that have followed what we considered an incidental effort, an effort made under stress and with
no intention other than to meet the needs of a particular moment. The only comment we can make is that we wrote better than we knew. . . .

I went down to Atlanta University on the tenth anniversary
of my graduation to receive an honorary degree. There it was
that I first met W. E. B. Du Bois, who was now one of the
professors. The year before, he had issued *The Souls of Black
Folk* (a work which, I think, has had a greater effect upon
and within the Negro race in America than any other single
book published in this country since *Uncle Tom's Cabin*) and
was already a national figure. I had been deeply moved and
influenced by the book, and was anxious to meet the author.
I met a quite handsome and unpedantic young man—Dr. Du
Bois was then thirty-six. Indeed, it was, at first, slightly difficult to reconcile the brooding but intransigent spirit of *The
Souls of Black Folk* with this apparently so light-hearted
man, this man so abundantly endowed with the gift of laughter. I noted then what, through many years of close association, I have since learned well, and what the world knows not
at all: that Du Bois in battle is a stern, bitter, relentless fighter, who, when he has put aside his sword, is among his par-
icular friends the most jovial and fun-loving of men. This
quality has been a saving grace for him, but his lack of the
ability to unbend in his relations with people outside the
small circle has gained him the reputation of being cold, stiff,
supercilious, and has been a cause of criticism amongst even
his adherents. This disposition, due perhaps to an inhibition
of spontaneous impulse, has limited his scope of leadership to
less than what it might have been, in that it has hindered his
attracting and binding to himself a body of zealous liegemen
—one of the essentials to the headship of a popular or an un-
popular cause. The great influence Du Bois has exercised has
been due to the concentrated force of his ideas, with next to
no reinforcement from that wide appeal of personal magne-
tism which is generally a valuable asset of leaders of
men. . . .

I began earnest work on *The Autobiography of an Ex-Colored Man,* of which I had already made a first draft of the opening. The story developed in my mind more rapidly than I had expected that it would; at times, outrunning my speed in getting it down. The use of prose as a creative medium was new to me; and its latitude, its flexibility, its comprehensiveness, the variety of approaches it afforded for surmounting technical difficulties gave me a feeling of exhilaration, exhilaration similar to that which goes with freedom of motion. I turned over in my mind again and again my original idea of making the book anonymous. I also debated with myself the aptness of *The Autobiography of an Ex-Colored Man* as a title. Brander Matthews had expressed a liking for the title, but my brother had thought it was clumsy and too long; he had suggested *The Chameleon.* In the end, I stuck to the original idea of issuing the book without the author's name, and kept the title that had appealed to me first. But I have never been able to settle definitely for myself whether I was sagacious or not in these two decisions. When I chose the title, it was without the slightest doubt that its meaning would be perfectly clear to anyone; there were people, however, to whom it proved confusing. When the book was published (1912) most of the reviewers, though there were some doubters, accepted it as a human document. This was a tribute to the writing, for I had done the book with the intention of its being so taken. But, perhaps, it would have been more far-sighted had I originally affixed my name to it as a frank piece of fiction. But I did get a certain pleasure out of anonymity, that no acknowledged book could have given me. The authorship of the book excited the curiosity of literate colored people, and there was speculation among them as to who the writer might be—to every such group some colored man who had married white, and so coincided with the main point on which the story turned, is known. I had the experience of listening to some of these discussions. I had a rarer experience, that of being introduced to and talking with one man who tacitly admitted to those present that he was the author of the book. Only two or three people knew that I was the writer of the story—the publishers themselves never knew me personally; yet the fact gradually leaked out and spread. The first printed statement was made by George A. Towns, my classmate at Atlanta University, who wrote a piece in which he gave his reasons for thinking I was the man. When the book was republished,* I affixed my name to it, and Carl

* Alfred A. Knopf, New York, 1925.

Van Vechten was good enough to write an Introduction, and
in it to inform the reader that the story was not the story of
my life. Nevertheless, I continue to receive letters from persons who have read the book inquiring about this or that
phase of my life as told in it. That is, probably, one of the
reasons why I am writing the present book. . . .

Nineteen-seventeen was a busy year for me. Yet I made the
time to collect my published and unpublished poems and
issue them in a little volume entitled *Fifty Years and Other
Poems.* Brander Matthews wrote a word of introduction for
the book. In the middle of the summer, I attended a three-
day conference of the Intercollegiate Socialist Society that was
held at Belleport, Long Island. I was on the program, but I
did not make a talk on economic or social conditions; instead, I read a paper on the contribution of the Negro to
American culture.

Some of the contributions that the Negro has made to
America are quite obvious—for example, his contribution of
labor—and their importance, more or less, has long been recognized. But the idea of his being a generous contributor to
the common cultural store and a vital force in the formation
of American civilization was a new approach to the race
question.

The common-denominator opinion in the United States
about American Negroes is, I think, something like this:
these people are here; they are here to be shaped and
molded and made into something different and, of course,
better; they are here to be helped; here to be given something; in a word, they are beggars under the nation's table
waiting to be thrown the crumbs of civilization. However
true this may be, it is also true that the Negro has helped to
shape and mold and make America; that he has been a creator as well as a creature; that he has been a giver as well as a
receiver. It is, no doubt, startling to contemplate that America would not and could not be precisely the America it is,
except for the influence, often silent, but nevertheless potent,
that the Negro has exercised in its making. That influence has
been both active and passive. Any contemplation of the Negro's passive influence ought to make America uneasy. Estimate, if you can, the effect upon the making of the character
of the American people caused by the opportunity which the
Negro has involuntarily given the dominant majority to practice injustice, wrong, and brutality for three hundred years
with impunity upon a practically defenseless minority. There

can be no estimate of the moral damage done to every American community that has indulged in the bestial orgy of torturing and mutilating a human being and burning him alive. The active influences of the Negro have come out of his strength; his passive influences out of his weaknesses. And it would be well for the nation to remember that for the good of one's own soul, what he needs most to guard against, most to fear, in dealing with another, is that one's weakness, not his strength.

My paper, despite the fact that it was removed from the main topic of the conference, was received well, and gave rise to some interesting discussion. A young man, Herbert J. Seligmann, who was reporting the conference for the *New York Evening Post* was enthusiastic about it. He asked for my manuscript and made a summary of it for his newspaper. Paragraphs of his summary actually went round the world; they were copied in American and European periodicals, and I got clippings from as far away as South Africa and Australia. The statement that evoked the greatest interest—and some controversy—was that the only things artistic in America that have sprung from American soil, permeated American life, and been universally acknowledged as distinctively American, had been the creations of the American Negro.

I was, of course, speaking of the principal folk-art creations of the Negro—his folklore, collected by Joel Chandler Harris under the title of *Uncle Remus,* his dances, and his music, sacred and secular. Some years later, I modified that statement by excepting American skyscraper architecture. In making the original statement I certainly had no inention of disparaging the accomplishments of the other groups, the aboriginal Indians and the white groups. The Indians have wrought finely, and what they have done sprang from the soil of America; but it must be admitted that their art-creations have in no appreciable degree permeated American life. In all that the white groups have wrought, there is no artistic creation—with the exception noted above—born of the physical and spiritual forces at work peculiarly in America, none that has made a universal appeal as something distinctively American.

One other statement in Mr. Seligmann's summary of my paper which was widely copied was that the finest artistic contribution that this country could offer as its own to the world was the American Negro spirituals.

It is, however, in his lighter music that the Negro has given America its best-known distinctive form of art. I would make no extravagant claims for this music, but I say "form of art," without apology. This lighter music has been fused and then developed, chiefly by Jewish musicians, until it has become our national medium for expressing ourselves musically in popular form, and it bids fair to become a basic element in the future great American music. The part it plays in American life and its acceptance by the world at large cannot be ignored. It is to this music that America in general gives itself over in its leisure hours, when it is not engaged in the struggles imposed upon it by the exigencies of present-day American life. At these times, the Negro drags his captors captive. On occasions, I have been amazed and amused watching white people dancing to a Negro band in a Harlem cabaret; attempting to throw off the crusts and layers of inhibitions laid on by sophisticated civilization; striving to yield to the feel and experience of abandon; seeking to recapture a taste of primitive joy in life and living; trying to work their way back into that jungle which was the original Garden of Eden; in a word, doing their best to pass for colored. . . .

Often I am asked if I think the Negro will remain a racial entity or merge; and if I am in favor of amalgamation. I answer that, if I could have my wish, the Negro would retain his racial identity, with unhampered freedom to develop his own qualities—the best of those qualities American civilization is much in need of as a complement to its other qualities —and finally stand upon a plane with other American citizens. To convince America and the world that he was capable of doing this would be the greatest triumph he could wish and work for. But what *I* may wish and what others may not wish can have no effect on the elemental forces at work; and it appears to me that the result of those forces will, in time, be the blending of the Negro into the American Race of the future. It seems probable that, instead of developing them independently to the utmost, the Negro will fuse his qualities with those of the other groups in the making of the ultimate American people; and that he will add a tint to America's complexion and put a perceptible permanent wave in America's hair. It may be that nature plans to work out on the North American continent a geographical color scheme similar to that of Europe, with the Gulf of Mexico as our Mediterranean. My hope is that in the process the Negro will be not merely sucked up but, through his own advancement and development, will go in on a basis of equal partnership.

If I am wrong in these opinions and conclusions, if the Negro is always to be given a heavy handicap back of the common scratch, or if the antagonistic forces are destined to dominate and bar all forward movement, there will be only one way of salvation for the race that I can see, and that will be through the making of its isolation into a religion and the cultivation of a hard, keen, relentless hatred for everything white. Such a hatred would burn up all that is best in the Negro, but it would also offer the sole means that could enable him to maintain a saving degree of self-respect in the midst of his abasement.

But the damage of such a course would not be limited to the Negro. If the Negro is made to fail, America fails with him. If America wishes to make democratic institutions secure, she must deal with this question right and righteously. For it is in the nature of a truism to say that this country can actually have no more democracy than it accords and guarantees to the humblest and weakest citizen.

It is both a necessity and to the advantage of America that she deal with this question right and righteously; for the well-being of the nation as well as that of the Negro depends upon taking that course. And she must bear in mind that it is a question which can be neither avoided nor postponed; it is not distant in position or time; it is immediately at hand and imminent; it must be squarely met and answered. And it cannot be so met and answered by the mere mouthings of the worn platitudes of humanitarianism, of formal religion, or of abstract democracy. For the Negroes directly concerned are not in far-off Africa; they are in and within our midst.

RICHARD WRIGHT (1908–1960)

A biographical note on Richard Wright appears in the Fiction section (see p. 113-114). His autobiographical essay, which follows, was first published in 1937 in American Stuff, *a collection of writing by members of the Federal Writers' Project.*

The Ethics of Living Jim Crow: An Autobiographical Sketch

My first lesson in how to live as a Negro came when I was quite small. We were living in Arkansas. Our house stood behind the railroad tracks. Its skimpy yard was paved with black cinders. Nothing green ever grew in that yard. The only touch of green we could see was far away, beyond the tracks, over where the white folks lived. But cinders were good enough for me and I never missed the green growing things. And anyhow cinders were fine weapons. You could always have a nice hot war with huge black cinders. All you had to do was crouch behind the brick pillars of a house with your hands full of gritty ammunition. And the first woolly black head you saw pop out from behind another row of pillars was your target. You tried your very best to knock it off. It was great fun.

I never fully realized the appalling disadvantages of a cinder environment till one day the gang to which I belonged found itself engaged in a war with the white boys who lived beyond the tracks. As usual we laid down our cinder barrage, thinking that this would wipe the white boys out. But they replied with a steady bombardment of broken bottles. We doubled our cinder barrage, but they hid behind trees, hedges, and the sloping embankments of their lawns. Having no such fortifications, we retreated to the brick pillars of our homes. During the retreat a broken milk bottle caught me behind the ear, opening a deep gash which bled profusely. The sight of blood pouring over my face completely demoralized our ranks. My fellow-combatants left me standing paralyzed in the center of the yard, and scurried for their homes. A kind neighbor saw me and rushed me to a doctor, who took three stitches in my neck.

I sat brooding on my front steps, nursing my wound and waiting for my mother to come from work. I felt that a grave injustice had been done me. It was all right to throw cinders. The greatest harm a cinder could do was leave a bruise. But broken bottles were dangerous; they left you cut, bleeding, and helpless.

When night fell, my mother came from the white folks' kitchen. I raced down the street to meet her. I could just feel in my bones that she would understand. I knew she would tell me exactly what to do next time. I grabbed her hand and babbled out the whole story. She examined my wound, then slapped me.

"How come yuh didn't hide?" she asked me. "How come yuh awways fightin'?"

I was outraged, and bawled. Between sobs I told her that I didn't have any trees or hedges to hide behind. There wasn't a thing I could have used as a trench. And you couldn't throw very far when you were hiding behind the brick pillars of a house. She grabbed a barrel stave, dragged me home, stripped me naked, and beat me till I had a fever of one hundred and two. She would smack my rump with the stave, and while the skin was still smarting, impart to me gems of Jim Crow wisdom. I was never to throw cinders any more. I was never to fight any more wars. I was never, never, under any conditions, to fight *white* folks again. And they were absolutely right in clouting me with the broken milk bottle. Didn't I know she was working hard every day in the hot kitchens of the white folks to make money to take care of me? When was I ever going to learn to be a good boy? She couldn't be bothered with my fights. She finished by telling me that I ought to be thankful to God as long as I lived that they didn't kill me.

All that night I was delirious and could not sleep. Each time I closed my eyes I saw monstrous white faces suspended from the ceiling, leering at me.

From that time on, the charm of my cinder yard was gone. The green trees, the trimmed hedges, the cropped lawns grew very meaningful, became a symbol. Even today when I think of white folks, the hard, sharp outlines of white houses surrounded by trees, lawns, and hedges are present somewhere in the background of my mind. Through the years they grew into an overreaching symbol of fear.

It was a long time before I came in close contact with white folks again. We moved from Arkansas to Mississippi. Here we had the good fortune not to live behind the railroad tracks, or close to white neighborhoods. We lived in the very heart of the local Black Belt. There were black churches and black preachers; there were black schools and black teachers; black groceries and black clerks. In fact, everything was so solidly black that for a long time I did not even think of white folks, save in remote and vague terms. But this could not last forever. As one grows older one eats more. One's clothing costs more. When I finished grammar school I had to go to work. My mother could no longer feed and clothe me on her cooking job.

There is but one place where a black boy who knows no trade can get a job, and that's where the houses and faces are white, where the trees, lawns, and hedges are green. My first job was with an optical company in Jackson, Mississippi. The morning I applied I stood straight and neat before the boss, answering all his questions with sharp yessirs and nosirs. I was very careful to pronounce my *sirs* distinctly, in order that he might know that I was polite, that I knew where I was, and that I knew he was a *white* man. I wanted that job badly.

He looked me over as though he were examining a prize poodle. He questioned me closely about my schooling, being particularly insistent about how much mathematics I had had. He seemed very pleased when I told him I had had two years of algebra.

"Boy, how would you like to learn something around here?" he asked me.

"I'd like it fine, sir," I said, happy. I had visions of "working my way up." Even Negroes have those visions.

"All right," he said. "Come on."

I followed him to the small factory.

"Pease," he said to a white man of about thirty-five, "this is Richard. He's going to work for us."

Pease looked at me and nodded.

I was then taken to a white boy of about seventeen.

"Morrie, this is Richard, who's going to work for us."

"Whut yuy sayin' there, boy!" Morrie boomed at me.

"Fine!" I answered.

The boss instructed these two to help me, teach me, give me jobs to do, and let me learn what I could in my spare time.

My wages were five dollars a week.

I worked hard, trying to please. For the first month I got along O.K. Both Pease and Morrie seemed to like me. But one thing was missing. And I kept thinking about it. I was not learning anything and nobody was volunteering to help me. Thinking they had forgotten that I was to learn something about the mechanics of grinding lenses, I asked Morrie one day to tell me about the work. He grew red.

"Whut yuh tryin' t' do, nigger, get smart?" he asked.

"Naw; I ain' tryin' t' git smart," I said.

"Well, don't, if yuh know whut's good for yuh!"

I was puzzled. Maybe he just doesn't want to help me, I thought. I went to Pease.

"Say, are yuh crazy, you black bastard?" Pease asked me, his gray eyes growing hard.

I spoke out, reminding him that the boss had said I was to be given a chance to learn something.

"Nigger, you think you're *white*, don't you?"

"Naw, sir!"

"Well, you're acting mighty like it!"

"But, Mr. Pease, the boss said . . ."

Pease shook his fist in my face.

"This is a *white* man's work around here, and you better watch yourself!"

From then on they changed toward me. They said good-morning no more. When I was a bit slow performing some duty, I was called a lazy black son-of-a-bitch.

Once I thought of reporting all this to the boss. But the mere idea of what would happen to me if Pease and Morrie should learn that I had "snitched" stopped me. And after all the boss was a white man, too. What was the use?

The climax came at noon one summer day. Pease called me to his work-bench. To get to him I had to go between two narrow benches and stand with my back against a wall.

"Yes, sir," I said.

"Richard, I want to ask you something," Pease began pleasantly, not looking up from his work.

"Yes, sir," I said again.

Morrie came over, blocking the narrow passage between the benches. He folded his arms, staring at me solemnly.

I looked from one to the other, sensing that something was coming.

"Yes, sir," I said for the third time.

Pease looked up and spoke very slowly.

"Richard, *Mr.* Morrie here tells me you called me *Pease*."

I stiffened. A void seemed to open up in me. I knew this was the show-down.

He meant that I had failed to call him Mr. Pease. I looked at Morrie. He was gripping a steel bar in his hands. I opened my mouth to speak, to protest, to assure Pease that I had never called him simply *Pease*, and that I had never had any intentions of doing so, when Morrie grabbed me by the collar, ramming my head against the wall.

"Now, be careful, nigger!" snarled Morrie, baring his teeth. "*I* heard yuh call 'im *Pease!* 'N' if you say yuh didn't, yuh're callin' me a *lie*, see?" He waved the steel bar threateningly.

If I had said: No, sir, Mr. Pease, I never called you *Pease*, I would have been automatically calling Morrie a liar. And if I had said: Yes, sir, Mr. Pease, I called you *Pease*, I would have been pleading guilty to having uttered the worst insult that a Negro can utter to a southern white man. I stood hesitating, trying to frame a neutral reply.

"Richard, I asked you a question!" said Pease. Anger was creeping into his voice.

"I don't remember calling you *Pease*, Mr. Pease," I said cautiously. "And if I did, I sure didn't mean . . ."

"You black son-of-a-bitch! You called me *Pease*, then!" he spat, slapping me till I bent sideways over a bench. Morrie was on top of me, demanding:

"Didn't yuh call 'im *Pease?* If yuh say yuh didn't I'll rip yo' gut string loose with this bar, yuh black granny dodger! Yuh can't call a white man a lie 'n' git erway with it, you black son-of-a-bitch!"

I wilted. I begged them not to bother me. I knew what they wanted. They wanted me to leave.

"I'll leave," I promised. "I'll leave right *now*."

They gave me a minute to get out of the factory. I was warned not to show up again, or tell the boss.

I went.

When I told the folks at home what had happened, they called me a fool. They told me that I must never again attempt to exceed my boundaries. When you are working for white folks, they said, you got to "stay in your place" if you want to keep working.

2

My Jim Crow education continued on my next job, which was portering in a clothing store. One morning, while polishing brass out front, the boss and his twenty-year-old son got out of their car and half dragged and half kicked a Negro woman into the store. A policeman standing at the corner looked on, twirling his night-stick. I watched out of the corner of my eye, never slackening the strokes of my chamois upon the brass. After a few minutes, I heard shrill screams coming from the rear of the store. Later the woman stumbled out, bleeding, crying, and holding her stomach. When she reached the end of the block, the policeman grabbed her and accused her of being drunk. Silently, I watched him throw her into a patrol wagon.

When I went to the rear of the store, the boss and his son were washing their hands in the sink. They were chuckling. The floor was bloody and strewn with wisps of hair and clothing. No doubt I must have appeared pretty shocked, for the boss slapped me reassuringly on the back.

"Boy, that's what we do to niggers when they don't want to pay their bills," he said, laughing.

His son looked at me and grinned.

"Here, hava cigarette," he said.

Not knowing what to do, I took it. He lit his and held the match for me. This was a gesture of kindness, indicating that even if they had beaten the poor old woman, they would not beat me if I knew enough to keep my mouth shut.

"Yes, sir," I said, and asked no questions.

After they had gone, I sat on the edge of a packing box and stared at the bloody floor till the cigarette went out.

That day at noon, while eating in a hamburger joint, I told my fellow Negro porters what had happened. No one seemed surprised. One fellow, after swallowing a huge bite, turned to me and asked:

"Huh! Is tha' all they did t' her?"

"Yeah. Wasn't tha' enough?' I asked.

"Shucks! Man, she's a lucky bitch!" he said, burying his lips deep into a juicy hamburger. "Hell, it's a wonder they didn't lay her when they got through."

3

I was learning fast, but not quite fast enough. One day, while I was delivering packages in the suburbs, my bicycle tire was punctured. I walked along the hot, dusty road, sweating and leading my bicycle by the handle-bars.

A car slowed at my side.

"What's the matter, boy?" a white man called.

I told him my bicycle was broken and I was walking back to town.

"That's too bad," he said. "Hop on the running board."

He stopped the car. I clutched hard at my bicycle with one hand and clung to the side of the car with the other.

"All set?"

"Yes, sir," I answered. The car started.

It was full of young white men. They were drinking. I watched the flask pass from mouth to mouth.

"Wanna drink, boy?" one asked.

I laughed as the wind whipped my face. Instinctively obeying the freshly planted precepts of my mother, I said:

"Oh, no!"

The words were hardly out of my mouth before I felt something hard and cold smash me between the eyes. It was an empty whisky bottle. I saw stars, and fell backwards from the speeding car into the dust of the road, my feet becoming entangled in the steel spokes of my bicycle. The white men piled out and stood over me.

"Nigger, ain' yuh learned no better sense'n tha' yet?" asked the man who hit me. "Ain' yuh learned t' say *sir* t' a white man yet?"

Dazed, I pulled to my feet. My elbows and legs were bleeding. Fists doubled, the white man advanced, kicking my bicycle out of the way.

"Aw, leave the bastard alone. He's got enough," said one.

They stood looking at me. I rubbed my shins, trying to stop the flow of blood. No doubt they felt a sort of contemptuous pity, for one asked:

"Yuh wanna ride t' town now, nigger? Yuh reckon yuh know enough t' ride now?"

"I wanna walk," I said, simply.

Maybe it sounded funny. They laughed.

"Well, walk, yuh black son-of-a-bitch!"

When they left they comforted me with:

"Nigger, yuh sho better be damn glad it wuz us yuh talked t' tha' way. Yuh're a lucky bastard, 'cause if yuh'd said tha' t' somebody else, yuh might've been a dead nigger now."

4

Negroes who have lived South know the dread of being caught alone upon the streets in white neighborhoods after the sun has set. In such a simple situation as this the plight of the Negro in America is graphically symbolized. While white strangers may be in these neighborhoods trying to get home, they can pass unmolested. But the color of a Negro's skin makes him easily recognizable, makes him suspect, converts him into a defenseless target.

Late one Saturday night I made some deliveries in a white neighborhood. I was pedaling my bicycle back to the store as fast as I could, when a police car, swerving toward me, jammed me into the curbing.

"Get down and put up your hands!" the policemen ordered.

I did. They climbed out of the car, guns drawn, faces set, and advanced slowly.

"Keep still!" they ordered.

I reached my hands higher. They searched my pockets and packages. They seemed dissatisfied when they could find nothing incriminating. Finally, one of them said:

"Boy, tell your boss not to send you out in white neighborhoods after sundown."

As usual, I said:

"Yes, sir."

5

My next job was a hall-boy in a hotel. Here my Jim Crow education broadened and deepened. When the bell-boys were busy, I was often called to assist them. As many of the rooms in the hotel were occupied by prostitutes, I was constantly called to carry them liquor and cigarettes. These women were nude most of the time. They did not bother about clothing, even for bell-boys. When you went into their rooms, you were supposed to take their nakedness for granted, as though it startled you no more than a blue vase or a red rug. Your presence awoke in them no sense of shame, for you were not regarded as human. If they were alone, you could steal sidelong glimpses at them. But if they were receiving men, not a flicker of your eyelids could show. I remember one incident vividly. A new woman, a huge, snowy-skinned blonde, took a room on my floor. I was sent to wait upon her. She was in bed with a thick-set man; both were nude and uncovered. She said she wanted some liquor and slid out of bed and waddled across the floor to get her money from a dresser drawer. I watched her.

"Nigger, what in hell are you looking at?" the white man asked me, raising himself upon his elbows.

"Nothing," I answered, looking miles deep into the blank wall of the room.

"Keep your eyes where they belong, if you want to be healthy!" he said.

"Yes, sir."

6

One of the bell-boys I knew in this hotel was keeping steady company with one of the Negro maids. Out of a clear sky the police descended upon his home and arrested him, accusing him of bastardy. The poor boy swore he had had no intimate relations with the girl. Nevertheless, they forced him to marry her. When the child arrived, it was found to be much lighter in complexion than either of the two supposedly legal parents. The white men around the hotel made a great joke of it. They spread the rumor that some white cow must have scared the poor girl while she was carrying the baby. If you were in their presence when this explanation was offered, you were supposed to laugh.

7

One of the bell-boys was caught in bed with a white prostitute. He was castrated and run out of town. Immediately after this all the bell-boys and hall-boys were called together and warned. We were given to understand that the boy who had been castrated was a "mighty, mighty lucky bastard." We were impressed with the fact that next time the management of the hotel would not be responsible for the lives of "trouble-makin' niggers." We were silent.

8

One night just as I was about to go home, I met one of the Negro maids. She lived in my direction, and we fell in to walk part of the way home together. As we passed the white night-watchman, he slapped the maid on her buttock. I turned around, amazed. The watchman looked at me with a long, hard, fixed-under stare. Suddenly he pulled his gun and asked:

"Nigger, don't yuh like it?"

I hesitated.

"I asked yuh don't yuh like it?" he asked again, stepping forward.

"Yes, sir," I mumbled.

"Talk like it, then!"

"Oh, yes, sir!" I said with as much heartiness as I could muster.

Outside, I walked ahead of the girl, ashamed to face her. She caught up with me and said:

"Don't be a fool! Yuh couldn't help it!"

This watchman boasted of having killed two Negroes in self-defense.

Yet, in spite of all this, the life of the hotel ran with an amazing smoothness. It would have been impossible for a stranger to detect anything. The maids, the hall-boys, and the bell-boys were all smiles. They had to be.

9

I had learned my Jim Crow lessons so thoroughly that I kept the hotel job till I left Jackson for Memphis. It so happened that while in Memphis I applied for a job at a branch of the optical company. I was hired. And for some reason, as long as I worked there, they never brought my past against me.

Here my Jim Crow education assumed quite a different form. It was no longer brutally cruel, but subtly cruel. Here I learned to lie, steal, to dissemble. I learned to play that dual role which every Negro must play if he wants to eat and live.

For example, it was almost impossible to get a book to read. It was assumed that after a Negro had imbibed what scanty schooling the state furnished he had no further need for books. I was always borrowing books from men on the job. One day I mustered enough courage to ask one of the men to let me get books from the library in his name. Surprisingly, he consented. I cannot help but think that he consented because he was a Roman Catholic and felt a vague sympathy for Negroes, being himself an object of hatred. Armed with a library card, I obtained books in the following manner: I would write a note to the librarian, saying: "Please let this nigger boy have the following books." I would then sign it with the white man's name.

When I went to the library, I would stand at the desk, hat in hand, looking as unbookish as possible. When I received the books desired I would take them home. If the books listed in the note happened to be out, I would sneak into the lobby and forge a new one. I never took any chances guessing with the white librarian about what the fictitious white man would want to read. No doubt if any of the white patrons had suspected that some of the volumes they enjoyed had been in the home of a Negro, they would not have tolerated it for an instant.

The factory force of the optical company in Memphis was much larger than that in Jackson, and more urbanized. At least they liked to talk, and would engage the Negro help in conversation whenever possible. By this means I found that many subjects were taboo from the white man's point of view. Among the topics they did not like to discuss with Negroes were the following: American white women; the Ku Klux Klan; France, and how Negro soldiers fared while there; French women; Jack Johnson; the entire northern part of the United States; the Civil War; Abraham Lincoln; U. S. Grant; General Sherman; Catholics; the Pope; Jews; the Republican Party; slavery; social equality; Communism; Socialism; the 13th and 14th Amendments to the Constitution; or any topic calling for positive knowledge or manly self-assertion on the part of the Negro. The most accepted topics were sex and religion.

There were many times when I had to exercise a great deal of ingenuity to keep out of trouble. It is a southern custom that all men must take off their hats when they enter an elevator. And especially did this apply to us blacks with rigid force. One day I stepped into an elevator with my arms full of packages. I was forced to ride with my hat on. Two white men stared at me coldly. Then one of them very kindly lifted my hat and placed it upon my armful of packages. Now the most accepted response for a Negro to make under such circumstances is to look at the white man out of the corner of his eye and grin. To have said: "Thank you!" would have made the white man *think* that you *thought* you were receiving from him a personal service. For such an act I have seen Negroes take a blow in the mouth. Finding the first alternative distasteful, and the second dangerous, I hit upon an acceptable course of action which fell safely between these two poles. I immediately—no sooner than my hat was lifted—pretended that my packages were about to spill, and appeared deeply distressed with keeping them in my arms. In this fashion I evaded having to acknowledge his service, and, in spite of adverse circumstances, salvaged a slender shred of personal pride.

How do Negroes feel about the way they have to live? How do they discuss it when alone among themselves? I think this question can be answered in a single sentence. A friend of mine who ran an elevator once told me:

"Lawd, man! Ef it wuzn't fer them polices 'n' them ol' lynch-mobs, there wouldn't be nothin' but uproar down here!"

J. SAUNDERS REDDING (1906–   )

When Redding's autobiographical book No Day of Triumph *was published in 1942, it included a brief Introduction by Richard Wright, which opened with the following paragraph:*

It has long been my conviction that the next quarter of a century will disclose a tremendous struggle *among* the Negro people for self-expression, self-possession, self-consciousness, individuality, new values, new loyalties, and, above all, for a new leadership. My reading of Redding's *No Day of Triumph* has confirmed and strengthened this conviction, for his book contains honesty, integrity, courage, grownup thinking and feeling, all rendered in terms of vivid prose. *No Day of Triumph* is another hallmark in the coming-of-age of the modern Negro; it is yet another signal in the turn of the tide from sloppy faith and cheap cynicism to fruitful seeking and passionate questioning.

J. Saunders Redding was born in Delaware, received a B.A. from Lincoln University and a Ph.D. in English from Brown University. He established a national reputation with his essays, literary criticism, fiction, and educational activities as Professor of English at Hampton Institute. He left this post recently when he was named Director of the Division of Research and Publication of the National Foundation on the Arts and the Humanities in Washington, D. C. He has received Rockefeller and Guggenheim awards and won the Mayflower Award from the North Carolina Historical Society. We present here three chapters from Part 1 (subtitled "Troubled in Mind") of No Day of Triumph. *An address by Professor Redding at the First Conference of Negro Writers (March, 1959) appears in the Literary Criticism section.*

No Day of Triumph

Chapter One—Troubled in Mind

1

Consciousness of my environment began with the sound of talk. It was not hysterical talk, not bravado, though it might well have been, for my father had bought in a neighborhood formerly forbidden, and we lived, I realize now, under an armistice. But in the early years, when we were a young family, there was always talk at our house; a great deal of it mere talk, a kind of boundless and robustious overflow of family feeling. Our shouts roared through the house with the exuberant gush of flood waters through an open sluice, for talk, generated by any trifle, was the power that turned the wheels of our inner family life. It was the strength and that very quality of our living that made impregnable, it seemed, even to time itself, the walls of our home. But it was in the beginning of the second decade of the century, when the family was an institution still as inviolate as the swing of the earth.

There was talk of school, of food, of religion, of people. There were the shouted recitations of poems and Biblical passages and orations from Bryan, Phillips, and John Brown. My mother liked rolling apostrophes. We children were all trained at home in the declining art of oratory and were regular contestants for prizes at school. My father could quote with appropriate gestures bits from Beveridge, whom he had never heard, and from Teddy Roosevelt and Fred Douglass, whom he had. There was talk of the "race problem," reasonable and unembittered unless Grandma Redding was there, and then it became a kind of spiritual poison, its virulence destructive of its own immediate effects, almost its own catharsis. Some of the poison we absorbed.

I remember Grandma Redding coming on one of her visits and finding us playing in the back yard. My brother and sister were there and we were playing with Myrtle Lott and Elwood Carter, white children who were neighbors. Grandma came in the back way through the alley, as she always did, and when we heard the gate scrape against the bricks we stopped. She stepped into the yard and looked fixedly at us. Holding her ancient, sagging canvas bag under one arm, she slowly untied the ribbons of her black bonnet. The gate fell shut behind her. Her eyes were like lashes on our faces. Reaching out her long arm, she held open the gate. Then she said, "Git. You white trash, git!" Our companions, pale with fright, ducked and scampered past her. When they had gone, Grandma nodded curtly to us. "Chillen," she said, and went into the house.

Grandma Redding's visits were always unannounced. She came the fifty-odd miles up from Still Pond, Maryland, as casually as if she had come from around the nearest corner. A sudden cold silence would fall, and there would be Grandma. I do not know how she managed to give the impression of shining with a kind of deadly hard glare, for she was always clothed entirely in black and her black, even features were as hard and lightless as stone. I never saw a change of expression on her features. She never smiled. In anger her face turned slowly, dully gray, but her thin nostrils never flared, her long mouth never tightened. She was tall and fibrous and one of her ankles had been broken when she was a girl and never properly set, so that she walked with a defiant limp.

She hated white people. In 1858, as a girl of ten, she had escaped from slavery on the eastern shore of Maryland with a young woman of eighteen. They made their way to Camden, New Jersey, but there was no work and little refuge there. Across the river, bustling Philadelphia swarmed with slave hunters. By subterfuge or by violence even free people were sometimes kidnaped and sent south. Near Bridgeton, New Jersey, the runaways heard, there was a free Negro settlement, but one night they were stopped on the docks by a constable who asked them for papers. They had none. Within two weeks after their escape they were slaves again. When my grandmother tried to run away from the flogging that was her punishment, Caleb Wrightson, her master, flung a chunk of wood at her and broke her ankle.

It was not until we were quite large children that Grandma Redding told us this story. She did not tell it for our pleasure, as one tells harrowing tales to children. It was without the dramatic effects that Grandma Conway delighted in. What *she* would have done with such a tale! No. Grandma Redding's telling was as bare and imageless as a lesson recited from the head and as coldly furious as the whine of a shot.

"An' ol' man Calub flane a hick'ry chunk an' brist my anklebone."

I can see her now as she sits stooped in the wooden rocker by the kitchen stove, her sharp elbows on her sharp knees and her long black fingers with their immense purple nails clawing upward at the air. Her undimmed eyes whipped at ours, and especially at mine, it seemed to me; her thin lips scarcely parted. She had just come in or was going out, for she wore her bonnet and it sat on the very top of her harsh, dull hair. Hatred shook her as a strong wind shakes a bough-less tree.

"An' ol' man Calub stank lik'a pes'-house from the rottin' of his stomick 'fore he died an' went t' hell, an' his boys died in the wo' an' went to hell."

But her implacable hatred needed no historical recall, and so far as I remember, she never told the tale to us again.

But generally Grandma Redding's taciturnity was a hidden rock in the sea of our talk. The more swift the tide, the more the rock showed, bleak and unavoidable. At other times the talk flowed smoothly around her: the bursts of oratory and poetry, the chatter of people and events, the talk of schooling and sometimes of money and often of God. Even the talk of God did not arouse her. I think she was not especially religious; and in this, too, she was unlike Grandma Conway.

My grandmothers met at our house but once. They did not like each other. . . .

5

My mother was tall, with a smooth, rutilant skin and a handsome figure. Her hair began to whiten in her late twenties and whitened very rapidly. I especially liked to be on the street with her, for I enjoyed the compliment of staring which was paid to her. I think she was not aware of these stares. There was pride in her, a kind of glowing consciousness that showed in her carriage in exactly the same way that good blood shows in a horse. But she had no vanity. Her pride gave to everything she did a certain ritualistic élan.

It is surprising to me now how little I learned about my mother in the sixteen years she lived after my birth. It was not that I lacked opportunity, but insight. She was never withdrawn or restrained, purposefully shading out her personality from us. And her speech and actions seemed to have the simple directness and the sharp impact of thrown stones. But she was a woman of many humors, as if, knowing her time to be short, she would live many lives in one. Gaiety and soberness, anger and benignity, joy and woe possessed her with equal force. In all her moods there was an intensity as in a spinning top.

I vividly recall the day when in rage and tears she stormed because another Negro family moved into our neighborhood. When her rage had passed and she had dropped into that stilly tautness that sometimes kept her strained for days, she said to my father:

"That's all it takes, Fellow. Today our house is worth one-third of what it was last night. When those people . . ." She shrugged her wide shoulders and stared at my father.

"Oh, Girl! Girl!" my father said gently. "You mustn't be so hard on them. They may be respectable people."

"Hard! Hard! And respectable people!" She laughed brittlely. "What has respectability got to do with it?"

Then she tried to find the words for what she thought, for we children were present and she did not wish to appear unreasonable before us. The subject of race was for her a narrow bridge over a chasmal sea, and the walking of it was not a part of her daily living. Only when she felt she must save herself from the abyss did she venture to walk. At other times she ignored it, not only in word, but I think in thought as well. She knew the speeches of John Brown and Wendell Phillips, the poetry of Whittier and Whitman, but not as my father knew them; not as battering stones hurled against the strong walls of a prison. She was not imprisoned. Stones, perhaps, but dropped into a dark sea whose tides licked only at the farthest shores of her life. She took this for reasonableness.

I remember she laughed a brittle laugh and said, "The first thing they moved in was one of those pianola things. Oh, we shall have music," she said bitterly, "morning, noon, and midnight. And they're not buying. They're renting. Why can't they stay where they belong!"

"Belong?" my father said.

"Yes. Over the bridge."

"They are our people, Girl," my father said.

My mother looked at him, tears of vexation dewing her eyes. She blinked back the tears and looked fixedly at my father's dark face shining dully under the chandelier, his bald head jutting back from his forehead like a brown rock. As if the words were a bad taste to be rid of, she said:

"Yours maybe. But not mine."

"Oh, Girl. Girl!"

But Mother had already swept from the dining room.

It is strange how little my deep affection for my mother (and hers for all of us) taught me about her while she lived. I have learned much more about her since her death. It is as if the significance of remembered speech and action unfolded to me gradually a long time after. My mother was the most complex personality I have ever known.

But no will of my mother's could abate the heave of the social tide just then beginning to swell. Our new neighbors were the first that we saw of that leaderless mass of blacks that poured up from the South during and after the war years. It was a trickle first, and then a dark flood that soon inundated the east side and burbled restively at our street. Within five months of the time my mother had raged, the whites were gone. But rents and prices in our street were too high for the laborers in morocco and jute mills, shipyards and foundries, the ditch-diggers, coal-heavers, and the parasites. They crowded sometimes as many as eight to a room in the houses below us, and I knew of at least one house of six small rooms in which fifty-one people lived.

Our street and the diagonal street above it were a more exclusive preserve. A few middle-class Jews, a clannish community of Germans clustered about their Turn Hall, and some Catholic Irish lived there. But they were nudged out. The Germans first, for they became the victims of mass hatred during the war, and the last German home was stoned just before the day of the Armistice. Landlords and realtors inflated prices to profit by Negro buyers who clamored for houses as if for heaven. Into our street moved the prosperous class of mulattoes, a physician and a dentist, a minister, an insurance agent, a customs clerk, a well-paid domestic, and several school teachers. Nearly all of these were buying at prices three times normal.

The atmosphere of our street became purely defensive. No neighborhood in the city was so conscious of its position and none, trapped in a raw materialistic struggle between the well-being of the west side and the grinding poverty of the east, fought harder to maintain itself. This struggle was the satanic bond, the blood-pact that held our street together.

But there was also the spiritual side to this struggle. It remained for me for a long time undefined but real. It was not clear and cold in the brain as religion was and taxes and food to eat and paint to buy. It was in the throat like a warm clot of phlegm or blood that no expectorant could dislodge. It was in the bowels and bone. It was memory and history, the pound of the heart, the pump of the lungs. It was Weeping Joe making bursting flares of words on the Court House wall and murmuring like a priest in funeral mass on our back steps of summer evenings. It was east side, west side, the white and the black, the word nigger, the cry of exultation, of shame, of fear when black Lemuel Price shot and killed a white policeman. It was Paul Dunbar, whose great brooding eyes spirit-flowed from his drawn face in a photograph over our mantel. It was sleeping and waking. It was Wilson and Hughes in 1917, Harding and Cox in 1921. It was a science teacher saying sarcastically, "Yes. I know. They won't hire you because you're colored," and, "Moreover, the dog licked Lazarus' wounds," and getting very drunk occasionally and reeling about, his yellow face gone purple, blubbering, "A good chemist, God damn it. A Goddamn good chemist! And here I am teaching a school full of niggers. Oh, damn my unwhite skin! And God damn it!" It was the music of pianolas played from dusk to dawn. And it was books read and recited and hated and loved: fairy tales, *Up From Slavery, Leaves of Grass, Scaramouche, Othello, The Yoke, Uncle Tom's Cabin, The Heroic Story of the Negro in the Spanish-American War, The Leopard's Spots, Door of the Night, Sentimental Tommy, The Negro, Man or Beast?,* and the rolling apostrophes of the *World's Best Orations.*

And on this plane allegiances were confused, divided. There was absolute cleavage between those spiritual values represented by Grandma Conway, who thought and lived according to ideas and ideals inherited from a long line of free ancestors and intimates (her father had been white, her mother part Irish, Indian, Negro. Her first husband was a mulatto carriage maker with a tradition of freedom three generations old) and those ill-defined, uncertain values represented by Grandma Redding and which, somehow, seemed to be close to whatever values our neighbors on the east held. What these were I never knew, nor, I suspect, did Grandma Redding. Certainly she would have cast equal scorn on the east side's black Lizzie Gunnar, who ran a whore house and who two days before every Christmas gathered up all the Negro children she could find and led them to the Court House for the city's party to the poor, because, "Niggahs is jus' about de poores' folks dere is," and white and foreign-born Weeping Joe, who spoke of linking the spirits of men together in the solvent bond of Christ. Her closeness to them was more a sympathetic prepossession than an alliance. They were her people, whether their values were the same as hers or not. Blood was stronger than ideal, and the thing that was between them sprang from emotion rather than mind. It was unreasoning, and as ineluctable as the flight of time. Grandma Redding was the outright inheritor of a historical situation.

But not so Grandma Conway. She had assumed—not to say usurped—both the privileges and the penalties of a tradition that was hers only disingenuously, and therefore all the more fiercely held. The privileges gave her power; the penalties strength. She was certain of her values and she held them to be inviolate. She believed in a personal God and that He was in His heaven and all was right with the world. She believed in a rigid code of morality, but in a double standard, because she believed that there was something in the male animal that made him naturally incontinent, and that some women, always of a class she scornfully pitied, had no other purpose in life than to save good women from men's incontinence. In her notion, such women were not loose any more than rutting bitches were loose. A loose woman was a woman of her own class who had wilfully assumed the privileges and shunned the penalties of her birth. Such women she hated with face-purpling hatred. She believed in banks and schools and prisons. She believed that the world was so ordered that in the end his just desserts came to every man. This latter belief was very comprehensive, for she thought in terms of reciprocal responsibility of man and his class—that man did not live for himself alone and that he could not escape the general defections (she called it "sin") of the group into which he was born.

These beliefs must have been conspicuous to Grandma Conway's most casual acquaintance, but to me—and I have no doubt, to the rest of us long familiar with them—they were past both realizing and remarking, like the skin of one's body.

But realization of her most occult belief must have come quite early. Perhaps it came to me in 1917, when, on one of her visits, she first found the lower boundary of our neighborhood roiling with strange black folk and brazen with conspicuous life. It may have come to me imperceptibly, along with the consciousness of the stigma attaching to blackness of skin. But this stigma was a blemish, not a taint. A black skin was uncomely, but not inferior. My father was less beautiful than my mother, but he was not inferior to her. There were soot-black boys whom I knew in school who could outrun, outplay, and outthink me, but they were less personable than I. And certainly we did not think in any conscious way that Grandma Redding was a lesser person than Grandma Conway. The very core of awareness was this distinction.

But gradually, subtly, depressingly and without shock there entered into my consciousness the knowledge that Grandma Conway believed that a black skin was more than a blemish. In her notion it was a taint of flesh and bone and blood, varying in degree with the color of the skin, overcome sometimes by certain material distinctions and the grace of God, but otherwise fixed in the blood.

To Grandma Conway, as to my mother, our new neighbors on the east were a threat.

In our house a compromise was struck. No one ever talked about it. In the careless flow of our talk, it was the one subject avoided with meticulous concern. My parents were stern disciplinarians, and this subject was so fraught with punishable possibilities and yet so conscious a part of our living that by the time the three older ones of us were in grammar and high school our care for the avoidance of it took on at times an almost hysterical intensity. Many a time, as we heard schoolmates do and as we often did ourselves outside, one or the other of us wished to hurl the epithet "black" or "nigger," or a combination, and dared only sputter, "You, you . . . monkey!" For being called a monkey was not considered half so grave an insult as being called the other; and it was at least as grave a sin to avoid as using the Lord's name in vain. My parents, of course, never used either black or nigger, and avoided mentioning color in describing a person. One was either dark or light, never black or yellow—and between these two was that indeterminate group of browns of which our family was largely composed. We grew up in the very center of a complex.

I think my older brother and sister escaped most of the adolescent emotional conflict and vague melancholy (it came later to them, and especially to my brother, and in decidedly greater force) which were the winds of my course through teenhood. For me it was a matter of choices, secret choices really. For them there was no choice. And yet I had less freedom than they. They went off to a New England college in 1919. Up to then their associates had been first the white and then the mulatto children on our street. Even the children whom they met in high school were largely of the mulatto group, for the dark tide of migration had not then swept the schools. Going to school was distinctly an upper-class pursuit, and the public school was almost as exclusive as the summer playground which Miss Grinnage conducted along stubbornly select lines for "children of the best blood" (it was her favorite phrase), almost as exclusive as the Ethical Culture lectures we attended once each month, or the basement chapel of St. Andrews Episcopal church, where Father Tatnall held segregated services for us twice a month. For my older brother and sister, the road through childhood was straight, without sideroads or crossings.

But by the time I reached high school in the fall of 1919, life was undergoing a tumultuous change. It was as if a placid river had suddenly broken its banks and in blind and senseless rage was destroying old landmarks, leveling the face of the country farther and farther beyond the shore line.

The migrants not only discovered our neighborhood, they discovered the church where we went to Sunday school and where my father was superintendent. They discovered the vast, beautiful reaches of the Brandywine where we used to walk on fair Sundays. They discovered the school. I remember the sickening thrill with which I heard a long-headed black boy arraign the mulatto teachers for always giving the choice parts in plays, the choice chores, the cleanest books to mulatto children. He called the teachers "color-struck," a phrase that was new to me, and "sons-of-bitches," a phrase that was not. He was put out of school. Many black children were put out of school, or not encouraged to continue. Two incidents stand out in my mind.

In my first oratorical competiton, I knew—as everyone else knew—that the contestant to beat was a gangling dark fellow named Tom Cephus. He had a fervor that I did not have and for which I was taught to substitute craft. His voice, already changed, boomed with a vibrant quality that was impressive to hear. Moreover, he was controlled, self-possessed, and I was not. For days before the competition I was unable to rest, and when I did finally face the audience, I uttered a sentence or two and from sheer fright and nervous exhaustion burst into uncontrollable tears. Somehow, bawling like a baby, I got through. I was certain that I had lost.

Cephus in his turn was superb. The greater part of the audience was with him. Beyond the first rows of benches, which were friendly to me, stretched row after increasingly dark row of black faces and beaming eyes. It was more than an oratorical contest to them. It was a class and caste struggle as intense as any they would ever know, for it was immediate and possible of compromise and assuagement, if not of victory. Mouths open, strained forward, they vibrated against that booming voice, transfixed in ecstasy. The applause was deafening and vindicative. In the back of the crowded hall someone led three cheers for Cephus (a wholly unheard-of thing) and while the teacher-judges were conferring, cheer after cheer swelled from the audience like the approaching, humming, booming bursting of ocean waves.

A pulsing hush fell on them when the judges returned.

They watched the announcer as leashed and hungry dogs watch the approach of food. But the judge was shrewd. She wanted that excitement to simmer down. Flicking a smile at the first rows, she calmly announced the singing of a lullaby and waited, a set smile on her face, until three verses had been sung. Then icily, in sprung-steel Bostonian accents, she announced to an audience whose soft-skinned faces gradually froze in spastic bewilderment, "Third place, Edith Miller. Second place, Thomas Cephus. First place . . ." My name was lost in a void of silence. "Assembly dismissed!"

Stunned beyond expression and feeling, the back rows filed out. The front rows cheered. Cephus's lips worked and he looked at me. I could not look at him. I wanted to fall on my knees.

I was truant from school for a week. When my parents discovered it, I took my punishment without a word. A little later that year, Cephus dropped out of school.

But I was stubborn in my resistance to these lessons. My stubbornness was not a rational thing arrived at through intellection. It was not as simple and as hard as that. I was not a conscious rebel. I liked people, and, for all the straitening effects of environment, I was only lightly color-struck. A dark skin was perhaps not as comely as a brown or yellow, but it was sometimes attractive. In matters of class morality and custom and thought I was perhaps too young to make distinctions. I liked people. When I was sixteen and a senior in high school, I liked a doe-soft black girl named Viny. After school hours, Viny was a servant girl to kindly, dumpy, near-white Miss Kruse, the school principal, who lived across the street from us. I saw a good bit of Viny, for I ran Miss Kruse's confidential errands and did innumerable small things for her. There was nothing clandestine about my relations with her servant girl. We talked and joked in the kitchen. We sometimes walked together from school. We were frequently alone in the house.

But one day Miss Kruse called me to the front porch, where in fine, warm weather she ensconced herself in a rocker especially braced to support her flabby weight. She sat with her back turned squarely to the street. She was very fair, and because she ate heavily of rich, heavy foods, at forty-five she was heavy-jowled, with a broad, pleasant, doughy face. A sack of flesh swelled beneath her chin and seemed to hold her mouth open in a tiny O. She was reading.

"Sit down," she said.

I sat in the chair next to hers, but facing the street, so that we could look directly at each other. Both sides of the street were still lined with trees at that time, and it was June. Hedges were green. Miss Kruse read for a while longer, then she crumpled the paper against herself and folded her fingers over it.

"You like Viny, don't you?" she asked, looking at me with a heavy frown.

"Yes, ma'am," I said.

"Well, you be careful. She'll get you in trouble," she said.

"Trouble?"

"How would you like to marry her?"

I did not answer, for I did not know what to say.

"How?"

"I don't know'm."

This provoked her. She threw the newspaper on the floor. The network of fine pink veins on the lobes of her nose turned purple.

"Well, let her alone! Or she'll trap you to marry her. And what would you look like married to a girl like that?" she said bitingly. "No friends, no future. You might as well be dead! How would you like to spend the rest of your life delivering ice or cleaning outdoor privies? Don't you know girls like her haven't any shame, haven't any decency? She'll get you in trouble."

I stared stupidly at her. I do not know what my reaction was. I remember being confused and hotly embarrassed, and after that a kind of soggy lethargy settled in my stomach, like indigestible food. I distinctly remember that I felt no resentment and no shock, and that my confusion was due less to this first frank indictment of blackness than to the blunt reference to sex. Boys talked about sex in giggly whispers among themselves, but between male and female talk of sex was taboo. In the midst of my embarrassment, I heard Miss Kruse's voice again, calm and gentle now, persuasive, admonitory.

"You're going to college. You're going to get a fine education. You're going to be somebody. You'll be ashamed you ever knew Viny. There'll be fine girls for you to know, to marry."

She sighed, making a round sound of it through her O-shaped mouth, and rubbing her hands hard together as if they were cold.

"Viny. Well, Viny won't ever be anything but what she is already."

And what is she? And what and where are the others? One, who wore the flashy clothes and made loud laughter in the halls, is now a man of God, a solemn, earnest pulpiteer.

Cephus, the boy who won and lost, is dead. And Pogie Walker's dead. It is remarkable how many of those I came to know in 1919 are dead. Birdie, Sweetie Pie, and Oliver. Viny? After she quit and moved away, she used to write me once a year on cheap, lined paper. "I'm doing alrite." (She never learned to spell). "I'm living alrite. I gess I'm geting along alrite. How do these few lines fine you?" And Brunson, the smartest of that migrant lot, who outran, outfought, outthought all of us. He was expelled for writing a letter and passing it among the students. Most of the things he said were true—the exclusion of the very black from the first yearbook, the way one teacher had of referring to the black-skinned kids as "You, Cloudy, there," and never remembering their names. Well, Brunson is a week-end drunk. At other times he's very bitter. Not long ago I saw him. I spoke to him. "You don't remember me," I said. "Yeah. I remember you all right. So what?" He lives down on the east side, way down, where in the spring the river comes. . . .

7

In my senior year I met Lebman. For several lonely months I had been the only Negro in the college, and the sense of competitive enmity, which began to develop slowly in me in my second year, was now at its height. It was more than a sense of competition. It was a perverted feeling of fighting alone against the whole white world. I raged with secret hatred and fear. I hated and feared the whites. I hated and feared and was ashamed of Negroes. (The memory of it even now is painful to me.) I shunned contacts with the general run of the latter, confining myself to the tight little college group centered around Boston. But even this group was no longer as satisfying as once it had been, and I gradually withdrew from it, though the bond of frustration was strong. But my own desperation was stronger. I wished to be alone. My room in University Hall had almost no visitors, but it was peopled by a thousand nameless fears.

Furtively trying to burn out the dark, knotted core of emotion, I wrote acidulous verse and sent bitter essays and stories to various Negro magazines. One editor wrote, "You must be crazy!" Perhaps I was. I was obsessed by nihilistic doctrine. Democracy? It was a failure. Religion? A springe to catch woodcocks. Truth? There was no objective ground of truth, nothing outside myself that made morality a principle. Destroy and destroy, and perhaps, I remember writing cynically, "from the ashes of nothingness will spring a phoenix not alto-

gether devoid of beauty." All my thoughts and feelings were
but symptomatic of a withering, grave sickness of doubt.

And then I met Lebman.

He was a Jew. He had lived across the hall from me since
the fall, and I had seen him once or twice in only the most
casual way. Then late one night he knocked at my door.
When I opened it, he was standing there pale and smiling, a
lock of damp, dark hair falling across his wide, knotty forehead.

"I saw your light. Do you mind if I ask you something?"

"Come in," I said automatically; but all my defenses
immediately went up.

Still smiling shyly, he came into the room and stood in the
center of the floor. He carried a book in his hand, his longer
fingers marking the place. He was wearing pajamas and a
robe. I remember I did not close the door nor sit down at
first, but stood awkwardly waiting, trying to exorcise my suspicion and fear. He looked around the room with quiet,
friendly curiosity.

"I've been reading your stuff in the *Quarterly*," he said.
"It's good."

"Thanks," I said. And I remember thinking, 'Don't try to
flatter me, damn you. I don't fall for that stuff.' Then I tried
to get ahold of myself, groping at my tangled feelings with
clumsy fingers of thought in an action almost physical.
"Thanks."

"I think you're after something," he said. It was a cliché,
and I did not like talking about my writing. It was always
like undressing before strangers. But Lebman was sincere,
and now unembarrassed.

"You do?" I said, trying to say it in a tone that would end
it.

"Yes."

"Why?"

"Oh, it's plain in your writing. You know, I correct papers
in philosophy too. Your paper on Unamuno, it was plain
there. That paper was all right too."

"I wish I knew what I was after, or that I was after something," I said defensively, cynically. I closed the door. Then
in the still, sharp silence that followed, I moved to the desk
and turned the chair to face the other chair in the corner.
Lebman sat down.

"What I came in to see you about was this," he said, holding the book up. And in another moment, without really asking me anything, he had plunged into a brilliant, brooding
discussion of Rudolph Fisher's *Walls of Jericho*, the book he

held in his hand, and of men and books. I listened captiously at first. He did not speak in the rhapsodic way of one who merely loves books and life. He spoke as one who understands and both loves and hates. He sat in the chair in the corner, where the light from the reading lamp fell upon his pale face, his narrow, angular shoulders. Through the window at his elbow we could see the mist-shrouded lights outlining the walks of the middle campus. Lebman talked and talked. I listened.

I do not remember all he said between that midnight and dawn, but one thing I do remember.

"I'm a Jew. I tried denying it, but it was no use. I suppose everyone at some time or other tries to deny some part or all of himself. Suicides, some crazy people go all the way. But spiritual schizophrenes aren't so lucky as suicides and the hopelessly insane. I used to think that only certain Jews suffered from this—the Jews who turn Christian and marry Christian and change their names from Lowenstein to Lowe and Goldberg to Goldsborough and still aren't happy. But they're not the only ones. Fisher makes a point of that. I thought so until I read him. You ought to read him, if you haven't."

"I've read him," I said, trying to remember the point.

"Schizophrenia in the mind, that's the curse of God; but in the spirit, it's man's curse upon himself. It took me a long time—all through college, through three years of reading manuscripts for a publisher, through another two years of graduate school—it took me years to realize what a thing it is. I'm a thirty-six-year-old bird, and I've only just found my roost.

"That's what you want, a roost, a home. And not just a place to hang your hat, but someplace where your spirit's free, where you belong. That's what everybody wants. Not a place in space, you understand. Not a marked place, geographically bounded. Not a place at all in fact. It's hard to tell others," he said. "But it's a million things and people, a kind of life and thought that your spirit touches, absorbed and absorbing, understood and understanding, and feels completely free and whole and one."

That midnight conversation—though it was scarcely that —recurred to me many times in the years immediately following.

When I came up for graduation in 1928, it still had not occurred to me to think of finding work to do that would turn my education to some account. My brother had been graduated from Harvard Law, and I thought randomly of

earning money to follow him there. My credits were transferred. But I earned very little and I could discover in myself
no absorbing interest, no recognition of a purpose. The summer blazed along to August. Then, out of the blue, John
Hope offered me a job at Morehouse College in Atlanta. I
took it. I was twenty-one in October of that fall, a lonely,
random-brooding youth, uncertain, purposeless, lost, and yet
so tightly wound that every day I lived big-eyed as death in
sharp expectancy of a mortal blow or a vitalizing fulfillment
of the unnamable aching emptiness within me.

But Morehouse College and the southern environment disappointed me. The college tottered with spiritual decay. Its
students were unimaginative, predatory, pretentious. Theirs
was a naked, metal-hard world, stripped of all but its material values, and these glittered like artificial gems in the sun
of their ambition. An unwholesome proportion of the faculty
was effete, innocuous, and pretentious also, with a flabby
softness of intellectual and spiritual fiber and even a lack of
personal force. They clustered together like sheared sheep in
a storm. They were a sort of mass-man, conscious of no spiritual status even as men, much less as a people. They were a
futile, hamstrung group, who took a liberal education (they
despised mechanical and technical learning) to be a process
of devitalization and to be significant in extrinsics only. They
awarded a lot of medallions and watch charms. Try as I
might, I could feel no kinship with them. Obviously my home
was not among them.

I thought often of Lebman in the pre-dawn quiet of my
room, saying, "Not a place in geography, but a million things
and people your spirit touches, absorbed and absorbing." I
did not want sanctuary, a soft nest protected from the hard,
strengthening winds that blew hot and cold through the
world's teeming, turbulent valley. I wanted to face the wind. I
wanted the strength to face it to come from some inexpressi-
bly deep well of feeling of oneness with the wind, of belonging to something, some soul-force outside myself, bigger than
myself, but yet a part of me. Not family merely, or institution, or race; but a people and all their topless strivings; a
nation and its million destinies. I did not think in concrete
terms at first. Indeed, I had but the shadow of this thought
and feeling. But slowly the shadow grew, taking form and
outline, until at last I felt and knew that my estrangement
from my fellows and theirs from me was but a failure to realize that we were all estranged from something fundamentally
ours. We were all withdrawn from the heady, brawling, lusty
stream of culture which had nourished us and which was the

stream by whose turbid waters all of America fed. We were spiritually homeless, dying and alone, each on his separate hammock of memory and experience.

This was emotional awareness. Intellectual comprehension came slowly, painfully, as an abscess comes. I laid no blame beyond immediate experience. Through hurt and pride and fear, they of this class (and of what others I did not know) had deliberately cut themselves off not only from their historical past but also from their historical future. Life had become a matter of asylum in some extra time-sphere whose hard limits were the rising and setting sun. Each day was another and a different unrelated epoch in which they had to learn again the forgetting of ancestral memory, to learn again to bar the senses from the sights and sounds and tastes of a way of life that they denied, to close the mind to the incessant close roar of a world to which they felt unrelated. This vitiated them, wilted them, dwarfed their spirits, and they slunk about their gray astringent world like ghosts from the shores of Lethe.

I tried fumblingly to tell them something of this, for my desire for spiritual wholeness was great. I yearned for some closer association with these men and women, some bond that was not knit of frustration and despair. In impersonal terms I tried to tell them something of this. They snubbed me. They looked upon me as a pariah who would destroy their societal bond, their asylum. They called me fool—and perhaps I was. Certainly I was presumptuous. Their whispers and their sterile laughter mocked me. They were at pains to ridicule me before the students. They called me radical, and it was an expletive the way they used it, said in the same way that one calls another a snake. For three years I held on, and then I was fired.

But my seeking grew in intensity and the need to find became an ache almost physical. For seven, eight years after that I sought with the same frantic insatiability with which one lives through a brutal, lustful dream. It was planless seeking, for I felt then that I would not know the thing I sought until I found it. It was both something within and something without myself. Within, it was like the buried memory of a name that will not come to the tongue for utterance. Without, it was the muffled roll of drums receding through a darkling wood. And so, restricted in ways I had no comprehension of, I sought, and everywhere—because I sought among the things and folk I knew—I went unfinding.

JAMES BALDWIN (1924–   )

Notes of a Native Son, Nobody Knows My Name, and The Fire Next Time *established the reputation of James Baldwin as an undisputed master of the contemporary American essay. With his four novels, a collection of short stories, and two plays, Baldwin joined Ralph Ellison in the mainstream of contemporary American letters and in the limelight of critical attention as one of two Negro writers who share in the expression of the American literary zeitgeist of the 1950's and 1960's. He was born and brought up in New York City and lived in Europe for a number of years. The following autobiographical sketch opened his first collection of essays in book form,* Notes of a Native Son (1955). *Baldwin's views on many questions, literary and social, appear in "James Baldwin . . . in Conversation" in the Literary Criticism section.*

Autobiographical Notes

I was born in Harlem thirty-one years ago. I began plotting novels at about the time I learned to read. The story of my childhood is the usual bleak fantasy, and we can dismiss it with the unrestrained observation that I certainly would not consider living it again. In those days my mother was given to the exasperating and mysterious habit of having babies. As they were born, I took them over with one hand and held a book with the other. The children probably suffered, though they have since been kind enough to deny it, and in this way I read *Uncle Tom's Cabin* and *A Tale of Two Cities* over and over and over again; in this way, in fact, I read just about everything I could get my hands on—except the Bible, probably because it was the only book I was encouraged to read. I must also confess that I wrote—a great deal—and my first profes-

sional triumph, in any case, the first effort of mine to be seen
in print, occurred at the age of twelve or thereabouts, when a
short story I had written about the Spanish revolution won
some sort of prize in an extremely short-lived church newspaper. I remember the story was censored by the lady editor,
though I don't remember why, and I was outraged.

Also wrote plays, and songs, for one of which I received a
letter of congratulations from Mayor La Guardia, and poetry, about which the less said, the better. My mother was delighted by all these goings-on, but my father wasn't; he
wanted me to be a preacher. When I was fourteen I became a
preacher, and when I was seventeen I stopped. Very shortly
thereafter I left home. For God knows how long I struggled
with the world of commerce and industry—I guess they
would say they struggled with *me*—and when I was about
twenty-one I had enough done of a novel to get a Saxton Fellowship. When I was twenty-two the fellowship was over, the
novel turned out to be unsalable, and I started waiting on tables in a Village restaurant and writing book reviews—
mostly, as it turned out, about the Negro problem, concerning which the color of my skin made me automatically an expert. Did another book, in company with photographer Theodore Pelatowski, about the store-front churches in Harlem.
This book met exactly the same fate as my first—fellowship,
but no sale. (It was a Rosenwald Fellowship.) By the time I
was twenty-four I had decided to stop reviewing books about
the Negro problem—which, by this time, was only slightly
less horrible in print than it was in life—and I packed my
bags and went to France, where I finished, God knows how,
Go Tell It on the Mountain.

Any writer, I suppose, feels that the world into which he
was born is nothing less than a conspiracy against the cultivation of his talent—which attitude certainly has a great deal to
support it. On the other hand, it is only because the world
looks on his talent with such a frightening indifference that
the artist is compelled to make his talent important. So that
any writer, looking back over even so short a span of time as
I am here forced to assess, finds that the things which hurt
him and the things which helped him cannot be divorced
from each other; he could be helped in a certain way only
because he was hurt in a certain way; and his help is simply
to be enabled to move from one conundrum to the next—one
is tempted to say that he moves from one disaster to the next.
When one begins looking for influences one finds them by the
score. I haven't thought much about my own, not enough
anyway; I hazard that the King James Bible, the rhetoric of

the store-front church, something ironic and violent and perpetually understated in Negro speech—and something of Dickens' love for bravura—have something to do with me today; but I wouldn't stake my life on it. Likewise, innumerable people have helped me in many ways; but finally, I suppose, the most difficult (and most rewarding) thing in my life has been the fact that I was born a Negro and was forced, therefore, to effect some kind of truce with this reality. (Truce, by the way, is the best one can hope for.)

One of the difficulties about being a Negro writer (and this is not special pleading, since I don't mean to suggest that he has it worse than anybody else) is that the Negro problem is written about so widely. The bookshelves groan under the weight of information, and everyone therefore considers himself informed. And this information, furthermore, operates usually (generally, popularly) to reinforce traditional attitudes. Of traditional attitudes there are only two—For or Against—and I, personally, find it difficult to say which attitude has caused me the most pain. I am perfectly aware that the change from ill-will to good-will, however motivated, however imperfect, however expressed, is better than no change at all.

But it is part of the business of the writer—as I see it—to examine attitudes, to go beneath the surface, to tape the source. From this point of view the Negro problem is nearly inaccessible. It is not only written about so widely; it is written about so badly. It is quite possible to say that the price a Negro pays for becoming articulate is to find himself, at length, with nothing to be articulate about. ("You taught me the language," says Caliban to Prospero, "and my profit on't is I know how to curse.") Consider: the tremendous social activity that this problem generates imposes on whites and Negroes alike the necessity of looking forward, of working to bring about a better day. This is fine, it keeps the waters troubled; it is all, indeed, that has made possible the Negro's progress. Nevertheless, social affairs are not generally speaking the writer's prime concern, whether they ought to be or not; it is absolutely necessary that he establish between himself and these affairs a distance that will allow, at least, for clarity, so that before he can look forward in any meaningful sense, he must first be allowed to take a long look back. In the context of the Negro problem neither whites nor blacks, for excellent reasons of their own, have the faintest desire to look back; but I think that the past is all that makes the present coherent, and further, that the past will remain horrible for exactly as long as we refuse to assess it honestly.

I know, in any case, that the most crucial time in my own development came when I was forced to recognize that I was a kind of bastard of the West; when I followed the line of my past I did not find myself in Europe but in Africa. And this meant that in some subtle way, in a really profound way, I brought to Shakespeare, Bach, Rembrandt, to the stones of Paris, to the cathedral at Chartres, and to the Empire State Building, a special attitude. These were not really my creations, they did not contain my history; I might search in them in vain forever for any reflection of myself. I was an interloper; this was not my heritage. At the same time I had no other heritage which I could possibly hope to use—I had certainly been unfitted for the jungle or the tribe. I would have to appropriate these white centuries, I would have to make them mine—I would have to accept my special attitude, my special place in this scheme—otherwise I would have no place in *any* scheme. What was the most difficult was the fact that I was forced to admit something I had always hidden from myself, which the American Negro has had to hide from himself as the price of his public progress; that I hated and feared white people. This did not mean that I loved black people; on the contrary, I despised them, possibly because they failed to produce Rembrandt. In effect, I hated and feared the world. And this meant, not only that I thus gave the world an altogether murderous power over me, but also that in such a self-destroying limbo I could never hope to write.

One writes out of one thing only—one's own experience. Everything depends on how relentlessly one forces from this experience the last drop, sweet or bitter, it can possibly give. This is the only real concern of the artist, to recreate out of the disorder of life that order which is art. The difficulty then, for me, of being a Negro writer was the fact that I was, in effect, prohibited from examining my own experience too closely by the tremendous demands and the very real dangers of my social situation.

I don't think the dilemma outlined above is uncommon. I do think, since writers work in the disastrously explicit medium of language, that it goes a little way towards explaining why, out of the enormous resources of Negro speech and life, and despite the example of Negro music, prose written by Negroes has been generally speaking so pallid and so harsh. I have not written about being a Negro at such length because I expect that to be my only subject, but only because it was the gate I had to unlock before I could hope to write about anything else. I don't think that the Negro problem in Amer-

ica can be even discussed coherently without bearing in mind
its context; its context being the history, traditions, customs,
the moral assumptions and preoccupations of the country; in
short, the general social fabric. Appearances to the contrary,
no one in America escapes its effects and everyone in America bears some responsibility for it. I believe this the more
firmly because it is the overwhelming tendency to speak of
this problem as though it were a thing apart. But in the work
of Faulkner, in the general attitude and certain specific passages in Robert Penn Warren, and, most significantly, in the
advent of Ralph Ellison, one sees the beginnings—at least—
of a more genuinely penetrating search. Mr. Ellison, by the
way, is the first Negro novelist I have ever read to utilize in
language, and brilliantly, some of the ambiguity and irony of
Negro life.

About my interests: I don't know if I have any, unless the
morbid desire to own a sixteen-millimeter camera and make
experimental movies can be so classified. Otherwise, I love to
eat and drink—it's my melancholy conviction that I've
scarcely ever had enough to eat (this is because it's *impossible* to eat enough if you're worried about the next meal)—
and I love to argue with people who do not disagree with me
too profoundly, and I love to laugh. I do *not* like bohemia, or
bohemians, I do not like people whose principal aim is pleasure, and I do not like people who are *earnest* about anything. I don't like people who like me because I'm a Negro;
neither do I like people who find in the same accident
grounds for contempt. I love America more than any other
country in the world, and, exactly for this reason, I insist on
the right to criticize her perpetually. I think all theories are
suspect, that the finest principles may have to be modified, or
may even be pulverized by the demands of life, and that one
must find, therefore, one's own moral center and move
through the world hoping that this center will guide one
aright. I consider that I have many responsibilities, but none
greater than this: to last, as Hemingway says, and get my
work done.

I want to be an honest man and a good writer.

ARNA BONTEMPS (1902–   )

A biographical note on Arna Bontemps appears in the Fiction section (see p. 87). The autobiographical essay which follows first appeared in "The South Today . . . 100 Years After Appomattox," a Special Supplement to Harper's *magazine, April, 1965.*

Why I Returned

At our request Arna Bontemps, whose books include American Negro Poetry, Story of the Negro, *and* 100 Years of Negro Freedom, *explains why he finally came South to live. These reminiscences of his father, his Uncle Buddy, the Scottsboro trials, and the early assaults on Jim Crow provide a fresh perspective on the present struggle for Negro rights.*

The last time I visited Louisiana, the house in which I was born was freshly painted. To my surprise, it seemed almost attractive. The present occupants, I learned, were a Negro minister and his family. Why I expected the place to be run down and the neighborhood decayed is not clear, but somewhere in my subconscious the notion that rapid deterioration was inevitable where Negroes live had been planted and allowed to grow. Moreover, familiar as I am with the gloomier aspects of living Jim Crow, this assumption did not appall me. I could reject the snide inferences. Seeking my birthplace again, however, after many years, I felt apologetic on other grounds.

Mine had not been a varmint-infested childhood so often the hallmark of Negro American autobiography. My parents and grandparents had been well-fed, well-clothed, and well-housed, although in my earliest recollections of the corner at Ninth and Winn in Alexandria both streets were rutted and

sloppy. On Winn there was an abominable ditch where water
settled for weeks at a time. I can remember Crazy George,
the town idiot, following a flock of geese with the bough of a
tree in his hand, standing in slush while the geese paddled
about or probed into the muck. So fascinated was I, in fact,
I did not hear my grandmother calling from the kitchen door.
It was after I felt her hand on my shoulder shaking me out
of my daydream that I said something that made her laugh.
"You called me Arna," I protested, when she insisted on
knowing why I had not answered. "My name is George." But
I became Arna for the rest of her years.

I had already become aware of nicknames among the people we regarded as members of the family. Teel, Mousie,
Buddy, Pinkie, Ya-ya, Mat, and Pig all had other names
which one heard occasionally. I got the impression that to be
loved intensely one needed a nickname. I was glad my grandmother, whose love mattered so much, had found one she
liked for me.

As I recall, my hand was in my grandmother's a good part
of the time. If we were not standing outside the picket gate
waiting for my young uncles to come home from school, we
were under the tree in the front yard picking up pecans after
one of the boys had climbed up and shaken the branches. If
we were not decorating a backyard bush with eggshells, we
were driving in our buggy across the bridge to Pineville on
the other side of the Red River.

This idyll came to a sudden, senseless end at a time when
everything about it seemed flawless. One afternoon my
mother and her several sisters had come out of their sewing
room with thimbles still on their fingers, needles and thread
stuck to their tiny aprons, to fill their pockets with pecans.
Next, it seemed, we were at the railroad station catching a
train to California, my mother, sister, and I, with a young
woman named Susy.

The story behind it, I learned, concerned my father. When
he was not away working at brick or stone construction,
other things occupied his time. He had come from a family
of builders. His oldest brother had married into the Metoyer
family on Cane River, descendants of the free Negroes who
were the original builders of the famous Melrose plantation
mansion. Another brother older than my father went down to
New Orleans, where his daughter married one of the prominent jazzmen. My father was a bandman himself and, when
he was not working too far away, the chances were he would
be blowing his horn under the direction of Claiborne Williams, whose passion for band music awakened the impulse

that worked its way up the river and helped to quicken American popular music.

My father was one of those dark Negroes with "good" hair, meaning almost straight. This did not bother anybody in Avoyelles Parish, where the type was common and "broken French" accents expected, but later in California people who had traveled in the Far East wondered if he were not a Ceylonese or something equally exotic. In Alexandria his looks, good clothes, and hauteur were something of a disadvantage in the first decade of this century.

He was walking on Lee Street one night when two white men wavered out of a saloon and blocked his path. One of them muttered, "Let's walk over the big nigger." My father was capable of fury, and he might have reasoned differently at another time, but that night he calmly stepped aside, allowing the pair to have the walk to themselves. The decision he made as he walked on home changed everything for all of us.

My first clear memory of my father as a person is of him waiting for us outside the Southern Pacific Depot in Los Angeles. He was shy about showing emotion, and he greeted us quickly on our arrival and let us know this was the place he had chosen for us to end our journey. We had tickets to San Francisco and were prepared to continue beyond if necessary.

We moved into a house in a neighborhood where we were the only colored family. The people next door and up and down the block were friendly and talkative, the weather was perfect, there wasn't a mud puddle anywhere, and my mother seemed to float about on the clean air. When my grandmother and a host of others followed us to this refreshing new country, I began to pick up comment about the place we had left, comment which had been withheld from me while we were still in Louisiana.

They talked mainly about my grandmother's younger brother, nicknamed Buddy. I could not remember seeing him in Louisiana, and I now learned he had been at the Keeley Institute in New Orleans taking a cure for alcoholism. A framed portrait of Uncle Buddy was placed in my grandmother's living room in California, a young mulatto dandy in elegant cravat and jeweled stickpin. All the talk about him gave me an impression of style, grace, éclat.

That impression vanished a few years later, however, when we gathered to wait for him in my grandmother's house; he entered wearing a detachable collar without a tie. His clothes did not fit. They had been slept in for nearly a week on the train. His shoes had come unlaced. His face was pock-marked. Nothing resembling the picture in the living room.

Two things redeemed the occasion, however. He opened his makeshift luggage and brought out jars of syrup, bags of candy my grandmother had said in her letters that she missed, pecans, and filé for making gumbo. He had stuffed his suitcase with these instead of clothes; he had not brought an overcoat or a change of underwear. As we ate the sweets, he began to talk. He was not trying to impress or even enter-tain us. He was just telling how things were down home, how he had not taken a drink or been locked up since he came back from Keeley the last time, how the family of his em-ployer and benefactor had been scattered or died, how the schoolteacher friend of the family was getting along, how high the Red River had risen along the levee, and such things.

Someone mentioned his white employer's daughter. A rumor persisted that Buddy had once had a dangerous crush on her. This, I took it, had to be back in the days when the picture in the living room was made, but the dim suggestion of interracial romance had an air of unreality. It was all mostly gossip, he commented, with only a shadow of a smile. Never had been much to it, and it was too long ago to talk about now. He did acknowledge, significantly, I thought, that his boss's daughter had been responsible for his enjoyment of poetry and fiction and had taught him perhaps a thousand songs, but neither of these circumstances had undermined his life-long employment in her father's bakery, where his spe-cialty was fancy cakes. Buddy had never married. Neither had the girl.

When my mother became ill, a year or so after Buddy's arrival, we went to live with my grandmother in the country for a time. Buddy was there. He had acquired a rusticity wholly foreign to his upbringing. He had never before worked out of doors. Smoking a corncob pipe and wearing oversized clothes provided by my uncles, he resembled a scare-crow in the garden, but the dry air and the smell of green vegetables seemed to be good for him. I promptly became his companion and confidant in the corn rows.

At mealtime we were occasionally joined by my father, home from his bricklaying. The two men eyed each other with suspicion, but they did not quarrel immediately. Mostly they reminisced about Louisiana. My father would say, "Sometimes I miss all that. If I was just thinking about myself, I might want to go back and try it again. But I've got the children to think about—their education."

"Folks talk a lot about California," Buddy would reply thoughtfully, "but I'd a heap rather be down home than here, if it wasn't for the *conditions*."

Obviously their remarks made sense to each other, but they left me with a deepening question. Why was this exchange repeated after so many of their conversations? What was it that made the South—excusing what Buddy called the *conditions* —so appealing for them?

There was less accord between them in the attitudes they revealed when each of the men talked to me privately. My father respected Buddy's ability to quote the whole of Thomas Hood's "The Vision of Eugene Aram," praised his reading and spelling ability, but he was concerned, almost troubled, about the possibility of my adopting the old derelict as an example. He was horrified by Buddy's casual and frequent use of the word *nigger*. Buddy even forgot and used it in the presence of white people once or twice that year, and was soundly criticized for it. Buddy's new friends, moreover, were sometimes below the level of polite respect. They were not bad people. They were what my father described as don't-care folk. To top it all, Buddy was still crazy about the minstrel shows and minstrel talk that had been the joy of his young manhood. He loved dialect stories, preacher stories, ghost stories, slave and master stories. He half-believed in signs and charms and mumbo-jumbo, and he believed wholeheartedly in ghosts.

I took it that my father was still endeavoring to counter Buddy's baneful influence when he sent me away to a white boarding school during my high school years, after my mother had died. "Now don't go up there acting colored," he cautioned. I believe I carried out his wish. He sometimes threatened to pull me out of school and let me scuffle for myself the minute I fell short in any one of several ways he indicated. Before I finished college, I had begun to feel that in some large and important areas I was being miseducated, and that perhaps I should have rebelled.

How dare anyone, parent, schoolteacher, or merely literary critic, tell me not to act *colored*? White people have been enjoying the privilege of acting like Negroes for more than a hundred years. The minstrel show, their most popular form of entertainment in America for a whole generation, simply epitomized, while it exaggerated, this privilege. Today nearly everyone who goes on a dance floor starts acting colored immediately, and this had been going on since the cakewalk was picked up from Negroes and became the rage. Why should I be ashamed of such influences? In popular music, as in the music of religious fervor, there is a style that is unmistakable, and its origin is certainly no mystery. On the playing field a Willie Mays could be detected by the way he catches a ball, even if his face were hidden. Should the way some Negroes walk be changed or emulated? Sometimes it is possible to tell whether or not a cook is a Negro without going into the kitchen. How about this?

In their opposing attitudes toward roots my father and my great uncle made me aware of a conflict in which every educated American Negro, and some who are not educated, must somehow take sides. By implication at least, one group advocates embracing the riches of the folk heritage; their opposites demand a clean break with the past and all it represents. Had I not gone home summers and hobnobbed with Negroes, I would have finished college without knowing that any Negro other than Paul Laurence Dunbar ever wrote a poem. I would have come out imagining that the story of the Negro could be told in two short paragraphs: a statement about jungle people in Africa and an equally brief account of the slavery issue in American history.

So what did one do after concluding that for him a break with the past and the shedding of his Negro-ness were not only impossible but unthinkable? First, perhaps, like myself, he went to New York in the 'twenties, met young Negro writers and intellectuals who were similarly searching, learned poems like Claude McKay's "Harlem Dancer" and Jean Toomer's "Song of the Son," and started writing and publishing things in this vein himself.

My first book was published just after the Depression struck. Buddy was in it, conspicuously, and I sent him a copy, which I imagine he read. In any case, he took the occasion to celebrate. Returning from an evening with his don't-care friends, he wavered along the highway and was hit and killed by an automobile. He was sixty-seven, I believe.

Alfred Harcourt, Sr. was my publisher. When he invited me to the office, I found that he was also to be my editor. He explained with a smile that he was back on the job doing editorial work because of the hard times. I soon found out what he meant. Book business appeared to be as bad as every other kind, and the lively and talented young people I had met in Harlem were scurrying to whatever brier patches they could find. I found one in Alabama.

It was the best of times and the worst of times to run to that state for refuge. Best, because the summer air was so laden with honeysuckle and spiraea it almost drugged the senses at night. I have occasionally returned since then but never at a time when the green of trees, of countryside, or even of swamps seemed so wanton. While paying jobs were harder to find here than in New York, indeed scarcely existed, one did not see evidences of hunger. Negro girls worked in kitchens not for wages but for the toting privilege —permission to take home leftovers.

The men and boys rediscovered woods and swamps and streams with which their ancestors had been intimate a century earlier, and about which their grandparents still talked wistfully. The living critters still abounded. They were as wild and numerous as anybody had ever dreamed, some small, some edible, some monstrous. I made friends with these people and went with them on possum hunts, and I was astonished to learn how much game they could bring home without gunpowder, which they did not have. When the possum was treed by the dogs, a small boy went up and shook him off the limb, and the bigger fellows finished him with sticks. Nets and traps would do for birds and fish. Cottontail rabbits driven into a clearing were actually run down and caught by barefoot boys.

Such carryings-on amused them while it delighted their palates. It also took their minds off the hard times, and they were ready for church when Sunday came. I followed them there, too, and soon began to understand why they enjoyed it so much. The preaching called to mind James Weldon Johnson's "The Creation" and "Go Down Death." The long-meter singing was from another world. The shouting was ecstasy itself. At a primitive Baptist foot washing I saw bench-walking for the first time, and it left me breathless. The young woman who rose from her seat and skimmed from the front of the church to the back, her wet feet lightly touching the tops of the pews, her eyes upward, could have astounded me no more had she walked on water. The members fluttered and wailed, rocked the church with their singing, accepted the miracle for what it was.

It was also the worst times to be in northern Alabama. That was the year, 1931, of the nine Scottsboro boys and their trials in nearby Decatur. Instead of chasing possums at night and swimming in creeks in the daytime, this group of kids without jobs and nothing else to do had taken to riding empty boxcars. When they found themselves in a boxcar with two white girls wearing overalls and traveling the same way, they knew they were in bad trouble. The charge against them was rape, and the usual finding in Alabama, when a Negro man was so much as remotely suspected, was guilty; the usual penalty, death.

To relieve the tension, as we hoped, we drove to Athens one night and listened to a program of music by young people from Negro high schools and colleges in the area. A visitor arrived from Decatur during the intermission and reported shocking developments at the trial that day. One of the girls involved had given testimony about herself which reasonably should have taken the onus from the boys. It had only succeeded in infuriating the crowd around the courthouse. The rumor that reached Athens was that crowds were spilling along the highway, lurking in unseemly places, threatening to vent their anger. After the music was over, someone suggested nervously that those of us from around Huntsville leave at the same time, keep our cars close together as we drove home, be prepared to stand by, possibly help, if anyone met with mischief.

We readily agreed. Though the drive home was actually uneventful, the tension remained, and I began to take stock with a seriousness comparable to my father's when he stepped aside for the Saturday night bullies on Lee Street in Alexandria. I was younger than he had been when he made his move, but my family was already larger by one. Moreover, I had weathered a Northern as well as a Southern exposure. My education was different, and what I was reading in newspapers differed greatly from anything he could have found in the Alexandria *Town Talk* in the first decade of this century.

With Ghandi making world news in India while the Scottsboro case inflamed passions in Alabama and awakened consciences elsewhere, I thought I could sense something beginning to shape up, possibly something on a wide scale. As a matter of fact, I had already written a stanza foreshadowing the application of a nonviolent strategy to the Negro's efforts in the South:

We are not come to wage a strife
   With swords upon this hill;
It is not wise to waste the life
   Against a stubborn will.
Yet would we die as some have done:
Beating a way for the rising sun.

Even so, deliverance did not yet seem imminent, and it was becoming plain that an able-bodied young Negro with a healthy family could not continue to keep friends in that community if he sat around trifling with a typewriter on the shady side of his house when he should have been working or at least trying to raise something for the table. So we moved on to Chicago.

Crime seemed to be the principal occupation of the South Side at the time of our arrival. The openness of it so startled us we could scarcely believe what we saw. Twice our small apartment was burglarized. Nearly every week we witnessed a stickup, purse-snatching, or something equally dismaying in the street. Once I saw two men get out of a car, enter one of those blinded shops around the corner from us, return dragging a resisting victim, slam him into the back seat of the car, and speed away. We had fled from the jungle of Alabama's Scottsboro era to the jungle of Chicago's crime-ridden South Side, and one was as terrifying as the other.

Despite literary encouragement, and the heartiness of a writing clan that adopted me and bolstered my courage, I never felt that I could settle permanently with my family in Chicago. I could not accept the ghetto, and ironclad residential restrictions against Negroes situated as we were made escape impossible, confining us to neighborhoods where we had to fly home each evening before darkness fell and honest people abandoned the streets to predators. Garbage was dumped in alleys around us. Police protection was regarded as a farce. Corruption was everywhere.

When I inquired about transfers for two of our children to integrated schools which were actually more accessible to our address, I was referred to a person not connected with the school system or the city government. He assured me he could arrange the transfers—at an outrageous price. This represented ways in which Negro leadership was operating in the community at that time and by which it had been reduced to impotence.

I did not consider exchanging this way of life for the institutionalized assault on Negro personality one encountered in the Alabama of the Scottsboro trials, but suddenly the campus of a Negro college I had twice visited in Tennessee began to seem attractive. A measure of isolation, a degree of security seemed possible there. If a refuge for the harassed Negro could be found anywhere in the 1930s, it had to be in such a setting.

Fisk University, since its beginnings in surplus barracks, provided by a general of the occupying army six months after the close of the Civil War, had always striven to exemplify racial concord. Integration started immediately with children of white teachers and continued till state laws forced segregation after the turn of the century. Even then, a mixed faculty was retained, together with a liberal environment, and these eventually won a truce from an outside community that gradually changed from hostility to indifference to acceptance and perhaps a certain pride. Its founders helped fight the battle for public schools in Nashville, and donated part of the college's property for this purpose. Its students first introduced Negro spirituals to the musical world. The college provided a setting for a continuing dialogue between scholars across barriers and brought to the city before 1943 a pioneering Institute of Race Relations and a Program of African Studies, both firsts in the region. When a nationally known scholar told me in Chicago that he found the atmosphere *yeasty*, I thought I understood what he meant.

We had made the move, and I had become the Librarian at Fisk when a series of train trips during World War II gave me an opportunity for reflections of another kind. I started making notes for an essay to be called "Thoughts in a Jim Crow Car." Before I could finish it, Supreme Court action removed the curtains in the railway diners, and the essay lost its point. While I had been examining my own feelings and trying to understand the need men have for customs like this, the pattern had altered. Compliance followed with what struck me, surprisingly, as an attitude of relief by all concerned. White passengers, some of whom I recognized by their positions in the public life of Nashville, who had been in a habit of maintaining a frozen silence until the train crossed the Ohio River, now nodded and began chatting with Negroes before the train left the Nashville station. I wanted to stand up and cheer. When the Army began to desegregate its units, I was sure I detected a fatal weakness in our enemy. Segregation, the monster that had terrorized my parents and driven them out of the green Eden in which they had been born, was itself vulnerable and could be attacked, possibly destroyed. I felt as if I had witnessed the first act of a spectacular drama. I wanted to stay around for the second.

Without the miseries of segregation, the South as a homeplace for a Negro of my temperament had clear advantages. In deciding to wait and see how things worked out, I was also betting that progress toward this objective in the Southern region would be more rapid, the results more satisfying, than could be expected in the metropolitan centers of the North, where whites were leaving the crumbling central areas to Negroes while they themselves moved into restricted suburbs and began setting up another kind of closed society.

The second act of the spectacular on which I had focused began with the 1954, decision of the Supreme Court. While this was a landmark, it provoked no wild optimism. I had no doubt that the tide would now turn, but it was not until the freedom movement began to express itself that I felt reassured. We were in the middle of it in Nashville. Our little world commenced to sway and rock with the fury of a resurrection. I tried to discover just how the energy was generated. I think I found it. The singing that broke out in the ranks of protest marchers, in the jails where sit-in demonstrators were held, in the mass meetings and boycott rallies, was gloriously appropriate. The only American songs suitable for a resurrection—or a revolution, for that matter—are Negro spirituals. The surge these awakened was so mighty it threatened to change the name of our era from the "space age" to the "age of freedom."

The Southern Negro's link with his past seems to me worth preserving. His greater pride in being himself, I would say, is all to the good, and I think I detect a growing nostalgia for these virtues in the speech of relatives in the North. They talk a great deal about "Soulville" nowadays, when they mean "South." "Soulbrothers" are simply the homefolks. "Soulfood" includes black-eyed peas, chitterlings, grits, and gravy. Aretha Franklin, originally from Memphis, sings, "Soulfood—it'll make you limber; it'll make you quick." Vacations in Soulville by these expatriates in the North tend to become more frequent and to last longer since times began to get better.

Colleagues of mine at Fisk who like me have pondered the question of staying or going have told me their reasons. The effective young Dean of the Chapel, for example, who since has been wooed away by Union Theological Seminary, felt constrained mainly by the opportunities he had here to guide a large number of students and by the privilege of identifying with them. John W. Work, the musicologist and composer, finds the cultural environment more stimulating than any he could discover in the North. Aaron Douglas, an art professor, came down thirty-four years ago to get a "real, concrete experience of the touch and feel of the South." Looking back, he reflects, "If one could discount the sadness, the misery, the near-volcanic intensity of Negro life in most of the South, and concentrate on the mild, almost tropical climate and the beauty of the landscape, one is often tempted to forget the senseless cruelty and inhumanity the strong too often inflict on the weak."

For my own part, I am staying on in the South to write something about the changes I have seen in my lifetime, and about the Negro's awakening and regeneration. That is my theme, and this is where the main action is. There is also the spectacular I am watching. Was a climax reached with the passage of the Civil Rights Act last year? Or was it with Martin Luther King's addressing Lyndon B. Johnson as "my fellow Southerner"? Having stayed this long, it would be absurd not to wait for the third act—and possibly the most dramatic.

MALCOLM X (1925–1965)

The legend, aura, and mystique surrounding Malcolm X, an epitome of the new black nationalism, was clearly reflected in 1967 with the publication of For Malcolm, *an anthology of poems on the life and death of Malcolm X, edited by Dudley Randall and Margaret G. Burroughs. Malcolm X was born in Omaha, Nebraska, the seventh child of Reverend Earl Little, a Baptist minister from the West Indies and an organizer for Marcus Garvey's Universal Negro Improvement Association. The family was continually on the move, and the young Malcolm's early years were spent in Omaha, Milwaukee, Lansing, Michigan, and Roxbury, a suburb of Boston. He became a Black Muslim, was an assistant minister in Detroit and a founder of Muslim temples throughout the United States. He rose to prominence in the hierarchy of the black Islamic movement, second only to the prophet, Elijah Muhammed. Malcolm visited Mecca and made two trips to Africa. In 1964 he broke with Elijah Muhammed, formed his own organization—the Organization of Afro-American Unity—to con-*

centrate on political rights for black Americans and also organized his own Islamic religious center, the Muslim Mosque, Inc. On February 21, 1965, during a meeting of his political organization in the Audubon Ballroom in Harlem, he was shot and killed. The Autobiography of Malcolm X, *published in 1965, has become a classic of contemporary black nationalist thinking. Following is the first chapter of the book.*

The Autobiography of Malcolm X

Chapter One—Nightmare

When my mother was pregnant with me, she told me later, a party of hooded Ku Klux Klan riders galloped up to our home in Omaha, Nebraska, one night. Surrounding the house, brandishing their shotguns and rifles, they shouted for my father to come out. My mother went to the front door and opened it. Standing where they could see her pregnant condition, she told them that she was alone with her three small children, and that my father was away, preaching, in Milwaukee. The Klansmen shouted threats and warnings at her that we had better get out of town because "the good Christian white people" were not going to stand for my father's "spreading trouble" among the "good" Negroes of Omaha with the "back to Africa" preachings of Marcus Garvey.

My father, the Reverend Earl Little, was a Baptist minister, a dedicated organizer for Marcus Aurelius Garvey's U.N.I.A. (Universal Negro Improvement Association). With the help of such disciples as my father, Garvey, from his headquarters in New York City's Harlem, was raising the banner of black-race purity and exhorting the Negro masses to return to their ancestral African homeland—a cause which had made Garvey the most controversial black man on earth.

Still shouting threats, the Klansmen finally spurred their horses and galloped around the house, shattering every window pane with their gun butts. Then they rode off into the night, their torches flaring, as suddenly as they had come.

My father was enraged when he returned. He decided to wait until I was born—which would be soon—and then the family would move. I am not sure why he made this decision, for he was not a frightened Negro, as most then were, and many still are today. My father was a big, six-foot-four, very black man. He had only one eye. How he had lost the other one I have never known. He was from Reynolds, Georgia, where he had left school after the third or maybe fourth grade. He believed, as did Marcus Garvey, that freedom, independence and self-respect could never be achieved by the Negro in America, and that therefore the Negro should leave America to the white man and return to his African land of origin. Among the reasons my father had decided to risk and dedicate his life to help disseminate this philosophy among his people was that he had seen four of his six brothers die by violence, three of them killed by white men, including one by lynching. What my father could not know then was that of the remaining three, including himself, only one, my Uncle Jim, would die in bed, of natural causes. Northern white police were later to shoot my Uncle Oscar. And my father was finally himself to die by the white man's hands.

It has always been my belief that I, too, will die by violence. I have done all that I can to be prepared. . . .

One afternoon in 1931 when Wilfred, Hilda, Philbert, and I came home, my mother and father were having one of their arguments. There had lately been a lot of tension around the house because of Black Legion threats. Anyway, my father had taken one of the rabbits which we were raising, and ordered my mother to cook it. We raised rabbits, but sold them to whites. My father had taken a rabbit from the rabbit pen. He had pulled off the rabbit's head. He was so strong, he needed no knife to behead chickens or rabbits. With one twist of his big black hands he simply twisted off the head and threw the bleeding-necked thing back at my mother's feet.

My mother was crying. She started to skin the rabbit, preparatory to cooking it. But my father was so angry he slammed on out of the front door and started walking up the road toward town.

It was then that my mother had this vision. She had always been a strange woman in this sense, and had always had a strong intuition of things about to happen. And most of her children are the same way, I think. When something is about to happen, I can feel something, sense something. I never have known something to happen that has caught me completely off guard—except once. And that was when, years later, I discovered facts I couldn't believe about a man who, up until that discovery, I would gladly have given my life for.

My father was well up the road when my mother ran screaming out onto the porch. *"Early! Early!"* She screamed his name. She clutched up her apron in one hand, and ran down across the yard and into the road. My father turned around. He saw her. For some reason, considering how angry he had been when he left, he waved at her. But he kept on going.

She told me later, my mother did, that she had a vision of my father's end. All the rest of the afternoon, she was not herself, crying and nervous and upset. She finished cooking the rabbit and put the whole thing in the warmer part of the black stove. When my father was not back home by our bedtime, my mother hugged and clutched us, and we felt strange, not knowing what to do, because she had never acted like that.

I remember waking up to the sound of my mother's screaming again. When I scrambled out, I saw the police in the living room; they were trying to calm her down. She had snatched on her clothes to go with them. And all of us children who were staring knew without anyone having to say it that something terrible had happened to our father.

My mother was taken by the police to the hospital, and to a room where a sheet was over my father in a bed, and she wouldn't look, she was afraid to look. Probably it was wise that she didn't. My father's skull, on one side, was crushed in, I was told later. Negroes in Lansing have always whispered that he was attacked, and then laid across some tracks for a streetcar to run over him. His body was cut almost in half.

He lived two and a half hours in that condition. Negroes then were stronger than they are now, especially Georgia Negroes. Negroes born in Georgia had to be strong simply to survive.

It was morning when we children at home got the word that he was dead. I was six. I can remember a vague commotion, the house filled up with people crying, saying bitterly that the white Black Legion had finally gotten him. My mother was hysterical. In the bedroom, women were holding smelling salts under her nose. She was still hysterical at the funeral.

I don't have a very clear memory of the funeral, either. Oddly, the main thing I remember is that it wasn't in a church, and that surprised me, since my father was a preacher, and I had been where he preached people's funerals in churches. But his was in a funeral home.

And I remember that during the service a big black fly came down and landed on my father's face, and Wilfred sprang up from his chair and he shooed the fly away, and he came groping back to his chair—there were folding chairs for us to sit on—and the tears were streaming down his face. When we went by the casket, I remember that I thought that it looked as if my father's strong black face had been dusted with flour, and I wished they hadn't put on such a lot of it.

Back in the big four-room house, there were many visitors for another week or so. They were good friends of the family, such as the Lyons from Mason, twelve miles away, and the Walkers, McGuires, Liscoes, the Greens, Randolphs, and the Turners, and others from Lansing, and a lot of people from other towns, whom I had seen at the Garvey meetings.

We children adjusted more easily than our mother did. We couldn't see, as clearly as she did, the trials that lay ahead. As the visitors tapered off, she became very concerned about collecting the two insurance policies that my father had always been proud he carried. He had always said that families should be protected in case of death. One policy apparently paid off without any problem—the smaller one. I don't know the amount of it. I would imagine it was not more than a thousand dollars, and maybe half of that.

But after that money came, and my mother had paid out a lot of it for the funeral and expenses, she began going into town and returning very upset. The company that had issued the bigger policy was balking at paying off. They were claiming that my father had committed suicide. Visitors came again, and there was bitter talk about white people: how could my father bash himself in the head, then get down across the streetcar tracks to be run over?

So there we were. My mother was thirty-four years old now, with no husband, no provider or protector to take care of her eight children. But some kind of a family routine got going again. And for as long as the first insurance money lasted, we did all right.

Wilfred, who was a pretty stable fellow, began to act older than his age. I think he had the sense to see, when the rest of us didn't, what was in the wind for us. He quietly quit school and went to town in search of work. He took any kind of job he could find and he would come home, dog-tired, in the evenings, and give whatever he had made to my mother.

Hilda, who always had been quiet, too, attended to the babies. Philbert and I didn't contribute anything. We just fought all the time—each other at home, and then at school we would team up and fight white kids. Sometimes the fights would be racial in nature, but they might be about anything.

Reginald came under my wing. Since he had grown out of the toddling stage, he and I had become very close. I suppose I enjoyed the fact that he was the little one, under me, who looked up to me.

My mother began to buy on credit. My father had always been very strongly against credit. "Credit is the first step into debt and back into slavery," he had always said. And then she went to work herself. She would go into Lansing and find different jobs—in housework, or sewing—for white people. They didn't realize, usually, that she was a Negro. A lot of white people around there didn't want Negroes in their houses.

She would do fine until in some way or other it got to people who she was, whose widow she was. And then she would be let go. I remember how she used to come home crying, but trying to hide it, because she had lost a job that she needed so much.

Once when one of us—I cannot remember which—had to go for something to where she was working, and the people saw us, and realized she was actually a Negro, she was fired on the spot, and she came home crying, this time not hiding it.

When the state Welfare people began coming to our house, we would come from school sometimes and find them talking with our mother, asking a thousand questions. They acted and looked at her, and at us, and around in our house, in a way that had about it the feeling—at least for me—that we were not people. In their eyesight we were just *things*, that was all.

My mother began to receive two checks—a Welfare check and, I believe, a widow's pension. The checks helped. But they weren't enough, as many of us as there were. When they came, about the first of the month, one always was already owed in full, if not more, to the man at the grocery store. And, after that, the other one didn't last long.

We began to go swiftly downhill. The physical downhill wasn't as quick as the psychological. My mother was, above everything else, a proud woman, and it took its toll on her that she was accepting charity. And her feelings were communicated to us.

She would speak sharply to the man at the grocery store for padding the bill, telling him that she wasn't ignorant, and he didn't like that. She would talk back sharply to the state

Welfare people, telling them that she was a grown woman, able to raise her children, that it wasn't necessary for them to keep coming around so much, meddling in our lives. And they didn't like that.

But the monthly Welfare check was their pass. They acted as if they owned us, as if we were their private property. As much as my mother would have liked to, she couldn't keep them out. She would get particularly incensed when they began insisting upon drawing us older children aside, one at a time, out on the porch or somewhere, and asking us questions, or telling us things—against our mother and against each other.

We couldn't understand why, if the state was willing to give us packages of meat, sacks of potatoes and fruit, and cans of all kinds of things, our mother obviously hated to accept. We really couldn't understand. What I later understood was that my mother was making a desperate effort to preserve her pride—and ours.

Pride was just about all we had to preserve, for by 1934, we really began to suffer. This was about the worst depression year, and no one we knew had enough to eat or live on. Some old family friends visited us now and then. At first they brought food. Though it was charity, my mother took it.

Wilfred was working to help. My mother was working, when she could find any kind of job. In Lansing, there was a bakery where, for a nickel, a couple of us children would buy a tall flour sack of day-old bread and cookies, and then walk the two miles back out into the country to our house. Our mother knew, I guess, dozens of ways to cook things with bread and out of bread. Stewed tomatoes with bread, maybe that would be a meal. Something like French toast, if we had any eggs. Bread pudding, sometimes with raisins in it. If we got hold of some hamburger, it came to the table more bread than meat. The cookies that were always in the sack with the bread, we just gobbled down straight.

But there were times when there wasn't even a nickel and we would be so hungry we were dizzy. My mother would boil a big pot of dandelion greens, and we would eat that. I remember that some small-minded neighbor put it out, and children would tease us, that we ate "fried grass." Sometimes, if we were lucky, we would have oatmeal or cornmeal mush three times a day. Or mush in the morning and cornbread at night.

Philbert and I were grown up enough to quit fighting long enough to take the .22 caliber rifle that had been our father's, and shoot rabbits that some white neighbors up or down the road would buy. I know now that they just did it to help us, because they, like everyone, shot their own rabbits. Sometimes, I remember, Philbert and I would take little Reginald along with us. He wasn't very strong, but he was always so proud to be along. We would trap muskrats out in the little creek in back of our house. And we would lie quiet until unsuspecting bullfrogs appeared, and we could spear them, cut off their legs, and sell them for a nickel a pair to people who lived up and down the road. The whites seemed less restricted in their dietary tastes.

Then, about in late 1934, I would guess, something began to happen. Some kind of psychological deterioration hit our family circle and began to eat away our pride. Perhaps it was the constant tangible evidence that we were destitute. We had known other families who had gone on relief. We had known without anyone in our home ever expressing it that we had felt prouder not to be at the depot where the free food was passed out. And, now, we were among them. At school, the "on relief" finger suddenly was pointed at us, too, and sometimes it was said aloud.

It seemed that everything to eat in our house was stamped Not To Be Sold. All Welfare food bore this stamp to keep the recipients from selling it. It's a wonder we didn't come to think of Not To Be Sold as a brand name.

Sometimes, instead of going home from school, I walked the two miles up the road into Lansing. I began drifting from store to store, hanging around outside where things like apples were displayed in boxes and barrels and baskets, and I would watch my chance and steal me a treat. You know what a treat was to me? Anything!

Or I began to drop in about dinnertime at the home of some family that we knew. I knew that they knew exactly why I was there, but they never embarrassed me by letting on. They would invite me to stay for supper, and I would stuff myself.

Especially, I liked to drop in and visit at the Gohannas' home. They were nice, older people, and great churchgoers. I had watched them lead the jumping and shouting when my father preached. They had, living with them—they were raising him—a nephew whom everyone called "Big Boy," and he and I got along fine. Also living with the Gohannas was old Mrs. Adcock, who went with them to church. She was always trying to help anybody she could, visiting anyone she heard was sick, carrying them something. She was the one who, years later, would tell me something that I remembered a long time: "Malcolm, there's one thing I like about you.

You're no good, but you don't try to hide it. You are not a hypocrite."

The more I began to stay away from home and visit people and steal from the stores, the more aggressive I became in my inclinations. I never wanted to wait for anything.

I was growing up fast, physically more so than mentally. As I began to be recognized more around the town, I started to become aware of the peculiar attitude of white people toward me. I sensed that it had to do with my father. It was an adult version of what several white children had said at school, in hints, or sometimes in the open, which really expressed what their parents had said—that the Black Legion or the Klan had killed my father, and the insurance company had pulled a fast one in refusing to pay my mother the policy money.

When I began to get caught stealing now and then, the state Welfare people began to focus on me when they came to our house. I can't remember how I first became aware that they were talking of taking me away. What I first remember along that line was my mother raising a storm about being able to bring up her own children. She would whip me for stealing, and I would try to alarm the neighborhood with my yelling. One thing I have always been proud of is that I never raised my hand against my mother.

In the summertime, at night, in addition to all the other things we did, some of us boys would slip out down the road, or across the pastures, and go "cooning" watermelons. White people always associated watermelons with Negroes, and they sometimes called Negroes "coons" among all the other names, and so stealing watermelons became "cooning" them. If white boys were doing it, it implied that they were only acting like Negroes. Whites have always hidden or justified all of the guilts they could by ridiculing or blaming Negroes.

One Halloween night, I remember that a bunch of us were out tipping over those old country outhouses, and one old farmer—I guess he had tipped over enough in his day—had set a trap for us. Always, you sneak up from behind the outhouse, then you gang together and push it, to tip it over. This farmer had taken his outhouse off the hole, and set it just in *front* of the hole. Well, we came sneaking up in single file, in the darkness, and the two white boys in the lead fell down into the outhouse hole neck deep. They smelled so bad it was all we could stand to get them out, and that finished us all for that Halloween. I had just missed falling in myself. The whites were so used to taking the lead, this time it had really gotten them in the hole.

Thus, in various ways, I learned various things. I picked strawberries, and though I can't recall what I got per crate for picking, I remember that after working hard all one day, I wound up with about a dollar, which was a whole lot of money in those times. I was so hungry, I didn't know what to do. I was walking away toward town with visions of buying something good to eat, and this older white boy I knew, Richard Dixon, came up and asked me if I wanted to match nickels. He had plenty of change for my dollar. In about a half hour, he had all the change back, including my dollar, and instead of going to town to buy something, I went home with nothing, and I was bitter. But that was nothing compared to what I felt when I found out later that he had cheated. There is a way that you can catch and hold the nickel and make it come up the way you want. This was my first lesson about gambling: if you see somebody winning all the time, he isn't gambling, he's cheating. Later on in life, if I were continuously losing in any gambling situation, I would watch very closely. It's like the Negro in America seeing the white man win all the time. He's a professional gambler; he has all the cards and the odds stacked on his side, and he has always dealt to our people from the bottom of the deck.

About this time, my mother began to be visited by some Seventh Day Adventists who had moved into a house not too far down the road from us. They would talk to her for hours at a time, and leave booklets and leaflets and magazines for her to read. She read them, and Wilfred, who had started back to school after we had begun to get the relief food supplies, also read a lot. His head was forever in some book.

Before long, my mother spent much time with the Adventists. It's my belief that what influenced her was that they had even more diet restrictions than she always had taught and practiced with us. Like us, they were against eating rabbit and pork; they followed the Mosaic dietary laws. They ate nothing of the flesh without a split hoof, or that didn't chew a cud. We began to go with my mother to the Adventist meetings that were held further out in the country. For us children, I know that the major attraction was the good food they served. But we listened, too. There were a handful of Negroes, from small towns in the area, but I would say that it was ninety-nine percent white people. The Adventists felt that we were living at the end of time, that the world soon was coming to an end. But they were the friendliest white people I had ever seen. In some ways, though, we children noticed, and, when we were back at home, discussed, that they were different from us—such as the lack of enough seasoning in their food, and the different way that white people smelled.

Meanwhile, the state Welfare people kept after my mother. By now, she didn't make it any secret that she hated them, and didn't want them in her house. But they exerted their right to come, and I have many, many times reflected upon how, talking to us children, they began to plant the seeds of division in our minds. They would ask such things as who was smarter than the other. And they would ask me why I was "so different."

I think they felt that getting children into foster homes was a legitimate part of their function, and the result would be less troublesome, however they went about it.

And when my mother fought them, they went after her—first, through me. I was the first target. I stole; that implied that I wasn't being taken care of by my mother.

All of us were mischievous at some time or another, I more so than any of the rest. Philbert and I kept a battle going. And this was just one of a dozen things that kept building up the pressure on my mother.

I'm not sure just how or when the idea was first dropped by the Welfare workers that our mother was losing her mind.

But I can distinctly remember hearing "crazy" applied to her by them when they learned that the Negro farmer who was in the next house down the road from us had offered to give us some butchered pork—a whole pig, maybe even two of them—and she had refused. We all heard them call my mother "crazy" to her face for refusing good meat. It meant nothing to them even when she explained that we had never eaten pork, that it was against her religion as a Seventh Day Adventist.

They were as vicious as vultures. They had no feelings, understanding, compassion, or respect for my mother. They told us, "She's crazy for refusing food." Right then was when our home, our unity, began to disintegrate. We were having a hard time, and I wasn't helping. But we could have made it, we could have stayed together. As bad as I was, as much trouble and worry as I caused my mother, I loved her.

The state people, we found out, had interviewed the Gohannas family, and the Gohannas' had said that they would take me into their home. My mother threw a fit, though, when she heard that—and the home wreckers took cover for a while.

It was about this time that the large, dark man from Lansing began visiting. I don't remember how or where he and my mother met. It may have been through some mutual friends. I don't remember what the man's profession was. In 1935, in Lansing, Negroes didn't have anything you could call a profession. But the man, big and black, looked something like my father. I can remember his name, but there's no need to mention it. He was a single man, and my mother was a widow only thirty-six years old. The man was independent; naturally she admired that. She was having a hard time disciplining us, and a big man's presence alone would help. And if she had a man to provide, it would send the state people away forever.

We all understood without ever saying much about it. Or at least we had no objection. We took it in stride, even with some amusement among us, that when the man came, our mother would be all dressed up in the best that she had—she still was a good-looking woman—and she would act differently, lighthearted and laughing, as we hadn't seen her act in years.

It went on for about a year, I guess. And then, about 1936, or 1937, the man from Lansing jilted my mother suddenly. He just stopped coming to see her. From what I later understood, he finally backed away from taking on the responsibility of those eight mouths to feed. He was afraid of so many of us. To this day, I can see the trap that Mother was in, saddled with all of us. And I can also understand why he would shun taking on such a tremendous responsibility.

But it was a terrible shock to her. It was the beginning of the end of reality for my mother. When she began to sit around and walk around talking to herself—almost as though she was unaware that we were there—it became increasingly terrifying.

The state people saw her weakening. That was when they began the definite steps to take me away from home. They began to tell me how nice it was going to be at the Gohannas' home, where the Gohannas' and Big Boy and Mrs. Adcock had all said how much they liked me, and would like to have me live with them.

I liked all of them, too. But I didn't want to leave Wilfred. I looked up to and admired my big brother. I didn't want to leave Hilda, who was like my second mother. Or Philbert; even in our fighting, there was a feeling of brotherly union. Or Reginald, especially, who was weak with his hernia condition, and who looked up to me as his big brother who looked out for him, as I looked up to Wilfred. And I had nothing, either, against the babies, Yvonne, Wesley, and Robert.

As my mother talked to herself more and more, she gradually became less responsive to us. And less responsible. The house became less tidy. We began to be more unkempt. And usually, now, Hilda cooked.

We children watched our anchor giving way. It was something terrible that you couldn't get your hands on, yet you couldn't get away from. It was a sensing that something bad was going to happen. We younger ones leaned more and more heavily on the relative strength of Wilfred and Hilda, who were the oldest.

When finally I was sent to the Gohannas' home, at least in a surface way I was glad. I remember that when I left home with the state man, my mother said one thing: "Don't let them feed him any pig."

It was better, in a lot of ways, at the Gohannas'. Big Boy and I shared his room together, and we hit it off nicely. He just wasn't the same as my blood brothers. The Gohannas' were very religious people. Big Boy and I attended church with them. They were sanctified Holy Rollers now. The preachers and congregations jumped even higher and shouted even louder than the Baptists I had known. They sang at the top of their lungs, and swayed back and forth and cried and moaned and beat on tambourines and chanted. It was spooky, with ghosts and spirituals and "ha'nts" seeming to be in the very atmosphere when finally we all came out of the church, going back home.

The Gohannas' and Mrs. Adcock loved to go fishing, and some Saturdays Big Boy and I would go along. I had changed schools now, to Lansing's West Junior High School. It was right in the heart of the Negro community, and a few white kids were there, but Big Boy didn't mix much with any of our schoolmates, and I didn't either. And when we went fishing, neither he nor I liked the idea of just sitting and waiting for the fish to jerk the cork under the water—or make the tight line quiver, when we fished that way. I figured there should be some smarter way to get the fish—though we never discovered what it might be.

Mr. Gohannas was close cronies with some other men who, some Saturdays, would take me and Big Boy with them hunting rabbits. I had my father's .22 caliber rifle; my mother had said it was all right for me to take it with me. The old men had a set rabbit-hunting strategy that they had always used. Usually when a dog jumps a rabbit, and the rabbit gets away, that rabbit will always somehow instinctively run in a circle and return sooner or later past the very spot where he originally was jumped. Well, the old men would just sit and wait in hiding somewhere for the rabbit to come back, then get their shots at him. I got to thinking about it, and finally I thought of a plan. I would separate from them and Big Boy and I would go to a point where I figured that the rabbit, returning, would have to pass me first.

It worked like magic. I began to get three and four rabbits before they got one. The astonishing thing was that none of the old men ever figured out why. They outdid themselves exclaiming what a sure shot I was. I was about twelve, then. All I had done was to improve on their strategy, and it was the beginning of a very important lesson in life—that anytime you find someone more successful than you are, especially when you're both engaged in the same business—you know they're doing something that you aren't.

I would return home to visit fairly often. Sometimes Big Boy and one or another, or both, of the Gohannas' would go with me—sometimes not. I would be glad when some of them did go, because it made the ordeal easier.

Soon the state people were making plans to take over all of my mother's children. She talked to herself nearly all of the time now, and there was a crowd of new white people entering the picture—always asking questions. They would even visit me at the Gohannas'. They would ask me questions out on the porch, or sitting out in their cars.

Eventually my mother suffered a complete breakdown, and the court orders were finally signed. They took her to the State Mental Hospital at Kalamazoo.

It was seventy-some miles from Lansing, about an hour and a half on the bus. A Judge McClellan in Lansing had authority over me and all of my brothers and sisters. We were "state children," court wards; he had the full say-so over us. A white man in charge of a black man's children! Nothing but legal, modern slavery—however kindly intentioned.

My mother remained in the same hospital at Kalamazoo for about twenty-six years. Later, when I was still growing up in Michigan, I would go to visit her every so often. Nothing that I can imagine could have moved me as deeply as seeing her pitiful state. In 1963, we got my mother out of the hospital, and she now lives there in Lansing with Philbert and his family.

It was so much worse than if it had been a physical sickness, for which a cause might be known, medicine given, a cure effected. Every time I visited her, when finally they led her—a case, a number—back inside from where we had been sitting together, I felt worse.

My last visit, when I knew I would never come to see her again—there—was in 1952. I was twenty-seven. My brother Philbert had told me that on his last visit, she had recognized him somewhat. "In spots," he said.

But she didn't recognize me at all.

She stared at me. She didn't know who I was.

Her mind, when I tried to talk, to reach her, was somewhere else. I asked, "Mama, do you know what day it is?"

She said, staring, "All the people have gone."

I can't describe how I felt. The woman who had brought me into the world, and nursed me, and advised me, and chastised me, and loved me, didn't know me. It was as if I was trying to walk up the side of a hill of feathers. I looked at her. I listened to her "talk." But there was nothing I could do.

I truly believe that if ever a state social agency destroyed a family, it destroyed ours. We wanted and tried to stay together. Our home didn't have to be destroyed. But the Welfare, the courts, and their doctor, gave us the one-two-three punch. And ours was not the only case of this kind.

I knew I wouldn't be back to see my mother again because it could make me a very vicious and dangerous person—knowing how they had looked at us as numbers and as a case in their book, not as human beings. And knowing that my mother in there was a statistic that didn't have to be, that existed because of a society's failure, hypocrisy, greed, and lack of mercy and compassion. Hence I have no mercy or compassion in me for a society that will crush people, and then penalize them for not being able to stand up under the weight.

I have rarely talked to anyone about my mother, for I believe that I am capable of killing a person, without hesitation, who happened to make the wrong kind of remark about my mother. So I purposely don't make any opening for some fool to step into.

Back then when our family was destroyed, in 1937, Wilfred and Hilda were old enough so that the state let them stay on their own in the big four-room house that my father had built. Philbert was placed with another family in Lansing, a Mrs. Hackett, while Reginald and Wesley went to live with a family called Williams, who were friends of my mother's. And Yvonne and Robert went to live with a West Indian family named McGuire.

Separated though we were, all of us maintained fairly close touch around Lansing—in school and out—whenever we could get together. Despite the artificially created separation and distance between us, we still remained very close in our feelings toward each other.

STANLEY SANDERS (1942–)

Born and educated in the Watts district of Los Angeles, Stanley Sanders became president of the student body at Whittier College, went to Oxford University as a Rhodes Scholar in 1965, and is presently studying at the Yale Law School. He was a co-founder of the Watts Summer Festival in 1966 and the director of the Summer Work Project for Youth, also in Watts, in 1967. He has published articles in The Nation *and in numerous educational journals. The following autobiographical article is reprinted from the special issue of* Ebony *magazine (August, 1967) devoted to "Negro Youth in America."*

"I'll Never Escape the Ghetto"

I was born, raised and graduated from high school in Watts. My permanent Los Angeles home address is in Watts. My father, a brother and sister still live in Watts. By ordinary standards these are credentials enough to qualify one as coming from Watts.

But there is more to it than that. I left Watts. After I was graduated from the local high school I went away to college. A college venture in Watts terms is a fateful act. There are no retractions or future deliverances. Watts, like other black ghettos across the country, is, for ambitious youths, a transient status. Once they have left, there is no returning. In this sense, my credentials are unsatisfactory. To some people, I am not from Watts. I can never be.

The Watts-as-a-way-station mentality has a firm hold on both those who remain and those who leave. Such as it is, the ghetto is regarded as no place to make a career for those who have a future. Without exception, the prime American values underscore the notion. Negroes, inside it or out, and whites too, behave toward the ghetto like travelers.

Accordingly, I was considered one of the lucky ones. My scholarship to college was a ticket. People did not expect me to return. Understanding this, I can understand the puzzlement in the minds of those in Watts when I was home last summer, working in the local poverty program. Rumors spread quickly that I was an FBI agent. I was suspect because I was not supposed to return. Some people said I was either a federal agent or a fool, for no reasonable man, they said, returns to Watts by choice. Outside of Watts, reports stated that I had "given up" a summer vacation to work in Watts. For my part, I had come home to work in my community, but to some people I could not come home to Watts. To them I was no longer from Watts.

My own state of mind, when I left Watts eight years ago to take up the freshman year at Whittier College, was different. It was to me less of a departure; it was the stepping-off point of an Odyssey that was to take me through Whittier College and Oxford University, to Yale Law School, and back to Watts. I had intended then, as now, to make Watts my home.

A career in Watts had been a personal ambition for many years. In many ways the career I envisioned was antithetical to ghetto life. In the ghetto, a career was something on the outside. In Los Angeles, this meant a pursuit founded in a world beyond Alameda street, at a minimum in the largely Negro middle-class Westside of Los Angeles. The talk among the ambitious and future-minded youth in Watts was on getting out so that careers could begin. And they did just that. The talented young people left Watts in droves. The one skill they had in common was the ability to escape the ghetto.

I was especially intrigued by a career in Watts because it was supposed to be impossible. I wanted to demonstrate that it could be done more than anything else. I recall a moment during a city-wide high school oratorical contest when one of the judges asked whether anything good could come out of Watts. Our high school won the contest. We showed that judge. I saw that achievement as a possible pattern for the entire ghetto. I was pleased.

I had not realized in leaving for Whittier College that, however worthy my intention of returning was, I was nevertheless participating in the customary exodus from Watts. It was not long after leaving that my early ambitions began to wear thin. The stigma of Watts was too heavy to bear. I could easily do without the questioning looks of my college classmates. I did not want my being from Watts to arouse curiosity.

I followed the instructions of those who fled Watts. I adopted the language of escape. I resorted to all the devices of those who wished to escape. I was from South Los Angeles, thereafter, not Watts. "South Los Angeles," geographically identical to Watts, carried none of the latter's stigma. South Los Angeles was a cleaner—safer—designation. It meant having a home with possibilities.

It never occurred to me at the time what I was doing. I thought of it only as being practical. It was important to me to do well in college. Community identity was secondary, if a consideration at all. Somehow, the Watts things interfered with my new college life. Moreover, Negro college youth during those undergraduate years had none of its present mood. Its theme was campus involvement. Good grades, athletics, popularity—these were the things that mattered. The word "ghetto" had not even entered the lexicon of race relations. Students were not conscious of the ghetto as a separate phenomenon. Civil rights, in the Southern sense, was academically fashionable. But the ghetto of the North was not. The concern for the ghetto was still in the future.

It was to occur to me later, at the time of the Watts riots, two years after I graduated from college, if my classmates at Whittier realized that the epochal conflagration taking place was in the home of one of their very own student body presidents. They had no reason to think it was. I had never told them that I was from Watts.

A lot of things changed during the two years at Oxford. My attitude toward home was one of them. It was there, ironically enough, that the Odyssey turned homeward. Those years were bound to be meaningful as a Yankee foreign student or Rhodes Scholar. I knew that much. But I would never have imagined when receiving the award that Oxford would be significant as a Negro experience. After all, it was part of the faith gained during four years at Whittier that everything concerning me and Watts would remain conveniently buried.

It emerged in an odd context. England then, for the most part, was free of the fine distinctions between blacks and whites traditionally made in America. Except for some exclusive clubs in London, there were few occasions where racial lines were drawn. The color-blindness of England was especially true in the student life at Oxford. (This relatively mild racial climate in England during the last three years has, with the large influx of blacks from the West Indies and Southern Asia, adopted some very American-like features. It was in such a relaxed racial atmosphere that all my defenses, about race and home, came down. At Oxford, I could reflect on the American black man.

My ghetto roots became crucially important in this examination. Englishmen were not concerned about the distinctions I was making in my own mind, between Watts and "South Los Angeles," between Watts and Whittier. They were not imagined distinctions. I was discovering that I could not escape the ghetto after all. A fundamental change was taking place in the ghettos, the Wattses, across the country. These changes were making the distinction. I realized I was a part of them, too.

By far the most traumatic of the new changes was ghetto rioting. I was studying at the University of Vienna, between semesters at Oxford, during the summer of 1964. News of Harlem rioting jolted the multi-national student community there. The typical European response was unlike anything I had seen before. They had no homes or businesses to worry about protecting. They wanted to know why Negroes did not riot more often. As the only Negro in the summer session I felt awkward for a time. I was being asked questions about the black man in America that no one had ever asked me before. I was embarrassed because I did not have any answers.

My own lack of shame in the rioting then taking place in America surprised me. In one sense, I was the archetype of the ghetto child who through hard work and initiative, was pulling himself toward a better life. I was the example, the exception. It was my life that was held up to Watts youth to emulate.

In another sense, however, my feelings toward the rioting were predictable. I had always been bothered by the passivity of the ghetto. The majority of black men in the North had remained outside the struggle. Nothing was happening in the ghettos. No one was making it happen. Ghetto rioting then was the first representation I perceived of movement and activity among the mass of Negroes in the North. It marked a break with the passive tradition of dependency and indifference. The ghetto was at least no longer content with its status as bastard child of urban America. The currents set in motion had a hopeful, irreversible quality about them. The ghetto wanted legitimation. That was a beginning.

The parallel between a single individual's success and the

boot-strap effort of the mass of ghetto youth is and remains too tenuous to comport with reality. This was made clear to me during the discussions of the Harlem riots on those hot summer days in Vienna. It shattered the notion that my individual progress could be hailed as an advance for all Negroes. Regrettably, it was an advance only for me. Earlier I had thought the success I had won satisfied an obligation I had to all Negroes. It is part of the lip service every successful Negro is obliged to pay to the notion of race progress whenever he achieves. In the face of mass rioting, the old shibboleths were reduced to embarrassing emptiness. I was enjoying the privileges of studying at the world's finest universities; Negroes at home were revolting against their miserable condition. To them, my experience and example were as remost as if I had never lived or been there. At best, only the top students could identify with my example—but they were few. And besides, the top students were not the problem.

When I returned to Oxford in the fall, following a spate of summer rioting in Eastern cities, I was convinced that some momentous changes had been wrought for all Negroes, not just those in the ghetto. It certainly meant a new militancy and a militancy of action, not the passive fulminations of the demi-militants. This was for Watts.

I returned home in August, 1965, from two years at Oxford just in time for the beginning of the Watts riots. As I walked the streets I was struck by the sameness of the community. There were few changes. Everything seemed to be in the same place where I had last seen it. It was unsettling for me to recall so easily the names of familiar faces I saw on the street. It was that feeling one gets when he feels he has done this one same thing before.

Streets remained unswept; sidewalks, in places, still unpaved. During this same time the growth rate in the rest of Southern California had been phenomenal, one of the highest in the country. L. A. suburbs had flourished. Watts, however, remained an unacknowledged child in an otherwise proud and respectable family of new towns.

The intellectual journey back to Watts after the Vienna summer and during the last year at Oxford had partly prepared me for what was soon to erupt into revolutionary scale violence. My first reaction after the riot began was to have it stopped. But I was not from Watts for the past six years. I, nor anyone outside of Watts, was in no moral position to condemn this vicious expression of the ghetto.

I enrolled in Yale Law School in the fall after the riots. This time I did not leave Watts. Nor did I wish to leave

Watts. Watts followed me to Yale. In fact, Watts was at Yale before I was. The discussions about riots and ghettos were more lively and compelling than the classroom discussions on the law. There were no word games or contrived problems. The questions raised were urgent ones.

Not surprisingly, Watts, too, was in the throes of painful discussion about the riots. It was beginning to look as though the deepest impact of the riots was on the people of Watts themselves. Old attitudes about the community were in upheaval. There were no explanations that seemed complete. No one knew for sure how it all began. There was no agreement on how it was continued as long as it was—and why. We only knew it happened. What I had often mistaken for pointless spoutings was in reality a manifestation of this desperate search for a truth about the riots.

The new intellectual climate in Watts was hard-wrought. It was rich enough to support even a communist bookstore. Writers, poets, artists flourished. I was handed full manuscripts of unpublished books by indigenous writers and asked to criticize them. I have not seen during eight years of college life as many personal journals kept and sketches written than in Watts since the 1965 riots. A new, rough wisdom of the street corner was emerging.

I suspected at the time and now realize that the riots were perhaps the most significant massive action taken by Northern Negroes. It was a watershed in the ghetto's history. Before the riots, the reach of the Negro movement in America seemed within the province of a small civil rights leadership. Now Watts, and places like Watts, were redefining the role of black men in their city's life.

I have affectionate ties to Watts. I bear the same mark as a son of Watts now that I did during that oratorical contest in high school. I may be personally less vulnerable to it today, but I am nevertheless influenced by it. While a group in Whittier, Calif. may regard it as unfortunate that its college's first Rhodes Scholar comes from Watts, I, for my part, could not feel more pride about that than I do now. I feel no embarrassment for those who think ill of Watts. I had once felt it. Now I only feel the regret for once having been embarrassed. "South Los Angeles" is a sour memory. Watts is my home.

Then I have my logical ties to Watts, too. My interest in the law stems from a concern for the future of Watts. The problem of the poor and of the city in America, simplified, is the problem of the ghetto Negro. I regard it as *the* problem of the last third of this century. Plainly, Watts is where the action is. The talents and leadership which I saw leave Watts as a child are the very things it needs most today. Many of the ghetto's wandering children are choosing a city to work in. My choice was made for me—long ago.

There is a difference between my schooling and the wisdom of the street corner. I know the life of a black man in Watts is larger than a federal poverty program. If there is no future for the black ghetto, the future of all Negroes is diminished. What affects it, affects me, for I am a child of the ghetto. When they do it to Watts, they do it to me, too. I'll never escape from the ghetto. I have staked my all on its future. Watts is my home.

3.

Poetry

PAUL LAURENCE DUNBAR (1872–1906)

Although the first Negro poet of record in America is Lucy Terry, a woman who wrote poems in the 1740's, and the names of Jupiter Hammon and Phillis Wheatley stand out in the history of Negro poetry in the eighteenth century, Paul Laurence Dunbar was the first Negro poet to win national recognition and full acceptance in America. Born and educated in Dayton, Ohio, the son of former slaves, he began writing verse as a youth. His first book of poems, Oak and Ivy *(1893) was distributed and sold by the poet, but his second volume,* Majors and Minors *(1895), also very much a private venture, was very favorably reviewed by William Dean Howells. This led to the publication of his third volume,* Lyrics of Lowly Life *(1896), by Dodd, Mead and Company, with an introduction by Howells, which was an instant success and made him a celebrity. James Weldon Johnson, in the revised edition of* The Book of American Negro Poetry *(1931), noted:*

There have been many changes in the estimates of Negro poetry since Dunbar died [February 9, 1906], but he still holds his place as the first American Negro poet of real literary distinction. There are some who will differ with this statement, feeling that it should be made about Phillis Wheatley. It is true that Phillis Wheatley did measure up to the best of her contemporaries; but it must be remembered that not one of her contemporaries was a poet of real literary distinction. Dunbar was the first to demonstrate a high degree of poetic talent combined with literary training and technical proficiency. In the field in which he became best known, Negro dialect poetry, his work has not been excelled. . . . Much of the poetry on which Dunbar's fame rests has passed; just as much of the poetry of his even more popular contemporary, Riley, has passed. Dialect poetry still holds a place in American literature, but the place itself is no longer considered an important one.

His poems and short stories were in demand by the best American magazines, and before his death, at the age of thirty-four, he wrote four novels and numerous stories. We present four of Dunbar's poems, two in the literary English he wanted to be known for, and two of his dialect poems.

We Wear the Mask

We wear the mask that grins and lies,
It hides our cheeks and shades our eyes,—
This debt we pay to human guile;
With torn and bleeding hearts we smile,
And mouth with myriad subtleties.

Why should the world be overwise,
In counting all our tears and sighs?
Nay, let them only see us, while
    We wear the mask.

We smile, but, O great Christ, our cries
To Thee from tortured souls arise.
We sing, but oh, the clay is vile
Beneath our feet, and long the mile;
But let the world dream otherwise,
    We wear the mask.

A Death Song

Lay me down beneaf de willers in de grass,
Whah de branch 'll go a-singin' as it pass.
  An' w'en I's a-layin' low,
  I kin hyeah it as it go
Singin', "Sleep, my honey, tek yo' res' at las'."

Lay me nigh to whah hit meks a little pool,
An' de watah stan's so quiet lak an' cool,
  Whah de little birds in spring,
  Ust to come an' drink an' sing,
An' de chillen waded on dey way to school.

Let me settle w'en my shouldahs draps dey load
Nigh enough to hyeah de noises in de road;
  Fu' I t'ink de las' long res'
  Gwine to soothe my sperrit bes'
Ef I's layin' 'mong de t'ings I's allus knowed.

Sympathy

I know what the caged bird feels, alas!
When the sun is bright on the upland slopes;
When the wind stirs soft through the springing grass,
And the river flows like a stream of glass;
When the first bird sings and the first bud opes,
And the faint perfume from its chalice steals—
I know what the caged bird feels!

I know why the caged bird beats his wing
Till its blood is red on the cruel bars;
For he must fly back to his perch and cling
When he fain would be on the bough a-swing;
And a pain still throbs in the old, old scars
And they pulse again with a keener sting—
I know why he beats his wing!

I know why the caged bird sings, ah me,
When his wing is bruised and his bosom sore,—
When he beats his bars and he would be free;

It is not a carol of joy or glee,
But a prayer that he sends from his heart's deep core,
But a plea, that upward to Heaven he flings—
I know why the caged bird sings!

A Negro Love Song

Seen my lady home las' night,
    Jump back, honey, jump back.
Hel' huh han' an' sque'z it tight,
    Jump back, honey, jump back.
Hyeahd huh sigh a little sigh,
Seen a light gleam f'om huh eye,
An' a smile go flittin' by—
    Jump back, honey, jump back.

Hyeahd de win' blow thoo de pine,
    Jump back, honey, jump back.
Mockin'-bird was singin' fine,
    Jump back, honey, jump back.
An' my hea't was beatin' so,
When I reached my lady's do',
Dat I couldn't ba' to go—
    Jump back, honey, jump back.

Put my ahm aroun' huh wais',
    Jump back, honey, jump back.
Raised huh lips an' took a tase,
    Jump back, honey, jump back.
Love me, honey, love me true?
Love me well ez I love you?
An' she answe'd, " 'Cose I do"—
    Jump back, honey, jump back.

WILLIAM EDWARD BURGHART DuBOIS (1868–1963)

It is no exaggeration to say that, in many respects, W. E. B. DuBois is the intellectual father of modern Negro scholarship, modern Negro militancy and self-consciousness, and modern Negro cultural development. His figure looms large as writer, editor, scholar, educator, historian, sociologist, and student of Africa. He was born in Great Barrington, Massachusetts, and graduated from Fisk University in 1888. He completed four years of graduate studies at Harvard, and his Ph.D. dissertation, The Suppression of the African Slave Trade, *was hailed as the "first scientific historical work" written by a Negro. It achieved publication as the first volume of the then new series of Harvard Historical Studies (1896). His* The Philadelphia Negro: A Social Study, *published by the University of Pennsylvania in 1899, is a pioneer work in the sociological study of the American Negro. He was a professor at Atlanta University from 1896 to 1910. In 1905 he founded the Niagara Movement, an early expression of the fight to end racial discrimination and segregation in the United States. In 1908 he was among the founders of the N.A.A.C.P. DuBois was the founder and served as the first editor of* The Crisis. *In an article in this journal in April, 1915, he stated the cultural program which was to be realized in the Negro Renaissance of the following decade: "In art and literature we should try to loose the tremendous emotional wealth of the Negro and the dramatic strength of his problems through writing, the stage, pageantry, and other forms of art. We should resurrect forgotten ancient Negro art and history, and we should set the black man before the world as both a creative artist and a strong subject for artistic treatment." He edited* The Atlanta Studies *(see Bibliography) and founded and edited* Phylon, *the famous scholarly "Atlanta University Review of Race and Culture." DuBois was the founder of the Pan-African Congresses and first director of the Secretariat for* Encyclopaedia Africana. *In addition to his scholarly studies and essays, he wrote fiction (see Bibliography) and poetry. We present two of his poems: "The Song of the Smoke," a poem written in 1899, which appeared anew in the special DuBois Memorial Issue of the quarterly review* Freedomways *(Winter, 1965) and has never before been anthologized, and the widely reprinted "A Litany at Atlanta," written after the Atlanta race riot in 1906. Two chapters from DuBois's classic,* The Souls of Black Folk, *appear in the Literary Criticism section.*

The Song of the Smoke

I am the smoke king,
I am black.
I am swinging in the sky.
I am ringing worlds on high:
I am the thought of the throbbing mills,
I am the soul toil kills,
I am the ripple of trading rills,

Up I'm curling from the sod,
I am whirling home to God.
I am the smoke king,
I am black.

I am the smoke king,
I am black.
I am wreathing broken hearts,
I am sheathing devils' darts;
Dark inspiration of iron times,
Wedding the toil of toiling climes
Shedding the blood of bloodless crimes.

Down I lower in the blue,
Up I tower toward the true,
I am the smoke king,
I am black.

I am the smoke king,
I am black.

I am darkening with song,
I am hearkening to wrong;
I will be black as blackness can,

The blacker the mantle the mightier the man,
My purpl'ing midnights no day dawn may ban.

I am carving God in night,
I am painting hell in white.
I am the smoke king,
I am black.

I am the smoke king,
I am black.

I am cursing ruddy morn,
I am nursing hearts unborn;
Souls unto me are as mists in the night,
I whiten my blackmen, I beckon my white,
What's the hue of a hide to a man in his might!

Sweet Christ, pity toiling lands!
Hail to the smoke king,
Hail to the black!

A Litany at Atlanta

Done at Atlanta, in the Day of Death, 1906.
O Silent God, Thou whose voice afar in mist and mystery
hath left our ears an-hungered in these fearful days—
Hear us, good Lord!

Listen to us, Thy children: our faces dark with doubt are
made a mockery in Thy sanctuary. With uplifted hands we
front Thy heaven, O God, crying:
We beseech Thee to hear us, good Lord!

We are not better than our fellows, Lord, we are but weak
and human men. When our devils do deviltry, curse Thou the
doer and the deed: curse them as we curse them, do to them
all and more than ever they have done to innocence and
weakness, to womanhood and home.
Have mercy upon us, miserable sinners!

And yet whose is the deeper guilt? Who made these devils?
Who nursed them in crime and fed them on injustice? Who
ravished and debauched their mothers and their grandmoth-

ers? Who bought and sold their crime, and waxed fat and rich on public iniquity?
Thou knowest, good God!

Is this Thy justice, O Father, that guile be easier than innocence, and the innocent crucified for the guilt of the untouched guilty?
Justice, O judge of men!

Wherefore do we pray? Is not the God of the fathers dead? Have not seers seen in Heaven's halls Thine hearsed and lifeless forms stark amidst the black and rolling smoke of sin, where all along bow bitter forms of endless dead?
Awake, Thou that sleepest!

Thou art not dead, but flown afar, up hills of endless light through blazing corridors of suns, where worlds do swing of good and gentle men, of women strong and free—far from the cozenage, black hypocrisy, and chaste prostitution of this shameful speck of dust!
Turn again, O Lord, leave us not to perish in our sin!

From lust of body and lust of blood,
    Great God, deliver us!

From lust of power and lust of gold,
    Great God, deliver us!

From the leagued lying of despot and of brute,
    Great God, deliver us!

A city lay in travail, God our Lord, and from her loins sprang twin Murder and Black Hate. Red was the midnight; clang, crack and cry of death and fury filled the air and trembled underneath the stars when church spires pointed silently to Thee. And all this was to sate the greed of greedy men who hide behind the veil of vengeance!
Bend us Thine ear, O Lord!

In the pale, still morning we looked upon the deed. We stopped our ears and held our leaping hands, but they—did they not wag their heads and leer and cry with bloody jaws: *Cease from Crime!* The word was mockery, for thus they train a hundred crimes while we do cure one.
Turn again our captivity, O Lord!

Behold this maimed and broken thing; dear God, it was an humble black man who toiled and sweat to save a bit from the pittance paid him. They told him: *Work and Rise.* He worked. Did this man sin? Nay, but some one told how some one said another did—one whom he had never seen nor known. Yet for that man's crime this man lieth maimed and murdered, his wife naked to shame, his children, to poverty and evil.

Hear us, O heavenly Father!

Doth not this justice of hell stink in Thy nostrils, O God? How long shall the mounting flood of innocent blood roar in Thine ears and pound in our hearts for vengeance? Pile the pale frenzy of blood-crazed brutes who do such deeds high on Thine altar, Jehovah Jireh, and burn it in hell forever and forever.

Forgive us, good Lord; we know not what we say!

Bewildered we are, and passion-tost, mad with the madness of a mobbed and mocked and murdered people; straining at the armposts of Thy Throne, we raise our shackled hands and charge Thee, God, by the bones of our stolen fathers, by the tears of our dead mothers, by the very blood of Thy crucified Christ: *What meaneth this? Tell us the Plan; give us the Sign!*

Keep not Thou silence, O God!

Sit no longer blind, Lord God, deaf to our prayer and dumb to our dumb suffering. Surely Thou too art not white, O Lord, a pale, bloodless, heartless thing?

Ah! Christ of all the Pities!

Forgive the thought! Forgive these wild, blasphemous words. Thou art still the God of our black fathers, and in Thy soul's soul sit some soft darkenings of the evening, some shadowings of the velvet night.

But whisper—speak—call, great God, for Thy silence is white terror to our hearts! The way, O God, show us the way and point us the path.

Whither? North is greed and South is blood; within, the coward, and without the liar. Whither? To Death?

Amen! Welcome dark sleep!

Whither? To life? But not this life, dear God, not this. Let the cup pass from us, tempt us not beyond our strength, for there is that clamoring and clawing within, to whose voice we

would not listen, yet shudder lest we must,—and it is red,
Ah! God! It is a red and awful shape.
> *Selah!*

> In yonder East trembles a star.
>> *Vengeance is mine; I will repay, saith the
>> Lord!*

> Thy will, O Lord, be done!
>> *Kyrie Eleison!*

> Lord, we have done these pleading, wavering
> words
>> *We beseech Thee to hear us, good Lord!*

> We bow our heads and hearken soft to the sob-
> bing of women and little children.
>> *We beseech Thee to hear us, good Lord!*

> Our voices sink in silence and in night.
>> *Hear us, good Lord!*

> In night, O God of a godless land!
>> *Amen!*

> In silence, O silent God.
>> *Selah!*

JAMES WELDON JOHNSON (1871–1938)

*A biographical note on James Weldon Johnson appears in the
Autobiography section (see pp. 269–270). Johnson's poem,
"The Creation," is reprinted from* God's Trombones *(1927).*

The Creation

A Negro Sermon

And God stepped out on space,
And He looked around and said,
"I'm lonely—
I'll make me a world."

And far as the eye of God could see
Darkness covered everything,
Blacker than a hundred midnights
Down in a cypress swamp.

Then God smiled,
And the light broke,
And the darkness rolled up on one side,
And the light stood shining on the other,
And God said, *"That's good!"*

Then God reached out and took the light in His hands,
And God rolled the light around in His hands,
Until He made the sun;
And He set that sun a-blazing in the heavens.
And the light that was left from making the sun
God gathered up in a shining ball
And flung against the darkness,
Spangling the night with the moon and stars.

Then down between
The darkness and the light
He hurled the world;
And God said, *"That's good!"*

Then God himself stepped down—
And the sun was on His right hand,
And the moon was on His left;
The stars were clustered about His head,
And the earth was under His feet.
And God walked, and where He trod
His footsteps hollowed the valleys out
And bulged the mountains up.

Then He stopped and looked and saw
That the earth was hot and barren.
So God stepped over to the edge of the world
And He spat out the seven seas;
He batted His eyes, and the lightnings flashed;
He clapped His hands, and the thunders rolled;
And the waters above the earth came down,
The cooling waters came down.

Then the green grass sprouted,
And the little red flowers blossomed,
The pine-tree pointed his finger to the sky,
And the oak spread out his arms;
The lakes cuddled down in the hollows of the ground,
And the rivers ran down to the sea;
And God smiled again,
And the rainbow appeared,
And curled itself around His shoulder.

Then God raised His arm and He waved His hand
Over the sea and over the land,
And He said, *"Bring forth! Bring forth!"*
And quicker than God could drop His hand,
Fishes and fowls
And beast and birds
Swam the rivers and the seas,
Roamed the forests and the woods,
And split the air with their wings,
And God said, *"That's good!"*

Then God walked around
And God looked around

On all that He had made.
He looked at His sun,
And He looked at His moon,
And He looked at His little stars;
He looked on His world
With all its living things,
And God said, *"I'm lonely still."*

Then God sat down
On the side of a hill where He could think;
By a deep, wide river He sat down;
With His head in His hands,
God thought and thought,
Till He thought, *"I'll make me a man!"*

Up from the bed of the river
God scooped the clay;
And by the bank of the river
He kneeled Him down;
And there the great God Almighty,
Who lit the sun and fixed it in the sky,
Who flung the stars to the most far corner of the night,
Who rounded the earth in the middle of His hand—
This Great God,
Like a mammy bending over her baby,
Kneeled down in the dust
Toiling over a lump of clay
Till He shaped it in His own image;

Then into it He blew the breath of life,
And man became a living soul.
Amen. Amen.

FENTON JOHNSON (1888–1958)

From beginnings with verse in conventional forms and often trite in content, Fenton Johnson became one of the very first Negro poets to turn to the revolutionary "new poetry" move-

ment in America. In 1918 and 1919 he published poems in Poetry *magazine and Alfred Kreymborg's* Others, *where he appeared along with William Carlos Williams, Wallace Stevens, and Marianne Moore. He never became a major figure, but he cultivated his own distinctive voice and a fatalistic, nihilistic vision of life which was very rare in Negro American literature. He was born and raised in Chicago, attended the University of Chicago, and was active in the Chicago literary circles. In an autobiographical note that he prepared for* Caroling Dusk, An Anthology of Verse by Negro Poets *(1927), edited by Countee Cullen, Johnson wrote:*

> Taught school one year and repented. Having scribbled since the age of nine, had some plays produced on the stage of the old Pekin Theatre, Chicago, at the time I was nineteen. When I was twenty-four my first volume *A Little Dreaming* was published. Since then *Visions of the Dusk* (1915) and *Songs of the Soil* (1916) represent my own collections of my work. Also published a volume of short stories *Tales of Darkest America* and a group of essays on American politics *For the Highest Good* . . . Edited two or three magazines and published one or two of them myself.

The Negro Collection of the Fisk University Library has an unpublished collection of Fenton Johnson poems in manuscript. The eight poems that follow are from Johnson's published works.

The Daily Grind

If Nature says to you,
"I intend you for something fine,
For something to sing the song
That only my whirling stars can sing,
For something to burn in the firmament
With all the fervor of my golden sun,
For something to moisten the parched souls
As only my rivulets can moisten the parched,"

What can you do?

If the System says to you,
"I intend you to grind and grind
Grains of corn beneath millstones;
I intend you to shovel and sweat

Before a furnace of Babylon;
I intend you for grist and meat
To fatten my pompous gods
As they wallow in an alcoholic nectar,"

What can you do?

Naught can you do
But watch that eternal battle
Between Nature and the System.
You cannot blame God,
You cannot blame man;
For God did not make the System,
Neither did man fashion Nature.
You can only die each morning,
And live again in the dreams of the night.
If Nature forgets you,
If the System forgets you,
God has blest you.

The World Is a Mighty Ogre

I could love her with a love so warm
You could not break it with a fairy charm;
I could love her with a love so bold
It would not die, e'en tho' the world grew cold.

I cannot cross the bridge, nor climb the tower,—
I cannot break the spell of magic power;
The rules of man forbid me raise my sword—
Have mercy on a humble bard, O Lord!

A Negro Peddler's Song

(The pattern of this song was sung by a Negro peddler in a Chicago alley.)

Good Lady,
I have corn and beets,
Onions, too, and leeks,
And also sweet potat-y.

Good Lady,
Buy for May and John;
And when work is done
Give a bite to Sadie.

Good Lady,
I have corn and beets,
Onions, too, and leeks,
And also sweet potat-y.

The Old Repair Man

God is the Old Repair Man.
When we are junk in Nature's storehouse he takes us apart.
What is good he lays aside; he might use it some day.
What has decayed he buries in six feet of sod to nurture the
    weeds.
Those we leave behind moisten the sod with their tears;
But their eyes are blind as to where he has placed
    the good.
Some day the Old Repair Man
Will take the good from its secret place
And with his gentle, strong hands will mold
A more enduring work—a work that will defy Nature—
And we will laugh at the old days, the troubled days,
When we were but a crude piece of craftsmanship,
When we were but an experiment in Nature's labora-
    tory. . . .
It is good we have the Old Repair Man.

Rulers

It is said that many a king in troubled Europe would sell his
    crown for a day of happiness.
I have seen a monarch who held tightly the jewel of happi-
    ness.
Oh Lombard Street in Philadelphia, as evening dropped to
    earth, I gazed upon a laborer duskier than a sky devoid
    of moon. He was seated on a throne of flour bags, waving
    his hand imperiously as two small boys played on their
    guitars the ragtime tunes of the day.

God's blessing on the monarch who rules on Lombard Street
   in Philadelphia.

The Scarlet Woman

Once I was good like the Virgin Mary and the Minister's
   wife.
My father worked for Mr. Pullman and white people's tips;
   but he died two days after his insurance expired.
I had nothing, so I had to go to work.
All the stock I had was a white girl's education and a face
   that enchanted the men of both races.
Starvation danced with me.
So when Big Lizzie, who kept a house for white men, came
   to me with tales of fortune that I could reap from the
   sale of my virtue I bowed my head to Vice.
Now I can drink more gin than any man for miles around.
Gin is better than all the water in Lethe.

Tired

I am tired of work; I am tired of building up somebody else's
   civilization.
Let us take a rest, M'Lissy Jane.
I will go down to the Last Chance Saloon, drink a gallon or
   two of gin, shoot a game or two of dice and sleep the rest
   of the night on one of Mike's barrels.
You will let the old shanty go to rot, the white people's
   clothes turn to dust, and the Calvary Baptist Church sink
   to the bottomless pit.
You will spend your days forgetting you married me and
   your nights hunting the warm gin Mike serves the ladies
   in the rear of the Last Chance Saloon.
Throw the children into the river; civilization has given us
   too many. It is better to die than to grow up and find that
   you are colored.
Pluck the stars out of the heavens. The stars mark our destiny. The stars marked my destiny.
I am tired of civilization.

Aunt Jane Allen

State Street is lonely today. Aunt Jane Allen has driven her
chariot to Heaven.

I remember how she hobbled along, a little woman, parched
of skin, brown as the leather of a satchel and with eyes
that had scanned eighty years of life.

Have those who bore her dust to the last resting place buried
with her the basket of aprons she went up and down State
Street trying to sell?

Have those who bore her dust to the last resting place buried
with her the gentle word *Son* that she gave to each of the
seed of Ethiopia?

CLAUDE McKAY (1891–1948)

*A prominent figure in the "Harlem Renaissance" of the
1920's and the American radical press of post-World War I
vintage, Claude McKay was born in a village in the island of
Jamaica. He was the youngest of eleven children of "a
peasant proprietor who owned his own land," as McKay described his father, who cultivated large tracts of coffee,
cocoa, bananas, and sugarcane. His first book of poetry,
Songs of Jamaica, consists of dialect verse which became
very popular in Jamaica. In 1912 he was the first Negro
awarded the medal of the Institute of Arts and Sciences in
Jamaica. He left the West Indies for the United States in the
same year to attend Tuskegee Institute. After three months
he went on to Kansas State University where he remained for
two years. Then he left for New York City. McKay devoted
the rest of his life to literary and editorial activities. His first
poems in America, "harbinger" notes of the Harlem Renaissance, were published in The Seven Arts Magazine in 1917,
in Pearson's in 1918 (when Frank Harris edited it), and in*

The Liberator. *In 1919 he traveled to Europe and lived in London for more than a year. There he published* Spring in New Hampshire *(1920), his second collection of poems. McKay returned to the U. S. in 1921 and worked with Max Eastman as associate editor of* The Liberator. *His first American volume of poetry,* Harlem Shadows, *was published in 1922, and in that same year he visited the Soviet Union for six months. After visits to Berlin and Paris, McKay remained in Europe for about ten years, often in contact with the prominent American expatriate writers of the 1920's. His first novel,* Home to Harlem *(1928), was a best seller and won the Harmon Gold Award for Literature. He wrote two additional novels,* Banjo *and* Banana Bottom, *and published a collection of short stories,* Gingertown. *A mixture of autobiography and travel,* A Long Way from Home *was published in 1937, and* Selected Poems of Claude McKay *(1953) was published posthumously with an Introduction by John Dewey and a biographical note by Max Eastman. The seven poems that follow are reprinted from this last volume.*

Baptism

Into the furnace let me go alone;
Stay you without in terror of the heat.
I will go naked in—for thus 'tis sweet—
Into the weird depths of the hottest zone.
I will not quiver in the frailest bone,
You will not note a flicker of defeat;
My heart shall tremble not its fate to meet,
My mouth give utterance to any moan.
The yawning oven spits forth fiery spears;
Red aspish tongues shout wordlessly my name.
Desire destroys, consumes my mortal fears,
Transforming me into a shape of flame.
I will come out, back to your world of tears,
A stronger soul within a finer frame.

If We Must Die

If we must die, let it not be like hogs
Hunted and penned in an inglorious spot,
While round us bark the mad and hungry dogs,

Making their mock at our accursed lot.
If we must die, O let us nobly die,
So that our precious blood may not be shed
In vain; then even the monsters we defy
Shall be constrained to honor us though dead!
O kinsmen! we must meet the common foe!
Though far outnumbered let us show us brave,
And for their thousand blows deal one deathblow!
What though before us lies the open grave?
Like men we'll face the murderous, cowardly pack,
Pressed to the wall, dying, but fighting back!

Outcast

For the dim regions whence my fathers came
My spirit, bondaged by the body, longs.
Words felt, but never heard, my lips would frame;
My soul would sing forgotten jungle songs.
I would go back to darkness and to peace,
But the great western world holds me in fee,
And I may never hope for full release
While to its alien gods I bend my knee.
Something in me is lost, forever lost,
Some vital thing has gone out of my heart,
And I must walk the way of life a ghost
Among the sons of earth, a thing apart.

For I was born, far from my native clime,
Under the white man's menace, out of time.

The Negro's Tragedy

It is the Negro's tragedy I feel
Which binds me like a heavy iron chain,
It is the Negro's wounds I want to heal
Because I know the keenness of his pain.
Only a thorn-crowned Negro and no white
Can penetrate into the Negro's ken,
Or feel the thickness of the shroud of night
Which hides and buries him from other men.

So what I write is urged out of my blood.

There is no white man who could write my book,
Though many think their story should be told
Of what the Negro people ought to brook.
Our statesmen roam the world to set things right.
This Negro laughs and prays to God for light!

America

Although she feeds me bread of bitterness,
And sinks into my throat her tiger's tooth,
Stealing my breath of life, I will confess
I love this cultured hell that tests my youth!
Her vigor flows like tides into my blood,
Giving me strength erect against her hate.
Her bigness sweeps my being like a flood.
Yet as a rebel fronts a king in state,
I stand within her walls with not a shred
Of terror, malice, not a word of jeer.
Darkly I gaze into the days ahead,
And see her might and granite wonders there,
Beneath the touch of Time's unerring hand,
Like priceless treasures sinking in the sand.

The White City

I will not toy with it nor bend an inch.
Deep in the secret chambers of my heart
I muse my life-long hate, and without flinch
I bear it nobly as I live my part.
My being would be a skeleton, a shell,
If this dark Passion that fills my every mood,
And makes my heaven in the white world's hell,
Did not forever feed me vital blood.
I see the mighty city through a mist—
The strident trains that speed the goaded mass,
The poles and spires and towers vapor-kissed,
The fortressed port through which the great ships
        pass,

The tides, the wharves, the dens I contemplate,
Are sweet like wanton loves because I hate.

The White House*

Your door is shut against my tightened face,
And I am sharp as steel with discontent;
But I possess the courage and the grace
To bear my anger proudly and unbent.
The pavement slabs burn loose beneath my feet,
A chafing savage, down the decent street;
And passion rends my vitals as I pass,
Where boldly shines your shuttered door of glass,
Oh, I must search for wisdom every hour,
Deep in my wrathful bosom sore and raw,
And find in it the superhuman power
To hold me to the letter of your law!
Oh, I must keep my heart inviolate
Against the potent poison of your hate.

JEAN TOOMER (1894–1967)

A biographical note on Jean Toomer appears in the Fiction section (see p. 63). The first three of the poems that follow are from Toomer's book Cane, *a mosaic of fiction and poetry. The fourth poem, "Brown River, Smile," is reprinted from the anthology* American Negro Poetry, *edited by Arna Bontemps.*

* "My title was symbolic . . . it had no reference to the official residence of the President of the United States. . . . The title 'White Houses' changed the whole symbolic intent and meaning of the poem, making it appear as if the burning ambition of the black malcontent was to enter white houses in general." Claude McKay: *A Long Way from Home* (1937), pp. 313-314.

Harvest Song

I am a reaper whose muscles set at sundown. All my oats are
  cradled.
But I am too chilled, and too fatigued to bind them. And I
  hunger.

I crack a grain between my teeth. I do not taste it.
I have been in the fields all day. My throat is dry. I hunger.

My eyes are caked with dust of oatfields at harvest-time.
I am a blind man who stares across the hills, seeking stack'd
  fields of other harvesters.

It would be good to see them . . . crook'd, split, and iron-
  ring'd handles of the scythes. It would be good to see
  them, dust-caked and blind. I hunger.

(Dusk is a strange fear'd sheath their blades are dull'd in.)
My throat is dry. And should I call, a cracked grain like the
  oats . . . eoho—

I fear to call. What should they hear me, and offer me their
  grain, oats, or wheat, or corn? I have been in the fields
  all day. I fear I could not taste it. I fear knowledge of
  my hunger.

My ears are caked with dust of oatfields at harvest-time.
I am a deaf man who strains to hear the calls of other
  harvesters whose throats are also dry.

It would be good to hear their songs . . . reapers of the
  sweet-stalk'd cane, cutters of the corn . . . even though
  their voices deafened me.

I hunger. My throat is dry. Now that the sun has set and I
  am chilled, I fear to call. (Eoho, my brothers!)

I am a reaper. (Eoho!) All my oats are cradled. But I am too
  fatigued to bind them. And I hunger. I crack a grain. It
  has no taste to it. My throat is dry. . . .

O my brothers, I beat my palms, still soft, against the stubble of my harvesting. (You beat your soft palms, too.) My pain is sweet. Sweeter than the oats or wheat or corn. It will not bring me knowledge of my hunger.

Song of the Son

Pour O pour that parting soul in song,
O pour it in the sawdust glow of night,
Into the velvet pine-smoke air to-night,
And let the valley carry it along.
And let the valley carry it along.

O land and soil, red soil and sweet-gum tree,
So scant of grass, so profligate of pines,
Now just before an epoch's sun declines
Thy son, in time, I have returned to thee,
Thy son, I have in time returned to thee.

In time, for though the sun is setting on
A song-lit race of slaves, it has not set;
Though late, O soil, it is not too late yet
To catch thy plaintive soul, leaving, soon gone,
Leaving, to catch thy plaintive soul soon gone.

O Negro slaves, dark purple ripened plums,
Squeezed, and bursting in the pine-wood air,
Passing, before they stripped the old tree bare
One plum was saved for me, one seed becomes

An everlasting song, a singing tree,
Caroling softly souls of slavery,
What they were, and what they are to me,
Caroling softly souls of slavery.

Cotton Song

Come, brother, come. Lets lift it;
Come now, hewit! roll away!
Shackles fall upon the Judgment Day
But lets not wait for it.

God's body's got a soul,

Bodies like to roll the soul,
Cant blame God if we dont roll,
Come, brother, roll, roll!

Cotton bales are the fleecy way
Weary sinner's bare feet trod,
Softly, softly to the throne of God,
"We aint agwine t wait until th Judgment Day!

Nassur; nassur,
Hump.
Eoho, eoho, roll away!
We aint agwine t wait until th Judgment Day!"

God's body's got a soul,
Bodies like to roll the soul,
Cant blame God if we dont roll,
Come, brother, roll, roll!

Brown River, Smile

It is a new America,
To be spiritualized by each new American.

Lift, lift, thou waking forces!
Let us feel the energy of animals,
The energy of rumps and bull-bent heads
Crashing the barrier to man.
It must spiral on!
A million million men, or twelve men,
Must crash the barrier to the next higher form.

Beyond plants are animals,
Beyond animals is man.
Beyond man is the universe.

The Big Light,
Let the Big Light in!

O thou, Radiant Incorporeal,
The I of earth and of mankind, hurl
Down these seaboards, across this continent,
The thousand-rayed discus of thy mind,
And above our walking limbs unfurl

Spirit-torsos of exquisite strength!

The Mississippi, sister of the Ganges,
Main artery of earth in the western world,
Is waiting to become
In the spirit of America, a sacred river.
Whoever lifts the Mississippi
Lifts himself and all America;
Whoever lifts himself
Makes that great brown river smile.
The blood of earth and the blood of man
Course swifter and rejoice when we spiritualize.

The old gods, led by an inverted Christ,
A shaved Moses, a blanched Lemur,
And a moulting thunderbird,
Withdrew into the distance and soon died,
Their dust and seed falling down
To fertilize the five regions of America.

We are waiting for a new God.

The old peoples—
The great European races sent wave after wave
That washed the forests, the earth's rich loam,
Grew towns with the seeds of giant cities,
Made roads, laid golden rails,
Sang once of its swift achievement,
And died congested in machinery.
They say that near the end
It was a world of crying men and hard women,
A city of goddam and Jehovah
Baptized in industry
Without benefit of saints,
Of dear defectives
Winnowing their likenesses from weathered rock
Sold by national organizations of undertakers.

Someone said:
    Suffering is impossible
    On cement sidewalks, in skyscrapers,
    In motorcars;
    Steel cannot suffer—
    We die unconsciously
    Because possessed by a nonhuman symbol.

Another cried:
>   It is because of thee, O Life,
>   That the first prayer ends in the last curse.

Another sang:
>   Late minstrels of the restless earth,
>   No muteness can be granted thee,
>   Lift thy laughing energies
>   To that white point which is a star.

The great African races sent a single wave
And singing riplets to sorrow in red fields,
Sing a swan song, to break rocks
And immortalize a hiding water boy.

>   I'm leaving the shining ground, brothers,
>   I sing because I ache,
>   I go because I must,
>   Brothers, I am leaving the shining ground;
>   Don't ask me where,
>   I'll meet you there,
>   I'm leaving the shining ground.

The great red race was here.
In a land of flaming earth and torrent-rains,
Of red sea-plains and majestic mesas,
At sunset from a purple hill
The Gods came down;
They serpentined into pueblo,
And a white-robed priest
Danced with them five days and nights;
But pueblo, priest, and Shalicos
Sank into the sacred earth
To fertilize the five regions of America.

>   Hi-ye, hi-yo, hi-yo
>   Hi-ye, hi-yo, hi-yo,
>   A lone eagle feather,
>   An untamed Navaho,
>   The ghosts of buffaloes,
>   Hi-ye, hi-yo, hi-yo,
>   Hi-ye, hi-yo, hi-yo.

We are waiting for a new people.

O thou, Radiant Incorporeal,

The I of earth and of mankind, hurl
Down these seaboards, across this continent,
The thousand-rayed discus of thy mind,
And above our walking limbs unfurl
Spirit-torsos of exquisite strength!
The east coast is masculine,
The west coast is feminine,
The middle region is the child—
Forces of reconciling
And generator of symbols.

 Thou, great fields, waving thy growths across the
  world,
 Couldest thou find the seed which started thee?
 Can you remember the first great hand to sow?
 Have you memory of His intention?
 Great plains, and thou, mountains,
 And thou, stately trees, and thou,
 America, sleeping and producing with the seasons,
 No clever dealer can divide,
 No machine can undermine thee.

The prairie's sweep is flat infinity,
The city's rise is perpendicular to farthest star,
I stand where the two directions intersect,
At Michigan Avenue and Walton Place,
Parallel to my countrymen,
Right-angled to the universe.

It is a new America,
To be spiritualized by each new American.

COUNTEE CULLEN (1903–1946)

*A classicist in poetic forms and inherently a romantic in his
thematic interests, acknowledging Keats as a central
influence, Countee Cullen was another central figure of the
Negro Renaissance. There was no single school of writing to*

which the Renaissance writers belonged. In poetry the "Harlem Renaissance" included the conventional forms of Countee Cullen and Claude McKay, along with the experimentations in free verse and jazz and blues rhythms of Langston Hughes. Cullen was born in New York City, "reared in the conservative atmosphere of a Methodist Parsonage," as he expressed it, and educated in the New York schools. He received his B. A. and Phi Beta Kappa key from New York University, and his M.A. from Harvard. Among the courses he took at Harvard was the one in verse forms taught by Robert Hillyer. In his book In Pursuit of Poetry *(1940), Professor Hillyer recalled "my friend and student" Countee Cullen and wrote:*

He was enrolled in the course in versification that I gave for many years at Harvard. In that course, I had the students practice writing in all the different forms of English verse. In Cullen's third book, *Copper Sun,* he published his exercises. Since he was a good poet, they were well worth preserving. He included them in a section called "At Cambridge" which, 'with grateful appreciation,' he dedicated to me. There they all are, ballad stanzas, heroic couplets, four-stress couplets, blank verse, Spenserian stanzas—he must have liked the Spenserian stanzas, for he wrote an extra poem in it—and rime royal. . . . As far as I know, the first rime royals in America were Countee Cullen's.

Cullen published his first collection of poems, Color *(1925), while he was still an undergraduate; it received the Harmon Gold Award. After graduating from Harvard, he became Assistant Editor of* Opportunity, *which, along with* The Crisis, *was an important medium of expression for the Negro writers of the Harlem Renaissance. He edited an anthology of verse by Negro poets,* Caroling Dusk *(1927), and wrote* The Black Christ *(1929) in France while on a Guggenheim Fellowship. Cullen also wrote a novel, as well as verse and stories for children. He taught in Harlem from 1934 to 1945. Cullen collaborated with his friend Arna Bontemps in writing the play* St. Louis Woman, *based on Bontemps' novel* God Sends Sunday; *it became a popular Broadway musical in 1946 with music by Vernon Duke. On These I Stand, Cullen's volume of collected poems, was published in 1947, a year after his death. Nine of his poems, written in different stages of his poetic development, are included here.*

Yet Do I Marvel

I doubt not God is good, well-meaning, kind.
And did He stoop to quibble could tell why
The little buried mole continues blind,
Why flesh that mirrors Him must some day die,
Make plain the reason tortured Tantalus
Is baited by the fickle fruit, declare
If merely brute caprice dooms Sisyphus
To struggle up a never-ending stair.
Inscrutable His ways are, and immune
To catechism by a mind too strewn
With petty cares to slightly understand
What awful brain compels His awful hand.
Yet do I marvel at this curious thing:
To make a poet black, and bid him sing!

[handwritten annotation: frustration of intellectual]

A Song of Praise

(For one who praised his lady's being fair.)

You have not heard my love's dark throat,
   Slow-fluting like a reed,
Release the perfect golden note
   She caged there for my need.

Her walk is like the replica
   Of some barbaric dance
Wherein the soul of Africa
   Is winged with arrogance.

And yet so light she steps across
   The ways her sure feet pass,
She does not dent the smoothest moss
   Or bend the thinnest grass.

My love is dark as yours is fair,
   Yet lovelier I hold her
Than listless maids with pallid hair,
   And blood that's thin and colder.

You-proud-and-to-be-pitied one,

Gaze on her and despair;
Then seal your lips until the sun
Discovers one as fair.

A Brown Girl Dead

With two white roses on her breasts,
    White candles at head and feet,
Dark Madonna of the grave she rests;
    Lord Death has found her sweet.

Her mother pawned her wedding ring
    To lay her out in white;
She'd be so proud she'd dance and sing
    To see herself tonight.

From the Dark Tower

(To Charles S. Johnson)

We shall not always plant while others reap
The golden increment of bursting fruit,
Not always countenance, abject and mute,
That lesser men should hold their brothers cheap;
Not everlastingly while others sleep
Shall we beguile their limbs with mellow flute,
Not always bend to some more subtle brute;
We were not made eternally to weep.

The night whose sable breast relieves the stark,
White stars is no less lovely being dark,
And there are buds that cannot bloom at all
In light, but crumple, piteous, and fall;
So in the dark we hide the heart that bleeds,
And wait, and tend our agonizing seeds.

Incident

Once riding in old Baltimore,
    Heart-filled, head-filled with glee,
I saw a Baltimorean

Keep looking straight at me.

Now I was eight and very small,
    And he was no whit bigger,
And so I smiled, but he poked out
    His tongue and called me, "Nigger."

I saw the whole of Baltimore
    From May until December:
Of all the things that happened there
    That's all that I remember.

Scottsboro, Too, Is Worth Its Song

(A poem to American poets)

I said:
Now will the poets sing,—
Their cries go thundering
Like blood and tears
Into the nation's ears,
Like lightning dart
Into the nation's heart.
Against disease and death and all things fell,
And war,
Their strophes rise and swell
To jar
The foe smug in his citadel.

Remembering their sharp and pretty
Tunes for Sacco and Vanzetti,
I said:
Here too's a cause divinely spun
For those whose eyes are on the sun,
Here in epitome
Is all disgrace
And epic wrong,
Like wine to brace
The minstrel heart, and blare it into song.

Surely, I said,
Now will the poets sing.
    But they have raised no cry.
    I wonder why.

Three Epitaphs

For My Grandmother

This lovely flower fell to seed;
Work gently sun and rain;
She held it as her dying creed
That she would grow again.

For Paul Laurence Dunbar

Born of the sorrowful of heart
Mirth was a crown upon his head;
Pride kept his twisted lips apart
In jest, to hide a heart that bled.

For a Lady I Know

She even thinks that up in heaven
Her class lies late and snores,
While poor black cherubs rise at seven
To do celestial chores.

MELVIN B. TOLSON (1898–1966)

In an angry article in Book Week, *which later became the Introduction to M. B. Tolson's last volume of verse,* Harlem Gallery *(1965) poet-critic Karl Shapiro wrote: "A great poet has been living in our midst for decades and is almost totally unknown. . . . Can this be possible in the age of criticism and of publications unlimited?" Tolson's obscurity was particularly paradoxical in the light of the fact that major American critics and poets hailed him as a significant modern. Tolson's second book of poetry,* Libretto for the Republic of

Liberia *(1953), had a preface by Allen Tate observing that "there is a great gift of language, a profound historical sense, and a first-rate intelligence at work in this poem from first to last." William Carlos Williams, in the fourth book of* Pater-*son, saluted Tolson and "his ode" to* Liberia. *Robert Frost, Theodore Roethke, Selden Rodman, John Ciardi and Stanley Edgar Hyman, in the words of Karl Shapiro, "tried to bring Tolson to the general literary consciousness, but with little success." Tolson was born in Moberly, Missouri, and was educated at Fisk, Lincoln, and Columbia universities. He received fellowships in literature from the Omega Psi Phi Fraternity and the Rockefeller Foundation. He taught at various colleges in the South and for several decades was associated with Langston University in Oklahoma, where he directed the campus Dust Bowl Theater and was Professor of Creative Literature. He wrote several plays. No ivory tower intellectual, Tolson participated actively in the political affairs of the community and was elected Mayor of Langston four times. "Dark Symphony," one of the poems included here, won the National Poetry Contest conducted by the American Negro Exposition in Chicago and was published in* The Atlantic Monthly. *Tolson was commissioned to write a poem for the Liberian Centennial and International Exposition and produced* Libretto for the Republic of Liberia, *for which he was designated Poet Laureate of Liberia. In 1952 he received the Bess Hokin Award of the Modern Poetry Association. We present three of his poems. The first two are from his first volume of verse,* Rendezvous with America *(1944), and the third is from his last book,* Harlem Gallery *(1965).*

An Ex-Judge at the Bar

Bartender, make it straight and make it two—
One for the you in me and the me in you.
Now let us put our heads together: one
Is half enough for malice, sense, or fun.

I know, Bartender, yes, I know when the Law
Should wag its tail or rip with fang and claw.
When Pilate washed his hands, that neat event
Set for us judges a Caesarean precedent.

What I shall tell you now, as man is man,
You'll find in neither Bible nor Koran.

It happened after my return from France
At the bar in Tony's Lady of Romance.

We boys drank pros and cons, sang *Dixie;* and then,
The bar a Sahara, we pledged to meet again.
But lo, on the bar there stood in naked scorn
The Goddess Justice, like September Morn.

Who blindfolds Justice on the courthouse roof
While the lawyers weave the sleight-of-hand of proof?
I listened, Bartender, with my heart and head,
As the Goddess Justice unbandaged her eyes and said:

"To make the world safe for Democracy,
You lost a leg in Flanders fields—*oui, oui?*
To gain the judge's seat, you twined the noose
That swung the Negro higher than a goose."

Bartender, who has dotted every *i?*
Crossed every *t?* Put legs on every *y?*
Therefore, I challenged her: "Lay on, Macduff,
And damned be him who first cries, 'Hold, enough!'"

The boys guffawed, and Justice began to laugh
Like a maniac on a broken phonograph.
Bartender, make it straight and make it three—
One for the Negro . . . one for you and me.

Dark Symphony

1
Allegro Moderato

Black Crispus Attucks taught
                    Us how to die
Before white Patrick Henry's bugle breath
Uttered the vertical
                    Transmitting cry:
"Yea, give me liberty or give me death."

Waifs of the auction block,
                    Men black and strong
The juggernauts of despotism withstood,
Loin-girt with faith that worms

Equate the wrong
And dust is purged to create brotherhood.

No Banquo's ghost can rise
                    Against us now,
Aver we hobnailed Man beneath the brute,
Squeezed down the thorns of greed
                    On Labor's brow,
Garroted lands and carted off the loot.

2
Lento Grave

The centuries-old pathos in our voices
Saddens the great white world,
And the wizardry of our dusky rhythms
Conjures up shadow-shapes of ante-bellum years:

Black slaves singing *One More River to Cross*
In the torture tombs of slave-ships,
Black slaves singing *Steal Away to Jesus*
In jungle swamps,
Black slaves singing *The Crucifixion*
In slave-pens at midnight,
Black slaves singing *Swing Low, Sweet Chariot*
In cabins of death,
Black slaves singing *Go Down, Moses*
In the canebrakes of the Southern Pharaohs.

3
Andante Sostenuto

They tell us to forget
The Golgotha we tread . . .
We who are scourged with hate,
A price upon our head.
They who have shackled us
Require of us a song,
They who have wasted us
Bid us condone the wrong.

They tell us to forget
Democracy is spurned.
They tell us to forget
The Bill of Rights is burned.
Three hundred years we slaved,

We slave and suffer yet:
Though flesh and bone rebel,
They tell us to forget!

Oh, how can we forget
Our human rights denied?
Oh, how can we forget
Our manhood crucified?
When Justice is profaned
And plea with curse is met,
When Freedom's gates are barred,
Oh, how can we forget?

4
Tempo Primo

The New Negro strides upon the continent
In seven-league boots . . .
The New Negro
Who sprang from the vigor-stout loins
Of Nat Turner, gallows-martyr for Freedom,
Of Joseph Cinquez, Black Moses of the Amistad Mutiny,
Of Frederick Douglass, oracle of the Catholic Man,
Of Sojourner Truth, eye and ear of Lincoln's legions,
Of Harriet Tubman, Saint Bernard of the Underground
    Railroad.

The New Negro
Breaks the icons of his detractors,
Wipes out the conspiracy of silence,
Speaks to *his* America:

"My history-moulding ancestors
Planted the first crops of wheat on these shores,
Built ships to conquer the seven seas,
Erected the Cotton Empire,
Flung railroads across a hemisphere,
Disemboweled the earth's iron and coal,
Tunneled the mountains and bridged rivers,
Harvested the grain and hewed forests,
Sentineled the Thirteen Colonies,
Unfurled Old Glory at the North Pole,
Fought a hundred battles for the Republic."

The New Negro:
His giant hands fling murals upon high chambers,
His drama teaches a world to laugh and weep,

His music leads continents captive,
His voice thunders the Brotherhood of Labor,
His science creates seven wonders,
His Republic of Letters challenges the Negro-baiters.

The New Negro,
Hard-muscled, Fascist-hating, Democracy-ensouled,
Strides in seven-league boots
Along the Highway of Today
Toward the Promised Land of Tomorrow!

5
Larghetto

None in the Land can say
To us black men Today:
You send the tractors on their bloody path,
And create Okies for *The Grapes of Wrath.*
You breed the slum that breeds a *Native Son*
To damn the good earth Pilgrim Fathers won.

None in the Land can say
To us black men Today:
You dupe the poor with rags-to-riches tales,
And leave the workers empty dinner pails.
You stuff the ballot box, and honest men
Are muzzled by your demagogic din.

None in the Land can say
To us black men Today:
You smash stock markets with your coined blitzkriegs,
And make a hundred million guinea pigs.
You counterfeit our Christianity,
And bring contempt upon Democracy.

None in the Land can say
To us black men Today:
You prowl when citizens are fast asleep,
And hatch Fifth Column plots to blast the deep
Foundations of the State and leave the Land
A vast Sahara with a Fascist brand.

6
Tempo di Marcia

Out of abysses of Illiteracy,
Through labyrinths of Lies,

Across waste lands of Disease . . .
We advance!

Out of dead-ends of Poverty,
Through wildernesses of Superstition,
Across barricades of Jim Crowism . . .
We advance!

With the Peoples of the World . . .
We advance!

PSI

Black Boy,
let me get up from the white man's Table of Fifty Sounds
in the kitchen; let me gather the crumbs and cracklings
of this autobio-fragment,
before the curtain with the skull and bones descends.

Many a *t* in the ms.
I've left without a cross,
many an *i* without a dot.
A dusky Lot
with a third degree and a second wind and a seventh turn
of pitch-and-toss,
my psyche escaped the Sodom of Gylt
and the Big White Boss.

Black Boy,
you stand before your heritage,
naked and agape;
cheated like a mockingbird
pecking at a Zuexian grape,
pressed like an awl to do
duty as a screw-
driver, you
ask the American Dilemma in you:
"If the trying plane
of Demos fail,
what will the trowel
of Uncle Tom avail?"

Black Boy,
in this race, at this time, in this place,

to be a Negro artist is to be
a flower of the gods, whose growth
is dwarfed at an early stage—
a Brazilian owl moth,
a giant among his own in an acreage
dark with the darkman's designs,
where the milieu moves back downward like the sloth.

Black Boy,
true—you
have not
dined and wined
(*ignoti nulla cupido*)
in the El Dorado of aeried Art,
for unreasoned reasons;
and your artists, not so lucky as the Buteo,
find themselves without a
skyscrape sanctuary
in the
season of seasons:
in contempt of the contemptible,
refuse the herb of grace, the rue
of Job's comforter;
take no
lie-tea in lieu
of Broken Orange Pekoe.
Doctor Nkomo said: "*What* is he who smacks
his lips when dewrot eats away the golden grain
of self-respect exposed like flax
to the rigors of sun and rain?"

Black Boy
every culture,
every caste,
every people,
every class,
facing the barbarians
with lips hubris-curled,
believes its death rattle omens
the *Dies Irae* of the world.

Black Boy,
summon Boas and Dephino,
Blumenbach and Koelreuter,
from their posts
around the gravestone of Bilbo,
who, with cancer in his mouth,

orated until he quaked the magnolias of the South,
while the pocketbooks of his weeping black serfs
        shriveled in the drouth;
            summon the ghosts
of scholars with rams' horns from Jericho
and facies in letters from Jerusalem,
            so
        we may ask them:
        "What is a Negro?"

        Black Boy,
what's in a people's name that wries the brain
        like the neck of a barley bird?
        Can sounding brass create
        an ecotype with a word?

        Black Boy,
    beware of the thin-bladed mercy
stroke, for one drop of Negro blood
    (V. *The Black Act of the F. F. V.*)
        opens the flood-
    gates of the rising tide of color
        and jettisons
the D. A. R. in the Heraclitean flux
        with Uncle Tom and
        Crispus Attucks.
    The Black Belt White,
    painstaking as a bedbug in
    a tenant farmer's truckle bed,
    rabbit-punched old Darrow
        because
he quoted Darwin's sacred laws
(instead of the Lord God Almighty's)
and gabbled that the Catarrhine ape
(the C from a Canada goose nobody knows)
        appears,
    after X's of years,
    in the vestigial shape
of the Nordic's thin lips, his aquiline nose,
        his straight hair,
orangutanish on legs and chest and head.
Doctor Nkomo, a votary of touch-and-go,
    who can stand the gaff
of Negrophobes and, like Aramis,
    parry a thrust with a laugh,
        said:
"In spite of the pig in the python's coils,

in spite of Blake's lamb in the jaws of the tiger,
Nature is kind, even in the raw: she toils
. . . aeons and aeons and aeons . . .
gives the African a fleecy canopy
to protect the seven faculties of the brain
from the burning convex lens of the sun;
she foils
whiteness
(without disdain)
to bless the African
(as Herodotus marvels)
with the birthright of a burnt skin for work or fun;
she roils
the Aryan
(as his eye and ear repose)
to give the African an accommodation nose
that cools the drying-up air;
she entangles the epidermis in broils
that keep the African's body free from lice-infested hair.
As man to man,
the Logos is
Nature is on the square
with the African.
If a black man circles the rim
of the Great White World, he will find
(even if Adamness has made him half blind)
the bitter waters of Marah *and*
the fresh fountains of Elim."

Although his transition
was a far cry
from Shakespeare to Sardou,
the old Africanist's byplay gave
no soothing feverfew
to the Dogs in the Zulu Club;
said he:
"A Hardyesque artistry
of circumstance
divides the Whites and Blacks in life,
like the bodies of the dead
eaten by vultures
in a Tower of Silence.
Let, then, the man with a maggot in his head
lean . . . lean . . . lean
on race or caste or class,
for the wingless worms of blowflies shall grub,
dry and clean,

the stinking skeletons of these,
when the face of the macabre weather-
cock turns to the torrid wind of misanthropy;
and later their bones shall be swept together
(like the Parsees')
in the Sepulchre of Anonymity."
A Zulu Wit cleared away his unsunned
mood with dark laughter;
but I sensed the thoughts of Doctor Nkomo
pacing nervously to and fro
like Asscher's, after
he'd cleaved the giant Cullinan Diamond.

Black Boy,
the vineyard is the fittest place
in which to booze (with Omar) and study
soil and time and integrity—
the telltale triad of grape and race.

Palates that can read the italics
of *salt* and *sugar* know
a grapevine
transplanted from Bordeaux
to Pleasant Valley
cannot give grapes that make a Bordeaux wine.

Like the sons of the lone mother of dead empires,
who boasted their ancestors,
page after page—
wines are peacocky
in their vintage and their age,
disdaining the dark ways of those engaging
in the profits
of chemical aging.
When the bluebirds sing
their perennial anthem
a capriccio, in the Spring,
the sap begins to move up the stem
of the vine, and the wine in the bed of the deep
cask stirs in its winter sleep.
Its bouquet
comes with the years, dry or wet;
so the connoisseurs say:
"The history of the wine
is repeated by the vine."

Black Boy,

beware of wine labels,
for the Republic does not guarantee
what the phrase "Château Bottled" means—
the estate, the proprietor, the quality.
This ignominy will baffle you, Black Boy,
because the white man's law
has raked your butt many a time
with fang and claw.
Beware of the waiter who wraps
a napkin around your Clos Saint Thierry,
if Chance takes you into high-hat places
open to all creeds and races
born to be or not to be.
Beware of the pop
of a champagne cork:
like the flatted fifth and octave jump in Bebop,
it is theatrical
in Vicksburg or New York.
Beware of the champagne cork
that does not swell up like your ma when she had you—that
comes out flat,
because the bottle of wine
is dead . . . dead
like Uncle Tom and the Jim Crow Sign.
Beware . . . yet
your dreams in the Great White World
shall be unthrottled
by pigmented and unpigmented lionhearts,
for we know *without no*
every people, by and by, produces its "Château Bottled."

White Boy,
as regards the ethnic origin
of Black Boy and me,
the *What* in Socrates' *"Tò tí?"*
is for the musk-ox habitat of anthropologists;
but there is another question,
dangerous as a moutaba tick,
secreted in the house
of every Anglo-Saxon sophist and hick:

Who is a Negro?
(I am a White in deah ole Norfolk.)
Who is a White?
(I am a Negro in little old New York.)
Since my mongrelization is invisible

and my Negroness a state of mind conjured up
by Stereotypus, I am a chameleon
on *that* side of the Mason-Dixon
that a white man's conscience
is not on.
My skin is as white
as a Roman's toga when he sought an office on the sly;
my hair is as blond
as xanthein;
my eyes are as blue
as the hawk's-eye.
At the Olympian powwow of curators,
when I revealed my Negroness,
my peers became shocked like virgins in a house
where satyrs tattooed on female thighs heralds of success.

White Boy,
counterfeit scholars have used
the newest brush-on Satinlac,
to make our ethnic identity
crystal clear for the lowest IQ
in every mansion and in every shack.
Therefore,
according to the myth that Negrophobes bequeath
to the Lost Gray Cause, since Black Boy is the color
of betel-stained teeth,
he and I
(from ocular proof
that cannot goof)
belong to races
whose dust-of-the-earth progenitors
the Lord God Almighty created
of different bloods,
in antipodal places.
However,
even the F. F. V. pate
is aware that laws defining a Negro
blackjack each other with*in* and with*out* a state.
The Great White World, White Boy, leaves you in a sweat
like a pitcher with three runners on the bases;
and, like Kant, you seldom get
your grammar straight—yet,
you are the wick that absorbs the oil in my lamp,
in all kinds of weather;
and we are teeth in the pitch wheel
that work together.

White Boy,
when I hear the word *Negro* defined,
why does it bring to mind
the chef, the gourmand, the belly-god,
the disease of kings, the culinary art
in alien lands, Black Mammy in a Dixie big house,
and the dietitian's chart?
Now, look at Black Boy scratch his head!
It's a stereotypic gesture of Uncle Tom,
a learned Gentleman of Color said
in his monumental tome,
The *Etiquette of the New Negro,*
which,
the publishers say,
by the way,
should be in every black man's home.

The Negro is a dish in the white man's kitchen—
a potpourri,
an ola-podrida,
a mixie-maxie,
a hotchpotch of lineal ingredients;
with UN guests at his table,
the host finds himself a Hamlet on the spot,
for, in spite of his catholic pose,
the Negro dish is a dish nobody knows:
to some ... tasty,
like an exotic condiment—
to others ... unsavory
and inelegant.

White Boy,
the Negro dish is a mix
like ... and *un*like
pimiento bisque, chop suey,
eggs à la Goldenrod, and eggaroni;
tongue-and-corn casserole, mulligan stew,
baked fillets of halibut, and cheese fondue;
macaroni milanaise, egg-milk shake,
mullagatawny soup, and sour-milk cake.

Just as the Chinese lack
an ideogram for "to be,"
our lexicon has no definition
for an ethnic amalgam like Black Boy and me.

Behold a Gordian knot without
the *beau geste* of an Alexander's sword!
Water, O Modern Mariner, water, everywhere,
unfit for *vitro di trina* glass
or the old-oaken-bucket's gourd!

For dark hymens on the auction block,
the lord of the mansion knew the macabre score:
not a dog moved his tongue,
not a lamb lost a drop of blood to protect a door,
O
Xenos of Xanthos,
what midnight-to-dawn lecheries,
in cabin and big house,
produced these brown hybrids and yellow motleys?

White Boy,
Buchenwald is a melismatic song
whose single syllable is sung to blues notes
to dark wayfarers who listen for the gong
at the crack of doom along
. . . that Lonesome Road . . .
before they travel on.

A Pelagian with the *raison d'être* of a Negro,
I cannot say I have outwitted dread,
for I am conscious of the noiseless tread
of the Yazoo tiger's ball-like pads behind me
in the dark
as I trudge ahead,
up and up . . . that Lonesome Road . . . up and up.

In a Vision in a Dream,
from the frigid seaport of the proud Xanthochroid,
the good ship *Défineznegro*
sailed fine, under an unabridged moon,
to reach the archipelago
Nigeridentité.
In the Strait of Octoroon,
off black Scylla,
after the typhoon Phobos, out of the Stereotypus Sea,
had rived her hull and sail to a T,
the *Défineznegro* sank the rock
and disappeared in the abyss
(*Vanitas vanitatum!*)
of white Charybdis.

FRANK HORNE (1899–   )

Born in New York City, and distinguished as a track athlete when he attended the College of the City of New York, Frank Horne is best known for the poems he wrote in the 1920's. He won The Crisis poetry prize in 1925. He graduated from the Northern Illinois College of Ophthalmology and was a Doctor of Optometry. He practiced in Chicago and New York and for many years served as an official with the United States Housing Authority. Widely anthologized, his only collection of poems, Haverstraw, *was published in Paul Breman's Heritage Series in London in 1963.*

Kid Stuff

The wise guys
tell me that Christmas
is Kid Stuff . . .
Maybe they've got
something there—
Two thousand years ago
three wise guys
chased a star
across a continent
to bring
frankincense and myrrh
to a Kid
born in a manger
with an idea in his head . . .

And as the bombs
crash
all over the world
today

                    the real wise guys
                    know
                    that we've all
                    got to go chasing stars
                    again
                    in the hope
                    that we can get back
                    some of that
                    Kid Stuff
                    born two thousand years ago—

Nigger
A Chant for Children

Little Black boy
Chased down the street—
"Nigger, nigger never die
Black face an' shiney eye,
Nigger . . . nigger . . . nigger . . ."

Hannibal . . . Hannibal
Bangin' thru the Alps
Licked the proud Romans,
Ran home with their scalps—
"Nigger . . . nigger . . . nigger . . ."

Othello . . . black man
Mighty in war
Listened to Iago
Called his wife a whore—
"Nigger . . . nigger . . . nigger . . ."

Crispus . . . Attucks
Bullets in his chest
Red blood of freedom
Runnin' down his vest
"Nigger . . . nigger . . . nigger . . ."

Toussant . . . Toussant
Made the French flee
Fought like a demon
Set his people free—
"Nigger . . . nigger . . . nigger . . ."

Jesus . . . Jesus
Son of the Lord

—Spit in his face
—Nail him on a board
"Nigger . . . nigger . . . nigger . . ."

Little Black boy
Runs down the street—
"Nigger, nigger never die
Black face an' shiney eye,
Nigger . . . nigger . . . nigger . . ."

STERLING A. BROWN (1901–   )

More than thirty years ago, in The Book of American Negro Poetry, *James Weldon Johnson described Sterling A. Brown as "one of the outstanding poets of the younger group." Johnson also wrote: "More than any other American poet he has made thematic use of the Negro folk epics and ballads. . . . He has perceived that one of the cardinal traits of Negro folk poetry is terseness—a trait at complete variance with the general idea of Negro diffuseness—and strictly adhered to it. He has, in fact, done the only thing that justifies the individual artist in taking material of this sort: he has worked it into original and genuine poetry." To Negro critics today, Brown is "the dean of American Negro poets," as John Henrik Clarke describes him in* American Negro Short Stories (1966). *In an interview published in* Negro Digest (May, 1967), *Leopold Senghor, the African poet, philosopher of Negritude, and President of Senegal, cited Sterling Brown and Langston Hughes as "the most Negro" poets in American literature. Brown was born and brought up in Washington, D. C. He went to Williams College, was elected to Phi Beta Kappa in 1921, and received his M.A. from Harvard in 1923. Since then he has been teaching, writing, and editing, with a long and distinguished career as professor of English at Howard University. He has been a visiting professor at New York University, Atlanta University, and Vassar College. From 1936 to 1939 he served as the Editor on Negro Affairs for the Federal Writers' Project. In 1939 he was a staff member of the Carnegie-Myrdal Study of the Negro. He was a Guggenheim Fellow in 1937–1938. His first book,* Southern Road

*(1932), is a collection of his early poems. He has published
two volumes of literary criticism (see Bibliography) and was
Senior Editor of The Negro Caravan (1941), a comprehensive
anthology of Negro American writing. Sterling Brown has
contributed poetry, book reviews, essays, and critical studies
to numerous publications, and his essay "A Century of Negro
Portraiture in American Literature" appears in the Literary
Criticism section.*

Sister Lou

Honey
When de man
Calls out de las' train
You're gonna ride,
Tell him howdy.

Gather up yo' basket
An' yo' knittin' an' yo' things,
An' go on up an' visit
Wid frien' Jesus fo' a spell.

Show Marfa
How to make yo' greengrape jellies,
An' give po' Lazarus
A passel of them Golden Biscuits.

Scald some meal
Fo' some rightdown good spoonbread
Fo' li'l box-plunkin' David.

An' sit aroun'
An' tell them Hebrew Chillen
All yo' stories. • • •

Honey
Don't be feared of them pearly gates,
Don't go 'round to de back,
No mo' dataway
Not evah no mo'.

Let Michael tote yo' burden
An' yo' pocketbook an' evah thing
'Cept yo' Bible,
While Gabriel blows somp'n
Solemn but loudsome
On dat horn of his'n.

Honey
Go Straight on to de Big House,
An' speak to yo' God
Widout no fear an' tremblin'.

Then sit down
An' pass de time of day awhile.

Give a good talkin' to
To yo' favorite 'postle Peter,
An' rub the po' head
Of mixed-up Judas,
An' joke awhile wid Jonah.

Then, when you gits de chance,
Always rememberin' yo' raisin',
Let 'em know youse tired
Jest a mite tired.

Jesus will find yo' bed fo' you
Won't no servant evah bother wid yo' room.
Jesus will lead you
To a room wid windows
Openin' on cherry trees an' plum trees
Bloomin' everlastin'.

An' dat will be yours
Fo' keeps.

Den take yo' time . . .
Honey, take yo' bressed time.

Memphis Blues

1

Nineveh, Tyre
Babylon,
Not much lef'
Of either one.
All dese cities
Ashes and rust,
De win' sing sperrichals
Through deir dus'. . . .
Was another Memphis
Mongst de olden days,
Done been destroyed
In many ways. . . .
Dis here Memphis

It may go
Floods may drown it;
Tornado blow;
Mississippi wash it
Down to sea—
Like de other Memphis in
History.

2

Watcha gonna do when Memphis on fire,
    Memphis on fire, Mistah Preachin' Man?
Gonna pray to Jesus and nebber tire,
    Gonna pray to Jesus, loud as I can,
        Gonna pray to my Jesus, oh, my Lawd!

Watcha gonna do when de tall flames roar,
    Tall flames roar, Mistah Lovin' Man?
Gonna love my brownskin better'n before—
    Gonna love my baby lak a do right man,
        Gonna love my brown baby, oh, my Lawd!

Watcha gonna do when Memphis falls down,
    Memphis falls down, Mistah Music Man?
Gonna plunk on dat box as long as it soun',
    Gonna plunk dat box fo' to beat de ban',
        Gonna tickle dem ivories, oh, my Lawd!

Watcha gonna do in de hurricane,
    In de hurricane, Mistah Workin' Man?
Gonna put dem buildings up again,
    Gonna put em up dis time to stan',
        Gonna push a wicked wheelbarrow, oh, my Lawd!

Watcha gonna do when Memphis near gone,
    Memphis near gone, Mistah Drinkin' Man?
Gonna grab a pint bottle of Mountain Corn,
    Gonna keep de stopper in my han',
        Gonna get a mean jag on, oh, my Lawd!

Watcha gonna do when de flood roll fas',
    Flood roll fas', Mistah Gamblin' Man?
Gonna pick up my dice fo' one las' pass—
    Gonna fade my way to de lucky lan',
        Gonna throw my las' seven—oh, my Lawd!

3

Memphis go
By Flood or Flame;
Nigger won't worry
All de same—
Memphis go
Memphis come back,
Ain' no skin
Off de nigger's back.
All dese cities
Ashes, rust. . . .
De win' sing sperrichals
Through deir dus'.

Slim in Hell

1

Slim Greer went to heaven;
St. Peter said, "Slim,
You been a right good boy."
An' he winked at him.

"You been a travelin' rascal
In yo' day.
You kin roam once mo';
Den you comes to stay.

"Put dese wings on yo' shoulders,
An' save yo' feet."
Slim grin, and he speak up,
"Thankye, Pete."

Den Peter say, "Go
To Hell an' see,
All dat is doing, and
Report to me.

"Be sure to remember
How everything go."
Slim say, "I be seein' yuh
On de late watch, bo."

Slim got to cavortin'
    Swell as you choose
Like Lindy in de Spirit
    Of St. Louis Blues.

He flew an' he flew,
    Till at last he hit
A hangar wid de sign readin'
    DIS IS IT.

Den he parked his wings
    An' strolled aroun',
Gittin' used to his feet
    On de solid ground.

2

Big bloodhound came aroarin'
    Like Niagry Falls,
Sicked on by white devils
    In overhalls.

Now Slim warn't scared,
    Cross my heart, it's a fac',
An de dog went on a bayin'
    Some po' devil's track.

Den Slim saw a mansion
    An' walked right in;
De Devil looked up
    Wid a sickly grin.

"Suttinly didn't look
    Fo' you, Mr. Greer,
How it happens you comes
    To visit here?"

Slim say—"Oh, jes' thought
    I'd drap by a spell."
"Feel at home, seh, an' here's
    De keys to hell."

Den he took Slim around
    An' showed him people
Raisin' hell as high as
    De First Church Steeple.

Lots of folks fightin'
    At de roulette wheel,
Like old Rampart Street,
    Or leastwise Beale.

Showed him bawdy houses
    An' cabarets,
Slim thought of New Orleans
    An' Memphis days.

Each devil was busy
    Wid a devilish broad,
An' Slim cried, "Lawdy,
    Lawd, Lawd, Lawd."

Took him in a room
    Where Slim see
De preacher wid a brownskin
    On each knee.

Showed him giant stills,
    Going everywhere,
Wid a passel of devils
    Stretched dead drunk there.

Den he took him to de furnace
    Dat some devils was firing,
Hot as hell, an' Slim start
    A mean presspirin'.

White devils wid pitchforks
    Threw black devils on,
Slim thought he'd better
    Be gittin' along.

An' he say—"Dis makes
    Me think of home—
Vicksburg, Little Rock, Jackson,
    Waco and Rome."

Den de devil gave Slim
    De big Ha-Ha;
An' turned into a cracker,
    Wid a sheriff's star.

Slim ran fo' his wings,

                Lit out from de groun'
            Hauled it back to St. Peter,
                Safety boun'.

                        3

                St. Peter said, "Well,
                    You got back quick.
                How's de devil? An' what's
                    His latest trick?"

            An' Slim say, "Peter,
                I really cain't tell,
            The place was Dixie
                That I took for hell."

                Then Peter say, "You must
                    Be crazy, I vow,
                Where'n hell dja think Hell *was*,
                    Anyhow?

            "Git on back to de yearth,
                Cause I got de fear,
            You'se a leetle too dumb,
                Fo' to stay up here . . ."

Remembering Nat Turner

(For R. C. L.)

We saw a bloody sunset over Courtland, once Jerusalem,
As we followed the trail that old Nat took
When he came out of Cross Keys down upon Jerusalem,
In his angry stab for freedom a hundred years ago.
The land was quiet, and the mist was rising,
Out of the woods and the Nottaway swamp,
Over Southampton the still night fell,
As we rode down to Cross Keys where the march began.

When we got to Cross Keys, they could tell us little of him,
The Negroes had only the faintest recollections:
    "I ain't been here so long, I come from up roun' New-
        some;
    Yassah, a town a few miles up de road,

The old folks who coulda told you is all dead an' gone.
I heard something, sometime; I doan jis remember what.
'Pears lak I heard that name somewheres or other.
So he fought to be free. Well. You doan say."

An old white woman recalled exactly
How Nat crept down the steps, axe in his hand,
After murdering a woman and child in bed,
"Right in this here house at the head of these stairs"
(In a house built long after Nat was dead).
She pointed to a brick store where Nat was captured,
(Nat was taken in the swamp, three miles away)
With his men around him, shooting from the windows
(She was thinking of Harper's Ferry and old John Brown).
She cackled as she told how they riddled Nat with bullets
(Nat was tried and hanged at Courtland, ten miles away).
She wanted to know why folks would comes miles
Just to ask about an old nigger fool.
      "Ain't no slavery no more, things is going all right,
      Pervided thar's a good goober market this year.
      We had a sign post here with printing on it,
      But it rotted in the hole, and thar it lays,
      And the nigger tenants split the marker for kindling.
      Things is all right, naow, ain't no trouble with the nig-
            gers
      Why they make this big to-do over Nat?"

As we drove from Cross Keys back to Courtland,
Along the way that Nat came down upon Jerusalem,
A watery moon was high in the cloud-filled heavens,
The same moon he dreaded a hundred years ago.
The tree they hanged Nat on is long gone to ashes,
The trees he dodged behind have rotted in the swamps.

The bus for Miama and the trucks boomed by,
And touring cars, their heavy tires snarling on the pavement.
Frogs piped in the marshes, and a hound bayed long,
And yellow lights glowed from the cabin windows.

As we came back the way that Nat led his army,
Down from Cross Keys, down to Jerusalem,
We wondered if his troubled spirit still roamed the Nottaway,
Or if it fled with the cock-crow at daylight,
Or lay at peace with the bones in Jerusalem,
Its restlessness stifled by Southampton clay.

We remembered the poster rotted through and falling,
The marker split for kindling a kitchen fire.

Southern Road

Swing dat hammer—hunh—
Steady, bo';
Swing dat hammer—hunh—
Steady, bo';
Ain't no rush, bebby,
Long ways to go.

Burner tore his—hunh—
Black heart away;
Burner tore his—hunh—
Black heart away;
Got me life, bebby,
An' a day.

Gal's on Fifth Street—hunh—
Son done gone;
Gal's on Fifth Street—hunh—
Son done gone;
Wife's in de ward, bebby,
Babe's not bo'n.

My ole man died—hunh—
Cussin' me;
My ole man died—hunh—
Cussin' me;
Ole lady rocks, bebby,
Huh misery.

Doubleshackled—hunh—
Guard behin';
Doubleshackled—hunh—
Guard behin';
Ball and chain, bebby,
On my min'.

White man tells me—hunh—
Dam yo' soul;
White man tells me—hunh—
Dam yo' soul;

Got no need, bebby,
To be tole.

Chain gang nevah—hunh—
Let me go;
Chain gang nevah—hunh—
Let me go;
Po' los' boy, bebby,
Evahmo' . . . .

Southern Cop

Let us forgive Ty Kendricks
The place was Darktown. He was young.
His nerves were jittery. The day was hot.
The Negro ran out of the alley.
And so Ty shot.

Let us understand Ty Kendricks
The Negro must have been dangerous,
Because he ran;
And here was a rookie with a chance
To prove himself man.

Let us condone Ty Kendricks
If we cannot decorate.
When he found what the Negro was running for,
It was all too late;
And all we can say for the Negro is
It was unfortunate.

Let us pity Ty Kendricks
He has been through enough,
Standing there, his big gun smoking,
Rabbit-scared, alone,
Having to hear the wenches wail
And the dying Negro moan.

The Young Ones

With cotton to the doorstep
No place to play;

No time:what with chopping cotton
All the day.

In the broken down car
They jounce up and down
Pretend to be steering
On the way to town.

It's as far as they'll get
For many a year;
Cotton brought them
And will keep them here.

The spare-ribbed yard-dog
Has gone away;
The kids, just as hungry,
Have to stay.

In the two-roomed shack
Their mammy is lying,
With a little new brother
On her arm, crying.

Another mouth to feed
Another body to bed,
Another to grow up
Underfed.

But their pappy's happy
And they hear him say:
"The good Lord giveth,
And taketh away.

"It's two more hands
For to carry a row;
Praise God from whom
All blessings flow."

The Ballad of Joe Meek

1

You cain't never tell
How far a frog will jump,

When you jes' see him planted
  On his big broad rump.

    Nor what a monkey's thinking
      By the working of his jaws—
    You jes' cain't figger;
      And I knows, because

Had me a buddy,
  Soft as pie
Joe Meek they called him
  And they didn't lie.

    The good book say
      "Turn the other cheek,"
    But that warn't no turning
      To my boy Joe Meek.

He turned up all parts,
  And baigged you to spank,
Pulled down his breeches,
  And supplied the plank.

    The worm that didn't turn
      Was a rattlesnake to Joe:
    Wasn't scary—jes' meek, suh,
      Was made up so.

                2

It was late in August
  What dey calls dog days,
Made even beetle hounds
  Git bulldog ways.

    Would make a pet bunny
      Chase a bad blood-hound,
    Make a new-born baby
      Slap his grandpa down.

The air it was muggy
  And heavy with heat,
The people all sizzled
  Like frying meat.

The icehouse was heaven
The pavements was hell
Even Joe didn't feel
So agreeable.

Strolling down Claiborne
In the wrong end of town
Joe saw two policemen
Knock a po' gal down.

He didn't know her at all,
Never saw her befo'
But that didn't make no difference,
To my ole boy Joe.

Walks up to the cops,
And, very polite,
Ast them ef they thought
They had done *just right.*

One cracked him with his billy
Above the left eye,
One thugged him with his pistol
And let him lie.

3

When he woke up, and knew
What the cops had done,
Went to a hockshop,
Got hisself a gun.

Felt mo' out of sorts
Than ever befo',
So he went on a rampage
My ole boy Joe.

Shot his way to the station house,
Rushed right in,
Wasn't nothing but space
Where the cops had been.

They called the reserves,
And the national guard,
Joe was in a cell
Overlooking the yard.

The machine guns sputtered,
  Didn't faze Joe at all—
But evvytime *he* fired
  A cop would fall.

    The tear-gas made him laugh
      When they let it fly,
    Laughing gas made him hang
      His head an' cry.

He threw the hand grenades back
  With a outshoot drop,
An' evvytime he threw
  They was one less cop.

    The Chief of Police said
      "What kinda *man* is this?"
    And held up his shirt
      For a armistice.

"Stop gunning, black boy,
  And we'll let you go."
"I thank you very kindly,"
  Said my ole boy Joe.

    "We promise you safety
      If you'll leave us be—"
    Joe said: "That's agreeable
      Sir, by me. . . ."

4

The sun had gone down
  The air it was cool,
Joe stepped out on the pavement
  A fighting fool.

    Had walked from the jail
      About half a square,
    When a cop behind a post
      Let him have it fair.

Put a bullet in his left side
  And one in his thigh,
But Joe didn't lose
  His shootin' eye.

Drew a cool bead
  On the cop's broad head;
"I return's you yo' favor"
  And the cop fell dead.

The next to last words
  He was heard to speak,
Was just what you would look for
  From my boy Joe Meek.

Spoke real polite
  To de folks standing by:
"Would you please do me one kindness,
  Fo' I die?"

"Won't be here much longer
  To bother you so,
Would you bring me a drink of water,
  Fo' I go?"

The very last words
  He was heard to say,
Showed a different Joe talking
  In a different way.

"Ef my bullets weren't gone,
  An' my strength all spent—
I'd send the chief something
  With a compliment."

"And we'd race to hell,
  And I'd best him there,
Like I would of done here
  Ef he'd played me fair."

5

So you cain't never tell
  How fas' a dog can run
When you see him a-sleeping,
  In the sun.

Strong Men

The strong men keep coming—Sandburg

>They dragged you from homeland,
>They chained you in coffles,
>They huddled you spoon-fashion in filthy hatches,
>They sold you to give a few gentlemen ease.
>
>They broke you in like oxen,
>They scourged you,
>They branded you,
>They made your women breeders,
>They swelled your numbers with bastards . . .
>They taught you the religion they disgraced.
>
>You sang:
>>Keep a-inchin' along
>>Lak a po' inch worm . . .
>
>You sang:
>>Bye and bye
>>I'm gonna lay down dis heaby load . . .
>
>You sang:
>>Walk togedder, chillen,
>>Dontcha git weary . . .
>>>*The strong men keep a-comin' on*
>>>*The strong men git stronger.*
>
>They point with pride to the roads you built for them,
>They ride in comfort over the rails you laid for them.
>They put hammers in your hands
>And said—Drive so much before sundown.
>
>You sang:
>>Ain't no hammah
>>In dis lan',
>>Strikes lak mine, bebby,
>>Strikes lak mine.
>
>They cooped you in their kitchens,
>They penned you in their factories,

They gave you the jobs that they were too good for,
They tried to guarantee happiness to themselves
By shunting dirt and misery to you.

You sang:
    Me an' muh baby gonna shine, shine
    Me an' muh baby gonna shine.
        The strong men keep a-comin' on
        The strong men git stronger . . .

They bought off some of your leaders
You stumbled, as blind men will . . .
They coaxed you, unwontedly soft-voiced . . .
You followed a way.
Then laughed as usual.

They heard the laugh and wondered;
Uncomfortable;
Unadmitting a deeper terror . . .
        The strong men keep a-comin' on
        Gittin' stronger . . .

What, from the slums
Where they have hemmed you,
What, from the tiny huts
They could not keep from you—
What reaches them
Making them ill at ease, fearful?
Today they shout prohibition at you
"Thou shalt not this"
"Thou shalt not that"
"Reserved for whites only"
You laugh.

One thing they cannot prohibit—
        The strong men . . . coming on
        The strong men gittin' stronger.
        Strong men . . .
        STRONGER . . .

ARNA BONTEMPS (1902–   )

*A biographical note on Arna Bontemps appears in the Fiction
section (see p. 87). The poems which follow were written
in the 1920's.*

A Note of Humility

When all our hopes are sown on stony ground
and we have yielded up the thought of gain,
long after our last songs have lost their sound
we may come back, we may come back again.

When thorns have choked the last green thing we loved
and we have said all that there is to say,
when love that moved us once leaves us unmoved
then men like us may come to have a day.

For it will be with us as with the bee,
the meagre ant, the sea-gull and the loon—
we may come back to triumph mournfully
an hour or two, but it will not be soon.

Gethsemane

All that night I walked alone and wept.
I tore a rose and dropped it on the ground.
My heart was lead; all that night I kept
Listening to hear a dreadful sound.

A tree bent down and dew dripped from its hair.
The earth was warm; dawn came solemnly.

I stretched full-length upon the grass and there
I said your name but silence answered me.

Southern Mansion

Poplars are standing there still as death
and ghosts of dead men
meet their ladies walking
two by two beneath the shade
and standing on the marble steps.

There is a sound of music echoing
through the open door
and in the field there is
another sound tinkling in the cotton:
chains of bondmen dragging on the ground.

The years go back with an iron clank,
a hand is on the gate,
a dry leaf trembles on the wall.
Ghosts are walking.
They have broken roses down
and poplars stand there still as death.

My Heart Has Known Its Winter

A little while spring will claim its own,
in all the land around for mile on mile
tender grass will hide the rugged stone.
My still heart will sing a little while,

And men will never think this wilderness
was barren once when grass is over all,
hearing laughter they may never guess
my heart has known its winter and carried gall.

Nocturne at Bethesda

I thought I saw an angel flying low.
I thought I saw the flicker of a wing

above the mulberry trees—but not again.
Bethesda sleeps. This ancient pool that healed
a host of bearded Jews does not awake.
This pool that once the angels troubled does not move.
No angel stirs it now, no Saviour comes
with healing in His hands to raise the sick
and bid the lame man leap upon the ground.

The golden days are gone. Why do we wait
so long upon the marble steps, blood
falling from our open wounds? And why
do our black faces search the empty sky?
Is there something we have forgotten? some precious thing
we have lost, wandering in strange lands?

There was a day, I remember now,
I beat my breast and cried 'Wash me God,
wash me with a wave of wind upon
the barley; O quiet One, draw near, draw near!
walk upon the hills with lovely feet
and in the waterfall stand and speak.

Dip white hands in the lily pool and mourn
upon the harps still hanging in the trees
near Babylon along the river's edge,
but oh, remember me, I pray, before
the summer goes and rose leaves lose their red.'

The old terror takes my heart, the fear
of quiet waters and of faint twilights.
There will be better days when I am gone
and healing pools where I cannot be healed.
Fragrant stars will gleam forever and ever
above the place where I lie desolate.

Yet I hope, still I long to live.
And if there can be returning after death
I shall come back. But it will not be here:
if you want me you must search for me
beneath the palms of Africa. Or if
I am not there you may call to me
across the shining dunes, perhaps I shall
be following a desert caravan.

I may pass through centuries of death
with quiet eyes, but I'll remember still

a jungle tree with burning scarlet birds.
There is something I have forgotten, some precious thing.
I shall be seeking ornaments of ivory,
I shall be dying for a jungle fruit.

You do not hear, Bethesda.
O still green water in a stagnant pool!
Love abandoned you and me alike.
There was a day you held a rich full moon
upon your heart and listened to the words
of men now dead and saw the angels fly.
There is a simple story on your face:
years have wrinkled you. I know, Bethesda!
You are sad. It is the same with me.

A Black Man Talks of Reaping

I have sown beside all waters in my day.
I planted deep, within my heart the fear
that wind or fowl would take the grain away.
I planted safe against this stark, lean year.

I scattered seed enough to plant the land
in rows from Canada to Mexico
but for my reaping only what the hand
can hold at once is all that I can show.

Yet what I sowed and what the orchard yields
my brother's sons are gathering stalk and root;
small wonder then my children glean in fields
they have not sown, and feed on bitter fruit.

The Day-Breakers

We are not come to wage a strife
with swords upon this hill:
it is not wise to waste the life
against a stubborn will.

Yet would we die as some have done:
beating a way for the rising sun.

LANGSTON HUGHES (1902–1967)

A biographical note on Langston Hughes appears in the Fiction section (see p. 96). We present ten of his poems. The first four are from his Selected Poems. *The next five, starting with "Dream Boogie," are from his remarkable cycle of Harlem poems* Montage of a Dream Deferred *(1951). The last poem, "Ballad of the Landlord," achieved notoriety recently when a Boston school teacher, Jonathan Kozol, was fired by the Boston school system for using this poem in a class in a ghetto school.*

Afro-American Fragment

So long,
So far away
Is Africa.
Not even memories alive
Save those that history books create,
Save those that songs
Beat back into the blood—
Beat out of blood with words sad-sung
In strange un-Negro tongue—
So long,
So far away
Is Africa.

Subdued and time-lost
Are the drums—and yet
Through some vast mist of race
There comes this song
I do not understand,
This song of atavistic land,
Of bitter yearnings lost

Without a place—
So long,
So far away
Is Africa's
Dark face.

As I Grew Older

It was a long time ago.
I have almost forgotten my dream.
But it was there then,
In front of me,
Bright as a sun—
My dream.

And then the wall rose,
Rose slowly,
Slowly,
Between me and my dream.
Rose slowly, slowly,
Dimming,
Hiding,
The light of my dream.
Rose until it touched the sky—
The wall.

Shadow.
I am black.

I lie down in the shadow.
No longer the light of my dream before me,
Above me.
Only the thick wall.
Only the shadow.

My hands!
My dark hands!
Break through the wall!
Find my dream!
Help me to shatter this darkness,
To smash this night,
To break this shadow
Into a thousand lights of sun,
Into a thousand whirling dreams
Of sun!

Dream Variations

To fling my arms wide
In some place of the sun,
To whirl and to dance
Till the white day is done.
Then rest at cool evening
Beneath a tall tree
While night comes on gently,
    Dark like me—
That is my dream!

To fling my arms wide
In the face of the sun,
Dance! Whirl! Whirl!
Till the quick day is done.
Rest at pale evening . . .
A tall, slim tree . . .
Night coming tenderly
    Black like me.

Daybreak in Alabama

When I get to be a composer
I'm gonna write me some music about
Daybreak in Alabama
And I'm gonna put the purtiest songs in it
Rising out of the ground like a swamp mist
And falling out of heaven like soft dew.
I'm gonna put some tall tall trees in it
And the scent of pine needles
And the smell of red clay after rain
And long red necks
And poppy colored faces
And big brown arms
And the field daisy eyes
Of black and white black white black people
And I'm gonna put white hands
And black hands and brown and yellow hands
And red clay earth hands in it
Touching everybody with kind fingers

And touching each other natural as dew
In that dawn of music when I
Get to be a composer
And write about daybreak
In Alabama.

Dream Boogie

Good morning, daddy!
Ain't you heard
The boogie-woogie rumble
Of a dream deferred?

Listen closely:
You'll hear their feet
Beating out and beating out a—

*You think
It's a happy beat?*

Listen to it closely:
Ain't you heard
something underneath
like a—

What did I say?

Sure,
I'm happy!
Take it away!

*Hey, pop!
Re-bop!
Mop!*

Y-e-a-h!

Children's Rhymes

When I was a chile we used to play,
"One—two—buckle my shoe!"
and things like that. But now, Lord,
listen at them little varmints!

> *By what sends*
> *the white kids*
> *I ain't sent:*
> *I know I can't*
> *be President.*

There is two thousand children
in this block, I do believe!

> *What don't bug*
> *them white kids*
> *sure bugs me:*
> *We knows everybody*
> *ain't free!*

Some of these young ones is cert'ly bad—
One batted a hard ball right through my window
and my gold fish et the glass.

> *What's written down*
> *for white folks*
> *ain't for us a-tall:*
> *"Liberty And Justice—*
> *Huh—For All."*

> *Oop-pop-a-da!*
> *Skee! Daddle-de-do!*
> *Be-bop!*

> Salt'peanuts!

> *De-dop!*

Theme for English B

The instructor said,

> *Go home and write*
> *a page tonight.*
> *And let that page come out of you—*
> *Then, it will be true.*

I wonder if it's that simple?

I am twenty-two, colored, born in Winston-Salem.
I went to school there, then Durham, then here
to this college on the hill above Harlem.
I am the only colored student in my class.
The steps from the hill lead down into Harlem,
through a park, then I cross St. Nicholas,
Eighth Avenue, Seventh, and I come to the Y,
the Harlem Branch Y, where I take the elevator
up to my room, sit down, and write this page:

It's not easy to know what is true for you or me
at twenty-two, my age. But I guess I'm what
I feel and see and hear, Harlem, I hear you:
hear you, hear me—we two—you, me, talk on this page.
(I hear New York, too.) Me—who?
Well, I like to eat, sleep, drink, and be in love.
I like to work, read, learn, and understand life.
I like a pipe for a Christmas present,
or records—Bessie, bop, or Bach.
I guess being colored doesn't make me *not* like
the same things other folks like who are other races.
So will my page be colored that I write?
Being me, it will not be white.
But it will be
a part of you, instructor.
You are white—
yet a part of me, as I am a part of you.
That's American.
Sometimes perhaps you don't want to be a part of me.
Nor do I often want to be a part of you.
But we are, that's true!
As I learn from you,
I guess you learn from me—
although you're older—and white—
and somewhat more free.

This is my page for English B.

                                                    Harlem

What happens to a dream deferred?

    Does it dry up
    like a raisin in the sun?

Or fester like a sore—
And then run?
Does it stink like rotten meat?
Or crust and sugar over—
like a syrupy sweet?

Maybe it just sags
like a heavy load.

Or does it explode?

Same in Blues

I said to my baby,
Baby, take it slow.
I can't, she said, I can't!
I got to go!

> *There's a certain*
> *amount of traveling*
> *in a dream deferred.*

Lulu said to Leonard,
I want a diamond ring.
Leonard said to Lulu,
You won't get a goddamn thing!

> *A certain*
> *amount of nothing*
> *in a dream deferred.*

Daddy, daddy, daddy,
All I want is you.
You can have me, baby—
but my lovin' days is through.

> *A certain*
> *amount of impotence*
> *in a dream deferred.*

Three parties
On my party line—
But that third party,
Lord, ain't mine!

There's liable
to be confusion
in a dream deferred.

From river to river,
Uptown and down,
There's liable to be confusion
when a dream gets kicked around.

Ballad of the Landlord

Landlord, landlord,
My roof has sprung a leak.
Don't you 'member I told you about it
Way last week?

Landlord, landlord,
These steps is broken down.
When you come up yourself
It's a wonder you don't fall down.

Ten Bucks you say I owe you?
Ten Bucks you say is due?
Well, that's Ten Bucks more'n I'll pay you
Till you fix this house up new.

What? You gonna get eviction orders?
You gonna cut off my heat?
You gonna take my furniture and
Throw it in the street?

Um-huh! You talking high and mighty.
Talk on—till you get through.
You ain't gonna be able to say a word
If I land my fist on you.

Police! Police!
Come and get this man!
He's trying to ruin the government
And overturn the land!

Copper's whistle!
Patrol bell!
Arrest.

Precinct Station.
Iron cell.
Headlines in press:

MAN THREATENS LANDLORD

.

.   .

TENANT HELD NO BAIL

.   .

JUDGE GIVES NEGRO 90 DAYS IN COUNTY JAIL

FRANK MARSHALL DAVIS (1905–   )

*With the publication of two volumes of poetry in the 1930's
and a third book of poems in 1948, Frank Marshall Davis
established his reputation as a socially minded poet employ-
ing free-verse forms. Davis was born in Arkansas City, Kansas, studied journalism at Kansas State College, and, for a
long period, was active as a journalist. After his initiation
into newspaper work in Chicago, he went to Georgia in 1931
to help start the Atlanta Daily World. Later he returned to
Chicago and worked with the Associated Negro Press. Davis
was awarded a Rosenwald Fellowship in creative writing in
1937. He is now living in Hawaii.*

Four Glimpses of Night

1

    Eagerly
    Like a woman hurrying to her lover
    Night comes to the room of the world
    And lies, yielding and content
    Against the cool round face
    Of the moon.

2

Night is a curious child, wandering
Between earth and sky, creeping
In windows and doors, daubing
The entire neighborhood
With purple paint.
Day
Is an apologetic mother
Cloth in hand
Following after.

3

Peddling
From door to door
Night sells
Black bags of peppermint stars
Heaping cones of vanilla moon
Until
His wares are gone
Then shuffles homeward
Jingling the gray coins
Of daybreak.

4

Night's brittle song, silver-thin
Shatters into a billion fragments
Of quiet shadows
At the blaring jazz
Of a morning sun.

I Sing No New Songs

Once I cried for new songs to sing . . . a black rose . . .
a brown sky . . . the moon for my buttonhole . . . pink
dreams for the table

Later I learned life is a servant girl . . . dusting the same
pieces yesterday, today, tomorrow . . . a never ending
one two three one two three one two three

The dreams of Milton were the dreams of Lindsay . . . drinking corn liquor, wearing a derby, dancing a foxtrot . . . a saxophone for a harp

Ideas rise with new mornings but never die . . . only names, places, people change . . . you are born, love, fight, tire and stop being . . . Caesar died with a knife in his guts . . . Jim Colosimo from revolver bullets

So I shall take aged things . . . bearded dreams . . . a silver dollar moon worn thin from the spending . . . model a new dress for this one . . . get that one a new hat . . . teach the other to forget the minuet . . . then I shall send them into the street

And if passersby stop and say "Who is that? I never saw this pretty girl before" or if they say . . . "Is that old woman still alive? I thought she died years ago" . . . if they speak these words, I shall neither smile nor swear . . . those who walked before me, those who come after me, may make better clothes, teach a more graceful step . . . but the dreams of Homer neither grow nor wilt. . . .

Robert Whitmore

Having attained success in business
possessing three cars
one wife and two mistresses
a home and furniture
talked of by the town
and thrice ruler of the local Elks
Robert Whitmore
died of apoplexy
when a stranger from Georgia
mistook him
for a former Macon waiter.

Flowers of Darkness

Slowly the night blooms, unfurling
Flowers of darkness, covering

The trellised sky, becoming
A bouquet of blackness
Unending
Touched with sprigs
Of pale and budding stars

Soft the night smell
Among April trees
Soft and richly rare
Yet commonplace
Perfume on a cosmic scale

I turn to you Mandy Lou
I see the flowering night
Cameo condensed
Into the lone black rose
Of your face

The young woman-smell
Of your poppy body
Rises to my brain as opium
Yet silently motionless
I sit with twitching fingers
Yea, even reverently
Sit I
With you and the blossoming night
For what flower, plucked,
Lingers long?

RICHARD WRIGHT (1908–1960)

*A biographical note on Richard Wright appears in the Fiction
section (see p. 113-114). The following poem first appeared in
Partisan Review in the summer of 1935.*

lynching

Between the World and Me

And one morning while in the woods I stumbled suddenly
    upon the thing,
Stumbled upon it in a grassy clearing guarded by scaly oaks
    and elms.
And the sooty details of the scene rose, thrusting themselves
    between the world and me. . . .

There was a design of white bones slumbering forgottenly
    upon a cushion of ashes.
There was a charred stump of a sapling pointing a blunt finger
    accusingly at the sky.
There were torn tree limbs, tiny veins of burnt leaves, and a
    scorched coil of greasy hemp;
●A vacant shoe, an empty tie, a ripped shirt, a lonely hat, and a
    pair of trousers stiff with black blood.
And upon the trampled grass were buttons, dead matches,
    butt-ends of cigars and cigarettes, peanut shells, a
    drained gin-flask, and a whore's lipstick;
Scattered traces of tar, restless arrays of feathers, and the lin-
    gering smell of gasoline.
And through the morning air the sun poured yellow surprise
    into the eye sockets of a stony skull. . . .
And while I stood my mind was frozen with a cold pity for
    the life that was gone.
The ground gripped my feet and my heart was circled by icy
    walls of fear—
The sun died in the sky; a night wind muttered in the grass
    and fumbled the leaves in the trees; the woods
    poured forth the hungry yelping of hounds; the
    darkness screamed with thirsty voices; and the wit-
    nesses rose and lived:
The dry bones stirred, rattled, lifted, melting themselves into
    my bones.
The grey ashes formed flesh firm and black, entering into my
    flesh.
The gin-flask passed from mouth to mouth; cigars and ciga-
    rettes glowed, the whore smeared the lipstick red
    upon her lips,
And a thousand faces swirled around me, clamoring that my
    life be burned. . . .

And then they had me, stripped me, battering my teeth into
    my throat till I swallowed my own blood.

My voice was drowned in the roar of their voices, and my
    black wet body slipped and rolled in their hands as
    they bound me to the sapling.

And my skin clung to the bubbling hot tar, falling from me
    in limp patches.

And the down and quills of the white feathers sank into my
    raw flesh, and I moaned in my agony.

Then my blood was cooled mercifully, cooled by a baptism
    of gasoline.

And in a blaze of red I leaped to the sky as pain rose like
    water, boiling my limbs.

Panting, begging I clutched childlike, clutched to the hot
    sides of death.

Now I am dry bones and my face a stony skull staring in yel-
    low surprise at the sun. . . .

ROBERT HAYDEN (1913–   )

*The Grand Prize for Poetry at the First World Festival of
Negro Arts, held in Dakar, Senegal, in 1965, was awarded to
Robert Hayden for his book of poetry A Ballad for Remembrance, published in the limited edition Heritage series
of Paul Breman, London. Hayden was born in Detroit, did
his undergraduate work at Wayne State University, and received his M. A. from the University of Michigan, where he
subsequently taught English for two years. He joined the faculty of Fisk University in 1946 and is now Professor of English there. He has received several American prizes and fellowships for his poetry: the Hopwood Award from the University of Michigan in 1938 and again in 1942, a Rosenwald
Fellowship in 1947, and a Ford Foundation grant in 1954.
He is poetry editor of the Baha'i magazine,* World Order.
Hayden edited the anthology Kaleidoscope: Poems by American Negro Poets *(1967), where, in an autobiographical note,
he wrote: "Opposed to the chauvinistic and the doctrinaire, he*

sees no reason why a Negro poet should be limited to 'racial
utterance' or to having his writing judged by standards different from those applied to the work of other poets."

Tour 5

The road winds down through autumn hills
in blazonry of farewell scarlet and
recessional gold, past cedar groves, through static
villages whose names are all that's left of Choctaw,

Chickasaw. We stop a moment
in a town watched over by Confederate
sentinels, buy gas and ask directions
of a rawboned man whose eyes revile us as

the enemy, as menace to
the shambling innocents who are the thankless
guardians of his heritage. Shrill gorgon
silence breathes behind his taut civility

and in the ever-tautening
air that's dark for us despite the Indian
summer glow. We drive on, following
the route of phantoms, highwaymen, of slaves and armies.

Children, wordless and remote,
wave at us from kindling porches. And now
the land is flat for miles, the landscape lush,
metallic, flayed; its brightness harsh as bloodstained swords.

On the Coast of Maine

Sebasco Estates

1

Ancestral, alone, under stone they lie
    who from granite hewed foundation for
this house, where now darklong darklong
    what once they must have heard I hear:

the foghorn's veering. Where o where o—
    a racked lonely sound,

in sea-reverberant night
the only man-created sound.

2

In sunken light,
through stalker's quiet
we walk.
Past stone walls that keep
the restless from
old granite-weary farmers' sleep,
between Puritan shadow,
Indian dark we go,
moving in a hush of time
where dead lichened
boughs like blackened
fishbones prong
the vibrant green
of spruce and pine.
And ghostly thunders are
remotely near.

3

In brightness-whetted
  morning,
the dropped gull
  splayed
on sand,
  wind
at its feathers
  picking.

Over the headlong
  toppling
rush and leashed-back
  mica'd
fall of the sea,
  gulls,
scouting and
  crying.

Figure

for Jeanette

He would slump to his knees, now that his agonies

are accomplished, would fall but for the chain that binds
  him to the tall columnar tree.

His head hangs heavily away to one side; we
cannot see his face. The dead weight of
  the quelled head has pulled

the haltering chain tight. A clothesline nooses
both wrists, forcing his arms in an arrowing angle
  out behind him. Stripes

of blood like tribal markings run from naked
shoulder to naked waist. We observe that his jeans are torn
  at the groin;

that the lower links of the chain cut deeply into
the small of his back and counter the sag, the downthrust.
  And the chain, we observe the chain—

the kind that a farmer might have had use for or a man with
a vicious dog. We have seen its like in hardware
  stores; it is cheap but strong

and it serves and except for the doubled length of it lashing
him to the blighted tree, he would slump to his knees, in total
  subsidence fall.

He is a scythe in daylight's clutch. Is gnomon.
Is metaphor of a place, a time. Is our
  time geometrized

In Light Half Nightmare and Half Vision

From the corpse woodpiles, from the ashes and staring pits
  of Dachau and Buchenwald they come—
  o David, Hirschel, Eva, cops and robbers with
  me once, their faces are like yours—
from Johannesburg, from Seoul. Their struggles are all
  horizons,
  their deaths encircle me. Through ruins,
through target streets I run, fleeing what I cannot
  flee; in light half nightmare and
half vision reach that cold cloacal dripping place
  where He, who is man beatified
and Godly mystery, lies chained in criminal darkness.
  The anguish of the multitudes
is in His eyes; His suffering transilluminates
  the suffering of an age.

Market

Ragged boys
lift sweets, haggle
for venomgreen
and scarlet gelatins.
A broken smile
dandles its weedy
cigarette
over papayas too ripe
and pyramids
of rotting oranges.
Turkeys like feather-
duster flowers
lie trussed in bunchy smother.
The barefoot cripple
foraging crawls
among rinds, orts,
chewed butts, trampled
peony droppings—
his hunger litany
and suppliant before
altars of mamey,
pineapple, mango.
Turistas pass.
Por caridad, por caridad.
Lord, how they stride
on the hard good legs
money has made them.
Ay! you creatures
who have walked
on seas of money all
your foreign lives!
Por caridad.
Odor of a dripping
flyblown carcass moans
beneath the hot
fragrance of carnations,
cool scent of lilies.
Starveling dogs
hover in the reek
of frying; ashy feet
(the twistfoot beggar laughs)

kick at them in vain.
Aloft the Fire King's
flashing mask of tin
looks down with eyes
of sunstruck glass.

Homage to the Empress of the Blues

Because there was a man somewhere in a candystripe silk shirt,
gracile and dangerous as a jaguar and because a woman moaned
for him in sixty-watt gloom and mourned him Faithless Love
Twotiming Love Oh Love Oh Careless Aggravating Love,

    She came out on the stage in yards of pearls, emerging like
    a favorite scenic view, flashed her golden smile and sang.

Because grey laths began somewhere to show from underneath
torn hurdygurdy lithographs of dollfaced heaven;
and because there were those who feared alarming fists of snow
on the door and those who feared the riot-squad of statistics,

    She came out on the stage in ostrich feathers, beaded satin.
    and shone that smile on us and sang.

Mourning Poem for the Queen of Sunday

Lord's lost Him His mockingbird,
His fancy warbler;
Satan sweet-talked her,
four bullets hushed her.
Who would have thought
she'd end that way?

Four bullets hushed her. And the world a-clang with evil.
Who's going to make old hardened sinner men tremble now
and the righteous rock?
Oh who and oh who will sing Jesus down
to help with struggling and doing without and being colored
all through blue Monday?
Till way next Sunday?

    All those angels
    in their cretonne clouds and finery

the true believer saw
when she rared back her head and sang,
all those angels are surely weeping.
Who would have thought
she'd end that way?

Four holes in her heart. The gold works wrecked.
But she looks so natural in her big bronze coffin
among the Broken Hearts and Gates-Ajar,
it's as if any moment she'd lift her head
from its pillow of chill gardenias
and turn this quiet into shouting Sunday
and make folks forget what she did on Monday.

Oh, Satan sweet-talked her,
and four bullets hushed her.
Lord's lost Him His diva,
His fancy warbler's gone.
Who would have thought,
who would have thought she'd end that way?

Middle Passage

1

Jesús, Estrella, Esperanza, Mercy :

Sails flashing to the wind like weapons,
sharks following the moans the fever and the dying;
horror the corposant and compass rose.

Middle Passage:
          voyage through death
                    to life upon these shores.

"10 April 1800—
Blacks rebellious. Crew uneasy. Our linguist says
their moaning is a prayer for death,
ours and their own. Some try to starve themselves.
Lost three this morning leaped with crazy laughter
to the waiting sharks, sang as they went under."

Desire, Adventure, Tartar, Ann:

Standing to America, bringing home
black gold, black ivory, black seed.

Deep in the festering hold thy father lies,
of his bones New England pews are made,
those are altar lights that were his eyes.

Jesus Saviour Pilot Me
Over Life's Tempestuous Sea

We pray that Thou wilt grant, O Lord,
safe passage to our vessels bringing
heathen souls unto Thy chastening.

Jesus Saviour

"8 bells. I cannot sleep, for I am sick
with fear, but writing eases fear a little
since still my eyes can see these words take shape
upon the page & so I write, as one
would turn to exorcism. 4 days scudding,
but now the sea is calm again. Misfortune
follows in our wake like sharks (our grinning
tutelary gods). Which one of us
has killed an albatross? A plague among
our blacks—Ophthalmia: blindness—& we
have jettisoned the blind to no avail.
It spreads, the terrifying sickness spreads.
Its claws have scratched sight from the Capt.'s eyes
& there is blindness in the fo'c'sle
& we must sail 3 weeks before we come
to port."

What port awaits us, Davy Jones'
or home? I've heard of slavers drifting, drift-
ing,
playthings of wind and storm and chance,
their crews
gone blind, the jungle hatred
crawling up on deck.

Thou Who Walked On Galilee

"Deponent further sayeth *The Bella J*
left the Guinea Coast
with cargo of five hundred blacks and odd
for the barracoons of Florida:

"That there was hardly room 'tween-decks for half
the sweltering cattle stowed spoon-fashion there;

that some went mad of thirst and tore their flesh
and sucked the blood:

"That Crew and Captain lusted with the comeliest
of the savage girls kept naked in the cabins;
that there was one they called The Guinea Rose
and they cast lots and fought to lie with her:

"That when the Bo's'n piped all hands, the flames
spreading from starboard already were beyond
control, the negroes howling and their chains
entangled with the flames:

"That the burning blacks could not be reached,
that the Crew abandoned ship,
leaving their shrieking negresses behind,
that the Captain perished drunken with the wenches:

"Further Deponent sayeth not."

Pilot Oh Pilot Me

2

Aye, lad, and I have seen those factories,
Gambia, Rio Pongo, Calabar;
have watched the artful mongos baiting traps
of war wherein the victor and the vanquished

Were caught as prizes for our barracoons.
Have seen the nigger kings whose vanity
and greed turned wild black hides of Fellatah,
Mandingo, Ibo, Kru to gold for us.

And there was one—King Anthracite we named him—
fetish face beneath French parasols
of brass and orange velvet, impudent mouth
whose cups were carven skulls of enemies:

He'd honor us with drum and feast and conjo
and palm-oil-glistening wenches deft in love,
and for tin crowns that shone with paste,
red calico and German-silver trinkets

Would have the drums talk war and send
his warriors to burn the sleeping villages

and kill the sick and old and lead the young
in coffles to our factories.

Twenty years a trader, twenty years,
for there was wealth aplenty to be harvested
from those black fields, and I'd be trading still
but for the fevers melting down my bones.

3

Shuttles in the rocking loom of history,
the dark ships move, the dark ships move,
their bright ironical names
like jests of kindness on a murderer's mouth;
plough through thrashing glister toward
fata morgana's lucent melting shore,
weave toward New World littorals that are
mirage and myth and actual shore.

Voyage through death,
              voyage whose chartings are unlove.

A charnel stench, effluvium of living death
spreads outward from the hold,
where the living and the dead, the horribly dying,
lie interlocked, lie foul with blood and excrement.

> *Deep in the festering hold thy father lies,*
> *the corpse of mercy rots with him,*
> *rats eat love's rotten gelid eyes.*

> *But, oh, the living look at you*
> *with human eyes whose suffering accuses you,*
> *whose hatred reaches through the swill of dark*
> *to strike you like a leper's claw.*

> *You cannot stare that hatred down*
> *or chain the fear that stalks the watches*
> *and breathes on you its fetid scorching breath;*
> *cannot kill the deep immortal human wish,*
> *the timeless will.*

> "But for the storm that flung up barriers
> of wind and wave, *The Amistad*, señores,
> would have reached the port of Príncipe in
>   two,

three days at most; but for the storm we
    should
have been prepared for what befell.
Swift as the puma's leap it came. There was
that interval of moonless calm filled only
with the water's and the rigging's usual sounds,
then sudden movement, blows and snarling
    cries
and they had fallen on us with machete
and marlinspike. It was as though the very
air, the night itself were striking us.
Exhausted by the rigors of the storm,
we were no match for them. Our men went
    down
before the murderous Africans. Our loyal
Celestino ran from below with gun
and lantern and I saw, before the cane-
knife's wounding flash, Cinquez,
that surly brute who calls himself a prince,
directing, urging on the ghastly work.
He hacked the poor mulatto down, and then
he turned on me. The decks were slippery
when daylight finally came. It sickens me
to think of what I saw, of how these apes
threw overboard the butchered bodies of
our men, true Christians all, like so much jet-
    sam.
Enough, enough. The rest is quickly told:
Cinquez was forced to spare the two of us
you see to steer the ship to Africa,
and we like phantoms doomed to rove the sea
voyaged east by day and west by night,
deceiving them, hoping for rescue,
prisoners on our own vessel, till
at length we drifted to the shores of this
your land, America, where we were freed
from our unspeakable misery. Now we
demand, good sirs, the extradition of
Cinquez and his accomplices to La
Havana. And it distresses us to know
there are so many here who seem inclined
to justify the mutiny of these blacks.
We find it paradoxical indeed
that you whose wealth, whose tree of liberty
are rooted in the labor of your slaves
should suffer the august John Quincy Adams

to speak with so much passion of the right
of chattel slaves to kill their lawful masters
and with his Roman rhetoric weave a hero's
garland for Cinquez. I tell you that
we are determined to return to Cuba
with our slaves and there see justice done. Cin-
    quez—
    or let us say 'the Prince'—Cinquez shall
    die."

The deep immortal human wish,
the timeless will:

    Cinquez its deathless primaveral image,
    life that transfigures many lives.

Voyage through death
                to life upon these shores.

Frederick Douglass

When it is finally ours, this freedom, this liberty, this beautiful
and terrible thing, needful to man as air,
usable as earth; when it belongs at last to all,
when it is truly instinct, brain matter, diastole, systole,
reflex action; when it is finally won; when it is more
than the gaudy mumbo jumbo of politicians:
this man, this Douglass, this former slave, this Negro
beaten to his knees, exiled, visioning a world
where none is lonely, none hunted, alien,
this man, superb in love and logic, this man
shall be remembered. O, not with statues' rhetoric,
not with legends and poems and wreaths of bronze alone,
but with the lives grown out of his life, the lives
fleshing his dream of the beautiful, needful thing.

OWEN DODSON (1914–   )

*Born in Brooklyn, New York, and educated at Bates College
and Yale University, Owen Dodson has achieved distinction
in poetry, fiction, and playwriting. His verse plays,* Divine
Comedy *and* Garden of Time, *were performed at Yale University and elsewhere. He has received the Maxwell Anderson
Verse Play Award. For many years he has been associated
with the Drama Department of Howard University. In
1949 he took the Howard University Players on a successful
tour of Scandinavia and Germany sponsored by the State Department. Dodson published a volume of poetry in 1946, and
a novel,* Boy at the Window *(1950). His short story, "The
Summer Fire," won a Paris Review prize and appeared in the
volume* Best Short Stories from the Paris Review *(1961). Dodson has been a Rosenwald Fellow and traveled to Italy on a
Guggenheim grant in 1953 for a year of writing. Seven of his
poems follow.*

Guitar

Ma six string guitar with the lonesome sound
Can't hold its own against a Georgia hound.

O mamma when the sun goes the downstairs way
And the night spreads out an the moon make day,

I sits with ma feet raised to the rail
And sings the song bout ma buddy in jail:
     In the red-dirt land,
     And the pine tree high,
     Gonna find me peace
     By-an-by.

Gonna find me a baby
Some pretty-eye gal
To be ma mother
Ma wife an pal.

Ain't had nobody
To call me home
From the electric cities
Where I roam.

Yes, I been travelin
Over all
To find a place
What I could call
Home, baby,
Sweet cotton-field home. . . .

When I gets to the place where a cracker got mad,
Struck ma fine buddy, struck all I had,
The hound start howlin till the stars break down
An make ma song like a boat what's drown.

Ma six string guitar with the lonesome sound
Can't hold its own against that Georgia hound.

Black Mother Praying

My great God, You been a tenderness to me,
Through the thick and through the thin;
You been a pilla to my soul;
You been like the shinin light a mornin in the black dark,
A elevator to my spirit.

Now there's a fire in this land like a last judgment,
And I done sat down by the rivers of Babylon
And wept deep when I remembered Zion,
Seein the water that can't quench fire
And the fire that burn up rivers.
Lord, I'm gonna say my say real quick and simple:

You know bout this war that's bitin the skies
        and gougin out the earth.
Last month, Lord, I bid my last boy away to fight.

I got all my boys fightin now for they country.
Didn't think bout it cept it were for freedom;
Didn't think cause they was black they wasn't American;
Didn't think a thing cept that they was my only sons,
And there was mothers all over the world
Sacrificin they sons like You let Yours be nailed
To the wood for men to behold the right.

Now I'm a black mother, Lord, I knows that now,
Black and burnin in these burnin times.
I can't hold my peace cause peace ain't fit to mention
When they's fightin right here in our streets
Like dogs—mongrel dogs and hill cats.
White is fightin black right here where hate abides
          like a cancer wound
And Freedom is writ big and crossed out:
Where, bless God, they's draggin us outta cars
In Texas and California, in Newark, Detroit,

Blood on the darkness, Lord, blood on the pavement,
Leavin us moanin and afraid.
What has we done?
Where and when has we done?
They's plantin the seeds of hate down in our bone marrow
When we don't want to hate.

We don't speak much in the street where I live, my God,
Nobody speak much, but we thinkin deep
Of the black sons in lands far as the wind can go,
Black boys fightin this war with them.

We thinkin deep bout they sisters stitchin airplane canvas,
And they old fathers plowin for wheat,
And they mothers bendin over washtubs,
They brothers at the factory wheels:
They all is bein body beat and spirit beat and
          heart sore and wonderin.

Listen, Lord, they ain't nowhere for black mothers to turn.
Won't You plant Your Son's goodness in this land
Before it too late?
Set Your stars of sweetness twinklin over us
          like winda lamps
Before it too late?
Help these men to see they losin while they winnin

Long as they allow theyselves to lynch in the city streets
　　　　and on country roads?

When can I pray again,
View peace in my own parlor again?
When my sons come home
How can I show em my broken hands?
How can I show em they sister's twisted back?
How can I present they land to them?
How, when they been battlin in far places for freedom?
Better let them die in the desert drinkin sand
Or holdin onto water and shippin into death
Than they come back and see they sufferin for vain.

I done seen a man runnin for his life,
Runnin like the wind from a mob, to no shelter.
Where were a hidin place for him?
Saw a dark girl nine years old
Cryin cause her father done had
The light scratched from his eyes in the month of June.
Where the seein place for him?
A black boy lyin with his arms huggin the pavement in pain.
What he starin at?
Good people hands up, searched for guns and razors
　　　　and pipes.
When they gonna pray again?

How, precious God, can I watch my son's eyes
When they hear this terrible?
How can I pray again when my tongue
Is near cleavin to the roof of my mouth?
Tell me, Lord, how?

Every time they strike us, they strikin Your Son;
Every time they shove us in, they cornerin they own
　　　　children.
I'm gonna scream before I hope again.
I ain't never gonna hush my mouth or lay down this
　　　　heavy, black, weary, terrible load
Until I fights to stamp my feet with my black sons
On a freedom solid rock and stand there peaceful
And look out into the star wilderness of the sky
And the land lyin about clean, and secure land,
And people not afraid again.
Lord, let us all see the golden wheat together,
Harvest the harvest together,

Touch the fulness and the hallelujah together.
                              Amen.

Drunken Lover

This is the stagnant hour:
The dead communion between mouth and mouth,
The drunken kiss lingered,
The dreadful equator south.

This is the hour of impotence
When the unfulfilled is unfulfilled.
Only the stale breath is anxious
And warm. All else is stilled.

Why did I come to this reek,
This numb time, this level?
Only for you, my love, only for you
Could I endure this devil.

I dreamed when I was
A pimply and urgent adolescent
Of these hours when love would be fire
And you the steep descent.

My mouth's inside is like cotton,
Your arm is dead on my arm.
What I pictured so lovely and spring
Is August and fungus calm.

O lover, draw away, grow small, go magic,
O lover, disappear into the tick of this bed;
Open all the windows to the north
For the wind to cool my head.

The Reunion

I loved the apple-sweetness of the air
And pines that settled slanting on the hill,
Indians old and soft with needles there,
Where once we stood, and both so strangely still.

We must have surely known what other days
Would come in other flaming autumn's flame.
And even though we walk through different ways
To different hills that hill remains the same.
Watch every splendor, envy all the sky,
But recognize the days we knew, and hear
The simple sounds we heard. As birds that fly
Southward to warmth, we shall come back one year.
The little teeth of time will make no mark
On any stone, on any leaf or bark.

Jonathan's Song

A Negro Saw the Jewish Pageant, "We Will Never Die"

(*For Sol Gordon*)

I am a part of this:
Four million starving
And six million dead:
I am flesh and bone of this.

I have starved
In the secret alleys of my heart
And died in my soul
Like Ahab at the white whale's mouth.

The twisted cross desire
For final annihilation
Of my race of sufferers:
I am Abel, too.

Because my flesh is whole
Do not think that it signifies life.
I am the husk, believe me.
The rest is dead, remember.

I am a part of this
Memorial to suffering,
Militant strength:
I am a Jew.

Jew is not a race

Any longer—but a condition.
All the desert flowers have thorns;
I am bleeding in the sand.

Take me for your own David:
My father was not cruel,
I will sing your psalms,
I have learned them by heart.

I have loved you as a child,
We pledged in blood together.
The union is not strange,
My brother and my lover.

There was a great scent of death
In the garden when I was born.
Now it is certain:
Love me while you can.

The wedding is powerful as battle,
Singular, dread, passionate, loud,
Ahab screaming and the screaming whale
And the destination among thorns.

Love is a triple desire:
Flesh, freedom, hope:
No wanton thing is allowed.
I will sing thy psalms, all thy psalms,
Take me while you can.

Yardbird's Skull (For Charlie Parker)

The bird is lost,
Dead, with all the music:
Whole sunsets heard the brain's music
Faded to last horizon notes.
I do not know why I hold
This skull, smaller than a walnut's,
Against my ear,
Expecting to hear
The smashed fear
Of childhood from . . . bone;
Expecting to see
Wind nosing red and purple,

Strange gold and magic
On bubbled windowpanes
Of childhood. Shall I hear?
I should hear: this skull
Has been with violets
Not Yorick, or the gravedigger,
Yapping his yelling story,
This skull has been in air,
Sensed his brother, the swallow,
(Its talent for snow and crumbs).
Flown to lost Atlantis islands,
Places of dreaming, swimming lemmings.
O I shall hear skull skull,
Hear your lame music,
Believe music rejects undertaking,
Limps back.
Remember tiny lasting, we get lonely:
Come sing, come sing, come sing sing
And sing.

Sailors on Leave

No boy chooses war.
Dear let me show
The picket fence
Around my heart
Where loves are hung
In pairs of pain
And joy: the piercing revellers.

Here in this bar, the Cosycue,
I hear my darling singer moan,
Lower lights within my mind,
Admit a surer light
To see, to die by.

Here so specially set
For me, I am amazed,
Are target lovers all lines
For me to break,
To leave them, to die by.

No boy chooses war
But then we go

And in a cause find causes
To regret the summer and
The easy girl or boy
We drift to exist,
To battle for, to die.

MARGARET WALKER (1915–   )

*In 1942 the first book of poems by Margaret Walker, For My
People, was published as the selection of the year in the Yale
University Series of Younger Poets. Margaret Abigail Walker
was born in Birmingham, Alabama, the daughter of a Methodist minister. After her early education in denominational
schools, she went on to study at Northwestern University and
received her M.A from the University of Iowa in 1940 and a
Ph.D., based on her work in the Writers' Workshop of the
University of Iowa, in 1965. Her novel Jubilee, awarded a
Houghton Mifflin Literary Fellowship in 1966, was the work
she submitted in lieu of a dissertation for her Ph.D. in creative writing. She has taught English in Livingstone College
and West Virginia State College and, since 1949, has been a
member of the faculty at Jackson State College in Mississippi.
She received a Rosenwald Fellowship for creative writing in
1944. For My People charted new paths in Negro poetry and
Jubilee added something distinctively new to the historical
novel of the Old South and the Civil War: the (fictional) point
of view of the slave. Jubilee has been translated into French,
German, and Swedish. She is presently working on another
novel, more short stories, and a new collection of poems. The
title poem of her first collection, which originally appeared in
Poetry magazine in 1937, follows.*

For My People

For my people everywhere singing their slave songs repeatedly: their dirges and their ditties and their blues and jubilees, praying their prayers nightly to an unknown god, bending their knees humbly to an unseen power;

For my people lending their strength to the years, to the gone years and the now years and the maybe years, washing ironing cooking scrubbing sewing mending hoeing plowing digging planting pruning patching dragging along never gaining never reaping never knowing and never understanding;

For my playmates in the clay and dust and sand of Alabama backyards playing baptizing and preaching and doctor and jail and soldier and school and mama and cooking and playhouse and concert and store and hair and Miss Choomby and company;

For the cramped bewildered years we went to school to learn to know the reasons why and the answers to and the people who and the places where and the days when, in memory of the bitter hours when we discovered we were black and poor and small and different and nobody cared and nobody wondered and nobody understood;

For the boys and girls who grew in spite of these things to be man and woman, to laugh and dance and sing and play and drink their wine and religion and success, to marry their playmates and bear children and then die of consumption and anemia and lynching;

For my people thronging 47th Street in Chicago and Lenox Avenue in New York and Rampart Street in New Orleans, lost disinherited dispossessed and happy people filling the cabarets and taverns and other people's pockets needing bread and shoes and milk and land and money and something—something all our own;

For my people walking blindly spreading joy, losing time being lazy, sleeping when hungry, shouting when bur-

dened, drinking when hopeless, tied and shackled and
tangled among ourselves by the unseen creatures who
tower over us omnisciently and laugh;

For my people blundering and groping and floundering in
the dark of churches and schools and clubs and societies,
associations and councils and committees and conventions,
distressed and disturbed and deceived and devoured by
money-hungry glory-craving leeches, preyed on by facile
force of state and fad and novelty, by false prophet and
holy believer;

For my people standing staring trying to fashion a better
way from confusion, from hypocrisy and misunderstanding, trying to fashion a world that will hold all the people,
all the faces, all the adams and eves and their countless
generations;

Let a new earth rise. Let another world be born. Let a
bloody peace be written in the sky. Let a second generation full of courage issue forth; let a people loving freedom come to growth. Let a beauty full of healing and
strength of final clenching be the pulsing in our spirits
and our blood. Let the martial songs be written, let the
dirges disappear. Let a race of men now rise and take
control.

GWENDOLYN BROOKS (1917–   )

*In 1950, Gwendolyn Brooks became the first Negro poet in
the United States to win the Pulitzer Prize, for her second volume of poetry,* Annie Allen *(1949). She was born in Topeka,
Kansas, and grew up and was educated in Chicago. Asked in
an interview published as a pamphlet by Illinois Bell Telephone, "Why do you write poetry?" she replied: "I like the
concentration, the crush; I like working with language, as others like working with paints and clay, or notes." Asked further, "Has much of your poetry a racial element?" she answered, "Yes. It is organic, not imposed. It is my privilege to
present Negroes not as curios but as people." And to the question, "What is your 'Poet's Premise'?" she answered: " 'Vivify
the contemporary fact,' said Whitman. I like to vivify the uni-*

versal *fact, when it occurs to me. But the universal wears contemporary clothing very well.*" In 1946 Gwendolyn Brooks
*received an award from the American Academy of Arts and
Letters. In 1964 she was awarded both the Friends Literature
Award for Poetry and the Thormod Monsen Award for Literature. She has been teaching creative writing and poetry in
three colleges in Chicago: Columbia College, Elmhurst College, and Northeastern Illinois State College. She has published three volumes of poetry to date; a short novel,* Maud
Martha *(1953); and a volume of verse for children. In
1963 her* Selected Poems *was published. She is a member of
the advisory board of the Institute for International Education, the Society for Midland Authors, and the Illinois Art
Council. Six of her poems follow.*

The Artists' and Models' Ball

(*For Frank Shepherd*)

Wonders do not confuse. We call them that
And close the matter there. But common things
Surprise us. They accept the names we give
With calm, and keep them. Easy-breathing then
We brave our next small business. Well, behind
Our backs they alter. How were we to know.

The Mother

Abortions will not let you forget.
You remember the children you got that you did not get,
The damp small pulps with a little or with no hair,
The singers and workers that never handled the air.
You will never neglect or beat
Them, or silence or buy with a sweet.
You will never wind up the sucking-thumb
Or scuttle off ghosts that come.
You will never leave them, controlling your luscious sigh,
return for a snack of them, with gobbling mother-eye.

I have heard in the voices of the wind the voices of my dim
        killed children.
I have contracted. I have eased
My dim dears at the breasts they could never suck.

I have said, Sweets, if I sinned, if I seized
Your luck
And your lives from your unfinished reach,
If I stole your births and your names,
Your straight baby tears and your games,
Your stilted or lovely loves, your tumults, your marriages,
      aches, and your deaths,
If I poisoned the beginnings of your breaths,
Believe that even in my deliberateness I was not deliberate.
Though why should I whine,
Whine that the crime was other than mine?—
Since anyhow you are dead.
Or rather, or instead,
You were never made.
But that too, I am afraid,
Is faulty: oh, what shall I say, how is the truth to be said?
You were born, you had body, you died.
It is just that you never giggled or planned or cried.

Believe me, I loved you all.
Believe me, I knew you, though faintly, and I loved,
      I loved you all.

The Preacher Ruminates Behind the Sermon

I think it must be lonely to be God.
Nobody loves a master. No. Despite
The bright hosannas, bright dear-Lords, and bright
Determined reverence of Sunday eyes.

Picture Jehovah striding through the hall
Of His importance, creatures running out
From servant-corners to acclaim, to shout
Appreciation of His merit's glare.

But who walks with Him?—dares to take His arm,
To slap Him on the shoulder, tweak His ear,
Buy Him a Coca-Cola or a beer,
Pooh-pooh His politics, call Him a fool?

Perhaps—who knows?—He tires of looking down.
Those eyes are never lifted. Never straight.
Perhaps sometimes He tires of being great
In solitude. Without a hand to hold.

The Children of the Poor

1

People who have no children can be hard:
Attain a mail of ice and insolence:
Need not pause in the fire, and in no sense
Hesitate in the hurricane to guard.
And when wide world is bitten and bewarred
They perish purely, waving their spirits hence
Without a trace of grace or of offense
To laugh or fail, diffident, wonder-starred.
While through a throttling dark we others hear
The little lifting helplessness, the queer
Whimper-whine; whose unridiculous
Lost softness softly makes a trap for us.
And makes a curse. And makes a sugar of
The malocclusions, the inconditions of love.

2

What shall I give my children? who are poor,
Who are adjudged the leastwise of the land,
Who are my sweetest lepers, who demand
No velvet and no velvety velour;
But who have begged me for a brisk contour,
Crying that they are quasi, contraband
Because unfinished, graven by a hand
Less than angelic, admirable or sure.
My hand is stuffed with mode, design, device.
But I lack access to my proper stone.
And plenitude or plan shall not suffice
Nor grief nor love shall be enough alone
To ratify my little halves who bear
Across an autumn freezing everywhere.

3

And shall I prime my children, pray, to pray?
Mites, come invade most frugal vestibules
Spectered with crusts of penitents' renewals
And all hysterics arrogant for a day.
Instruct yourselves here is no devil to pay.

Children, confine your lights in jellied rules;
Resemble graves; be metaphysical mules;
Learn Lord will not distort nor leave the fray.
Behind the scurryings of your neat motif
I shall wait, if you wish: revise the psalm
If that should frighten you: sew up belief
If that should tear: turn, singularly calm
At forehead and at fingers rather wise,
Holding the bandage ready for your eyes.

4

First fight. Then fiddle. Ply the slipping string
With feathery sorcery; muzzle the note
With hurting love; the music that they wrote
Bewitch, bewilder. Qualify to sing
Threadwise. Devise no salt, no hempen thing
For the dear instrument to bear. Devote
The bow to silks and honey. Be remote
A while from malice and from murdering.
But first to arms, to armor. Carry hate
In front of you and harmony behind.
Be deaf to music and to beauty blind.
Win war. Rise bloody, maybe not too late
For having first to civilize a space
Wherein to play your violin with grace.

5

When my dears die, the festival-colored brightness
That is their motion and mild repartee
Enchanted, a macabre mockery
Charming the rainbow radiance into tightness
And into a remarkable politeness
That is not kind and does not want to be,
May not they in the crisp encounter see
Something to recognize and read as rightness?
I say they may, so granitely discreet,
The little crooked questionings inbound,
Concede themselves on most familiar ground,
Cold an old predicament of the breath:
Adroit, the shapely prefaces complete,
Accept the university of death.

6

Life for my child is simple, and is good.
He knows his wish. Yes, but that is not all.
Because I know mine too.
And we both want joy of undeep and unabiding things,
Like kicking over a chair or throwing blocks out of a window
Or tipping over an icebox pan
Or snatching down curtains or fingering an electric outlet
Or a journey or a friend or an illegal kiss.
No. There is more to it than that.
It is that he has never been afraid.
Rather, he reaches out and lo the chair falls with a
       beautiful crash,
And the blocks fall, down on the people's heads,
And the water comes slooshing sloppily out across the floor.
And so forth.
Not that success, for him, is sure, infallible.
But never has he been afraid to reach.
His lesions are legion.
But reaching is his rule.

We Real Cool

The Pool Players.
Seven at the Golden Shovel.

We real cool. We
Left school. We

Lurk late. We
Strike straight. We

Sing sin. We
Thin gin. We

Jazz June. We
Die soon.

The Chicago Defender Sends a Man
to Little Rock

Fall, 1957

In Little Rock the people bear
Babes, and comb and part their hair
And watch the want ads, put repair
To roof and latch. While wheat toast burns
A woman waters multiferns.

Time upholds or overturns
The many, tight, and small concerns.

In Little Rock the people sing
Sunday hymns like anything,
Through Sunday pomp and polishing.

And after testament and tunes,
Some soften Sunday afternoons
With lemon tea and Lorna Doones.

I forecast
And I believe
Come Christmas Little Rock will cleave
To Christmas tree and trifle, weave,
From laugh and tinsel, texture fast.

In Little Rock is baseball; Barcarolle.
That hotness in July . . . the uniformed figures raw and
          implacable
And not intellectual,
Batting the hotness or clawing the suffering dust.
The Open Air Concert, on the special twilight green. . . .
When Beethoven is brutal or whispers to lady-like air.
Blanket-sitters are solemn, as Johann troubles to lean
To tell them what to mean. . . .

There is love, too, in Little Rock. Soft women softly
Opening themselves in kindness,
Or, pitying one's blindness,
Awaiting one's pleasure

In azure
Glory with anguished rose at the root. . . .
To wash away old semi-discomfitures.
They re-teach purple and unsullen blue.
The wispy soils go. And uncertain
Half-havings have they clarified to sures.

In Little Rock they know
Not answering the telephone is a way of rejecting life,
That it is our business to be bothered, is our business
To cherish bores or boredom, be polite
To lies and love and many-faceted fuzziness.
I scratch my head, massage the hate-I-had.
I blink across my prim and pencilled pad.
The saga I was sent for is not down.
Because there is a puzzle in this town.
The biggest News I do not dare
Telegraph to the Editor's chair:
"They are like people everywhere."

The angry Editor would reply
In hundred harryings of Why.

And true, they are hurling spittle, rock,
Garbage and fruit in Little Rock.
And I saw coiling storm a-writhe
On bright madonnas. And a scythe
Of men harassing brownish girls.
(The bows and barrettes in the curls
And braids declined away from joy.)

I saw a bleeding brownish boy. . . .

The lariat lynch-wish I deplored.

The loveliest lynchee was our Lord.

DUDLEY RANDALL (1914–   )

Born in Washington, D. C., Dudley Randall is prominent in the Detroit group of Negro poets. He received his B.A. in English from Wayne University in 1949 and his Master's degree in Library Science from the University of Michigan in 1951. He has published poems, short stories, and articles in numerous journals. In 1962 he won a Tompkins Award for fiction and poetry and in 1966 a Tompkins Award for poetry. From 1962 to 1964 he worked with Margaret Danner and other Negro poets in the Boone House cultural center in Detroit. In 1965, Randall founded the Broadside Press, which publishes individually designed "broadsides" of single poems by black poets, suitable for framing, for personal collection, or for classroom use. To date, eighteen broadsides—a number of them illustrated—have appeared. Broadside Press has also begun to publish books of poetry. In the summer of 1966, Randall visited Paris, Prague, and the Soviet Union, with a delegation of Afro-American artists. He has translated Latin, French, and Russian poetry into English and in Moscow read his own translations of Russian poems into English. He is currently working on a novel and on a volume of poems, While Cities Flame. *Four of his poems follow: the first three are from the book* Poem Counterpoem, *and the fourth is a revised version of a poem which appeared originally in* The Journal of Black Poetry, *Spring, 1967.*

The Southern Road

There the black river, boundary to hell,
And here the iron bridge, the ancient car,
And grim conductor, who with surly yell
Forbids white soldiers where the black ones are.
And I re-live the enforced avatar

Of desperate journey to a dark abode
Made by my sires before another war;
And I set forth upon the southern road.

To a land where shadowed songs like flowers swell
And where the earth is scarlet as a scar
Friezed by the bleeding lash that fell (O fell)
Upon my fathers' flesh. O far, far, far
And deep my blood has drenched it. None can bar
My birthright to the loveliness bestowed
Upon this country haughty as a star.
And I set forth upon the southern road.

This darkness and these mountains loom a spell
Of peak-roofed town where yearning steeples soar
And the holy holy chanting of a bell
Shakes human incense on the throbbing air
Where bonfires blaze and quivering bodies char.
Whose is the hair that crisped, and fiercely glowed?
I know it; and my entrails melt like tar
And I set forth upon the southern road.

O fertile hillsides where my fathers are,
From which my griefs like troubled streams have
      flowed,
I have to love you, though they sweep me far.
And I set forth upon the southern road.

Legacy: My South

What desperate nightmare rapts me to this land
Lit by a bloody moon, red on the hills,
Red in the valleys? Why am I compelled
To tread again where buried feet have trod,
To shed my tears where blood and tears have flowed?
Compulsion of the blood and of the moon
Transports me. I was molded from this clay.
My blood must ransom all the blood shed here,
My tears redeem the tears. Cripples and monsters
Are here. My flesh must make them whole and hale.
I am the sacrifice.

                    See where the halt
Attempt again and again to cross a line

Their minds have drawn, but fear snatches them back
Though health and joy wait on the other side.
And there another locks himself in a room
And throws away the key. A ragged scarecrow
Cackles an antique lay, and cries himself
Lord of the world. A naked plowman falls
Famished upon the plow, and overhead
A lean bird circles.

Booker T. and W. E. B.

(Booker T. Washington and W. E. B. Du Bois)

"It seems to me," said Booker T.,
"It shows a mighty lot of cheek
To study chemistry and Greek
When Mister Charlie needs a hand
To hoe the cotton on his land,
And when Miss Ann looks for a cook,
Why stick your nose inside a book?"

"I don't agree," said W. E. B.
"If I should have the drive to seek
Knowledge of chemistry or Greek,
I'll do it. Charles and Miss can look
Another place for hand or cook.
Some men rejoice in skill of hand,
And some in cultivating land,
But there are others who maintain
The right to cultivate the brain."

"It seems to me," said Booker T.,
"That all you folks have missed the boat
Who shout about the right to vote,
And spend vain days and sleepless nights
In uproar over civil rights.
Just keep your mouths shut, do not grouse,
But work, and save, and buy a house."

"I don't agree," said W. E. B.,
"For what can property avail
If dignity and justice fail?
Unless you help to make the laws,
They'll steal your house with trumped-up clause.

A rope's as tight, a fire as hot,
No matter how much cash you've got.
Speak soft, and try your little plan,
But as for me, I'll be a man."

"It seems to me," said Booker T.—

"I don't agree,"
Said W. E. B.

The Idiot

"That cop was powerful mean.
First he called me, 'Black boy.'
Then he punched me in the face
and drug me by the collar to a wall
and made me lean against it with my hands spread
while he searched me,
and all the time he searched me
he kicked me and cuffed me and cussed me.

I was mad enough
to lay him out,
and would've did it, only
I didn't want to hurt his feelings,
and lose the good will
of the good white folks downtown,
who hired him."

LERONE BENNETT, JR.

As Senior Editor of Ebony, *the large-circulation Negro picto-rial monthly, Lerone Bennett, Jr., is a leading Afro-American journalist. He has written extensively on the history, life, and attitudes of black men in America (see Bibliography). He was* born in Clarksdale, Mississippi, grew up in Jackson (the state capital), and graduated from Morehouse College in Atlanta. Bennett was City Editor of the Atlanta Daily World and in 1953 went to Chicago to work with the Johnson publications, first on Jet and then on Ebony. The following poem is reprinted from New Negro Poets U.S.A., the collection edited by Langston Hughes in 1964.

Blues and Bitterness

For Billy Holiday

Ice tinkled in glasses,
froze and rolled away
from hearts
in tombs where she slept.
Smoke noosed,
coiled and dangled from ceilings
in caves where she wept.

I woke up this morning
Just befo' the break of day.
I was bitter, blue and black, Lawd.
There ain't nothing else to say.

In saloons
festooned with trumpets
she prayed—sang
love songs to dead men
waiting with hammers
at the bottom of syringes.
She sang it in a song
before Sartre put it into a book.
She was Bigger
before Wright wrote,
was with Nekeela
in a slave coffle,
was stripped, branded
and eaten by the sharks
and rose again
on the third day in Georgia.

I wondered why God made me.
I wondered why He made me black.

I wondered why Mama begat me—
And I started to give God His ticket back.

LANCE JEFFERS (1919–   )

*Spanning the West and the East of the United States, Nebras-
ka-born Lance Jeffers grew up in Stromsberg, Nebraska, and
in San Francisco, and after serving as an officer in World
War II, received his B.A.* (cum laude) *and his M.A. from Columbia University in New York City. His poems have appeared in Phylon, The Tamarack Review, Burning Spear, and
the anthology Beyond the Blues. His short story "The Dawn
Swings In" was included in The Best American Short Stories
—1948. He is now a member of the faculty at Indiana University—Kokomo Campus. The poems that follow are making their initial appearance in print in this anthology.*

The Night Rains Hot Tar

The night rains hot tar into my throat,
the taste is good to my heart's tongue,
into my heart the night pours down its moon
like a yellow molten residue of dung,
the night pours down the sea into my throat,
my heart drains off its blood in love and pain,
the night pours a Negro song into my throat:
bloodred is the color of this rain:

like a bowstring of song across my throat,
the wind through the pine-trees behind the shack,
the loneliness I wear like a torn coat,
the ghetto-terror kneeling thief-like on my back,
the prayer to my genius, its power to survive,
the coaldust in my veins to come to fire before I die!

On Listening to the Spirituals

When the master lived a king and I a starving hutted slave
  beneath the lash, and

when my five-year-old son was driven at dawn to cottonfield
  to pick until he could no longer see the sun, and

when master called my wife to the big house when mistress
  was gone, took her against her will and gave her a dollar
  to be still, and when she turned upon her pride and cleav-
  ered it, cursed her dignity and stamped on it, came back to
  me with his evil on her thighs, hung her head when I condemned her with my eyes,

what broken mettle of my soul wept steel, cracked teeth in
  self-contempt upon my flesh, crept underground to seek
  new roots and secret breathing place?

When all the hatred of my bones was buried in a forgotten
  county of my soul,
then from beauty muscled from the degradation of my oaken
  bread,
I stroked on slavery soil the mighty colors of my song,
  a passionate heaven rose no God in heaven could create!

Grief Streams Down My Chest

Grief streams down my chest
like spittle from the baby's mouth,
and in the corridors behind my eyes,
  Vietnamese mothers dry-eyed walk and hand me stone
  tablets and motion me to inscribe my name thereon that
  I have seen and dimly understood their suffering.
My black grief's a pygmy pyramid beside the grassy mountain of their thorn as high as the Asian continent is long.

The Unknown

A river of slush runs through my heart,
this river I leave behind.

A blighted pine cringes in my heart,
a tree for pain to climb.

A vein of gold seeps through my heart,
molten, sweet, and live.

A field of wheat thrives in my heart,
blacksoil to the womb-blue sky.

A blacktop road's paved through my heart
that pilgrims love to ride.

A forest path winds through my heart,
ends by the redwood's thigh.

But where the wood goes black as night
and trees thick out my sight,
my heart will fire a dangered new path
for my song to fling its cry.

NAOMI LONG MADGETT (1923–   )

Prominent as one of the Detroit group of poets, Naomi Long Madgett was born in Norfolk, Virginia, the youngest of three children of a Baptist minister. She was educated in the public schools of East Orange, New Jersey, and St. Louis, Missouri, and did her undergraduate work at Virginia State College. In Detroit she received a Master's degree in English Education at Wayne State University, and has done further graduate work at Wayne State and at the University of Detroit. Mrs.

Madgett has been teaching English at Northwestern High School in Detroit since 1955. She has published three volumes of poetry, has been widely anthologized, and is also the author of two textbooks. In 1965 she became the first recipient of the $10,000 Mott Fellowship in English at Oakland University. Named "Distinguished English Teacher of the Year" in 1967 by the Metropolitan Detroit English Club, Naomi Long Madgett is a member of the National Writers Club, the Detroit Women Writers, and the Michigan State Council for the Arts (Literature Committee). The three poems which follow are from her latest collection of poems, Star By Star (1965).

Native

Down the unspun swerve of trackless weeds
I travel unaware,
Propelled by sudden vengeances of seeds
Of anywhere
Whose hues I never learned nor whose design.
Unmindful of intent,
I wander where the knowing roots entwine
The innocent,
And suck the pungent juice into my vein,
And do not question why.
Expect no definition to explain
Or deify.
For blessed or damned, inherent in my lust
And native to my need
Is this same potent urgency that dust
Conveys to seed.

Her Story

They gave me the wrong name, in the first place.
They named me Grace and waited for a light and agile
    dancer.
But some trick of the genes mixed me up
And instead I turned out big and black and burly.

In the second place, I fashioned the wrong dreams.
I wanted to dress like Juliet and act

Before applauding audiences on Broadway.
I learned more about Shakespeare than he knew about
    himself.
But of course, all that was impossible.
"Talent, yes," they would tell me,
"But an actress has to look the part."
So I ended up waiting on tables in Harlem
And hearing uncouth men yell at me:
"Hey, momma, you can cancel that hamburger
And come on up to 102."

In the third place, I tried the wrong solution.
The stuff I drank made me deathly sick
And someone called a doctor.
Next time I'll try a gun.

The Race Question

(For one whose fame depends on keeping The Problem a problem)
    Would it please you if I strung my tears
    In pearls for you to wear?
    Would you like a gift of my hands' endless beating
    Against old bars?

    This time I can forget my Otherness,
    Silence my drums of discontent awhile
    And listen to the stars.

    Wait in the shadows if you choose.
    Stand alert to catch
    The thunder and first sprinkle of unrest
    Your insufficiency demands.
    But you will find no comfort.
    I will not feed your hunger with my blood
    Nor crown your nakedness
    With jewels of my elegant pain.

MARI EVANS

In the work of Mari Evans, we hear a voice of the new generation of black poets. Born in Toledo, Ohio, and educated at the University of Toledo, she now lives in Indianapolis, where she edits an industrial magazine. She has worked as a musician, choir director, and church organist. Her poems have been published in a wide array of journals and anthologies, have been broadcast in the United States and England, and were included in the Broadway production "A Hand Is on the Gate." Her first volume of verse, a collection of twenty-four poems, is being prepared for publication in Paul Breman's Heritage series in London. Of her five poems that follow, the first appeared in Negro Digest, two have previously been anthologized, and the last two were received by the editor in manuscript form from the poet.

Coventry

there is a thin wall
gossamer thin
and
clear with limpid
clearness
against whose sides
dreams
bruise themselves and
voiceless
man implores . . .

there is a wall
gossamer thin
limpidly clear
unpenetrable . . .

before which my
aloneness
stands looking up

Status Symbol

i
Have Arrived

i
am the
New Negro

i
am the result of
President Lincoln
World War I
and Paris
the
Red Ball Express
white drinking fountains
sitdowns and
sit-ins
Federal Troops
Marches on Washington
and
prayer meetings . . .

today
They hired me
it
is a status
job . . .
along
with my papers
They
gave me my
Status Symbol
the
key
to the
White . . . Locked . . .
John

The Emancipation of George-Hector
(a colored turtle)

George-Hector
. . . is
spoiled.
formerly he stayed
well up in his
shell . . . but now
he hangs arms and legs
sprawlingly
in a most languorous fashion . . .
head reared back
to

be
admired.

he didn't use to
talk . . .
but
he does now.

My Man Let Me Pull Your Coat . . .

All praise be to
Allah
only the
mistakes . . .
are mine
the otherness
the cries
the implorations
all
the blue smoke
the acrid stink
the white bodies
the cold cell
and the outstretched hands
unbelieving
opening
learning

                    grasping
                    sharing
                    pounding
                    tearing
                    splintering
                    shrieking upraised proud
         cacophony of hate love
         salvation
         to lie smeared
         blood-red over the hearts
         and cobblestones
         of a nation shamed
         slinking silently from the
                        love beats
         expiring softly
         before the brethren
         Labbayka! *
         My Man—let me. . . .

Black Jam for Dr. Negro

Pullin me in off the corner to wash my face an
cut my afro turn
my collar
down
when that aint my
thang I
walk heels first
nose round an tilted
up
my ancient
eyes
see your thang
baby
an it aint
shit
your thang
puts my eyes out baby
turns my seeking fingers

* "'Labbayka! Labbayka!' (Here I come, O Lord!)—the cry of every orthodox Muslim after he has entered the state of Ihram (a spiritual and physical state of consecration) and as he begins the traditional Hajj, or journey to Mecca." (This was the poet's explanation of the word in response to a query from the editor.)—Ed.

into splintering fists
messes up my head
an I scream you out
your thang
is whats wrong
   an you keep
   pilin it on rubbin it
   in
   smoothly
   doin it
   to death

what you sweatin
baby
        your guts
puked an rotten
waitin
to be defended

LeROI JONES (1934–   )

*Poet, playwright, novelist, essayist, and polemicist, LeRoi
Jones started out in literature as an avant-garde writer with
a primarily aesthetic interest but has since become an active,
controversial black nationalist. He believes that it is the function of black writers to be "missionaries of Blackness," to reject the aesthetics and culture of white America, to study the
African and Arabic languages, and to bring black people together as a separate group and force in the United States. He
was born in Newark, New Jersey, and attended the public
schools there. He did his undergraduate work at Howard
University and graduate work at the New School for Social
Research and Columbia University. He served in the Air
Force from 1954 to 1957. Jones was awarded a Whitney fel-
lowship in 1961–62 and a Guggenheim award in 1964–65.
His play* Dutchman *received the Obie award for the best off-
Broadway play of 1964. Jones has published two volumes of*

poetry and a mimeographed collection of new poems (see Bibliography); a novel; six plays; a collection of essays; Blues People, *a study of "the Negro experience in white America and the music that developed from it"; and* Tales (1967), *a collection of sixteen short stories. The five poems that follow are from his first book of poems,* Preface to a Twenty Volume Suicide Note (1961). *On January 4, 1968, LeRoi Jones was sentenced, in Newark, to two and a half to three years in jail on a charge of illegally possessing a gun. He was subsequently released on $25,000 bail pending an appeal. At the trial, the judge cited his disagreement with the ideas expressed in a poem by Jones as part of the motivation for the sentence. P.E.N., the international association of writers, has voiced protest against the sentence as a violation of freedom of expression. The United Black Artists (UBA), a group of more than two hundred Afro-American artists, writers, and intellectuals, has rallied to the defense of LeRoi Jones and has declared that "as long as the right of free expression and the dictates of individual conscience are violated, we will continue as black people to fearlessly affirm these rights and to support our brother LeRoi Jones and the principles of conscience and free expression which he so courageously exemplifies for mankind."*

Preface to a Twenty Volume Suicide Note

(For Kellie Jones, Born 16 May, 1959)
Lately, I've become accustomed to the way
The ground opens up and envelops me
Each time I go out to walk the dog.
Or the broad-edged silly music the wind
Makes when I run for a bus . . .

Things have come to that.

And now, each night I count the stars,
And each night I get the same number.
And when they will not come to be counted,
I count the holes they leave.

Nobody sings anymore.

And then last night, I tiptoed up
To my daughter's room and heard her

Talking to someone, and when I opened
The door, there was no one there . . .
Only she on her knees, peeking into

Her own clasped hands.

The Invention of Comics

I am a soul in the world: in
the world of my soul the whirled
light from the day
the sacked land
of my father.

In the world, the sad
nature of
myself. In myself
nature is sad. Small
prints of the day. Its
small dull fires. Its
sun, like a greyness
smeared on the dark.

The day of my soul, is
the nature of that
place. It is a landscape. Seen
from the top of a hill. A
grey expanse; dull fires
throbbing on its seas.

The man's soul, the complexion
of his life. The menace
of its greyness. The
fire throbs, the sea
moves. Birds shoot
from the dark. The edge
of the waters lit
darkly for the moon.

And the moon, from the soul. Is
the world, of the man. The man
and his sea, and its moon, and
the soft fire throbbing. Kind

death. O
my dark and sultry
love.

Look For You Yesterday, Here You Come Today

Part of my charm:

        envious blues feeling
        separation of church & state
        grim calls from drunk debutantes

Morning never aids me in my quest.
I have to trim my beard in solitude.
I try to hum lines from "The Poet In New York".

People saw metal all around the house on Saturdays. The
                                      Phone rings.

terrible poems come in the mail. Descriptions of celibate parties

        torn trousers: Great Poets dying
        with their strophes on. & me
        incapable of a simple straightforward
        anger.

It's so diffuse
being alive. Suddenly one is aware
        that nobody really gives a damn.
        My wife is pregnant with *her* child.
        "It means nothing to me", sez Strindberg.

An avalanche of words
could cheer me up. Words from Great Sages.
        Was James Karolis a great sage??
        Why did I let Ora Matthews beat him up
        in the bathroom? Haven't I learned my lesson.
I would take up painting
if I cd think of a way to do it
better than Leonardo. Than Bosch.
Than Hogarth. Than Kline.

Frank walked off the stage, singing
"My silence is as important as Jack's incessant yatter."

I am a mean hungry sorehead.
Do I have the capacity for grace??
To arise one smoking spring
& find one's youth has taken off
for greener parts.

A sudden blankness in the day
as if there were no afternoon.
& all my piddling joys retreated
to their own dopey mythic worlds.

The hours of the atmosphere
grind their teeth like hags.

                    (When will world war two be over?)

I stood up on a mailbox
waving my yellow tee-shirt
watching the grey tanks
stream up Central Ave.

                    All these thots
                    are Flowers Of Evil
                    cold & lifeless
                    as subway rails ·

the sun like a huge cobblestone
flaking its brown slow rays
primititi
          once, twice, . My life
          seems over & done with.
          Each morning I rise
          like a sleep walker
          & rot a little more.

All the lovely things I've known have disappeared.
I have all my pubic hair & am lonely.
There is probably no such place as Battle Creek, Michigan!

Tom Mix dead in a Boston Nightclub
before I realized what happened.

People laugh when I tell them about Dickie Dare!

What is one to do in an alien planet
where the people breathe New Ports?

Where is my space helmet, I sent for it
3 lives ago . . . when there were box tops.

What has happened to box tops??

O, God . . . I must have a belt that glows green
in the dark. Where is my Captain Midnight decoder??
I can't understand what Superman is saying!

THERE *MUST* BE A LONE RANGER!!!

* * * *

but this also
is part of my charm.
A maudlin nostalgia
that comes on
like terrible thoughts about death.

How dumb to be sentimental about anything
To call it love
& cry pathetically
into the long black handkerchief
of the years.

> "Look for you yesterday
> Here you come today
> Your mouth wide open
> But what you got to say?"

—part of my charm

old envious   blues feeling
ticking like   a big cobblestone clock.

I hear the reel running out . . .
the spectators are impatient for popcorn:
It was only a selected short subject

F. Scott Charon
will soon be glad-handing me
like a legionaire

My silver bullets all gone
My black mask trampled in the dust

& Tonto way off in the hills
moaning like Bessie Smith.

The Death of Nick Charles

1

. . . And how much of this
do you understand? I hide
my face, my voice twisted
in the heavy winter fog. If I
came to you, left this wet island
& came to you; now, when I am young,
& have strength in my fingers. To say,
I love you, & cannot even recognize
you. How much of me
could you understand? (Only
that I love colour, motion, thin high air
at night? The recognizable parts
of yourself?)

We love only heroes. Glorious
death in battle. Scaling walls,
burning bridges behind us, destroying
all ways back. All retreat. As if
some things were fixed. As if the moon
would come to us each night (&
we could watch
from the battlements). As if
there were anything certain
or lovely
in our lives.

Sad
long
motion of air
pushing in my face. Lies,
weakness, hatred
of myself. Of you
for not understanding
this. Or not
despising me
for the right causes. I am
sick as, OH,
the night is. As
cold days are,

when we must watch them
grow old
& dark.

2

I am thinking
of a dance. One I could
invent, if there
were music. If you
would play for me, some
light music. Couperin
with yellow hillsides. Ravel
as I kiss your hair. Lotions
of Debussy.
I am moved by what? Angered at its whine;
the quiet delicacy of my sadness. The elements.
My face torn by wind, faces, desire, lovely chinese ladies
sweeping the sidewalks. (And this is not
what I mean. Not the thing I wanted for you. Not, finally.
Music, only terror at this lightly scribbled day.

Emotion. Words.
Waste. No clear delight.
No light under my fingers. The room, The
walls, silent & deadly. Not
Music.

If there were
a dance. For us
to make; your fingers
on my face, your face wet
with tears (or silence. For us
to form upon this heavy air. Tearing
the silence, hurting the darkness
with the colour of our movement! Nakedness?
Great leaps
into the air? Huge pirouettes; the moon blurred
on ancient lakes. Thin horns
and laughter.

3

Can you hear this? Do you know
who speaks to you? Do you
know me? (Not even

your lover. Afraid of you, your sudden
disorder. Your ringless
hands. Your hair
disguised. Your voice
not even real. Or
beautiful.

          (What we had
I cannot even say. Something
like loathing
covers your words.

4

It grows dark
around you. And these words
are not music. They make no motions
for a dance. (Standing awkwardly
before the window, watching
the moon. The ragged smoke
lifting against
grey sheaths
of night.
You shimmer like words
I barely hear. Your face
twisted into words. "Love, Oh,
Love me." The window facing night, & always
when we cannot speak.

What shapes stream through the glass?
Only shadows
on the wall. Under
my fingers, trailing me
with a sound like
glass on slate. You cry out
in the night,
& only the moon
answers.

5

The house sits
between red buildings. And a bell
rocks against the night air. The moon
sits over the North river, underneath
a blue bridge. Boats & old men

move through the darkness. Needing
no eyes. Moving slowly
towards the long black line
of horizon. Footfalls, the
twisting dirty surf. Sea birds
scalding the blackness.

I sit inside alone, without
thoughts. I cannot lie
& say I think of you. I merely sit
& grow weary, not even watching
the sky lighten with morning.

                    & now

I am sleeping
& you will not be able
to wake me.

The Bridge

for wieners & mcclure

I have forgotten the head
of where I am. Here at the bridge. 2
bars, down the street, seeming
to wrap themselves around my fingers, the day,
screams in me; pitiful like a little girl
you sense will be dead before the winter
is over.

I can't see the bridge now, I've past
it, its shadow, we drove through, headed out
along the cold insensitive roads to what
we wanted to call "ourselves."
"How does the bridge go?" Even tho
you find yourself in its length
strung out along its breadth, waiting
for the cold sun to tear out your eyes. Enamoured
of its blues, spread out in the silk clubs of
this autumn tune. The changes are difficult, when
you hear them, & know they are all in you, the chords

of your disorder meddle with your would be disguises.

Sifting in, down, upon your head, with the sun & the insects.

(Late feeling) Way down till it barely, after that rush of
wind & odor reflected from hills you have forgotten the color
when you touch the water, & it closes, slowly, around your
    head.

The bridge will be behind you, that music you know, that
    place,
you feel when you look up to say, it is me, & I have forgotten,
all the things, you told me to love, to try to understand, the
bridge will stand, high up in the clouds & the light, & you,

(when you have let the song run out) will be sliding through
unmentionable black.

4.

Literary Criticism

W. E. B. DuBOIS (1868–1963)

A biographical note on W. E. B. DuBois appears in the Poetry section (see pp. 358–359). The Souls of Black Folk has been published in about thirty editions in the United States since its initial publication in 1903. James Weldon Johnson observed that it had "a greater effect upon and within the Negro race in America than any other single book published in this country since Uncle Tom's Cabin." Professor Sterling A. Brown, in an essay elsewhere in this section, says it "is still one of the best interpretations of Negro life and aspirations." Langston Hughes noted that "one of the first books I read on my own was The Souls of Black Folk." In an Introduction to a paperback edition of this classic, Professor Saunders Redding wrote:

The Souls of Black Folk may be seen as fixing that moment in history when the American Negro began to reject the idea of the world's belonging to white people only, and to think of himself, in concert, as a potential force in the organization of society. With its publication, Negroes of training and intelligence, who had hitherto pretended to regard the race problem as of strictly personal concern and who sought invididual salvation in a creed of detachment and silence, found a bond in their common grievances and a language through which to express them.

Following are the first and final chapters, or essays, of this landmark book.

The Souls of Black Folk

1

Of Our Spiritual Strivings

> O water, voice of my heart, crying in the sand,
>   All night long crying with a mournful cry,
> As I lie and listen, and cannot understand
>   The voice of my heart in my side or the voice
>   of the sea,
>   O water, crying for rest, is it I, is it I?
>   All night long the water is crying to me.
>
> Unresting water, there shall never be rest
>   Till the last moon droop and the last tide fail,
> And the fire of the end begin to burn in the west;
>   And the heart shall be weary and wonder and cry
>   like the sea,
>   All life long crying without avail,
>   As the water all night long is crying to me.
>   ARTHUR SYMONS.

Between me and the other world there is ever an unasked question: unasked by some through feelings of delicacy; by others through the difficulty of rightly framing it. All, nevertheless, flutter round it. They approach me in a half-hesitant sort of way, eye me curiously or compassionately, and then, instead of saying directly, How does it feel to be a problem? they say, I know an excellent colored man in my town; or, I fought at Mechanicsville; or, Do not these Southern outrages make your blood boil? At these I smile, or am interested, or reduce the boiling to a simmer, as the occasion may require. To the real question, How does it feel to be a problem? I answer seldom a word.

And yet, being a problem is a strange experience,—peculiar even for one who has never been anything else, save perhaps in babyhood and in Europe. It is in the early days of rollicking boyhood that the revelation first bursts upon one, all in a day, as it were. I remember well when the shadow swept across me. I was a little thing, away up in the hills of New England, where the dark Housatonic winds between Hoosac and Taghkanic to the sea. In a wee wooden schoolhouse, something put it into the boys' and girls' heads to buy gorgeous visiting-cards—ten cents a package—and exchange. The exchange was merry, till one girl, a tall newcomer, refused my card,—refused it peremptorily, with a glance. Then it dawned upon me with a certain suddenness that I was different from the others; or like, mayhap, in heart and life and longing, but shut out from their world by a vast veil. I had thereafter no desire to tear down that veil, to creep through; I held all beyond it in common contempt, and lived above it in a region of blue sky and great wandering shadows. That sky was bluest when I could beat my mates at examination-time, or beat them at a foot-race, or even beat their stringy heads. Alas, with the years all this fine contempt began to fade; for the worlds I longed for, and all their dazzling opportunities, were theirs, not mine. But they should not keep these prizes, I said; some, all, I would wrest from them. Just how I would do it I could never decide: by reading law, by healing the sick, by telling the wonderful tales that swam in my head,—some way. With other black boys the strife was not so fiercely sunny: their youth shrunk into tasteless sycophancy, or into silent hatred of the pale world about them and mocking distrust of everything white; or wasted itself in a bitter cry, Why did God make me an outcast and a stranger in mine own house? The shades of the prison-house closed round about us all: walls strait and stubborn to the whitest, but relentlessly narrow, tall, and unscalable to sons of night who must plod darkly on in resignation, or beat unavailing palms against the stone, or steadily, half hopelessly, watch the streak of blue above.

After the Egyptian and Indian, the Greek and Roman, the Teuton and Mongolian, the Negro is a sort of seventh son, born with a veil, and gifted with second-sight in this American world,—a world which yields him no true self-consciousness,

but only lets him see himself through the revelation of the
other world. It is a peculiar sensation, this double-conscious-
ness, this sense of always looking at one's self through the eye
of others, of measuring one's soul by the tape of a world that
looks on in amused contempt and pity. One ever feels his two-
ness,—an American, a Negro; two souls, two thoughts, two
unreconciled strivings; two warring ideals in one dark body,
whose dogged strength alone keeps it from being torn asun-
der.

The history of the American Negro is the history of this
strife,—this longing to attain self-conscious manhood, to
merge his double self into a better and truer self. In this merging he wishes neither of the older selves to be lost. He would
not Africanize America, for America has too much to teach
the world and Africa. He would not bleach his Negro soul in
a flood of white Americanism, for he knows that Negro blood
has a message for the world. He simply wishes to make it possible for a man to be both a Negro and an American, without
being cursed and spit upon by his fellows, without having the
doors of Opportunity closed roughly in his face.

This, then, is the end of his striving; to be a co-worker in
the kingdom of culture, to escape both death and isolation, to
husband and use his best powers and his latent genius. These
powers of body and mind have in the past been strangely
wasted, dispersed, or forgotten. The shadow of a mighty
Negro past flits through the tale of Ethiopia the Shadowy and
of Egypt the Sphinx. Throughout history, the powers of single
black men flash here and there like falling stars, and die sometimes before the world has rightly gauged their brightness.
Here in America, in the few days since Emancipation, the
black man's turning hither and thither in hesitant and doubtful striving has often made his very strength to lose effectiveness, to seem like absence of power, like weakness. And yet it
is not weakness,—it is the contradiction of double aims. The
double-aimed struggle of the black artisan—on the one hand
to escape white contempt for a nation of mere hewers of
wood and drawers of water, and on the other hand to plough
and nail and dig for a poverty-stricken horde—could only result in making him a poor craftsman, for he had but half a
heart in either cause. By the poverty and ignorance of his people, the Negro minister or doctor was tempted toward quack-
ery and demagogy; and by the criticism of the other world,
toward ideals that made him ashamed of his lowly tasks. The
would-be black *savant* was confronted by the paradox that the
knowledge his people needed was a twice-told tale to his white
neighbors, while the knowledge which would teach the white

world was Greek to his own flesh and blood. The innate love
of harmony and beauty that set the ruder souls of his people
a-dancing and a-singing raised but confusion and doubt in the
soul of the black artist; for the beauty revealed to him was the
soul-beauty of a race which his larger audience despised, and
he could not articulate the message of another people. This
waste of double aims, this seeking to satisfy two unreconciled
ideals, has wrought sad havoc with the courage and faith and
deeds of ten thousand thousand people,—has sent them often
wooing false gods and invoking false means of salvation, and
at times has even seemed about to make them ashamed of
themselves.

Away back in the days of bondage they thought to see in
one divine event the end of all doubt and disappointment; few
men ever worshipped Freedom with half such unquestioning
faith as did the American Negro for two centuries. To him, so
far as he thought and dreamed, slavery was indeed the sum of
all villainies, the cause of all sorrow, the root of all prejudice;
Emancipation was the key to a promised land of sweeter
beauty than ever stretched before the eyes of wearied Israelites. In song and exhortation swelled one refrain—Liberty; in
his tears and curses the God he implored had Freedom in his
right hand. At last it came,—suddenly, fearfully, like a
dream. With one wild carnival of blood and passion came the
message in his own plaintive cadences:—

"Shout O children!
 Shout, you're free!
 For God has bought your liberty!"

Years have passed away since then,—ten, twenty, forty;
forty years of national life, forty years of renewal and development, and yet the swarthy spectre sits in its accustomed seat
at the Nation's feast. In vain do we cry to this our vastest social problem:—

"Take any shape but that, and my firm nerves
 Shall never tremble!"

The Nation has not yet found peace from its sins; the freedman has not yet found in freedom his promised land. Whatever of good may have come in these years of change, the
shadow of a deep disappointment rests upon the Negro people,—a disappointment all the more bitter because the unat-
tained ideal was unbounded save by the simple ignorance of a
lowly people.

The first decade was merely a prolongation of the vain
search for freedom, the boon that seemed ever barely to elude
their grasp,—like a tantalizing will-o'-the-wisp, maddening
and misleading the headless host. The holocaust of war, the
terrors of the Ku-Klux Klan, the lies of carpet-baggers, the
disorganization of industry, and the contradictory advice of
friends and foes, left the bewildered serf with no new watch-
word beyond the old cry for freedom. As the time flew, however, he began to grasp a new idea. The ideal of liberty demanded for its attainment powerful means, and these the Fif-
teenth Amendment gave him. The ballot, which before he had
looked upon as a visible sign of freedom, he now regarded as
the chief means of gaining and perfecting the liberty with
which war had partially endowed him. And why not? Had not
votes made war and emancipated millions? Had not votes en-
franchised the freedmen? Was anything impossible to a power
that had done all this? A million black men started with renewed zeal to vote themselves into the kingdom. So the decade flew away, the revolution of 1876 came, and left the
half-free serf weary, wondering but still inspired. Slowly but
steadily, in the following years, a new vision began gradually
to replace the dream of a political power,—a powerful movement, the rise of another ideal to guide the unguided, another
pillar of fire by night after a clouded day. It was the ideal of
"book-learning"; the curiosity, born of compulsory ignorance,
to know and test the power of the cabalistic letters of the
white man, the longing to know. Here at last seemed to have
been discovered the mountain path to Canaan; longer than the
highway of Emancipation and law, steep and rugged, but
straight, leading to heights high enough to overlook life.

Up the new path the advance guard toiled, slowly, heavily,
doggedly; only those who have watched and guided the falter-
ing feet, the misty minds, the dull understandings, of the dark
pupils of these schools know how faithfully, how piteously,
this people strove to learn. It was weary work. The cold statis-
tician wrote down the inches of progress here and there, noted
also where here and there a foot had slipped or some one had
fallen. To the tired climbers, the horizon was ever dark, the
mists were often cold, the Canaan was always dim and far
away. If, however, the vistas disclosed as yet no goal, no rest-
ing-place, little but flattery and criticism, the journey at least
gave leisure for reflection and self-examination; it changed the
child of Emancipation to the youth with dawning self-consciousness, self-realization, self-respect. In those sombre forests of his striving his own soul rose before him, and he saw
himself,—darkly as through a veil; and yet he saw in himself

some faint revelation of his power, of his mission. He began
to have a dim feeling that, to attain his place in the world, he
must be himself, and not another. For the first time he sought
to analyze the burden he bore upon his back, that deadweight
of social degradation partially masked behind a half-named
Negro problem. He felt his poverty; without a cent, without a
home, without land, tools, or savings, he had entered into
competition with rich, landed, skilled neighbors. To be a poor
man is hard, but to be a poor race in a land of dollars is the
very bottom of hardships. He felt the weight of his ignorance,
—not simply of letters, but of life, of business, of the humanities; the accumulated sloth and shirking and awkwardness of
decades and centuries shackled his hands and feet. Nor was
his burden all poverty and ignorance. The red stain of bastardy, which two centuries of systemic legal defilement of
Negro women had stamped upon his race, meant not only the
loss of ancient African chastity, but also the hereditary weight
of a mass of corruption from white adulterers, threatening almost the obliteration of the Negro home.

A people thus handicapped ought not to be asked to race
with the world, but rather allowed to give all its time and
thought to its own social problems. But alas! while sociologists
gleefully count his bastards and his prostitutes, the very soul
of the toiling, sweating black man is darkened by the shadow
of a vast despair. Men call the shadow prejudice, and
learnedly explain it as the natural defence of culture against
barbarism, learning against ignorance, purity against crime,
the "higher" against the "lower" races. To which the Negro
cries Amen! and swears that to so much of this strange prejudice as is founded on just homage to civilization, culture, righteousness, and progress, he humbly bows and meekly does ob-
eisance. But before that nameless prejudice that leaps beyond
all this he stands helpless, dismayed, and well-nigh speechless;
before that personal disrespect and mockery, the ridicule and
systematic humiliation, the distortion of fact and wanton license of fancy, the cynical ignoring of the better and the bois-
terous welcoming of the worse, the all-pervading desire to in-
culcate disdain for everything black, from Toussaint to the
devil,—before this there rises a sickening despair that would
disarm and discourage any nation save that black host to
whom "discouragement" is an unwritten word.

But the facing of so vast a prejudice could not but bring
inevitable self-questioning, self-disparagement, and lowering
of ideals which ever accompany repression and breed in an atmosphere of contempt and hate. Whispering and portents
came borne upon the four winds: Lo! we are diseased and

dying, cried the dark hosts; we cannot write, our voting is in vain; what need of education, since we must always cook and serve? And the Nation echoed and enforced this self-criticism, saying: Be content to be servants, and nothing more; what need of higher culture for half-men? Away with the black man's ballot, by force or fraud,—and behold the suicide of a race! Nevertheless, out of the evil came something of good, —the more careful adjustment of education to real life, the clearer perception of the Negroes' social responsibilities, and the sobering realization of the meaning of progress.

So dawned the time of *Sturm und Drang:* storm and stress to-day rocks our little boat on the mad waters of the world-sea; there is within and without the sound of conflict, the burning of body and rending of soul; inspiration strives with doubt, and faith with vain questionings. The bright ideals of the past,—physical freedom, political power, the training of brains and the training of hands,—all these in turn have waxed and waned, until even the last grows dim and overcast. Are they all wrong,—all false? No, not that, but each alone was oversimple and incomplete,—the dreams of a credulous race-childhood, or the fond imaginings of the other world which does not know and does not want to know our power. To be really true, all these ideals must be melted and welded into one. The training of the schools we need to-day more than ever,—the training of deft hands, quick eyes and ears, and above all the broader, deeper, higher culture of gifted minds and pure hearts. The power of the ballot we need in sheer self-defence,—else what shall save us from a second slavery? Freedom, too, the long-sought, we still seek,—the freedom of life and limb, the freedom to work and think, the freedom to love and aspire. Work, culture, liberty,—all these we need, not singly but together, not successively but together each growing and aiding each, and all striving toward that vaster ideal that swims before the Negro people, the ideal of human brotherhood, gained through the unifying ideal of Race; the ideal of fostering and developing the traits and talents of the Negro, not in opposition to or contempt for other races, but rather in large conformity to the greater ideals of the American Republic, in order that some day on American soil two world-races may give each to each those characteristics both so sadly lack. We the darker ones come even now not altogether empty-handed: there are to-day no truer exponents of the pure human spirit of the Declaration of Independence than the American Negroes; there is no true American music but the wild sweet melodies of the Negro slave; the American fairy tales and folk-lore are Indian and African;

and, all in all, we black men seem the sole oasis of simple faith and reverence in a dusty desert of dollars and smartness. Will America be poorer if she replace her brutal dyspeptic blundering with light-hearted but determined Negro humility? or her coarse and cruel wit with loving jovial good-humor? or her vulgar music with the soul of the Sorrow Songs?

Merely a concrete test of the underlying principles of the great republic is the Negro Problem, and the spiritual striving of the freedmen's sons is the travail of souls whose burden is almost beyond the measure of their strength, but who bear it in the name of an historic race, in the name of this the land of their fathers' fathers, and in the name of human opportunity.

And now what I have briefly sketched in large outline let me on coming pages tell again in many ways, with loving emphasis and deeper detail, that men may listen to the striving in the souls of black folk.

14

Of the Sorrow Songs

I walk through the churchyard
    To lay this body down;
I know moon-rise, I know star-rise;
I walk in the moonlight, I walk in the starlight;
I'll lie in the grave and stretch out my arms,
I'll go to judgment in the evening of the day,
And my soul and thy soul shall meet that day,
    When I lay this body down.
          NEGRO SONG.

They that walked in darkness sang songs in the olden days— Sorrow Songs—for they were weary at heart. And so before each thought that I have written in this book I have set a phrase, a haunting echo of these weird old songs in which the soul of the black slave spoke to men. Ever since I was a child these songs have stirred me strangely. They came out of the South unknown to me, one by one, and yet at once I knew them as of me and of mine. Then in after years when I came to Nashville I saw the great temple builded of these songs towering over the pale city. To me Jubilee Hall seemed ever made of the songs themselves, and its bricks were red with the blood and dust of toil. Out of them rose for me morning, noon, and night, bursts of wonderful melody, full of the voices of my brothers and sisters, full of the voices of the past.

Little of beauty has America given the world save the rude grandeur God himself stamped on her bosom; the human spirit in this new world has expressed itself in vigor and ingenuity rather than in beauty. And so by fateful chance the Negro folk-song—the rhythmic cry of the slave—stands today not simply as the sole American music, but as the most beautiful expression of human experience born this side the seas. It has been neglected, it has been, and is, half despised, and above all it has been persistently mistaken and misunderstood; but notwithstanding, it still remains as the singular spiritual heritage of the nation and the greatest gift of the Negro people.

Away back in the thirties the melody of these slave songs stirred the nation, but the songs were soon half forgotten. Some, like "Near the lake where drooped the willow," passed into current airs and their source was forgotten; others were caricatured on the "minstrel" stage and their memory died away. Then in war-time came the singular Port Royal experiment after the capture of Hilton Head, and perhaps for the first time the North met the Southern slave face to face and heart to heart with no third witness. The Sea Islands of the Carolinas, where they met, were filled with a black folk of primitive type, touched and moulded less by the world about them than any others outside the Black Belt. Their appearance was uncouth, their language funny, but their hearts were human and their singing stirred men with a mighty power. Thomas Wentworth Higginson hastened to tell of these songs, and Miss McKim and others urged upon the world their rare beauty. But the world listened only half credulously until the Fisk Jubilee Singers sang the slave songs so deeply into the world's heart that it can never wholly forget them again.

There was once a blacksmith's son born at Cadiz, New York, who in the changes of time taught school in Ohio and helped defend Cincinnati from Kirby Smith. Then he fought at Chancellorsville and Gettysburg and finally served in the Freedman's Bureau at Nashville. Here he formed a Sunday-school class of black children in 1866, and sang with them and taught them to sing. And then they taught him to sing, and when once the glory of the Jubilee songs passed into the soul of George L. White, he knew his life-work was to let those Negroes sing to the world as they had sung to him. So in 1871 the pilgrimage of the Fisk Jubilee Singers began. North to Cincinnati they rode,—four half-clothed black boys and five girl-women,—led by a man with a cause and a purpose. They stopped at Wilberforce, the oldest of Negro schools, where a black bishop blessed them. Then they went, fighting cold and starvation, shut out of hotels, and cheerfully sneered at, ever northward; and ever the magic of their song kept thrilling hearts, until a burst of applause in the Congregational Council at Oberlin revealed them to the world. They came to New York and Henry Ward Beecher dared to welcome them, even though the metropolitan dailies sneered at his "Nigger Minstrels." So their songs conquered till they sang across the land and across the sea, before Queen and Kaiser, in Scotland and Ireland, Holland and Switzerland. Seven years they sang, and brought back a hundred and fifty thousand dollars to found Fisk University.

Since their day they have been imitated—sometimes well, by the singers of Hampton and Atlanta, sometimes ill, by straggling quartettes. Caricature has sought again to spoil the quaint beauty of the music, and has filled the air with many debased melodies which vulgar ears scarce know from the real. But the true Negro folk-song still lives in the hearts of those who have heard them truly sung and in the hearts of the Negro people.

What are these songs, and what do they mean? I know little of music and can say nothing in technical phrase, but I know something of men, and knowing them, I know that these songs are the articulate message of the slave to the world. They tell us in these eager days that life was joyous to the black slave, careless and happy. I can easily believe this of some, of many. But not all the past South, though it rose from the dead, can gainsay the heart-touching witness of these songs. They are the music of an unhappy people, of the children of disappointment; they tell of death and suffering and unvoiced longing toward a truer world, of misty wanderings and hidden ways.

The songs are indeed the siftings of centuries; the music is far more ancient than the words, and in it we can trace here and there signs of development. My grandfather's grandmother was seized by an evil Dutch trader two centuries ago; and coming to the valleys of the Hudson and Housatonic, black, little, and lithe, she shivered and shrank in the harsh north winds, looked longingly at the hills, and often crooned a heathen melody to the child between her knees, thus:

Do ba-na co-ba, ge-ne me, ge-ne me!

Do ba-na co-ba, ge-ne me, ge-ne me!

Ben d' nu-li, nu-li, nu-li, nu-li, ben d'   le.

The child sang it to his children and they to their children's children, and so two hundred years it has travelled down to us and we sing it to our children, knowing as little as our fathers what its words may mean, but knowing well the meaning of its music.

This was primitive African music; it may be seen in larger form in the strange chant which heralds "The Coming of John":

"You may bury me in the East,
 You may bury me in the West,
 But I'll hear the trumpet sound in that morning,"

—the voice of exile.

Ten master songs, more or less, one may pluck from this forest of melody—songs of undoubted Negro origin and wide popular currency, and songs peculiarly characteristic of the slave. One of these I have just mentioned. Another whose strains begin this book is "Nobody knows the trouble I've seen." When, struck with a sudden poverty, the United States refused to fulfil its promises of land to the freedmen, a brigadier-general went down to the Sea Islands to carry the news. An old woman on the outskirts of the throng began singing this song; all the mass joined with her, swaying. And the soldier wept.

The third song is the cradle-song of death which all men know,—"Swing low, sweet chariot,"—whose bars begin the life story of "Alexander Crummell." Then there is the song of many waters, "Roll, Jordon, roll," a mighty chorus with minor cadences. There were many songs of the fugitive like that which opens "The Wings of Atalanta," and the more familiar "Been a-listening." The seventh is the song of the End and the Beginning—"My Lord, what a mourning! when the stars begin to fall"; a strain of this is placed before "The Dawn of Freedom." The song of groping—"My way's cloudy"—begins "The Meaning of Progress"; the ninth is the song of this chapter—"Wrestlin' Jacob, the day is a-breaking,"—a pæan of hopeful strife. The last master song is the song of songs—"Steal away,"—sprung from "The Faith of the Fathers."

There are many others of the Negro folk-songs as striking and characteristic as these, as, for instance, the three strains in the third, eighth, and ninth chapters; and others I am sure could easily make a selection on more scientific principles. There are, too, songs that seem to be a step removed from the more primitive types: there is the maze-like medley, "Bright sparkles," one phrase of which heads "The Black Belt"; the Easter carol, "Dust, dust and ashes"; the dirge, "My mother's took her flight and gone home"; and that burst of melody hovering over "The Passing of the First-Born"—"I hope my mother will be there in that beautiful world on high."

These represent a third step in the development of the slave song, of which "You may bury me in the East" is the first, and songs like "March on" (chapter six) and "Steal away" are the second. The first is African music, the second Afro-American, while the third is a blending of Negro music with the music heard in the foster land. The result is still distinctively Negro and the method of blending original, but the elements are both Negro and Caucasian. One might go further and find a fourth step in this development, where the songs of white America have been distinctively influenced by the slave songs or have incorporated whole phrases of Negro melody, as "Swanee River" and "Old Black Joe." Side by side, too, with the growth has gone the debasements and imitations—the Negro "minstrel" songs, many of the "gospel" hymns, and some of the contemporary "coon" songs,—a mass of music in which the novice may easily lose himself and never find the real Negro melodies.

In these songs, I have said, the slave spoke to the world. Such a message is naturally veiled and half articulate. Words and music have lost each other and new and cant phrases of a dimly understood theology have displaced the older sentiment. Once in a while we catch a strange word of an unknown tongue, as the "Mighty Myo," which figures as a river of death; more often slight words or mere doggerel are joined to music of singular sweetness. Purely secular songs are few in number, partly because many of them were turned into hymns by a change of words, partly because the frolics were seldom heard by the stranger, and the music less often caught. Of nearly all the songs, however, the music is distinctly sorrowful. The ten master songs I have mentioned tell in word and music of trouble and exile, of strife and hiding; they grope toward some unseen power and sigh for rest in the End.

The words that are left to us are not without interest, and, cleared of evident dross, they conceal much of real poetry and meaning beneath conventional theology and unmeaning rhapsody. Like all primitive folk, the slave stood near to Nature's heart. Life was a "rough and rolling sea" like the brown Atlantic of the Sea Islands; the "Wilderness" was the home of God, and the "lonesome valley" led to the way of life. "Winter'll soon be over," was the picture of life and death to a tropical imagination. The sudden wild thunderstorms of the South awed and impressed the Negroes,—at times the rumbling seemed to them "mournful," at times imperious:

"My Lord calls me,
  He calls me by the thunder,
  The trumpet sounds it in my soul."

The monotonous toil and exposure is painted in many words. One sees the ploughmen in the hot, moist furrow, singing:

"Dere's no rain to wet you,
  Dere's no sun to burn you,
  Oh, push along, believer,
  I want to go home."

The bowed and bent old man cries, with thrice-repeated wail:

"O Lord, keep me from sinking down,"

and he rebukes the devil of doubt who can whisper:

"Jesus is dead and God's gone away."

Yet the soul-hunger is there, the restlessness of the savage, the wail of the wanderer, and the plaint is put in one little phrase:

My soul wants something that's new, that's new

Over the inner thoughts of the slaves and their relations one with another the shadow of fear ever hung, so that we get but glimpses here and there, and also with them, eloquent omissions and silences. Mother and child are sung, but seldom father; fugitive and weary wanderer call for pity and affection, but there is little of wooing and wedding; the rocks and the mountains are well known, but home is unknown. Strange blending of love and helplessness sings through the refrain:

"Yonder 's my ole mudder,
  Been waggin' at de hill so long;
'Bout time she cross over,
  Git home bime-by."

Elsewhere comes the cry of the "motherless" and the "Farewell, farewell, my only child."

Love-songs are scarce and fall into two categories—the frivolous and light, and the sad. Of deep successful love there is ominous silence, and in one of the oldest of these songs there is a depth of history and meaning:

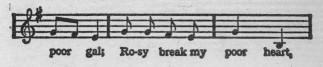

Poor Ro-sy, poor gal; Poor Ro-sy,

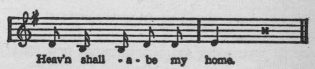

poor gal; Ro-sy break my poor heart,

Heav'n shall - a - be my home.

A black woman said of the song, "It can't be sung without a full heart and a troubled sperrit." The same voice sings here that sings in the German folk-song:

"Jetz Geh i' an's brunele, trink' aber net."

Of death the Negro showed little fear, but talked of it familiarly and even fondly as simply a crossing of the waters, perhaps—who knows?—back to his ancient forests again. Later days transfigured his fatalism, and amid the dust and dirt the toiler sang:

"Dust, dust and ashes, fly over my grave,
  But the Lord shall bear my spirit home."

The things evidently borrowed from the surrounding world undergo characteristic change when they enter the mouth of the slave. Especially is this true of Bible phrases. "Weep, O captive daughter of Zion," is quaintly turned into "Zion, weep-a-low," and the wheels of Ezekiel are turned every way in the mystic dreaming of the slave, till he says:

"There's a little wheel a-turnin' in-a-my heart."

As in olden time, the words of these hymns were improvised by some leading minstrel of the religious band. The circumstances of the gathering, however, the rhythm of the songs, and the limitations of allowable thought, confined the poetry for the most part to single or double lines, and they seldom were expanded to quatrains or longer tales, although there are some few examples of sustained efforts, chiefly paraphrases of the Bible. Three short series of verses have always attracted me,—the one that heads this chapter, of one line of which Thomas Wentworth Higginson has fittingly said, "Never, it seems to me, since man first lived and suffered was his infinite longing for peace uttered more plaintively." The second and third are descriptions of the Last Judgment,—the one a late improvisation, with some traces of outside influence:

"Oh, the stars in the elements are falling,
  And the moon drips away into blood,
  And the ransomed of the Lord are returning unto God,
  Blessed be the name of the Lord."

And the other earlier and homelier picture from the low coast lands:

"Michael, haul the boat ashore,
  Then you'll hear the horn they blow,
  Then you'll hear the trumpet sound,
  Trumpet sound the world around,
  Trumpet sound for rich and poor,
  Trumpet sound the Jubilee,
  Trumpet sound for you and me."

Through all the sorrow of the Sorrow Songs there breathes a hope—a faith in the ultimate justice of things. The minor cadences of despair change often to triumph and calm confidence. Sometimes it is faith in life, sometimes a faith in death, sometimes assurance of boundless justice in some fair world beyond. But whichever it is, the meaning is always clear: that sometime, somewhere, men will judge men by their souls and not by their skins. Is such a hope justified? Do the Sorrow Songs sing true?

The silently growing assumption of this age is that the probation of races is past, and that the backward races of to-day are of proven inefficiency and not worth the saving. Such an assumption is the arrogance of peoples irreverent toward Time and ignorant of the deeds of men. A thousand years ago such an assumption, easily possible, would have made it difficult for the Teuton to prove his right to life. Two thousand years ago such dogmatism, readily welcome, would have scouted the idea of blond races ever leading civilization. So woefully unorganized is sociological knowledge that the meaning of progress, the meaning of "swift" and "slow" in human doing, and the limits of human perfectability, are veiled, unanswered sphinxes on the shores of science. Why should Æschylus have sung two thousand years before Shakespeare was born? Why has civilization flourished in Europe, and flickered, flamed, and died in Africa? So long as the world stands meekly dumb before such questions, shall this nation proclaim its ignorance and unhallowed prejudices by denying freedom of opportunity to those who brought the Sorrow Songs to the Seats of the Mighty?

Your country? How came it yours? Before the Pilgrims landed we were here. Here we have brought our three gifts and mingled them with yours: a gift of story and song—soft, stirring melody in an ill-harmonized and unmelodious land; the gift of sweat and brawn to beat back the wilderness, conquer the soil, and lay the foundations of this vast economic empire two hundred years earlier than your weak hands could have done it; the third, a gift of the Spirit. Around us the history of the land has centred for thrice a hundred years; out of the nation's heart we have called all that was best to throttle and subdue all that was worst; fire and blood, prayer and sacrifice, have billowed over this people, and they have found peace only in the altars of the God of Right. Nor has our gift of the Spirit been merely passive. Actively we have woven ourselves with the very warp and woof of this nation, —we fought their battles, shared their sorrow, mingled our blood with theirs, and generation after generation have pleaded with a headstrong, careless people to despise not Justice, Mercy, and Truth, lest the nation be smitten with a curse. Our song, our toil, our cheer, and warning have been given to this nation in blood-brotherhood. Are not these gifts worth the giving? Is not this work and striving? Would America have been America without her Negro people?

Even so is the hope that sang in the songs of my fathers well sung. If somewhere in this whirl and chaos of things there dwells Eternal Good, pitiful yet masterful, then anon in His good time America shall rend the Veil and the prisoned shall go free. Free, free as the sunshine trickling down the morning into these high windows of mine, free as yonder fresh young voices welling up to me from the caverns of brick and mortar below—swelling with song, instinct with life, tremulous treble and darkening bass. My children, my little children, are singing to the sunshine, and thus they sing:

Let us cheer the wea-ry trav-el-ler,

Cheer the wea-ry trav-el-ler, Let us

cheer the wea-ry trav-el-ler A-

long the heav-en-ly way.

And the traveller girds himself, and sets his face toward the Morning, and goes his way.

ALAIN LOCKE (1886–1954)

As a philosopher, writer, critic, scholar in the social sciences, cultural mentor, and editor of The New Negro—*the landmark collection of writing which registered the arrival of the "Negro Renaissance"—Alain Locke was a major force and figure in the development of modern Negro American literature and culture. Born in Philadelphia, Alain LeRoy Locke was educated at the Philadelphia School of Pedagogy, at Oxford University (as a Rhodes scholar), and at the University of Berlin. He received his Ph.D. from Harvard in 1918. For forty-one years he was associated with Howard University, where he became Professor of Philosophy and head of the Department of Philosophy. He was Exchange Professor at Fisk University in 1927, Inter-American Exchange Professor to Haiti in 1943 and Visiting Professor at the University of Wisconsin in 1945–46. He founded the Associates in Negro Folk Education, edited its series of Bronze Booklets, and throughout his life combined studies in philosophy, education, the social sciences, and the arts with wide-ranging studies on the Negro in American culture. He published pioneer studies on Negro writers and literature and on African and Negro American art, drama, and music. Two of his essays of the 1920's follow: the first appeared in* The New Negro *in 1925 and the second appeared originally in* Carolina Magazine *and was subsequently published in the* Modern Library Anthology of American Negro Literature *(1929).*

The New Negro

In the last decade something beyond the watch and guard of statistics has happened in the life of the American Negro and the three norns who have traditionally presided over the Negro problem have a changeling in their laps. The Sociologist, the Philanthropist, the Race-leader are not unaware of the New Negro, but they are at a loss to account for him. He simply cannot be swathed in their formulae. For the younger generation is vibrant with a new psychology; the new spirit is awake in the masses, and under the very eyes of the professional observers is transforming what has been a perennial problem into the progressive phases of contemporary Negro life.

Could such a metamorphosis have taken place as suddenly as it has appeared to? The answer is no; not because the New Negro is not here, but because the Old Negro had long become more of a myth than a man. The Old Negro, we must remember, was a creature of moral debate and historical controversy. His has been a stock figure perpetuated as an historical fiction partly in innocent sentimentalism, partly in deliberate reactionism. The Negro himself has contributed his share to this through a sort of protective social mimicry forced upon him by the adverse circumstances of dependence. So for generations in the mind of America, the Negro has been more of a formula than a human being—a something to be argued about, condemned or defended, to be "kept down," or "in his place," or "helped up," to be worried with or worried over, harassed or patronized, a social bogey or a social burden. The thinking Negro even has been induced to share this same general attitude, to focus his attention on controversial issues, to see himself in the distorted perspective of a social problem. His shadow, so to speak, has been more real to him than his personality. Through having had to appeal from the unjust stereotypes of his oppressors and traducers to those of his liberators, friends and benefactors he has had to subscribe to the traditional positions from which his case has been viewed. Little true social or self-understanding has or could come from such a situation.

But while the minds of most of us, black and white, have thus burrowed in the trenches of the Civil War and Reconstruction, the actual march of development has simply flanked these positions, necessitating a sudden reorientation of view. We have not been watching in the right direction; set North and South on a sectional axis, we have not noticed the East till the sun has us blinking.

Recall how suddenly the Negro spirituals revealed themselves; suppressed for generations under the stereotypes of Wesleyan hymn harmony, secretive, half-ashamed, until the courage of being natural brought them out—and behold, there was folk-music. Similarly the mind of the Negro seems suddenly to have slipped from under the tyranny of social intimidation and to be shaking off the psychology of imitation and implied inferiority. By shedding the old chrysalis of the Negro problem we are achieving something like a spiritual emancipation. Until recently, lacking self-understanding, we have been almost as much of a problem to ourselves as we still are to others. But the decade that found us with a problem has left us with only a task. The multitude perhaps feels as yet only a strange relief and a new vague urge, but the thinking few know that in the reaction the vital inner grip of prejudice has been broken.

With this renewed self-respect and self-dependence, the life of the Negro community is bound to enter a new dynamic phase, the buoyancy from within compensating for whatever pressure there may be of conditions from without. The migrant masses, shifting from countryside to city, hurdle several generations of experience at a leap, but more important, the same thing happens spiritually in the life-attitudes and self-expression of the Young Negro, in his poetry, his art, his education and his new outlook, with the additional advantage, of course, of the poise and greater certainty of knowing what it is all about. From this comes the promise and warrant of a new leadership. As one of them has discerningly put it:

We have tomorrow
Bright before us
Like a flame.

Yesterday, a night-gone thing
A sun-down name.

And dawn today
Broad arch above the road we came.
We march!

This is what, even more than any "most creditable record of fifty years of freedom," requires that the Negro of to-day be seen through other than the dusty spectacles of past controversy. The day of "aunties," "uncles" and "mammies" is equally gone. Uncle Tom and Sambo have passed on, and even the "Colonel" and "George" play barnstorm rôles from which they escape with relief when the public spotlight is off. The popular melodrama has about played itself out, and it is time to scrap the fictions, garret the bogeys and settle down to a realistic facing of facts.

First we must observe some of the changes which since the traditional lines of opinion were drawn have rendered these quite obsolete. A main change has been, of course, that shift-

ing of the Negro population which has made the Negro problem no longer exclusively or even predominantly Southern.
Why should our minds remain sectionalized, when the problem itself no longer is? Then the trend of migration has not
only been toward the North and the Central Midwest, but
city-ward and to the great centers of industry—the problems
of adjustment are new, practical, local and not peculiarly racial. Rather they are an integral part of the large industrial
and social problems of our present-day democracy. And
finally, with the Negro rapidly in process of class differentia-
tion, if it ever was warrantable to regard and treat the Negro
en masse it is becoming with every day less possible, more
unjust and more ridiculous.

In the very process of being transplanted, the Negro is becoming transformed.

The tide of Negro migration, northward and city-ward, is
not to be fully explained as a blind flood started by the demands of war industry coupled with the shutting off of foreign migration, or by the pressure of poor crops coupled with
increased social terrorism in certain sections of the South and
Southwest. Neither labor demand, the boll-weevil nor the Ku
Klux Klan is a basic factor, however contributory any or all
of them may have been. The wash and rush of this human
tide on the beach line of the northern city centers is to be
explained primarily in terms of a new vision of opportunity,
of social and economic freedom, of a spirit to seize, even in
the face of an extortionate and heavy toll, a chance for the
improvement of conditions. With each successive wave of it,
the movement of the Negro becomes more and more a mass
movement toward the larger and the more democratic chance
—in the Negro's case a deliberate flight not only from countryside to city, but from medieval America to modern.

Take Harlem as an instance of this. Here in Manhattan is
not merely the largest Negro community in the world, but
the first concentration in history of so many diverse elements
of Negro life. It has attracted the African, the West Indian,
the Negro American; has brought together the Negro of the
North and the Negro of the South; the man from the city
and the man from the town and village; the peasant, the student, the business man, the professional man, artist, poet,
musician, adventurer and worker, preacher and criminal, ex-
ploiter and social outcast. Each group has come with its own
separate motives and for its own special ends, but their greatest experience has been the finding of one another. Proscription and prejudice have thrown these dissimilar elements into
a common area of contact and interaction. Within this area,

race sympathy and unity have determined a further fusing of sentiment and experience. So what began in terms of segregation becomes more and more, as its elements mix and react, the laboratory of a great race-welding. Hitherto, it must be admitted that American Negroes have been a race more in name than in fact, or to the exact, more in sentiment than in experience. The chief bond between them has been that of a common condition rather than a common consciousness; a problem in common rather than a life in common. In Harlem, Negro life is seizing upon its first chances for group expression and self-determination. It is—or promises at least to be—a race capital. That is why our comparison is taken with those nascent centers of folk-expression and self-determination which are playing a creative part in the world today. Without pretense to their political significance, Harlem has the same rôle to play for the New Negro as Dublin has had for the New Ireland or Prague for the New Czechoslovakia.

Harlem, I grant you, isn't typical—but it is significant, it is prophetic. No sane observer, however sympathetic to the new trend, would contend that the great masses are articulate as yet, but they stir, they move, they are more than physically restless. The challenge of the new intellectuals among them is clear enough—the "race radicals" and realists who have broken with the old epoch of philanthropic guidance, sentimental appeal and protest. But are we after all only reading into the stirrings of a sleeping giant the dreams of an agitator? The answer is in the migrating peasant. It is the "man farthest down" who is most active in getting up. One of the most characteristic symptoms of this is the professional man, himself migrating to recapture his constituency after a vain effort to maintain in some Southern corner what for years back seemed an established living and clientele. The clergyman following his errant flock, the physician or lawyer trailing his clients, supply the true clues. In a real sense it is the rank and file who are leading, and the leaders who are following. A transformed and transforming psychology permeates the masses.

When the racial leaders of twenty years ago spoke of developing race-pride and stimulating race-consciousness, and of the desirability of race solidarity, they could not in any accurate degree have anticipated the abrupt feeling that has surged up and now pervades the awakened centers. Some of the recognized Negro leaders and a powerful section of white opinion identified with "race work" of the older order have indeed attempted to discount this feeling as a "passing phase," an attack of "race nerves" so to speak, an "aftermath of the war," and the like. It has not abated, however, if we are to gauge by the present tone and temper of the Negro press, or by the shift in popular support from the officially recognized and orthodox spokesmen to those of the independent, popular, and often radical type who are unmistakable symptoms of a new order. It is a social disservice to blunt the fact that the Negro of the Northern centers has reached a stage where tutelage, even of the most interested and well-intentioned sort, must give place to new relationships, where positive self-direction must be reckoned with in ever increasing measure. The American mind must reckon with a fundamentally changed Negro.

The Negro too, for his part, has idols of the tribe to smash. If on the one hand the white man has erred in making the Negro appear to be that which would excuse or extenuate his treatment of him, the Negro, in turn, has too often unnecessarily excused himself because of the way he has been treated. The intelligent Negro of to-day is resolved not to make discrimination an extenuation for his shortcomings in performance, individual or collective; he is trying to hold himself at par, neither inflated by sentimental allowances nor depreciated by current social discounts. For this he must know himself and be known for precisely what he is, and for that reason he welcomes the new scientific rather than the old sentimental interest. Sentimental interest in the Negro has ebbed. We used to lament this as the falling off of our friends; now we rejoice and pray to be delivered both from self-pity and condescension. The mind of each racial group has had a bitter weaning, apathy or hatred on one side matching disillusionment or resentment on the other; but they face each other to-day with the possibility at least of entirely new mutual attitudes.

It does not follow that if the Negro were better known, he would be better liked or better treated. But mutual understanding is basic for any subsequent coöperation and adjustment. The effort toward this will at least have the effect of remedying in large part what has been the most unsatisfactory feature of our present stage of race relationships in America, namely the fact that the more intelligent and representative elements of the two race groups have at so many points got quite out of vital touch with one another.

The fiction is that the life of the races is separate, and increasingly so. The fact is that they have touched too closely at the unfavorable and too lightly at the favorable levels.

While inter-racial councils have sprung up in the South,

drawing on forward elements of both races, in the Northern cities manual laborers may brush elbows in their everyday work, but the community and business leaders have experienced no such interplay or far too little of it. These segments must achieve contact or the race situation in America becomes desperate. Fortunately this is happening. There is a growing realization that in social effort the co-operative basis must supplant long-distance philanthropy, and that the only safeguard for mass relations in the future must be provided in the carefully maintained contacts of the enlightened minorities of both race groups. In the intellectual realm a renewed and keen curiosity is replacing the recent apathy; the Negro is being carefully studied, not just talked about and discussed. In art and letters, instead of being wholly caricatured, he is being seriously portrayed and painted.

To all of this the New Negro is keenly responsive as an augury of a new democracy in American culture. He is contributing his share to the new social understanding. But the desire to be understood would never in itself have been sufficient to have opened so completely the protectively closed portals of the thinking Negro's mind. There is still too much possibility of being snubbed or patronized for that. It was rather the necessity for fuller, truer self-expression, the realization of the unwisdom of allowing social discrimination to segregate him mentally, and a counter-attitude to cramp and fetter his own living—and so the "spite-wall" that the intellectuals built over the "color-line" has happily been taken down. Much of this reopening of intellectual contacts has centered in New York and has been richly fruitful not merely in the enlarging of personal experience, but in the definite enrichment of American art and letters and in the clarifying of our common vision of the social tasks ahead.

The particular significance in the re-establishment of contact between the more advanced and representative classes is that it promises to offset some of the unfavorable reactions of the past, or at least to re-surface race contacts somewhat for the future. Subtly the conditions that are molding a New Negro are molding a new American attitude.

However, this new phase of things is delicate; it will call for less charity but more justice; less help, but infinitely closer understanding. This is indeed a critical stage of race relationships because of the likelihood, if the new temper is not understood, of engendering sharp group antagonism and a second crop of more calculated prejudice. In some quarters, it has already done so. Having weaned the Negro, public opinion cannot continue to paternalize. The Negro to-day is inevitably moving forward under the control largely of his own objectives. What are these objectives? Those of his outer life are happily already well and finally formulated, for they are none other than the ideals of American institutions and democracy. Those of his inner life are yet in process of formation, for the new psychology at present is more of a consensus of feeling than of opinion, of attitude rather than of program. Still some points seem to have crystallized.

Up to the present one may adequately describe the Negro's "inner objectives" as an attempt to repair a damaged group psychology and reshape a warped social perspective. Their realization has required a new mentality for the American Negro. And as it matures we begin to see its effects; at first, negative, iconoclastic, and then positive and constructive. In this new group psychology we note the lapse of sentimental appeal, then the development of a more positive self-respect and self-reliance; the repudiation of social dependence, and then the gradual recovery from hyper-sensitiveness and "touchy" nerves, the repudiation of the double standard of judgment with its special philanthropic allowances and then the sturdier desire for objective and scientific appraisal; and finally the rise from social disillusionment to race pride, from the sense of social debt to the responsibilities of social contribution, and offsetting the necessary working and commonsense acceptance of restricted conditions, the belief in ultimate esteem and recognition. Therefore the Negro to-day wishes to be known for what he is, even in his faults and shortcomings, and scorns a craven and precarious survival at the price of seeming to be what he is not. He resents being spoken of as a social ward or minor, even by his own, and to being regarded a chronic patient for the sociological clinic, the sick man of American Democracy. For the same reasons, he himself is through with those social nostrums and panaceas, the so-called "solutions" of his "problem," with which he and the country have been so liberally dosed in the past. Religion, freedom, education, money—in turn, he has ardently hoped for and peculiarly trusted these things; he still believes in them, but not in blind trust that they alone will solve his life-problem.

Each generation, however, will have its creed, and that of the present is the belief in the efficacy of collective effort, in race co-operation. This deep feeling of race is at present the mainspring of Negro life. It seems to be the outcome of the reaction to proscription and prejudice; an attempt, fairly successful on the whole, to convert a defensive into an offensive position, a handicap into an incentive. It is radical in tone, but not in purpose and only the most stupid forms of opposition, misunderstanding or persecution could make it otherwise. Of course, the thinking Negro has shifted a little toward the left with the world-trend, and there is an increasing group who affiliate with radical and liberal movements. But fundamentally for the present the Negro is radical on race matters, conservative on others, in other words, a "forced radical," a social protestant rather than a genuine radical. Yet under further pressure and injustice iconoclastic thought and motives will inevitably increase. Harlem's quixotic radicalisms call for their ounce of democracy to-day lest to-morrow they be beyond cure.

The Negro mind reaches out as yet to nothing but American wants, American ideas. But this forced attempt to build his Americanism on race values is a unique social experiment, and its ultimate success is impossible except through the fullest sharing of American culture and institutions. There should be no delusion about this. American nerves in sections unstrung with race hysteria are often fed the opiate that the trend of Negro advance is wholly separatist, and that the effect of its operation will be to encyst the Negro as a benign foreign body in the body politic. This cannot be—even if it were desirable. The racialism of the Negro is no limitation or reservation with respect to American life; it is only a constructive effort to build the obstructions in the stream of his progress into an efficient dam of social energy and power. Democracy itself is obstructed and stagnated to the extent that any of its channels are closed. Indeed they cannot be selectively closed. So the choice is not between one way for the Negro and another way for the rest, but between American institutions frustrated on the one hand and American ideals progressively fulfilled and realized on the other.

There is, of course, a warrantably comfortable feeling in being on the right side of the country's professed ideals. We realize that we cannot be undone without America's undoing. It is within the gamut of this attitude that the thinking Negro faces America, but with variations of mood that are if anything more significant than the attitude itself. Sometimes we have it taken with the defiant ironic challenge of McKay:

Mine is the future grinding down to-day
Like a great landslip moving to the sea,
Bearing its freight of débris far away
Where the green hungry waters restlessly
Heave mammoth pyramids, and break and roar
Their eerie challenge to the crumbling shore.

Sometimes, perhaps more frequently as yet, it is taken in the fervent and almost filial appeal and counsel of Weldon Johnson's:

O Southland, dear Southland!
Then why do you still cling
To an idle age and a musty page,
To a dead and useless thing?

But between defiance and appeal, midway almost between cynicism and hope, the prevailing mind stands in the mood of the same author's *To America*, an attitude of sober query and stoical challenge:

How would you have us, as we are?
  Or sinking 'neath the load we bear,
Our eyes fixed forward on a star,
  Or gazing empty at despair?

Rising or falling? Men or things?
  With dragging pace or footsteps fleet?
Strong, willing sinews in your wings,
  Or tightening chains about your feet?

More and more, however, an intelligent realization of the great discrepancy between the American social creed and the American social practice forces upon the Negro the taking of the moral advantage that is his. Only the steadying and sobering effect of a truly characteristic gentleness of spirit prevents the rapid rise of a definite cynicism and counter-hate and a defiant superiority feeling. Human as this reaction would be, the majority still deprecate its advent, and would gladly see it forestalled by the speedy amelioration of its causes. We wish our race pride to be a healthier, more positive achievement than a feeling based upon a realization of the shortcomings of others. But all paths toward the attainment of a sound social attitude have been difficult; only a relatively few enlightened minds have been able as the phrase puts it "to rise above" prejudice. The ordinary man has had until recently only a hard choice between the alternatives of supine and humiliating submission and stimulating but hurtful counter-prejudice. Fortunately from some inner, desperate resourcefulness has recently sprung up the simple expedient of fighting prejudice by mental passive resistance, in other words by trying to ignore it. For the few, this manna may perhaps be effective, but the masses cannot thrive upon it.

Fortunately there are constructive channels opening out

into which the balked social feelings of the American Negro can flow freely.

Without them there would be much more pressure and danger than there is. These compensating interests are racial but in a new and enlarged way. One is the consciousness of acting as the advance-guard of the African peoples in their contact with Twentieth Century civilization; the other, the sense of a mission of rehabilitating the race in world esteem from that loss of prestige for which the fate and conditions of slavery have so largely been responsible. Harlem, as we shall see, is the center of both these movements; she is the home of the Negro's "Zionism." The pulse of the Negro world has begun to beat in Harlem. A Negro newspaper carrying news material in English, French and Spanish, gathered from all quarters of America, the West Indies and Africa has maintained itself in Harlem for over five years. Two important magazines, both edited from New York, maintain their news and circulation consistently on a cosmopolitan scale. Under American auspices and backing, three pan-African congresses have been held abroad for the discussion of common interests, colonial questions and the future co-operative development of Africa. In terms of the race question as a world problem, the Negro mind has leapt, so to speak, upon the parapets of prejudice and extended its cramped horizons. In so doing it has linked up with the growing group consciousness of the dark-peoples and is gradually learning their common interests. As one of our writers has recently put it: "It is imperative that we understand the white world in its relations to the non-white world." As with the Jew, persecution is making the Negro international.

As a world phenomenon this wider race consciousness is a different thing from the much asserted rising tide of color. Its inevitable causes are not of our making. The consequences are not necessarily damaging to the best interests of civilization. Whether it actually brings into being new Armadas of conflict or argosies of cultural exchange and enlightenment can only be decided by the attitude of the dominant races in an era of critical change. With the American Negro, his new internationalism is primarily an effort to recapture contact with the scattered peoples of African derivation. Garveyism may be a transient, if spectacular, phenomenon, but the possible rôle of the American Negro in the future development of Africa is one of the most constructive and universally helpful missions that any modern people can lay claim to.

Constructive participation in such causes cannot help giving the Negro valuable group incentives, as well as increased prestige at home and abroad. Our greatest rehabilitation may possibly come through such channels, but for the present, more immediate hope rests in the revaluation by white and black alike of the Negro in terms of his artistic endowments and cultural contributions, past and prospective. It must be increasingly recognized that the Negro has already made very substantial contributions, not only in his folk-art, music especially, which has always found appreciation, but in larger, though humbler and less acknowledged ways. For generations the Negro has been the peasant matrix of that section of America which has most undervalued him, and here he has contributed not only materially in labor and in social patience, but spiritually as well. The South has unconsciously absorbed the gift of his folk-temperament. In less than half a generation it will be easier to recognize this, but the fact remains that a leaven of humor, sentiment, imagination and tropic nonchalance has gone into the making of the South from a humble, unacknowledged source. A second crop of the Negro's gifts promises still more largely. He now becomes a conscious contributor and lays aside the status of a beneficiary and ward for that of a collaborator and participant in American civilization. The great social gain in this is the releasing of our talented group from the arid fields of controversy and debate to the productive fields of creative expression. The especially cultural recognition they win should in turn prove the key to that revaluation of the Negro which must precede or accompany any considerable further betterment of race relationships. But whatever the general effect, the present generation will have added the motives of self-expression and spiritual development to the old and still unfinished task of making material headway and progress. No one who understandingly faces the situation with its substantial accomplishment or views the new scene with its still more abundant promise can be entirely without hope. And certainly, if in our lifetime the Negro should not be able to celebrate his full initiation into American democracy, he can at least, on the warrant of these things, celebrate the attainment of a significant and satisfying new phase of group development, and with it a spiritual Coming of Age.

The Negro in American Culture

The position of the Negro in American culture is indeed a paradox. It almost passes understanding how and why a group of people can be socially despised, yet at the same time artistically esteemed and culturally influential, can be both an oppressed minority and a dominant cultural force. Yet this is their position, at least at present. Some of the most characteristic American things are Negro or Negroid, derivatives of the folk life of this darker tenth of the population, and America at home basks in their influence, thrives upon their consumption and vulgarization, and abroad at least must accept their national representativeness. This because these things are among the most distinctive products of the American soil, and because too they have a contagious and almost irresistible hold upon human psychology—since, being soundly primitive, they are basically and universally human. Even now, much of what is characteristically Negro is representatively American; and as the contemporary cultural and artistic expression of the Negro spirit develops, this will be so more and more.

Unfortunately, but temporarily, what is best known are the vulgarizations; and of these "Jazz" and by-products are in the ascendancy. We must not, cannot, disclaim the origin and characteristic quality of "Jazz"; it is an important racial derivative. But it does not follow that it is spiritually representative. It is in the first place not a pure Negro folk thing, but a hybrid product of the reaction of the elements of Negro folk song and dance upon popular and general elements of contemporary American life. "Jazz" is one-third Negro folk idiom, one-third ordinary middle class American idea and sentiment, and one-third spirit of the "machine-age" which, more and more, becomes not American but Occidental. Because the basic color of the mixture is Negro, we attribute jazz, more largely than we should, to Negro life. Rather we should think of it this way,—jazz represents Negro life in its technical elements, American life in general in its intellectual content. This may seem an unwarrantable statement, and will remain so for those who only know American life superficially. The truth becomes evident, however, only to those who contrast the pure and serious forms of Negro art, which are less known, with the popular vulgarized forms which, with the modern vogue of jazz, are world-known. The serious folk art of the older Negro generation is best represented by the so-called "Spirituals," a body of real and genuine folk-song of great musical and spiritual importance; while the serious art which can best represent to the world the Negro of the present generation is contemporary Negro poetry. In this article, we shall use Negro poetry as a means of indicating the present cultural position of the Negro in American life.

Properly to do so, we should first see a little of the historical background. Slavery, for generations the lot of nine-tenths of the Negro population, put upon the Negro the conditions and stigma of a peasant class: conditions which as economic and civic handicaps and as race prejudice still hamper, in spite of considerable improvement, the position of the Negro masses, emancipated only since 1863. In spite of rapid assimilation of American standards and ways of life, and phenomenal educational advance (only 11 per cent of the Negro population is now illiterate), and in spite of much philanthropic interest and help from a minority of the white population, the general attitude of public opinion in America has set the Negro off to himself as a class apart. It has been an inconsistent ostracism from the beginning, even under the slave régime. For then, while the Negro was most despised, he was as domestic menial ensconced in the very heart of the family life of the landowning aristocracy; a situation which accounts in part for his rapid assimilation of American modes. Since emancipation, American race prejudice has been just as capricious; it has segregated the Negro socially but not culturally in the broad sense of the word culture, and while making him a submerged class economically and politically, has not isolated or differentiated his institutional life.

The consequence has been that the Negro today is a typical American with only a psychological sense of social difference; a minority that, having no political vent for its collective ambitions—since political participation and equal civil rights are the goal of its practical aspirations—has an enormous amount of accumulated self-determination. Social prejudice, which was meant to hamper the Negro,—and which has hampered him in economic, political and social ways,—has turned out to be a great spiritual discipline and a cultural blessing in disguise. For it has preserved the Negro sense of a peculiar folk-solidarity, preserved the peculiar folk-values and intensified their modes of expression; so that now they stand out in the rather colorless amalgam of the general population as the most colorful and distinctive spiritual things in American life. This is the root of the paradox we referred to at the beginning; the stone that was socially rejected in the practical aspects of the American democracy has become a corner stone spiritually in the making of a distinctive American culture. For when America began to tire of being culturally merely a province of Europe, and turned to the artistic development of native things, among the most distinctive to hand were the folk-things of the Negro which prejudice had isolated from the materializing and standardizing process of general American conditions.

This was the position that confronted the cultural nationalists in America a decade ago:—the aboriginal Indian things had been ruthlessly pushed aside and all but exterminated, the native white elements were for the most part different only in size, number and tempo from their European derivatives; and there, characteristically different and colorful, were the Negro folk-products,—an alluring, undeveloped source of native materials and local color. We had a wholesale adoption of these elements in popular dance and music; then as European appreciation pointed the way—(we must not forget the rôle of Dvořák, Delius and Darius Milhaud in this), a second wave of this influence spread to serious music. In another field, after a popular craze for "dialect poetry" led in the nineties by a Negro poet, Paul Laurence Dunbar, serious American poetry began with Vachel Lindsay to turn to jazz rhythms and background for inspiration. The climax of this movement, naturally, has been with the contemporary Negro poets whom we shall soon discuss. Then in the development of native American drama, Ridgely Torrence started a vogue for Negro folk-plays, and Edward Sheldon and Eugene O'Neill discovered the unique possibilities of the Negro problem-play, as "The Emperor Jones." Paul Green, late Pulitzer prize winner, discovered the importance of the Southern Negro folk-types in the series of plays which have made him a figure in the development of native American drama. Lately, too, a whole school of American fiction has been turning to the exploitation of the Negro milieu and its folk-values; one school with an exotic approach,—Ronald Firbank, Haldane McFall, Carl Van Vechten, and another still more important school of Southern realism, Ellen Glasgow, Julia Peterkin ("Green Thursday" and "Black April") climaxing with Du Bose Heyward's famous story of Charleston life, "Porgy." These have been supplemented later by a school of Negro writers of fiction, among which the recent successes of Claude McKay's "Home to Harlem," and Rudolph Fisher's "The Walls of Jericho," have given us, by all odds, the most representative Negro fiction up to date. We can thus trace the reasons why, in recent American art, the Negro has had proportionately more than his tenth share of space and influence, and how, as an unexpected but very appreciable gift to the national spiritual life,—a veritable treasure of the humble—the Negro elements have given new values and fresh momentum to the contemporary cultural self-expression of America.

But the greatest and most representative development of Negro folk-experience and its values must come from Negro artists themselves. This situation, after generations of artistic impotence except in folk-lore and folk-song, is now being capitalized by the young Negro intellectuals. And contemporary Negro poetry is its best articular expression. In it we can see more clearly than anywhere else the ideals and objectives of the "New Negro," and the movement for cultural self-expression that has been aptly termed the "Negro Renaissance." A Negro editor of the new school, Charles S. Johnson, says: "The new racial poetry of the Negro is the expression of something more than experimentation in a new technique. It marks the birth of a new racial consciousness and self-conception. It is first of all a frank acceptance of race, but the recognition of this difference without the usual implications of disparity. It lacks apology, the wearying appeals to pity, and the conscious philosophy of defense. In being itself it reveals its greatest charm; and in accepting its distinctive life, invests it with a new meaning." Mr. Johnson is further right in saying that "the poetry of Langston Hughes is without doubt the finest expression of this new Negro poetry. It is also a significant part of the poetry of new America, recording its beauty in its own idiom." Langston Hughes has written this manifesto of the movement: "We younger Negro artists who create now intend to express our individual dark-skinned selves without fear or shame. If white people are pleased we are glad. If they are not, it does not matter. We know we are beautiful. And ugly too. The tom-tom cries and the tom-tom laughs. If colored people are pleased we are glad. If they are not, their displeasure doesn't matter either. We build our temples for tomorrow, strong as we know how, and we stand on top of the mountain, free within ourselves." This is the young Negro's spiritual declaration of independence; and marks the attainment, nearly two generations after physical freedom, of spiritual emancipation.

But what, we may now ask, is Negro Poetry? Certainly not merely poetry by Negro writers. There is a considerable amount of abstract lyricism on universal themes, written by Negro poets. This vein of expression serves as a demostration of the Negro's participation in the national culture common to all, of his share in modern thought in fact. Neither is Negro poetry the older dialect poetry of a peasant patois and a Ghetto world of restricted and genre types and sentiment. Negro poetry today represents many strains, having only one common factor,—the fact of reflecting some expression of the emotional sense of race or some angle of the peculiar group tradition and experience. In the case of the American Negro the sense of race is stronger than that of nationality; and in some form or other is a primary factor in the consciousness of the Negro poet.

Race has many diverse ways of reflecting itself in the equation of life; each temperament reflects it just a bit differently and reacts to it just a bit differently. We too frequently neglect this important point, that the racial factors may reside in the overtones of artistic expression and that there is often more of race in its sublimations than in its crude reportorial expression. Of course, to begin with, we have the direct portrayal of Negro folk-life and folk-types, with their characteristic idioms of thought, feeling and speech, but contemporary Negro poetry has opened up many other veins of subtler racial expression. There is, for example, the poetry of derived emotional coloring that merely reflects in a secondary way the tempo and moods of Negro life, the school that reflects not a race substance but a race temperament. There is too the vein that emphasizes the growing historical sense of a separate cultural tradition; a racialist trend that is the equivalent of a nationalist background and spirit in Europe. Again, we have the poetry of personal expression in which the racial situations induce a personal reaction and a particular philosophy of life. Finally we have the vein that directly expresses the sense of group and its common experiences, and partly as poetry of social protest, partly as poetry of social exhortation and propaganda, directly capitalizes the situations and dilemmas of racial experience. For the analysis of Negro poetry these strains of race consciousness and their modes of expression are more important, if anything, than the formal and technical distinctions of a poetic school. It is upon this basis, at last, that we shall proceed in this present analysis.

A basic point for the interpretation of contemporary Negro poetry is the realization that the traditional dialect school is now pretty generally regarded as the least representative in any intimate racial sense. To the Negro poet of today, it represents a "minstrel tradition," imposed from without and reflecting, even in its apparent unsophistication, conscious posing and self-conscious sentimentality. If Negro poetry of this type had addressed primarily its own audience, it would have been good poetry in the sense that the "Spirituals" are. But for the most part it has been a "play-up" to set stereotypes and an extraverted appeal to the amusement complex of the overlords. Rarely, as in the case of a true folk-ballad or work-song, lullaby or love-song, do we have in Negro dialect poetry the genuine brew of naïve folk-products.

Rather have these things presented the Negro spirit in distorted, histrionic modifications, tainted with the attitude of "professional entertainment." Of course, one may argue, the poetry of the Troubadours was that of professional entertainers,—and so it was, but with this difference—that the tradition was completely shared by the audiences and that there was no dissociation of attitude between those who sang and those who listened.

So in the revision of the dialect tradition which the younger Negro poets are trying to bring about, there is first of all James Weldon Johnson's well-known criticism of dialect as a limited medium of expression, "with but two stops,—pathos and humor." There is also the attempt to reinstate the authentic background, and the naïve point of view, as is successfully achieved at times in Mr. Johnson's "sermons in verse" of the "God's Trombones" volume. Here we have the folk-spirit attempting at least the "epic rôle," and speaking in the grand manner, as in the Judgment Day sermon of the old ante-bellum Negro preacher:

Too late, sinner! Too late!
Good bye, sinner! Good bye!
In hell, sinner! In hell!
Beyond the reach of the love of God.

And I hear a voice, crying, crying;
Time shall be no more!
Time shall be no more!
Time shall be no more!
And the sun will go out like a candle in the wind,
The moon will turn to dripping blood,
The stars will fall like cinders,
And the sea will burn like tar;
And the earth shall melt away and be dissolved,
And the sky will roll up like a scroll.
With a wave of his hand God will blot out time,
And start the wheel of eternity.

Sinner, oh, sinner,
Where will you stand
In that great day when God's a-going to rain down fire?

The contemporary dialect school insists on true and objective folk-values: though not always on the serious, bardic note which is sounded here. But even in comic portrayal the younger school tries equally to purge the false sentimentality and clownishness, and has been successful. The folk-lyrics of Langston Hughes have spontaneous moods and rhythms, and

carry irresistible conviction. They are our really most successful efforts up to this date to recapture the folk-soul; he ranges
from the deep spirituality of:

At de feet o' Jesus,
Sorrow like a sea.
Lordy, let yo' mercy
Come driftin' down on me.

At de feet o' Jesus,
At yo' feet I stand
O, ma little Jesus,
Please reach out yo' hand—

to the quizzical humor of

I'm gonna walk to de graveyard
'Hind ma friend, Miss Cora Lee.
Gonna walk to de graveyard
'Hind ma dear friend, Cora Lee,
Cause when I'm dead some
Body'll have to walk behind me.

And again to the homely, secular folkliness of

De railroad bridge's
A sad song in de air.
De railroad bridge's
A sad song in de air.
Ever' time de trains pass
I wants to go somewhere.

This work of Hughes in the folk-forms has started up an
entire school of younger Negro poetry: principally in the
blues form and in the folk-ballad vein. It is the latter that
seems to me most promising, in spite of the undeniable interest of the former in bringing into poetry some of the song
and dance rhythms of the Negro. But this is, after all, a technical element: it is the rich substance of Negro life that
promises to rise in recreated outlines from the folk-ballads of
the younger writers. And much as the popular interest in the
preservation of this peasant material owes to Paul Laurence
Dunbar, to "When Malindy Sings" and "When de Co'n
Pone's Hot," nevertheless there is no comparison in authenticity or naïve beauty in the more objective lyrics of today.
For example, Lucy Williams' "No'thboun' ":

O'de wurl' ain't flat,
An' de wurl' ain't round

H'its one long strip
Hangin' up an' down—
Jes' Souf an' Norf;
Jes' Norf an' Souf.
Since Norf is up
An' Souf is down,
An' Hebben is up,
I'm upward boun'.

Or Joseph Cotter's "Tragedy of Pete" or Sterling Brown's
"Odyssey of Big Boy" or "Maumee Ruth." As a matter of
fact, this latter poet is, with Hughes, a genius of folk-values,
the most authentic evocation of the homely folk-soul. His importance warrants quotation at length. "Tornado Blue," contemporary though it is, is graphically authentic:

Black wind came aspeedin' down de river from de Kansas plains,
Black wind came aspeedin' down de river from de Kansas plains,
Black wind came aroarin' like a flock of giant aeroplanes.

Destruction was adrivin' it, and close beside was Fear.
Destruction drivin', pa'dner at his side was Fear,
Grinnin' Death and skinny Sorrow was abringin' up de rear. . . .

Newcomers dodged de mansions, an' knocked on de po' folks, do'.
Dodged most of de mansions, an' knocked down de po' folks' do'.
Never knew us po' folks so popular befo'.

Foun' de moggidge unpaid, foun' de insurance long past due,
Moggidge unpaid, de insurance very long pas' due,
De home we wukked so hard fo' goes back to de Fay an' Jew.

"Memphis Blues" is inimitably fine:

Nineveh. Tyre.
Babylon,
Not much lef'
Of either one.
All dese cities
Ashes and rust
De wind sings sperrichals
Through deir dus'.
Was another Memphis
'Mongst de olden days,
Done been destroyed
In many ways. . . .
Dis here Memphis
It may go.
Floods may drown it,
Tornado blow,
Mississippi wash it

Down to sea—
Like de other Memphis in
History.

The modern dialect school—if it may so be styled—has thus
developed a simplicity and power unknown to the earlier dialect writers, and has revealed a psychology so much more
profound and canny than the peasant types with which we
were so familiar and by which we were so amused and ca-
joled that we are beginning to doubt today the authenticity of
what for years has passed as the typical Negro.

Another remove from the plain literal transcription of
folk-life is the work of the "Jazz school," which as a matter
of fact is not native in origin. Vachel Lindsay it was who
brought it into prominence at a time when it was only a submerged and half-inarticulate motive in Negro doggerel.
Today it too often degenerates back into this mere trickery of
syncopation. Yet there is powerful and fresh poetic technique
in its careful transposition to poetic idiom. But it will never
come into its own with an eye-reading public or until its close
competitor, the school of free verse, begins to lose some of its
vogue. For essentially it is not a school of irregular rhythm
like the free verse technique, but a more varied and quantita-
tive scansion based on musical stresses and intervals inseparable from the ear control of chant and oral delivery. Only
elaborate analysis will do it justice, but an obvious and masterful example will have to suffice us in a quotation from
Jean Toomer:

Pour, O pour that parting soul in song,
O pour it in the sawdust glow of night,
Into the velvet pine-smoke air to-night,
And let the valley carry it along.
And let the valley carry it along. . . .

O land and soil, red soil and sweet gum-tree,
So scant of grass, so profligate of pines,
Now just before an epoch's sun declines,
Thy son, in time, I have returned to thee,
Thy son, I have in time returned to thee.

There is more Negro rhythm here, and in a line like "Caroling softly souls of slavery," than in all the more exaggerated
jazz of the sensationalists, black and white, who beat the
bass-drum and trapping cymbals of American jazz rather
than the throbbing tom-tom and swaying lilt of the primitive
voice and body surcharged with escaping emotion. Negro
rhythms, even in their gay moods, are rhapsodic; they quiver

more than they clash, they glide more than they march. So except in occasional patches, the rhythmic expression of Negro idioms in poetry awaits a less sensation-loving audience than we now have, and subtler musicianship than even our contemporary poets have yet attained.

We come now to the more sophisticated expressions of race in American Negro poetry. For a long while the racial sense of the Negro poet was hectic and forced: it was self-consciously racial rather than normally so. These were the days of rhetoric and apostrophe. The emotional identification was at best dramatic, and often melodramatic. As with the greater group-pride and assurance of the present-day Negro, race becomes more of an accepted fact, his racial feelings are less constrained. Countee Cullen's calmly stoical sonnet "From the Dark Tower," Arna Bontemps' "A Black Man Talks of Reaping," Langston Hughes' "Dream Variation" or "The Negro Speaks of Rivers" are characteristic now. Yesterday it was the rhetorical flush of partisanship, challenged and on the defensive. This was the patriotic stage through which we had to pass. Nothing is more of a spiritual gain in the life of the Negro than the quieter assumption of his group identity and heritage; and contemporary Negro poetry registers this incalculable artistic and social gain. Occasionally dramatic still, and to advantage, as in Cullen's "Simon the Cyrenian Speaks" or Lewis Alexander's sonnets "Africa" and "The Dark Brother," the current acceptance of race is quiet with deeper spiritual identification and supported by an undercurrent of faith rather than a surface of challenging pride.

Thus, as in Gwendolyn Bennett's:

I love you for your brownness
And the rounded darkness of your breast.
I love you for the breaking sadness in your voice
And shadows where your wayward eyelids rest. . . .

Oh, little brown girl, born for sorrow's mate,
Keep all you have of queenliness,
Forgetting that you once were slave,
And let your full lips laugh at Fate!

Or again, Countee Cullen's:

My love is dark as yours is fair,
Yet lovelier I hold her
Than listless maids with pallid hair,
And blood that's thin and colder.

You-proud-and-to-be-pitied one,

Gaze on her and despair;
Then seal your lips until the sun
Discovers one as fair.

A subtler strain of race consciousness flows in a more mystical sense of race that is coming to be a favorite mood of Negro poetry. This school was born in the lines of Claude McKay to "The Harlem Dancer":

But looking at her falsely smiling face,
I knew herself was not in that strange place.

This mood springs from the realization that the Negro experience has bred something mystical and strangely different in the Negro soul. It is a sublimation of the fact of race, conjured up nowhere more vividly than in these lines of Langston Hughes:

I've known rivers:
Ancient, dusky rivers.
My soul has grown deep like the rivers.

However, this mystical transposition of race into pure feeling is often so sublimated as not to be explicit at all: many a reader would not detect it in the following two poems, except as it was pointed out to him as a veiled statement of racial emotion or racial experience. Lewis Alexander's "Transformation" refers to racial largesse and Negro social forgiveness:

I return the bitterness,
Which you gave to me;
When I wanted loveliness
Tantalant and free.

I return the bitterness.
It is washed by tears;
Now it is a loveliness
Garnished through the years.

I return it loveliness,
Having made it so;
For I wore the bitterness
From it long ago.

This is all the more effective because it might just as well be a romantic lyric of unrequited love or a poem of Christian forgiveness; though very obviously it is the old miracle of the deepest particularity finding the universal. The same is true, I think, of another fine lyric, "I Think I See Him There," by

Waring Cuney that almost needs the conscious recall of the Negro spiritual

Were you there
When they nailed Him to the cross

to sense the background of its particular Negro intensity of feeling and compassion:

I think I see Him there
With a stern dream on His face
I see Him there—
Wishing they would hurry
The last nail in place.
And I wonder, had I been there,
Would I have doubted too?
Or would the dream have told me,
What this man speaks is true.

One would, of course, not foolishly claim for the race a monopoly of this sort of spiritual discipline and intensification of mood, but at the same time there is no more potent and potential source of it in all modern experience.

We next come to that strain of Negro poetry that reflects social criticism. With the elder generation, this strain was prominent, more so even than today, but it began and ended in humanitarian and moral appeal. It pled for human rights and recognition, was full of pathos and self-pity, and threatened the wrath of God, but in no very commanding way. Finally in bitter disillusionment it turned to social protest and revolt. The challenge vibrated within our own generation to the iron notes and acid lines of Claude McKay. Weldon Johnson's title poem, "Fifty Years and After," represents a transition point between the anti-slavery appeal and the radical threat. To the extent that the radical challenge is capable of pure poetry, Claude McKay realized it. But contemporary Negro poetry has found an even more effective weapon and defense than McKay's

If we must die—let it not be like hogs
Hunted and penned in an inglorious spot.

Or the mood of his terrific indictment, "The Lynching":

All night a bright and solitary star
Hung pitifully o'er the swinging char.
Day dawned, and soon the mixed crowds came to view
The ghastly body swaying in the sun:

The women thronged to look, but never a one
Showed sorrow in her eyes of steely blue;
And little lads, lynchers that were to be,
Danced round the dreadful thing in fiendish glee.

For Negro protest has found a true catharsis in a few inspired notes, and has discovered the strength of poetic rather
than intellectual irony. As a point of view this promises perhaps a more persuasive influence than any literary and artistic force yet brought to bear upon the race question in all the
long debate of generations. Certainly we have that note in
Langston Hughes' "Song for a Dark Girl":

Way down South in Dixie
(Break the heart of me)
They hung my black young lover
To a cross-roads tree.

Way down South in Dixie
(Bruised body high in air)
I asked the white Lord Jesus
What was the use of prayer?

Way down South in Dixie
(Break the heart of me)
Love is a naked shadow
On a gnarled and naked tree.

Finally we come to the most sophisticated of all race motives
—the conscious and deliberate threading back of the historic
sense of group tradition to the cultural backgrounds of Africa. Undoubtedly this motive arose in a purely defensive and
imitative reaction. But it has grown stronger and more positive year by year. Africa is naturally romantic. It is poetic
capital of the first order, even apart from the current mode
of idealizing the primitive and turning toward it in the reaction from the boredom of ultra-sophistication. There is some
of this Caucasian strain in the Negro poet's attitude toward
Africa at the present time. But it is fortunately not dominant
with the Negro poet. It is interesting to notice the different
approaches from which the younger Negro poets arrive at a
spiritual espousal of Africa. Of course, with the minor poetical talents, it is rhetorical and melodramatically romantic, as
it has always been. But our better poets are above this. Mr.
Cullen, who has a dormant but volcanically potential "pagan-
ism of blood"—(he himself puts it, "My chief problem has
been that of reconciling a Christian upbringing with a pagan
inclination")—is torn between the dilemma of the primitive

and the sophisticated in more poems than the famous "Heritage" which dramatizes the conflict so brilliantly. For him the African mood comes atavistically, and with something of a sense of pursuing Furies: he often eulogizes the ancestral spirits in order to placate them:

So I lie, who find no peace
Night or day, no slight release
From the unremittent beat
Made by cruel padded feet
Walking through my body's street.
Up and down they go, and back,
Beating out a jungle track.

But if Cullen has given us the exotic, emotional look on the race past, Hughes has given us what is racially more significant,—a franker, more spiritual loyalty, without sense of painful choice or contradiction, a retrospective recall that is intimate and natural. For him,

We should have a land of trees
Bowed down with chattering parrots
Brilliant as the day,
And not this land where birds are gray.

The moods of Africa, the old substances of primitive life, are for this growing school of thought a precious heritage, acceptable as a new artistic foundation; the justification of the much discussed racial difference, a source of new inspiration in the old Antæan strength. But if there is to be any lasting restatement of the African tradition, it cannot be merely retrospective. That is why even this point of view must merge into a transposition of the old elemental values to modern modes of insight. This is just on the horizon edge in Negro poetry and art, and is one of the goals of racialism in the new æsthetic of Negro life. No better advance statement has been made than Mae Cowdery's lines:

I will take from the hearts
Of black men—
Prayers their lips
Are 'fraid to utter
And turn their coarseness
Into a beauty of the jungle
Whence they came.

If and when this is achieved the last significance of race in our art and poetry will have manifested itself beyond question or challenge.

To trace Negro poetry in the way we have done, does some necessary violence to the unity of individual writers who combine several strands in their poetic temperaments. It also overlooks some of the purely universal and general poetry which others have contributed. But it will give some definite impression of the recent racial and cultural revival which Negro poets are expressing and of the interesting and unique developments that the interaction of the white and black races in America is producing. And incontestably the artistic product of this generation gauges the rising tide of Negro culture and the deep artistic potentialities of Negro art. The position of the Negro in American culture today is strategic and promising; it is his spiritual recompense for generations of long-suffering and will for some generations yet furnish the basis of his contribution to the spiritual treasury of the nation.

RICHARD WRIGHT (1908–1960)

A biographical note on Richard Wright appears in the Fiction section (see pp. 113–114). The following is Richard Wright's full critical statement on his novel, Native Son. *It was first delivered as a lecture in a New York Public Library in Harlem, a part of it appeared in* The Saturday Review of Literature (*June, 1940*), *and subsequently it was published as a pamphlet.*

How "Bigger" Was Born

I am not so pretentious as to imagine that it is possible for me to account completely for my own book, *Native Son*. But I am going to try to account for as much of it as I can, the sources of it, the material that went into it, and my own years' long changing attitude toward that material.

In a fundamental sense, an imaginative novel represents the merging of two extremes; it is an intensely intimate expression on the part of a consciousness couched in terms of the most objective and commonly known events. It is at once something private and public by its very nature and texture. Confounding the author who is trying to lay his cards on the table is the dogging knowledge that his imagination is a kind of community medium of exchange: what he has read, felt, thought, seen, and remembered is translated into extensions as impersonal as a worn dollar bill.

The more closely the author thinks of why he wrote, the more he comes to regard his imagination as a kind of self-generating cement which glued his facts together, and his emotions as a kind of dark and obscure designer of those facts. Always there is something that is just beyond the tip of the tongue that could explain it all. Usually, he ends up by discussing something far afield, an act which incites skepticism and suspicion in those anxious for a straight-out explanation.

Yet the author is eager to explain. But the moment he makes the attempt his words falter, for he is confronted and defied by the inexplicable array of his own emotions. Emotions are subjective and he can communicate them only when he clothes them in objective guise; and how can he ever be so arrogant as to know when he is dressing up the right emotion in the right Sunday suit? He is always left with the uneasy notion that maybe *any* objective drapery is as good as *any* other for any emotion.

And the moment he does dress up an emotion, his mind is confronted with the riddle of that "dressed up" emotion, and he is left peering with eager dismay back into the dim reaches of his own incommunicable life. Reluctantly, he comes to the conclusion that to account for his book is to account for his life, and he knows that that is impossible. Yet, some curious, wayward motive urges him to supply the answer, for there is the feeling that his dignity as a living being is challenged by something within him that is not understood.

So, at the outset, I say frankly that there are phases of *Native Son* which I shall make no attempt to account for. There are meanings in my book of which I was not aware until they literally spilled out upon the paper. I shall sketch the outline of how I *consciously* came into possession of the materials that went into *Native Son*, but there will be many things I shall omit, not because I want to, but simply because I don't know them.

The birth of Bigger Thomas goes back to my childhood, and there was not just one Bigger, but many of them, more than I could count and more than you suspect. But let me start with the first Bigger, whom I shall call Bigger No. 1.

When I was a bareheaded, barefoot kid in Jackson, Mississippi, there was a boy who terrorized me and all of the boys I played with. If we were playing games, he would saunter up and snatch from us our balls, bats, spinning tops, and marbles. We would stand around pouting, sniffling, trying to keep back our tears, begging for our playthings. But Bigger would refuse. We never demanded that he give them back; we were afraid, and Bigger was bad. We had seen him clout boys when he was angry and we did not want to run that risk. We never recovered our toys unless we flattered him and made him feel that he was superior to us. Then, perhaps, if he felt like it, he condescended, threw them at us and then gave each of us a swift kick in the bargain, just to make us feel his utter contempt.

That was the way Bigger No.1 lived. His life was a continuous challenge to others. At all times he *took* his way, right or wrong, and those who contradicted him had him to fight. And never was he happier than when he had someone cornered and at his mercy; it seemed that the deepest meaning of his squalid life was in him at such times.

I don't know what the fate of Bigger No.1 was. His swaggering personality is swallowed up somewhere in the amnesia of my childhood. But I suspect that his end was violent. Anyway, he left a marked impression upon me; maybe it was because I longed secretly to be like him and was afraid. I don't know.

If I had known only one Bigger I would not have written *Native Son*. Let me call the next one Bigger No.2; he was about seventeen and tougher than the first Bigger. Since I, too, had grown older, I was a little less afraid of him. And the hardness of this Bigger No.2 was not directed toward me or the other Negroes, but toward the whites who ruled the South. He bought clothes and food on credit and would not pay for them. He lived in the dingy shacks of the white landlords and refused to pay rent. Of course, he had no money, but neither did we. We did without the necessities of life and starved ourselves, but he never would. When we asked him why he acted as he did, he would tell us (as though we were little children in a kindergarten) that the white folks had everything and he had nothing. Further, he would tell us that we were fools not to get what we wanted while we were alive in this world. We would listen and silently agree. We longed to believe and act as he did, but we were afraid. We were Southern Negroes and we were hungry and we wanted to live, but we were more willing to tighten our belts than risk conflict. Bigger No.2 wanted to live and he did; he was in prison the last time I heard from him.

There was Bigger No.3, whom the white folks called a "bad nigger." He carried his life in his hands in a literal fashion. I once worked as a ticket-taker in a Negro movie house (all movie houses in' Dixie are Jim Crow; there are movies for whites and movies for blacks), and many times Bigger No.3 came to the door and gave my arm a hard pinch and walked into the theater. Resentfully and silently, I'd nurse my bruised arm. Presently, the proprietor would come over and ask how things were going, I'd point into the darkened theater and say: "Bigger's in there." "Did he pay?" the proprietor would ask. "No, sir," I'd answer. The proprietor would pull down the corners of his lips and speak through his teeth: "We'll kill that goddamn nigger one of these days." And the episode would end right there. But later on Bigger No.3 was killed during the days of Prohibition: while delivering liquor to a customer he was shot through the back by a white cop.

And then there was Bigger No.4, whose only law was death. The Jim Crow laws of the South were not for him. But as he laughed and cursed and broke them, he knew that some day he'd have to pay for his freedom. His rebellious spirit made him violate all the taboos and consequently he always oscillated between moods of intense elation and depression. He was never happier than when he had outwitted some foolish custom, and he was never more melancholy than when brooding over the impossibility of his ever being free. He had no job, for he regarded digging ditches for fifty cents a day as slavery. "I can't live on that," he would say. Ofttimes I'd find him reading a book; he would stop and in a joking, wistful, and cynical manner ape the antics of the white folks. Generally, he'd end his mimicry in a depressed state and say: "The white folks won't let us do nothing." Bigger No.4 was sent to the asylum for the insane.

Then there was Bigger No.5, who always rode the Jim Crow streetcars without paying and sat wherever he pleased. I remember one morning his getting into a streetcar (all streetcars in Dixie are divided into two sections: one section is for whites and is labeled——FOR WHITES; the other section is for Negroes and is labeled—FOR COLORED) and sitting in the white section. The conductor went to him and said:

"Come on, nigger. Move over where you belong. Can't you read?" Bigger answered: "Naw, I can't read." The conductor flared up: "Get out of that seat!" Bigger took out his knife, opened it, held it nonchalantly in his hand, and replied: "Make me." The conductor turned red, blinked, clenched his fists, and walked away, stammering: "The goddam scum of the earth!" A small angry conference of white men took place in the front of the car and the Negroes sitting in the Jim Crow section overheard: "That's that Bigger Thomas nigger and you'd better leave 'im alone." The Negroes experienced an intense flash of pride and the streetcar moved on its journey without incident. I don't know what happened to Bigger No.5. But I can guess.

The Bigger Thomases were the only Negroes I know of who consistently violated the Jim Crow laws of the South and got away with it, at least for a sweet brief spell. Eventually, the whites who restricted their lives made them pay a terrible price. They were shot, hanged, maimed, lynched, and generally hounded until they were either dead or their spirits broken.

There were many variations to this behavioristic pattern. Later on I encountered other Bigger Thomases who did not react to the locked-in Black Belts with this same extremity and violence. But before I use Bigger Thomas as a springboard for the examination of milder types, I'd better indicate more precisely the nature of the environment that produced these men, or the reader will be left with the impression that they were essentially and organically bad.

In Dixie there are two worlds, the white world and the black world, and they are physically separated. There are white schools and black schools, white churches and black churches, white businesses and black businesses, white graveyards and black graveyards, and, for all I know, a white God and a black God. . . .

This separation was accomplished after the Civil War by the terror of the Ku Klux Klan, which swept the newly freed Negro through arson, pillage, and death out of the United States Senate, the House of Representatives, the many state legislatures, and out of the public, social, and economic life of the South. The motive for this assault was simple and urgent. The imperialistic tug of history had torn the Negro from his African home and had placed him ironically upon the most fertile plantation areas of the South; and, when the Negro was freed, he outnumbered the whites in many of these fertile areas. Hence, a fierce and bitter struggle took place to keep the ballot from the Negro, for had he had a chance to vote, he would have automatically controlled the richest lands of the South and with them the social, political, and economic destiny of a third of the Republic. Though the South is politically a part of America, the problem that faced her was peculiar and the struggle between the whites and the blacks after the Civil War was in essence a struggle for power, ranging over thirteen states and involving the lives of tens of millions of people.

But keeping the ballot from the Negro was not enough to hold him in check; disfranchisement had to be supplemented by a whole panoply of rules, taboos, and penalties designed not only to insure peace (complete submission), but to guarantee that no real threat would ever arise. Had the Negro lived upon a common territory, separate from the bulk of the white population, this program of oppression might not have assumed such a brutal and violent form. But this war took place between people who were neighbors, whose homes adjoined, whose farms had common boundaries. Guns and disfranchisement, therefore, were not enough to make the black neighbor keep his distance. The white neighbor decided to limit the amount of education his black neighbor could receive; decided to keep him off the police force and out of the local national guards; to segregate him residentially; to Jim Crow him in public places; to restrict his participation in the professions and jobs; and to build up a vast, dense ideology of racial superiority that would justify any act of violence taken against him to defend white dominance; and further, to condition him to hope for little and to receive that little without rebelling.

But, because the blacks were so *close* to the very civilization which sought to keep them out, because they could not *help* but react in some way to its incentives and prizes, and because the very tissue of their consciousness received its tone and timbre from the strivings of that dominant civilization, oppression spawned among them a myriad variety of reactions, reaching from outright blind rebellion to a sweet, otherworldly submissiveness.

In the main, this delicately balanced state of affairs has not greatly altered since the Civil War, save in those parts of the South which have been industrialized or urbanized. So volatile and tense are these relations that if a Negro rebels against rule and taboo, he is lynched and the reason for the lynching is usually called "rape," that catchword which has garnered such vile connotations that it can raise a mob anywhere in the South pretty quickly, even today.

Now for the variations in the Bigger Thomas pattern.

Some of the Negroes living under these conditions got religion, felt that Jesus would redeem the void of living, felt that the more bitter life was in the present the happier it would be in the hereafter. Others, clinging still to that brief glimpse of post-Civil War freedom, employed a thousand ruses and stratagems of struggle to win their rights. Still others projected their hurts and longings into more naive and mundane forms —blues, jazz, swing—and, without intellectual guidance, tried to build up a compensatory nourishment for themselves. Many labored under hot suns and then killed the restless ache with alcohol. Then there were those who strove for an education, and when they got it, enjoyed the financial fruits of it in the style of their bourgeois oppressors. Usually they went hand in hand with the powerful whites and helped to keep their groaning brothers in line, for that was the safest course of action. Those who did this called themselves "leaders." To give you an idea of how completely these "leaders" worked with those who oppressed, I can tell you that I lived the first seventeen years of my life in the South without so much as hearing of or seeing one act of rebellion from *any* Negro, save the Bigger Thomases.

But why did Bigger revolt? No explanation based upon a hard and fast rule of conduct can be given. But there were always two factors psychologically dominant in his personality. First, through some quirk of circumstance, he had become estranged from the religion and the folk culture of his race. Second, he was trying to react to and answer the call of the dominant civilization whose glitter came to him through the newspapers, magazines, radios, movies, and the mere imposing sight and sound of daily American life. In many respects his emergence as a distinct type was inevitable.

As I grew older, I became familiar with the Bigger Thomas conditioning and its numerous shadings no matter where I saw it in Negro life. It was not, as I have already said, as blatant or extreme as in the originals; but it was there, nevertheless, like an undeveloped negative.

Sometimes, in areas far removed from Mississippi, I'd hear a Negro say: "I wish I didn't have to live this way. I feel like I want to burst." Then the anger would pass; he would go back to his job and try to eke out a few pennies to support his wife and children.

Sometimes I'd hear a Negro say: "God, I wish I had a flag and a country of my own." But that mood would soon vanish and he would go his way placidly enough.

Sometimes I'd hear a Negro ex-soldier say: "What in hell did I fight in the war for? They segregated me even when I was offering my life for my country." But he, too, like the others, would soon forget, would become caught up in the tense grind of struggling for bread.

I've even heard Negroes, in moments of anger and bitterness, praise what Japan is doing in China, not because they believed in oppression (being objects of oppression themselves), but because they would suddenly sense how empty their lives were when looking at the dark faces of Japanese generals in the rotogravure supplements of the Sunday newspapers. They would dream of what it would be like to live in a country where they could forget their color and play a responsible role in the vital processes of the nation's life.

I've even heard Negroes say that maybe Hitler and Mussolini are all right; that maybe Stalin is all right. They did not say this out of any intellectual comprehension of the forces at work in the world, but because they felt that these men "did things," a phrase which is charged with more meaning than the mere words imply. There was in the back of their minds, when they said this, a wild and intense longing (wild and intense because it was suppressed!) to belong, to be identified, to feel that they were alive as other people were, to be caught up forgetfully and exultingly in the swing of events, to feel the clean, deep, organic satisfaction of doing a job in common with others.

It was not until I went to live in Chicago that I first thought seriously of writing of Bigger Thomas. Two items of my experience combined to make me aware of Bigger as a meaningful and prophetic symbol. First, being free of the daily pressure of the Dixie environment, I was able to come into possession of my own feelings. Second, my contact with the labor movement and its ideology made me see Bigger clearly and feel what he meant.

I made the discovery that Bigger Thomas was not black all the time; he was white, too, and there were literally millions of him, everywhere. The extension of my sense of the personality of Bigger was the pivot of my life; it altered the complexion of my existence. I became conscious, at first dimly, and then later on with increasing clarity and conviction, of a vast, muddied pool of human life in America. It was as though I had put on a pair of spectacles whose power was that of an x-ray enabling me to see deeper into the lives of men. Whenever I picked up a newspaper, I'd no longer feel that I was reading of the doings of whites alone (Negroes are rarely mentioned in the press unless they've committed some crime!), but of a complex struggle for life going on in my country, a struggle in which I was involved. I sensed, too,

that the Southern scheme of oppression was but an append-
age of a far vaster and in many respects more ruthless and
impersonal commodity-profit machine.

Trade-union struggles and issues began to grow meaningful
to me. The flow of goods across the seas, buoying and de-
pressing the wages of men, held a fascination. The pro-
nouncements of foreign governments, their policies, plans,
and acts were calculated and weighed in relation to the lives
of people about me. I was literally overwhelmed when, in
reading the works of Russian revolutionists, I came across descriptions of the "holiday energies of the masses," "the loco-
motives of history," "the condition's prerequisite for revolution," and so forth. I approached all of these new revelations
in the light of Bigger Thomas, his hopes, fears, and despairs;
and I began to feel far-flung kinships, and sense, with fright
and abashment, the possibilities of *alliances* between the
American Negro and other people possessing a kindred consciousness.

As my mind extended in this general and abstract manner,
it was fed with even more vivid and concrete examples of the
lives of Bigger Thomas. The urban environment of Chicago,
affording a more stimulating life, made the Negro Bigger
Thomases react more violently than even in the South. More
than ever I began to see and understand the environmental
factors which made for this extreme conduct. It was not that
Chicago segregated Negroes more than the South, but that
Chicago had more to offer, that Chicago's physical aspect—
noisy, crowded, filled with the sense of power and fulfillment
—did so much more to dazzle the mind with a taunting sense
of possible achievement that the segregation it did impose
brought forth from Bigger a reaction more obstreperous than
in the South.

So the concrete picture and the abstract linkages of relationships fed each other, each making the other more meaningful and affording my emotions an opportunity to react to
them with success and understanding. The process was like a
swinging pendulum, each to and fro motion throwing up its
tiny bit of meaning and significance, each stroke helping to
develop the dim negative which had been implanted in my
mind in the South.

During this period the shadings and nuances which were
filling in Bigger's picture came, not so much from Negro life,
as from the lives of whites I met and grew to know. I began
to sense that they had their own kind of Bigger Thomas behavioristic pattern which grew out of a more subtle and
broader frustration. The waves of recurring crime, the silly

fads and crazes, the quicksilver changes in public taste, the hysteria and fears—all of these had long been mysteries to me. But now I looked back on them and felt the pinch and pressure of the environment that gave them their pitch and peculiar kind of being. I began to feel with my mind the inner tensions of the people I met. I don't mean to say that I think that environment *makes* consciousness (I suppose God makes that, if there is a God), but I do say that I felt and still feel that the environment supplies the instrumentalities through which the organism expresses itself, and if that environment is warped or tranquil, the mode and manner of behavior will be affected toward deadlocking tensions or orderly fulfillment and satisfaction.

Let me give examples of how I began to develop the dim negative of Bigger. I met white writers who talked of their responses, who told me how whites reacted to this lurid American scene. And, as they talked, I'd translate what they said in terms of Bigger's life. But what was more important still, I read their novels. Here for the first time, I found ways and techniques of gauging meaningfully the effects of American civilization upon the personalities of people. I took these techniques, these ways of seeing and feeling, and twisted them, bent them, adapted them, until they became *my* ways of apprehending the locked-in life of the Black Belt areas. This association with white writers was the life preserver of my hope to depict Negro life in fiction, for my race possessed no fictional works dealing with such problems, had no background in such sharp and critical testing of experience, no novels that went with a deep and fearless will down to the dark roots of life.

Here are examples of how I culled information relating to Bigger from my reading:

There is in me a memory of reading an interesting pamphlet telling of the friendship of Gorky and Lenin in exile. The booklet told of how Lenin and Gorky were walking down a London street. Lenin turned to Gorky and, pointing, said: "Here is *their* Big Ben." "There is *their* Westminster Abbey." "There is *their* library." And at once, while reading that passage, my mind stopped, teased, challenged with the effort to remember, to associate widely disparate but meaningful experiences in my life. For a moment nothing would come, but I remained convinced that I had heard the meaning of those words sometime, somewhere before. Then, with a sudden glow of satisfaction of having gained a little more knowledge about the world in which I lived, I'd end up by saying: "That's Bigger. That's the Bigger Thomas reaction."

In both instances the deep sense of exclusion was identical. The feeling of looking at things with a painful and unwarrantable nakedness was an experience, I learned, that transcended national and racial boundaries. It was this intolerable sense of feeling and understanding so much, and yet living on a plane of social reality where the look of a world which one did not make or own struck one with a blinding objectivity and tangibility, that made me grasp the revolutionary impulse in my life and the lives of those about me and far away.

I remember reading a passage in a book dealing with old Russia which said: "We must be ready to make endless sacrifices if we are to be able to overthrow the Czar." And again I'd say to myself: "I've heard that somewhere, sometime before." And again I'd hear Bigger Thomas, far away and long ago, telling some white man who was trying to impose upon him: "I'll kill you and go to hell and pay for it." While living in America I heard from far away Russia the bitter accents of tragic calculation of how much human life and suffering it would cost a man to live as a man in a world that denied him the right to live with dignity. Actions and feelings of men ten thousand miles from home helped me to understand the moods and impulses of those walking the streets of Chicago and Dixie.

I am not saying that I heard any talk of revolution in the South when I was a kid there. But I did hear the lispings, the whispers, the mutters which some day, under one stimulus or another, will surely grow into open revolt unless the conditions which produce Bigger Thomases are changed.

In 1932 another source of information was dramatically opened up to me and I saw data of a surprising nature that helped to clarify the personality of Bigger. From the moment that Hitler took power in Germany and began to oppress the Jews, I tried to keep track of what was happening. And on innumerable occasions I was startled to detect, either from the side of the Fascists or from the side of the oppressed, reactions, moods, phrases, attitudes that reminded me strongly of Bigger, that helped to bring out more clearly the shadowy outlines of the negative that lay in the back of my mind.

I read every account of the Fascist movement in Germany I could lay my hands on, and from page to page I encountered and recognized familiar emotional patterns. What struck me with particular force was the Nazi preoccupation with the construction of a society in which there would exist among all people (*German* people, of course!) *one* solidarity of ideals, *one* continuous circulation of fundamental beliefs, notions, and assumptions. I am not now speaking of the popular idea of regimenting people's thought; I'm speaking of the implicit, almost unconscious, or pre-conscious, assumptions and ideals upon which whole nations and races act and live. And while reading these Nazi pages I'd be reminded of the Negro preacher in the South telling of a life beyond this world, a life in which the color of men's skins would not matter, a life in which each man would know what was deep down in the hearts of his fellow man. And I could hear Bigger Thomas standing on a street corner in America expressing his agonizing doubts and chronic suspicions, thus: "I ain't going to trust nobody. Everything is a racket and everybody is out to get what he can for himself. Maybe if we had a true leader, we could do something." And I'd know that I was still on the track of learning about Bigger, still in the midst of the modern struggle for solidarity among men.

When the Nazis spoke of the necessity of a highly ritualized and symbolized life, I could hear Bigger Thomas on Chicago's South Side saying: "Man, what we need is a leader like Marcus Garvey. We need a nation, a flag, an army of our own. We colored folks ought to organize into groups and have generals, captains, lieutenants, and so forth. We ought to take Africa and have a national home." I'd know, while listening to these childish words, that a white man would smile derisively at them. But I could not smile, for I knew the truth of those simple words from the facts of my own life. The deep hunger in those childish ideas was like a flash of lightning illuminating the whole dark inner landscape of Bigger's mind. Those words told me that the civilization which had given birth to Bigger contained no spiritual sustenance, had created no culture which could hold and claim his allegiance and faith, had sensitized him and had left him stranded, a free agent to roam the streets of our cities, a hot and whirling vortex of undisciplined and unchannelized impulses. The results of these observations made me feel more than ever estranged from the civilization in which I lived, and more than ever resolved toward the task of creating with words a scheme of images and symbols whose direction could enlist the sympathies, loyalties, and yearnings of the millions of Bigger Thomases in every land and race. . . .

But more than anything else, as a writer, I was fascinated by the similarity of the emotional tensions of Bigger in America and Bigger in Nazi Germany and Bigger in old Russia. All Bigger Thomases, white and black, felt tense, afraid, nervous, hysterical, and restless. From far away Nazi Germany and old Russia had come to me items of knowledge that told me that certain modern experiences were creating types of personalities whose existence ignored racial and national lines of demarcation, that these personalities carried with them a more universal drama-element than anything I'd ever encountered before; that these personalities were mainly imposed upon men and women living in a world whose fundamental assumptions could no longer be taken for granted: a world ridden with national and class strife; a world whose metaphysical meanings had vanished; a world in which God no longer existed as a daily focal point of men's lives; a world in which men could no longer retain their faith in an ultimate hereafter. It was a highly geared world whose nature was conflict and action, a world whose limited area and vision imperiously urged men to satisfy their organisms, a world that existed on a plane of animal sensation alone.

It was a world in which millions of men lived and behaved like drunkards, taking a stiff drink of hard life to lift them up for a thrilling moment, to give them a quivering sense of wild exultation and fulfillment that soon faded and let them down. Eagerly they took another drink, wanting to avoid the dull, flat look of things, then still another, this time stronger, and then they felt that their lives had meaning. Speaking figuratively, they were soon chronic alcoholics, men who lived by violence, through extreme action and sensation, through drowning daily in a perpetual nervous agitation.

From these items I drew my first political conclusions about Bigger: I felt that Bigger, an American product, a native son of this land, carried within him the potentialities of either Communism or Fascism. I don't mean to say that the Negro boy I depicted in *Native Son* is either a Communist or a Fascist. He is not either. But he is product of a dislocated society; he is a dispossessed and disinherited man; he is all of this, and he lives amid the greatest possible plenty on earth and he is looking and feeling for a way out. Whether he'll follow some gaudy, hysterical leader who'll promise rashly to fill the void in him, or whether he'll come to an understanding with the millions of his kindred fellow workers under trade-union or revolutionary guidance depends upon the future drift of events in America. But, granting the emotional state, the tensity, the fear, the hate, the impatience, the sense of exclusion, the ache for violent action, the emotional and cultural hunger, Bigger Thomas, conditioned as his organism is, will not become an ardent, or even a lukewarm, supporter of the *status quo*.

The difference between Bigger's tensity and the German variety is that Bigger's, due to America's educational restrictions on the bulk of her Negro population, is in a nascent state, not yet articulate. And the difference between Bigger's longing for self-identification and the Russian principle of self-determination is that Bigger's, due to the effects of American oppression, which has not allowed for the forming of deep ideas of solidarity among Negroes, is still in a state of individual anger and hatred. Here, I felt was *drama!* Who will be the first to touch off these Bigger Thomases in America, white and black?

For a long time I toyed with the idea of writing a novel in which a Negro Bigger Thomas would loom as a symbolic figure of American life, a figure who would hold within him the prophecy of our future. I felt strongly that he held within him, in a measure which perhaps no other contemporary type did, the outlines of action and feeling which we would encounter on a vast scale in the days to come. Just as one sees when one walks into a medical research laboratory jars of alcohol containing abnormally large or distorted portions of the human body, just so did I see and feel that the conditions of life under which Negroes are forced to live in America contain the embryonic emotional prefigurations of how a large part of the body politic would react under stress.

So, with this much knowledge of myself and the world gained and known, why should I not try to work out on paper the problem of what will happen to Bigger? Why should I not, like a scientist in a laboratory, use my imagination and invent test-tube situations, place Bigger in them, and, following the guidance of my own hopes and fears, what I had learned and remembered, work out in fictional form an emotional statement and resolution of this problem?

But several things militated against my starting to work. Like Bigger himself, I felt a mental censor—product of the fears which a Negro feels from living in America—standing over me, draped in white, warning me not to write. This censor's warnings were translated into my own thought processes thus: "What will white people think if I draw the picture of such a Negro boy? Will they not at once say: 'See, didn't we tell you all along the niggers are like that? Now, look, one of their own kind has come along and drawn the picture for us!' " I felt that if I drew the picture of Bigger truthfully, there would be many reactionary whites who would try to make of him something I did not intend. And yet, and this was what made it difficult, I knew that I could not write of Bigger convincingly if I did not depict him as he *was:* that is, resentful toward whites, sullen, angry, ignorant, emotionally unstable, depressed and unaccountably elated at times, and unable even, because of his own lack of inner organization which American oppression has fostered in him, to unite with the members of his own race. And would not whites misread Bigger and, doubting his authenticity, say: "This man is preaching hate against the whole white race"?

The more I thought of it the more I became convinced that if I did not write of Bigger as I saw and felt him, if I did not try to make him a living personality and at the same time a symbol of all the larger things I felt and saw in him, I'd be reacting as Bigger himself reacted: that is, I'd be acting out of *fear* if I let what I thought whites would say constrict and paralyze me.

As I contemplated Bigger and what he meant, I said to myself: "I must write this novel, not only for others to read, but to free *myself* of this sense of shame and fear." In fact, the novel, as time passed, grew upon me to the extent that it became a necessity to write it; the writing of it turned into a way of living for me.

Another thought kept me from writing. What would my own white and black comrades in the Communist party say? This thought was the most bewildering of all. Politics is a hard and narrow game; its policies represent the aggregate desires and aspirations of millions of people. Its goals are rigid and simply drawn, and the minds of the majority of politicians are set, congealed in terms of daily tactical maneuvers. How could I create such complex and wide schemes of associational thought and feeling, such filigreed webs of dreams and politics, without being mistaken for a "smuggler of reaction," "an ideological confusionist," or "an individualistic and dangerous element"? Though my heart is with the collectivist and proletarian ideal, I solved this problem by assuring myself that honest politics and honest feeling in imaginative representation ought to be able to meet on common healthy ground without fear, suspicion, and quarreling. Further, and more importantly, I steeled myself by coming to the conclusion that whether politicians accepted or rejected Bigger did not really matter; my task, as I felt it, was to free myself of this burden of impressions and feelings, recast them into the image of Bigger and make him *true*. Lastly, I felt that a right more immediately deeper than that of politics or race was at stake; that is, a *human* right, the right of a man to think and feel honestly. And especially did this personal and human right bear hard upon me, for temperamentally I am inclined to satisfy the claims of my own ideals rather than the expectations of others. It was this obscure need that had pulled me into the labor movement in the beginning and by exercising it I was but fulfilling what I felt to be the laws of my own growth.

There was another constricting thought that kept me from work. It deals with my own race. I asked myself: "What will Negro doctors, lawyers, dentists, bankers, school teachers, so-cial workers and business men, think of me if I draw such a picture of Bigger?" I knew from long and painful experience that the Negro middle and professional classes were the peo-ple of my own race who were more than others ashamed of Bigger and what he meant. Having narrowly escaped the Big-ger Thomas reaction pattern themselves—indeed, still retain-ing traces of it within the confines of their own timid person-alities—they would not relish being publicly reminded of the lowly, shameful depths of life above which they enjoyed their bourgeois lives. Never did they want people, especially *white* people, to think that their lives were so much touched by anything so dark and brutal as Bigger.

Their attitude toward life and art can be summed up in a single paragraph: "But, Mr. Wright, there are so many of us who are *not* like Bigger? Why don't you portray in your fic-tion the *best* traits of our race, something that will show the white people what we have done in spite of oppression? Don't represent anger and bitterness. Smile when a white per-son comes to you. Never let him feel that you are so small that what he has done to crush you has made you hate him! Oh, above all, save your *pride!*"

But Bigger won over all these claims; he won because I felt that I was hunting on the trail of more exciting and thrilling game. What Bigger meant had claimed me because I felt with all of my being that he was more important than what any person, white or black, would say or try to make of him, more important than any political analysis designed to explain or deny him, more important, even, than my own sense of fear, shame, and diffidence.

But Bigger was still not down upon paper. For a long time I had been writing of him in my mind, but I had yet to put him into an image, a breathing symbol draped out in the guise of the only form of life my native land had allowed me to know intimately, that is, the ghetto life of the American Negro. But the basic reason for my hesitancy was that an-other and far more complex problem had risen to plague me. Bigger, as I saw and felt him, was a snarl of many realities; he had in him many levels of life.

First, there was his personal and private life, that intimate existence that is so difficult to snare and nail down in fiction, that elusive core of being, that individual data of consciousness which in every man and woman is like that in no other. I had to deal with Bigger's dreams, his fleeting, momentary sensations, his yearning, visions, his deep emotional responses.

Then I was confronted with that part of him that was dual in aspect, dim, wavering, that part of him which is so much a part of *all* Negroes and *all* whites that I realized that I could put it down upon paper only by feeling out its meaning first within the confines of my own life. Bigger was attracted and repelled by the American scene. He was an American, because he was a native son; but he was also a Negro nationalist in a vague sense because he was not allowed to live as an American. Such was his way of life and mine; neither Bigger nor I resided fully in either camp.

Of this dual aspect of Bigger's social consciousness, I placed the nationalistic side first, not because I agreed with Bigger's wild and intense hatred of white people, but because his hate had placed him, like a wild animal at bay, in a position where he was most symbolic and explainable. In other words, his nationalist complex was for me a concept through which I could grasp more of the total meaning of his life than I could in any other way. I tried to approach Bigger's *snarled* and *confused* nationalist feelings with *conscious* and *informed* ones of my own. Yet, Bigger was not nationalist enough to feel the need of religion or the folk culture of his own people. What made Bigger's social consciousness most complex was the fact that he was hovering unwanted between two worlds—between powerful America and his own stunted place in life—and I took upon myself the task of trying to make the reader feel this No Man's Land. The most that I could say of Bigger was that he felt the *need* for a whole life and *acted* out of that need; that was all.

Above and beyond all this, there was that American part of Bigger which is the heritage of us all, that part of him which we get from our seeing and hearing, from school, from the hopes and dreams of our friends; that part of him which the common people of America never talk of but take for granted. Among millions of people the deepest convictions of life are never discussed openly; they are felt, implied, hinted at tacitly and obliquely in their hopes and fears. We live by idealism that makes us believe that the Constitution is a good document of government, that the Bill of Rights is a good legal and humane principle to safeguard our civil liberties, that every man and woman should have the opportunity to realize himself, to seek his own individual fate and goal, his own peculiar and untranslatable destiny. I don't say that

Bigger knew this in the terms in which I'm speaking of it; I don't say that any such thought ever entered his head. His emotional and intellectual life was never that articulate. But he knew it emotionally, intuitively, for his emotions and his desires were developed, and he caught it, as most of us do, from the mental and emotional climate of our time. Bigger had all of this in him, dammed up, buried, implied, and I had to develop it in fictional form.

There was still another level of Bigger's life that I felt bound to account for and render, a level as elusive to discuss as it was to grasp in writing. Here again, I had to fall back upon my own feeling as a guide, for Bigger did not offer in his life any articulate verbal explanations. There seems to hover somewhere in that dark part of all our lives, in some more than in others, an objectless, timeless, spaceless element of primal fear and dread, stemming, perhaps, from our birth (depending upon whether one's outlook upon personality is Freudian or non-Freudian!), a fear and dread which exercises an impelling influence upon our lives all out of proportion to its obscurity. And, accompanying this *first fear*, is, for the want of a better name, a reflex urge toward ecstasy, complete submission, and trust. The springs of religion are here, and also the origins of rebellion. And in a boy like Bigger, young, unschooled, whose subjective life was clothed in the tattered rags of American "culture," this primitive fear and ecstasy were naked, exposed, unprotected by religion or a framework of government or a scheme of society whose final faiths would gain his love and trust; unprotected by trade or profession, faith or belief; opened to every trivial blast of daily or hourly circumstance.

There was yet another level of reality in Bigger's life: the impliedly political. I've already mentioned that Bigger had in him impulses which I had felt were present in the vast upheavals of Russia and Germany. Well, somehow, I had to make these political impulses felt by the reader in terms of Bigger's daily actions, keeping in mind as I did so the probable danger of my being branded as a propagandist by those who would not like the subject matter.

Then there was Bigger's relationship with white America, both North and South, which I had to depict, which I had to make known once again, alas; a relationship whose effects are carried by every Negro, like scars, somewhere in his body and mind.

I had also to show what oppression had done to Bigger's relationships with his own people, how it had split him off from them, how it had baffled him; how oppression seems to

hinder and stifle in the victim those very qualities of character which are so essential for an effective struggle against the
oppressor.

Then there was the fabulous city in which Bigger lived, an
indescribable city, huge, roaring, dirty, noisy, raw, stark,
brutal; a city of extremes: torrid summers and sub-zero win-
ters, white people and black people, the English language and
strange tongues, foreign born and native born, scabby poverty
and gaudy luxury, high idealism and hard cynicism! A city so
young that, in thinking of its short history, one's mind, as it
travels backward in time, is stopped abruptly by the barren
stretches of wind-swept prairie! But a city old enough to have
caught within the homes of its long, straight streets the symbols and images of man's age-old destiny, of truths as old as
the mountains and seas, of dramas as abiding as the soul of
man itself! A city which has become the pivot of the Eastern,
Western, Northern, and Southern poles of the nation. But a
city whose black smoke clouds shut out the sunshine for
seven months of the year; a city in which, on a fine balmy
May morning one can sniff the stench of the stockyards; a
city where people have grown so used to gangs and murders
and graft that they have honestly forgotten that government
can have a pretense of decency!

With all of this thought out, Bigger was still unwritten.
Two events, however, come into my life and accelerated the
process, made me sit down and actually start work on the
typewriter, and just stop the writing of Bigger in my mind as
I walked the streets.

The first event was my getting a job in the South Side
Boys' Club, an institution which tried to reclaim the thousands of Negro Bigger Thomases from the dives and the alleys of the Black Belt. Here, on a vast scale, I had an opportunity to observe Bigger in all of his moods, actions, haunts.
Here I felt for the first time that the rich folk who were paying my wages did not really give a good goddamn about Bigger, that their kindness was prompted at the bottom by a selfish motive. They were paying me to distract Bigger with
ping-pong, checkers, swimming, marbles, and baseball in
order that he might not roam the streets and harm the valuable white property which adjoined the Black Belt. I am not
condemning boys' clubs and ping-pong as such; but these little stopgaps were utterly inadequate to fill up the centuries-
long chasm of emptiness which American civilization had
created in these Biggers. I felt that I was doing a kind of
dressed-up police work, and I hated it.

I would work hard with these Biggers, and when it would

come time for me to go home I'd say to myself under my breath so that no one could hear: "Go to it, boys! Prove to the bastards that gave you these games that life is stronger than ping-pong. . . . Show them that full-blooded life is harder and hotter than they suspect, even though that life is draped in a black skin which at heart they despise. . . ."

They did. The police blotters of Chicago are testimony to how *much* they did. That was the only way I could contain myself for doing a job I hated; for a moment I'd allow myself, vicariously, to feel as Bigger felt—not much, just a little, just a *little*—but, still, there it was.

The second event that spurred me to write of Bigger was more personal and subtle. I had written a book of short stories which was published under the title of *Uncle Tom's Children*. When the reviews of that book began to appear, I realized that I had made an awfully naive mistake. I found that I had written a book which even bankers' daughters could read and weep over and feel good about. I swore to myself that if I ever wrote another book, no one would weep over it; that it would be so hard and deep that they would have to face it without the consolation of tears. It was this that made me get to work in dead earnest.

Now, until this moment I did not stop to think very much about the plot of *Native Son*. The reason I did not is because I was not for one moment ever worried about it. I had spent years learning about Bigger, what had made him, what he meant; so, when the time came for writing, *what had made him and what he meant* constituted my plot. But the far-flung items of his life had to be couched in imaginative terms, terms known and acceptable to a common body of readers, terms which would, in the course of the story, manipulate the deepest held notions and convictions of their lives. That came easy. The moment I began to write, the plot fell out, so to speak. I'm not trying to oversimplify or make the process seem oversubtle. At bottom, what happened is very easy to explain.

Any Negro who has lived in the North or the South knows that times without number he has heard of some Negro boy being picked up on the streets and carted off to jail and charged with "rape." This thing happens so often that to my mind it had become a representative symbol of the Negro's uncertain position in America. Never for a second was I in doubt as to what kind of social reality or dramatic situation I'd put Bigger in, what kind of test-tube I'd set up to evoke his deepest reactions. Life had made the plot over and over again, to the extent that I knew it by heart. So frequently do these acts recur that when I was halfway through the first draft of *Native Son* a case paralleling Bigger's flared forth in the newspapers of Chicago. (Many of the newspaper items and some of the incidents in *Native Son* are but fictionalized versions of the Robert Nixon case and rewrites of news stories from the *Chicago Tribune*.) Indeed, scarcely was *Native Son* off the press before Supreme Court Justice Hugo L. Black gave the nation a long and vivid account of the American police methods of handling Negro boys.

Let me describe this stereotyped situation: A crime wave is sweeping a city and citizens are clamoring for police action. Squad cars cruise the Black Belt and grab the first Negro boy who seems to be unattached and homeless. He is held for perhaps a week without charge or bail, without the privilege of communicating with anyone, including his own relatives. After a few days this boy "confesses" anything that he is asked to confess, any crime that handily happens to be unsolved and on the calendar. Why does he confess? After the boy has been grilled night and day, hanged up by his thumbs, dangled by his feet out of twenty-story windows, and beaten (in places that leave no scars—cops have found a way to do that), he signs the papers before him, papers which are usually accompanied by a verbal promise to the boy that he will not go to the electric chair. Of course, he ends up by being executed or sentenced for life. If you think I'm telling tall tales, get chummy with some white cop who works in a Black Belt district and ask him for the lowdown.

When a black boy is carted off to jail in such a fashion, it is almost impossible to do anything for him. Even well-disposed Negro lawyers find it difficult to defend him, for the boy will plead guilty one day and then not guilty the next, according to the degree of pressure and persuasion that is brought to bear upon his frightened personality from one side or the other. Even the boy's own family is scared to death; sometimes fear of police intimidation makes them hesitate to acknowledge that the boy is blood relation of theirs.

Such has been America's attitude toward these boys that if one is picked up and confronted in a police cell with ten white cops, he is intimidated almost to the point of confessing anything. So far removed are these practices from what the average American citizen encounters in his daily life that it takes a huge act of his imagination to believe that it is true; yet, this same average citizen, with his kindness, his American sportsmanship and good will, would probably act with the mob if a self-respecting Negro family moved into his apartment building to escape the Black Belt and its terrors and limitations. . . .

Now, after all of this, when I sat down to the typewriter, I could not work; I could not think of a good opening scene for the book. I had definitely in mind the kind of emotion I wanted to evoke in the reader in that first scene, but I could not think of the type of concrete event that would convey the motif of the entire scheme of the book, that would sound, in varied form, the note that was to be resounded throughout its length, that would introduce to the reader just what kind of an organism Bigger's was and the environment that was bearing hourly upon it. Twenty or thirty times I tried and failed; then I argued that if I could not write the opening scene, I'd start with the scene that followed. I did. The actual writing of the book began with the scene in the pool room.

Now, for the writing. During the years in which I had met all of those Bigger Thomases, those varieties of Bigger Thomases, I had not consciously gathered material to write of them; I had not kept a notebook record of their sayings and doings. Their actions had simply made impressions upon my sensibilities as I lived from day to day, impressions which crystallized and coagulated into clusters and configurations of memory, attitudes, moods, ideas. And these subjective states, in turn, were automatically stored away somewhere in me. I was not even aware of the process. But, excited over the book which I had set myself to write, under the stress of emotion, these things came surging up, tangled, fused, knotted, entertaining me by the sheer variety and potency of their meaning and suggestiveness.

With the whole theme in mind, in an attitude almost akin to prayer, I gave myself up to the story. In an effort to capture some phase of Bigger's life that would not come to me readily, I'd jot down as much of it as I could. Then I'd read it over and over, adding each time a word, a phrase, a sentence until I felt that I had caught all the shadings of reality I felt dimly were there. With each of these rereadings and re-writings it seemed that I'd gather in facts and facets that tried to run away. It was an act of concentration, of trying to hold within one's center of attention all of that bewildering array of facts which science, politics, experience, memory, and imagination were urging upon me. And, then, while writing, a new and thrilling relationship would spring up under the drive of emotion, coalescing and telescoping alien facts into a known and felt truth. That was the deep fun of the job: to feel within my body that I was pushing out to new areas of feeling, strange landmarks of emotion tramping upon foreign soil, compounding new relationships of perceptions, making new and—until that very split second of time!—unheard-of and unfelt effects with words. It had a buoying and tonic impact upon me; my senses would strain and seek for more and more of such relationships; my temperature would rise as I worked. That is writing as I feel it, a kind of significant living.

The first draft of the novel was written in four months, straight through, and ran to some 576 pages. Just as a man rises in the morning to dig ditches for his bread, so I'd work daily. I'd think of some abstract principle of Bigger's conduct and at once my mind would turn it into some act I'd seen Bigger perform, some act which I hoped would be familiar enough to the American reader to gain his credence. But in the writing of scene after scene I was guided by but one criterion: to tell the truth as I saw it and felt it. That is, to objectify in words some insight derived from my living in the form of action, scene, and dialogue. If a scene seemed improbable to me, I'd not tear it up, but ask myself: "Does it reveal enough of what I feel to stand in spite of its unreality?" If I felt it did, it stood. If I felt that it did not, I ripped it out. The degree of morality in my writing depended upon the degree of felt life and truth I could put down upon the printed page. For example, there is a scene in *Native Son* where Bigger stands in a cell with a Negro preacher, Jan, Max, the State's Attorney, Mr. Dalton, Mrs. Dalton, Bigger's mother, his brother, his sister, Al, Gus, and Jack. While writing the scene, I knew that it was unlikely that so many people would ever be allowed to come into a murderer's cell. But I wanted those people in that cell to elicit a certain important emotional response from Bigger. And so the scene stood. I felt that what I wanted that scene to say to the reader was *more important than its surface reality or plausibility.*

Always, as I wrote, I was both reader and writer, both the conceiver of the action and the appreciator of it. I tried to write so that, in the same instant of time, the objective and subjective aspects of Bigger's life would be caught in a focus of prose. And always I tried to *render, depict*, not merely to tell the story. If a thing was cold, I tried to make the reader *feel cold*, and not just tell about it. In writing in this fashion, sometimes I'd find it necessary to use a stream of consciousness technique, then rise to an interior monologue, descend to a direct rendering of a dream state, then to a matter-of-fact depiction of what Bigger was saying, doing, and feeling. Then I'd find it impossible to say what I wanted to say without stepping in and speaking outright on my own; but when doing this I always made an effort to retain the mood of the story, explaining everything only in terms of Bigger's life and, if possible, in the rhythms of Bigger's thought (even though the words would be mine). Again, at other times, in the guise of the lawyer's speech and the newspaper items, or in terms of what Bigger would overhear or see from afar, I'd give what others were saying and thinking of him. But always, from the start to finish, it was Bigger's story, Bigger's fears, Bigger's flight, and Bigger's fate that I tried to depict. I wrote with the conviction in mind (I don't know if this is right or wrong; I only know that I'm temperamentally inclined to feel this way) that the main burden of all serious fiction consists almost wholly of character-destiny and the items, social, political, and personal, of that character-destiny.

As I wrote I followed, almost unconsciously, many principles of the novel which my reading of the novels of other writers had made me feel were necessary for the building of a well-constructed book. For the most part the novel is rendered in the present; I wanted the reader to feel that Bigger's story was happening *now*, like a play upon the stage or a movie unfolding upon the screen. Action follows action, as in a prize fight. Wherever possible, I told of Bigger's life in close-up, slow-motion, giving the feel of the grain in the passing of time. I had long had the feeling that this was the best way to "enclose" the reader's mind in a new world, to blot out all reality except that which I was giving him.

Then again, as much as I could, I restricted the novel to what Bigger saw and felt, to the limits of his feeling and thoughts, even when I was conveying *more* than that to the reader. I had the notion that such a manner of rendering made for a sharper effect, a more pointed sense of the character, his peculiar type of being and consciousness. Throughout there is but one point of view: Bigger's. This, too, I felt, made for a richer illusion of reality.

I kept out of the story as much as possible, for I wanted the reader to feel that there was nothing between him and Bigger; that the story was a special *première* given in his own private theater.

I kept the scenes long, made as much happen within a short space of time as possible; all of which, I felt, made for greater density and richness of effect.

In a like manner I tried to keep a unified sense of background throughout the story; the background would change, of course, but I tried to keep before the eyes of the reader at all times the forces and elements against which Bigger was striving.

And because I had limited myself to rendering only what Bigger saw and felt, I gave no more reality to the other characters than that which Bigger himself saw.

This, honestly, is all I can account for in the book. If I attempted to account for scenes and characters, to tell why certain scenes were written in certain ways, I'd be stretching facts in order to be pleasantly intelligible. All else in the book came from my feelings reacting upon the material, and any honest reader knows as much about the rest of what is in the book as I do; that is, if, as he reads, he is willing to let his emotions and imagination become as influenced by the materials as I did. As I wrote, for some reason or other, one image, symbol, character, scene, mood, feeling evoked its opposite, its parallel, its complimentary, and its ironic counterpart. Why? I don't know. My emotions and imagination just like to work that way. One can account for just so much of life, and then no more. At least, not yet.

With the first draft down, I found that I could not end the book satisfactorily. In the first draft I had Bigger going smack to the electric chair; but I felt that two murders were enough for one novel. I cut the final scene and went back to worry about the beginning. I had no luck. The book was one-half finished, with the opening and closing scenes unwritten. Then, one night, in desperation—I hope that I'm not disclosing the hidden secrets of my craft!—I sneaked out and got a bottle. With the help of it, I began to remember many things which I could not remember before. One of them was that Chicago was overrun with rats. I recalled that I'd seen many rats on the streets, that I'd heard and read of Negro children being bitten by rats in their beds. At first I rejected the idea of Bigger battling a rat in his room; I was afraid that the rat would "hog" the scene. But the rat would not leave me; he presented himself in many attractive guises. So, cautioning myself to allow the rat scene to disclose *only* Bigger, his family, their little room, and their relationships, I let the rat walk in, and he did his stuff.

Many of the scenes were torn out as I reworked the book. The mere rereading of what I'd written made me think of the possibility of developing themes which had been only hinted at in the first draft. For example, the entire guilt theme that runs through *Native Son* was woven in *after* the first draft was written.

At last I found out how to end the book; I ended it just as I had begun it, showing Bigger living dangerously, taking his life into his hands, accepting what life had made him. The lawyer, Max, was placed in Bigger's cell at the end of the novel to register the moral—or what *I* felt was the moral— horror of Negro life in the United States.

The writing of *Native Son* was to me an exciting, enthralling, and even a romantic experience. With what I've learned in the writing of this book, with all of its blemishes, imperfections, with all of its unrealized potentialities, I am launching out upon another novel, this time about the status of women in modern American society. This book, too, goes back to my childhood just as Bigger went, for, while I was storing away impressions of Bigger, I was storing away impressions of many other things that made me think and wonder. Some experience will ignite somewhere deep down in me the smoldering embers of new fires and I'll be off again to write yet another novel. It is good to live when one feels that such as that will happen to one. Life becomes sufficient unto life; the rewards of living are found in living.

I don't know if *Native Son* is a good book or a bad book. And I don't know if the book I'm working on now will be a good book or a bad book. And I really don't care. The mere writing of it will be more fun and a deeper satisfaction than any praise or blame from anybody.

I feel that I'm lucky to be alive to write novels today, when the whole world is caught in the pangs of war and change. Early American writers, Henry James and Nathaniel Hawthorne, complained bitterly about the bleakness and flatness of the American scene. But I think that if they were alive, they'd feel at home in modern America. True, we have no great church in America; our national traditions are still of such a sort that we are not wont to brag of them; and we have no army that's above the level of mercenary fighters; we have no group acceptable to the whole of our country upholding certain humane values; we have no rich symbols, no colorful rituals. We have only a money-grabbing, industrial civilization. But we do have in the Negro the embodiment of a past tragic enough to appease the spiritual hunger of even a James; and we have in the oppression of the Negro a shadow athwart our national life dense and heavy enough to satisfy even the gloomy broodings of a Hawthorne. And if Poe were alive, he would not have to invent horror; horror would invent him.

New York, March 7, 1940

STERLING A. BROWN (1901–   )

*A biographical note on Sterling Brown appears in the Poetry
section (see p. 403). The following critical study is reprinted
from* The Massachusetts Review, Winter, 1966.

A Century of Negro Portraiture
in American Literature

1

Over a century ago, in November, 1863, Harriet Beecher
Stowe wrote that she was going to Washington to satisfy herself that "the Emancipation Proclamation was a reality and a
substance not to fizzle out. . . ." She meant to talk to "Father Abraham himself." When she was ushered into his study,
her frailty startled President Lincoln. As his big knotted hand
took her small one, he quizzed: "So this is the little lady who
made this big war." Pressed by her eagerness, Lincoln assured
Harriet Beecher Stowe that he was determined to issue the
Emancipation Proclamation on New Year's Day.

In spite of Lincoln's gallant exaggeration, his estimate of
the impact of *Uncle Tom's Cabin* showed his old canniness.
His secretary of state, not so given to overstatement, said that
"without *Uncle Tom's Cabin* there would have been no Abraham Lincoln"; and here William Seward also spoke cannily.
For the novel had been an instantaneous success here and
abroad. Many of Father Abraham's hundred thousand strong
had read it a decade earlier in their forming years; many carried it in their knapsacks, and it had dramatized for both
North and South the American moral dilemmas and something of the humanity involved in the controversy over slavery.

Herman Melville had expressed antislavery opinions even
earlier in *Mardi*. The approach, however, was oblique, and
the antislavery sections were only a small part of a murky al-

legory, which was to be largely unread in contrast to Mrs. Stowe's popular success. Still, *Mardi* is pertinent here for Melville's clear indictment of slavery, his dread and prophecy of the inevitable clash of the irreconcilable viewpoints about slavery and the Negro. Describing the Capitol of Vivenza (his name for the United States) Melville singled out the creed "All Men are born Free and Equal," noting that an addition, in minute hieroglyphics, read: "all except the tribe of Hamo." On the flag being hoisted over the Capitol, red stripes corresponded to marks on the back of the slave who was doing the hoisting. Strangers visiting the South of Vivenza discovered that the slaves were men. For this a haughty spokesman denounced them as "firebrands come to light the flame of revolt." This grim prophet, a fictionalized Calhoun properly named Nullo, swore that the first blow struck for the slaves would "dissolve the Union of Vivenza's vales." Like his allegorical visitors, Melville was troubled over what seemed an irrepressible conflict between North and South and, dreading war, concluded that only Time "must befriend these thralls." In spite of his doubts about the best course, he was nevertheless certain that slavery was "a blot, foul as the crater pool of hell."

These two significant novelists of a century ago indicate how influential the treatment of Negro life and character has been in American history and literature. From the outset of our national life "Negro character," if such a loose term may be used at the beginning of this essay, has intrigued American authors. Their portraits have evinced varying degrees of sympathy and understanding, skill and power. Their motives have been manifold. Their success has not been marked.

Before the Civil War creative literature dealing with Negro life was abundant, though not distinguished. Minor efforts at real characterizations—some perceptive, some vague, some tentative guesses about half-strangers—occur in Cooper, Poe, William Gilmore Simms, and the southern humorists. By and large, however, the Negro in the literature of this period was a mere pawn in the growing debate over slavery. With the overwhelming success of *Uncle Tom's Cabin* in 1852 the battle of the books was joined, and torrents of proslavery replies rushed from the presses. These were ungainly books, crude sentimentalizings and melodramatizings of the proslavery argument of Dew and Harper, of Calhoun and Fitzhugh. Slaves chanted paeans to the Arcadian existence of the old South; others walked the woods as embodiments of the various Bible Defenses of Slavery—one of them, for instance, pulling a much thumbed copy of the Sacred Book out of his overalls to confound a Yankee abolitionist who was haunting this Eden. The wisest slaves rejected freedom; the maladjusted and the half-wits ran away to the North where they either died in snow drifts (they needed master to tell them to come in out of the snow) or else they saw the light, and stole away, back to the Southland and slavery (a kind of Underground Railroad in reverse). One novel, *Life at the South, or Uncle Tom's Cabin As It Is* * closes with another Tom, disillusioned with the North, heading back South. "And if the reader shall chance to travel the high road, as it winds up the valley of the Shenandoah, above Winchester, he will find no slave more contented than Uncle Tom." A tall, tall order. Carry me back to old Virginny.

They would have to carry him back to get him there, was what a Negro like Frederick Douglass thought; and this opinion was shared by such other stout-hearted fugitives as Martin Delany, David Ruggles, Sojourner Truth, Harriet Tubman, and William Wells Brown. These and many other Negroes fought in the antislavery crusade; several used stirring autobiographies, pamphlets, journalism and oratory in the battle. Creative literature, however, was the exception with them; an embattled people used literature as a weapon, as propaganda; not as exploration, but as exposé of injustice. There were a few short stories and novels, and hortatory poetry. The truth of Negro life and character, however, is in such an autobiography as Douglass's *My Bondage and My Freedom* more than in the fiction and poetry of the time.

---

* To illustrate some of the absurdities cited and the repetition that really amounted to plagiarism, compare this novel with one that preceded it by twenty years. In *The Yemassee* (1832), by William Gilmore Simms, a heroic slave, the properly named Hector, is offered his freedom:

"I d--n to h---, maussa if I gwine to be free!" roared the adhesive black, in a tone of unrestrainable determination . . ."'Tis onpossible, maussa, and dere's no use for to talk about it. Enty I know wha' kind of ting freedom is wid black man? Ha! you make Hector free, he turn wuss than poor buckra, he tief out of de shop—he git drunk and lie in de ditch—den if sick come, he roll, he toss in de wet grass of de stable. You come in de morning, Hector dead . . ."

Twenty years later, in 1852, in *Life at the South, or Uncle Tom's Cabin As It Is*, the author, W. L. G. Smith, has a character also named Hector, who is also offered his freedom. And he also says:

"I damn to hell, massa, if I gwine to be free, roared the adhesive black in a tone of unrestrainable determination . . ." etc. *ad literatim et ad nauseum.*

Also engaged in this crusade were white abolitionist poets —Bryant, Longfellow, Whittier—and novelists like Harriet Beecher Stowe. Their hearts were better than their circumstantial material; they, as Lowell said of Mrs. Stowe, "instinctively went right to the organic elements of human nature, whether under a white skin or black"; they knew the right thing—that men should be free. But they lacked realistic knowledge of Negro life and experience, and for this lack sentimental idealism could not compensate. Before the Civil War, therefore, the characterization of the Negro was far from the complexity that we now know was there; it was oversimplified—the contented slave, and his corollary, the wretched freedman; the comic minstrel on the one hand, and the persecuted victim, the noble savage, the submissive Christian, the tragic octoroon on the other.*

2

If, before Appomattox, *Uncle Tom's Cabin* was undoubtedly the champion in the battle of the books, for a long time afterwards the proslavery defense was victorious. The plantation tradition, glorifying slavery as a benevolent guardianship, crystallized. Negro and white characters were neatly packaged. Inevitable were old marse, the essence of chivalry; young missy, 100% southern womanhood, the essence of charm; and young marse, chip off the old block, the essence of dash and courage; all essences. Negro characters were grooved also: the mammy, proud of her quality whitefolks, the wise upbringer of their children (there is little mention of her own); her male counterpart, also worshipful of his whitefolks, devoted to their glory and service; and the clown, the razor-toting, watermelon-eating singer and dancer, with a

* "I swear their nature is beyond my comprehension. A strange people!—merry 'mid their misery—laughing through their tears, like the sun shining through the rain. Yet what simple philosophers they! They tread life's path as if 'twere strewn with roses devoid of thorns, and make the most of life with natures of sunshine and song."

"Natures of sunshine and song." Most readers of this passage would take it to refer to the American Negro. Instead it is about the Irish, spoken by an English officer in a play dealing with one of the most tragic periods in the history of the persecution of the Irish. (From Sterling A. Brown, *The Negro in American Fiction* [Washington, D.C., 1931], p. 1.)

Stereotyping is a thrice-told tale. The treatment of the Jewish character in English, European, and American literature, is certainly another instance. Years ago, a perceptive commentator on our popular art, Issac Goldberg, pointed to the startling fact that the three most popular butts of comedy on our vaudeville stage were the Irishman, the Negro, and the Jew, the three most persecuted minorities at that moment of American History.

penchant for big words he could neither understand nor pronounce, whom the thriving black-face minstrel shows made
one of America's favorite theatrical personages.

Among the authors who established the plantation tradition, Thomas Nelson Page and Joel Chandler Harris were
most persuasive. These and their fellows were children when
the Civil War broke out; they had known Negro children as
playmates; they remembered their grandfathers and fathers
and uncles with ancestral pride; they saw the old South
through the haze of retrospect; they invested the Lost Cause
with the glamor of the defeated and the departed. They combined the chuckling of humorous, philosophical slaves with
the pathos of ill-starred aristocrats. Frequenters of the Negro
quarters, rapt listeners to old Negro yarn spinners in their absorptive years, blessed with sharp eyes and ears and retentive
memories, these authors were able to convey the plausible,
surface realism of local color. The dialect, often meticulously
rendered, rang true; if the words were right, the thoughts behind them had to be right. A Negro folkline, "You can read
my letters, but you sho' cain't read my mind," should have
caused them and their readers some doubt—but for all of
their claim that they knew the Negro, *that* was *one* line, and
one aspect of his character that they did not know.

So Page has his inveterate old uncles reminiscing on the
good old days before the war, to a white stranger who asks
just the right question and then stands back while the torrent
leaps: a stranger who never for a moment suspects guile or
irony or forgetfulness or inaccuracy. "Dem was good ole
times, Marster, de bes' Sam ever see," is one refrain that is
repeated. These old uncles are more ventriloquist's dummies
than people, but to the readers of the eighties, they were appealing and persuasive. A vouched-for legend tells us that
Thomas Wentworth Higginson, the abolitionist friend of John
Brown, the man who was wounded in a fight in Boston to
keep a fugitive slave from being returned to the South, the
colonel of a Negro regiment in the Civil War, this man, the
legend goes, who had fought so strenuously for the Negro,
was discovered thirty years after the war in his study, in tears
from reading *In Ole Virginia* by Thomas Page.*

Joel Chandler Harris was readier to show some harshness
in the antebellum South, but his picture remains one of mutual affection and kindness. A surly, intractable Blue Dave is
rehabilitated when he finds another master as good as his first

* Paul H. Buck, *The Road to Reunion* (1865–1900) (Boston, 1937), p.
235.

one, who had died; Free Joe, who has no one to look after
him, a misfit among the happier slaves, dies disconsolate, and
ineffectual, and free. Harris contributed minor masterpieces
in his Br'er Rabbit Tales; these are his garnerings of rich
yield, and without his perceptiveness some of the world's best
folk literature might have perished. But despite his disclaim-
er, Harris *did* doctor the tales he picked up in the slave
quarters; they are not genuinely folk—of the folk, by the
folk, to the folk, for the folk—but they are told by an old
uncle to entertain a little white boy. The framework in which
they are told is the plantation tradition. When Harris used
Uncle Remus as a kind of columnist for the *Atlanta Constitution*, as he often did, Uncle Remus is closer kin to Henry
Grady and the New South than to Remus's African forebears. Still in his inimitable speech he deplores education of
Negroes as the "ruination of this country . . . a barrel stave
[he says] can fling mo' sense into [his] people in one minute
than all de schoolhouses betwixt dis and de State er Midgi-
gan." There are two Uncle Remuses. The inferior one was a
dialect-talking version of a Georgia politician, and for all of
his pithiness he is more cracker-box philosopher than sage of
the quarters.

But Page and Harris, and a horde of followers were popular in the leading Northern magazines and converted much of
the North, which was ready to forget the late grueling contest. They presented a glowing picture of the kindlier aspects
of slavery. Their cardinal principles were mutual affection between the races; and the peculiar endowment of each race to
occupy its role: one race the born master, one race the born
slave. The road to reunion was opening; tension was relaxing;
the troubled past could be forgotten, the wrongs could be
covered over, perhaps they had not been so bad, perhaps they
could go away. So the Plantation Tradition became fixed.

During the Reconstruction, other stereotypes were added
to those of the contented slave, the comic minstrel, and the
wretched freedman.* These were the brute Negro and the
tragic mulatto. Page contrasted the old issue Negro, loyal and
contented (in Page's version), with the new issue, who were
disloyal, ungrateful, and discontented, ruined by emancipa-

---

* The effect, of course, was not confined to the last century. In the
first doctoral dissertation written on this subject, the critic pontificates
that in one twenty-six line sketch by Joel Chandler Harris about Br'er
Fox and Br'er Mud Turtle (I quote): "the whole range of the Negro
character is revealed thoroughly." John Herbert Nelson, *The Negro
Character in American Literature* (Lawrence, Kansas: The Department
of Journalism Press, 1926), p. 118.

tion. These new Negroes were shown as insulting swaggerers. They were often in Federal uniforms, or they engaged in politics. The docile mastiffs had become mad dogs; the carriers of the rabies were carpetbaggers, scalawags, Union troops, and Yankee schoolmarms. A sort of Ku Klux Klan fiction emerged; insolent Negroes, often rapists, were shown in atrocity stories, and the knightly Klan rode, white sheeted, to restore southern civilization and to protect southern womanhood.* As a colleague, E. Franklin Frazier, used to quip: "The closer a Negro got to the ballot box, the more he looked like a rapist."

The tragic mulatto stereotype stemmed from the antislavery crusade, whose authors used it, partly to show miscegenation as an evil of slavery, partly as an attempt to win readers' sympathies by presenting central characters who were physically very like the readers. Antislavery authors, Harriet Beecher Stowe included, held to a crude kind of racism. Their near-white characters are the intransigent, the resentful, the mentally alert—for biological, not social, reasons. In the proslavery argument, the mixed blood characters are victims of a divided inheritance * and proof of the disastrous results

---

* Two of the most widely known Hollywood motion pictures have made great use of the formulas of the plantation tradition and especially of the brute Negro. These are D. W. Griffith's *The Birth of a Nation* (based upon the melodramatic novels of Thomas Dixon, *The Clansman* and *The Leopard Spots*) and Margaret Mitchell's *Gone With The Wind*, in which the glamor of Scarlett O'Hara and Rhett Butler should not blind us to the trite stereotyping of character and social background.

---

* What might be called the fractional theory of personality gets its *reductio ad absurdum* in Roark Bradford's *This Side of Jordan* (1929).

> "The blade of a razor flashed . . . Her Negro Blood sent it unerringly between two ribs. Her Indian blood sent it back for an unnecessary second and third slash."

It might be hazarded that her Eskimo blood kept her from being chilled with horror.

Fannie Hurst's *Imitation of Life* contains another gem. Of the fair-skinned heroine, Peola, we get this analysis from her mother:

> "It may be mixed up wid plenty of white blood . . . but thin out chicken gravy wid water an' it remains [sic!] chicken gravy, only not so good. . . ."

She prays for her octoroon daughter:

> "Lord git de white horses drove out of her blood. Kill de curse—shame de curse her light-colored pap lef' for his baby. . . . Chase

of amalgamation. Most of the villains in reconstruction fiction are mixed bloods, "inheriting the vices of both races and the virtues of neither." The mulatto, or quadroon, or octoroon heroine has been a favorite for a long time; in books by white authors the whole desire of her life is to find a white lover; then balked by the dictates of her society, she sinks to a tragic end. In our century, Negro authors have turned the story around; now after restless searching, she finds peace only after returning to her own people. In both cases, however, the mulatto man or woman is presented as a lost, unhappy, woebegone abstraction.

The fiction of George Washington Cable pays great attention to the free people of color of old Louisiana, whose rigid caste restrictions brought tragedy to quadroon and octoroon heroines. But Cable did not limit his sympathy for the victims of slavery to this unfortunate caste; his picture of old Louisiana was colorful but crowded with authoritative antiquarian detail. Whether educated free man of color, or illiterate field hand, or captured African Prince Bras-Coupé, who killed rather than serve as slave, Cable gave shrewd, knowing interpretations of Negro character. The first genuine southern liberal, Cable knew too much about slavery to idealize the old regime, and he was sensitively aware of the dark shadows of the past on the South of his day. The best local colorist of Louisiana, he found his social sympathies too broad for his native section, and he spent his last years in self-imposed exile.

One of Cable's services to American literature lies in his re-enforcing of Mark Twain's growing liberality concerning Negroes. *Huckleberry Finn* is more telling an indictment of slavery than patently antislavery novels are. The callousness of a small God-fearing town toward Negroes, the conditioning of a small boy, so that the word "abolitionist" is the worst insult he can imagine; the topsy-turvyness of Huck's self-condemnation when he decides that he will help Jim escape only because he hasn't been brought up right and is in the devil's grip; the characterization of Jim, superstitious but shrewd,

---

de wild white horses tramplin' on my chile's happiness. . . . It's de white horses dat's wild, a-swimmin in de blood of mah chile."

It is submitted that with all those horses running wild in Peola's aorta, she could hardly be a stable character. From this novel, of which Hollywood has made two increasingly saccharine versions, oral tradition among Negroes has taken the name of Peola for a fair skinned girl; not in respect, however, but in burlesque.

kindly, self-sacrificial, but determined to be free, not contented in slavery—all of these are vividly rendered. A single passage of dialogue and the pretensions of the plantation tradition are shredded away. Consider this scene: Jim is on the raft; Huck sets off in the canoe, ostensibly to learn the name of the town they are passing but really to betray Jim to the slavehunters.

> "Putty soon I'll be a-shout'n for joy, and I'll say its all on account o'Huck I's a free man; en I couldn't ever been free if it hadn't been for Huck; Huck done it . . . Dah you goes, de ole true Huck, de on'y white gen'lman dat ever kep' his promise to ole Jim."

This tobacco-chewing, pipe-smoking, barefooted one-gallused Missouri kid, this truant from learning, the delinquent son of the town drunk—now on his way to betray his buddy—becomes "the only white gentleman that ever kept his promise to old Jim." Twain's irony does not leave the old tradition of noblesse oblige much to stand on.

Negro writers at the turn of the century also deepened the portraiture. According to William Dean Howells, Paul Laurence Dunbar was the "first American Negro to feel the Negro life aesthetically and express it lyrically." Influenced almost inevitably by the powerful plantation tradition, most of his poems about slavery echo Irwin Russell, Page and Joel Chandler Harris, but his poems about the Negro life of his own day are affectionate, sympathetic, and winning. Characters that had been treated as clownish were now revealed as more richly human. Dunbar was of the school of James Whitcomb Riley—of the happy hearthside and pastoral contentment. He was a gentle person, and even if publishing conditions had permitted it, he probably would not have chosen the prevalent harshness to write about. In a few short stories and poems in standard English he showed bitterness, but this is typically oblique as in "We Wear the Mask," a poem containing a true metaphor but more plaintive than revealing.

Dunbar's contemporary, Charles Waddell Chesnutt, was concerned with the harsher—and more typical aspects—of life in the South, and with the problems of the color line. His volume of folk tales (*The Conjure Woman*, 1899) seems to resemble the tales of Page and Harris, but on close reading Chesnutt is quite different. His tales are told by a shrewd, self-serving Uncle, whose characterizations of both Negroes and whites is salty—and no nonsense about the good old days. Chesnutt based one of his strongest novels, *The Mar-row of Tradition* (1901) on the riot in Wilmington, North Carolina. This novel and *The Colonel's Dream* (1905) show a grasp of social reality, and a powerful ability to dramatize his material.

The novels of Albion Tourgee, who served as an officer in the Union Army and remained in North Carolina as a "car-petbagger," are informed and powerful, and with the fiction of Chesnutt, are necessary correctives to the Ku Klux Klan fiction of the post-war South. *A Fool's Errand* (1879) and *Bricks Without Straw* (1880) are melodramatic—fighting fire with fire—but they come closer to the complex realities of the time and anticipate the fiction of the twentieth century more than those of any other writer save Chesnutt.

3

At the turn of the century W. E. B. Dubois started his distin-guished career with *The Souls of Black Folk,* which is still one of the best interpretations of Negro life and aspirations. On the creative side, Dubois continued to write poems, short stories, novels, autobiographies and essays, but none of these excel this pioneering work which was marked by impassioned polemics against compromise, incisive irony at hypocrisy, sensitive brooding over the dilemmas of democracy, and af-firmation of race pride and solidarity.

A key essay by Dubois, called "The Sorrow Songs," was one of the earliest and best interpretations of the spirituals. Dubois' awareness of the dignity and beauty of Negro folk music was broadened and deepened by James Weldon John-son. In addition to editing two comprehensive volumes of spirituals with his brother, J. Rosamond Johnson, he com-mented upon Negro musical shows, ragtime, and the begin-nings of jazz from the vantage point of a participant in their history. His novel, *Autobiography of an Ex-Colored Man* (1912), was the first to deal with Negro life on several levels, from the folk to the sophisticated. It is rather more a chart of Negro life than a novel, but it contains informed analysis and valid interpretation. Johnson's Preface to the *Book of Ameri-can Negro Poetry* (1922) boldly advanced the claims of the Negro's creativeness. Johnson's own earlier poems, collected in *Fifty Years and Other Poems* (1917), looked backward in genre pieces of the school of Dunbar, and looked at the pres-ent and towards the future in hortatory and lyrical verse. In the commemorative title poem, Johnson insisted on the Neg-ro's belonging to America, on his services, and on his potential. As with Dubois, creative literature for Johnson was the other arm to propagandistic work for the NAACP.

Johnson's hope for more adequate and accurate presentation of Negro life was not long in coming. The time—the post-war decade, with its revolt against squeamishness, repression, and Babbittry—was favorable. The lost generation seemed to find itself in Harlem or the Caribbean or Africa; youth rekindled the flame in Harlem where a magazine blazed forth for one issue with the name "Fire!" Carl Van Doren felt that the decided need of American literature for "color, music, gusto, the free expression of gay or desperate moods" could best be filled by the exploration of Negro life and character. Exploitation, however, rather than exploration, was as often as not the result. Eugene O'Neill's *The Emperor Jones* (1920) ushered in the decade: the play was theatrically effective, with a Negro of some aggressiveness and truculence, until then a rarity on the stage, at the tragic center instead of in comic relief, but it relied overly on tomtoms and atavism. So did O'Neill's generally unconvincing *All God's Chillun Got Wings*, which caused a tremendous imbroglio on Broadway, for all of its essential conformism to racial myths.

The technical facility of Vachel Lindsay's *The Congo* (1914) made it too popular; its repetend:

Then I saw the Congo, creeping through the black
Cutting through the jungle with a golden track

seemed to be the marching song of the white writers on safari to the newly discovered Harlem and other *terras incognitas*. Even as humane an author as Waldo Frank in *Holiday* defined white and Negro "consciousness" too schematically and too expeditiously. Sherwood Anderson's *Dark Laughter* used "the Negro way of life of levee loungers" to beat such whipping boys and girls as American neuroticism and acquisitiveness. John W. Vandercook brought back from Haiti and Surinam inspiring romances of heroism and noble savagery but, not content with these, he lectured the American Negro for having degenerated from his distinguished forebears in the Surinam bush. In *Tom-Tom* (1926), Vandercook related how the spectacle of a quadroon-octoroon chorus and "several wealthy well-educated mulatto families" in the choice seats—upon his one visit to a Harlem theatre—awoke him to "the supreme tragedy of the Negro." The chorus and the audience clarified race differences for him. "We [the whites]," he states, "are optical—intellectual. They are auricular—emotional." W. B. Seabrook's books on Haiti exploited the orgiastic and voodooistic. The French novelist Paul Morand

wrote a group of stories called *Magie Noire* (1928), in which
atavism was luridly and absurdly expressed; in one story, for
instance, a Negro intellectual attending a Pan-African con-
vention in Brussels visits a Negro Museum and immediately
runs berserk. Ronald Firbank's Mayfair burlesque, *Prancing
Nigger* (1924), was exactly titled. Perhaps the epitome of the
trend was Carl Van Vechten's *Nigger Heaven* (1925), in
which Harlem, the heaven, was flamboyant and erotic.

The craft and viewpoint of Carl Van Vechten and his fellows influenced Negro writers, and the frequent interracial
parties compounded the interest. Only a few of the Harlem
indigènes withstood the blandishments of the aesthetes and
the hedonists: the best of those who wrote about Harlem
were Rudolph Fisher, an insouciant O. Henry of Baghdad-
on-the-Hudson, and Claude McKay, an unvarnished realist.
But even these accented the instinctual, hedonistic, and peculiar.

The Harlemites that emerged from the pages of novels by
both white and Negro authors in this period were exotic pri-
mitives, whose dances—the Charleston, the "black bottom,"
the "snake hips," the "walking the dog"—were tribal rituals;
whose music with wa-wa trumpets and trombones and drum
batteries doubled for tom-toms; whose chorus girls with
bunches of bananas girdling their shapely middles nurtured
tourists' delusions of the "Congo creeping through the black."
Joie de vivre was a racial monopoly: rhythm and gaiety were
on one side—the darker—of the racial line. "That's why dar-
kies were born" sang a Negro jazz musician who should have
known better. "The whites have only money, privilege,
power; Negroes have cornered the joy" was the theme of a
Negro novelist, who did know better.

The amorality and irresponsibility of the youthful rebels
was reproved by such genteel critics as Benjamin Brawley.
The burgeoning jazz met with disfavor among the Negro
middle-class, who wished to conform to socially-approved
standards. The leaders of the NAACP felt that the characterization of Harlem sweet-backs and hot mammas did injustice
to their propaganda and purposes. After chiding younger
Negro authors, Dubois turned in *Dark Princess* (1928) to
what he considered the proper study of writers: the rising
tide of color. Though idealized and contrived, this novel handled Pan-Africanism and the emergence of Asia and Africa
with prescience. Walter White's *Fire in the Flint* (1925, an
anti-lynching novel) and *Flight* (1926, an anti-passing-for-
white novel) were also idealized and tractarian, though informed and somewhat new in material. To Jessie Fauset and

Nella Larsen, delineators of Negro middle-class life, proving
a point meant more than presenting people. Properly resentful of the nonsense about inherent racial traits; irked by the
theories of "race differences," such novelists blinked at the
realities of differences (social and cultural) between the
races. Occasionally, in their novels about passing Negroes,
especially Jessie Fauset's *Comedy: American Style* (1933),
the intraracial color snobbishness and the latent self-hatred of
anti-Negro Negroes could be glimpsed, but these glimpses
were rare, and the usual picture was bland, at once self-pi-
tying and self-congratulatory.

Such novelists, according to Wallace Thurman's *Infants of
the Spring* (1932), write only to "apprise white humanity of
the better classes among Negro humanity." A sharp-eyed,
nay-saying young Negro, Thurman also lampooned the pho-
ney primitivism of his confrères. One of the best satires of
the pretense and sham rife at this time came from E. Simms
Campbell, whose talent for cartooning extended to pen as
well as to brush and palette. He remembered:

> intellectual parties where Negroes who were in the theatre
> were looked upon as social plums and the dumbest and most
> illiterate were fawned over by Park Avenue . . . [and where]
> the intellectual stink could have been cut with a knife—a
> dull knife.*

The poets of the period spoke more deeply than the novelists. Claude McKay's *Harlem Shadows* (1922) was original
and authentic in its controlled craftsmanship and in its revelation of a personality: an independent, angry radical—now
excoriating America for its injustices, now rousing race solidarity, now setting nostalgic vignettes of his native Jamaica
against the tragic but fascinating Harlem. Less militant, but
as deeply engaged by "race," Countee Cullen also brought
disciplined technique to the revelation of a subtle, sophisticated consciousness, as in "Heritage," "The Shroud of
Color," and various cutting epigrams. Langston Hughes was
less conventional in technique than these two poets, and less
subjective, taking the Negro folk—particularly the urban
masses—for his subject. For over three decades, in more than
a dozen books, Hughes has told their story, interpreted their
lives, and made use of their language, lore, and song to point
up his own commentary on America.

Among others, Waring Cuney, Frank Horne, and three

* "Blues," in *Jazzmen*, ed. by F. Ramsey, Jr. and C. E. Smith (New
York, 1939), pp. 103–104.

women poets—Georgia Douglass Johnson, Angelina Grimke, and Ann Spencer—wrote truthfully about themselves, and thereby widened and deepened the self-portraiture of Negroes. One of the finest books of poems of the twenties was James Weldon Johnson's *God's Trombones* (1927), in which he recreated the eloquence of the old Negro preacher. This work not only marked a development from apologistic rhetoric and sentimentalized genre poetry, but also in its respect for the intrinsic dignity of folk-stuff showed younger writers the way to go, much as Yeats and Synge had previously shown young Irish writers.

Two striking books of this movement were Jean Toomer's *Cane* (1923) and Eric Walrond's *Tropic Death* (1926). These authors were alike in being masters of their craft and, unfortunately, in falling silent after the publication of one book each. Toomer is a poet in the few lyrics in *Cane*, and even more so in his evocative prose. No imaginative work since *The Souls of Black Folk* had so deeply explored Negro life in the deep South, in border cities, in the North, among the folk, the urban masses, the bourgeoisie, the intellectuals; and none had revealed it so beautifully. Walrond's *Tropic Death* is a brilliantly impressionistic, obliquely, subtly communicated series of portraits of the author's native West Indies.

In 1925 Du Bose Heyward wrote a poetic novel about a crippled beggar named Porgy of Catfish Row, Charleston, S. C. Through the success of the novel, its dramatization by the Theater Guild, its several versions in moving pictures, and the folk opera (by Du Bose and his wife Dorothy Heyward, and George and Ira Gershwin), Porgy is the most widely known Negro character (nationally and internationally) since Uncle Tom. Heyward, a white South Carolinian, was a sensitive and sympathetic observer of Negroes, especially on the waterfront. His poem "Jazzbo Brown" and his second novel *Mamba's Daughters* (1925) were fresh and honest. Julia Peterkin, another South Carolinian, was also a careful and absorptive observer of life on the plantations in such books as *Green Thursday* (1924) and *Scarlet Sister Mary* (1928). Both Heyward and Mrs. Peterkin veered toward the exotic primitive, however; a fellow South Carolinian, E. C. L. Adams, gave a fuller picture of the workaday life of Negroes, with none of the harshness minimized, in two books of dialogues: *Congaree Sketches* (1927) and *Nigger to Nigger* (1928). These books, with their vividness of folkspeech, the irony, starkness and knowingness of the talkers, added a new dimension to the treatment of the Negro folk. No white folk-

lorist (not even Harris) no Negro folklorist (not even Chesnutt) knew so much and rendered it so well as this white
country doctor in the Congaree River section of South Carolina. Howard Odum and Guy Johnson at the University of
North Carolina studied Negro folk songs for clues to understanding Negro life; as by-products, Odum produced three
novels about a synthesized roustabout, Left Wing Gordon,
who attains a certain convincingness and complexity; and
Johnson wrote the first and best study of the steel driver John
Henry, who is now in the pantheon of American folk heroes.

John Henry was debunked and belittled in Roark Bradford's *John Henry* (1932), from which a bad musical was
made. Bradford was born on a plantation worked by
Negroes, had a Negro nurse, and several Negroes as boyhood
friends. He had watched them (in his words) "at work in the
fields, in the levee camps, and on the river . . . at home, in
church, at their picnics and their funerals." A gifted mimic,
like Harris, he was able to reproduce the folk vocabulary and
syntax, and books like *Ol' Man Adam An' His Chillun*
(1928) and *King David and the Philistine Boys* (1930) are
burlesque masterpieces. Dividing Negroes into three types,
"the nigger, the colored person, and the Negro—upper case
N." Bradford takes his stand by the first type, and though delighted to be in his company, sees him solely as primitive and
uproariously funny.* Bradford could hardly have respected
John Henry who was a steel-driving *man*.

Since Bradford also did not respect the folk-Negro's religion, it is strange that his travesties of the Bible in *Ol' Man
Adam An' His Chillun* served as a springboard for Marc
Connelly's play *The Green Pastures*. Connelly, however,
though not so soaked in local color as Bradford, was wise
enough to know that there was more than farce to the folk,
was humane enough to see the true values of material that
Bradford underestimated, and was a canny stage artificer. He
made full use of the understanding and advice of Richard
Harrison and his fine troupe of Negro actors, and finally was
inspired to set the play in a framework of spirituals sung au-
thentically by the Hall Johnson choir. A miracle in two
senses of the word, *The Green Pastures*, according to Kenneth Burke, exploited the "child symbol":

> The Negroes of "The Green Pastures" with their heavenly
> clambakes, mildly disconsolate "Lawd," the incongruous Afri-
> canization of the Biblical legends, can carry one into a region

* *Ol' Man Adam An' His Chillun* (New York, 1938), p. x.

of gentleness that is in contrast with the harsh demands of our day, caressing.

In contrast to this play, Burke set Hall Johnson's *Run, Little Chillun!*, a play written from within about a Negro religious cult, which "brings out an aspect of the Negro-symbol with which our theatre-going public is not theatrically at home: the power side of the Negro." * Burke was not surprised at the sluggishness of the general public's interest, but he deplored it. In the three decades since, *The Green Pastures* has been revived as a play and movie and has been much anthologized, but the text of *Run, Little Chillun!* is unavailable.

4

Even while Burke was so writing, however, stress was being shifted from quaint philosophers of the quarters in the good old days to the oppressed victims or the aroused laborers in the troublesome, workaday present. Recognition that the Negro was crucial in labor's march to democracy and that the Negro *belongs*, or must belong, here and now, supplanted delusions of his "special endowment," special behavior and special niche in American life. It was important for writers, both Negro and white, to recognize these truths, though today they may seem truisms. The thirties had this healthy influence in thought about *the* Negro: unfortunately, however, enforcement of economic and political creeds interfered (as did antislavery convictions earlier) with complex and convincing characterization. A new type of Negro did emerge in the forceful plays of Paul Green, whose dramaturgy, combined with Richard Wright's fervor and understanding, produced *Native Son*, one of America's few distinguished tragedies dealing with racial materials.

In the depression various brands of radicalism, whether derived from Socialism, Communism, Garveyism, the IWW or just grass-roots dissidence, found Negro life and character to be unworked mines. The old firehouse, Scott Nearing, after writing the grim *Black America* (1929), piled the woes of that exposé on the head of a Negro family in *Freeborn* (1932), the first revolutionary novel of Negro life. For all of its veracity the momentum of the novel was lessened by the fact that it was "unpublishable by any commercial concern." A journalistic radical, John Spivak exposed the chain gang system in *Georgia Nigger* (1932), but here as in so many

* "Negro's Pattern of Life," *Saturday Review of Literature*, X (July 29, 1933), pp. 10–14.

"proletarian" novels characterization was strangled by radical theory, with the last twist given by melodramatic clichés. The best "proletarian" works on Negro life were Grace Lumpkin's novel *A Sign for Cain* (1935) and Paul Peters' and George Sklar's drama *Stevedore* (1934). Both set at the center of the stage a self-respecting, virile, quiet but strong hero, slowly but surely awakened, capable of the greatest trust, willing and ready to die for the causes of race advance and economic brotherhood. From the nobility of an Uncle Tom we now get the nobility of the working-class hero. We also get repetitions of the despicable hat-in-hand tattling Negro, the strong matriarch, and the supposed clown, whose mask is irony; and on the white side, the brutal sheriff, the wishy-washy liberal and (counterpart to the Negro hero) the courageous organizer. One of the stock incidents in these works is the consummation of the triumphant march, hand in hand, and rank by rank, of the white and black workers of the world. After thirty years such a march still occurs far less in life than it did in the novels and plays of the thirties.

That there were such people and such events in America goes without saying, but that the actuality of Negro experience and its literary representation do not always coincide should also at this point go without saying. The Negro author most influenced by neo-Marxist literary canons was Richard Wright. After, and even during, his brief visitation with the Communist Party, Wright was uncomfortable with the working-class hero, however, and was more at home artistically portraying lower-class victims and arraigning American injustices: mob violence in the South, ghetto deprivations and frustrations in the North. From "Big Boy" to Bigger Thomas, Wright presented in such dynamic books as *Uncle Tom's Children, Native Son* and *Black Boy* the searing effects of poverty and prejudice on sensitive Negro youths. Wright's indignation was enormous and his power to communicate the violence and shock was great. Carrying a personal anger too deep for him to master through art, he sought Europe for a resting place. There he became increasingly the interpreter of the American Negro to the European intellectuals, and also, increasingly, he lost touch with the realities of the racial situation in the states. The native son died before he could return home; had he returned he would have found himself not so lost, so alienated, so outside. His own insight, dedication and craft have helped bring about this changed situation.

At a crucial point in his career, Wright was aided by the John Reed Clubs (leftist writing groups) and the Federal Writers' Project. A child of the New Deal (more accurately a stepchild), the Federal Writers' Project gave employment to Negro authors as diverse as Claude McKay and Frank Yerby; Ted Poston and Willard Motley; Arna Bontemps and Roi Ottley; Zora Neale Hurston and Henry Lee Moon. One achievement of the Writers' Project, through its city, county, state and regional guides, was the sponsorship of local history and lore, both current and historic. Negro writers benefited from these interests. Far more revelatory than the Harlem fad were Zora Neale Hurston's rewarding novels of her native Florida: *Jonah's Gourd Vine* (1934) and *Their Eyes Were Watching God* (1937), and best of all, *Mules and Men* (1935), in which Miss Hurston, a trained anthropologist, becomes the first Negro to join the many authors who have ploughed the fertile fields of Negro folk life. From a horde of narratives by living ex-slaves, the folklorist B. A. Botkin assembled the indispensable *Lay My Burden Down* (1945), a folk history of slavery of surprising worth; and Roscoe E. Lewis collected a mass of material and fashioned it into *The Negro in Virginia*, the pioneer in a series, doomed by the short life of the project, that would have dealt regionally with Negro life. Sufficient material was salvaged from the excellent notes on Negroes in New York to supply Roi Ottley's bright, informative narratives, *New World A-Coming* (1943) and *Black Odyssey* (1948). Arna Bontemps in his first-rate novel of a Negro insurrection, *Black Thunder* (1936), turned away from the hedonistic fiction that he exploited in *God Sends Sunday* (1931), to a more important interest in the history of the American Negro—a subject that has busied him fruitfully ever since.

The population of William Faulkner's Yoknapatawpha County contains many Negroes, and they are certainly not the least interesting persons to William Faulkner's readers, or to himself. Faulkner's depth in characterizing Negroes increased with the years; whereas in an earlier novel, *Soldier's Pay,* he accepted the myths of *his* own tribal past, soon he steadily began to see Negroes whole, and with *Go Down, Moses* he defied several of his region's set beliefs concerning the Negro. In his last years, Faulkner was rejected by his fellow Oxonians as too liberal, and accepted (gingerly) by Negro intellectuals as not liberal enough. His essential liberalism on race can be questioned (his correspondence to his "new Southern" spokesman Gavin Stevens, a lawyer who grows in good will to the Negro, but also and better in good understanding, needs study). There is no questioning, however, that in ploughing deeply into the soil of his single county, Faulkner was wise, prescient, and rewarded. What seems at first glance the familiar stereotyping becomes, on true reading, complex and revelatory, e.g., Dilsey is far more than the old mammy; Joe Christmas more than the tragic mulatto; Nancy Manigault more than the depraved "wench." But Faulkner also presents new people, unnoticed before but here candidly portrayed: the admirable Lucius Beauchamps, Sam Fathers, and the Centaur in Brass. When spouting the Southern liberal's ambivalent credo (cf. Gavin Stevens' long-windedness in *Intruder in the Dust*) Faulkner is unconvincing or wrong, but when he stands back and lets his Negro character speak out and act out, Faulkner is right, and often superb.

Faulkner's éclat has dimmed the achievement of several other Southern novelists, who, in dealing with the Negro, often did what Faulkner could not or would not do. One example is Erskine Caldwell, a genuine liberal, who in such stories as "The People Vs. Abe Latham, Colored," "Kneel to the Rising Sun," and "Candy Man Beechum," and in a novel, *Trouble in July*, has snapshots and photographs that are fresh and authentic. Other examples are Hamilton Basso, especially in his *Courthouse Square* (1936), and William March in *Come In at the Door*. Both deal with areas of Negro experience untouched by Faulkner, as does, to cite a current example Harper Lee's *To Kill a Mockingbird*. A historical novelist, T. S. Stribling has written a trilogy of a Southern family —both branches, Negro and white—in *The Forge* (1931), *The Store* (1933), and *Unfinished Cathedral* (1934). This masterpiece of re-creating the past is most unfairly neglected today.

Another underestimated novel on race relations is *Strange Fruit* (1944), by Lillian Smith. Here, like Faulkner, Miss Smith explores the conventionally stereotyped liaison between Negro woman and white man. Miss Smith's psychological probing results in much that is clarifying and revealing. The ambivalence of the white youth is dramatized in *Strange Fruit;* it is analyzed and substantiated in *Killers of the Dream* (1949). This book also is neglected by the "southern critical establishment," though were some of its members to read it they might learn about themselves. *Strange Fruit* was made into a play and created a stir. At the same time, *Deep are the Roots* by Arnaud D'Usseau and James Gow handled an interracial liaison on a higher level than had been usual. Other dramas getting to grips with the reality of Negro experience were *Jeb,* and a Negro adaptation of a play on Polish life, *Anna Lucasta* by Philip Yordan. The griefs of a Polish family were easily transposed to a Negro family.

The Negro intellectual—as intellectual, not merely victim or malcontent—is missing from American fiction. Even college life has been scanted as a subject. An underestimated book, Bucklin Moon's *Without Magnolias* (1949) is a well-done, serious presentation of a Southern Negro college. It includes sharp *aperçus* and insights, surprising at first when one realizes that the author was a white man, but not surprising when one recalls that George Washington Cable, Mark Twain, Albion Tourgee and Lillian Smith also wore their color lightly.

Moon's book on Negro academics is broader and more firmly based than J. Saunders Redding's novel on college life, *Stranger and Alone* (1950). More revealing autobiographically than fictionally, *Stranger and Alone* lacks the power and insight that mark *No Day of Triumph*, Redding's distinguished work of reportage, whose gallery of people—Southern, Northern, Negro, white—and whose searching commentary deserve to be better known. Redding's *On Being Negro in America* has the ambitious reach of books so titled; it grasps both truths and truisms. Although Redding terms it his valedictory to "race," it is no such thing, of course, nor could it be. Instead it signaled the beginning of a career as a sort of Negro roving ambassador, depriving us of one of the sharpest and best informed observers of the American scene. Carl Rowan's career is similar: after keen and persuasive reportage on the Negro in America in *South of Freedom* and *Go Down to Sorrow,* he then traveled and reported on India, Pakistan and Southeast Asia in *The Pitiful and the Proud.*

While as Director of the United States Information Agency Rowan presented America's cause to the world in Washington, D. C., Chester Himes raged at America's ways in Paris. As rebellious as Richard Wright but even more nihilistic and despairing, Himes has most fully presented the misanthropic, frustrated, furious young Negro, insulted and injured, uprooted and lost in the novels, *If He Hollers* (1945), *Lonely Crusade* (1947), and the largely autobiographical *Third Generation* (1954), a searing attack on the Negro bourgeoisie. No one can stay long near Himes's characters and feel at all easy with such "racialistic" abstractions as humility, forgivingness, cheerfulness and contentment.

Another expatriate, Julian Mayfield, wrote three significant novels before departing for the greener fields of Ghana. These were *The Hit, The Long Night* (1958) and *The Grand Parade* (1960). The first two, with Ann Petry's *The Street* (1946), are authentic slices of Harlem life, refuting the repeated lie of Harlem the playground. Many young Negro novelists have found that one novel in everyman's life and have written it in sociological and naturalistic terms, generally in urban settings, under the influence of Dreiser, Farrell, and especially Wright and Himes. William Gardner Smith's *The Last of the Conquerors* centers around the life of Negroes in the armed forces occupying Germany, and the outlook is new and sharp. John O. Killens, in what might be considered a "proletarian novel" showed a man's upbringing in *Youngblood*, a powerful but more hopeful book than any by Wright or Himes. Killens's *And Then We Heard the Thunder* (1962) is so far the best treatment of the Negro soldier in fiction. It is an angry book but rich in sardonic humor and a wide gallery of interesting, diversified people. Similarly sardonic and powerful though less successful as a novel is Hari Rhodes's *A Chosen Few* which deals with Negroes in the Marine Corps. The same qualities of rage, violence, and honesty mark the novels of John Williams, whose novels *Sissie* (1963) and *The Angry Ones,* and the anthology *The Angry Black* (1962), mark a newcomer of promise and strength.

Of fiction dealing with Negro life during the last two decades, Ralph Ellison's *Invisible Man* has invited most critical attention. This picaresque novel, something of a black *Candide,* stirred so much interest and belief in its variety and authenticity of characters, both Negro and white, that the old stereotypes were shaken. Carrying his naive hero from boyhood in Oklahoma to manhood in Harlem, Ellison gives a wonderful series of vignettes, rich in farce, comedy, irony, satire, melodrama, tragedy and grotesquerie, all set solidly in Negro experience. Like Voltaire's Candide, Ellison's hero ends up by cultivating his garden in an underground hole in Gotham. Though he is defeated, his creator is triumphant, and one of his triumphs is that it will be hard for cardboard heroes and villains to occupy the fictional stage any longer.

Because of Ellison's silence since *Invisible Man,* broken intermittently, of course, by his perceptive essays, James Baldwin is today the best known Negro writer, and partly because of the paper-back revolution is probably the best known American Negro writer in history. *Go Tell It On the Mountain* is a winning novel, rich in emotion and understanding, leaning heavily upon Baldwin's autobiography, as almost all of his work does, including his latest, the widely discussed *Another Country.* Baldwin's essays, especially *The Fire Next Time,* mark him as the most powerful and prophetic voice of the young militants in SNCC and CORE. There is such a bond between him and the youngsters that one hopes he has at last come home again. Gifted as a novelist and essayist, he has written two startling plays: *Blues for Mr. Charlie*, a play written in the wake of Birmingham, exacerbated and ferocious, but to at least one critic less lasting than *Amen Corner*, which the gifted Frank Silvera has staged on both coasts.

When *Amen Corner* had its premier several years ago at Howard University it seemed to some that here was the finest grasp of Negro life and character yet encountered on a stage. Lorraine Hansberry's *Raisin in the Sun* belongs in its fine company, for presentation of people, people who happen to be Negroes, people of a different category from Porgy and Scarlet Sister Mary and Lulu Belle and Uncle Tom and The Octoroon. And Ossie Davis's hilarious *Purlie Victorious* also has people in it, of a different section, hemisphere, world, universe from Amos an' Andy, Stepin Fetchit and Uncle Remus. Incidentally, the humor of Dick Gregory, Jackie Mabley and Godfrey Cambridge belongs with this type of genuine Negro humor, as remote from the usual radio, movie farce as Charlie Chaplin is from the Katzenjammer Kids.

The plays of LeRoi Jones have also caused a stir. In spite of the considerable talents of this young poet-playwright, the unadulterated hatred of his plays seems factitious, not real. That white Greenwich Village audiences are titillated by *The Toilet, Dutchman* and *The Slave* is certain, but this says more about them than about Negro life in America. A wave of masochism swings in; cries of *peccavi, peccavimus* fill the air; but this does not mean that the cause is art or insight or revelation.

A healthier kind of writing, less desperate, less frenetic, but as concerned with injustice is the developing literature of the freedom movement. Times of gestation, conception, birth and early nurturing of a revolution are not necessarily times that produce creative literature. The types of writing for these activists are tracts, pamphlets, advertisements, slogans, squibs, lampoons, parodies, burlesques. Closest to fiction and drama are the autobiographical narratives, fragments recollected in whatever tranquillity is permitted by jail sentences or returns to campuses and jobs. There are signs of such autobiographical renderings from such activists as Michael Thelwell, Len Holt, Claude Brown, Bill Mahoney, and Charles Cobb, to name only the few freedom fighters whom the author knows best. A good anthology has just been issued by *Freedomways* which is called *Mississippi: Opening the Closed Society*. This issue is earnest that the novels and poems and plays will come. As long as these young people hold fiercely to their hope, and to their conviction, singingly proclaimed, that "We Shall Overcome," the good writing will someday come. We can wait. These young people are in a worthy tradition: that of David Walker, David Ruggles, Frederick Douglass, Harriet Tubman, Sojourner Truth, William Nell, Martin Delany, Henry Highland Garnet, Samuel Ringgold Ward and William Wells Brown, that driving wedge of Negro propagandists who functioned so ably a century ago.

5

But this, it seems, is where I came in. The images of Negroes in fiction and drama have increased in number, and their manifold identities have been further recognized. More readers and writers seem aware of the humanist's concern "that the discovery and explanation of the individual . . . in space and time shall not be reduced to a point where his particular character is lost": where he becomes

> indistinguishable from any other person who possesses the same race, milieu and moment. . . . Even when we turn . . . to the study of communities and states, cultures and civilizations, we are equally anxious to make every possible distinction, to recognize every qualitative difference. In the humanist's quest, similarities, whether between individual human beings or between cultural patterns, are useful only insofar as they lead to the discovery of differences; these resemblances are never absolute, they are merely means to discourse, and they have a way of disappearing just as soon as one turns from the larger group to examine the individuals in whom a fleeting resemblance has been caught.*

Stereotyping is on the way out. Besides the enormous, comprehensive literature on races and cultures, readers, theatregoers, creative writers and critics have developed a sophistication boding ill for the allegorical, the simplistic, the superficial characterization of the past. The dangers and unreality of schematic, too well-made plotting; the weakness of flat and one-sided characters in distinction to round and complex characters; the pronounced effect of setting on character so that setting itself becomes a character; the ineffectuality of thesis-ridden novels; all of these have grown clearer. Readers and writers learn that deductive, expository and direct delineation is patently inferior to inductive, indirect delineation;

---

* Harcourt Brown, "Science and the Human Comedy: Voltaire," in *Science and the Modern Mind*, ed. by G. Holton (Boston, 1958), p. 20.

that readers welcome discovery instead of indoctrination; that showing, in fiction, is better than telling. So the expounding, grouping, consigning, assuming, relegating phases of stereotyping disappear.

Fiction and drama have led in the destruction or at least the displacement of the stereotypes. The social revolution at home and the emergent nations abroad have had repercussions in the cultural world.** A willingness—nay, an eagerness —to learn the truth is coupled with a willingness to grant dignity to others. Even Hollywood has made a belated start toward pictures of genuine Negro life. It is television, however, that has rushed in where movies and even Broadway long feared to tread.

Nevertheless, stereotyping is not altogether out. The hipster generation, Norman Mailer pontificates, was attracted to what *the Negro* had to offer (italics mine, but let Mailer take over):

> In such places as Greenwich Village, a *ménage-à-trois* was completed—the bohemian and the juvenile delinquent came face-to-face with the Negro, and the hipster was a fact in American life—And in this wedding of the white and black it was the Negro who brought the cultural dowry. Any Negro who wishes to live must live with danger from his first day, and no experience can be casual to him, no Negro can saunter down a street with any real certainty that violence will not visit him on his walk. The cameos of security for the average white: mother and the home, job and the family, are not even a mockery to millions of Negroes; they are impossi-

----

** As one instance: nearly forty years ago, when a Negro husband was to be seen kissing his white wife's hand in O'Neill's *All God's Chillun Got Wings*, a mob was threatened in New York City. Today both on and off Broadway interracial liaisons are common in plays, e.g.: *The Owl and the Pussy Cat, No Strings, The Slave*. Odets's *Golden Boy* was wrenched from a play about an Italian pugilist violinist to one about a Negro pugilist-song-and-dance-man whose sweetheart is a white woman.

Concerning television: one single Negro viewer, glowing when he sees his people in unfamiliar roles, still wearies of the word "dignity" in its millionth application and wishes (1) that the Negro lawyer might lose at least one case (Perry Mason did); (2) that Negroes might be arrested for some crimes that they did commit; (3) that some Negroes not so unfailingly noble and sacrificial might also be shown; and (4) that Negroes might be allowed to use language not so stilted—that like other characters, they might be permitted one slave expression, one split verb, one modifier that dangles, and God save us one—just one dialectical trope. Nevertheless if one has to choose between the ennoblement and Aunt Jemima, this reviewer will have to endure the ennoblement.

ble. The Negro has the simplest of alternatives: live a life of
constant humility or ever-threatening danger. In such a pass
where paranoia is as vital to survival as blood, the Negro had
stayed alive and begun to grow by following the need of his
body where he could. Knowing in the cells of his existence
that life was war, nothing but war, the Negro (all exceptions
admitted) could rarely afford the sophisticated inhibitions of
civilization, and so he kept for his survival the art of the primitive, he lived in the enormous present, he subsisted for his
Saturday night kicks, relinquishing the pleasures of the mind
for the more obligatory pleasures of the body, and in his
music he gave voice to the character and quality of his existence, to his rage and the infinite variations of joy, lust, lan-
guor, growl, cramp, pinch, scream and despair of his orgasm.*

To which, astounded, one Negro at least can only say, slipping into a consonant Freudian argot: "Poppycock." This is a
Greenwich Village refurbishing of old stereotypes.** The
ménage-à-trois of which Mailer speaks derives from this earlier trio (1) the Abolitionist insistence on the utter debasement of slavery, (2) the Marxst theory of the class struggle
transferred to race, and (3) the glorification of the exotic primitive rife in the miscalled Jazz Age. If Mailer seeks the real
ménage-à-trois that birthed this monstrosity let him seek out
Harriet Beecher Stowe, Earl Browder, and Carl Van Vechten,
with James Ford dropping in. What an unholy triangle that
turned out to be!

Concerning stereotyping even Robert Penn Warren has his
quandaries; uncertain as to who speaks today for the Negro,
he admits to a bewildering diversity among the subjects of his
long search. This is a promising sign, for Warren once was
sure about the Negro, using a buzzard to speak for him the
prognostication: "Nigger, your breed ain't metaphysical."
Today while discussing a Negro metaphysical novelist, Warren praises Ralph Ellison for theorizing about "the basic
unity of experience . . ." and also about "the rich variety"
of Negroes and their experience in American life. He quotes
Ellison approvingly:

For even as his life toughens the Negro, even as it brutal-
izes him, sensitizes him, dulls him, goads him to anger,
moves him to irony, sometimes fracturing and sometimes af-

---

* *Advertisements for Myself* (New York: Signet, 1959), p. 306.
** The quadroon, octoroon hedonists who throng the fiction of the
Beats are merely the granddaughters of the tragic mulattoes of the old
stereotype. Kerouac's *Subterraneans* has a close cousin to the Tawny
Messalina of Seventh Avenue in Van Vechten's *Nigger Heaven*. She
has been here before.

firming his hopes . . . it *conditions* him to deal with *his* life, and no mere abstraction in somebody's head.*

Warren finds Ellison refreshing for reinspecting the "standard formulations," the "mere stereotypes" of the Revolution. Well, the sun do move.

But the writer feels no need to default to Warren, even though Warren is currently the authority on the Civil War and Segregation and, in some quarters, of the Civil Rights Revolution. For this is where I came in. Over thirty years ago I wrote

One manifest truth, however, is this: the sincere, sensitive artist, willing to go beneath the clichés of popular belief to get at an underlying reality, will be wary of confining a race's entire character to a half-dozen narrow grooves. He will hardly have the temerity to say that his necessarily limited observation of a few Negroes in a restricted environment can be taken as the last word about some mythical *the* Negro. He will hesitate to do this, even though he had a Negro mammy, or spent a night in Harlem, or has been a Negro all his life. The writer submits that such an artist is the only one worth listening to, although the rest are legion.**

In the intervening years there have been many writers worth listening to, though not so many as hoped for, who saw Negro life steadily and whole. Nevertheless, clichés and stereotypes linger, and even burgeon. The conclusion, in these much later years, still holds. It is here that I take my stand.

* *Who Speaks for the Negro* (New York, 1965), p. 351.
** "Negro Character as Seen by White Authors," *Journal of Negro Education*, II, 2 (April, 1933), p. 203.

JAMES BALDWIN (1924–   )

*A biographical note on James Baldwin appears in the Auto-
biography section (see p. 316). The following essay is reprinted from his first volume of essays,* Notes of a Native Son
(1955).

Many Thousands Gone

It is only in his music, which Americans are able to admire
because a protective sentimentality limits their understanding
of it, that the Negro in America has been able to tell his
story. It is a story which otherwise has yet to be told and
which no American is prepared to hear. As is the inevitable
result of things unsaid, we find ourselves until today oppressed with a dangerous and reverberating silence; and the
story is told, compulsively, in symbols and signs, in hieroglyphics; it is revealed in Negro speech and in that of the
white majority and in their different frames of reference. The
ways in which the Negro has affected the American psychology are betrayed in our popular culture and in our morality;
in our estrangement from him is the depth of our estrangement from ourselves. We cannot ask: what do we *really* feel
about him—such a question merely opens the gates on chaos.
What we really feel about him is involved with all that we
feel about everything, about everyone, about ourselves.

The story of the Negro in America is the story of America
—or, more precisely, it is the story of Americans. It is not a
very pretty story: the story of a people is never very pretty.
The Negro in America, gloomily referred to as that shadow
which lies athwart our national life, is far more than that. He
is a series of shadows, self-created, intertwining, which now
we helplessly battle. One may say that the Negro in America
does not really exist except in the darkness of our minds.

This is why his history and his progress, his relationship to all other Americans, has been kept in the social arena. He is a social and not a personal or a human problem; to think of him is to think of statistics, slums, rapes, injustices, remote violence; it is to be confronted with an endless cataloguing of losses, gains, skirmishes; it is to feel virtuous, outraged, help-less, as though his continuing status among us were somehow analogous to disease—cancer, perhaps, or tuberculosis—which must be checked, even though it cannot be cured. In this arena the black man acquires quite another aspect from that which he has in life. We do not know what to do with him in life; if he breaks our sociological and sentimental image of him we are panic-stricken and we feel ourselves be-trayed. When he violates this image, therefore, he stands in the greatest danger (sensing which, we uneasily suspect that he is very often playing a part for our benefit); and, what is not always so apparent but is equally true, we are then in some danger ourselves—hence our retreat or our blind and immediate retaliation.

Our dehumanization of the Negro then is indivisible from our dehumanization of ourselves: the loss of our own identity is the price we pay for our annulment of his. Time and our own force act as our allies, creating an impossible, a fruitless tension between the traditional master and slave. Impossible and fruitless because, literal and visible as this tension has be-come, it has nothing to do with reality.

Time has made some changes in the Negro face. Nothing has succeeded in making it exactly like our own, though the general desire seems to be to make it blank if one cannot make it white. When it has become blank, the past as thor-oughly washed from the black face as it has been from ours, our guilt will be finished—at least it will have ceased to be visible, which we imagine to be much the same thing. But, paradoxically, it is we who prevent this from happening; since it is we, who, every hour that we live, reinvest the black face with our guilt; and we do this—by a further paradox, no less ferocious—helplessly, passionately, out of an unrealized need to suffer absolution.

Today, to be sure, we know that the Negro is not biologi-cally or mentally inferior; there is no truth in those rumors of his body odor or his incorrigible sexuality; or no more truth than can be easily explained or even defended by the social sciences. Yet, in our most recent war, his blood was segre-gated as was, for the most part, his person. Up to today we are set at a division, so that he may not marry our daughters or our sisters, nor may he—for the most part—eat at our ta-

bles or live in our houses. Moreover, those who do, do so at
the grave expense of a double alienation: from their own
people, whose fabled attributes they must either deny or,
worse, cheapen and bring to market; from us, for we require
of them, when we accept them, that they at once cease to be
Negroes and yet not fail to remember what being a Negro
means—to remember, that is, what it means to us. The
threshold of insult is higher or lower, according to the people
involved, from the bootblack in Atlanta to the celebrity in
New York. One must travel very far, among saints with nothing to gain or outcasts with nothing to lose, to find a place
where it does not matter—and perhaps a word or a gesture
or simply a silence will testify that it matters even there.

For it means something to be a Negro, after all, as it
means something to have been born in Ireland or in China,
to live where one sees space and sky or to live where one sees
nothing but rubble or nothing but high buildings. We cannot
escape our origins, however hard we try, those origins which
contain the key—could we but find it—to all that we later
become. What it means to be a Negro is a good deal more
than this essay can discover; what it means to be a Negro in
America can perhaps be suggested by an examination of the
myths we perpetuate about him.

Aunt Jemima and Uncle Tom are dead, their places taken
by a group of amazingly well-adjusted young men and
women, almost as dark, but ferociously literate, well-dressed
and scrubbed, who are never laughed at, who are not likely
ever to set foot in a cotton or tobacco field or in any but the
most modern of kitchens. There are others who remain, in
our odd idiom, "underprivileged"; some are bitter and these
come to grief; some are unhappy, but, continually presented
with the evidence of a better day soon to come, are speedily
becoming less so. Most of them care nothing whatever about
race. They want only their proper place in the sun and the
right to be left alone, like any other citizen of the republic.
We may all breathe more easily. Before, however, our joy at
the demise of Aunt Jemima and Uncle Tom approaches the
indecent, we had better ask whence they sprang, how they
lived? Into what limbo have they vanished?

However inaccurate our portraits of them were, these portraits do suggest, not only the conditions, but the quality of
their lives and the impact of this spectacle on our consciences. There was no one more forbearing than Aunt Jemima, no one stronger or more pious or more loyal or more
wise; there was, at the same time, no one weaker or more
faithless or more vicious and certainly no one more immoral.

Uncle Tom, trustworthy and sexless, needed only to drop the title "Uncle" to become violent, crafty, and sullen, a menace to any white woman who passed by. They prepared our feast tables and our burial clothes; and, if we could boast that we understood them, it was far more to the point and far more true that they understood us. They were, moreover, the only people in the world who did; and not only did they know us better than we knew ourselves, but they knew us better than we knew them. This was the piquant flavoring to the national joke, it lay behind our uneasiness as it lay behind our benevolence: Aunt Jemima and Uncle Tom, our creations, at the last evaded us; they had a life—their own, perhaps a better life than ours—and they would never tell us what it was. At the point where we were driven most privately and painfully to conjecture what depths of contempt, what heights of indifference, what prodigies of resilience, what untamable superiority allowed them so vividly to endure, neither perishing nor rising up in a body to wipe us from the earth, the image perpetually shattered and the word failed. The black man in our midst carried murder in his heart, he wanted vengeance. We carried murder too, we wanted peace.

In our image of the Negro breathes the past we deny, not dead but living yet and powerful, the beast in our jungle of statistics. It is this which defeats us, which continues to defeat us, which lends to interracial cocktail parties their rattling, genteel, nervously smiling air: in any drawing room at such a gathering the beast may spring, filling the air with flying things and an unenlightened wailing. Wherever the problem touches there is confusion, there is danger. Wherever the Negro face appears a tension is created, the tension of a silence filled with things unutterable. It is a sentimental error, therefore, to believe that the past is dead; it means nothing to say that it is all forgotten, that the Negro himself has forgotten it. It is not a question of memory. Oedipus did not remember the thongs that bound his feet; nevertheless the marks they left testified to that doom toward which his feet were leading him. The man does not remember the hand that struck him, the darkness that frightened him, as a child; nevertheless, the hand and the darkness remain with him, indivisible from himself forever, part of the passion that drives him wherever he thinks to take flight.

The making of an American begins at that point where he himself rejects all other ties, any other history, and himself adopts the vesture of his adopted land. This problem has been faced by all Americans throughout our history—in a way it *is* our history—and it baffles the immigrant and sets on edge the second generation until today. In the case of the Negro the past was taken from him whether he would or no; yet to forswear it was meaningless and availed him nothing, since his shameful history was carried, quite literally, on his brow. Shameful; for he was heathen as well as black and would never have discovered the healing blood of Christ had not we braved the jungles to bring him these glad tidings. Shameful; for, since our role as missionary had not been wholly disinterested, it was necessary to recall the shame from which we had delivered him in order more easily to escape our own. As he accepted the alabaster Christ and the bloody cross—in the bearing of which he would find his redemption, as, indeed, to our outraged astonishment, he sometimes did—he must, henceforth, accept that image we then gave him of himself: having no other and standing, moreover, in danger of death should he fail to accept the dazzling light thus brought into such darkness. It is this quite simple dilemma that must be borne in mind if we wish to comprehend his psychology.

However we shift the light which beats so fiercely on his head, or *prove,* by victorious social analysis, how his lot has changed, how we have both improved, our uneasiness refuses to be exorcized. And nowhere is this more apparent than in our literature on the subject—"problem" literature when written by whites, "protest" literature when written by Negroes —and nothing is more striking than the tremendous disparity of tone between the two creations. *Kingsblood Royal* bears, for example, almost no kinship to *If He Hollers Let Him Go,* though the same reviewers praised them both for what were, at bottom, very much the same reasons. These reasons may be suggested, far too briefly but not at all unjustly, by observing that the presupposition is in both novels exactly the same: black is a terrible color with which to be born into the world.

Now the most powerful and celebrated statement we have yet had of what it means to be a Negro in America is unquestionably Richard Wright's *Native Son.* The feeling which prevailed at the time of its publication was that such a novel, bitter, uncompromising, shocking, gave proof, by its very existence, of what strides might be taken in a free democracy; and its indisputable success, proof that Americans were now able to look full in the face without flinching the dreadful facts. Americans, unhappily, have the most remarkable ability to alchemize all bitter truths into an innocuous but piquant confection and to transform their moral contradictions, or public discussion of such contradictions, into a proud decoration, such as are given for heroism on the field of battle. Such a book, we felt with pride, could never have been written before—which was true. Nor could it be written today. It bears already the aspect of a landmark; for Bigger and his brothers have undergone yet another metamorphosis; they have been accepted in baseball leagues and by colleges hitherto exclusive; and they have made a most favorable appearance on the national screen. We have yet to encounter, nevertheless, a report so indisputably authentic, or one that can begin to challenge this most significant novel.

It is, in a certain American tradition, the story of an unremarkable youth in battle with the force of circumstance; that force of circumstance which plays and which has played so important a part in the national fables of success or failure. In this case the force of circumstance is not poverty merely but color, a circumstance which cannot be overcome, against which the protagonist battles for his life and loses. It is, on the surface, remarkable that this book should have enjoyed among Americans the favor it did enjoy; no more remarkable, however, than that it should have been compared, exuberantly, to Dostoevsky, though placed a shade below Dos Passos, Dreiser, and Steinbeck; and when the book is examined, its impact does not seem remarkable at all, but becomes, on the contrary, perfectly logical and inevitable.

We cannot, to begin with, divorce this book from the specific social climate of that time: it was one of the last of those angry productions, encountered in the late twenties and all through the thirties, dealing with the inequities of the social structure of America. It was published one year before our entry into the last world war—which is to say, very few years after the dissolution of the WPA and the end of the New Deal and at a time when bread lines and soup kitchens and bloody industrial battles were bright in everyone's memory. The rigors of that unexpected time filled us not only with a genuinely bewildered and despairing idealism—so that, because there at least was *something* to fight for, young men went off to die in Spain—but also with a genuinely bewildered self-consciousness. The Negro, who had been during the magnificent twenties a passionate and delightful primitive, now became, as one of the things we were most self-conscious about, our most oppressed minority. In the thirties, swallowing Marx whole, we discovered the Worker and realized—I should think with some relief—that the aims of the Worker and the aims of the Negro were one. This theorem

—to which we shall return—seems now to leave rather too much out of account; it became, nevertheless, one of the slogans of the "class struggle" and the gospel of the New Negro.

As for this New Negro, it was Wright who became his most eloquent spokesman; and his work, from its beginning, is most clearly committed to the social struggle. Leaving aside the considerable question of what relationship precisely the artist bears to the revolutionary, the reality of man as a social being is not his only reality and that artist is strangled who is forced to deal with human beings solely in social terms; and who has, moreover, as Wright had, the necessity thrust on him of being the representative of some thirteen million people. It is a false responsibility (since writers are not congressmen) and impossible, by its nature, of fulfillment. The unlucky shepherd soon finds that, so far from being able to feed the hungry sheep, he has lost the wherewithal for his own nourishment: having not been allowed—so fearful was his burden, so present his audience!—to recreate his own experience. Further, the militant men and women of the thirties were not, upon examination, significantly emancipated from their antecedents, however bitterly they might consider themselves estranged or however gallantly they struggled to build a better world. However they might extol Russia, their concept of a better world was quite helplessly American and betrayed a certain thinness of imagination, a suspect reliance on suspect and badly digested formulae, and a positively fretful romantic haste. Finally, the relationship of the Negro to the Worker cannot be summed up, nor even greatly illuminated, by saying that their aims are one. It is true only insofar as they both desire better working conditions and useful only insofar as they unite their strength as workers to achieve these ends. Further than this we cannot in honesty go.

In this climate Wright's voice first was heard and the struggle which promised for a time to shape his work and give it purpose also fixed it in an ever more unrewarding rage. Recording his days of anger he has also nevertheless recorded, as no Negro before him had ever done, that fantasy Americans hold in their minds when they speak of the Negro: that fantastic and fearful image which we have lived with since the first slave fell beneath the lash. This is the significance of *Native Son* and also, unhappily, its overwhelming limitation.

Native Son begins with the *Brring!* of an alarm clock in the squalid Chicago tenement where Bigger and his family live. Rats live there too, feeding off the garbage, and we first encounter Bigger in the act of killing one. One may consider that the entire book, from the harsh *Brring!* to Bigger's weak "Good-by" as the lawyer, Max, leaves him in the death cell, is an extension, with the roles inverted, of this chilling metaphor. Bigger's situation and Bigger himself exert on the mind the same sort of fascination. The premise of the book is, as I take it, clearly conveyed in these first pages: we are confronting a monster created by the American republic and we are, through being made to share his experience, to receive illumination as regards the manner of his life and to feel both pity and horror at his awful and inevitable doom. This is an arresting and potentially rich idea and we would be discussing a very different novel if Wright's execution had been more perceptive and if he had not attempted to redeem a symbolical monster in social terms.

One may object that it was precisely Wright's intention to create in Bigger a social symbol, revelatory of social disease and prophetic of disaster. I think, however, that it is this assumption which we ought to examine more carefully. Bigger has no discernible relationship to himself, to his own life, to his own people, nor to any other people—in this respect, perhaps, he is most American—and his force comes, not from his significance as a social (or anti-social) unit, but from his significance as the incarnation of a myth. It is remarkable that, though we follow him step by step from the tenement room to the death cell, we know as little about him when this journey is ended as we did when it began; and, what is even more remarkable, we know almost as little about the social dynamic which we are to believe created him. Despite the details of slum life which we are given. I doubt that anyone who has thought about it, disengaging himself from sentimentality, can accept this most essential premise of the novel for a moment. Those Negroes who surround him, on the other hand, his hard-working mother, his ambitious sister, his poolroom cronies, Bessie, might be considered as far richer and far more subtle and accurate illustrations of the ways in which Negroes are controlled in our society and the complex techniques they have evolved for their survival. We are limited, however, to Bigger's view of them, part of a deliberate plan which might not have been disastrous if we were not also limited to Bigger's perceptions. What this means for the novel is that a necessary dimension has been cut away; this dimension being the relationship that Negroes bear to one another, the depth of involvement and unspoken recognition of shared experience which creates a way of life. What the novel reflects—and at no point interprets—is the isolation of the Negro within his

own group and the resulting fury of impatient scorn. It is this
which creates its climate of anarchy and unmotivated and un-
apprehended disaster; and it is this climate, common to most
Negro protest novels, which has led us all to believe that in
Negro life there exists no tradition, no field of manners, no
possibility of ritual or intercourse, such as may, for example,
sustain the Jew even after he has left his father's house. But
the fact is not that the Negro has no tradition but that there
has as yet arrived no sensibility sufficiently profound and
tough to make this tradition articulate. For a tradition expresses, after all, nothing more than the long and painful experience of a people; it comes out of the battle waged to
maintain their integrity or, to put it more simply, out of their
struggle to survive. When we speak of the Jewish tradition we
are speaking of centuries of exile and persecution, of the
strength which endured and the sensibility which discovered
in it the high possibility of the moral victory.

This sense of how Negroes live and how they have so long
endured is hidden from us in part by the very speed of the
Negro's public progress, a progress so heavy with complexity,
so bewildering and kaleidoscopic, that he dare not pause to
conjecture on the darkness which lies behind him; and by the
nature of the American psychology which, in order to appre-
hend or be made able to accept it, must undergo a metamorphosis so profound as to be literally unthinkable and which
there is no doubt we will resist until we are compelled to
achieve our own identity by the rigors of a time that has yet
to come. Bigger, in the meanwhile, and all his furious kin,
serve only to whet the notorious national taste for the sensational and to reinforce all that we now find it necessary to
believe. It is not Bigger whom we fear, since his appearance
among us makes our victory certain. It is the others, who
smile, who go to church, who give no cause for complaint,
whom we sometimes consider with amusement, with pity,
even with affection—and in whose faces we sometimes surprise the merest arrogant hint of hatred, the faintest, withdrawn, speculative shadow of contempt—who make us uneasy; whom we cajole, threaten, flatter, fear; who to us remain unknown, though we are not (we feel with both relief
and hostility and with bottomless confusion) unknown to
them. It is out of our reaction to these hewers of wood and
drawers of water that our image of Bigger was created.

It is this image, living yet, which we perpetually seek to
evade with good works; and this image which makes of all
our good works an intolerable mockery. The "nigger," black,
benighted, brutal, consumed with hatred as we are consumed

with guilt, cannot be thus blotted out. He stands at our shoulders when we give our maid her wages, it is his hand which we fear we are taking when struggling to communicate with the current "intelligent" Negro, his stench, as it were, which fills out mouths with salt as the monument is unveiled in honor of the latest Negro leader. Each generation has shouted behind him, *Nigger!* as he walked our streets; it is he whom we would rather our sisters did not marry; he is banished into the vast and wailing outer darkness whenever we speak of the "purity" of our women, of the "sanctity" of our homes, of "American" ideals. What is more, he knows it. He is indeed the "native son": he is the "nigger." Let us refrain from inquiring at the moment whether or not he actually exists; for we *believe* that he exists. Whenever we encounter him amongst us in the flesh, our faith is made perfect and his necessary and bloody end is executed with a mystical ferocity of joy.

But there is a complementary faith among the damned which involves their gathering of the stones with which those who walk in the light shall stone them; or there exists among the intolerably degraded the perverse and powerful desire to force into the arena of the actual those fantastic crimes of which they have been accused, achieving their vengeance and their own destruction through making the nightmare real. The American image of the Negro lives also in the Negro's heart; and when he has surrendered to this image life has no other possible reality. Then he, like the white enemy with whom he will be locked one day in mortal struggle, has no means save this of asserting his identity. This is why Bigger's murder of Mary can be referred to as an "act of creation" and why, once this murder has been committed, he can feel for the first time that he is living fully and deeply as a man was meant to live. And there is, I should think, no Negro living in America who has not felt, briefly or for long periods, with anguish sharp or dull, in varying degrees and to varying effect, simple, naked and unanswerable hatred; who has not wanted to smash any white face he may encounter in a day, to violate, out of motives of the cruelest vengeance, their women, to break the bodies of all white people and bring them low, as low as that dust into which he himself has been and is being trampled; no Negro, finally, who has not had to make his own precarious adjustment to the "nigger" who surrounds him and to the "nigger" in himself.

Yet the adjustment must be made—rather, it must be attempted, the tension perpetually sustained—for without this he has surrendered his birthright as a man no less than his birthright as a black man. The entire universe is then peopled only with his enemies, who are not only white men armed with rope and rifle, but his own far-flung and contemptible kinsmen. Their blackness is his degradation and it is their stupid and passive endurance which makes his end inevitable.

Bigger dreams of some black man who will weld all blacks together into a mighty fist, and feels, in relation to his family, that perhaps they had to live as they did precisely because none of them had ever done anything, right or wrong, which mattered very much. It is only he who, by an act of murder, has burst the dungeon cell. He has made it manifest that *he* lives and that his despised blood nourishes the passions of a man. He has forced his oppressors to see the fruit of that oppression: and he feels, when his family and his friends come to visit him in the death cell, that they should not be weeping or frightened, that they should be happy, *proud* that he has dared, through murder and now through his own imminent destruction, to redeem their anger and humiliation, that he has hurled into the spiritless obscurity of their lives the lamp of his passionate life and death. Henceforth, they may remember Bigger—who has died, as we may conclude, for them. But they do not feel this; they only know that he has murdered two women and precipitated a reign of terror; and that now he is to die in the electric chair. They therefore weep and are honestly frightened—for which Bigger despises them and wishes to "blot" them out. What is missing in his situation and in the representation of his psychology—which makes his situation false and his psychology incapable of development —is any revelatory apprehension of Bigger as one of the Negro's realities or as one of the Negro's roles. This failure is part of the previously noted failure to convey any sense of Negro life as a continuing and complex group reality. Bigger, who cannot function therefore as a reflection of the social illness, having, as it were, no society to reflect, likewise refuses to function on the loftier level of the Christ-symbol. His kinsmen are quite right to weep and be frightened, even to be appalled: for it is not his love for them or for himself which causes him to die, but his hatred and his self-hatred; he does not redeem the pains of a despised people, but reveals, on the contrary, nothing more than his own fierce bitterness at having been born one of them. In this also he is the "native son," his progress determinable by the speed with which the distance increases between himself and the auction-block and all that the auction-block implies. To have penetrated this phenomenon, this inward contention of love and hatred, blackness and whiteness, would have given him a stature more nearly human and an end more nearly tragic; and would have given us a document more profoundly and genuinely bitter and less harsh with an anger which is, on the one hand, exhibited and, on the other hand, denied.

Native Son finds itself at length so trapped by the American image of Negro life and by the American necessity to find the ray of hope that it cannot pursue its own implications. This is why Bigger must be at the last redeemed, to be received, if only by rhetoric, into that community of phantoms which is our tenaciously held ideal of the happy social life. It is the socially conscious whites who receive him—the Negroes being capable of no such objectivity—and we have, by way of illustration, that lamentable scene in which Jan, Mary's lover, forgives him for her murder; and, carrying the explicit burden of the novel, Max's long speech to the jury. This speech, which really ends the book, is one of the most desperate performances in American fiction. It is the question of Bigger's humanity which is at stake, the relationship in which he stands to all other Americans—and, by implication, to all people—and it is precisely this question which it cannot clarify, with which it cannot, in fact, come to any coherent terms. He is the monster created by the American republic, the present awful sum of generations of oppression; but to say that he is a monster is to fall into the trap of making him subhuman and he must, therefore, be made representative of a way of life which is real and human in precise ration to the degree to which it seems to us monstrous and strange. It seems to me that this idea carries, implicitly, a most remarkable confession: that is, that Negro life is in fact as debased and impoverished as our theology claims; and, further, that the use to which Wright puts this idea can only proceed from the assumption—not entirely unsound—that Americans, who evade, so far as possible, all genuine experience, have therefore no way of assessing the experience of others and no way of establishing themselves in relation to any way of life which is not their own. The privacy or obscurity of Negro life makes that life capable, in our imaginations, of producing anything at all; and thus the idea of Bigger's monstrosity can be presented without fear of contradiction, since no American has the knowledge or authority to contest it and no Negro has the voice. It is an idea, which, in the framework of the novel, is dignified by the possibility it promptly affords of presenting Bigger as the herald of disaster, the danger signal of a more bitter time to come when not Bigger alone but all his kindred will rise, in the name of the many thousands who have perished in fire and flood and by rope and torture, to demand their rightful vengeance.

But it is not quite fair, it seems to me, to exploit the national innocence in this way. The idea of Bigger as a warning boomerangs not only because it is quite beyond the limit of probability that Negroes in America will ever achieve the means of wreaking vengeance upon the state but also because it cannot be said that they have any desire to do so. *Native Son* does not convey the altogether savage paradox of the American Negro's situation, of which the social reality which we prefer with such hopeful superficiality to study is but, as it were, the shadow. It is not simply the relationship of oppressed to oppressor, of master to slave, nor is it motivated merely by hatred; it is also, literally and morally, a *blood* relationship, perhaps the most profound reality of the American experience, and we cannot begin to unlock it until we accept how very much it contains of the force and anguish and terror of love.

Negroes are Americans and their destiny is the country's destiny. They have no other experience besides their experience on this continent and it is an experience which cannot be rejected, which yet remains to be embraced. If, as I believe, no American Negro exists who does not have his private Bigger Thomas living in the skull, then what most significantly fails to be illuminated here is the paradoxical adjustment which is perpetually made, the Negro being compelled to accept the fact that this dark and dangerous and unloved stranger is part of himself forever. Only this recognition sets him in any wise free and it is this, this necessary ability to contain and even, in the most honorable sense of the word, to *exploit* the "nigger," which lends to Negro life its high element of the ironic and which causes the most well-meaning of their American critics to make such exhilarating errors when attempting to understand them. To present Bigger as a warning is simply to reinforce the American guilt and fear concerning him, it is most forcefully to limit him to that previously mentioned social arena in which he has no human validity, it is simply to condemn him to death. For he has always been a warning, he represents the evil, the sin and suffering which we are compelled to reject. It is useless to say to the courtroom in which this heathen sits on trial that he is their responsibility, their creation, and his crimes are theirs; and that they ought, therefore, to allow him to live, to make articulate to himself behind the walls of prison the meaning of his existence. The meaning of his existence has already been most adequately expressed, nor does anyone wish, particularly not in the name of democracy, to think of it any more; as for the possibility of articulation, it is this possibility which above all others we most dread. Moreover, the court-room, judge, jury, witnesses and spectators, recognize immediately that Bigger is their creation and they recognize this not only with hatred and fear and guilt and the resulting fury of self-righteousness but also with that morbid fullness of pride mixed with horror with which one regards the extent and power of one's wickedness. They know that death is his portion, that he runs to death; coming from darkness and dwelling in darkness, he must be, as often as he rises, ban-ished, lest the entire planet be engulfed. And they know, finally, that they do not wish to forgive him and that he does not wish to be forgiven; that he dies, hating them, scorning that appeal which they cannot make to that irrecoverable hu-manity of his which cannot hear it; and that he *wants* to die because he glories in his hatred and prefers, like Lucifer, rather to rule in hell than serve in heaven.

For, bearing in mind the premise on which the life of such a man is based, *i.e.*, that black is the color of damnation, this is his only possible end. It is the only death which will allow him a kind of dignity or even, however horribly, a kind of beauty. To tell this story, no more than a single aspect of the story of the "nigger," is inevitably and richly to become in-volved with the force of life and legend, how each perpe-tually assumes the guise of the other, creating that dense, many-sided and shifting reality which is the world we live in and the world we make. To tell his story is to begin to liber-ate us from his image and it is, for the first time, to clothe this phantom with flesh and blood, to deepen, by our under-standing of him and his relationship to us, our understanding of ourselves and of all men.

But this is not the story which *Native Son* tells, for we find here merely, repeated in anger, the story which we have told in pride. Nor, since the implications of this anger are evaded, are we ever confronted with the actual or potential signifi-cance of our pride; which is why we fall, with such a positive glow of recognition, upon Max's long and bitter summing up. It is addressed to those among us of good will and it seems to say that, though there are whites and blacks among us who hate each other, we will not; there are those who are be-trayed by greed, by guilt, by blood lust, but not we; we will set our faces against them and join hands and walk together into that dazzling future when there will be no white or black. This is the dream of all liberal men, a dream not at all dishonorable, but, nevertheless, a dream. For, let us join hands on this mountain as we may, the battle is elsewhere. It proceeds far from us in the heat and horror and pain of life itself where all men are betrayed by greed and guilt and blood lust and where no one's hands are clean. Our good will, from which we yet expect such power to transform us, is thin, passionless, strident: its roots, examined, lead us back to our forebears, whose assumption it was that the black man, to become truly human and acceptable, must first become like us. This assumption once accepted, the Negro in America can only acquiesce in the obliteration of his own personality, the distortion and debasement of his own experience, surrendering to those forces which reduce the person to anonymity and which make themselves manifest daily all over the darkening world.

THREE PAPERS FROM THE FIRST CONFERENCE OF NEGRO WRITERS (MARCH, 1959)

Following are three papers, by Arthur P. Davis, Saunders Redding, and Langston Hughes, delivered at the First Conference of Negro Writers in March, 1959. Professor Davis' paper was first published as an article in Phylon *in 1956. The three papers are reprinted from the volume of selected papers delivered at this Conference,* The American Negro Writer and His Roots, *published by the American Society of African Culture in 1960.*

ARTHUR P. DAVIS (1904–   )

Critic, writer, educator, and co-editor of the famous anthology The Negro Caravan, *Arthur P. Davis was born and raised in Hampton, Virginia, and has been Professor of English at Howard University since 1944. He began his own undergraduate studies at Howard, went on to Columbia College in New York, where he was elected to Phi Beta Kappa in 1927, and received his M.A. and Ph.D. at Columbia University. He started out as Professor of English at North Carolina College in Durham in 1927, and before he went to Howard he was on the faculty of Virginia Union University for more than a decade. He conducted a weekly column for the Norfolk* Journal and Guide *for about seventeen years (1933–1950). His book* Isaac Watts: His Life and Works, *published in New York and later in London, was hailed by* The Times Literary Supplement *of London for its "careful scholarship" and style. Professor Davis has published numerous scholarly articles and*

*book reviews, many of them on American Negro literature
and writers. [For biographical notes on Saunders Redding and
Langston Hughes see the Autobiography section (p. 299) and
the Fiction section (pp. 96–97).]*

1. Integration and Race Literature

Integration is the most vital issue in America today. The
word is on every tongue, and it has acquired all kinds of
meanings and connotations. The idea—not the fact obviously
—but the idea of integration threatens to split the nation into
two hostile camps. As the Negro is the center of this violent
controversy, his reaction to it is of supreme importance. In
this paper I wish to examine one segment of that reaction—
that of the Negro creative artist. How has the integration
issue affected him? It is my belief that the concept of integration has already produced a major trend or change in our literature, and that as integration becomes a reality, it will
transform Negro writing even more drastically. The rest of
this article will be an attempt to illustrate and uphold this
thesis.

But before we explore these changes, let us examine the
peculiar period in which the Negro writer finds himself because of the integration movement. In the phrase of Matthew
Arnold, he is actually living "between two worlds"—one not
yet dead, the other not fully born. It is obvious to even the
most rabid critic that racial conditions in America are far
better than they have ever been before. Barriers are falling in
all areas. The armed forces are integrated. Most Southern
universities have Negro students, and the Supreme Court has
sounded the legal death knell of segregation in public schools.
The State Department and the better Northern schools are
vying with each other to enlist the services of outstanding
race scholars. In practically all states Negroes can now vote
without risking their lives; and though the Till Case may
seem to deny it, lynching is a dead practice. In short, despite
the last desperate and futile efforts of frightened and panicky
Southerners, the country has committed itself spiritually to
integration. As yet, it is still largely a spiritual commitment,
but it has changed radically the racial climate of America.

This change of climate, however, has inadvertently dealt
the Negro writer a crushing blow. Up to the present decade,
our literature has been predominantly a protest literature.
Ironical though it may be, we have capitalized on oppression

(I mean, of course, in a literary sense). Although we may deplore and condemn the cause, there is great creative motivation in a movement which brings all members of a group together and cements them in a common bond. And that is just what segregation did for the Negro, especially during the 'Twenties and 'Thirties when full segregation was not only practiced in the South but tacitly condoned by the whole nation. As long as there was this common enemy, we had a common purpose and a strong urge to transform into artistic terms our deep-rooted feelings of bitterness and scorn. When the enemy capitulated, he shattered our most fruitful literary tradition. The possibility of imminent integration has tended to destroy the protest element in Negro writing.

And one must always keep in mind the paradox involved. We do not have actual integration anywhere. We have surface integration and token integration in many areas, but the everyday pattern of life for the overwhelming majority of Negroes is unchanged, and probably will be for the next two or three decades. But we do have—and this is of the utmost importance—we do have the spiritual climate which will eventually bring about complete integration. The Negro artist recognizes and acknowledges that climate; he accepts it on good faith; and he is resolved to work with it at all costs. In the meantime, he will have to live between worlds, and that for any artist is a disturbing experience. For the present-day Negro artist—especially the writer in his middle years—it becomes almost a tragic experience because it means giving up a tradition in which he has done his apprentice and journeyman work, giving it up when he is prepared to make use of that tradition as a master craftsman.

Another disturbing factor which must be considered here is that this change of climate came about rather suddenly. Perhaps it would be more exact to say that the full awareness came suddenly because there were signs of its approach all during the 'Forties, and Negro writers from time to time showed that they recognized these signs. But the full awareness did not come until the present decade, and it came with some degree of abruptness. For example, all through World War II, all through the 'Forties, the Negro writer was still grinding out protest and Problem novels, most of them influenced by *Native Son*. The list of these works is impressive: *Blood on the Forge* (1941), *White Face* (1943), *If He Hollers* (1943), *The Street* (1946), *Taffy* (1951), and there were others—practically all of them naturalistic novels with the same message of protest against America's treatment of its black minority. The poets wrote in a similar vein. *For My*

People (1942), *Freedom's Plow* (1943), *A Street in Bronzeville* (1945), and *Powerful Long Ladder* (1946) all had strong protest elements, all dealt in part with the Negro's fight against segregation and discrimination at home and in the armed forces. Noting the dates of these works, one realizes that, roughly speaking, up to 1950 the protest tradition was in full bloom, and that most of our best writers were still using it. And then with startling swiftness came this awareness of a radical change in the nation's climate; and with it the realization that the old protest themes had to be abandoned. The new climate tended to date the Problem works of the 'Forties as definitely as time had dated the New Negro "lynching-passing" literature of the 'Twenties and 'Thirties. In other words, protest writing has become the first casualty of the new racial climate.

Faced with the loss of his oldest and most cherished tradition, the Negro writer has been forced to seek fresh ways to use his material. First of all, he has attempted to find new themes within the racial framework. Retaining the Negro character and background, he has shifted his emphasis from the protest aspect to Negro living and placed it on the problems and conflicts within the group itself. For example, Chester Himes, pursuing this course in his latest novel, *Third Generation,* explores school life in the Deep South. His main conflict in this work is not concerned with interracial protest but with discord within a Negro family caused by color differences. The whole racial tone of this novel is quite different from that of *If He Hollers,* which, as stated above, is a typical protest work. One came out in 1943, the other in 1953. The two books are a good index to the changes which took place in the decade separating them.

In like manner, Owen Dodson and Gwendolyn Brooks in their novels, *Boy at the Window* and *Maud Martha,* respectively, show this tendency to find new themes within the racial framework. Both of these publications are "little novels," written in the current style, giving intimate and subtle vignettes of middle class living. Their main stress is on life within the group, not on conflict with outside forces. Taking a different approach, William Demby, in *Beetlecreek,* completely reversed the protest pattern by showing the black man's inhumanity to his white brother. In *The Outsider,* Richard Wright has taken an even more subtle approach. He uses a Negro main character, but by adroitly and persistently minimizing that character's racial importance, he succeeds in divorcing him from any association with the traditional protest alignment. And Langston Hughes in his latest work,

Sweet Flypaper of Life, though using all Negro characters, does not even remotely touch on the matter of interracial protest. All of these authors, it seems to me, show their awareness of the new climate by either playing down or avoiding entirely the traditional protest approach.

Another group of writers have elected to show their awareness by avoiding the Negro character. Among them are William Gardner Smith (*Anger at Innocence*), Ann Petry (*Country Place*), Richard Wright (*Savage Holiday*), and Willard Motley (*Knock on Any Door*). None of these works has Negro main characters. With the exception of *Knock on Any Door*, each is a "second" novel, following a work written in the 'Forties which has Negro characters and background, and which is written in the protest vein. In each case the first work was highly popular, and yet each of these novelists elected to avoid the theme which gave him his initial success. The effect of the changed climate, it seems to me, is obvious here.

I realize that Frank Yerby with his ten or more best sellers in a row should be listed in this group. Yerby, however, has never used a Negro background or Negro principal characters for his novels. His decision not to make use of the Negro protest tradition came so early in his career, we cannot use it as a case in point at this time. But it is interesting to note that Yerby's first published work, a short story, was written in the protest tradition.

So far I have spoken only of the novelists, but the Negro poets have also sensed the change of climate in America and have reacted to it. Incidentally, several of our outstanding protest poets of the 'Thirties and 'Forties have simply dropped out of the picture as poets. I cannot say, of course, that the new climate alone has silenced them, but I do feel that it has been a contributing cause. It is hard for a mature writer to slough off the tradition in which he has worked during all of his formative years. Acquiring a new approach in any field of art is a very serious and trying experience. One must also remember that the protest tradition was no mere surface fad with the Negro writer. It was part of his self-respect, part of his philosophy of life, part of his inner being. It was almost a religious experience with those of us who came up through the dark days of the 'Twenties and 'Thirties. When a tradition so deeply ingrained is abandoned, it tends to leave a spiritual numbness—a kind of void not easily filled with new interests or motivations. Several of our ablest poets —and novelists too, for that matter—have not tried to fill that void.

But a few of our poets have met the challenge of the new climate, among them Langston Hughes, M. B. Tolson, Robert Hayden, and several others. A comparison of their early and later works will show in each case a tendency either to avoid protest themes entirely or to approach them much more subtly and obliquely. Compare, for example, Tolson's *Rendezvous with America* (1944) with a *Libretto for the Republic of Liberia* (1953). The thumping rhythms of the protest verse in the former work have given way in the latter to a new technique, one that is influenced largely by Hart Crane. With this work, Tolson has turned his back on the tradition in which he came to maturity, and he has evidently done so successfully. Concerning the work, Allen Tate feels that: "For the first time . . . a Negro poet has assimilated completely the full poetic language of his time and, by implication, the language of the Anglo-American poetic tradition." A younger poet like Gwendolyn Brooks, in her poetic career, as brief as it is, also illustrates this change in attitude. There is far more racial protest in *A Street in Bronzeville* than in her latest Pulitzer-Prize-winning volume, *Annie Allen*. Moreover, the few pieces in the latter book which concern the Problem are different in approach and in technique from those in the first work. This tendency to avoid too much emphasis on Problem poetry is also seen, curiously enough, in a very recent anthology, *Lincoln University Poets*, edited by Waring Cuney, Langston Hughes, and Bruce Wright. Several of the Lincoln poets were writing during the New Negro period when the protest tradition was at its height, but these editors, two of them New Negro poets themselves, took great pains to keep the protest pieces down to the barest minimum; and those which they included are relatively mild.

Summing up then, I think we can safely say that the leaven of integration is very much at work. It has forced the Negro creative artist to play down his most cherished tradition; it has sent him in search of new themes; it has made him abandon, at least on occasion, the Negro character and background; and it has possibly helped to silence a few of the older writers now living.

The course of Negro American literature has been highlighted by a series of social and political crises over the Negro's position in America. The Abolition Movement, the Civil War, Reconstruction, World War I, and the Riot-Lynching Period of the 'Twenties all radically influenced Negro writing. Each crisis in turn produced a new tradition in our literature; and as each crisis has passed, the Negro writer has dropped the special tradition which the occasion demanded and moved towards the main stream of American literature. The Integration Controversy is another crisis and from it we hope that the Negro will move permanently into full participation in American life—social, economic, political and literary.

But what about the literature of this interim between two worlds—between a world of dying segregation and one of a developing integration? It is my belief that this period will produce for a while a series of "good-will books"—novels and short stories for the most part in which the emphasis will be on what the Negro journalists now call "positive reporting." In an all-out effort to make integration become a reality, the Negro writer will tend to play down the remaining harshness in Negro American living and to emphasize the progress towards equality. This new type of work will try to do in fiction what Roi Ottley has done in *No Green Pastures*. May I say in passing that I do not imply any praise of this work. It simply illustrates for me a trend which I feel will become more and more popular during this interim period. May I also add that this type of good-will publication will lend itself to all kinds of abuse at the hands of mercenary charlatans; it will create other stereotypes more unbelievable than those we already have, but it will be immensely popular.

During this interim there will also come into fashion another type of racial publication—racial fiction that, without using the Problem, will do for the internal life of Negroes what *Marty* has done for New York Italian-American family and group life and what a host of works in recent years have done for Irish-American life. With the pressure of segregation lightened, the Negro artist will find it easy to draw such pictures of his people. He will discover, what we all know in our objective moments, that there are many facets of Negro living—humorous, pathetic, and tragic—which are not directly touched by the outside world. Hughes' *Sweet Flypaper of Life* is, I believe, a forerunner of many more works of this type.

And when we finally reach that stage in which we can look at segregation in the same way that historians now regard the Inquisition or the Hitler Era in Germany or any other evil period of the past, we shall then do naturally and without self-consciousness what the Joyces and Dostoevskys of the world have always done—write intimately and objectively of our own people in universal human terms.

SAUNDERS REDDING

2. The Negro Writer and His Relationship to His Roots

I do not feel in the least controversial or argumentative about the announced subject. Indeed, I have touched upon it so often in one way or another that I long ago exhausted my store of arguments, and if I now revert to a kind of expressionistic way of talking, my excuse for it is patent. "The Negro Writer and his Relationship to his Roots" is the kind of subject which, if one talked directly on it for more than' twenty minutes, he would have to talk at least a year. I shan't talk directly on it, and I shan't talk a year. An exhaustive treatment? Heaven forbid—or anything near it. Suggestive? Well, I can only hope.

And anyway, I realize now that my position' here is that of the boy who, through native disability, cannot himself play but is perfectly willing to furnish the ball for others to play in exchange for the pleasure of watching the game.

Since my theme is that the American situation has complex and multifarious sources and that these sources sustain the emotional and intellectual life of American Negro writers, let me take as my starting point a classic oversimplification. This is that the meaning of American society and of the American situation to the Negro is summed up in such works as *Native Son, Invisible Man,* and the *Ordeal of Mansart,* and in two or three volumes of poetry, notably *Harlem Shadows, The Black Christ,* and *The Weary Blues,* and that the American Negro writer's entire spirit is represented by such writers as Richard Wright, Ralph Ellison and William Burghardt Du Bois—by realists, surrealists, and romantic idealists.

Please understand me. Wright, Ellison and Du Bois are not mendacious men, and they are doing what writers must always do. They are telling the truth as they see it, which happens to be largely what it is, and they are producing from the examined, or at least the observed causes, the predictable effects; and no one should blame them if the impression they give of the American situation is deplorable. They have been blamed, you know. But let those who blame these writers blame themselves for forgetting that fiction is fiction, and that no novel can pretend to be an exact photographic copy of a country or of the people in a country.

Moreover, dishonor, bigotry, hatred, degradation, injustice, arrogance and obscenity do flourish in American life, and especially in the prescribed and proscriptive American Negro life; and it is the right and the duty of the Negro writer to say so—to complain. He has cause. The temptation of the moral enthusiast is not only strong in him; it is inevitable. He never suspends social and moral judgment. Few actions and events that touch him as a man fail to set in motion his machinery as an artist. History is as personal to him as the woman he loves; and he is caught in the flux of its events, the currents of its opinion and the tides of its emotion; and he believes that the mood is weak which tolerates an impartial presentment of these, and that this weak mood cannot be indulged in a world where the consequences of the actions of a few men produce insupportable calamities for millions of humble folk. He is one of the humble folk. He forages in the cause of righteousness. He forgets that he is also one of Apollo's company.

On the one hand, the jungle; on the other, the resourceful hunter to clear it. The jungle, where lurk the beasts, nourishes the hunter. It is there that he has that sum of relationships that make him what he is. It is where he lives. It is precisely because the jungle is there and is terrible and dangerous that the Negro writer writes and lives at all.

But first, I suppose you must grant me, if only for the sake of this brief expositon, that the American Negro writer is not just an American with a dark skin. If he were, I take it, the theme of this conference would be mighty silly and the conference itself superfluous. This granted, you want to know what the frame of reference is, and about this I shall be dogmatic.

Neither the simplest nor the subtlest scrutiny reveals to an honest man that he has two utterly diverse kinds of experience, that of sense data and that of purpose. Psychology seems to have no difficulty establishing the natural gradation of impulse to purpose. In varying degrees, all our experiences are complications of physical processes.

Shifting from the dogmatic to the apologetic, I must eliminate from view a period of nearly three hundred years from 1619 to 1900. It was the period that saw the solid establishment here in America of a tradition of race relations and of the concepts that supported the tradition. It was a period that need not be rehearsed. Within the frame of reference thus established, let us look at a certain chain of events.

In 1902 came Thomas Dixon's *The Leopard's Spots*, and three years later *The Clansman*. Both were tremendously popular, and both were included in the repertoires of traveling theatrical companies; and I think it is significant—though we will only imply how—that even a colored company, The Lafayette Players, undertook an adaptation of *The Leopard's Spots*. In 1903 there was a race riot in New York. In 1906 race riots occurred in Georgia and Texas; in 1908 in Illinois. By this latter year, too, all the Southern states had disfranchised the Negro, and color caste was legalized or had legal status everywhere. The Negro's talent for monkeyshines had been exploited on the stage, and some of the music that accompanied the monkeyshines was created by James Weldon Johnson and his brother Rosamond. Meantime, in 1904, Thomas Nelson Page had written the one true canonical book of the law and the prophets, *The Negro, The Southerner's Problem*. And, most cogent fact of all, Booker Washington, having sworn on this bible of reactionism, had been made the undisputed leader of American Negroes because, as he had pledged to do, he advocated a race policy strictly in line with the tradition and the supporting concepts of race relations.

If there had been a time when this tradition seemed to promise the Negro a way out, that time was not now. He had been laughed at, tolerated, amusingly despaired of, but all his own efforts were vain. All the instruments of social progress —schools, churches, lodges—adopted by colored people were the subjects of ribald jokes and derisive laughter. "Mandy, has you studied yo' Greek?" "I's sewing, Ma." "Go naked, Gal. Git Dat Greek!"

Any objective judgment of Booker Washington's basic notion must be that it was an extension of the old tradition framed in new terms. Under the impact of social change, the concept was modified to include the stereotype of the Negro as a happy peasant, a docile and satisfied laborer under the stern but kindly eye of the white boss, a creature who had a place and knew it and loved it and would keep it unless he got bad notions from somewhere. The once merely laughable coon had become now also the cheap farm grub or city laborer who could be righteously exploited for his own good and for the greater glory of America. By this addition to the concept, the Negro-white status quo, the condition of inferior-superior race and caste could be maintained in the face of profound changes in the general society.

What this meant to the Negro writer was that he must, if he wished an audience, adhere to the old forms and the acceptable patterns. It meant that he must create within the limitations of the concept, or that he must dissemble completely, or that he must ignore his racial kinship altogether and leave unsounded the profoundest depths of the peculiar experiences which were his by reason of that kinship. Some chose the first course; at least one—Dunbar—chose the second (as witness his sickly, sticky novels of white love life and his sad epithalamium to death); and a good many chose the third: Braithwaite's anthologies of magazine verse, James Weldon Johnson's contributions to the *Century Magazine*, and the writing of Alice Dunbar, Anne Spenser, and Angelina Grimke.

But given the whole web of circumstances—empirical, historic, psychological—these writers must have realized that they could not go on and that the damps and fevers, chills and blights, terrors and dangers of the jungle could not be ignored. They must have realized that, with a full tide of race-consciousness bearing in upon them, they could not go on forever denying their racehood and that to try to do this at all was a symptom of psychotic strain. Rather perish now than escape only to die of slow starvation.

What had happened was that Booker Washington, with the help of the historic situation and the old concepts, had so thoroughly captured the minds of white people that his was the only Negro voice that could be heard in the jungle. Negro schools needing help could get it only through Booker Washington. Negro social thought wanting a sounding board could have it only on Washington's say-so. Negro political action was weak and ineffective without his strength. Many Negro writers fell silent, and for the writer, silence is death.

Many, not but all. There were stubborn souls and courageous, and the frankly mad among them. There was the Boston *Guardian*, and the Chicago *Defender*, and the Atlanta University Pamphlets, and *The Souls of Black Folk*, and finally the *Crisis;* and this latter quickly developed a voice of multi-range and many tones. It roared like a lion and cooed like a dove and screamed like a monkey and laughed like a hyena. And always it protested. Always the sounds it made were the sounds of revolt in the jungle, and protestation and revolt were becoming—forgive me for changing my figure—

powerful reagents in the social chemistry that produced the "new" Negro.

Other factors contributed to this generation too. The breath of academic scholarship was just beginning to blow hot and steadily enough to wither some of the myths about the Negro. The changes occurring with the onset of war in Europe sloughed off other emotional and intellectual accretions. The Negro might be a creature of "moral debate," but he was also something more. "I ain't a problem," a Negro character was made to say, "I's a person." And that person turned out to be a seeker after the realities in the American dream. When he was called upon to protect that dream with his blood, he asked questions and demanded answers. Whose dream was he protecting, he wanted to know, and why and wherefore? There followed such promises as only the less scrupulous politicians had made to him before. Then came the fighting and the dying, and finally came a thing called peace.

By this time, the Negro was already stirring massively along many fronts. He cracked Broadway wide open. The Garvey movement swept the country like wildfire. *Harlem Shadows, The Gift of Black Folk, Color, Fire in the Flint, The Autobiography of an Ex-coloured Man.* The writers of these and other works were declared to be irresponsible. A polemical offensive was launched against them, and against such non-artist writers as Philip Randolph, Theophilus Lewis, William Patterson, Angelo Herndon. They were accused of negativism; they were called un-American. Cultural nationalism raised its head and demanded that literature be patriotic, optimistic, positive, uncritical, like *Americans All*, and *American Ideals*, and *America Is Promises*, and *It Takes a Heap O'Living*, which were all written and published in the period of which I speak. But democracy encourages criticism, and it is true that even negative criticism implies certain positive values like veracity, for instance, and these Negro writers had positive allegiances. Their sensibilities were violently irritated, but their faith and imaginations were wonderfully nourished by the very environment which they saw to be and depicted as being bad.

Fortunately there was more than faith and fat imagination in some of these works. There was also talent. Had this not been so, Negro writing would have come to nothing for perhaps another quarter century, for the ground would not have been plowed for the seeds of later talents. But DuBois, Johnson, McKay, Fisher, Cullen, Hughes knew what they were about. Their work considerably furthered the interest of white writers and critics. Whatever else O'Neill, Rosenfeld, Connelly, Calverton and Heyward did, they gave validity to the notion that the Negro was material for serious literary treatment.

Beginning then and continuing into the forties, Negro writing had two distinct aspects. The first of these was arty, self-conscious, somewhat precious, experimental, and not truly concerned with the condition of man. Some of the "little reviews" printed a lot of nonsense by Negro writers, including the first chapter of a novel which was to be entirely constructed of elliptical sentences. Then there was *Cane:* sensibility, inwardness, but much of it for the purpose of being absorbed into the universal oneness. Nirvana. Oblivion. Transcendence over one's own personality through the practice of art for art's sake. The appropriate way of feeling and thinking growing out of a particular system of living. And so eventually Gurdjieff.

But the second aspect was more important. The pathos of man is that he hungers for personal fulfillment and for a sense of community with others. And these writers hungered. There is no American national character. There is only an American situation, and within this situation these writers sought to find themselves. They had always been alienated, not only because they were Negroes, but because democracy in America decisively separates the intellcetual from everyone else. The intellectual in America is a radically alienated personality, the Negro in common with the white, and both were hungry and seeking, and some of the best of both found food and an identity in communism. But the identity was only partial and, the way things turned out, further emphasized their alienation. So—at least for the Negro writers among them— back into the American situation, the jungle where they could find themselves. A reflex of the natural gradation of impulse to purpose.

Surely this is the meaning of *Native Son.* "Bigger Thomas was not black all the time," his creator says. "He was white too, and there were literally millions of him. . . . Modern experiences were creating types of personalities whose existence ignored racial . . . lines." Identity. Community. Surely this is the meaning of *Invisible Man* and the poignant, pain-filled, pain-relieving humor of simple Jesse B. It is the meaning of *Go Tell It on the Mountain,* and it is explicitly the meaning of four brilliant essays in part three of a little book of essays called *Notes of a Native Son.* (How often that word "native" appears, and how meaningful its implications!) Let me quote a short, concluding passage from one of these essays.

"Since I no longer felt that I could stay in this cell forever, I was beginning to be able to make peace with it for a time. On the 27th . . . I went again to trial . . . and the case . . . was dismissed. The story of the *Drap De Lit*, . . . caused great merriment in the courtroom. . . . I was chilled by their merriment, even though it was meant to warm me. It could only remind me of the laughter I had often heard at home. . . . This laughter is the laughter of those who consider themselves to be at a safe remove from all the wretched, for whom the pain of living is not real. I had heard it so often in my native land that I had resolved to find a place where I would never hear it anymore. In some deep, black, stony and liberating way, my life, in my own eyes, began during that first year in Paris, when it was borne in on me that this laughter is universal and never can be stilled." Explicit.

The human condition, the discovery of self. Community. Identity. Surely this must be achieved before it can be seen that a particular identity has a relation to a common identity, commonly described as human. This is the ultimate that the honest writer seeks. He knows that the dilemmas, the perils, the likelihood of catastrophe in the human situation are real and that they have to do not only with whether men understand each other but with the quality of man himself. The writer's ultimate purpose is to use his gifts to develop man's awareness of himself so that he, man, can become a better instrument for living together with other men. This sense of identity is the root by which all honest creative effort is fed, and the writer's relation to it is the relation of the infant to the breast of the mother.

LANGSTON HUGHES

3. Writers: Black and White

Even to sell *bad* writing you have to be good.

There was a time when, if you were colored, you might sell bad writing a little easier than if you were white. But no more. The days of the Negro's passing as a writer and getting by purely because of his "negritude" are past.

Even pure Africans find it hard to get published in the U.S.A. You have to be a Nadine Gordimer or an Alan Paton. For the general public, "the blacker the berry, the sweeter the juice" may be true in jazz, but not in prose. These days I would hate to be a Negro writer depending on race to get somewhere.

To create a market for your writing you have to be consistent, professional, a continuing writer—not just a one-article or a one-story or a one-book man. Those expert vendors, the literary agents, do not like to be bothered with a one-shot writer. No money in them. Agents like to help build a career, not light a flash in the pan. With one-shot writers, literary hucksters cannot pay their income taxes. Nor can publishers get their money back on what they lose on the first book. Even if you are a good writer, but *not* consistent, you probably will not get far. Color has nothing to do with writing as such. So I would say, in your mind don't be a *colored* writer even when dealing in racial material. Be a *writer* first. Like an egg: first, egg; then an Easter egg, the color applied.

To write about yourself, you should first be outside yourself—objective. To write well about Negroes, it might be wise, occasionally at least, to look at them with white eyes—then the better will you see how distinctive we are. Sometimes I think whites are more appreciative of our *uniqueness* than we are ourselves. The white "black" artists—dealing in Negro material—have certainly been financially more successful than any of us real Negroes have ever been. Who wrote the most famous "Negro" (in quotes) music? George Gershwin, who looked at Harlem from a downtown penthouse, while Duke Ellington still rode the "A" train. Who wrote the best selling plays and novels and thereby made money's mammy? White Eugene O'Neill, white Paul Green, white Lillian Smith, white Marc Connelly, and Du Bose Heyward: *Emperor Jones, In Abraham's Bosom, Strange Fruit, Green Pastures, Porgy*. Who originated the longest running Negro radio and TV show? The various white authors of the original *Amos and Andy* scripts, not Negroes. Who wrote all those Negro and interracial pictures that have swept across the Hollywood screen from *Hallelujah* to *Anna Lucasta*, from *Pinky* to *Porgy and Bess*? Not Negroes. Not you, not I, not any colored-body here.

Our eyes are not white enough to look at Negroes clearly in terms of popular commercial marketing. Not even white enough to see as Faulkner sees—through Mississippi-Nobel-Prize-winning-Broadway eyes in his play "Requiem for a Nun." There his "nigger dope-fiend whore" of a mammy, Nancy Manningoe, "cullud," raises the curtain with three traditional "Yas, Lawd's," and when asked later by a white actor, "What would a person like you be doing in heaven?" humbly replies, "Ah kin work." Since Faulkner repeatedly calls Nancy "a nigger dope-fiend whore," all I can add is she is also a liar—because the *last* thing a Negro thinks of doing in heaven is working. Nancy knows better, even if Faulkner doesn't.

Nigger dope-fiend Nancy, Porgy's immoral Bess, Mamba's immoral daughter, street-walking Anna Lucasta, whorish Carmen Jones! Lawd, let me be a member of the wedding! "White folks Ah kin work!" In fact, yas, Lawd, I have to work because—

You've done taken my blues and gone—
Sure have! You sing 'em on Broadway,
And you sing 'em in Hollywood Bowl.
You mixed 'em up with symphonies,
And you fixed 'em so they don't sound like me.
Yep, you done taken my blues and gone!
You also took my spirituals and gone.
Now you've rocked-and-rolled 'em to death!
You put me in *Macbeth,*
In *Carmen Jones,* and *Anna Lucasta,*
And all kinds of *Swing Mikados*
And in everything but what's about me—
But someday somebody'll
Stand up and talk about me,
And write about me—
Black and beautiful—
And sing about me,
And put on plays about me!
I reckon it'll be me myself!
Yes, it'll be me.

Of course, it may be a long time before we finance big Broadway shows or a seven-million-dollar movie like *Porgy and Bess* on which, so far as I know, not a single Negro writer was employed. The *Encyclopaedia Britannica* declares *Porgy and Bess* "the greatest American musical drama ever written." The *Encyclopaedia Britannica* is white. White is right. So shoot the seven million! 7 come 11! Dice, gin, razors, knives, dope, watermelon, whores—7-11! Come 7!

Yet, surely Negro writing, even when commercial, need not be in terms of stereotypes. The interminable crap game at the beginning of *Porgy and Bess* is just because its authors could not see beyond the *surface* of Negro color. But the author of the original novel did see, with his white eyes, wonderful, poetic human qualities in the inhabitants of Catfish Row that made them come alive in his book, half alive on the stage, and I am sure, bigger than life on the screen. Du Bose Heyward was a *writer* first, white second, and this you will have to be, too: *writer* first, *colored* second. That means losing nothing of your racial identity. It is just that in the great sense of the word, anytime, any place, good art transcends land, race, or nationality, and color drops away. If you are a good writer, in the end neither blackness nor whiteness makes a difference to readers.

Greek the writer of *Oedipus* might have been, but *Oedipus* shakes Booker T. Washington High School. Irish was Shaw, but he rocks Fisk University. Scottish was Bobby Burns, but kids like him at Tuskegee. The more regional or national an art is in its origins, the more universal it may become in the end. What could be more Spanish than *Don Quixote:* yet what is more universal? What more Italian than Dante? Or more English than Shakespeare? Advice to Negro writers: Step *outside yourself*, then look back—and you will see how human, yet how beautiful and black you are. How very black —even when you're integrated.

As to marketing, however, blackness seen through black eyes may be too black for wide white consumption—unless coupled with greatness or its approximation. What should a Negro writer do, then, in a land where we have no black literary magazines, no black publishers, no black producers, no black investors able to corral seven million dollars to finance a movie? Sell what writing you can, get a job teaching, and give the rest of your talent away. Or else try becoming a good *bad* writer or a black *white* writer, in which case you might, with luck, do as well as white *black* writers do. If you are good enough in a *bad* way, or colored enough in a *good* way, you stand a chance perhaps, maybe, of becoming *even* commercially successful. At any rate, I would say, keep writing. Practice will do you no harm.

Second, be not dismayed! Keep sending your work out, magazine after magazine, publisher after publisher. Collect rejection slips as some people collect stamps. When you achieve a publication or two, try to get a literary agent—who will seek to collect checks for you instead of rejection slips. See along the way how few editors or agents will ask what color you are physically if you have something good to sell. I would say very few or NONE. Basically they do not care about race, if what you write is readable, new, different, exciting, alive on the printed page. Almost nobody knows Frank Yerby is colored. Few think about Willard Motley's complexion. Although how you treat the materials of race may narrow your market, I do not believe your actual race will. Certainly racial or regional subject matter has its marketing limitations. Publishers want only so many Chinese books a year. The same is true of Negro books.

However, if you want a job as a free-lance writer in Hollywood, on radio, or in TV, that now is sometimes possible—in contrast to the years before the War. But in the entertainment field, regular full-time staff jobs are still not too easy to come by if you are colored. Positions are valuable in the U.S.A., so commercial white culture would rather allow a colored writer a book than a job, even fame rather than an ordinary, decent, dependable living. But if you are so constituted as to wish a dependable living, with luck you might possibly nowadays achieve that too, purely as a writer. I hope so—because *starving* writers are stereotypes. And a stereotype is the last thing a Negro wants to be.

But you can't be a member of the Beat Generation, the fashionable word at the moment in marketing, *unless* you starve a little. Yet who wants to be "beat?" Not Negroes. That is what this conference is all about—how *not* to be "beat." So don't worry about beatness. That is easy enough to come by. Instead, let your talent bloom! You say you are mired in manure? Manure fertilizes. As the old saying goes, "Where the finest roses bloom, there is always a lot of manure around."

Of course, to be highly successful in a white world—commercially successful—in writing or anything else, you really should *be* white. But until you get white, *write*.

BLYDEN JACKSON (1910–   )

Literary critic, educator and editor, Blyden Jackson was born in Paducah, Kentucky, and began his teaching career in the public schools of Louisville. He did his undergraduate work at Wilberforce University, was a Rosenwald Fellow (1947–49), and received his M.A. and Ph.D. from the University of Michigan. Following a decade of teaching at Fisk University, Jackson joined the faculty of Southern University in 1954, where he was head of the English Department. He has been Dean of Graduate Studies at Southern University since 1962. Dean Jackson is a past president of the College Language Association, a former book review editor of Phylon, *and is currently Associate Editor of* CLA Journal. *He has published articles in a wide variety of periodicals. The following critical study is reprinted from* CLA Journal, September, 1960.

The Negro's Image of the Universe As Reflected in His Fiction

Among the most notable effects of fiction is its capacity for producing within the limits of the illusion it creates a world which, even in the sense of the goegrapher and historian, can seem, almost literally, very true. So, there is undoubtedly a real England with a real past, a real present, and still, apparently, a quite respectable real future. But there is also, as many devoted readers know, an England of English fiction, a complete and separate world unlike any other fictional reality, built out of a set of distinctively English sensibilities recollected, if in tranquillity, surely in some distinctively English versions of that often admirable psychic state. Just so, too, there is, within American literary tradition, a world of Negro fiction, within itself as singular a phenomenon as any other fictive world, and as representative, as any other fictive world, of a peculiar reaction to the objective facts of actual existence.

Three things seem, above all, to impart to this world of Negro fiction its distinctive character. One of these things is a matter of the physical shape which that world assumes under the Negro writer's analytic eye. Another, somewhat harder to label, but no harder to ascertain within the fundamental constitution of the universe, has to do with a power which seems to preside, like the ruling spirit in Hardy's *Wessex*, over all chains of consequence, and thus to control them in keeping with its own prescriptive intent and in a mood, an atmospheric tone, which becomes thereby the prevailing temper of the whole universe. The other, hardest of the three to give a name and hardest to describe precisely, is a matter of process, a sort of special law of the conservation of energy, ending in its own special pattern of circumscribed variability and its own special maintenance of a special *status quo*. Let us look, then, at each of these three things in order—at the way, that is, to speak most simply, this universe looks, the way it feels, and at what may well be called its peculiar eschatology.

First, then, our glance at the way this universe looks.

Surely the two most celebrated of Negro novels are Richard Wright's *Native Son* and Ralph Ellison's *Invisible Man*. In one of them, *Native Son*, the physical setting is Chicago. But no reader can be so obtuse as not to notice that the Chicago which establishes every point of reference in *Native Son* is the Chicago of the Negro ghetto. It is the only Chicago with which Bigger Thomas, the novel's black protagonist, can identify himself. Indeed, all creation, in the perspective of his well-conditioned reflexes, takes essential shape simply and clearly as ghetto and non-ghetto, an extension of himself, as it were, into me and not me. And in this uncompromising dichotomy of his physical environment to Bigger it is the ghetto, always the ghetto, which constitutes the prime reality. The non-ghetto is the obligatory second term, the meaningful opposite without which the ghetto could not be seen for what it is. But as Chicago serves *Native Son*, so does New York serve *Invisible Man*. There are some minor differences. In *Invisible Man* the action does not open in New York, but it arrives there soon enough, and while its protagonist does see this metropolis outside of Harlem as Bigger Thomas never quite sees Chicago beyond the Southside, the fact remains that it is Harlem which pervades the book, just as it is Harlem, or its equivalent, which establishes the same radical division for the Invisible Man as Chicago's Southside does for Bigger Thomas, the division of the physical world in its totality into ghetto and non-ghetto, that division which accounts alike for the Invisible Man's unique kind of invisibility and the Native Son's unique kind of native sonness.

That the two best known of Negro novels should put the emphasis which they do upon the two largest Negro ghettos is an informative circumstance. Harlem and Chicago's Southside are ghettos easily allied with the classic pattern. Give each of them a wall. They then should conform in every substantial respect to those famed quarters set aside for Jews in medieval towns from which ghettos have derived their name and definition. And it is only literally that Harlem and the Southside lack a wall. So, too, it is only in the most literal terms that the campus on which the Invisible Man spends the most credulous and most hopeful period of his youth fails to be what it undoubtedly effectively is, merely another ghetto. Surely this campus differs much in outward show from the single squalid and sadly down-at-heel tenement room into which Bigger, his brother, his mother and his sister compress all the activities of their life as a domestic household. It has green lawns, clean buildings, a quiet bourgeois atmosphere, and, when the moonlight broods upon its broad expanse, the sort of beauty which Matthew Arnold noted in his Oxford of the dreaming spires. Nevertheless Mr. Norton, the white trustee, comes into it as a visitor from an altogether alien world. Thus would he have entered Harlem. Thus, too, would he have come into the Negro quarter of any small town, be it in the Kansas of Langston Hughes' *Not Without Laughter* or the Georgia of John Oliver Killens' *Youngblood*. And thus, too, would he have entered the agrarian South of Negro peasants such as George Wylie Henderson's Jule or Ollie Miss. For what has happened in virtually every piece of Negro fiction brooks of but one interpretation, whether its creator was working as a conscious artist or whether his divided landscape comes unwittingly into focus under his spontaneous hand. All Negro fiction tends to conceive of its physical world as a sharp dichotomy, with the ghetto as its central figure and its symbolic truth, and with all else comprising a non-ghetto which throws into high relief the ghetto itself as the fundamental fact of life for Negroes as a group.

This has been consistently the case with fiction by Negro authors since the earliest novel of Negro authorship, William Wells Brown's *Clotelle*, itself a travelogue through much of the extensive ghetto formed by the *mise-en-scène* of American slavery. A few exceptions to this general condition do exist. I instance as examples of such exceptions Charles W. Chesnutt's short story, "Baxter's Procrustes," basically a *jeu d'esprit*, and Ann Petry's novel, *Country Place*, one of the several sustained fictions of Negro authorship in which a Negro writer has attempted to write of the predominantly white world as a white person would. But I should not want to concede as exceptions of significant worth such novels about white life as Frank Yerby's sensational fantasies, which make no pretense at seriousness, nor even those works similarly oriented, as Willard Motley's *Knock on Any Door*, about which one can hardly escape the conclusion voiced recently by Robert Bone that it is a lesser *Native Son* masquerading as a treatment of Skid Row. Moreover, so firmly holds this rule of the ghetto over the landscape of Negro fiction that one may be sure of the exceptions to it as exceptions. As with all true exceptions they disprove no generalizations. They only prove the rule.

But so much, now, for this universe as physical shape. Let us consider briefly its special feel.

There is a word in our language, *irony*, which a strong tradition in American life has been at great pains never to associate with the Negro character. Negroes, avers this strong tradition, are comic, primitive, savage in ways sometimes gay, sometimes brutal, but never so mature, so complex, so civilized as to be capable of making the subtle distinctions required of a practitioner of irony. For *irony* derives from classical Greek, the language of a people themselves mature, complex and highly civilized, a people, that is, separated by many generations of superior culture from the barbaric innocence and crudity of the Negro collective consciousness. Moreover, the first great ironist of historic note was Socrates, thinker par excellence and master of dialectic. Only the wildest heresy would link him with the typical representative of anything having to do with Negroes.

It must be admitted that irony could hardly consort with children or with minstrel men. It requires a certain refinement of perception. It depends upon that nice derangement of affairs in which an outcome is incongruous to an expectation. In addition, within some observer it must produce a very special kind of emotional discord. It must cause that observer, at one and the same time, pleasure and pain. He must want, at one and the same instant, to laugh and cry. In art, of course, form is a necessary adjunct, and students of irony have noted that, once given the proper ironic incongruity, that incongruity may express itself in three ways. It may be of speech, when what is said carries a meaning incongruous to its meaning on first examination, the incongruity producing the proper emotional discord. It may be irony of character, when what a person actually is turns out to be incongruous to what he seems to be, again with the proper emotional effect. Parenthetically, here, of course, Socrates belongs, who seemed so stupid and was so wise, as here, too, belong all dissemblers of his ilk, including a long line of Uncle Toms. For ironic dissimulation, the concealing of superior knowledge on the part of the ironist, a special skill of Socrateses as of Uncle Toms, is inseparable from irony of character. Finally, it may be irony of events, when a train of events ends with an outcome incongruous to the expectation, still, of course, with the attendant proper emotional effect of conjunctive pain and laughter in the observer.

To think of some of the titles of Negro novels, especially

with the contents of those novels clearly in mind, is at once
to begin to suspect, no matter how subtle an ironist is supposed to be, that irony may play a large role in the universe
of Negro fiction. *Native Son* is certainly an irony of speech,
in view of the conditions which lawyer Max contends made
Bigger Thomas the logical outcome, the true son, of his environment, and so is *One Way to Heaven*, for where does Sam
Lucas go, and how does he get there? So, also, are *Last of
the Conquerors*, with its double, if not triple, puns on *Last*
and *Conquerors*, *The Blacker the Berry*, whose Emmy Lou
does not find the juice of life sweet in any regard, *Comedy,
American Style; If He Hollers, Let Him Go; Tambourines to
Glory; The Walls of Jericho*, which have yet to tumble; *God
Sends Sunday, The Living Is Easy*, even *The Autobiography
of an Ex-Colored Man*. But it is only when one begins to
probe Negro fiction beyond its titles that one truly initiates
himself into the great extent to which the presiding genius in
the universe of Negro fiction is the ogre of an irony—or, to
be more specific, the ogre of one particular irony, so ubiqui-
tous in the Negro world that it seems to be every Negro's
vade mecum and so gross in its proportions that, in strong
contradiction to the inherent logic of ironic perception, no
exquisiteness of sensibility is required to feel the dry mock of
its incongruity. This particular irony is, of course, bound up
with American color caste. All over America life is lived,
officially and otherwise, only in the name of democracy. It is
that way now. It has been that way since there was an America, for the Declaration of Independence, which proclaimed
American nationhood, also proclaimed American democracy.
But all over America how different from the name of Democracy are the practices of color caste! How incongruous
to an expectation is this ironic outcome!

And so, well-nigh as omnipresent in the world of Negro fiction as the figure of the ghetto is the irony of color caste. Repeatedly in Negro fiction not to see exactly this one irony is
really not to see what is present there at all. But to see this
irony is to become one with the Negro writer and to prove
upon one's emotional pulse the Negro writer's world exactly
in the manner of the Negro writer himself. Thus, in Ann Petry's *The Street*, the protagonist, Lutie Johnson, has a special
reaction to a main street in one of those Connecticut towns
where the right men in gray flannel suits live with their wives,
their relatives and in-laws, their pets and their often secretly
bitter domestics, of whom Lutie a while was one. That Connecticut street is to Lutie an all too tangible reminder of a
condition she pines to attain, but from which she is forever

barred. It is the suppressed term of an irony given the substance of an objective correlative. Against that street, that objective correlative, Lutie may later put, in her own mind, the
street on which she comes to live in Harlem with her son and
only child, Bub. Where the Connecticut street is clean, the
Harlem street, *the* street, incidentally, of the novel's title, is
foul. Where the Connecticut street is open and free and radiant to Lutie's inner eye, the Harlem street is hemmed in and
furtive and drab in its meannesses and its makeshifts. Where
the Connecticut street is a bourgeois heaven, the Harlem
street is a bourgeois hell. And to make especially this latter
contrast, the most important of them all, as forceful as it can
be made, Ann Petry has done all she can to project an image
of Lutie Johnson's psychology as the psychology of an un-
abashed and uncritical bourgeois. Lutie is one of the faithful.
She has bargained her soul on getting ahead. Does she not
take a course at night, and then an examination, to get the job
which frees her from servitude in the white man's household?
She is strong—Mrs. Petry provides her with a magnificent
physique—young, intelligent, determined and willing to work
hard in the best tradition of Alexander Hamilton, Stephen
Girard, John D. Rockefeller and General Motors. Not one
tiniest trace of skepticism corrupts her orthodoxy. The wholeness of her devotion nothing mars. Marx would be unthinkable for her, Veblen, a tiresome dilettante. And certainly she
would have only bewildered contempt for the kind of rebellion against Philistia with which the modern artist has as-
saulted Mrs. Grundy since the earliest days of modern art's
many isms.

By all odds the outcome of Lutie's expectations should be
the street in the Connecticut town. By the irony of color
caste it is the street in the Harlem ghetto, directly the descen-
dant of the row of slave cabins in the ante-bellum plantation
for which the idiom of the slave South often used the generic
name, "the street," and even more directly the ironically incongruous outcome to the expectations of an American democrat like Lutie. As it is with *The Street*, so is it with the
overwhelming bulk of Negro fiction. The scene is not always
Harlem. The characters are not always as naïvely trustful as
Lutie Johnson of the democratic dream. But the irony is virtually always present, changing its incidental details, never
changing its fundamental terms, a distinctive component of
the universe of Negro fiction and a component without which
the universe would be very materially altered in significance
and value.

But now I want to proceed to the third, and final, major

feature I have chosen to cite in the universe of Negro fiction. About this feature one may not, because of its very nature, speak as categorically as one may about the other two features cited here. And yet it is, I am convinced, a feature which should not be ignored.

All universes subject to human observation seem to operate according to some principle which determines the character of the universe. Conceivably the principle may be actually more subjective than it is anything else. Nevertheless the men who inhabit the universe believe in its reality, and tend to accommodate their actions and their thoughts to their belief. For example, to the Vikings whose world appears in the Norse sagas the great principle which governed process in the universe was conflict. Indeed the end of all things was to come in a battle between the Frost Giants and the Gods and the passport to Valhalla was death in combat. And so the world of Viking culture flames with the burnings of halls and clangs with the weapons of warriors feuding in obedience to custom. On the other hand, the world of medieval Christendom, for all of St. Augustine's *City of God*, is relatively tensionless. It is basically a holding action, the keeping in place of a great chain of being proceeding downwards from God, the Unmoved Mover, through the lowest realm of an hierarchical order and back again to its source, a closed circuit in which the decisive process is not change, but rather, the maintenance of the established pattern. In the American tradition, however, change rather than a holding action has been the historic process. This nation was not born until after the idea of progress, no sop to the Cerberus of any *ancien régime*. If Physiocratic thought with its Newtonian science got into this nation's Constitution, at least by the Age of Jackson this nation's politics, in theory and practice, reflected also the Godwinian optimism which assumed that the Watchmaker Universe was wound up to bring on, be it ever so gradually, the sometime utopia of the perfectibility of man. For generations of American life, moreover, what this benevolent philosophy of cosmic process hypostasized, the moving frontier, unfolding the bounty of a rich continent, tended to confirm. To a New England Brahmin, or to one of Edith Wharton's old New Yorkers, that frontier may not have been an unmixed blessing. But to humbler folk, until the last homestead vanished and the great corporations captured the national economy, it must have seemed a welcome evidence that opportunity, all any one needed in America to improve himself, was built in in the grand design. Even a fierce old aristocrat like James Fenimore Cooper, romancing the brief past America had accumulated in his, to our nation, youthful day, cannot fail but produce in his fiction an America in which change plays an important role. Or even more curiously, a Willa Cather, intoning elegies for that golden time which she always located in the American past, could not have lamented as she lamented had she not premised as the indispensable background for her sweet moan a changing social order. But the world of Negro fiction is as static as the world of the medieval synthesis. It is a world in which the distinctive cosmic process is not change, but a holding action. In the typical Negro novel, after all the sound and fury dies, one finds things substantially as they were when the commotion all began. At the end of *Native Son* the world of Bigger Thomas does not differ from that he has always known. It was, and is, a world in which, season in and season out, the elemental process is a holding action, the maintenance of a continuing unaffected relationship of caste to caste in the American pattern of color caste. We know, at the end, that Bigger has made an effort to re-define his relationship with this world. We know that he has not succeeded in meaningful terms. But we know also that his failure does not involve the reconciliation of variables except as he has undergone an intensification of his own ability to perceive. And in *Invisible Man*, again, the world with which we deal is static. When the Invisible Man keeps asking himself his question about Tod Clifton—keeps wanting to know, that is, why Clifton has dropped out of history—the language deceives no one. There is no history in *Invisible Man* in the sense that history is change. All that Tod Clifton has dropped out of is a picture, not a process, at least not a process rendered operational by its function as change. I should say offhand that in major pieces of Negro fiction only in Langston Hughes' *Not Without Laughter* and John Oliver Killens' *Youngblood* is the phenomenon of change to be discerned in the constitution of the fictional universe. To an overwhelming degree the universe of Negro fiction is panoramic, not dramatic. It is a still picture, the unchanging backdrop against which actors are paraded to show how fixed is a setting which should be, but has not, altered its essential features. It is, in short, the limited universe of a literature of protest, a universe that, with its quality of *stasis*, can well be seen as the same universe which Negroes see, but only from two different angles, when they see first in it either the ghetto or the irony of color caste.

And now let me finish off this brief excursion into the world of Negro fiction with a final observation. It seems to me that few, if any, literary universes are as impoverished as the universe of Negro fiction. I have spoken of some things that can be found there. Of greater moment, conceivably, are the things that cannot be found there. In a famous passage in his *Hawthorne* Henry James once bemoaned the things America lacked. Much more can a sympathetic critic bemoan the absence of a plethora of things devoutly to be desired in the world of Negro fiction. And of even greater moment, it may well be, is the circumstance that, in the final analysis, all that is in this universe of Negro fiction seems too easily convertible into one primal substance. To look for any length of time at this world is to see the ghetto melt into the irony of color caste, the irony of color caste melt into the holding action that is this universe's law of *stasis*, this holding action melt into the ghetto, and so on until all is one and one is all. But should universes be quite so monolithic? Not, I think, even when they are fictional. There must be much about the universe, even about the Negro universe which is their special care, that Negroes have not said in their fiction. Who can say, who looks soberly at what has been done, that Othello's occupation is anything but far from being gone?

JOHN HENRIK CLARKE (1915–   )

A New Yorker and Harlemite since 1933, John Henrik Clarke, editor of The Best Short Stories by Negro Writers, *was born in Union Springs, Alabama, and raised in Columbus, Georgia. Best known as a critic, editor, and anthologist, he has also published poetry and short stories. For many years he wrote a syndicated book review column for the Associated Negro Press. Clarke was co-founder of* Harlem Quarterly, *book review editor of* Negro History Bulletin, *and feature writer on African and American Negro subjects for the Pittsburgh* Courier *and* Ghana Evening News, *and has served on the editorial staffs of five different publications. He is now Associate Editor of* Freedomways; A Quarterly Review of the*

Negro Freedom Movement *and has contributed to numerous periodicals in the United States and abroad. The following article is a new and revised version of a study, "Transition in the American Negro Short Story," which was first published in Phylon in 1960. It appeared in its present revised form in Negro Digest, December, 1967.*

The Origin and Growth of Afro-American Literature

Africans were great story tellers long before their first appearance in Jamestown, Virginia, in 1619. The rich and colorful history, art and folklore of West Africa, the ancestral home of most Afro-Americans, present evidence of this, and more.

Contrary to a misconception which still prevails, the Africans were familiar with literature and art for many years before their contact with the Western world. Before the breaking up of the social structure of the West African states of Ghana, Melle (Mali) and Songhay, and the internal strife and chaos that made the slave trade possible, the forefathers of the Africans who eventually became slaves in the United States lived in a society where university life was fairly common and scholars were beheld with reverence.

There were in this ancestry rulers who expanded their kingdoms into empires, great and magnificent armies whose physical dimensions dwarfed entire nations into submission, generals who advanced the technique of military science, scholars whose vision of life showed foresight and wisdom, and priests who told of gods that were strong and kind. To understand fully any aspect of Afro-American life, one must realize that the black American is not without a cultural past, though he was many generations removed from it before his achievements in American literature and art commanded any appreciable attention.

I have been referring to the African Origin of Afro-American Literature and history. This preface is essential to every meaningful discussion of the role of the Afro-American in every major aspect of American life, past and present. Before getting into the main body of this talk I want to make it clear that the Black Race did not come to the United States culturally empty-handed.

I will elaborate very briefly on my statement to the effect

that "the forefathers of the Africans who eventually became slaves in the United States once lived in a society where university life was fairly common and scholars were beheld with reverence."

During the period in West African history—from the early part of the fourteenth century to the time of the Moorish invasion in 1591, the City of Timbuktu, with the University of Sankore in the Songhay Empire, was the intellectual center of Africa. Black scholars were enjoying a renaissance that was known and respected throughout most of Africa and in parts of Europe. At this period in African history, the University of Sankore, at Timbuktu, was the educational capital of the Western Sudan. In his book *Timbuktu the Mysterious*, Felix DuBois gives us the following description of this period:

"The scholars of Timbuktu yielded in nothing, to the saints in their sojourns in the foreign universities of Fez, Tunis and Cairo. They astounded the most learned men of Islam by their erudition. That these Negroes were on a level with the Arabian Savants is proved by the fact that they were installed as professors in Morocco and Egypt. In contrast to this, we find that the Arabs were not always equal to the requirements of Sankore."

I will speak of only one of the great black scholars referred to in the book by Felix DuBois.

Ahmed Baba was the last chancellor of the University of Sankore. He was one of the greatest African scholars of the late sixteenth century. His life is a brilliant example of the range and depth of West African intellectual activity before the colonial era. Ahmed Baba was the author of more than 40 books; nearly every one of these books had a different theme. He was in Timbuktu when it was invaded by the Moroccans in 1592, and he was one of the first citizens to protest this occupation of his beloved home town. Ahmed Baba, along with other scholars, was imprisoned and eventually exiled to Morocco. During his expatriation from Timbuktu, his collection of 1,600 books, one of the richest libraries of his day, was lost.

Now, West Africa entered a sad period of decline. During the Moorish occupation, wreck and ruin became the order of the day. When the Europeans arrived in this part of Africa and saw these conditions, they assumed that nothing of order and value had ever existed in these countries. This mistaken impression, too often repeated, has influenced the interpretation of African and Afro-American life in history for over 400 years.

Negroes played an important part in American life, history
and culture long before 1619. Our relationship to this country is as old as the country itself.

Africans first came to the new world as explorers. They
participated in the exploratory expeditions of Balboa, the dis-
coverer of the Pacific, and Cortes, the conqueror of Mexico.
An African explorer helped to open up New Mexico and Ari-
zona and prepared the way for the settlement of the Southwest. Africans also accompanied French Jesuit missionaries
on their early travels through North America.

In the United States, the art and literature of the Negro
people has had an economic origin. Much that is original in
black American folklore, or singular in "Negro spirituals"
and blues, can be traced to the economic institution of slavery and its influence upon the Negro's soul.

After the initial poetical debut of Jupiter Hammon and
Phillis Wheatley, the main literary expression of the Negro
was the slave narrative. One of the earliest of these narratives
came from the pen of Gustavas Vassa, an African from
Nigeria. This was a time of great pamphleteering in the
United States. The free Africans in the North, and those who
had escaped from slavery in the South, made their mark
upon this time and awakened the conscience of the nation.
Their lack of formal educational attainments gave their narratives a strong and rough-hewed truth, more arresting than
scholarship.

Gustavas Vassa established his reputation with an autobiography, first printed in England. Vassa, born in 1745, was
kidnapped by slavers when he was 11 years old and taken to
America. He was placed in service on a plantation in Virginia. Eventually, he was able to purchase his freedom. He
left the United States, made his home in England and became
active in the British anti-slavery movement. In 1790, he presented a petition to Parliament to abolish the slave trade. His
autobiography, *The Interesting Narrative of the Life of Gustavas Vassa,* was an immediate success and had to be published in five editions.

At the time when slave ships were still transporting Africans to the New World, two 18th century Negroes were writing and publishing works of poetry. The first of these was Jupiter Hammon, a slave in Queens Village, Long Island. In
1760, Hammon published *An Evening Thought: Salvation by
Christ, With Penitential Cries . . .* In all probability this was
the first poem published by an American Negro. His most remarkable work, "An address to the Negroes of New York,"
was published in 1787. Jupiter Hammon died in 1800.

Phillis Wheatley (1753–1784), like Hammon, was influenced by the religious forces of the Wesley-Whitefield revival. Unlike Hammon, however, she was a writer of unusual talent. Though born in Africa, she acquired in an uncredibly short time both the literary culture and the religion of her New England masters. Her writings reflect little of her race and much of the age in which she lived. She was a New England poet of the third quarter of the 18th century, and her poems reflected the poetic conventions of the Boston Puritans with whom she lived. Her fame continued long after her death in 1784 and she became one of the best known poets of New England.

Another important body of literature came out of this period. It is the literature of petition, written by free black men in the North, who were free in name only. Some of the early petitioners for justice were Caribbean-Americans who saw their plight and the plight of the Afro-Americans as one and the same.

In 18th century America, two of the most outstanding fighters for liberty and justice were the West Indians—Prince Hall and John B. Russwurm. When Prince Hall came to the United States, the nation was in turmoil. The colonies were ablaze with indignation. Britain, with a series of revenue acts, had stoked the fires of colonial discontent. In Virginia, Patrick Henry was speaking of liberty or death. The cry, "No Taxation Without Representation," played on the nerve strings of the nation. Prince Hall, then a delicate-looking teenager, often walked through the turbulent streets of Boston, an observer unobserved.

A few months before these hectic scenes, he had arrived in the United States from his home in Barbados, where he was born about 1748, the son of an Englishman and a free African woman. He was, in theory, a free man, but he knew that neither in Boston nor in Barbados were persons of African descent free in fact. At once, he questioned the sincerity of the vocal white patriots of Boston. It never seemed to have occurred to them that the announced principles motivating their action was stronger argument in favor of destroying the system of slavery. The colonists held in servitude more than a half million human beings, some of them white; yet they engaged in the contradiction of going to war to support the theory that all men were created equal.

When Prince Hall arrived in Boston, that city was the center of the American slave trade. Most of the major leaders of revolutionary movement, in fact, were slaveholders or investors in slave-supported businesses. Hall, like many other

Americans, wondered: what did these men mean by freedom?

The condition of the free black men, as Prince Hall found them, was not an enviable one. Emancipation brought neither freedom nor relief from the stigma of color. They were still included with slaves, indentured servants, and Indians in the slave codes. Discriminatory laws severely circumscribed their freedom of movement.

By 1765, Prince Hall saw little change in the condition of the blacks, and though a freeman, at least in theory, he saw his people debased as though they were slaves still in bondage. These things drove him to prepare himself for leadership among his people. So, through diligence and frugality, he became a property owner, thus establishing himself in the eyes of white people as well as the blacks.

But the ownership of property was not enough. He still had to endure sneers and insults. He went to school at night, and later became a Methodist preacher. His church became the forum for his people's grievances. Ten years after his arrival in Boston, he was the accepted leader of the black community.

In 1788, Hall petitioned the Massachusetts Legislature, protesting the kidnapping of free Negroes. This was a time when American patriots were engaged in a constitutional struggle for freedom. They had proclaimed the inherent rights of all mankind to life, liberty and the pursuit of happiness. Hall dared to remind them that the black men in the United States were human beings and as such were entitled to freedom and respect for their human personality.

Prejudice made Hall the father of African secret societies in the United States. He is the father of what is now known as Negro Masonry. Hall first sought initiation into the white Masonic Lodge in Boston, but was turned down because of his color. He then applied to the Army Lodge of an Irish Regiment. His petition was favorably received. On March 6, 1775, Hall and fourteen other black Americans were initiated in Lodge Number 441. When, on March 17, the British were forced to evacuate Boston, the Army Lodge gave Prince Hall and his colleagues a license to meet and function as a Lodge. Thus, on July 3, 1776, African Lodge No. 1 came into being. This was the first Lodge in Masonry established in America for men of African descent.

The founding of the African Lodge was one of Prince Hall's greatest achievements. It afforded the Africans in the

New England area a greater sense of security, and contributed to a new spirit of unity among them. Hall's interest did not end with the Lodge. He was deeply concerned with improving the lot of his people in other ways. He sought to have schools established for the children of the free Africans in Massachusetts. Of prime importance is the fact that Prince Hall worked to secure respect for the personality of his people and also played a significant role in the downfall of the Massachusetts slave trade. He helped to prepare the groundwork for the freedom fighters of the 19th and 20th centuries, whose continuing efforts have brought the black American closer to the goal of full citizenship.

The literature of petition was continued by men like David Walker whose *Appeal,* an indictment of slavery, was published in 1829. Dynamic ministers like Samuel Ringgold Ward and Henry Highland Garnet joined the ranks of the petitioners at the time a journalist literature was being born.

Frederick Douglass, the noblest of American black men of the 19th century, was the leader of the journalist group. He established the newspaper *North Star* and, later, the magazine *Douglass Monthly.* John B. Russwurm and Samuel Cornish founded the newspaper *Freedom's Journal* in 1827.

In 1829, a third poet, George Moses Horton, published his book, *The Hope of Liberty.* In his second volume, *Naked Genius* (1865), he expressed his anti-slavery convictions more clearly. George Moses Horton was the first slave poet to openly protest his status.

Throughout the early part of the 19th century, the slave narrative became a new form of American literary expression.

The best known of these slave narratives came from the pen of Frederick Douglass, the foremost Negro in the anti-slavery movement. His first book was *The Narrative of the Life of Frederick Douglass* (1845). Ten years later, an improved and enlarged edition, *My Bondage and My Freedom,* was published. His third autobiography, *Life and Times of Frederick Douglass,* was published in 1881 and enlarged in 1892. Douglass fought for civil rights and against lynching and the Ku Klux Klan. No abuse of justice escaped his attention and his wrath.

It was not until 1887 that an Afro-American writer emerged who was fully a master of the short story as a literary form. This writer was Charles W. Chesnutt. Chesnutt, an Ohioan by birth, became a teacher in North Carolina while still in his middle teens. He studied the traditions and superstitions of the people that he taught and later made this material into the ingredient of his best short stories. In August 1887, his short story, "The Goophered Grapevine," appeared in *The Atlantic Monthly*. This was the beginning of a series of stories which were later brought together in his first book, *The Conjure Woman* (1899). "The Wife of His Youth" also appeared in the *Atlantic* (July 1898) and gave the title to his second volume, *The Wife of His Youth and Other Stories of the Color Line* (1899). Three more stories appeared later: "Baxter's Procrustes" in the *Atlantic* (June, 1904), and "The Doll" and "Mr. Taylor's Funeral" in *The Crisis* magazine (April, 1912 and April-May, 1915).

Chesnutt's novel did not measure up to the standards he had set with his short stories, though they were all compe- tently written. In 1928, he was awarded the Spingarn Medal for his "pioneer work as a literary artist depicting the life and struggle of Americans of Negro descent."

Paul Laurence Dunbar, a contemporary of Charles W. Chesnutt, made his reputation as a poet before extending his talent to short stories. Both Dunbar and Chesnutt very often used the same subject matter in their stories. Chesnutt was by far the better writer, and his style and attitude differed radi- cally from Dunbar's.

Dunbar's pleasant folk tales of tradition-bound plantation black folk were more acceptable to a large white reading audience with preconceived ideas of "Negro characteristics." In all fairness, it must be said that Dunbar did not cater to this audience in all of his stories. In such stories as "The Tragedy at Three Forks," "The Lynching of Jube Benson" and "The Ordeal of Mt. Hope," he showed a deep concern and understanding of the more serious and troublesome as- pects of Afro-American life. Collections of his stories are: *Folks from Dixie* (1898), *The Strength of Gideon* (1900), *In Old Plantation Days* (1903), and *The Heart of Happy Hollow* (1904). Only one of his novels, *The Sport of the Gods* (1902), is mainly concerned with Afro-American char- acters.

Chesnutt and Dunbar, in their day, reached a larger general reading audience than any of the black writers who came be- fore them. The period of the slave narratives had passed. Yet, the black writer was still an oddity and a stepchild in the eyes of most critics. This attitude continued in a lessening degree throughout one of the richest and most productive periods in Afro-American writing in the United States—the period called "the Negro Renaissance." The community of Harlem was the center and spiritual godfather and midwife for this renaissance. The cultural emancipation of the Afro-American that began before the first World War was now in full force. The black writer discovered a new voice within himself and liked the sound of it. The white writers who had been interpreting our life with an air of authority and a preponderance of error looked at last to the black writer for their next cue. In short story collections like Jean Toomer's *Cane* (1923) and Langston Hughes' *The Ways of White Folks* (1934) heretofore untreated aspects of Afro-American life were presented in an interesting manner that was unreal to some readers because it was new and so contrary to the stereotypes they had grown accustomed to.

In her book *Mules and Men* (1935), Zora Neale Hurston presented a collection of folk tales and sketches that showed the close relationship between humor and tragedy in Afro-American life. In doing this, she also fulfilled the first requirement of all books—to entertain and guide the reader through an interesting experience that is worth the time and attention it takes to absorb it. In other stories like *The Gilded Six Bits, Drenched in Light* and *Spunk* another side of Miss Hurston's talent was shown.

In the midst of this renaissance, two strong voices from the West Indians were heard. Claude McKay, in his books *Ginger-Town* (1932) and *Banana Bottom* (1933), wrote of life in his Jamaican homeland in a manner that debunked the travelogue exoticism usually attributed to Negro life in the Caribbean area. Before the publication of these books, Harlem and its inhabitants had already been the subject matter for a group of remarkable short stories by McKay and the inspiration for his book, *Home to Harlem,* still the most famous novel ever written about that community.

In 1926, Eric Walrond, a native of British Guiana, explored and presented another side of West Indian life in his book, *Tropic Death,* a near classic. In these 10 naturalistic stories, Eric Walrond concerns himself mostly with labor and living conditions in the Panama Canal Zone where a diversity of people and ways of life meet and clash, while each tries to survive at the expense of the other. Clear perception and strength of style enabled Mr. Walrond to balance form and content in such a manner that the message was never intruded upon the unfolding of the stories.

Rudolph Fisher, another bright star of the Harlem literary renaissance, was first a brilliant young doctor. The new and light touch he brought to his stories of Afro-American life did not mar the serious aspect that was always present. The message in his comic realism was more profound because he was skillful enough to weave it into the design of his stories without destroying any of their entertainment value. His stories "Blades of Steel," "The City of Refuge" and "The Promised Land" were published in *The Atlantic Monthly*. "High Yaller" appeared in *The Crisis* magazine during the hey-day of that publication, and was later reprinted in the O'Brien anthology, *Best Short Stories of 1934*. Unfortunately, he died before all of his bright promise was fulfilled.

The Harlem literary renaissance was studded with many names. Those already mentioned are only a few of the most outstanding. During the period of this literary flowering among black writers, Harlem became the Mecca, the stimulating Holy City, drawing pilgrims from all over the country and from some places abroad. Talented authors, playwrights, painters and sculptors came forth eagerly showing their wares.

Three men, W. E. B. Du Bois, James Weldon Johnson and Alain Locke, cast a guiding influence over this movement without becoming a part of the social climbing and pseudo-intellectual aspect of it. W. E. B. Du Bois, by continuously challenging the old concepts and misinterpretations of Afro-American life, gave enlightened new directions to a whole generation. As editor of *The Crisis*, he introduced many new black writers and extended his helpful and disciplining hand when it was needed. Following the death of Booker T. Washington and the decline of the Booker T. Washington school of thought, he became the spiritual father of the new black intelligentsia.

James Weldon Johnson moved from Florida to New York. His diversity of talent established his reputation long before the beginning of the "New Negro literary movement." Later, as a participant in and historian of the movement, he helped to appraise and preserve the best that came out of it. In his books, *Autobiography of an Ex-Colored Man* (1912), *The Book of American Negro Poetry* (1922), *Black Manhattan* (1930), and *Along This Way*, an autobiography (1933), James Weldon Johnson showed clearly that Negro writers have made a distinct contribution to the literature of the United States. His own creative talent made him one of the most able of these contributors.

Alain Locke is the writer who devoted the most time to the interpretation of the "New Negro literary movement" and to Afro-American literature in general. In 1925, he expanded the special Harlem issue of the magazine *Survey Graphic* (which he edited) into the anthology, *The New Negro*. This book is a milestone and a guide to Afro-American thought, literature and art in the middle twenties. The objective of the volume "to register the transformation of the inner and outer life of the Negro in America that had so significantly taken place in the last few preceding years," was ably achieved. For many years, Mr. Locke's annual appraisal of books by and about Negroes, published in *Opportunity* magazine, was an eagerly awaited literary event.

Early in the Harlem literary renaissance period, the black ghetto became an attraction for a varied assortment of white celebrities and just plain thrill-seeking white people lost from their moorings. Some were insipid rebels, defying the mores of their upbringing by associating with Negroes on a socially equal level. Some were too rich to work, not educated enough to teach, and not holy enough to preach. Others were searching for the mythological "noble savage"—the "exotic Negro."

These professional exotics were generally college educated Negroes who had become estranged from their families and the environment of their upbringing. They talked at length about the great books within them waiting to be written. Their white sponsors continued to subsidize them while they "developed their latent talent." Of course the "great books" of these camp followers never got written and, eventually, their white sponsors realized that they were never going to write—not even a good letter. Ironically, these sophisticates made a definite contribution to the period of the "New Negro literary renaissance." In socially inclined company, they proved that a black American could behave with as much attention to the details of social protocol as the best bred and richest white person in the country. They could balance a cocktail glass with expertness. Behind their pretense of being writers they were really actors—and rather good ones. They were generally better informed than their white sponsors and could easily participate in a discussion of the writings of Marcel Proust in one minute, and the music of Ludwig Von Beethoven the next. As social parasites, they conducted themselves with a smoothness approaching an artistic accomplishment. Unknown to them, their conduct had done much to eliminate one of the major prevailing stereotypes of Afro-American life and manners.

Concurrently with the unfolding of this mildly funny comedy, the greatest productive period in Afro-American literature continued. The more serious and talented black writers were actually writing their books and getting them published.

Opportunity magazine, then edited by Charles Johnson, and *The Crisis,* edited by W. E. B. Du Bois, were the major outlets for the new black writers.

Opportunity short story contests provided a proving ground for a number of competent black writers. Among the prize winners were Cecil Blue, John F. Matheus, Eugene Gordon and Marita Bonner.

Writers like Walter White, Jessie Fauset, Wallace Thurman, Nella Larsen, George S. Schuyler, Sterling A. Brown and Arna Bontemps had already made their debut and were accepted into the circle of the matured.

The stock market collapse of 1929 marked the beginning of the depression and the end of the period known as "The Negro Renaissance." The "exotic Negro," professional and otherwise, became less exotic now that a hungry look was upon his face. The numerous white sponsors and well-wishers who had begun to flock to Harlem ten years before no longer had time or money to explore and marvel over Harlem life. Many Harlem residents lived and died in Harlem during this period without once hearing of the famous literary movement that had flourished and declined within their midst. It was not a mass movement. It was a fad, partly produced in Harlem and partly imposed on Harlem. Most of the writers associated with it would have written just as well at any other time.

In the intervening years between the end of "The Negro Renaissance" and the emergence of Richard Wright, black writers of genuine talent continued to produce books of good caliber. The lack of sponsorship and pampering had made them take serious stock of themselves and their intentions. *The Crisis,* organ of the National Association for the Advancement of Colored People, and *Opportunity,* organ of the National Urban League, continued to furnish a publishing outlet for new black writers. The general magazines published stories by black writers intermittently, seemingly on a quota basis.

During this period writers like Ralph Ellison, Henry B. Jones, Marian Minus, Ted Poston, Lawrence D. Reddick and Grace W. Thompkins published their first short stories.

In 1936 Richard Wright's first short story to receive any appreciable attention, "Big Boy Leaves Home," appeared in the anthology, *The New Caravan.* "The Ethics of Living Jim Crow: An Autobiographical Sketch" was published in *Ameri-*

can Stuff, anthology of the Federal Writers' Project, the next year. In 1938, when his first book, *Uncle Tom's Children,* won a $500 prize contest conducted by *Story Magazine,* his talent received national attention. With the publication of his phenomenally successful novel, *Native Son,* in 1940, a new era in Afro-American literature had begun. Here, at last, was a black writer who undeniably wrote considerably better than many of his white contemporaries. As a short story craftsman, he was the most accomplished black writer since Charles W. Chesnutt.

After the emergence of Richard Wright, the period of indulgence for Negro writers was over. Hereafter, black writers had to stand or fall by the same standards and judgments used to evaluate the work of white writers. The era of the patronized and pampered black writer had at last come to an end. The closing of this era may, in the final analysis, be the greatest contribution Richard Wright made to the status of Negro writers and to Negro literature.

When the United States entered the second World War, the active Negro writers, like most other writers in the country, turned their talents to some activity in relation to the war.

The first short stories of Ann Petry began to appear in *The Crisis. The Negro Caravan,* the best anthology of Negro literature since Alain Locke edited *The New Negro* sixteen years before, had already appeared with much new material. Chester B. Himes, a dependable writer during the depression period, managed to turn out a number of remarkable short stories while working in shipyards and war industries in California. In 1944, he received a Rosenwald Fellowship to complete his first novel, *If He Hollers Let Him Go.* In 1945, Frank Yerby won an O. Henry Memorial Award for his excellent short story, "Health Card," which had been published in *Harper's* magazine a year before.

A new crop of post-war black writers was emerging. In their stories they treated new aspects of Afro-American life or brought new insights to the old aspects. Principally, they were good story tellers, aside from any message they wanted to get across to their readers. The weepy sociological propaganda stories (so prevalent during the depression era) had had their day with the Negro writer and all others. There would still be protest stories, but the protest would now have to meet the standards of living literature.

Opportunity and *The Crisis,* once the proving ground for so many new black writers, were no longer performing that much needed service. The best of the new writers found acceptance in the general magazines. Among these are James

Baldwin, Lloyd Brown, Arthur P. Davis, Owen Dodson, Lance Jeffers, John O. Killens, Robert H. Lucas, Albert Murray, George E. Norford, Carl R. Offord, John H. Robinson, Jr., John Caswell Smith, Jr. and Mary E. Vroman.

With the rise of nationalism and independent states in Africa, and the rapid change of the status of the Negro in the United States, the material used by black writers and their treatment of it did, of necessity, reflect a breaking away from the old mooring.

Among black writers the period of the 1940's was the period of Richard Wright. The period of the 1960's was the period of James Baldwin.

The now flourishing literary talent of James Baldwin had no easy birth, and he did not emerge overnight, as some of his new discoverers would have you believe. For years this talent was in incubation in the ghetto of Harlem, before he went to Europe a decade ago in an attempt to discover the United States and how he and his people relate to it. The book in which that discovery is portrayed, *The Fire Next Time,* is a continuation of his search for place and definition.

Baldwin, more than any other writer of our times, has succeeded in restoring the personal essay to its place as a form of creative literature. From his narrow vantage point of personal grievance, he has opened a "window on the world." He plays the role traditionally assigned to thinkers concerned with the improvement of human conditions—that of alarmist. He calls national attention to things in the society that need to be corrected and things that need to be celebrated.

When Richard Wright died in Paris in 1960, a new generation of black writers, partly influenced by him, was beginning to explore, as Ralph Ellison said, "the full range of American Negro humanity." In the short stories and novels of such writers as Frank London Brown, William Melvin Kelly, LeRoi Jones, Paule Marshall, Rosa Guy and Ernest J. Gaines, both a new dimension and a new direction in writing are seen. They have questioned and challenged all previous interpretations of Afro-American life. In doing this, they have created the basis for a new American literature.

The black writer and his people are now standing at the crossroads of history. This is the black writer's special vantage point, and this is what makes the task and the mission of the black writer distinctly different from that of the white writer. The black writer, concerned with creating a work of art in a segregated society, has a double task. First; he has to explain the society to himself and create his art while opposing that society. Second: he cannot be honest with himself or his people without lending his support, at least verbally, to the making of a new society that respects the dignity of men.

The black writer must realize that his people are now entering the last phase of a transitional period between slavery and freedom. It is time for the black writer to draw upon the universal values in his people's experience, just as Sean O'Casey and Sholem Aleichem drew upon the universal values in the experiences of the Irish and the Jews. In the next phase of Afro-American writing, a literature of celebration must be created—not a celebration of oppression, but a celebration of survival in spite of it.

RICHARD G. STERN (1928–)

An author and educator, Richard Stern conducted the following interview with Ralph Ellison for the Chicago literary magazine december. *It was published in the Winter, 1961, issue of* december *under the title "That Same Pain, That Same Pleasure . . ." and was later included in Ellison's book of collected essays and articles* Shadow and Act.

An Interview with Ralph Ellison

STERN: Last night we were talking about the way in which your literary situation has been special, the way in which you as a Negro writer have valued the parochial limitations of most Negro fiction. Accepting this, not debating it, would you want to talk a bit about the sources of the strength by which you escaped them?

ELLISON: Well, to the extent that one cannot ever escape what is given I suppose it had less to do with writing per se than with my desire, beginning at a very early age, to be more fully a part of that larger world which surrounded the

Negro world into which I was born. It was a matter of attitude. Then there were the accidents through which so much of that world beyond the Negro community became available to me. Ironically, I would have to start with some of the features of American life which it has become quite fashionable to criticize in a most unthinking way—the mass media. Like so many kids of the Twenties, I played around with radio—building crystal sets and circuits consisting of a few tubes which I found published in the radio magazines. At the time we were living in a white middleclass neighborhood where my mother was custodian for some apartments, and it was while searching the trash for cylindrical ice cream cartons which were used by amateurs for winding tuning coils that I met a white boy who was looking for the same thing. I gave him some of those I'd found and we became friends. Oddly enough, I don't remember his family name even though his father was pastor of the leading Episcopal church in Oklahoma City at that time, but his nickname was Hulie and for kids of eight or nine that was enough. Due to a rheumatic heart Hulie was tutored at home and spent a great deal of time playing by himself and in taking his parents' elaborate radio apart and putting it back together again, and building circuits of his own. For all of his delicate health, he was a very intelligent and very alive boy. It didn't take much encouragement from his mother, who was glad to have someone around to keep him company, for me to spend much of my free time helping with his experiments. By the time I left the community, he had become interested in shortwave communication and was applying for a ham license. I moved back into the Negro community and began to concentrate on music, and was never to see him again, but knowing this white boy was a very meaningful experience. It had little to do with the race question as such, but with our mutual loneliness (I had no other playmates in that community) and a great curiosity about the growing science of radio. It was important for me to know a boy who could approach the intricacies of electronics with such daring and whose mind was intellectually aggressive. Knowing him led me to expect much more of myself and of the world.

The other accident from that period lay in my mother's bringing home copies of such magazines as *Vanity Fair* and of opera recordings which had been discarded by a family for whom she worked. You might say that my environment was extended by these slender threads into the worlds of white families whom personally I knew not at all. These magazines and recordings and the discarded books my mother brought home to my brother and me spoke to me of a life which was broader and more interesting, and although it was not really a part of my own life, I never thought they were not for me simply because I happened to be a Negro. They were things which spoke of a world which I could some day make my own.

STERN: Were you conscious at this time of peculiar limitations upon your freedom of action, perhaps even your freedom of feeling?

ELLISON: Well, now, remember that this was in Oklahoma, which is a border state and as the 46th state was one of the last of our territories to achieve statehood. Although opened to American settlers in 1889, at the time of my birth it had been a state only seven years. Thus it had no tradition of slavery and while it was segregated, relationships between the races were more fluid and thus more human than in the old slave states. My parents, like most of the other Negroes, had come to the new state looking for a broader freedom and had never stopped pushing against the barriers. Having arrived at the same time that most of the whites had, they felt that the restriction of Negro freedom was imposed unjustly through the force of numbers and that they had the right and obligation to fight against it. This was all to the good. It made for a tradition of aggressiveness and it gave us a group social goal which was not as limited as that imposed by the old slave states. I recognized limitations, yes; but I thought these limitations were unjust and I felt no innate sense of inferiority which would keep me from getting those things I desired out of life. There were those who stood in the way but you just had to keep moving toward whatever you wanted.

As a kid I remember working it out this way: there was a world in which you wore your everyday clothes on Sunday, and there was a world in which you wore your Sunday clothes everyday—*I* wanted the world in which you wore your Sunday clothes everyday. I wanted it because it represented something better, a more exciting and civilized and human way of living; a world which came to me through certain scenes of felicity which I encountered in fiction, in the movies, and which I glimpsed sometimes through the windows of great houses on Sunday afternoons when my mother took my brother and me for walks through the wealthy white sections of the city. I know it now for a boy's vague dream of possibility. Hulie was part of it, and shop window displays of elegant clothing, furniture, automobiles—those Lincolns and Marmons!—and of course music and books. And for me none of this was hopelessly beyond the reach of my Negro world, really; because if you worked and you fought for your rights, and so on, you could finally achieve it. This involved our American Negro faith in education, of course, and the idea of self-cultivation—although I couldn't have put it that way back during the days when the idea first seized me. Interesting enough, by early adolescence the idea of Renaissance Man had drifted down to about six of us and we discussed mastering ourselves and everything in sight as though no such thing as racial discrimination existed. As you can see, quite a lot of our living was done in the imagination.

STERN: At one part of your life you became conscious that there was something precious in being a Negro in this country at this time. Can you remember when you discovered this?

ELLISON: Well, part of it came from the affirmation of those things in the Negro environment which I found warm and meaningful. For instance, I had none of the agricultural experience of my mother, who had grown up on a farm in Georgia, and although in 20 minutes you could move from Oklahoma City into deep farm country, I shared none of the agricultural experience of many of my classmates. I was of the city, you see. But during the fall cotton picking season certain kids left school and went with their parents to work in the cotton fields. Now most parents wished their children to have no contact with the cotton patch, it was part of an experience which they wanted to put behind them. It was part of the Old South which they had come west to forget. Just the same those trips to the cotton patch seemed to me an enviable experience because the kids came back with such wonderful stories. And it wasn't the hard work which they stressed, but the communion, the playing, the eating, the dancing and the singing. And they brought back jokes, *our* Negro jokes—not those told about Negroes by whites—and they always returned with Negro folk stories which I'd never heard before and which couldn't be found in any books I knew about. This was something to affirm and I felt there was a richness in it. I didn't think too much about it but what my schoolmates shared in the country and what I felt in their accounts of it seemed much more real than the Negro middle-class values which were taught in school.

Or again: I grew up in a school in which music was emphasized and where we were taught harmony from the ninth through the twelfth grades and where much time was given to music appreciation and the study of the shorter classical

forms, but where jazz was considered disreputable. Of course
this is part of the story of jazz even today. So much of the
modern experimentation in jazz springs—as far as Negro
jazz modernists are concerned—from a misplaced shame over
the so called lowclass origins of jazz. These are usually men
of Negro middle-class background who have some formal
training in music and who would like for jazz to be a "respectable" form of expression tied up with other forms of revolt. They'd like to dry up the deep, rowdy stream of jazz
until it becomes a very thin trickle of respectable sound indeed. Be that as it may, despite my teachers, the preachers
and other leaders of the community, I was with those who
found jazz attractive, an important part of life. I hung
around the old Blue Devils orchestra out of which the famous Basie band was formed. I knew these people and admired them. I knew Jimmy Rushing, the blues singer who
then was not quite the hero of the middleclass people whom I
knew that he is today after years of popular success. But for
us, even when he was a very young man, a singer who came
home to the city once in a while, Jimmy represented, gave
voice to, something which was very affirming of Negro life;
feelings which you couldn't really put into words. Of course,
beyond jazz there was all the boasting, the bragging, that
went on when no one but ourselves was supposed to be listening, when you weren't really being judged by the white world.
At least when you *thought* you weren't being judged and
didn't care if you were. For instance, there is no place like a
Negro barbershop for hearing what Negroes really think.
There is more unself-conscious affirmation to be found here
on a Saturday than you can find in a Negro college in a
month, or so it seems to me.

Getting back to your question, I suppose my attitude toward these elements of Negro life became a discipline toward
affirming that which felt desirable to me over and beyond
anything which we were taught in school. It was more a matter of the heart than of the mind.

STERN: You found something precious, special, and associated it with jazz. Now between finding that jazz was a vehicle for special qualities which you admired in Negroes and finding that literature was a vehicle, you yourself wanted to employ—

ELLISON: I wanted to be a composer but not a jazz composer, interestingly enough. I wanted to be a symphonist.

STERN: How about that then?

ELLISON: Well, I had always listened to music and as far
back as I can remember I had the desire to create. I can't

remember when I first wanted to play jazz or to create classical music. I can't remember a time when I didn't want to make something, whether it was a small one-tube radio or a crystal set, or my own toys. This was a part of the neighborhood where I spent most of my childhood. There were a number of us who were that way.

STERN: Did your desire to be a symphony composer rather than a jazz instrumentalist stand for a sort of denial of your own cultural situation as a Negro?

ELLISON: No, No. You see, what is often misunderstood nowadays is that there wasn't always this division between the ambitions of jazz musicians and the standards of classical music; the idea was to master both traditions. In school the classics were pushed at us on all sides and if you danced, if you shared any of the social life of the young people, jazz was inescapable; it was all around you. And if you were a *musician* you were challenged by its sounds and by the techniques required to produce them. In fact, we admired such jazz men as the late bassist Walter Page and the trumpeter Icky Lawrence over all other local musicians, because although they usually played in jazz bands, they could go into any theater pit and play the scores placed before them. They played the arrangements for the silent movies at sight and we found this very impressive. Such men as Lawrence and Page—and there were several others—had conservatory training as well as a rich jazz experience and thus felt no need to draw a line between the two traditions. Following them our ideal was to master both. It wasn't a matter of wanting to do the classics because they denied or were felt to deny jazz, and I suppose my own desire to write symphonies grew out of an attraction to the bigger forms and my awareness that they moved many people as they did me in a different way. The range of mood was much broader.

STERN: Can you describe the difference in your own feelings about the two forms?

ELLISON: I can try, but since I shall be trying to recall emotions having to do with the non-verbal medium of music, and at a time when I was a very young and inarticulate boy, I can only give you vague impressions. You see, jazz was so much a part of our total way of life that it got not only into our attempts at playing classical music but into forms of activities usually not associated with it: into marching and into football games, where it has since become a familiar fixture. A lot has been written about the role of jazz in a certain type of Negro funeral marching, but in Oklahoma City it got into military drill. There were many Negro veterans from the

Spanish-American War who delighted in teaching the younger boys complicated drill patterns, and on hot summer evenings we spent hours on the Bryant school grounds (now covered with oil wells) learning to execute the commands barked
at us by our enthusiastic drill masters. And as we mastered
the patterns, the jazz feeling would come into it and no one
was satisfied until we were swinging. These men who taught
us had raised a military discipline to the level of a low art
form, almost a dance, and its spirit was jazz.

On the other hand, I became a member of the school band
while in the eighth grade and we played military music, the
classical marches, arrangements of symphonic music, over-
tures, snatches of opera and so on, and we sang classical sacred music and the Negro spirituals. So all this was a part of
it, and not only did we have classes in music appreciation
right through school, on May Day we filled the Western
League Ball Park wrapping maypoles and dancing European
folk dances. You really should see a field of little Negro kids
dancing an Irish gig or a Scottish fling. There must have been
something incongruous about it for the few whites who came
to see us, but there we were and for us the dance was the
thing. Culturally everything was mixed, you see, and beyond
all question of conscious choices there was a level where you
were claimed by emotion and movement and moods which
you couldn't put into words. Often we wanted to share both:
the classics and jazz, the charleston and the Irish reel, spirituals and the blues, the sacred and the profane. I remember
the breakfast dances, the matinee dances along with the tent
meetings and the more formal Afro-Methodist Episcopal
Christmas services which took place in our church; they all
had their special quality. During adolescence I remember attending sunrise services, which took place before Christmas
morning. It was a very sacred service but I remember my
mother permitting me to leave after the services were over to
attend a breakfast dance. She didn't attend dances herself and
was quite pious by that time, but there was no necessary
clash between these quite different celebrations of Christmas,
and for me the two forms added quite a bit to my sense of
the unity of the life I lived. Just the same there were certain
yearnings which I felt, certain emotions, certain needs for
other forms of transcendence and identification which I could
only associate with classical music. I heard it in Beethoven, I
heard it in Schumann. I used to hear it in Wagner—he is
really a young man's composer; especially a young bandsman
with plenty of brass. I was always a trumpeter so I was always listening for those composers who made the most use,

the loudest use, of the brass choir. Seriously though, you got glimpses, very vague glimpses of a far different world than that assigned by segregation laws and I was taken very early with a passion to link together all I loved within the Negro community and all those things I felt in the world which lay beyond.

STERN: So pretty early you had a sense of being a part of a larger social or cultural complex?

ELLISON: Put it this way: I learned very early that in the realm of the imagination all people and their ambitions and interests could meet. This was inescapable, given my reading and my daydreaming. But this notion, this vague awareness, was helped along by the people I came to know. On the level of race relations, my father had many white friends who came to the house when I was quite small so that any feeling of distrust I was to develop toward whites later on were modified by those with whom I had warm relations. Oklahoma offered many opportunities for such friendships. I remember also an English actress named Emma Bunting—I wonder what happened to her? Anyway, when I was a child, Emma Bunting used to bring over a repertory company each summer and when she performed in Oklahoma City her maid, a very handsome Negro woman named Miss Clark, used to stay with us. There was no segregation in the downtown theatres during that period—although it came later—and my mother went frequently to plays and was very proud of a lace bag which Emma Bunting had given her. You see there is always some connection. Miss Clark brought not only the theatre into our house but England as well. I guess it's the breaks in the pattern of segregation which count, the accidents. When I reached high school I knew Dr. Ludwig Hebestreit, a conductor who formed the nucleus of what became the Oklahoma Symphony—a German for whom I used to cut the grass in exchange for trumpet lessons. But these lessons were about everything else. He'd talk to me about all that lay behind music and after I'd performed my trumpet lesson and been corrected he'd say, "You like such and such a composition, don't you?" And I'd say, "Yes," and he'd sit down at a piano with a piece of scoring paper and in a few minutes he would have written out passages of the orchestration and show me bar by bar how the sounds were blended.

"The strings are doing this," he'd say, "and the trumpets are playing this figure against the woodwinds," and so on.

Most of it was over my head but he made it all so logical and, better still, he taught me how to attack those things I desired so that I could pierce the mystery and possess them. I came to feel, yes, that, if you want these things and master the technique, you could get with it. You could make it yours. I came to understand, in other words, that all that stood between me and writing symphonies was not simply a matter of civil rights—even though the civil rights struggle was all too real. At that time my mother was being thrown into jail every other day for violating a zoning ordinance by moving into a building in a section where Gov. Alfapha Bill Murray had decided Negroes shouldn't live . . .

STERN: You went on then to Tuskegee, and you studied music seriously, and came up to New York more or less intending to . . .

ELLISON: To go back to Tuskegee. I came up during my Junior year hoping to work and learn a little bit about sculpture. And although I did study a bit, I didn't get the job through which I hoped to earn enough money for my school expenses, so I remained in New York where I soon realized that although I had a certain facility with three-dimensional form I wasn't really interested in sculpture. So after a while I blundered into writing.

STERN: The music you had given up by this time?

ELLISON: No, no I was still trying to be a musician. I was doing some exercises in composition under Wallingford Reigger and although I was much behind his advanced students I stayed there and studied with him until I had to have a tonsillectomy. It turned out to be a pretty chronic case and caused a lot of trouble, and by the time I tried to go back to my classes my mother died out in Ohio and I left New York for a good while. It was during the period in Dayton I started trying seriously to write and that was the breaking point.

STERN: Can you remember why you started to write or how?

ELLISON: I can remember very vividly. Richard Wright had just come to New York and was editing a little magazine. I had read a poem of his which I liked and when we were introduced by a mutual friend he suggested that I try to review a novel for his magazine. My review was accepted and published and so I was hooked.

STERN: You were launched. . . .

ELLISON: Oh no, not really launched.

STERN: You were conscious that such a thing was possible. Was Wright famous at that time?

ELLISON: No, Wright hadn't written *Native Son.* He had published *Uncle Tom's Children,* which was the real beginning of his fame, and he was already working on *Native Son.* I remember the first scene that he showed me, it was the poolroom scene, it isn't the first scene but it was one of the first written and I was to read the rest of the book as it came out of the typewriter.

STERN: At that time were you dissatisfied with the sort of work Wright was doing?

ELLISON: Dissatisfied? I was too amazed with watching the process of creation. I didn't understand quite what was going on, but by this time I had talked with Wright a lot and he was very conscious of technique. He talked about it not in terms of mystification but as writing know-how. "You must read so-and-so," he'd say. "You have to go about learning to write *consciously*. People have talked about such and such a problem and have written about it. You must learn how Conrad, Joyce, Dostoievsky get their effects. . . ." He guided me to Henry James and to Conrad's prefaces, that type of thing. Of course, I knew that my own feelings about the world, about life, were different, but this was not even a matter to question. Wright knew what he was about, what he wanted to do, while I hadn't even discovered myself. I knew only that what I would want to express would not be an imitation of his kind of thing.

STERN: So what sort of thing did you feel Wright was not doing that you wanted to do?

ELLISON: Well, I don't suppose I judged. I am certain I did not judge in quite so conscious a way, but I think I felt more complexity in life and my background made me aware of a larger area of possibility. Knowing Wright himself and something of what he was doing increased that sense of the possible. Also, I think I was less interested in an ideological interpretation of Negro experience. For all my interest in music, I had been in love with literature for years and years —if a writer may make such a confession. I read everything. I must have read fairy tales until I was 13, and I was always taken with the magical quality of writing, with the poetry of it. When I came to discover a little more about what I wanted to express I felt that Wright was overcommitted to ideology—even though I too wanted many of the same things for our people. You might say that I was much less a social determinist. But I suppose that basically it comes down to a difference in our concepts of the individual. I, for instance, found it disturbing that Bigger Thomas had none of the finer qualities of Richard Wright, none of the imagination, none of the sense of poetry, none of the gaiety. And I preferred Richard Wright to Bigger Thomas. Do you see. Which gets you in on the—directs you back to the difference between what

Wright was himself and how he conceived of the individual; back to his conception of the quality of Negro humanity.

STERN: Did you think you might write stories in which Negroes did not appear?

ELLISON: No, there was never a time when I thought of writing fiction in which only Negroes appeared, or in which only whites appeared. And yet, from the very beginning I wanted to write about American Negro experience and I suspected that what was important, what made the difference lay in the perspective from which it was viewed. When I learned more and started thinking about this consciously I realized that it was a source of creative strength as well as a source of wonder. It's also a relatively unexplored area of American experience simply because our knowledge of it has been distorted through the over-emphasis of the sociological approach. Unfortunately, many Negroes have been trying to define their own predicament in exclusively sociological terms, a situation I consider quite shortsighted. Too many of us have accepted a statistical interpretation of our lives and thus much of that which makes us a source of moral strength to America goes unappreciated and undefined. Now when you try to trace American values as they find expression in the Negro community, where do you begin? To what books do you go? How do you account for Little Rock and the Sit-Ins? How do you account for the strength of those kids? You can find sociological descriptions of the conditions under which they live but few indications of their morale.

STERN: You felt as you were starting to get serious about writing that you had a special subject to write about?

ELLISON: Yes, I think so. Well, let's put it this way: Sometimes you get a sense of mission even before you are aware of it. An act is demanded of you but you're like a sleep-walker searching for some important object, and when you find it you wake up to discover that it is the agency through which that mission, assigned you long ago, at a time you barely understood the command, could be accomplished. Thus while there appeared to be no connection between my wanting to write fiction and my mother's insistence, from the time I was a small boy, that the hope of our group depended *not* upon the older Negroes but upon the young, upon me, as it were, this sense of obligation got into my work immediately. Of course these are very complicated matters, because I have no desire to write propaganda. Instead I felt it important to explore the full range of American Negro humanity and to affirm those qualities which are of value beyond any question of segregation, economics or previous condition of servitude. The obligation was always there and there is much to affirm. In fact, all Negroes affirm certain feelings of identity, certain foods, certain types of dancing, music, religious experiences, certain tragic attitudes toward experience and toward our situation as Americans. You see, we do this all within the community, but when it is questioned from without—that's when things start going apart. Like most Americans we are not yet fully conscious of our identity either as Negroes or Americans. This affirmation, of which I speak, this insistence upon achieving our social goal has been our great strength and also our great weakness because the terms with which we have tried to define ourselves have been inadequate. We know we're not the creatures which our enemies in the white South would have us be and we know too that neither color nor our civil predicament explain us adequately. Our strength is that with the total society saying to us, "NO, NO, NO, NO," we continue to move toward our goal. So when I came to write I felt moved to affirm and to explore all this—not as a social mission, but as the stuff of literature and as an expressive of the better part of my own sense of life.

STERN: Somebody has described a literary situation as one which commemorates what a man feels is passing or threatened. Did you feel that your work might be a commemoration of values which were disappearing as you wrote about them?

ELLISON: How shall I say? Yes, I do feel this. Now just how consciously I was concerned with it at the time I wrote I don't know. When I started writing *Invisible Man* I was reading Lord Raglan's *The Hero*, in which he goes into figures of history and myth to account for the fact that when the chips were down, Negro leaders did not represent the Negro community.

Beyond their own special interests they represented white philanthropy, white politicians, business interests, and so on. This was an unfair way of looking at it, perhaps, but there was something missing, something which is only now being corrected. It seemed to me that they acknowledged no final responsibility to the Negro community for their acts and implicit in their roles were constant acts of betrayal. This made for a sad, chronic division between their values and the values of those they were supposed to represent. And the fairest thing to say about it is that the predicament of Negroes in the United States rendered these leaders automatically impotent—until they recognized their true source of power—which lies, as Martin Luther King perceived, in the Negro's ability to suffer even death for the attainment of our beliefs. Back in the 40's only preachers had real power through which to effect their wills but most of these operated strictly within the Negro community. Only Adam Powell was using the power of the Negro Church to assert the Negro's political will. So at that time a thick fog of unreality separated the Negro group from its leaders—But let me tell you a story: At Tuskegee, during graduation week countless high-powered word artists, black and white, descended upon us and gathered in the gym and the chapel to tell us in high-flown words what the Negro thought, what our lives were and what our goals should be. The buildings would be packed with visitors and relatives and many guardians of race relations—Northern and Southern. Well, the Negro farm people from the surrounding countryside would also come to the campus at the same time. Graduation week was a festival time for the surrounding Negro community, and very often these people would have children and relatives taking part in the ceremonies in progress in the chapel and the gym. But do you know that while the big-shot word artists were making their most impressive speeches, the farm people would be out on the old athletic field dancing square dances, having picnics, playing baseball, and visiting among themselves as though the ceremonies across the wide lawns did not exist; or at best had no connection with the lives they led. Well, I found their celebrations much more attractive than the official ceremonies and I would leave my seat in the orchestra and sneak out to watch them; and while my city background had cut me off from the lives they led and I had no desire to live the life of a sharecropper, I found their unrhetorical activities on the old football field the more meaningful.

STERN: The familiar liberal hope is that any specialized form of social life which makes for invidious distinctions should disappear. Your view seems to be that anything that counts is the results of such specialization.

ELLISON: Yes.

STERN: Now a good many people, millions, are damaged permanently, viciously, unfairly by such distinctions. At the same time, they contribute, as you more than perhaps any writer in the world have seen, to something marvelous. Some sort of decision probably has to be made by an individual who is sensitive to this paradox, I wonder what yours is. Do you want the preservation of that which results in both the marvelous and the terrible, or do you feel that the marvelous should not endure while the terrible endures along with it?

ELLISON: I am going to say something very odd. In the

first place, I think that the mixture of the marvelous and the terrible is a basic condition of human life and that the persistence of human ideals represents the marvelous pulling itself up out of the chaos of the universe. In the fairy tale, beauty must be awakened by the beast, the beastly man can only regain his humanity through love. There are other terms for this but they come to much the same thing. Here the terrible represents all that hinders, all that opposes human aspiration, and the marvelous represents the triumph of the human spirit over chaos. While the terms and the conditions are different and often change, our triumphs are few and thus must be recognized for what they are and preserved. Besides I would be hard put to say where the terrible could be localized in our national experience, for I see in so much of American life which lies beyond the Negro community the very essence of the terrible.

STERN: Yes, but the last few days we have been talking about some of the particular meannesses which are characteristic of the Negro situation . . . Just the fact that there are four Negro congressmen, when adequate representation would mean that there'd be twenty . . .

ELLISON: Yes.

STERN: And hundreds of things of this sort, many of which result in crippling injustices and meannesses. Now, can this go on? And if it doesn't go on, will this mean the elimination of that which you have commemorated in fiction?

ELLISON: Well, what I have tried to commemorate in fiction is that which I believe to be enduring and abiding in our situation, especially those human qualities which the American Negro has developed despite and in rejection of the obstacles and meannesses imposed upon us. If the writer exists for any social good, his role is that of preserving in art those human values which can endure by confronting change. Our Negro situation is changing rapidly but so much which we've gleaned through the harsh discipline of Negro American life is simply too precious to be lost. I speak of the faith, the patience, the humor, the sense of timing, rugged sense of life and the manner of expressing it which all go to define the American Negro. These are some of the things through which we've confronted the obstacles and meannesses of which you speak and which we dare not fail to adapt to changed conditions lest we destroy ourselves. Times change but these possessions must endure forever—not simply because they define us as a group, but because they represent a further instance of man's triumph over chaos. You know, the skins of those thin-legged little girls who faced the mob in Little Rock marked them as Negro but the spirit which directed their feet is the old universal urge towards freedom. For better or worse, whatever there is of value in Negro life is an American heritage and as such it must be preserved. Besides, I am unwilling to see those values which I would celebrate in fiction as existing sheerly through terror; they are a result of a tragic-comic confrontation of life.

I think that art is a celebration of life even when life extends into death and that the sociological conditions which have made for so much misery in Negro life are not necessarily the only factors which make for the values which I feel should endure and shall endure. I see a period when Negroes are going to be wandering around because, you see, we have had this thing thrown at us for so long that we haven't had a chance to discover what in our own background is really worth preserving. For the first time we are given a choice, we are making a choice. And this is where the real trouble is going to start. The South could help. If it had a sense of humor, you know, the South could say, "All right, we will set aside six months and there will be complete integration—all right, you don't have to integrate the women—but there will be complete integration as far as anything else is concerned. Negroes may go anywhere, they may see how we entertain, how we spend our leisure, how we worship, and so on," and that would be the end of the whole problem. Because most Negroes could not be nourished by the life white Southerners live. It is too hag-ridden, it is too obsessed, it is too concerned with attitudes which could change everything that Negroes have been conditioned to expect of life. No, I believe in diversity, and I think that the real death of the United States will come when everyone is just alike.

As for my writer's necessity of cashing in on the pain undergone by my people (and remember I write of the humor as well), writing is my way of confronting, often for the hundredth time, that same pain and that same pleasure. It is my way of seeing that it be not in vain.

DAN GEORGAKAS (1938–   )

Greek-American poet, editor, and anthologist Dan Georgakas gathered the following conversations of James Baldwin. This selection is reprinted from Arts in Society *(Summer, 1966), the publication of the University Extension of the University of Wisconsin.*

James Baldwin . . . in Conversation

(The following is a collage of statements made by James Baldwin during his two weeks in Italy in late 1965. Some of the remarks were made in lectures, some for the various media, some to interviewers, most in private conversation. I have not put them in an order which suits my peculiar caprices but one which I feel accurately represents the writer's present mood and direction.)

I remember those times, now so remote, when young and scuffling and afraid, I took the great long shot at being a writer to save my family. I couldn't do anything else. No one could tell me what a writer looked like. I made money and bought them a house. What's happened is fantastic. I'm probably the most photographed writer in the world. That's what happened to me. The trick is to survive it and I'm going to survive it. I'm here to stay.

If my witness is true, a lot of America is dead; that is the reality no one is willing to face.

I'm not a Negro leader. I have never thought of myself as a Negro leader. It is impossible to be a writer and a public spokesman. I am a writer.

Writers can die in many ways. Some perish in obscurity and others in the light. They die in the street and in the Waldorf Astoria sipping champagne.

My generation died. I mean that literally. Of the kids who grew up with me on my block, only a handful are still alive. My generation died.

America is the ultimate product of Western Civilization. How else could we have evolved given the Western World?

You don't know how ruthless one has to be to become a Willie Mays, a Harry Belafonte, a James Baldwin.

Regarding the classic decline of American writers after an early success, especially the decline of novelists, I would say there is a great deal of truth in it but I intend to break that law. We all feel it.

The Western World has created me, given me my name, has hidden my truth as a permanent and historical fact. I may recover from this and I may not. I'm a grim man, old and insane enough to tell you that not many survive being born black in America and that America is a creation and descendent of Europe.

I might be willing to settle for a non-segregated seat or join a Board. The kids are not. They are not that foolish. They are betrayed and they know it.

America has created a state of mood which is dangerous for the world. In order to buy and sell men like cattle, one had to pretend they were cattle. Being Christian, knowing it was wrong, they had to pretend it was not done to me but to animals. What has happened is that America which used to buy and sell black men still isn't sure if they are animals or not. America hasn't made up her mind. What I say doesn't apply to one tenth a nation but to two thirds the globe. We treat the world like we do our Negroes.

The new novel, *Tell Me How Long the Train's Been Gone*, is almost finished. I thought it was going to be a short story when it broke off from a longer work. It starts in the first person with the decay of a Negro actor. His white mistress and a ruined older brother are important. In the third part a young Negro terrorist more or less takes over the book.

I miss New York but I can't work there. I can't write. I must have isolation in order to start again. Pressures are too much in New York. You spend all your time resisting. You don't find out what you are thinking or dreaming. It isn't personal. It's the city.

We have marines and money and diplomats to crush Cuba but not for South Africa.

I'd be interested in American theatre if we had one. I started writing plays to find out what can be learned from the human voice. I found out.

Johnson's war on poverty is a bullshit tip and everyone knows it, a bullshit tip that means nothing.

I'm popular now and I drink too much.
I know it.

The success of the Freedom Theatre in bringing Moliere and Brecht to the Mississippi Delta is not surprising. You get a direct and spontaneous response and creation. That's what makes theatre.

They've said I'm mad, bitter, possessed, but never that I was wrong.

What the Western World has done is believe that the people it has conquered are inferior to it and different from it. This is a deceit no one could have held for long without great effect on their reason.

I'm a good little soldier.

What deserts might be reborn, what cities built, what children saved with one third wasted to build bombs we can't afford to use.

I don't want to emphasize this but the State Department tried to stop *Blues for Mr. Charlie* from going to Europe. I almost had to cause a scandal to get my company over to England.

People keep saying I'm bitter and hate whites. I know that isn't true. I wonder why people need to think that?

It wasn't Floyd's fault. It wasn't Cassius' fault. It was our fault. We have done it to the two of them. It is possible to have a city without a ghetto. The reason for a ghetto is it is profitable to some. The reason Wallace is not in jail for insurrection is because he represented some interests at the price of not representing the people of Alabama. This is not mysterious.

I can't go out in New York. I can't go where I like to drink, to see people I like, to hang out. I'm a celebrity in New York.

"Blues" was a great success in Sweden at Bergman's theatre. They played it straight with all Swedes. No black face. They understood the play is about tribes, not races, about how we treat one another.

I had a terrible time to accept the fact that most people wanted to treat me as a dancing doll. Wow, he's black and he can write. Once I was bitter about this.

What one person has to go through is inhuman. Consider how many perish in the attempt. It's criminal. The bomb shelters ended at Central Park. People are playing with other people's lives. It's criminal.

Sometimes I feel like telling a method actor to just go on, walk across the damn stage without bumping into anything, talk loud enough to be heard in the cheap seats, remember your lines.

Sometimes I feel like telling one of them what Miles Davis advises me to say: Just what makes you think I think you can read?

A man is a man, a woman is a woman, a child is a child, no matter where and these are the fundamental things, the inalienable things.

My short story collection has gotten interesting reactions. Different critics like different stories. The ones some called the best the others thought were the worst. The general opinion seems to be I was a nice sweet cat with talent when I was twenty but now I'm bitter and it's had a terrible effect on my work.

My mail got so horrible I turned it over to the FBI. Maybe they were writing some of it. I went around a week with a bodyguard. I got mobbed in Foley Square. I was cut off from friends by about 10,000 people. Everyone was friendly but there were so many people I was afraid. Some big black cats jumped on stage and carried me away.

I want to get strength within traditional forms, to make elegant sentences do dirty work.

The day is coming when the tide will turn in Johannesburg and one fine day we will hear about it on the radio and on television. We will hear about stealing and massacres. The Western World will be shocked.

When I speak of seeing a development, people think I want it to happen or that I approve of it. Some officials in Washington actually believe *The Fire Next Time* caused Watts.

They hit the streets in Watts not because Negroes like to drink or to steal, but because they've been in jail too long. Because a new law had been passed making fair housing illegal. Looting went on all right. What was not said was who stole from whom first. It's a great thing to be in Sacramento devising laws locking people into a ghetto. It's another thing to be locked in that ghetto.

To get an apartment on the West Side I had to threaten headlines. If this is true for me and Lena Horne and Harry Belafonte, what about the local cat on the corner?

I'm not reading many contemporary novels. If they're any good you wish you had done it and try to keep from letting it interfere with your own work. If it is inferior to what you are doing, why bother?

Sexless people are trying to get together and they can't. As long as you don't treat me as a man, what can I do? The kids are reacting against it.

What is true for Washington is true for Paris, Rome, and London. The Western World must give up the idea it has anything to give me. A short time ago, we were concerned with landing marines in Santo Domingo to defend the people but the people being saved know better. We may believe the Congo was caused by savage cannibals but some must understand the Katanga mines were owned by Europeans. People want to take back their land.

I prefer to say little about other writers but I respect William Styron.

I'm terribly aware that whatever I do has public repercussions. The State Department thinks I'm unpatriotic, that I besmirch my government abroad.

What am I supposed to say when a church is burned down in Georgia and no one is punished?

William Burroughs is a very brave man.

I check in USIS libraries to see if they have my books and books by Wright, Ellison, Hughes, and Du Bois.

America had to invent Negro and White to hide the way we treat each other. I can't achieve belief in American democracy by watching American democracy or believe in the ideals of the Western World by watching what the Western World does. This is absolutely true.

Then Truman said to Jack in that sugary Southern drawl he has, "but Jack that ain't writin', that's typin'."

I'm reading lots of African and European history. A lot of Du Bois. I want to get into the past.

Ralph Ellison: I'm praying for him and I hope he prays for me.

To be born in a free society and not be born free is to be born into a lie. To be told by co-citizens and co-Christians that you have no value, no history, have never done anything that is worthy of human respect destroys you because in the beginning you believe it. Many Negroes die because they believe it.

Real writers question their age. They demand Yes and No answers. Typers collaborate. You collaborate or you question.

How hard it is to talk to young people. They don't believe what the White World says. They don't believe me either. Why should they believe me? They only have one life and their situation is indefensible. Don't take anybody's word. Check it out yourself. You'll find out. Then you may be able to change it.

I reread *Bleak House* a few years ago. It was preposterous but marvelous. I don't know how Dickens did it.

The trick is to accept what makes you good.

We have no right to be in Vietnam. They do not want to be "liberated."

"Everyone's Protest Novel" came out of two years of reviewing and writing for various magazines. I can see why Wright thought it was an attack. I was only trying to get at something. The essay destroyed our friendship. It did something for me too. I reread his *Native Son* and wrote another essay.

You must avoid believing that things *are* black and white—do you know what I mean?

The American white man has trapped himself into a weird kind of adolescent competition: I bet mine's bigger than yours. The Negro pays for this fantasy. There has got to be something weird going on in the mind of anybody who has to castrate another man.

One great difference between Wright and me is what I would call my eroticism. *Giovanni's Room* is not about homosexuality. *Another Country* is about the price you pay to make a human relationship.

I'm coming to the end of the tunnel.
I will get out of it.

I don't want Negro faces put in history books. I want American history taught. Unless I'm in that book, you're not in it either. History is not a procession of illustrious people. It's about what happens to a people. Millions of anonymous people is what history is about.

In the end Wright's heart was broken.

You face reality, not the lights. The lights go off as quickly as they go on.

Remember what they told Martin Luther King in Watts: We don't want no prayers. We don't want no dreams. We want jobs. And the economy cannot produce those jobs, not even for whites.

I'm also doing a play with music called *Our Fathers* which is set in Greece and deals with two Negro soldiers and a Greek girl.

I make a lot of money for other people. I'm what they call a property, a million dollar property.

In one of those Southern towns, the confederate flag flew over the federal courthouse. That's insurrection. We're told they lost the Civil War but the National Guardsmen had confederate flags sewn on their shoulders. By what right does Wallace sit in the state house? He doesn't represent the state at all because I can't vote in that state and a lot of whites are scared. How did we get today's South? The Northern industrialists needed a cheap labor pool. The segregation laws were written at the turn of the century. There's nothing irrational about it. If we meant what we said, we would not allow a Wallace. As long as Wallaces are tolerated neither King nor God Almighty will be able to convince any black cat anywhere that America is anything but a total fraud.

Great art can only be created out of love. To write in this age is a positive act.

One of the last times I saw him we had been talking about the children, not his in particular, but of all the children growing up, and Malcolm said, "I'm the warrior of this revolution and you're the poet." It's about the only compliment he ever gave me.

The duty of a writer in the United States is to write: that's all.

We will undo the South or it will undo America.

I can barely represent myself. I'm not a spokesman. No one is. I know something about whence I came. If you forget that then forget about everything, the party is over. I'm a black funky raggedyass shoeshine boy. If I forget that, it's the end of me.

When Malcolm returned from Mecca, he was a different man, a far greater man.

I want people to treat me as a writer, not a Negro writer. They'd like to label me red. My problem is to look at that paper and look at my life. That has no label.

Like all of us I've had difficulties and disappointments. I've got a long way to go. I seem to be marking time sometimes, but I'm crouching, in order to leap.

When you look at the jigsaw puzzle all the pieces fit: Congo, Watts, Cuba.

Sometimes writing is like giving birth. You need someone to give a name, to say, push, baby, push.

If we—and I mean the relatively conscious whites and the relatively conscious blacks, who must, like lovers, insist on, or create the consciousness of others—do not falter in our duty now, we may be able, handful that we are, to end the racial nightmare of our country and change the history of the world.

We are responsible for the people we call our leaders. We are responsible for their charters and treaties which support governments like South Africa, such that in fact subjugate man all the way from Los Angeles to the edge of China.

I feel terribly menaced by this present notoriety because it is antithetical to the kind of an endeavor which has to occur in silence and over a great period of time and which by definition is extremely dangerous precisely because one has to smash at all the existing definitions.

In any case, society will change. In any case one day, banks will fail again. In any case, the Western World that now owns the banks will either share with all or lose all. We will change society or it will be changed for us.

I would like to write very different things than the things I have written and go much further than I have so far gone. And I am sure that if I live, I will.

I believe in everybody. I think we're going to make it. But I know the price.

STERLING STUCKEY (1932–   )

A critic and educator of the younger generation, Sterling Stuckey was born in Memphis, Tennessee, and has lived in Chicago since 1945. He is currently a candidate for the Ph.D. degree at Northwestern University and is a Hearst Fellow in American history. He has taught in the Chicago public schools, at the University of Illinois—Chicago Circle and the Center for Inner City Studies in Chicago. Stuckey has published articles in Freedomways, Negro Digest, *and other publications and is a consultant in American history to Encyclopaedia Britannica Films, Inc. He is chairman of the Amistad Society, a committee on the history and culture of Americans of African descent, and has long been active in the civil rights movements and the freedom schools in Mississippi, Louisiana, Alabama, and Chicago. The following critical article was originally published in* New University Thought.

Frank London Brown

"The profoundest commitment possible to a black creator in this country today—beyond all creeds, crafts, classes and ideologies whatsoever—is to bring before his people the scent of freedom . . . (Ossie Davis in Purlie told me!)

Now and then artist and man of action merge, as with Malraux in *Man's Fate*, Silone in *Bread and Wine*. With the publication of Frank Brown's *Trumbull Park*, the reader was once more privileged to examine the work of such a man, for Brown lived in the racial battleground of Trumbull Park, suffered there, fought there; and though he did not write with the grace and authority of Silone or Malraux, he presented a first novel of extraordinary quality.

It has been almost four years since the publication of *Trumbull Park*. In these years Brown, although poised be-

tween life and death, continued to work as a university professor, write a novel, read his short stories before many
groups and, above all else, to defend the underdog. Seven
months ago, Frank Brown died of an incurable disease which
had drained away the strength of his body but which had
been absolutely defied by his spirit.

In his youth, Brown lived in the slums of Chicago's South
Side and attended Du Sable High School. Later he sang jazz,
worked as a machinist, organized textile workers, and in an
atmosphere charged with tension helped a Negro escape from
Mississippi shortly after Emmett Till was lynched. He was
filled with the joy of life and was conscious of its perils and
subterranean snares—of the deadly jolts that morphine and
heroin shot through the tired black bodies of many of his
contemporaries, of the cruel and perverse tangle of black and
white souls America had willed, of the style of life fashioned
by blacks to survive the fury of being a Negro in America.

Brown's experience was as varied as that of any novelist of
our time, though much of his life was confined to the bleak
and deadly jungle of the South Side, of which, for him, 58th
Street was the radiating center, receiving all and wasting all
but a few in its grinding, dehumanizing mills. It was here, in
this dark nether-world of crime, tenements, jacklegged preachers, shattered idealism, dogged hope, molasses and clothes
lines that Brown battered his way into manhood. It was here
that he dug Bird, the young Miles, the timeless Muddy Waters. It was here at the center of Negro life that he caught the
vision of life universal while feeling the sometimes throbbing,
sometimes faint, pulse of the human spirit under the eroding
forces of ghetto life. The apprenticeship on the 58th Street
"Stroll" prepared him for *Trumbull Park*, "McDougall," *The
Mythmakers*, and all that was to follow. Had Brown's life not
been stopped so cruelly short, he would surely have continued his explorations into the dark and somber Stroll, where
hip begins with the age of reason for so many and never ends
for those to whom it is the only defense against an oppres-
sive, painfully closed universe.

The fact that death came to Brown the man so early was
tragic in itself, for he was an unaffected, engaging, and self-
less person; that death would cut short the life of Brown the
artist was still more cruel. His major published work, *Trumbull Park*, and his superb short stories had marked him as a
writer of major talent. And *The Mythmakers*, a bleak novel
in which all the violence and fury of a cruelly lacerated soul
come screaming to the fore in a nightmare of murder in the
shadow of the "el" tracks that wind their way through The

Stroll, was hailed by John U. Nef as a novel "touched with genius."

One of my most vivid memories of Frank carries me back to the late summer of 1961, a time of racial strife at one of Chicago's public beaches. I was sitting in his office discussing the crisis and casually mentioned that I was going to wade-in with a group of friends, that we did not want police protection and therefore would not notify them of our plans. Frank said he would join us and indicated that he wanted to "pay his dues." Frank, on that sunny day at Rainbow Beach, gave not a hint of despair, showed no trace of tenseness or fear. He had faced angry mobs before, he had been stoned, had even come close to walking the last mile but he refused to give in. We did not realize then that he was living in the shadow of death. His affirmation of life, his strength in dealing with problems that would unnerve the average man, would not let him display weakness or behave ignobly even in the face of the grimmest of all antagonists.

A few months later Brown participated in a sit-in demonstration protesting discrimination in apartment buildings owned by the University of Chicago, the school where he taught. The demonstrations, which took place at the University's administration building, represented his last direct action effort.

The certain knowledge of imminent death must have been hard for Frank to bear, but he must have readied himself to meet death with the same courage that sustained him as he daily walked through screaming mobs of racists to his wife and three daughters at his besieged Trumbull Park apartment. Frank's life, like the lives of all Negroes, was destined to have a last mile or death-row quality about it. But for Frank the mile was shorter than usual and the approximate date was known. Every minute became more compelling in urgency as Frank demanded more of himself than ever: the speaking engagements scarcely abated up to the final minute; his teaching and studies went on with characteristic brilliance; the short stories and reviews continued to pour from his pen, the stride remained as steady as ever.

Creative Social Struggle

The key to understanding Frank Brown as man and writer lay in his commitment to creative social struggle and to the illumination of that world that is taken for granted or more often ignored by the white man. A product of that world, a native son, he loved much that is woven into its fabric. Frank

Brown realized instinctively what Eugene O'Neill was driven to by reason forty years ago:

> *"It seems to me that to be a Negro writer today must be a tremendously stimulating thing. They have within them an untouched world of deep reality. What greater boon can a true artist ask of fate?"*

For Brown it was a conscious boon and he gladly accepted it as *his* fate. He considered the folk experience of the Negro rich in revolutionary as well as aesthetic content. For Brown, the Negro artist and intellectual were to use it to provide for the masses of Negroes the basis for what Matthew Arnold called the instinct for human expansion. Brown saw no fundamental conflict in being both a Negro and an American, a situation that has caused great alarm among Negro intellectuals who have tried so desperately to escape their origins. And so when African intellectuals and artists Senghor, Diop, and Césaire began to write of *negritude* Brown did not fall back and exclaim in horror: "This is a species of fascism!" He considered the attempt on the part of black men to rediscover their roots natural and essential and, as does Sartre in his essay on *Black Orpheus,* a form of *anti-racist* racism. He never had the problem which has tortured so many Negro artists, causing them, out of an obsession with and shame of their very blackness, to write and paint white. His "reconciliation to being a nigger," to borrow a phrase from Baldwin, came not three thousand miles away on foreign soil, but on 43rd Street as a very young man while listening to Muddy Waters, a blues singer who eclipses Ray Charles in evocative, gut-bucket power. More precisely, it was never a reconciliation for Brown but a natural, happy realization. An awareness of this aspect of Brown's outlook is absolutely essential, for it explains the direction his writing took and reveals the vast gulf that separated him from James Baldwin.

There seems to be in Baldwin's fiction scarcely a trace of the social concern that engaged Brown. Baldwin's characters seldom, if ever, believe in the world around them. More interesting, his Negro characters not only do not believe in the white man's world (save for the protagonist in *Go Tell It on the Mountain*), they do not believe in themselves. They suffer from utter despair and futility and reflect none of the hope and militancy that inspires a generation of young Negroes to rebel against oppression. Baldwin, for all the strains of Billie Holiday, Handy, and Bessie Smith in *Another Country,* for all the scathing attacks against injustice in his essays, has yet to explore the new spirit to which *Trumbull Park* is a monument.

Brown's short stories reveal a writer of power and sensitivity. These stories are coherent, and careful planning brings off suprises when the reader least expects them. In "McDougal" he creates almost by implication a mood, tone, atmosphere, and set of relations upon which most short story writers would spend page after page of description and analysis. McDougal, a young and suffering white trumpet player, married to a black woman who has borne him four children, living on 47th Street and battling to prevent the landlords from bleeding the life out of his family, distils the essence of his experience in a trumpet solo that matches in intensity, intuitive perception, and execution the towering standards of Percy R. Brookins, Jake, Pro, and Little Jug, Negro jazzmen who "gig" with him.

The world of jazz and the Negroes who inhabit it has never been examined with greater perception and understanding. The diolgoue speaks for itself:

> Brookins: *"You know that cat's after us? I mean he's out to blow the real thing. You know what I mean? Like he's no Harry James? Do you know that?"*

> Little Jug: *"I been knowing that . . . he knows what's happening . . . I mean about where we get it, you dig? I mean with Leola and those kids and Forty Seventh Street and those jive landlords, you dig? The man's been burnt, Percy. Listen to that somitch listen to him!"*

Brown's description of Leola, McDougal's pregnant wife, is on any showing, superb:

> *"McDougall's eyes were closed and he did not see the dark woman with the dark cotton suit that ballooned away from the great bulge of her stomach. He didn't see her ease into a chair at the back of the dark smoky room. He did not see the smile on her face or the sweat upon her flat nose."*

A few months before his death Brown prefigured his own fate in "A Matter of Time," a short story in which the protagonist, a black mill hand, knows he is dying and that in spite of his death, life will continue as usual. There is little doubt that Brown was writing of himself. And so in the end, in "A Matter of Time," as in the beginning with *Trumbull Park*, Brown identified with the dispossessed.

But it was not enough for him to write of the struggles of

the dispossessed. It was natural, therefore, for Frank Brown to move from the slums of the South Side to Trumbull Park, a public housing project on the perimeter of Chicago near the Gary steel mills. Frank and his family moved into Trumbull Park after housing authorities had already allowed Arthur Davis, a light-skinned Negro, and his family to move in, thinking they were white. Before Davis and his wife came to know the feel of their new apartment, the mob began the frenzied chant: "Get out, nigger! Get out, nigger! We want the nigger!" They stoned the apartment and set off bomb after bomb. Davis prepared himself for the long fight ahead, and for a long time he fought alone—that is, until the Frank Browns and others moved into the project. The venom of the mob increased as it continued to jeer, bomb, and stone. The Negro tenants watched, planned, suffered, and even had a party or two while caught in the vortex of a special living hell.

Eventually millions of people knew about Trumbull Park. The Negro tenants in Trumbull Park knew they knew, and knew no one else would do anything about it. They knew that finally they would have to fall back upon themselves and war as best they could against those who would deny them the right to live as human beings, which was their only reason for taking flight from the tenements which stretch like an incubus across Chicago's South Side.

After the first fifty pages or so of *Trumbull Park*, it becomes clear to the reader that there is a certain directness of approach that calls forth characters who, though vibrant in their immediacy, are not quite like those we encounter daily. Somehow Brown has gotten inside these instruments of dialogue and action, explaining or making explicable, and ordering. He does not let his characters rock the boat; nor does he permit the plot to sap them of vitality. Buggie Martin, the martyr-hero of *Trumbull Park*, remains just shadowy enough to rise above and sometimes dominate the plot, just elusive enough to excite interest and yet remain credible. *Trumbull Park* begins in high gear when Brown describes the terrible living conditions in a slum building, the attacks of marauding rats, the rotting bannisters and congested living. With deft and powerful language, he evokes the pathetic image of Baby-doll, the little girl who topples to her death over a rotten bannister. One cannot forget the moving picture of Bertha, the little girl's mother, as she rushes down six flights of stairs and exclaims over the broken body of her child, "Oh Lordy, no! Oh Lordy, have mercy! Kind Jesus, have mercy! O Lordy, no! . . . My baby's gone!"

At another point, drawing upon the folk tradition of the Negro people—this time as expressed through the blues of Joe Williams—Brown presents the following exchange between the protagonist and his wife on the morning when Buggie, who had been receiving police protection, decides to walk to work like a man, facing the mob and possibly death rather than submit to the ignominy of riding in a squad car:

"It may take a little longer getting home today, so don't get worried if I'm not home at exactly five."

"Ain't nobody worried!"

"And it ain't nobody cryin!"

Buggie leaves singing under his breath:

"Every day . . . Every day I have the blues . . . Ev-ev'ry daaaaa-ay . . . Ev'ry day I have the bluuuu-es . . ."

Though Buggie encounters no difficulty on the way to work, he meets the mob face to face as he leaves the bus and begins the walk to his apartment after getting off work. Harry Harvey, a young but courageous Negro who had only recently moved into Trumbull Park, joined him and heard the two white women who had been riding the bus with them scream: "Niggers, niggers, niggers! Here come the niggers."

Buggie and Harry walked, with the police walking alongside imploring them to ride in the squad car. They refused and walked on in the face of the jeering, threatening mob which hurled bricks as well as curses. They walked all the way home, Buggie and Harry, singing with still greater vigor and clarity:

"Every day, every day . . . Well, it ain't nobody worried, and it ain't nobody cryin."

The most striking quality about the style of writing in *Trumbull Park* is its great simplicity, leanness and utter lack of affectation and phoniness. The philosophy of life that emerges and the dramatic tension that holds the novel together stem from the action of the characters and the deft juxtaposition of events.

The technique, so often used in Beat literature, of presenting a character who repeatedly bombards his audience with hipster talk, looks rather frail alongside the finished product of one who was a master of hip jargon. Brown presents not only the dialogue but also much of the description in his story in the vernacular of the characters who move in the novel. He realized that the language of The Stroll is rooted in the subsoil of life and cannot be abstracted from the tragic intensity of experience and paraded before the reader, in typical Beat fashion, as the occult and monotonous word-opiate of an enlightened elite. Brown has written an entire novel in which the language of the hipster is indigenous to the circumstances of the story. Therefore, the dialogue never seems false or forced but flows naturally, propelled by the demands of the story.

Trumbull Park met with a very warm reception, especially from many Negro writers and artists. They felt that it, along with Lorraine Hansberry's *Raisin in the Sun* and Ossie Davis' *Purlie Victorious*, signalled the advent of a new and brilliant flowering of creative effort on the part of Negro writers.

The appearance of Brown, Davis and Hansberry calls to mind the effort of Langston Hughes, Claude McKay and Sterling Brown during the Negro Renaissance of the 1920's to present unashamedly life among Negro common people while relying heavily, and with pride, upon their cultural heritage. The movement of the twenties, though of impressive proportions, was not viable, partly because many of the younger writers became interested in other themes and partly because many of them mistakenly felt they could not be writers as long as they wrote about Negroes.

There are those who will say that Frank Brown—because he wrote of Negro experience—was limited. But the courage, suffering, joy and violence of which he wrote are all part of the human landscape, and Brown, by giving vigorous expression to them, enables his reader, whatever his race, to identify.

It was precisely the ability of Brown to say "yes" through Buggie Martin which sets him apart from and against those writers who seem more enchanted by the sound of their voices than by the content of their words. He says "yes" to life in spite of its cruelty. He affirms and passionately voices the folk experiences, the blues, jazz, spirituals, and even a dash of Sunday afternoon Holy Roller rhythm. In a word, he embraces the mood and texture of life in The Stroll. Brown did this better than any other writer of his time. His bittersweet song, Brown's blues, expressed the will to victory over the agony in life and filled the air with the survival spirit of a people who, though schooled long and well in oppression, are determined to close the gap between promise and fulfillment.

DARWIN T. TURNER (1931–   )

Born and educated in Cincinnati, Ohio, Darwin Turner en-
tered the University of Cincinnati at the age of thirteen, was
elected to Phi Beta Kappa at fifteen, and received his B.A. at
sixteen and his M.A. in English at eighteen. He earned his
Ph.D. in English at the University of Chicago. Versatile, and
interested in a very wide range of literature, he has published
fiction and a volume of poetry, in addition to a long bibliog-
raphy of critical and scholarly articles. He has taught and
served as chairman of the English departments in predomi-
nantly Negro colleges in Georgia, Maryland, Florida, and
North Carolina, and is now Dean of the Graduate School at
North Carolina A. & T. State University in Greensboro. Pro-
fessor Turner is a past president of the College Language As-
sociation. He was awarded a study grant from the American
Council of Learned Societies (1965) and a Fellowship in the
North Carolina-Duke Universities Co-operative Program in
the Humanities. He is a member of the Board of Directors of
the National Council of Teachers of English, of the Execu-
tive Committee of the Conference on College Composition
and Communication, and of the Program Committee of the
Modern Language Association. The following article is re-
printed from CLA Journal, *December, 1961.*

The Negro Dramatist's Image of the Universe, 1920–1960

In drama, as in his other media of self-expression, the Negro
artist has retouched his image of the universe as the Negro's
shifting position in American society has afforded new per-
spectives. For the Negro, the stage represented, first, a pulpit
from which to denounce the injustices meted out to him in
America or a platform on which to parade idealized heroes

to supplant the grinning, dancing Jim Crows of the white playwrights. His universe was a checkerboard of black and white: the white purity lauding both the Negro and the benevolent people who struggled to elevate the Negro; the black of corruption castigating both the treacherous Uncle Toms and the people who chained the race in ignorance and deprivation. As the Negro has been guaranteed additional rights, however, the playwrights have perceived a universe of shades of grey, a universe of non-noble, non-villainous human beings who wrestle with life.

Beginning as a crusader, a preacher, an instructor, the Negro dramatist has become a delineator, a psychologist cognizant of his artistic responsibility to represent life faithfully. The maturing of the Negro dramatist to a standard-conscious, accurate painter of his universe can be observed by comparing characteristic images in Negro dramas of the Twenties and Thirties with similar images in dramas of the Fifties. In order to restrict the topic, the examination will be limited to the dramatist's delineating of the hero; his treatment of education, religion, and superstition; his attitude towards life in the North, and his discernment of the relationship between Negroes and the larger American society.

The Image of the Hero

Since most individuals view the universe as a macrocosm and themselves as the microcosm, the first aspect of the Negro's image of the universe which warrants study is his image of himself. To efface the Negro stereotype paraded in plantation novels of the "Old South" tradition and exhibited in minstrel shows, the Negro protest dramatists of the Twenties and Thirties created a counter stereotype: a dark-skinned, physically impressive adult—noble, courageous, rebellious, and proud.

Carving his characters to the "noble savage" Indian prototype of Aphra Behn and James Fenimore Cooper, Willis Richardson emphasized the physical strength, the nobility, and the courage of his heroes. In *The Flight of the Natives* (1927), Mose refuses to permit any man to flog him. When his master, cowed from the attempt, threatens to sell him "down the river," Mose reluctantly decides to escape without his wife, who is physically incapable of withstanding the rigors of flight. As he leaves, however, he swears to rescue her eventually. The heroes of *The Black Horseman* (1929) are tall, athletic Africans eulogized for their bravery. Massinissa, a tall, dark-skinned hero, contrasts with Syphax, his smaller, fairer antagonist. Massinissa unmasks a Roman spy by torturing him. An African, he argues, would never reveal secrets, no matter how severely he might be tortured. In both works, Richardson glorified qualities which he considered intrinsic virtues of the Negro: dignity, nobility, and courage.

Although John Matheus, in *Ti Yette* (1929), centered his story about a Creole quadroon, Matheus invested him with qualities typical of Richardson's heroes. Racine, the quadroon, idolizes Negroes who have died rather than submit to indignity. Determined to marry his sister to an African prince, Racine kills her when he learns that she plans to reject her African ancestor in order to marry a white man.

One of the most productive Negro dramatists of the Thirties, S. Randolph Edmonds, continued the pattern in such dramas as *Bad Man* and *Nat Turner*, both published in 1934. Thea Dugger, the Bad Man, leaps from the mold of Bret Harte's heroes. Although his animal savagery has wrenched fearful respect from Negro workers in a saw-mill camp, a girl's faith ennobles him. When the sister of one of the workers visits her lover in the camp, Thea, flattered by her admiration, protects her from the other workers. When a lynch mob attacks the camp to capture the murderer of a white man, Thea prefers to sacrifice himself rather than to risk endangering the girl's life in a fight.

Proud and courageous, he detests cowards. When the lynchers approach, he refuses to join the Negroes who seek escape. He will fight, or he will die; he will not run.

Edmonds' Nat Turner possesses Thea's courage although he lacks Thea's physical strength. Respected by some of his enslaved followers, feared as a witch-doctor by others, judged untrustworthy or even insane by still others, Nat desires to inspire the Virginia slaves with his pride and his fearlessness. "No real man," he tells them, "ain' willing tuh be wurked lak a mule in de field, whupped lak a dog, and tied tuh one farm and one master. . . . We mus' let dem know dat jes' because our skins is black we is not afraid tuh die."

Thea and Nat project a twin image dominant in the protest dramas of the Twenties and the Thirties. Thea typifies the hero whose pride and physical strength provoke his defying tyranny. He sometimes wins followers when others seek the protection of his strength; he sometimes becomes a martyr when he refuses to bend even though he stands alone. In contrast, Nat Turner typifies the leader who, less strong physically, uses religion and inspiration to teach other Negroes the necessity of rebelling.

The submissive Negro, trusting God and the white man to

resolve his problems, rarely is the protagonist of the protest dramas. Such a character can be observed in Frank Wilson's *Meek Mose* (1928). Scorned by his neighbors, who call him a white man's tool, Mose suffers eviction and an attempt upon his life. Continuing to advise faith in God, he triumphs when oil is discovered.

More often, however, the submissive Negro is the villain. In both *Nat Turner* and *Bad Man*, the despicable characters are the cowards who advise surrender.

Significantly, although they drew stereotypes, Negro dramatists revealed weaknesses in their heroes by the mid-thirties. Thea bullies weaker Negroes. Nat is fanatic. Their virtues are magnified, but their vices distinguish them from the noble savages of Richardson's dramas.

The hero image in the more recent dramas has been that of an ordinary human being rather than an idealized stereotype. Three significant developments merit attention.

First, although the hero or protagonist elicits sympathy, he does not necessarily arouse admiration. Richard Wright's Bigger Thomas, in *Native Son* (1941), embodies Thea Dugger's weaknesses with none of Thea's redeeming qualities. Uncouth and cowardly, he lies, rapes, and murders; yet he is the sympathetic protagonist of a protest drama.

Recognizing the unreality of both the "noble-savage" drawn by Negro polemicists and the "savage-beast" drawn by Dixon and other Negrophobes, Wright blended in Bigger the weaknesses for which the race has been criticized. Then he charged non-Negro America with the responsibility of breeding such individuals. Although he offered a stereotype as obvious as Massinissa had been, Wright evidenced the new confidence of the Negro writer in revealing the vices of the race, not in comedy, but in work intended to evoke sympathy.

In the Forties and the Fifties, Negro dramatists have delineated credible protagonists both in dramas intended to be produced before Negroes and in those intended to be produced before predominately non-Negro audiences. In A. Clifton Lamb's *Roughshod up the Mountain* (1956), the central figure, an uneducated minister desiring to retain his post, ignores his inability to guide his sophisticated, educated congregation.

The hero of Langston Hughes' *Simply Heavenly* (1957) is Jesse B. Semple. Ordinary—even weak in character, Semple carouses, squanders his money, and philanders. A comic and a pathetic figure, he typifies the dramatist's realistic appraisal of some Negroes who comprise the group which Hughes has described as the lower class of Negro society. But *Simply*

Heavenly does not dramatize the problems of all Negroes of that group: it tells the story of Jesse B. Semple. Hughes displayed Semple before the Broadway audience confident that the Negro had attained sufficient dignity in American life that the audience would not confuse Semple with all Negroes.

To point to Biggers and Semples is not to imply that the stereotyped noble Negro has disappeared from the stage. He lives in idealizations of school teachers who sacrifice life and love for their children and in idealizations of such leaders as Frederick Douglass. Nevertheless, the contemporary Negro dramatist exercises greater freedom in delineating the weaknesses of a character whom he wishes to have accepted as an individual rather than as a representative of a race.

A second development in the characterization of Negro protagonists has been that the educated Negro is no longer regarded as an individual significantly different from other Negroes. The development undoubtedly reflects the change in the Negro's position. Whereas in the Twenties and the Thirties, a college education was still considered an opportunity for only the "Talented Tenth" or those whose families possessed wealth, today a college education lies within the reach of many Negroes in urban communities.

Evidence of the earlier attitude toward the educated Negro appears in May Miller's *Riding the Goat* (1929). Jones, the antagonist of the play, dislikes Dr. Carter because he believes that Carter's education has enabled him to win the love of Ruth Chapman. Even Ann Hetty, Ruth's grandmother, suspects Carter's education. She says, "Course I thinks Doctor's all right in some ways, but them educated chaps always manages to think a little diff'rent."

In contrast, in *Simply Heavenly* (1957), Boyd, a young, educated Negro, gains respect as a person who will succeed in life. Significantly, however, the protagonist is not Boyd but Jesse Semple, who survives by means of common sense rather than formal education. Hughes has not ridiculed the educated Negro; at the same time, however, he has not pedestaled Boyd as the individual carrying the hopes of the race.

Third, recent dramatists have studied the intelligent or even intellectual hero as an individual rather than as a representative of the race. In *Bad Man,* Ted James had cried, "We ain't s'posed tuh pay no 'tention tuh a burnin' man . . . but ef de people wid larnin' can't do nothin' 'bout hit, 'tain nothing we can do." Implicit in the cry is a prayer for an educated Negro to solve the race's problems.

In *Simply Heavenly,* Boyd attracts not as a leader but as a respected individual.

In Louis Peterson's *Take a Giant Step* (1953), the hero is a sensitive, intelligent young Negro who acquires education routinely. Although he discerns a difference between himself and the people whom he encounters when he seeks companionship in a tavern, he does not envision himself as a person with a mission. He desires merely to adjust to a society which accepts him intellectually but not socially.

Education, Superstition, and Religion

The new attitude toward the education of the hero reflects a changed attitude towards a second area of his universe: education, superstition, and religion.

As has been suggested, most dramatists of the Twenties and Thirties, writing during a time in which the average Negro could not secure a college education, viewed education as the curse of individuals or as the hope of the race, an attitude still evidenced occasionally in such a work as William Robinson's *The Passing Grade* (1958), which castigates the unjust administration of the rural Negro schools in the South. Those who hailed education as the need of the race assumed ignorance to be a major cause of the Negro's inferior position and echoed Dr. W. E. B. DuBois' pleas for educated men and women to serve as spokesmen and as leaders. Those distrusting education demonstrated an anti-intellectualism characteristic of American society as a whole rather than of the Negro race alone. From the first American comedy, Royall Tyler's *The Contrast* (1787), through the era of Will Rogers, to the present disparagement of "eggheads," American society has mocked the college-bred, cultured individual and has praised the shrewd, ingenious wit educated in the school of hard knocks. Consequently, the reflection of that attitude in dramas by Negroes should surprise no one.

Negro playwrights of the Twenties and Thirties who pictured superstition as a characteristic of the race used it for three purposes: local color, criticism, and comedy. Significantly, however, by associating superstition with the older characters in the plays, they identified it with the past rather than with the future of the race.

In John Matheus's *'Cruiter,* for example, the grandmother superstitiously anticipates bad fortune for business begun on Friday. Matheus has characterized her, however, as one of the older Negroes bound to tradition. Although she sends her son and her daughter North to find a freedom impossible in the South, she refuses to accompany them.

Similarly, in Edmonds' *The New Window* (1934), Lizzie,

the middle-aged wife, superstitiously awaits fortuitous omens while Hester, her daughter, assists destiny. Offered an opportunity to free herself from sixteen years of marriage to a bully, Lizzie is impotent; but, knowing his intentions to fight a duel, Hester dulls the firing pin of his gun so that he will be killed.

The danger of depending upon superstitions provided a theme for Georgia D. Johnson's *Plumes*. Distrusting modern medical practice, Charity Brown, a middle-aged woman, debates the advisability of submitting her child to an operation. Before she decides whether to risk the operation, the child dies.

Often, a satirical treatment of superstition has distinguished the older generation from the younger generation. In James W. Butcher's *The Seer*, Bucephalus Wilson, a charlatan, has preyed upon the superstitions of older Negroes in order to further his selfish plans. When Wilson schemes to use Ivory Toles' fear of ghosts as an instrument to force Toles to consent to Wilson's marrying Toles' daughter, the girl's young suitor unmasks Wilson by posing as a ghost. All three of the comedy's older characters—Toles, Wilson, and Wilson's henchman—behave superstitiously. Even Wilson, who recognizes most of the ignorance of superstition, fears ghosts. In contrast, the intelligent, ingenious young hero and heroine fear nothing.

In *The Conjure Man Dies* (1936) Rudolph Fisher used voodoo and sorcery as a background for melodrama and horror. Although they have employed superstition for their dramatic purposes, most Negro dramatists have avoided picturing voodoo as a unique, important, or necessary part of the Negro's faith.

Perhaps because it has been considered characteristic of Negro thought, religion has been a popular element for dramatists, who have used it both as a theme and as background for the plot. Some dramatists have suggested the hope which Negroes have sought in religion. Mammy, in Edmonds' *Breeders* (1934), verbalizes the attitude: "Lawd, Ah don't want tuh question Yo' justice an' Murcy, but Ah kain't help but axe how long Yuh will let Yo' chilluns be sold down de river lak horses an' cows, and beat wussen de mules dey water down at de waterin' branch. . . . Stop it soon, Lawd! Stop it soon an' let Yo' chilluns drink of de water of freedom, an' put on de garments of righteousness."

Other dramatists, however, have criticized the delusion of accepting religion as a panacea. In *Meek Mose* (1928), Wilson suggested that religion is offered to Negroes to make them forget the discriminatory practices of American society. In *Bleeding Hearts* (1934), Edmonds revealed the despair of a Negro who could not find solace in religion. In *Divine Comedy* (1938), Owen Dodson castigated the religious fanatics who delude Negroes just as charlatans have deceived them with superstition.

Other dramatists have not suggested attitudes toward religion but have used it merely as background for purposes of humor, history, local color, or social criticism. In *Jedgement Day* Pawley contrasted Zeke's superstition with the sincere religious conviction of his wife and of the minister. George Norwood dramatized the Father Divine movement in *Joy Exceeding Glory*. A. Clifton Lamb, in *Roughshod up the Mountain* (1956), used religion as a vehicle for dramatizing the conflict in Negro society resulting from the transition of the race. Having ascended to the pulpit when "the call" has inspired him to leave his trade as a brick-layer, a Negro minister attempts unsuccessfully to prevent his congregation from replacing him with a young minister trained in the Harvard School of Divinity. To the author, however, the theme is not religious but social: it states the demand of the Negro populace for educated and rational, rather than emotional, leadership.

Two interesting aspects of the Negro dramatist's treatment of education and religion appear in the plays. First, dramatists have ignored the Negro's interest in culture and in the fine arts. Perhaps part of the reason for the neglect of this phase of Negro life lies in the dramatists' tendency to focus upon Negroes of lower economic positions.

Second, as protest drama has diminished, dramatists have become less constrained in their treatment of immorality. Many protest dramatists created images to refute the allegation that sexual immorality characterizes Negro behavior. In *The Flight of the Natives* the Negroes remain faithful to their mates even though they have not been married legally. In *Breeders* the heroine kills herself rather than submit to a relationship with the plantation stud.

Recent playwrights, however, have depicted immoral sexual relationships more objectively; sometimes they have even sanctioned such relationships. The young hero of *Take a Giant Step* attempts to prove his masculinity and to weld himself to Negro society by consummating a physical relationship with a prostitute after his desire for a more spiritual relationship has been rebuffed by a seemingly virtuous young woman who, weary of poverty, wishes to offer her body to any man who has enough money to escort her on a tour of nightclubs. In *Roughshod up the Mountain,* the young minister who represents the intelligence of the new Negro is romantically associated with a reformed prostitute, a twentieth century Mary Magdalene. Although the heroine of *Simply Heavenly* refuses to risk remaining alone with Semple before their marriage, the hero sometimes relapses into the arms of another woman, who wears morality more loosely.

Attitudes Towards the North

A third important facet of the Negro's image of his universe is his attitude towards life in the North, particularly Harlem. In much of the drama of the Twenties and the Thirties, the North represented a vaguely defined section of America in which the Negro might find freedom. Harlem, however, often symbolized a modern Babylon in which damnation awaited the unsuspecting Southern Negro.

The conflicting attitudes towards the North appear in Frank Wilson's *Sugar Cane* (1920). Paul Cain distrusts all Northern Negroes whereas his son envisions the North as a place where Negroes can acquire education. In Jean Toomer's *Balo* (1927), Balo's father desires to remain in Georgia to farm and preach. The mother, however, dreams of the happiness which she can find only in the North. Although Granny, in *'Cruiter,* sends her grandson North to find economic security in a munitions factory, she prefers to remain in the section which has been her home.

Historical, anti-slavery dramas, of course, pictured the North as a world of freedom for Negroes, to whom any place would have offered more happiness than the South offered. The same attitude persisted in early protest dramas. For instance, in *Bleeding Hearts,* embittered because his employer has refused to permit him to stop work to comfort his dying wife, Joggison Taylor leaves the South. He fears that he will kill his employer if he remains.

The contrasting attitude—suspicion of the North—is evident in *Harlem* (1922), by Wallace Thurman, a Negro, in collaboration with William J. Rapp. After their migration to Harlem from South Carolina, the Williams family experiences only misery. Cordelia, the daughter, prostitutes herself. Financial failure forces the family to give rent parties. Cordelia becomes involved in murder when her West Indian lover is accused of having murdered a gambler who had been a former suitor. Eulalie Spence, in *The Starter* (1927), satirized Negro life which spawns such individuals as T. J., indolent, conceited, dependent upon the support of Georgia, his industrious sweetheart. The most violent condemnation of the North in drama of the Twenties and Thirties, however, is Edmonds' *Old Man Pete*. Having come North at their children's invitation, Pete Collier and his wife offend their sophisticated children by shouting in church and by dressing and conducting themselves in rural, Southern ways which the children wish to forget. When the parents realize the children's feelings, they decide to return to the South. Trying to walk from Harlem to Grand Central Station on the coldest night in the history of New York, they freeze to death while resting in Central Park.

Recent dramatists, such as Hughes and Peterson, however, have depicted life in the North more objectively, revealing the vices of life among the lower classes but viewing the North neither as a heaven nor a hell.

Negro Society

The final aspect of Negro life to be examined is the Negro's picture of his society and of the relationship between that society and America.

Perhaps because they dramatized protest themes, many Negro playwrights of the Twenties and the Thirties saw Negro society only as it was affected by white society. In such works as *Sugar Cane* (1920), *'Cruiter*, *Ti Yette* (1929), *Bad Man* (1934), and *Bleeding Hearts* (1934)—as well as those works which condemn slavery, the basic conflict results from the inability of Negroes to protect themselves from unjust impingements by other Americans. In *Sugar Cane* and *Ti Yette*, white men exploit Negro women sexually. In *Bad Man*, friction between the races costs Negro life, and in *Bleeding Hearts*, the inhumanity of the white employer precipitates the conflict. The attitude of these dramatists is effectively expressed in *'Cruiter* when Sonny says, "Whatevah whi' folks wants o' we-all, we-all jes' nacherly got tuh do, Ah spose."

Interference with the lives of Negroes is dramatized effectively in Ransom Rideout's *Going Home* (1928). Having settled abroad after World War I, Israel Du Bois marries a European girl who believes him to be a wealthy American. When American troops pass through the town where Du Bois lives, Major Powell, the son of the family which reared Du Bois as a servant, foments a race war but finally persuades Du Bois to leave his wife and to return to America.

In some of the drama of the Twenties and the Thirties, however, and in more recent plays, the Negro playwright has considered conflicts caused by internal rather than external forces. Richardson's *The Broken Banjo* (1925) describes the problems of a Negro betrayed by his wife's parasitic relatives. Langston Hughes's *Soul Gone Home* (1938) introduces the ghost of a son who charges his mother with misconduct because she was not able to provide him with the food, the clothing, and the example of moral purity which a child should have.

Other dramatists have drawn their characters so racelessly that one cannot identify them as Negroes. In *The House of Sham* (1929), Richardson dramatized the problem of a real estate broker, who, by fraudulent practices, enables his wife and his daughter to live extravagantly. Thelma Duncan, in *Sacrifice* (1930), told the story of a youth who protects a friend by assuming the blame for stealing an examination. In *The Anger of One Young Man* (1959), William Robinson has described the frustration of a writer whose idealism is blighted by the mercenary materialism of the publishing trade.

Still other dramatists have emphasized the uniquely Negroid existence of their characters. In *Big White Fog* (1938), Theodore Ward dramatized problems of a Negro family affected by the depression, Communism, domestic quarrels, and anti-Semitism. As Americans they respond to issues which touch all Americans. As Negroes they react to such other matters as Garveyism and the attempt of a white man to buy the affection of one of the daughters.

The Harlemites of *Simply Heavenly* dwell in an isolated world. The central problem is Semple's effort to amass enough money to persuade Joyce to marry him. Conflicts within that society and the economic status of the characters remind the audience that the figures are lower class Negroes. Rather than being embarrassed about their lives, however, they defend their ways. When a Negro stranger condemns as stereotypes the other Negroes in a neighborhood tavern, Mamie justifies her enjoyment of watermelons, chitterlings, red dresses, gin, and black-eyed peas and rice. "I didn't come here to Harlem to get away from my people," she says. "I come here because ther's more of 'em. I loves my race. I loves my people."

In *Take a Giant Step*, Louis Peterson has dramatized the manner in which an educated Negro may become isolated from both Negro and white society. When he reaches the age at which he and his friends begin to seek the companionship of females, Spencer Scott, whose family is the only Negro one in the neighborhood, is rebuffed by his former playmates.

Seeking association within his race, he perceives equally his inability to adjust to the Negroes who visit taverns.

A. Clifton Lamb, in *Roughshod up the Mountain*, has pictured the chasm dividing the traditional Negro society from the new Negro society. On one side are the uneducated Negro laborers; on the other side are Negroes who, by means of education, have attained professional positions.

Perhaps the most dominant and the most important idea in recent drama by Negroes is the impossibility of typifying the Negro race. Lorraine Hansberry's *A Raisin in the Sun* (1959) effectively dramatizes this idea.

Lorraine Hansberry has not idealized the Younger family. Descended from five generations of slaves and sharecroppers, the Youngers, domestic laborers, have little which other people would covet. Desiring to free his wife and his mother from the burden of helping to support the family and desiring to provide his son with an inheritance of which he can be proud, Walter Lee Younger experiences bitter frustration because no one else in his family agrees to his scheme to invest his mother's insurance money in a liquor store. Far from epitomizing nobility, he searches for pride and for maturity. As he says, "I'm thirty-five years old; I been married eleven years and I got a boy who sleeps in the living room—and all I got to give him is stories about how rich white people live." He believes that the Negro who wishes to succeed must imitate white people.

In contrast, his sister, Beneatha (Bennie), inspired partly by racial pride and partly by the lectures of her African suitor, argues against the assimilation of the Negro race into the American culture. Whereas Walter materialistically concentrates upon acquiring money, Bennie wants to become a doctor because her desire since childhood has been to help other people.

Concerned neither with money nor with crusades, their mother desires merely to provide cleanliness and decency for her family. When she receives the insurance money left by her husband, she restrains herself from donating the ten thousand dollars to the church only because she wishes to help her children realize their dreams. She wants her children to respect themselves and to respect others. She refuses to consent to her son's purchasing a liquor store because she believes that it is morally wrong to sell liquor. She wants to maintain a household characterized by the simplicity of Christian ethics. She sees herself symbolized in a ragged plant which she has nursed and has treasured because, in the

North, she has never had sufficient space for the garden which she desires.

Separated by personality and belief, the members of the family conflict incessantly in their attitudes towards education and religion. Although Walter does not oppose education, he resents the fact that Bennie's desire to become a doctor rather than a nurse will necessitate expenses which he wishes to avoid. Bennie, an atheist, seeks education, not to help her race collectively, but to help individuals. Lena Younger, their mother, comforts herself with the belief that God helps the good.

The Youngers are basically moral. Walter would not commit adultery; in fact, he argues that wives are excessively suspicious in believing that their husbands are running to other women when the husbands merely want to be alone. Bennie refuses to become involved in a casual affair with a man to whom she is attracted. To save money, however, Walter's wife Ruth deliberates abortion, and Walter fails to oppose her.

The North has not brought prosperity to the Youngers, emigrants from the South. On the other hand, it has not harmed them. Life in the crowded slums of Southside Chicago has not been pleasant. They have shared a bathroom with other tenants, and they have lacked sufficient space for separate bedrooms or for a garden. Miss Hansberry has reported the situation, however, rather than used it as a basis for protest. The only major conflict with American society stems from the Youngers' decision to move into an all-white neighborhood because they cannot afford to purchase a home at the inflationary prices charged in suburban developments for Negroes.

The Youngers disagree even in their attitudes toward their race. Although Walter blames the backwardness of the race for the inferior economic status of the Negro, he responds to the rhythms of recordings of African music. Bennie recognizes the barrier which separates her from the snobbish Negroes who possess wealth; yet she considers herself a crusader for and a defender of her race. Individual in their characters and their attitudes towards life, the Youngers find unity only in their common belief in the importance of self-respect, a philosophy not unique to the Negro race.

The Future Images of Negro Drama

The changes in the Negro dramatist's image of his hero, his attitude toward education, his attitude toward the North, and his image of his society and its problems parallel those which can be observed in other media utilized by Negro literary artists; from idealization of Negroes to efface the caricatures created by white authors, to strident, self-conscious defense of the vices of Negroes, to objective appraisal. Unlike the Negro novelist, the dramatist cannot escape easily into a world of racelessness. If he employs Negroes to enact his stories, he identifies the characters with Negroes. For that reason, perhaps, the Negro dramatists, more than the novelists, have continued to emphasize problems unique to the Negro race. As reasons for protest have faded, however, they have become more concerned with dilemmas of individuals rather than of the entire race. They have created individuals in the confidence that America has become educated to a stage at which audiences will not assume these characters to typify the Negro race. The Negro dramatists of the present and of the future are no longer compelled to regard themselves as spokesmen for a race which needs educated and talented writers to plead its cause. Now they can regard themselves as artists, writing about the Negro race only because that is the group with which they are the most familiar.

GEORGE E. KENT (1920–   )

Educator and critic, George Kent was born and grew up in Columbus, Georgia. His father was a blacksmith and his mother a rural schoolteacher and principal. He completed his undergraduate studies at Savannah State College and, majoring in literary cirticism, earned both his M.A. and Ph.D. at Boston University. He has been Chairman of the English Department and Dean of the College at Delaware State College and is now Professor of English and Director of the Division of Liberal Arts at Quinnipiac College in Connecticut. He has been a visiting professor at Florida A. & M. University, Grambling State College, the University of Connecticut, and Wesleyan University. Professor Kent is now completing a book-length critical study of Faulkner, tentatively entitled

Faulkner and Racial Consciousness. *The following article is based on a paper delivered at the annual meeting of the College Language Association in 1967. It explains the literary subject matter explored in a course he taught on "The Ethnic Writer in Urban American Culture" at an NDEA Institute in English at Wesleyan University (Connecticut) in the summer of 1966. A full account of this institute and further reflections on this course are embodied in his article in* CLA Journal, *September, 1967.*

Ethnic Impact in American Literature
(Reflections on a Course)

When we speak of Negro cultural values, we encounter certain liberals and some Negroes who are wont to say that what we are talking about is habits deriving from slavery and the ghettos—and let's get rid of them real fast, wholesale. Their attitude accepts unconditionally those unrelieved sociological images of the maimed and the diseased and the perverted. The images are powerful because, like frozen food in the supermarkets, they package easily, market easily, and are arranged easily on the shelves of the compartments of our minds; but they seem to me to be insufficiently related to the density and complexity of reality. It is not necessary, either, to assume a complete dichotomy between Negro experience and the values of Western culture or to become shiny-eyed over some sort of mystique. Cultural values are won in the hard crucible of experience, the dirt and the grime, as well as the sky and the far horizon. Perhaps what Negroes are up against is the age-old problem of the necessity for, not casting out hard-won values, but rather a transvaluation of values. (Patience, for example, does make a good slave, but also, creatively and aggressively exercised, the builder, the inventor, and the revolutionist.) Here are some of the key values that seem frequently to be reflected by Negro folk literature and by outstanding Negro writers:

1. The insistence upon a tough-minded grip upon reality
2. A willingness to confront the self searchingly and even with laughter
3. Patience and endurance
4. Humor as a tool for transcendence
5. A sort of deadend courage, and not so deadend
6. An acceptance of the role of suffering in retaining one's

humanity and in retaining some perspective on the humanity of the oppressor
7. A high development of dissimulation and camouflage
8. A sense of something more than this world and of its
   rhythms
9. A deep sense of the inexorable limitations of life and
   all that we associate with the tragic and tragicomic vision
10. Ceremonies of poise in a non-rational universe (The
    hipsters and the cool-cats play an endless satire upon
    Western assumptions of rationality.)

"Who wills to be a Negro?" cries Ralph Ellison, the outstanding writer, in *Shadow and Act*. "I do!"*

And he is not alone.

Obviously, there is not time to illustrate in detail. I suggest
very careful attention to Ralph Ellison's *Shadow and Act*,
which despite some excesses in emphasizing the positive, is a
brilliant theory of culture. The varieties of folk expression—
slave narratives, spirituals, the blues, work songs, etc., tend to
embody some such set of values. They can be heard if one
listens not merely to the contents of the works but also to
what the *form* is saying. The better Negro writers frequently
express several of the values. Charles W. Chesnutt's Josh
Green in *The Marrow of Tradition* and Bud Johnson in his
The Colonel's Dream, the latter character a victim of the
convict lease system, are types of rock-bottom courage. Some
of the best poems of Langston Hughes reflect the poise
amidst the non-rationality of the Western system. Such conscious artists as Richard Wright, James Baldwin and Ralph
Ellison tend to occupy the whole spread of values. Richard
Wright's sharp negative approach to some Negro values, I
found very useful, since all values have negative aspects and
sometimes cut back at the possessor. In several short stories
in *Uncle Tom's Children*, Wright tended to see effectiveness
in the Negro culture, although the values are usually in tension with the mores of the broader culture and within the
Negro character, himself. In *Native Son* most Negro values
are seen negatively against the background of urban on-
slaught. In *Black Boy*, the viewpoint is negative, as Wright no-
toriously said:

> Whenever I thought of the essential bleakness of black life in
> America, I knew that Negroes had never been allowed to
> catch the full spirit of Western civilization, that they lived
> somehow in it but not of it. And when I brooded upon the
> cultural barrenness of black life, I wondered if clean, positive

* Ralph Ellison, *Shadow and Act* (New York, 1964), p. 132.

tenderness, love, honor, and the capacity to remember were native with man.*

Wright is particularly offended with the tendency to camouflage and dissimulation, the training away from curiosity, the otherworldliness, the repression, engendered in the culture. Certainly, one great value of Wright is that he very early saw the destructiveness of the modern city upon a people ill-supported by the institutions and devices, which most immigrant groups could count upon. He is particularly useful in his portrayal of the Negro cultural values under tension from their clash with the American middle-class structure.

Although I am sympathetic to Ellison's argument that his own inspiration comes from sources broader, more varied, and richer than Wright, and that black writers should not be considered as simply developing in a kind of black apostolic succession, I freely used him and Baldwin to illustrate a different and more positive approach to black cultural values. As early as 1945 in the *Antioch Review*, Ellison in "Richard Wright's Blues" tried to come to terms with Wright's viewpoint:

> Wright knows perfectly well that Negro life is a by-product of Western civilization, and that in it, if only one possesses the humanity and humility to see, are to be discovered all those impulses, tendencies, life and cultural forms to be found elsewhere in Western society.†

In an early short story, "That I Had the Wings," Ellison portrayed a young boy arising to a sense of self-consciousness and aspiration, who is rebuked for his aspirations by an aunt, who invokes the suppressive element of Negro culture. (That's for white folks.) In "Flying Home," a reverse situation occurs: a character who literally must crash his plane and land in the care of the folk values before he can gain the strength to confront Western culture. Incidentally, the airplane is a great Western symbol for both Wright and Ellison. In *Invisible Man*, we have a veritable textbook concerning the power of Negro cultural values, and a considerable satire focused upon the negative aspects: particularly the drive to dissimulation and camouflage. It may be said that the invisible narrator tends to gain power and identity as he negotiates a correct relationship with his own culture and learns the limitations of Western values—as well as their challenge.

* Richard Wright, *Black Boy* (New York, 1945), p. 33.
† Ralph Ellison, *Shadow and Act*, p. 93.

Despite the title of the course, The Ethnic Writer in Urban American Culture, I tried to make clear that the tensions of which America is now conscious did not spring to birth with the 1954 Supreme Court Decision on school desegregation. So, in relationship to the protest tradition, we read such works as *David Walker's Appeal*, a pre-Civil War book with a Malcolm X scream and venom; *Narrative of the Life of Frederick Douglass*, for some artistic sense of the meaning of slavery; *Up From Slavery* by Booker Washington, with the perspective broadened by Douglass's *Narrative* and Dubois's *The Souls of Black Folks* (for it is mandatory that the perspective be broadened). We read James Weldon Johnson's *The Autobiography of an Ex-Colored Man*, representative poets since 1900, and selections of prose where novels were out of print. Of the so-called Harlem Renaissance novelists, only Claude McKay's *Home to Harlem* is in print and thus available for general assignment, although individual members of the class read such other novels of the period as were available in the Wesleyan University Library. For the folk tradition, *The Book of Negro Folklore* edited by Langston Hughes and Arna Bontemps was essential. For contemporary writing, Wright, Ellison, and Baldwin, and Herbert Hill's anthology, *Soon One Morning*, were important sources.

For background, a history of the Negro is mandatory, since the American educational system fosters historical ignorance regarding Negroes and leaves most people unprepared for the simplest intelligent discussion of issues. John Hope Franklin's *From Slavery to Freedom* is, on all grounds, preferable. There were many reference works on literary and sociological background, and my preference, in sociology, was for some old-timers who do *not* make a fetish of a kind of statistical orientation that seems to flatten out both reality and humanity and to turn tendencies into absolutes with jet speed: *Shadow of the Plantation* by Charles S. Johnson, *After Freedom* by Hortense Powdermaker, *Deep South* by Allison Davis and *Black Metropolis* by St. Clair Drake and Horace Cayton. On slavery, *The Peculiar Institution* by Kenneth Stampp is extremely useful—as is *Slavery* by Stanley Elkins, although I think that his theory of a widespread existence of real-life Samboes founders in the face of a single simple question: How could his Samboes, of induced imbecility, have created the body of folk materials that we have, with its insights on the human condition and the Creator?

Although the attempt was made to place the literature in a variety of contexts, the stress was upon a rigorous literary criticism. The question that the class was supposed to answer for each work was whether the author seemed to have penetrated conventional assumptions about reality sufficiently to render the privateness and complexity of the Negro experience. Autobiography was useful in indicating objectively the complexity of Negro life, for often autobiography pointed to a complexity which the artist had not imaged fully in novels and other literary forms. The following autobiographies have very complex situations that have unexploited possibilities: James Weldon Johnson *Along This Way*; Claude McKay, *A Long Ways From Home*; Zora Neale Hurston's *Dust Tracks on a Road*; Richard Wright, *Black Boy* and "I Tried to Be a Communist"; Pauli Murray, *Proud Shoes*; Katherine Dunham, *A Touch of Innocence*; and Horace Cayton, *Long Old Road*. A particular value of the critical approach is that it tends to put such popular, misleading labels as "assimilationism" and "cultural dualism" into proper perspective, and lead to a deeper discovery of the literature.

Such were the inner patterns of the course, in its attempt to render the imaginative sense of minority groups' experiences as they mounted high points of self-consciousness. The pain of this consciousness is unalleviated by the fact that the group leaves its impress upon the dominant culture, even as it loses the one-to-one contact between its values and "reality." Later, it assumes outwardly the contours of the Anglo-Saxon, and a new generation arises which remembers only faintly the travails of Joseph and the tribe, and can center the tragic experience of the fathers only in the most external ceremonies. Certainly, a good deal of tragic meaning is lost which would deepen our lives.

The Negro minority stands out in stark uniqueness. Sociologically, we may well ponder the blunt words of Charles E. Silberman in *Crisis in Black and White*: "The European Ethnic groups . . . could move into the mainstream of American life without forcing before hand any drastic rearrangements of attitudes and institutions. For the Negro to do so, however, will require the most radical changes in the whole structure of American society."* Literarily, we may well ponder two symbols of terrifying power near the end of Chapter 10 in Ralph Ellison's *Invisible Man*: the iron bridge of technology which threatens to become autonomous to the destruction of all humanistic values and the nightmare of castration experienced by the invisible narrator:

But now they [all opponents to identity] came forward

* Charles E. Silberman, *Crisis in Black and White* (New York, 1964), p. 43.

with a knife, holding me; and I felt the bright red pain and they took the two bloody blobs and cast them over the bridge, and out of my anguish I saw them curve up and catch beneath the apex of the curving arch of the bridge, to hang there, dripping down through the sunlight into the dark red water. And while the others laughed, before my pain-sharpened eyes the whole world was slowly turning red.

"Now you're free of illusions," Jack said. . . .†

Without illusions, the invisible narrator feels painful and empty, but points out that it is not only "my generations wasting upon the water—"

"But your sun . . ."
"Yes?"
"And your moon . . ."
"He's crazy!"
"Your world. . ."
"I knew he was a mystic idealist!" Tobitt said.
"Still," I said, "there's your universe, and that drip-drop upon the water you hear is all the history you've made, all you're going to make."*

As slave of technology, the scene implies in part, the American idealistic struggles and proclamations become an exercise in narcissism and abstract universalism. One may hear this castration rage from the frustrated ghettoes crescendoing out of today's television news.

And finally, the adaptability of the course. The inter-disciplinary approach is very useful, although not indispensable. The materials combine easily with history or sociology or psychology. The full value of the course, I think, is best delivered if the instructors agree, from the outset, upon the kinds of faculties and truth which each discipline emphasizes: the more scientific emphasizing the rational, categorizing, and data-collecting faculties; the literary emphasizing imaginative sweep and the attempt to recapture the contradictory density and complexity of the stream of life. The Negro father or family in sociology, for example, is not interchangeable with the Negro father or family in literature, and the course is immediately reduced if the distinction is not clear. Obviously, the course can be offered in the conventional one-instructor pattern. Some version of the course, whichever approach is used, would fill an alarming gap in the high school curriculum where Negro and white students tend to

† Ralph Ellison, *Invisible Man* (New York, 1952), p. 493.
* *Ibid.*

confront the Negro experience as simply a blank or a problem.

Part of the adapting is in terms of people. For the white student, the sheer speed of change in public surface tends to make unrecognizable, quaint or esoteric tendencies and patterns that had their grip upon white lives well up into the Twentieth Century. Religious fundamentalism and extreme poverty are examples and may be placed in proper context by reference to various American writers of great power. The teacher should also be wary of any occasional tendency to substitute a stereotyped, push-button liberalism for literary understanding. For a black student, in integrated schools, the lethargy of social change may influence his reception of a particular work. The situations presented in the hard-hitting naturalistic style of many outstanding Negro writers may still be very close by, uncomfortably so—or conversely, the situations may seem very different from the particular high school student's middle-class environment. The answer is still the placement of the writing in the appropriate context, an effort required for teaching literature, anyway. One useful context is that of the folk values, but there are also plenty of general American contexts to be drawn upon.

The exciting aspect of the course is that it utilizes a very urgent motivation of both black and white students: to get a deeper than conventional sense of America and their own identities. The vanguard of students, in general, are seeking through a variety of confrontations: The campus and various public issues claim their passionate involvement. A growing number of black students are demanding the right to a positive identity that takes no upward slant toward middle class values. The polite search is over. The vanguard have sought their identity in the backroads of Mississippi, and often under the clubs of jailers who attempted to imprint their identity in blood. They have sought it in the souls of gnarled and starving share-croppers and head-ragged mothers. What they seem to be seeking is a means, not merely to fit into the Western world, but to negotiate manly terms with it. These actions of the vanguards have probably done little to shake up our lethargic curriculums. Maybe the question that we ought to face is whether through some courses that emphasize relevance, without abating a jot of universality, intellectual rigor, and critical analysis, academia can speak more intimately to some of the intellectual hunger of our students and time.

CLARENCE MAJOR (1936–   )

Very much a part of the vital "little magazine" movement of today, Clarence Major has edited his own literary journal Coercion Review *(1958–1961), been associate editor of half a dozen others, been book-review editor of* Anagogic *and* Paideumic Review, *and is a contributing editor of* The Journal of Black Poetry. *He was born in Atlanta, Georgia, and was raised and schooled in Chicago, where he attended the Art Institute of Chicago and later studied English and journalism. He has also worked as a welder in a steel plant in Omaha, Nebraska. His poems, short stories, and articles have appeared in numerous publications and he published two books of poems in the 60's. His short stories have appeared in* Olivant Annual Anthology of Short Stories *for 1957, 1959 and 1966, and his poems have been included in three anthologies. Major has taught creative writing both for the Harlem Education Programs and Columbia University's Teachers and Writers Collaborative and was writer in residence at the Pennsylvania Advancement School for two sessions (1967 and 1968). Clarence Major is now living in New York City and expects publication soon of a novel and a new collection of poems. The following article is reprinted from* The Journal of Black Poetry *(Spring, 1967).*

A Black Criterion

The black poet confronted with western culture and civilization must isolate and define himself in as bold a relief as he can. He must chop away at the white criterion and destroy its hold on his black mind because seeing the world through white eyes from a black soul causes death. The black poet must not attempt to create from a depth of black death. The true energy of black art must be brought fully into the possession of the black creator. The black poet must stretch his consciousness not only in the direction of other non-western people across the earth, but in terms of pure reason and expand the mind areas to the far reaches of creativity's endlessness to find new ways of seeing the world the black poet of the west is caught up in.

If we black poets see ourselves and our relationships with the deeper elements of life and with all mankind perhaps we can also break through the tangled ugly white energy of western fear and crime.

We are in a position to know at first hand the social and political machinery that is threatening to destroy the earth and we can use a creative and intellectual black criterion on it.

I believe the artist does owe something to the society in which he is involved; he should be involved fully. This is the measure of the poet, and the black poet in his—from a white point of view—invisibility must hammer away at his own world of creative criticism of this society. A work of art, a poem, can be a complete "thing"; it can be alone, not preaching, not trying to change men, and though it might change them, if the men are ready for it, the poem is not reduced in its artistic status. I mean we black poets can write poems of pure creative black energy right here in the white west and make them works of art without falling into the cheap market place of bullshit and propaganda. But it is a thin line to stand on.

We are the "eye" of the west really.

We must shake up not only our own black brothers but the superficial and shoddy people stumbling in the brainlessness of the western decline. We must use our black poetic energy to overthrow the western ritual and passion, the curse, the dark ages of this death, the original sin's impact on a people and their unjust projection of it upon us black people; we must lead ourselves out of this madness and if our journey brings out others—perhaps even white people—then it will be good for us all. We must use our magic, as brother Leroi says.

The nightmare of this western sadism must be fought with a superior energy and black poetic spirit is a powerful weapon.

With the poem, we must erect a spiritual black nation we all can be proud of. And at the same time we must try to do the impossible—always the impossible—by bringing the poem back into the network of man's social and political life.

Total life is what we want.

BIBLIOGRAPHY

JAMES BALDWIN

FICTION

Go Tell It on the Mountain, New York, Knopf, 1953. Dell paperback, 1965. (Novel)

Giovanni's Room, New York, Dial, 1956. Dell paperback, 1964. (Novel)

Another Country, New York, Dial, 1962. Dell paperback, 1963. (Novel)

Going to Meet the Man, New York, Dial, 1965, Dell paperback, 1970. (Short stories)

Tell Me How Long the Train's Been Gone, New York, Dial, 1968. (Novel)

If Beale Street Could Talk, New York, Dial, 1974. Signet paperback, 1975. (Novel)

Just Above My Head, New York, Dial, 1979. Dell paperback, 1980. (Novel)

ESSAYS AND MISCELLANEOUS PROSE

Notes of a Native Son, Boston, Beacon, 1955. New York, Bantam paperback, 1971.

Nobody Knows My Name, New York, Dial, 1961. Dell paperback, 1964; also Delta.

The Fire Next Time, New York, Dial, 1963. New York, Watts; Dell paperback, 1970.

Nothing Personal, Photographs by Richard Avedon, New York, Atheneum, 1964. Dell paperback, 1965. (Social commentary)

with Margaret Mead, *A Rap on Race,* Philadelphia, Lippincott, 1971.

No Name in the Street, New York, Dial, 1972. Dell paperback, 1973.

with Nikki Giovanni, *A Dialogue,* Philadelphia, Lippincott, 1973; also paperback.

The Devil Finds Work, New York, Dial, 1976.

DRAMA

Blues for Mister Charlie, New York, Dial, 1964. Dell paperback, 1964. (Three-act play)

The Amen Corner, New York, Dial, 1968. (Three act play)

LERONE BENNETT, JR.

HISTORY

Before the Mayflower: A History of the Negro in America, 1619–1964, Chicago, Johnson, 1964 and 1969. New York, Penguin paperback, 1966.

Black Power U.S.A.: The Human Side of Reconstruction 1867–1877, Chicago, Johnson, 1967.

Ed., *Ebony Pictorial History of Black America*, 4 volumes, Chicago, Johnson, 1971.

Made in the Water: Great Moments in Black American History, Chicago, Johnson, 1979.

Pioneers in Protest, Chicago, Johnson, 1968.

Shaping of Black America, Chicago, Johnson, 1975.

ESSAYS AND MISCELLANEOUS PROSE

The Negro Mood and Other Essays, Chicago, Johnson, 1964. New York, Ballantine paperback, 1965.

Confrontation: Black and White, Chicago, Johnson, 1965.

The Black Mood, New York, Barnes and Noble paperback, 1970.

The Challenge of Blackness, Chicago, Johnson, 1972.

BIOGRAPHY

What Manner of a Man: A Biography of Martin Luther King, Jr., Chicago, Johnson, 1965.

ARNA BONTEMPS

FICTION

God Sends Sunday, New York, Harcourt, Brace, 1931. New York, AMS Press. (Novel)

Black Thunder, New York, Macmillan, 1936. Beacon Press paperback, 1968. (Novel)

Drums at Dusk, New York, Macmillan, 1939. (Novel)

The Old South: A Summer Tragedy and Other Stories of the Thirties, New York, Dodd, Mead, 1973. (Short stories)

POETRY

Personals, London, Paul Breman, 1963. Detroit, Broadside paperback, 1974.

ANTHOLOGIES

and Langston Hughes, eds., *The Poetry of the Negro 1764–1949*. Garden City, N.Y., Doubleday, 1949.

and Langston Hughes, eds., *The Book of Negro Folklore,*
New York, Dodd, Mead, 1959.

Ed., *Great Slave Narratives,* Boston, Beacon Press, 1969; also
paperback.

Ed., *American Negro Poetry,* New York, Hill & Wang paperback, 1974; also paperback.

Ed., *The Harlem Renaissance Remembered,* New York, Dodd,
Mead, 1972.

HISTORY

with Jack Conroy, *They Seek a City,* Garden City, N.Y., Doubleday, 1945. (Study of Negro migration)

100 Years of Negro Freedom, New York, Dodd, Mead, 1961;
also paperback. Westport, Conn., Greenwood, 1980.

with Jack Conroy, *Anyplace But Here,* New York, Hill &
Wang paperback, 1966.

GWENDOLYN BROOKS

POETRY

A Street in Bronzeville, New York, Harper, 1945.

Annie Allen, New York, Harper, 1949. Westport, Conn.,
Greenwood, 1972.

The Bean Eaters, New York, Harper, 1960.

Selected Poems, New York, Harper and Row, 1963; also
paperback.

In the Mecca, New York, Harper, 1968.

Aloneness, Detroit, Broadside, 1971; also paperback.

Riot, Detroit, Broadside, 1969; also paperback.

Family Pictures, Detroit, Broadside, 1970; also paperback.

Beckonings, Detroit, Broadside paperback, 1975.

The Tiger Who Wore White Gloves, Chicago, Third World,
1974.

AUTOBIOGRAPHY

Report from Part One: An Autobiography, Detroit, Broadside,
1972.

World of Gwendolyn Brooks, New York, Harper, 1971. (Includes *A Street in Bronzeville, Annie Allen, Maud Martha,
The Bean Eaters, In the Mecca*)

FICTION

Maud Martha, New York, Harper, 1953. AMS Press. (Novel)

FRANK LONDON BROWN

FICTION

Trumbull Park, Chicago, Regnery, 1959. (Novel)

STERLING A. BROWN

POETRY

Southern Road, New York, Harcourt, Brace, 1932.
The Collected Poems of Sterling A. Brown, New York, Harper, 1980.
The Last Ride of Will Bill and Eleven Narrative Poems, Detroit, Broadside, 1975; also paperback.

CRITICISM

The Negro in American Fiction bound with *Negro Poetry and Drama*, New York, Arno. Atheneum paperback, 1969.

CHARLES W. CHESNUTT

FICTION

The Conjure Woman, Boston, Houghton, Mifflin, 1899. Ann Arbor, Mich., University of Michigan Press, 1969. New York, Scholarly, 1977. (Short stories)
The Wife of His Youth and Other Stories of the Color Line, Boston, Houghton, Mifflin, 1899. Ann Arbor, Mich., University of Michigan Press paperback, 1968. New York, Irvington; Scholarly, 1977. (Short stories)
The House Behind the Cedars, Boston, Houghton, Mifflin, 1900. Macmillan paperback, 1969. (Novel)
The Marrow of Tradition, Boston, Houghton, Mifflin, 1901. Boston, Dynamic Learn Corp., 1978. New York, Irvington; also paperback. Ann Arbor, Mich., University of Michigan Press paperback, 1969. New York, Arno, 1969; AMS Press. (Novel)
The Colonel's Dream, New York, Doubleday, Page, 1905. Miami, Mnemosyne paperback. New York, Arno. Westport, Conn., Negro University Press. New York, Irvington. (Novel)

BIOGRAPHY

Frederick Douglass, Boston, Small, Maynard, 1899. Chicago, Johnson, 1971.

JOHN HENRIK CLARKE

POETRY

Rebellion in Rhyme, Prairie City, Ill., Decker Press, 1948.

ANTHOLOGIES

Ed., *Harlem, U.S.A.*, Berlin, Seven Seas Books, 1965. New York, Macmillan paperback, 1971.
Ed., *Harlem, A Community in Transition*, New York, Citadel paperback, 1969.
Ed., *American Negro Short Stories*, New York, Hill & Wang, 1966; also paperback.

Ed., *William Styron's Nat Turner: Ten Black Writers Respond*, Boston, Beacon Press, 1968; also paperback.

Ed., *Malcolm X, the Man and His Times*, New York, Macmillan, 1969; also paperback.

et al., *Black Titan: W. E. B. DuBois*, Boston, Beacon Press, 1970.

Ed., *Marcus Garvey and the Vision of Africa*, New York, Random House paperback, 1974.

COUNTEE CULLEN

POETRY

Color, New York, Harper, 1925. New York, Arno, 1970.

The Ballad of the Brown Girl: An Old Ballad Retold, New York, Harper, 1927.

Copper Sun, New York, Harper, 1927.

The Black Christ and Other Poems, New York, Harper, 1929.

The Medea and Some Poems, New York, Harper, 1935. (A play and a collection of verse)

On These I Stand, New York, Harper, 1947. (Novel)

FICTION

One Way to Heaven, New York, Harper, 1932. New York, AMS Press. (Novel)

ANTHOLOGIES

Ed., *Caroling Dusk: An Anthology of Verse by Negro Poets*, New York, Harper, 1927. New York, Harper, 1974; Irvington.

ARTHUR P. DAVIS

ANTHOLOGIES

with Sterling A. Brown and Ulysses Lee, eds., *The Negro Caravan*, New York, Dryden, 1941.

with Saunders Redding, eds., *Cavalcade: Negro American Writing from 1760 to the Present*, Boston, Houghton, Mifflin, 1971.

From the Dark Tower; Afro-American Writers from 1900 to 1960, Washington, D.C., Howard University Press, 1974.

BIOGRAPHY

Isaac Watts: His Life and Works, New York, Dryden, 1943. Geneva, Alabama, Allenson.

FRANK MARSHALL DAVIS

POETRY

Black Man's Verse, Chicago, Black Cat Press, 1935.

I Am the American Negro, Chicago, Black Cat Press, 1937. New York, Arno.
47th Street, Prairie City, Ill., Decker Press, 1948.

OWEN DODSON

POETRY

Powerful Long Ladder, New York, Farrar, Straus, 1946. New York, Farrar, Straus, 1970; also paperback.

DRAMA

The Confession Stone, Detroit, Broadside paperback, 1970.

FICTION

Boy at the Window, New York, Farrar, Straus and Young, 1951. Madison, New Jersey, Chatham Bookseller, 1972. New York, Farrar, Straus, 1977. Also entitled *When Trees Are Green,* New York, Popular Library paperback, 1977.
Come Home Early, Child, New York, Popular Library paperback, 1977.

FREDERICK DOUGLASS

AUTOBIOGRAPHY

Narrative of the Life of Frederick Douglass, An American Slave, Written by Himself, Boston, Anti-Slavery Office, 1945. New York, Signet paperback, 1968. Cambridge, Mass., Harvard University Press, 1960; also paperback. New York, Doubleday paperback.
My Bondage and My Freedom, New York, Miller, Orton and Mulligan, 1855. Chicago, Johnson, Ebony Classic Series. New York, Dover paperback, 1969.
Life and Times of Frederick Douglass, Boston, 1892. Magnolia, Mass., Peter Smith.
Life and Times of Frederick Douglass: The Complete Autobiography, New York, Macmillan paperback, 1962.

COLLECTED WRITINGS

Ed., Philip Foner, *The Life and Writings of Frederick Douglass,* 4 vols., New York, International Publishers, 1975; also paperback.
Ed., Philip Foner, *The Life and Writings of Frederick Douglass: Supplementary Volume: 1844–1860,* New York, International Publishers, 1975; also paperback.
Ed., Philip Foner, *Frederick Douglass: Selections,* New York, International Publishers paperback, 1945.
Ed., Barbara Ritchie, *Life and Times of Frederick Douglass,* New York, Crowell, 1966.
Ed., Barbara Ritchie, *Mind and Heart of Frederick Douglass: Excerpts from Speeches of the Great Negro Orator,* New York, Crowell, 1968.

Ed., John W. Blessingame, *The Frederick Douglass Papers;
Series One: Speeches, Debates, and Interviews Volume I
1841–1846,* New Haven, Yale University Press, 1979.

W. E. B. DUBOIS*

FICTION

The Quest of the Silver Fleece, Chicago, McClurg, 1911. New
York, Arno 1970. Westport, Conn., Negro Universities
Press. New York, Kraus, 1975. Miami, Mnemosyne paper-
back. New York, AMS Press. (Novel)

Dark Princess: A Romance, New York, Harcourt, Brace,
1928. New York, Kraus, 1975. (Novel)

The Ordeal of Mansart, New York, Mainstream, 1957. New
York, Kraus, 1976. (The first novel in the Black Flame
trilogy)

Mansart Builds a School, New York, Mainstream, 1959. New
York, Kraus, 1976. (The second novel in the Black Flame
trilogy)

Worlds of Color, New York, Mainstream, 1961. New York,
Kraus, 1976. (The third novel in the Black Flame trilogy)

ESSAYS

The Souls of Black Folk: Essays and Sketches, Chicago, Mc-
Clurg, 1903. New York, Fawcett paperback. New York,
Kraus, 1973. Magnolia, Mass., Peter Smith. New York, Sig-
net paperback, 1969. Dodd, Mead, 1979. Included in *Three
Negro Classics,* ed., John Hope Franklin, Avon paperback,
1965.

Dusk of Dawn: An Essay Toward an Autobiography of a
Race Concept, New York, Harcourt, Brace, 1940. New
York, Kraus, 1975.

EDUCATION

The College-Bred Negro, Atlanta, Ga., Atlanta University
Press, 1900. New York, Kraus.

The Negro Common School, Atlanta, Ga., Atlanta University
Press, 1901.

The College-Bred Negro American, Atlanta, Ga., Atlanta University Press, 1910. New York, Kraus paperback.

The Common School and the Negro American, Atlanta, Ga.,
Atlanta University Press, 1911. New York, Kraus.

HISTORY

*The Suppression of the African Slave Trade to the United
States of America,* New York, Longmans Green, 1896. So-

---

*Based on "A Selected Bibliography of the Published Writings of
W. E. B. DuBois" by Ernest Kaiser, Published in *Freedomways,*
Winter, 1965.

cial Science Press, 1954. New York, Russell, 1965. Williamstown, Mass., Corner Hse., 1970. Baton Rouge, Louisiana State University Press paperback, 1970. New York, Schocken, 1969. Kraus, 1973. (version edited by Philip Foner, New York, Dover paperback, 1970)

The Gift of Black Folk: The Negroes in the Making of America, Boston, Stratford Co., 1924. New York, Kraus, 1975; AMS Press.

A Pageant in Seven Decades, 1868–1938, Atlanta, Ga., Atlanta University Press, 1938.

Black Reconstruction in America, 1860–1880, New York, Harcourt, Brace, 1935. New York, Russell, 1956. New York, Atheneum paperback, 1969.

The World and Africa: An Inquiry into the Part which Africa Has Played in World History, New York, Viking, 1947. International Publishers, 1965; also paperback. New York, Kraus.

AUTOBIOGRAPHY

The Autobiography of W. E. B. DuBois, New York, International Publishers, 1968; also paperback. New York, Kraus, 1976.

In Battle for Peace: The Story of My 83rd Birthday, New York, Masses and mainstream, 1952. New York, Kraus, 1976.

BIOGRAPHY

John Brown, Philadelphia, George W. Jacobs and Co., 1909. New York, International Publishers paperback, 1962. Arlington Heights, Ill., Metro Books, 1972. New York, Kraus.

SOCIOLOGY

The Conservation of Races, Washington, D.C., American Negro Academy, 1897.

The Social and Physical Condition of Negroes in Cities, Atlanta, Ga., Atlanta University Press, 1897.

Some Efforts of American Negroes for Their Own Social Betterment, Atlanta, Ga., Atlanta University Press, 1898.

The Negro in Business, Atlanta, Ga., Atlanta University Press, 1899. New York, AMS Press, 1971.

The Philadelphia Negro: A Social Study, Philadelphia, University of Pennsylvania, 1899. New York, Schocken, 1968; also paperback. New York, Kraus, 1973.

Black North in 1901: A Social Study, (series of *New York Times* articles), 1901. New York, Arno, 1970.

The Negro Artisan, Atlanta, Ga., Atlanta University Press, 1902. New York, Kraus.

Some Notes on Negro Crime, Particularly in Georgia, Atlanta, Ga., Atlanta University Press, 1904. New York, Kraus paperback.

The Health and Physique of the Negro American, Atlanta,
Ga., Atlanta University Press, 1906.
Economic Cooperation among Negro Americans, Atlanta, Ga.,
Atlanta University Press, 1907. New York, Kraus.
The Negro American Family, Atlanta, Ga., Atlanta Univer-
sity Press, 1908. Westport, Conn., Negro Universities Press.
New York, Kraus.
Efforts for Social Betterment among Negro Americans, At-
lanta, Ga., Atlanta University Press, 1909. New York, Kraus.
The Social Evolution of the Black South, Washington, D.C.,
American Negro Monograph Co., 1911.
The Negro American Artisan, Atlanta, Ga., Atlanta University
Press, 1912. New York, Kraus.
Morals and Manners among Negro Americans, Atlanta, Ga.,
Atlanta University Press, 1915. New York, Kraus paperback.
The Negro, New York, Henry Holt, 1915. New York, Kraus,
1975. New York, Oxford University Press paperback, 1970.
*Darkwater: The Twentieth Century Century Completion of
Uncle Tom's Cabin,* Washington, D.C., A. Jenkins Co.,
1920. Also another edition subtitled *Voices from Within the
Veil,* New York, Harcourt, Brace, 1930. New York, Kraus,
1975. New York, Schocken paperback, 1969. New York,
AMS Press, 1969.
*Black Folk, Then and Now: An Essay in the History and
Sociology of the Negro Race,* New York, Henry Holt, 1939.
New York, Kraus, 1975.
Color and Democracy: Colonies and Peace, New York, Har-
court, Brace, 1945. New York, Kraus, 1975.

RELIGION

The Negro Church, Atlanta, Ga., Atlanta University Press,
1903. New York, Scholarly.

SELECTED WRITINGS

*An ABC of Color: Selections from over a Half Century of the
Writings of W. E. B. DuBois,* Berlin, Seven Seas paperback,
1963. New York, International Publishers paperback, 1970.

COLLECTED WRITINGS

Ed., Philip Foner, *W. E. B. DuBois Speaks: Speeches and Ad-
dresses, 1890–1919,* New York, Path Press, 1977; also
paperback.
Ed., Philip Foner, *W. E. B. DuBois Speaks: Speeches and Ad-
dresses, 1920–1963,* New York, Path Press, 1977; also
paperback.
Ed., Herbert Aptheker, *The Education of Black People: Ten
Critiques, 1906–1960,* Amherst, Mass., University of Massachusetts Press, 1973. New York, Monthly Review Press,
paperback, 1975.
Ed., Herbert Aptheker, *The Correspondence of W. E. B. Du-*

Bois: Selections, 1877–1934, Amherst, Mass., University of Massachusetts Press, 1973.

Ed., Herbert Aptheker, *The Correspondence of W. E. B. Du-Bois: Selections, 1934–1944, Vol. 2.,* Amherst, Mass., University of Massachusetts Press, 1976.

Ed., Herbert Aptheker, *The Correspondence of W. E. B. Du-Bois: Selections, 1934–1944, Vol. 2,* Amherst, Mass., University of Massachusetts Press, 1978.

Ed., Herbert Aptheker, *The Book Reviews of W. E. B. Du-Bois,* New York, Kraus, 1967.

Ed., Herbert Aptheker, *Prayers for Dark People,* Amherst, Mass., University of Massachusetts Press, 1980; also paperback.

Eds., Dan S. Green and Edwin D. Driver, *W. E. B. DuBois on Sociology and the Black Community,* University of Chicago Press paperback, 1980.

PAUL LAURENCE DUNBAR

POETRY

Candle-Lightin' Time, New York, Dodd, Mead, 1901. New York, AMS Press.

Chris'mus is a Comin' and Other Poems, New York, Dodd, Mead, 1905.

The Complete Poems of Paul Laurence Dunbar, New York, Dodd, Mead, 1913. Dodd paperback, 1980. (Includes his earlier books of poetry)

Howdy, Honey, Howdy, Toronto, Musson, 1905. New York, Dodd, Mead, 1905. New York, AMS Press; Arno.

Joggin' erlong, New York, Dodd, Mead, 1906. New York, Arno.

Speakin' o' Christmas—and Other Christmas and Special Poems, New York, Dodd, Mead, 1914. New York, AMS Press.

Li'l Gal, New York, Dodd, Mead, 1904. New York, AMS Press; Arno. New York, Scholarly, 1977.

Lyrics of Lowly Life, New York, Dodd, Mead, 1896. New York, Arno, 1969. New York, Irvington; also paperback.

Lyrics of the Hearthside, New York, Dodd, Mead, 1899. New York, AMS Press; Arno.

Lyrics of Love and Laughter. New York, Dodd, Mead, 1903. New York, AMS Press; Arno.

Lyrics of Sunshine and Shadow. New York, Dodd, Mead, 1905. New York, AMS Press.

Majors and Minors, Toledo, Ohio, Hadley & Hadley, 1895. New York, Arno.

Oak and Ivy, Dayton, Ohio, United Brethren Publishing House, 1893.

A Plantation Portrait, New York, Dodd, Mead, 1905.

Poems of Cabin and Field, New York, Dodd, Mead, 1899. New York, AMS Press; Arno.

When Malindy Sings, New York, Dodd, Mead, 1903. New York, AMS Press; Arno.

FICTION

Folks from Dixie, New York, Dodd, Mead, 1898. London, J. Bowden. Westport, Conn., Negro Universities Press. New York, Arno; Irvington paperback. (Short stories)

The Uncalled, New York, Dodd, Mead, 1898. New York, Arno; AMS Press. Miami, Mnemosyne paperback. New York, Irvington. Westport, Conn., Negro Universities Press. (Novel)

The Love of Landry, New York, Dodd, Mead, 1900. New York, Arno. Boston, Gregg, 1970. Westport, Conn., Negro Universities Press. New York, Irvington. Miami, Mnemosyne paperback. (Novel)

The Strength of Gideon and Other Stories, New York, Dodd, Mead, 1900. New York, Arno, 1969. (Short stories)

The Fanatics, New York, Dodd, Mead, 1901. Boston, Gregg, 1971. New York, Arno. Westport, Conn., Negro Universities Press. Miami, Mnemosyne paperback. (Novel)

The Sport of the Gods, New York, Dodd, Mead, 1902. New York, Macmillan paperback, 1970. Miami, Mnemosyne paperback. New York, Arno, 1969. (Novel)

In Old Plantation Days, New York, Dodd, Mead, 1903. Westport, Conn., Negro Universities Press, (Short stories)

The Heart of Happy Hollow, New York, Dodd, Mead, 1904. New York, Arno. Westport, Conn., Negro Universities Press. (Short stories)

Best Stories, New York, Dodd, Mead, 1938.

COLLECTED WRITINGS

Eds., Jay Martin and Gossie Hudson, *The Paul Laurence Dunbar Reader,* New York, Dodd, Mead, 1975.

Collected Works, New York, Gordon Press.

RALPH ELLISON

FICTION

Invisible Man, New York, Random House, 1952; also paperback, 1972. New York, Modern Library paperback, 1963. (Novel)

ESSAYS

Shadow and Act, New York, Random House, 1964.

MARI EVANS

POETRY

Where Is All the Music? London, Paul Breman, 1968.

I Am a Black Woman, New York, Morrow paperback, 1970.

I Look at Me, Chicago, Third World, 1974; also paperback.

RUDOLPH FISHER

FICTION

The Walls of Jericho, New York, Knopf, 1928. New York, Arno, 1969. (Novel)

The Conjure-Man Dies, New York, Covici Friede, 1932. New York, Arno. (Novel)

ROBERT HAYDEN

POETRY

Heart-Shape in the Dust, Detroit, Falcon, 1940.

and Myron O'Higgins, *The Lion and the Archer,* Nashville, Tenn., Hemphill Press (Published privately, limited ed.), 1948.

Figure of Time, Nashville, Tenn., Hemphill Press, 1955.

A Ballad of Remembrance, London, Paul Breman, 1962. Distributed in the U.S. by Broadside Press.

Selected Poems, New York, October House, 1966.

The Night Blooming Cereus, Detroit, Broadside paperback, 1972.

Words in the Mourning Time: Poems, New York, October House, 1970.

Angle of Ascent: New and Selected Poems, New York, Liveright paperback, 1975.

American Journal, New York, Liveright, 1981; also paperback.

ANTHOLOGIES

Ed., *Kaleidoscope: Poems by American Negro Poets,* New York, Harcourt, Brace and World, 1967.

FRANK HORNE

POETRY

Haverstraw, London, Paul Breman, 1963.

LANGSTON HUGHES

FICTION

Not Without Laughter, New York, Knopf, 1930. New York, Macmillan paperback, 1969. (Novel)

The Ways of White Folks, New York, Knopf, 1934. Random paperback, 1971. (Short stories)

Simple Speaks His Mind, New York, Simon and Schuster, 1950.

Laughing to Keep from Crying, New York, Henry Holt, 1952. (Short stories)

Simple Takes a Wife, New York, Simon and Schuster, 1953.

Simple Stakes a Claim, New York, Simon and Schuster, 1957.

The Best of Simple, New York, Hill & Wang paperback, 1961.

(A selection of Simple sketches from the three previous volumes)

Something in Common and Other Stories, New York, Hill & Wang paperback, 1963. (Short stories)

Simple's Uncle Sam, New York, Hill & Wang, 1965; also paperback.

POETRY

The Weary Blues, New York, Knopf, 1926.

Fine Clothes to the Jew, New York, Knopf, 1927.

The Negro Mother, New York, Golden Stair Press, 1931. New York, Arno.

Dear Lovely Death, New York, Knopf, 1931.

The Dream-Keeper, New York, Knopf, 1932.

Scottsboro Limited: Four Poems and a Play in Verse, New York, Golden Stair Press, 1932.

New Song, New York, International Workers Order, 1938.

Shakespeare in Harlem, New York, Knopf, 1942.

Fields of Wonder, New York, Knopf, 1947.

One-Way Ticket, New York, Knopf, 1949.

Montage of a Dream Deferred, New York, Knopf, 1951.

Ask Your Mama; 12 Moods for Jazz, New York, Knopf, 1961.

Selected Poems of Langston Hughes, New York, Knopf, 1959. Random paperback, 1974.

The Panther and the Lash; Poems of Our Times, New York, Knopf paperback, 1967; also paperback.

DRAMA

with David Martin, *Simply Heavenly*, Chicago, Dramatists Publishing Co., 1957.

Tambourines to Glory, New York, John Day, 1958.

Ed., Webster Smalley, *Five Plays by Langston Hughes*, Bloomington, Ind., Indiana University Press, 1963; also paperback.

ESSAY

with Roy De Carava, *The Sweet Flypaper of Life*, New York, Hill & Wang, 1967. (A literary sketch accompanying photographs of Harlem by De Carava)

AUTOBIOGRAPHY

The Big Sea, New York, Knopf, 1940. Hill & Wang paperback, 1963.

I Wonder As I Wander, New York, Holt, Rinehart, 1965. Hill & Wang paperback, 1964. New York, Octagon, 1974.

HISTORY

with Milton Meltzer, *A Pictorial History of the Negro in America*, New York, Crown, 1956.

Fight for Freedom; The Story of the NAACP, New York, Norton 1962. New York, Berkley Publishing Co. paperback, 1962.

with Milton Meltzer, *Black Magic: A Pictorial History of the Negro in American Entertainment,* New York, Prentice-Hall, 1967.

SELECTED WORKS

The Langston Hughes Reader, New York, Braziller, 1958.
The Langston Hughes Reader, New York, Dodd, Mead, 1966.
Ed., Faith Berry, *Good Morning Revolution: Uncollected Writings of Social Protest,* Westport, Conn., Lawrence Hill, 1973; also paperback.

ANTHOLOGIES

and Arna Bontemps, eds., *Poetry of the Negro, Seventeen Forty-Six—Nineteen Seventy,* New York, Doubleday, 1970; also paperback.
Ed., *An African Treasury; Articles, Essays, Stories, Poems, by Black Africans,* New York, Crown, 1960. Pyramid paperback, 1961.
Ed., *Poems from Black Africa,* Bloomington, Ind., Indiana University Press, 1963; also paperback.
Ed., *New Negro Poets U.S.A.,* Bloomington, Ind., Indiana University Press, 1964.
Ed., *The Book of Negro Humor,* New York, Dodd, Mead, 1965.
Ed., *The Best Short Stories by Negro Writers,* Boston, Little, Brown, 1967; also paperback.

FENTON JOHNSON

POETRY

A Little Dreaming, Chicago, Peterson Linotyping Co., 1913.
Visions of the Dusk, New York, F.J., 1915. New York, Arno.
Songs of the Soil, New York, F.J., 1916. New York, AMS Press, 1975.

FICTION

Tales of Darkest America, Chicago, The Favorite Magazine, 1920. New York, Arno. (Short stories)

JAMES WELDON JOHNSON

FICTION

The Autobiography of an Ex-Colored Man, New York, Sherman French, 1912. New York, Knopf, 1927. Hill & Wang paperback, 1960. Darby, Penn., Arden Library, 1978. Included in *Three Negro Classics,* ed., John Hope Franklin, Avon paperback, 1965. (Novel)

POETRY

Fifty Years and Other Poems, Boston, Cornhill, 1917. New York, AMS Press.

God's Trombones: Seven Old-Time Negro Sermons in Verse,
New York, Viking, 1927. Penguin paperback, 1976.
St. Peter Relates an Incident of the Resurrection Day, New
York, Viking, 1930. New York, AMS Press.

AUTOBIOGRAPHY

*Along This Way: The Autobiography of James Weldon John-
son,* New York, Viking, 1933. New York, Da Capo, 1973.

MISCELLANEOUS PROSE

Black Manhattan, New York, Knopf, 1930. New York, Arno,
1968; Atheneum paperback, 1968.
Negro Americans, What Now?, New York, Viking, 1934. New
York, AMS Press, 1971. New York, Da Capo, 1973.

ANTHOLOGIES

Ed., *The Book of American Negro Poetry,* New York, Harcourt, Brace, rev. ed., 1931; also paperback, 1969.
and J. Rosamond Johnson, eds., *The Books of American Negro Spirituals,* 2 vols., New York, Viking, 1940. (Contains
The Book of American Negro Spirituals, 1925, and *The
Second Book of Negro Spirituals,* 1926)

LEROI JONES

POETRY

Preface to a Twenty Volume Suicide Note, New York, Cor-
inth/Citadel, 1961. Totem/Corinth paperback, 1967.
The Dead Lecturer, New York, Grove, 1964. Evergreen paper-
back.
Black Arts, Newark, N.J., Jihad, 1966, also 1967.
Selected Poetry of Amiri-Baraka—LeRoi Jones, New York,
Morrow, 1979; also paperback.

DRAMA

Dutchman and *The Slave,* New York, Morrow, 1964. Apollo
paperback. (Two plays)
Baptism and *The Toilet,* New York, Grove paperback, 1967.
(Two plays)
Slave Ship, Newark, N.J., Jihad, 1967.
The Motion of History and Other Plays, New York, Morrow,
1978; also paperback.

FICTION

System of Dante's Hell, New York, Grove, 1966. Grove paperback, 1976. (Novel)
Tales, New York, Grove, 1967; also paperback. (16 short
stories)

CRITICISM

Blues People: Negro Music in White America, New York,

Morrow, 1963; also paperback. Westport, Conn., Green-
wood, 1980.
Black Music, New York, Morrow, 1967; also paperback.
Westport, Conn., Greenwood, 1980.

ESSAYS AND MISCELLANEOUS PROSE

Home, New York, Morrow, 1966; also paperback, 1972.
with Billy Abernathy, *In Our Terribleness: Pictures of the Hip
World,* Indianapolis, Ind., Bobbs, 1969.
It's Nation Time, Chicago, Third World paperback, 1970. (Es-
says)
Raise Race Rays Raze: Essays Since 1965, New York, Univ.
Place, 1971.
A Collection of Critical Essays, Englewood Cliffs, N.J., Pren-
tice Hall, 1978; also paperback.

ANTHOLOGIES

Ed., *The Moderns: New Fiction in America,* New York, Cor-
inth/Citadel, 1963.
Ed., *Four Young Lady Poets,* New York, Corinth/Citadel,
1964; also paperback.
and Larry Neal, eds., *Black Fire: An Anthology of Afro-
American Writing,* New York, Morrow, 1968; also paperback.

ALAIN LOCKE

ANTHOLOGIES

Ed., *The New Negro: An Interpretation,* New York, Alfred
and Charles Boni, 1925. New York, Arno, 1968. Chicago,
Johnson, 1968. New York, Atheneum paperback, 1968.
and Montgomery Gregory, eds., *Plays of Negro Life; A Source
Book of Native American Drama,* New York, Harper, 1927.
Westport, Conn., Negro Universities Press.
Ed., *Four Negro Poets,* New York, Simon and Schuster, 1927.
(Claude McKay, Countee Cullen, Jean Toomer and Langston Hughes)
and Bernard Stern, eds., *When Peoples Meet: A Study in Race
and Culture Contacts,* New York, Progressive Education Association, 1942. New York, AMS Press, 1977.

LITERARY CRITICISM

A Decade of Negro Self-Expression, Charlottesville, Va., John
F. Slater Fund, 1928.
The Negro in America, Chicago, American Library Associa-
tion, 1933.

ART

*The Negro in Art: A Pictorial Record of the Negro Artist and
of the Negro Theme in Art,* Washington, D.C., Associates

in Negro Folk Education, 1940. Arlington Heights, Ill., Metro Books, 1969. New York, Hacker.

The Negro and His Music, bound with *Negro Art: Past and Present,* New York, Arno, 1969.

CLAUDE McKAY

POETRY

Songs of Jamaica, Kingston, Jamaica, Ashton W. Gardner & Co., 1912.

Constab' Ballads, London, Watts, 1912. New York, Gordon Press, 1977.

Spring in New Hampshire and Other Poems, London, G. Richards, 1920.

Harlem Shadows, New York, Harcourt, Brace, 1922.

Selected Poems of Claude McKay, New York, Bookman, 1953. New York, Harcourt, Brace paperback, 1969.

The Dialect Poetry of Claude McKay, (two volumes in one facsimile edition including Volume 1, *Songs of Jamaica;* Volume 2, *Constab Ballads*), New York, Arno.

FICTION

Home to Harlem, New York, Harper, 1928. Madison, New Jersey, Chatham Bookseller, 1973. (Novel)

Banjo, a Story without a Plot, New York, Harper, 1929. New York, Harcourt, Brace paperback, 1970. (Novel)

Gingertown, New York, Harper, 1932. New York, Arno. (Short stories)

Banana Bottom, New York, Harper, 1935. Madison, New Jersey, Chatham Bookseller, 1971. New York, Harcourt, Brace paperback, 1974. (Novel)

AUTOBIOGRAPHY

A Long Way from Home, New York, L. Furman, Inc., 1937. New York, Arno. New York, Harcourt, Brace paperback, 1970.

SOCIOLOGY

Harlem: Negro Metropolis, New York, Dutton, 1940.

Ed., Alan L. McLeod, *The Negroes in America,* (translated from the Russian by Robert J. Winter), New York, Kennikat, 1979.

NAOMI LONG MADGETT

POETRY

Songs to a Phantom Nightingale, New York, Fortuny's, 1941. (Published under the name of Naomi Cornelia Long)

One and the Many, New York, Exposition Press, 1956.

Star by Star, Detroit, Harlo Press, 1965. Detroit, Lotus paperback, 1965.

Exits and Entrances, Detroit, Lotus paperback, 1978.
Pink Ladies in the Afternoon, Detroit, Lotus paperback, 1972.

CLARENCE MAJOR

POETRY

Love Poems of a Black Man, Omaha, Nebraska, Coercion Press, 1964.

Human Juices, Omaha, Nebraska, Coercion Press, 1965.

All-Night Visitors, New York, University Place paperback, 1973.

Emergency Exit, New York, Fiction Collective, 1975; also paperback.

Reflex & Bone Structure, New York, Fiction Collective, 1975; also paperback.

Swallow the Lake, New York, Columbia University Press, 1970; also paperback.

Symptoms & Madness, New York, Corinth Books, 1971; also paperback.

The Syncopated Cakewalk, New York, Barlenmir, 1974.

ANTHOLOGIES

Ed., *New Black Poetry,* New York, International Publishers paperback, 1969.

MALCOLM X

AUTOBIOGRAPHY

with assistance of Alex Haley, *The Autobiography of Malcolm X,* New York, Grove, 1965; also paperback, 1966. New York, Ballantine paperback, 1977.

SELECTED WORKS

Ed., George Breitman, *Malcolm X Speaks: Selected Speeches and Statements,* New York, Merit, 1965. New York, Path Press, 1976.

Malcolm X on Afro-American History, New York, Merit paperback original, 1967. Expanded edition, New York, Path Press paperback, 1972.

Two Speeches by Malcolm X, New York, Pioneer Publishers paperback original, 1967. New York, Path Press.

PAULE MARSHALL

FICTION

Brown Girl, Brownstones, New York, Random House, 1959; also paperback. (Novel)

Soul Clap Hands and Sing, New York, Atheneum, 1961. Madison, New Jersey, Chatham Booksellers, 1971. (Four novellas)

ANN PETRY

FICTION
   The Street, Boston, Houghton, Mifflin, 1946. New York, BJ
      Publishing Group paperback, 1969. (Novel)
   Country Place, Boston, Houghton, Mifflin, 1947. Madison,
      New Jersey, Chatham Bookseller, 1971. (Novel)
   The Narrows, Boston, Houghton, Mifflin, 1953. Madison, New
      Jersey, Chatham Bookseller, 1973. (Novel)

DUDLEY RANDALL

POETRY
   After the Killing, Detroit, Broadside paperback, 1973.
   Broadside Memories: Poets I Have Known, Detroit, Broadside
      paperback, 1975.
   Cities Burning, Detroit, Broadside paperback, 1966.
   More to Remember, Chicago, Third World, 1971. Detroit,
      Broadside, 1971; also paperback.
   with Margaret Danner, *Poem Counterpoem*, Detroit, Broad-
      side Press, 1966.

ANTHOLOGIES
   and Margaret G. Burroughs, eds., *For Malcolm*, Detroit,
      Broadside Press, 1967, second edition, 1969; also paper-
      back. (Poems on the life and death of Malcolm X)
   Ed., *Black Poets*, New York, Bantam paperback, 1971.

J. SAUNDERS REDDING

AUTOBIOGRAPHY
   No Day of Triumph, New York, Harper, 1942.

FICTION
   Stranger and Alone, New York, Harcourt, Brace, 1950. (Novel)

CRITICISM
   To Make a Poet Black, Chapel Hill, North Carolina, Univer-
      sity of North Carolina Press, 1939.

HISTORY
   They Came in Chains: Americans from Africa, Philadelphia,
      Lippincott, 1950.
   *The Lonesome Road: The Story of the Negro's Part in Amer-
      ica*, Garden City, N.Y., Doubleday, 1958.
   The Negro, New York, Potomac Books, 1967.

ESSAYS
   On Being Negro in America, New York, Bobbs-Merrill, 1962.

ANTHOLOGY
   with Arthur P. Davis, eds., *Cavalcade: Negro American Writ-*

ing from 1760 to the Present, Boston, Houghton, Mifflin, 1971.

MELVIN B. TOLSON

POETRY

Rendezvous with America, New York, Dodd, Mead, 1944.

Libretto for the Republic of Liberia, New York, Twayne, 1953. Macmillan paperback, 1970; Twayne, 1971.

Harlem Gallery, New York, Twayne, 1965. Macmillan paperback, 1969.

JEAN TOOMER

FICTION AND POETRY

Cane, New York, Boni and Liveright, 1923. (After being out of print for many years, *Cane* was issued again in 1967 by University Place Press, 69 University Place, New York, N.Y. 10003). New York, Liveright, 1975; also paperback.

DARWIN T. TURNER

POETRY

Katharsis, Wellesley, Mass., Wellesley Press, 1964.

ANTHOLOGIES AND MISCELLANEOUS PROSE

Ed., *The Wayward and the Seeking: A Collection of Writings by Jean Toomer,* Washington, D.C., Howard University Press, 1980.

Ed., *Afro-American Writers,* New York, Appleton-Century-Crofts paperback, 1970.

Black American Literature: Essays, Poetry, Fiction, Drama, Columbus, Ohio, Merrill paperback, 1970.

MARGARET WALKER

POETRY

For My People, New Haven, Conn., Yale University Press, 1942. New York, Arno, 1969; AMS Press.

October Journey, Detroit, Broadside paperback, 1973.

Prophets for a New Day, Detroit, Broadside paperback, 1970.

FICTION

Jubilee, Boston, Houghton, Mifflin, 1966. New York, Bantam paperback, 1975.

RICHARD WRIGHT

FICTION

Uncle Tom's Children, New York, Harper, 1938. (Four short

stories). New York, Harper, 1940. Harper paperback, 1965.
(Five short stories)

Native Son, New York, Harper, 1940, and 1969; also paperback. (Novel)

The Outsider, New York, Harper, 1953. Harper paperback,
1965. (Novel)

The Long Dream, Garden City, N.Y., Doubleday, 1958. Madison, New Jersey, Chatham Bookseller, 1969. (Novel)

Eight Men, New York, World, 1961. New York, B. J. Publishing Group paperback, 1969. (Short stories)

Lawd Today, New York, Walker, 1963.

Savage Holiday, New York, Award Books paperback, 1965.
Madison, New Jersey, Chatham Bookseller, 1975. (Novel,
copyright in 1954, published posthumously)

AUTOBIOGRAPHY

Black Boy, New York, Harper, 1945, and 1969; also paperback.

American Hunger, New York, Harper, 1977; also paperback,
1979.

ESSAYS AND MISCELLANEOUS PROSE

Twelve Million Black Voices, New York, Viking, 1941. Arno,
1969. (History)

Black Power: A Record of Reactions in a Land of Pathos,
New York, Harper, 1954. Westport, Conn., Greenwood,
1974. (Reportage on Africa)

The Color Curtain: A Report on the Bandung Conference,
New York, World, 1956.

Pagan Spain, New York, Harper, 1957.

White Man, Listen, Garden City, N.Y., Doubleday, 1957.
Westport, Conn., Greenwood, 1978.

DRAMA

with Paul Green, *Native Son: The Biography of a Young
American*, New York, Harper, 1941.

SELECTED WRITINGS

Eds., Ellen Wright and Michel Fabre, *Richard Wright Reader*,
New York, Harper, 1978; also paperback.